READER'S DIGEST
SELECT EDITIONS

www.readersdigest.co.uk

The Reader's Digest Association Limited
11 Westferry Circus Canary Wharf London E14 4HE

For information as to ownership of
copyright in the material of this book,
and acknowledgments, see last page.

Printed in Germany
ISBN 0 276 42992 3

**SELECTED AND CONDENSED
BY READER'S DIGEST**

THE READER'S DIGEST ASSOCIATION LIMITED, LONDON

CONTENTS

If you haven't yet discovered Lee Child's thrillers, starring his charismatic hero Jack Reacher, we recommend that you dip into this one. Many critics have called the books addictive and Child's fan base continues to grow. *One Shot* starts with a shocking and inexplicable shooting in a town in middle America—a crime that soon has the local police scratching their heads in disbelief. Why has the marksman left such an obvious trail of clues in his wake? It's almost as if he wants to be caught. And why, when he's arrested, does the suspect say: 'Get Jack Reacher for me.'? A fascinating story that reveals a tantalising and more complex scenario than the police at first imagined.

Barry Pilton, a scriptwriter for television and radio, whose credits include *Week Ending* and *Spitting Image*, has produced his first novel, a humorous portrait of a small community in mid-Wales that is invaded by some 'incomers' with idealistic notions about life in the country. Locals—from Clydog the Knowledge, whose journalism is usually limited to reports of escaped heifers, to Gwillim, the grumpy landlord of a local pub—brace themselves for disaster. And when sophisticated ideas clash with a way of life that has remained unchanged for decades, they are, of course, proved right. Provocative and sharply observant, this is one of the funniest, liveliest books of the year.

BLACK TIDE
CAROLINE CARVER
315

Caroline Carver is an exciting new name in British fiction. Her latest novel has an ecological theme and will sweep you along from the freezing Southern Ocean to the sweltering outback of Western Australia. Journalist India Kane is on a Greenpeace ship when it is hit by a tanker and sinks, resulting in the loss of eight crew members including one of her close friends. Vowing to bring the vessel's owner to justice, India investigates, only to find that the tanker is something of a ghost ship, unregistered and untraceable. Her life is endangered when she follows a trail of greed and corruption across Australia in order to uncover the truth.

When you're in the mood for something a little thought-provoking, there's nothing quite as satisfying as a good courtroom drama. Few writers do them as well as Rose Connors, who is herself a lawyer and can draw on her own rich experience. In *Temporary Sanity*, Connors's heroine, Marty Nickerson, has her work cut out in her first defence case: the man she's representing freely admits he is guilty. Worse, it transpires that the crime was captured by TV cameras—a fact the prosecuting counsel will not hesitate to seize upon. Marty's position seems absolutely hopeless, but she is determined to win this seemingly impossible case.

TEMPORARY SANITY
ROSE CONNORS
467

TEMPORARY SANITY
ROSE CONNORS
'CONNORS IS A WONDERFUL NEW VOICE'
LINDA FAIRSTEIN

Five shots ring out in a downtown plaza. A sudden and brutal crime is committed by a lone sniper who disappears as swiftly and as silently as he came.

When police arrive on the scene they are puzzled by the marksman's random choice of target. More baffling still is the fact that he has left a clear trail of evidence behind.

CHAPTER ONE

F riday. Five o'clock in the afternoon. Maybe the hardest time to move unobserved through a city. Or maybe the easiest. Because at five o'clock on a Friday nobody pays attention to anything. Except the road ahead.

The man with the rifle drove north. Not fast, not slow. Not drawing attention. He was in a light-coloured minivan that had seen better days. He was alone. He was wearing a light-coloured raincoat and the kind of shapeless beanie hat that old guys wear on the golf course. It was pulled down low. The man was wearing sunglasses, even though the van had dark windows and the sky was cloudy. And he was wearing gloves, even though winter was three months away.

Traffic slowed to a crawl where First Street started up a hill. Then it stopped completely where two lanes became one because the blacktop was torn up for construction. There was construction all over town. Driving had been a nightmare for a year. Holes in the road, gravel trucks, concrete trucks, blacktop spreaders. The man with the rifle checked his watch.

Eleven minutes.

Be patient.

He took his foot off the brake and crawled ahead. Then he stopped again where the roadway narrowed and the sidewalks widened where the down-town shopping district started. There were big stores to the left and the right, each one set a little higher than the last, because of the hill.

A hundred yards later the congestion eased. First Street opened out and became slightly shabby again. There were bars and dollar stores. Then yet more construction where a parking garage was being extended. Then further ahead the street was blocked by a low wall. Behind it was a pedestrian plaza with an ornamental pool and a fountain. On the plaza's left, the old city library. On its right, a new office building. Behind it, a black glass tower. First Street turned an abrupt right angle in front of the plaza's boundary wall and ran away west, then on under the raised state highway.

But the man in the minivan slowed before he hit the turn in front of the plaza and made a left and entered the parking garage. There was no barrier, because each slot had its own parking meter. Therefore there was no cashier, no ticket, no witness, no paper trail. The man in the minivan knew all that. He wound round the ramps to the first level and headed for the far back corner of the structure. Left the van idling for a moment and slipped out of the seat and moved an orange traffic cone from the space he wanted. It was the last one in the old part of the building, right next to where the new part was being added on.

He drove the van into the space and shut it down. Sat still for a moment. The garage was quiet. It was completely full with silent cars. The space he had protected with the traffic cone had been the last one available. The garage was always packed. He knew that. That was why they were extending it. It was used by shoppers. That was why it was quiet. Nobody in their right mind would try to leave at five o'clock. Not into the rush-hour traffic. Either they would get out by four or wait until six.

The man in the minivan checked his watch.

Four minutes.

Easy.

He opened the door and slid out. Took a quarter from his pocket and put it in the meter. Twisted the handle and heard the coin fall and saw the clockwork give him an hour in exchange. There was no other sound. Nothing in the air except the smell of parked automobiles. Gasoline, rubber, cold exhaust.

He stood still next to the van. On his feet he had a pair of old desert boots. Khaki suede, single eyelets, white crepe soles, much favoured by Special Forces soldiers.

He opened the minivan's sliding rear door and unfolded a blanket and revealed the rifle. It was a Springfield M1A Super Match autoloader, American walnut stock, heavy premium barrel, ten-shot box magazine, chambered for the .308, the commercial equivalent of the rifle that the American military had used during his long-ago years in the service. It was a fine weapon. It was loaded with Lake City M852s, his favourite custom cartridges. Special Lake City Match brass, Federal powder, Sierra MatchKing 168-grain hollow-point boat-tail bullets.

He lifted the rifle off the rear bench. Carried it to where the old part of the garage finished and the new part began. There was a half-inch trench between the old concrete and the new. He guessed it was an expansion joint. For the summer heat. He guessed they were going to fill it with soft tar. Directly above it there was yellow and black CAUTION DO NOT ENTER tape strung between two pillars. He dropped to one knee and slid under it. Stood up again and walked on into the raw new construction.

Parts of the new concrete floor were trowelled smooth and parts were still rough. There were wooden planks laid here and there as walkways. There were more open expansion joints. There were strings of bare light bulbs, turned off. Empty wheelbarrows, crushed soda cans, silent concrete mixers. There was grey cement dust everywhere, as fine as talc.

The man with the rifle walked on until he came close to the new northeast corner. Then he stopped and put his back tight against a raw concrete pillar. Inched to his right with his head turned until he could see where he was. He was about eight feet from the garage's new perimeter wall. Looking due north. The unfinished wall was about waist-high.

The man with the rifle inched forward until he felt the corner of the pillar between his shoulder blades. He turned his head again. Now he was looking directly into the public plaza. The ornamental pool was a long narrow rectangle running away from him. It was maybe eighty feet by twenty. It was a large tank of water, just sitting there. Like a big above-ground swimming pool. It was bounded by four waist-high brick walls. His line of sight ran on an exact diagonal from its near front corner to its far back corner. The fountain splashed right in the centre of the pool. The front wall of the pool was about three feet behind the wall that separated the plaza from First Street. The two low walls ran close together and parallel for twenty feet, east to west, with just the width of a narrow walkway between them.

He was on the garage's first floor, but the way First Street ran uphill meant that the plaza was much less than one storey below him. There was a shallow downward angle. On the right of the plaza he could see the door of the new office building. It had been built and it hadn't been rented. So to preserve some kind of credibility for the new downtown, the state had filled it with government offices. The Department of Motor Vehicles was in there, and a joint Army–Navy–Air Force–Marine Corps recruiting office.

He dropped to his knees and then to his stomach. The low crawl was a sniper's principal mode of movement. In the service he had low-crawled a million miles. Knees and elbows and belly. He reached the base of the wall and squirmed up into a kneeling position. He folded his right leg underneath him. He planted his left foot flat and his left shin vertical. He propped his left elbow on his left knee. Raised the rifle. Rested the end·of the forestock on the top of the low concrete wall. Sawed it gently back and forth until it felt good and solid. He breathed in, breathed out. *One shot, one kill.* That was the sniper's credo. To succeed required control and stillness and calm. He breathed in, breathed out. Felt himself relax. Felt himself come home.

Ready. Infiltration successful.

Now wait until the time is right.

He waited about seven minutes, keeping still, breathing low, clearing his mind. He looked at the library on his left. Above it and behind it the raised highway curled in on stilts, then straightened a little and passed behind the black glass tower. It was about level with the fourth storey back there. The tower itself had the NBC peacock logo on a monolith near its main entrance, but the network affiliate didn't occupy the whole building.

A lot of people were coming out of the new building on the right. The government offices were closing. The people came out through the doors and walked right-to-left directly in front of him, funnelling into single file as they entered the narrow space and passed the short end of the ornamental pool between the two low walls. Like ducks in a shooting gallery. *A target-rich environment.* The range was less than thirty-five yards.

Very close.

He waited.

Now there were so many people coming all at once that they had to pause and shuffle to get into single file to pass between the two low walls. Just like the traffic had snarled at the bottom of First Street. A bottleneck.

The man with the rifle breathed in, and breathed out, and waited.

Then he stopped waiting.

He pulled the trigger, and kept on pulling.

His first shot hit a man in the head and killed him instantly. There was a supersonic *crack* from the bullet and a puff of pink mist from the head and the guy went straight down like a puppet with the strings cut.

A kill with the first cold shot.

Excellent.

He worked fast, left to right. The second shot hit the next man in the head. Same result as the first. The third shot hit a woman in the head. Same result. Three shots in maybe two seconds. Three targets down. Absolute surprise. No reaction for a split second. Then chaos broke out. There were twelve people caught in the narrow space between the plaza wall and the pool wall. Three were already down. The remaining nine ran. Four ran forward and five spun away from the corpses and ran back. Those five collided with the press of people still moving their way. There were sudden loud screams. There was a solid stalled mass of panicked humanity, right in front of the man with the rifle. Very close.

His fourth head shot killed a man in a suit. His fifth missed completely. The Sierra MatchKing passed straight into the ornamental pool and disappeared. He moved the Springfield's muzzle a fraction, and his sixth shot caught a guy on the bridge of his nose and blew his head apart.

The man with the rifle stopped firing.

He ducked low behind the garage wall and crawled backwards three feet. He lay on his stomach and swept his spent shell cases into a pile. He scooped five of them into his gloved hands but the sixth rolled away and fell into an unfinished expansion joint.

Leave it, surely.

No time.

He jammed the five cases he had in his raincoat pocket and crawled backwards. Then he came to his knees and stood up. Turned around and walked back the same way he had come. Back to his minivan.

The rear door was still open. He rewrapped the warm rifle in its blanket and slid the door shut. Got in and started the engine. Glanced at the parking meter. He had forty-four minutes left on it. He backed out and headed for the exit ramp. He had passed under the raised highway before he heard the first sirens. The sirens were heading east, and he was heading west.

Good work, he thought. *Covert infiltration, six shots fired, five targets down, successful exfiltration, as cool as the other side of the pillow.*

THE MEDIA reacted quickest. Not surprisingly, since the shootings took place right in front of the local NBC affiliate's window. First, even before a dozen panicked bystanders hit 911 on their cellphones, every minicam in the NBC office starting rolling. The cameras were grabbed up and switched on and pointed at the windows. Second, a local news anchor called Ann Yanni started rehearsing what she knew would be her very first network breaking-news report. She was sick and scared and badly shaken, but she knew an opportunity when she saw it. The words that came to her first were sniper and senseless and slaying. The alliteration was purely instinctive. And slaying was a great word. It communicated the randomness, the savagery. It was exactly the right word for the story. She ran for the door.

THE DOZEN simultaneous 911 calls lit up the emergency switchboard like a Christmas tree, and the local police and fire departments were rolling within forty seconds. Serious crimes were plainly involved, so the Serious Crimes Squad's lead detective was given temporary command. He was a high-quality twenty-year police department veteran. His name was Emerson. He was blasting through slow traffic with no way of knowing what had happened. He had an open channel with the 911 dispatcher.

'New guy on a cellphone now,' the dispatcher screamed.

'Who?' Emerson screamed back.

'Marine Corps, from the recruiting office.'

Emerson knew he needed eyes. 'OK,' he said. 'Patch the Marine through.'

There were loud clicks and electronic sounds and then Emerson heard screaming, the splash of water. The fountain, he thought.

A voice came through. 'This is Kelly,' it said. 'First Sergeant, United States Marine Corps.'

'Emerson, PD. I'm about ten minutes out. What have we got?'

'Five dead,' the Marine said.

'Injured?'

'None that I can see.'

'Five dead and no injured?'

'Affirmative,' the Marine said.

Emerson said nothing. Public-place shootings always produced injured along with the dead. Usually in a one-to-one ratio, at least.

'Who are the DOAs?'

'Civilians. Four males, one female.'

'Where were you?'

'In the recruiting office. I'm outside now.'

'What did you see?'

'Nothing.'

'What did you hear?'

'Incoming gunfire, six rounds. Long gun. Just one.'

'A *rifle*?'

'An autoloader, I think. It fired fast, but it wasn't on full automatic. The victims were all hit in the head.'

A sniper, Emerson thought. Shit. A crazy man with an assault weapon.

'Has he gone now?' he said.

'No further firing, sir.'

'Where are you?'

'Head down behind the plaza wall, sir. I've got a few people with me.'

'Where was he?'

'Maybe in the parking garage. The new part. People were pointing at it. There may have been some muzzle flash. And that's the only major structure directly facing the victims.'

'Are you in uniform?' Emerson asked.

'Full dress, sir. For the recruiting office.'

'OK, do your best to keep order until my guys get there.'

'Roger that, sir.'

Emerson hit the switch that gave him the all-cars radio net.

'All units, listen up,' he said. 'This was a lone nutcase with a long gun. Probably an automatic weapon. Indiscriminate firing in a public place. Possibly from the new part of the parking garage. So either he's still in there, or he's already in the wind. All units that are more than ten blocks out, lock down a perimeter. Nobody enters or exits, OK? No vehicles, no pedestrians, nobody under any circumstances. All units that are closer than ten blocks, proceed inward with extreme caution. But do not let him get away. Do *not* miss him. This is a must-win, people.'

Emerson double-parked two blocks from the plaza and told a uniformed sergeant to direct the search of the parking garage, from the top down, from the southwest corner. The uniforms cleared each level. The old part was badly lit and full of parked cars, and every car represented a potential hiding place. But they didn't find anybody. They had no real problem with the new construction. It wasn't lit, but there were no parked cars. The patrolmen simply came down the stairwell and swept each level in turn with flashlight beams. Nobody there. The sergeant called it in.

'Good work,' Emerson said.

And it *was* good work. The fact that they searched from the southwest corner outwards left the northeast corner untouched. Nothing was disturbed. So by good luck or good judgment the police department had turned in an immaculate performance in the first phase of what would eventually be seen as an immaculate investigation from beginning to end.

By SEVEN o'clock in the evening it was going dark and Ann Yanni had been on the air eleven times. Three of them network, eight of them local. Personally she was a little disappointed with that ratio. *If it bleeds, it leads* was any news organisation's credo, but this bleeding was way out there, far from New York or LA. It had a tinge of weirdo-from-the-heartland about it. Not really prime-time stuff. And in truth, Ann didn't have much to offer. None of the victims was identified yet. None of the *slain*. So she had no heart-warming background stories to share. She didn't have much to offer in the way of visuals, either. Just a gathering crowd held five blocks back by police barricades, and occasional close-ups of the parking garage, which was where everyone assumed the sniper had been.

By EIGHT o'clock Emerson's guys had taken hundreds of statements. Marine Corps First Sergeant Kelly was still sure he had heard six shots. Emerson was inclined to believe him. Then some other guy mentioned that his cell-phone must have been open the whole time, connected to another guy's voicemail. The cellular company retrieved the recording and six gunshots were faintly audible on it. But the medical examiners had counted only five entry wounds in the five DOAs. Therefore there was a bullet missing. Three other witnesses reported seeing a plume of water kick out of the pool.

Emerson ordered the pool to be drained. The fire department handled it, using a pumping engine to dump the water into the city storm drains. They figured there were about 80,000 gallons of water to move, and that the job would be complete in an hour.

Meanwhile crime-scene technicians used drinking straws and laser pointers to estimate the fatal trajectories. They figured that the most reliable evidence would come from the first victim. Presumably he was walking purposefully right-to-left across the plaza when the first shot came in. After that, it was possible that the subsequent victims were twisting or turning or moving in other unpredictable ways. So they based their conclusions solely on the first guy. The bullet had travelled slightly high-to-low and left-to-right as it passed through his head. One tech stood upright on the spot and another held a drinking straw against the side of his head at the correct angle and held it steady. Then the first guy ducked out of the way and a third fired a laser pointer through the straw. It put a tiny red spot on the northeast corner of the parking garage extension, first level. Witnesses had claimed they had seen muzzle flashes up there. Now science had confirmed their statements.

Emerson sent his crime-scene people into the garage and told them they had all the time they needed. But he told them not to come back with nothing.

ANN YANNI left the black glass tower at eight thirty and took a camera crew down to the barricades five blocks away. She figured she might be able to identify some of the victims by process of elimination. People whose relatives hadn't come home for dinner might be gathering there, desperate for information. She shot twenty minutes of tape. She got no specific information at all. Instead she got twenty minutes of crying and wailing and sheer stunned incredulity. The whole city was in pain and in shock. She started out secretly proud that she was in the middle of everything, and she ended up with tears in her eyes and sick to her stomach.

THE PARKING garage was where the case was broken. It was a treasure trove. A patrolman took a witness statement from a regular user of the garage saying that the last space on the first level had been blocked off with an orange traffic cone. Because of it, the witness had been forced to leave the garage and park elsewhere. He had been pissed about it. A guy from the city said the cone hadn't been there officially. So the cone was bagged for evidence. Then the city guy said there were discreet security cameras at the entrance and exit. The tape was taken away. Then the city guy said the new extension was stalled for funding and hadn't been worked on for two weeks. So anything in there less than two weeks old wasn't anything to do with him.

The crime-scene technicians started at the yellow and black CAUTION DO NOT ENTER tape. The first thing they found was a scuff of blue cotton material on the rough concrete directly underneath it. Like a guy had dropped to one knee to squirm underneath and had left a little of his blue jeans behind. They photographed the scuff and then picked it up whole with an adhesive sheet of clear plastic. Then they brought in klieg lights and angled them low across the floor. They saw perfect footprints. The lead tech called Emerson on his Motorola.

'He was wearing weird shoes,' he said.

'What kind of weird shoes?'

'You ever heard of crepe? It's a crude kind of rubber. It picks everything up. If we find this guy, we're going to find crepe-soled shoes with cement dust all over the soles. Also, we've got carpet fibres here, picked up by the crepe rubber earlier and scraped off where the concrete's rough. They're probably from his rugs at home and in his car.'

'Keep going,' Emerson said.

AT TEN TO NINE Emerson briefed his Chief of Police for a press conference.

'Six shots fired and five people dead,' Emerson said. 'All head shots. I'm betting on a trained shooter. Probably ex-military.'

'Were we right to keep this away from the FBI?' the Chief asked.

'It wasn't terrorism. It was a lone nut.'

'I want to sound confident about bringing this one in.'

'So far we've got good stuff, but not great stuff.'

The Chief nodded and said nothing.

At nine o'clock exactly, Emerson took a call from the pathologist. His staff had X-rayed all five heads. Massive tissue damage, entry and exit wounds, no lodged bullets.

'Hollow points,' the pathologist said. 'All of them through and through.'

Emerson turned and looked at the ornamental pool. Six bullets in there, he thought. Five through-and-throughs and one miss. The pool was finally empty by nine fifteen. All that was left was a quarter-inch of scummy grit, and a lot of trash. Emerson had the lights reangled and sent in twelve recruits from the Academy.

THE CRIME-SCENE techs in the parking garage extension logged forty-eight footprints going and forty-four coming back. The perp had taken longer strides on the way back. In a hurry. The footprints were size eleven. They found fibres on the last pillar before the northeast corner. Mercerised cotton, at a guess, from a pale-coloured raincoat, at shoulder-blade height. They found major dust disturbance on the floor between the pillar and the perimeter wall. Plus more blue fibres and more raincoat fibres, and tiny crumbs of crepe rubber, pale in colour, and old.

'He low-crawled,' the lead tech said.

They found where he must have stopped and knelt. They saw varnish scrapings on the lip of the wall.

'He rested his gun there,' the lead tech said. 'Sawed it back and forth, to get it steady.'

The tech aimed his gaze over the varnish scrapings, like he was aiming a rifle. What he saw in front of him was Emerson, pacing in front of the ornamental pool, less than thirty-five yards away.

THE ACADEMY recruits spent thirty minutes in the empty pool and came out with nearly eight dollars in pennies, and six bullets. Five of them were just misshapen blobs of lead, but one of them looked absolutely brand new. It was a boat-tail hollow-point, almost certainly a .308. Emerson called his lead crime-scene tech up in the garage.

'I need you down here,' he said.

'No, I need you up here,' the tech replied.

Emerson got up to the first level and found all the techs crouched with their flashlight beams pointing down into a narrow crack in the concrete.

'Expansion joint,' the lead tech said. 'And look what fell in it.'

Emerson shouldered his way in and looked down and saw the gleam of brass. 'A cartridge case,' he said.

'The guy took the others with him. But this one got away.'

The tech stood up and used his flashlight beam to locate an electrical box on the ceiling. He looked on the floor underneath and found a rat's nest of discarded trimmings. He chose an eighteen-inch length of ground wire, bent it into an L-shape. He jiggled the wire down into the open joint and slid it along until the end went neatly into the empty cartridge case. Then he lifted it out very carefully. He dropped it into a plastic evidence bag.

'Meet at the station,' Emerson said. 'In one hour. I'll scare up a DA.'

He walked away, then stopped next to the empty parking bay.

'Empty the meter,' he called. 'Fingerprint all the quarters.'

'Why?' the tech called back. 'You'd have to be crazy to pay for parking just before you blow five people away.'

'You don't blow five people away *unless* you're crazy.'

SOMEONE from the District Attorney's office always got involved at this point, because the responsibility for prosecution rested squarely on the DA's shoulders. So the DA's office made its own evaluation of the evidence. Did they have a case? Was the case weak or strong? It was like an audition. Like a trial before a trial. This time, because of the magnitude, Emerson was performing in front of the DA himself. The big cheese, the actual guy who had to run for election. And re-election.

They made it a three-man conference in Emerson's office. Emerson, the lead crime-scene tech and the DA. The DA was called Rodin, which was a contraction of a Russian name that had been a lot longer before his great-grandparents came to America. He was fifty years old, lean and fit, and very cautious. His office had an outstanding victory percentage, mostly due to the fact that he wouldn't prosecute anything less than a total certainty.

'I need good news,' Rodin said. 'The whole city is freaking out.'

'We know exactly how it went down,' Emerson told him. 'We can trace it every step of the way.'

'So walk me through it.'

'We've got monochrome security videotape of a light-coloured minivan entering the garage eleven minutes before the event. Can't see the plates for mud and the camera angle isn't great. But it's probably a Dodge Caravan, not new, with tinted windows. And we're also looking through old tapes because it's clear he entered the garage earlier and illegally blocked off a particular space with a traffic cone from a city construction site.'

Rodin nodded. 'So, he reserved himself a parking space?'

'Right where the new construction starts. Therefore the cone would have looked plausible. We have a witness who saw it in place at least an hour before. And the cone has fingerprints on it. The right thumb and index finger match prints on a quarter we took out of the parking meter.'

'He paid to park?'

'Evidently.'

Rodin paused. 'Won't stand up,' he said. 'Defence will claim he could have placed the cone for an innocent reason. You know, selfish but innocent. And the quarter could have been in the meter for days.'

'There's more,' Emerson said. 'He parked, and then he walked through the new construction. He left trace evidence behind, from his shoes and his clothing. And he'll have picked trace evidence up, cement dust mostly.'

Rodin shook his head. 'Ties him to the scene sometime during the last two weeks. That's all.'

'We've got a three-way lock on his weapon,' Emerson said.

That got Rodin's attention.

'He missed with one shot,' Emerson said. 'It went into the pool. And you know what? That's exactly how ballistics labs test-fire a gun. They fire into a long tank of water. The water slows and stops the bullet with absolutely no damage. So we've got a pristine bullet with all the grooves we need to tie it to an individual rifle. We've also got varnish scrapings from where he steadied it on the wall. We find the rifle and we'll match the varnish and the scratches. It's as good as DNA.'

'Are you going to find the rifle?'

'We found a shell case. It's got tool marks on it from the ejector mechanism. So we've got a bullet *and* a case. Together they tie the weapon to the crime. The scratches tie the weapon to the garage location. The garage location ties the crime to the guy who left the trace evidence behind.'

Rodin said nothing. Emerson knew he was thinking about the trial. Technical evidence was sometimes a hard sell.

'The shell case has got fingerprints on it,' Emerson said. 'From when he loaded the magazine. Same thumb and index finger as on the quarter in the parking meter and on the cone. So we can tie the crime to the gun, the gun to the ammo and the ammo to the guy who used it. It all connects.'

'The videotape shows the minivan leaving?'

'Ninety seconds after the first 911 call came in.'

'Who is he?'

'I think he was a military shooter,' Emerson said. 'All military personnel are in the data bases. So it's just a matter of time.'

IT WAS a matter of forty-nine minutes. A desk guy knocked and entered. He was carrying a sheaf of paper. The paper listed a name, an address and a history. Plus supplementary information from all over the system, including a driver's licence photo. Emerson smiled. Exactly six hours after the first shot was fired, the situation was nailed down tight.

'His name is James Barr,' Emerson said. 'He's forty-one years old. He lives twenty minutes from here. He served in the US army. Honourable discharge fourteen years ago. Infantry specialist, which I'm betting means a sniper. DMV says he drives a six-year-old Dodge Caravan, beige.'

He slid the papers across his desk to Rodin. Rodin picked them up and scanned them through, once, twice, carefully. Emerson watched his eyes. It was like watching a Vegas slot machine line up three cherries.

'James Barr,' Rodin said, like he was savouring the word. He gazed at the driver's licence photo. 'James Barr, welcome to a shitload of trouble, sir.'

'Amen to that,' Emerson said, waiting for a compliment.

'I'll get the warrants,' Rodin said. 'Arrest, and searches on his house and car. Judges will be lining up to sign them.'

He left, and Emerson called the Chief of Police with the good news. The Chief said he would schedule an eight o'clock press conference for the next morning. He wanted Emerson there.

The warrants were ready in an hour, but the arrest took three hours to set up. First, surveillance confirmed that Barr was home. His place was an unremarkable one-storey ranch. Lights were on and Barr himself was spotted briefly in a window. He seemed to be alone. Then he seemed to go to bed. Lights went off and the house went quiet. The PD SWAT team took charge. Emerson was detailed to make the actual arrest, wearing full body armour and a borrowed helmet. An assistant DA would be alongside him, to monitor the legality of the process. A paramedic team would be instantly available. Altogether, thirty-eight men were involved, and they were all tired. Most of them had been working nineteen hours straight. So there was a lot of nervous tension in the air. People figured that nobody owned just one automatic weapon. If a guy had one, he had more.

But in the event, the arrest was a walk in the park. James Barr barely woke up. They broke down his doors at three in the morning and found him asleep, alone in bed. He stayed asleep with fifteen armed men in his bedroom aiming fifteen submachine guns and fifteen flashlight beams at him. He stirred a little when the SWAT commander threw his blankets to the floor, searching for concealed weapons. He had none. He was a large man, with white skin and black hair that was going grey all over his body.

Emerson pushed his way through the crowd in the bedroom. Saw a three-quarters-full pint of Jack Daniel's on the night table, next to an orange prescription bottle that was also three-quarters full. He bent to look at it. Sleeping pills. Legal. Recently prescribed to someone called Rosemary Barr. The label said: ROSEMARY BARR. TAKE ONE FOR SLEEPLESSNESS.

'Who's Rosemary Barr?' the assistant DA asked. 'Is he married?'

Emerson glanced around the room. 'Doesn't look like it.'

'Suicide attempt?' the SWAT commander asked.

Emerson shook his head. 'He'd have swallowed them all. Plus the whole pint of JD. I guess Mr Barr had trouble getting off to sleep tonight, that's all.'

'We need to be careful,' the assistant DA said. 'He's impaired right now. His lawyer is going to say he's not capable of understanding Miranda. So we can't let him say anything.'

Emerson called for the paramedics. They fussed around Barr, listened to his heart, checked his pulse, read the prescription label. Then they pronounced him reasonably healthy, but fast asleep.

'Are we even sure this is the guy?' the assistant DA asked.

Emerson found a pair of suit trousers folded over a chair and checked the pockets. Came out with a wallet. Found the driver's licence. The name was right, and the address was right. And the photograph was right.

'OK, take him in,' Emerson said.

They wrapped him in a blanket and two cops dragged him out of the house and into a car. Emerson stayed in the house and started the search. He found the scuffed blue jeans in the bedroom closet. The crepe-soled shoes were placed neatly on the floor below them. They were dusty. The raincoat was in the hall closet. The beige Dodge Caravan was in the garage. The scratched rifle was in the basement. It was one of several resting on a rack. On a bench underneath it were five 9mm handguns. And boxes of ammunition, including a half-empty box of Lake City M852 168-grain boat-tail hollow-point .308s. Next to the boxes were glass jars with empty cartridge cases in them. The jar nearest the front of the bench held just five of them. Lake City brass. The jar's lid was still off. Emerson bent down and sniffed. The air in the jar smelt of gunpowder. Cold and old, but not very.

THE PRESS conference killed the story stone dead. A story needs the guy to be *still out there*. A story needs the guy roaming, sullen, hidden, dangerous. It needs fear. It needs to make everyday chores, like pumping gas or visiting the mall, exposed and hazardous. So to hear that the guy was found and arrested even before the start of the second news cycle was a disaster for Ann Yanni. She would get one more network news spot to recap the crime and report the arrest, and that would be it. Back to obscurity. So Yanni was disappointed, but she hid it well. She asked questions and made her tone admiring.

The Chief yielded the floor to Emerson after about ten minutes. Emerson filled in full details on the perp's identity and his history. He kept it dry. He outlined the investigation. He answered questions. He didn't boast.

Then Rodin stepped up. The DA made it sound like the police had been involved in some early minor skirmishing and that the real work was about to begin. His office would review everything and make the necessary determinations. And yes, Ms Yanni, because he thought the circumstances warranted it, he would certainly seek the death penalty for James Barr.

JAMES BARR woke up in his cell with a chemical hangover at nine o'clock Saturday morning. He was immediately fingerprinted and Mirandised once, and then twice. The right to remain silent, the right to a lawyer. He chose to remain silent. Not many people do. The urge to talk is usually overwhelming. But James Barr beat it. He just clamped his mouth shut and kept it that way. Plenty of people tried to talk to him, but he didn't answer. Not a word.

Emerson was relaxed about it. Truth was, he didn't really want Barr to say anything. He preferred to line up all the evidence, scrutinise it, test it, polish it, and get to a point where he could anticipate a conviction *without* a confession. Confessions were vulnerable to defence accusations of coercion. For Emerson, they were icing on the cake. Literally the *last* thing he wanted to hear, not the first. Not like on the TV cop shows, where relentless interrogation was a kind of performance art. So he just stayed out of the loop and let his forensics people complete their slow, patient work.

JAMES BARR'S sister was younger than him and unmarried and living in a rented downtown condo. Her name was Rosemary. She had seen the news Friday night, and again Saturday morning. She heard a police detective say her brother's name. At first she thought it was a mistake. But the guy kept on saying it. Rosemary burst into tears.

Then she forced herself to calm down, and got busy.

She worked as a secretary in an eight-man law firm. The salary wasn't spectacular, but there were intangibles to compensate. One was a promise that the firm would handle legal matters for its employees and their families free. Mostly that was about wills and divorce. It wasn't about defending adult siblings who were wrongly accused in notorious urban sniper slayings. But she felt she had to give it a try. Because she knew her brother, and she knew he couldn't be guilty.

She called the partner she worked for, at home. He was mostly a tax guy, so he called the firm's criminal litigator. The litigator called the managing partner, who called a meeting of all the partners. They held it over lunch at the country club. From the start, the agenda was about how to refuse Rosemary Barr's request in the most tactful way. A defence to a crime of this nature wasn't something they were equipped to handle. Or *inclined* to handle. There were public relations implications. They were all agreed on that. But Rosemary Barr was a good employee who had worked many years for them. They knew she had no money, because they did her taxes. They assumed her brother had no money, either. But the Constitution guaranteed competent counsel, and they didn't have a very high opinion of public defenders. So they were caught in a genuine ethical dilemma.

The litigator resolved it. His name was David Chapman, and he knew Rodin at the DA's office pretty well. So Chapman went to the smoking room and used his cellphone to call the DA at home. The two lawyers had a full and frank discussion. Then Chapman came back to the lunch table.

'It's a slam dunk,' he told the others. 'Ms Barr's brother is guilty all to hell and gone. Rodin's case is going to read like a textbook. All we would have to do is plead in mitigation. If we can get the lethal injection reduced to life without, there's a big win right there.'

'You happy to handle it?'

'Under the circumstances.'

'What grounds for mitigation?'

'He's a Gulf War vet. So there's probably chemical stuff going on. Or some kind of delayed post-traumatic thing.'

The managing partner nodded. Turned to the tax guy. 'Tell your secretary we'll do everything to help her brother in his hour of need.'

BARR WAS MOVED from the police station lockup to the county jail before either his sister or Chapman got a chance to see him. It wasn't a pleasant place to be. Men were stacked three to a cell and the guards were short-handed. New guys were called fish, and were left to fend for themselves.

Barr survived as a fish for two hours, and then he was escorted to an interview room. He found a table and two chairs bolted to the floor. In one of the chairs was a guy. On the table was a pocket tape recorder.

'My name is David Chapman,' the guy in the chair said. 'I'm a criminal defence attorney. A lawyer. Your sister works at my firm. She asked us to help you out.'

Barr said nothing.

'The charges are very serious.'

Barr stayed quiet.

'I'm recording this conversation,' Chapman said. 'Putting it on tape. I take it that's OK with you?'

Barr said nothing.

'Have the charges been explained to you?' Chapman asked.

Barr said nothing.

'I can't help you if you won't help yourself,' Chapman said.

Barr just stared at him. Then he leaned forward and spoke for the first time since the previous afternoon. He said, 'They got the wrong guy.' Then he said it again. 'They got the wrong guy.'

'So tell me about the right guy,' Chapman said, immediately.

But Barr just retreated back into silence.

'Are you *denying* it?' Chapman asked him.

No response.

'The evidence is all there,' Chapman said. 'It's just about overwhelming. So we need to talk about *why* you did it.'

Barr said nothing.

'You want me to help you?' Chapman said. 'Or not?'

Barr said nothing.

'Maybe it was your old wartime experience,' Chapman said. 'Or post-traumatic stress.'

Barr said nothing.

'The evidence is right there,' Chapman said. 'Denying it is not an option.'

'Get Jack Reacher for me,' Barr said.

'Who?'

'Jack Reacher.'

'Who's he? A friend?'

'Just get him for me.'

'Where is he? Is he a doctor?'

But Barr just got up and walked to the door and pounded on it until the jailer opened it and led him back to his overcrowded cell.

CHAPMAN ARRANGED to meet Rosemary Barr and the firm's investigator at his law offices. The investigator was a retired cop shared by most of the city's law firms. He was a private detective, with a licence. His name was Franklin. He did all his work at a desk, with phone books and computer data bases. He had no equal as a fact-checker or a skip-tracer and he still had plenty of friends in the police department.

'The evidence is rock solid,' he said. 'That's what I'm hearing. Emerson's pretty reliable. So is Rodin, but for a different reason. Emerson's a stiff and Rodin is a coward. Neither one of them would be saying what they're saying unless the evidence was there.'

'I just can't believe he did it,' Rosemary Barr said.

'Well, certainly he seems to be denying it,' Chapman said. 'And he's asking for someone called Jack Reacher. You know who he is?'

Rosemary Barr shook her head.

'My guess is he may be a psychiatrist. Mr Barr brought the name up right after I told him how strong the evidence is. So maybe Reacher is someone who can help us out with the mitigation.'

'My brother never saw a psychiatrist,' Rosemary Barr said.

'How long has he been in town?'

'Fourteen years. Since the army.'

'Were you close?'

'We lived in the same house. His house.'

'But you don't live there any more.'

'No,' Rosemary Barr said. She looked away. 'I moved out.'

'Might your brother have seen a shrink after you moved out?'

'He would have told me.'

Chapman turned back to Franklin. 'Maybe Reacher was his army doctor.'

'In which case I'll find him,' Franklin said.

'We shouldn't be talking about mitigation,' Rosemary said. 'We should be talking about reasonable doubt. About *innocence*.'

'The evidence is very strong,' Chapman said. 'He used his own gun.'

FRANKLIN FOUND Jack Reacher's name in the National Personnel Record Center's data base. Reacher had entered military service in 1984 and received an honourable discharge in 1997. James Barr himself had signed up in 1985 and mustered out in 1991. So there was a six-year overlap. But Reacher had been no kind of a doctor. No kind of a psychiatrist. He had been a military cop. A major. Maybe a high-level investigator. Barr had finished as a lowly Specialist E-4. Infantry, not military police. So what was the point of contact between a military police major and an infantry E-4?

At the end of three hours, Franklin figured he would never find out, because Reacher fell off the radar after 1997. Completely. There was no trace of him anywhere. He was still alive, according to the Social Security Administration. He wasn't in prison, according to the NCIC. But he had disappeared. He had no credit rating. He wasn't listed as title holder to any real estate, or automobiles, or boats. He had no debts. No warrants outstanding. No address. No phone number. He wasn't a husband. Wasn't a father. He was a ghost.

JAMES BARR spent the same three hours in serious trouble. It started when he stepped out of his cell to walk down to the payphones. The corridor was narrow. He bumped into another guy. Then he made a bad mistake. He glanced at the guy and apologised.

A bad mistake because a fish can't make eye contact with another prisoner. Not without implying disrespect. Barr didn't understand.

The guy he made eye contact with was a Mexican. He had gang tattoos.

'What are you looking at?' the Mexican said.

At that point, James Barr understood. *What are you looking at?* That was pretty much a standard opener. Barrack rooms, barrooms, dark alleys, it was not a phrase you wanted to hear.

'Nothing,' he said, then realised he had made the situation much worse.

'You calling me nothing?'

Barr put his eyes back on the floor and moved on, but it was way too late. He felt the Mexican's stare on his back and gave up on the payphone idea. The phones were in a dead-end lobby and he didn't want to feel trapped. So he headed back to his cell. He got there OK. Didn't look at anyone, didn't speak. He lay down on his bunk. About two hours later, he guessed he could handle a little macho bluster. And he was bigger than the Mexican.

He wanted to call his sister. He wanted to know she was OK. He set off for the payphones again.

He got there unmolested. There were four phones on the wall, four men talking, four lines of other men waiting behind them. Then the men in front of Barr vanished. Just melted out of sight.

James Barr turned round.

He saw the Mexican with the tattoos. He had a knife in his hand and twelve friends behind him. The knife was a plastic toothbrush handle wrapped with tape and sharpened to a point, like a stiletto. The friends were all stocky little guys, all with the same tattoos.

'Wait,' Barr said.

But the Mexicans didn't wait, and eight minutes later Barr was in a coma. He was found on the floor, with multiple stab wounds and a cracked skull and severe subdural bleeding. He was medevaced to the city hospital and sewn up and operated on to relieve pressure from a swollen brain. Then he was dumped in a secure intensive care unit, comatose. The doctors weren't sure when he would wake up again. Maybe in a day. Maybe in a week. Maybe in a month. Maybe never.

THE WARDEN at the jail called late at night and told Emerson. Then Emerson called and told Rodin. Then Rodin called and told Chapman. Then Chapman called and told Franklin.

'So what happens now?' Franklin asked him.

'It's on ice. You can't try a guy in a coma.'

'What about when he wakes up?'

'If he's OK, then they'll go ahead, I guess.'

'What if he isn't?'

'Then they won't. Can't try a vegetable.'

'So what do we do now?'

'Nothing,' Chapman said. 'We weren't taking it very seriously anyhow. Barr's guilty, and there's nothing much anyone can do for him.'

Franklin phoned Rosemary Barr, because he wasn't sure if anyone else would have taken the trouble. Nobody else had. So he broke the news himself. Rosemary Barr didn't have much of an outward reaction. She just went very quiet. It was like she was on emotional overload.

'I guess I should go to the hospital,' she said.

'If you want,' Franklin said.

'He's innocent, you know,' she said.' This is so unfair.'

'Did you see him yesterday?' Franklin asked.

'You mean, can I alibi him?'

'Can you?'

'No,' she said. 'I can't.'

'Are there places he goes regularly? Movies, bars?'

'Not really.'

'Friends he hangs with?'

'I'm not sure.'

'Girlfriends?'

'Not for a long time.'

'Other family he visits?'

'There's just the two of us. Him and me.'

Franklin said nothing. There was a long pause.

'Did you find that person he mentioned?' Rosemary Barr asked.

'Jack Reacher? No, I'm afraid not. No trace.'

'OK,' Rosemary Barr said. 'Then we'll have to manage without him.'

But even as they spoke, on the phone late at night on Saturday, Jack Reacher was on his way to them.

CHAPTER TWO

Reacher was on his way to them because of a woman. He had spent Friday night in South Beach, Miami, in a salsa club, with a dancer from a cruise ship. The boat was Norwegian, and so was the girl. They had met on the beach in the afternoon. Reacher was working on his tan. He didn't know what she was working on. But he felt her shadow fall across his face and opened his eyes to find her staring at him. Or maybe at his scars. She was pale, in a black bikini. A *small* black bikini.

They ended up having a late dinner together and then going out to the club. She was fun to be with. And she was a great dancer, obviously. Full of energy. She wore him out. At four in the morning she took him back to her hotel, eager to wear him out some more. Her hotel was a small Art Deco place near the ocean. Clearly the cruise line treated its people well. It was much more romantic than Reacher's own motel. And much closer.

And it had cable television, which Reacher's place didn't. He woke at eight on Saturday morning when he heard the dancer in the shower. He turned on the TV. He wanted Friday night's American League highlights. He never found them. He clicked his way through successive channels and then stopped dead on CNN because he heard the chief of an Indiana police department say a name he knew: *James Barr.* The picture was of a press conference. The caption at the top of the screen said: *Courtesy NBC.* There was a banner across the bottom that said: *Friday Night Massacre.* Then the police chief introduced a homicide detective called Emerson. Emerson said the name again: *James Barr.* Then, like he anticipated the exact question in Reacher's mind, he ran through a brief biography: *Forty-one years old, local Indiana resident, US army infantry specialist from 1985 to 1991, Gulf War veteran, currently unemployed.*

Reacher watched the screen. Emerson seemed like a concise type of a guy. Then he introduced a district attorney. This guy's name was Rodin, and he wasn't concise. He spent ten minutes claiming Emerson's credit for himself. Reacher knew how *that* worked. He had been a cop of sorts for thirteen years. Rodin said *James Barr* a few more times and then said the state was maybe looking to fry him.

For what?

Reacher waited.

A local anchor called Ann Yanni came on. She recapped the events of the night before. Sniper slaying. Senseless slaughter. An automatic weapon. A parking garage. A public plaza. Commuters on their way home. Five dead. A suspect in custody, but a city still grieving.

Reacher turned the TV off. The dancer came out of the bathroom. She was pink and fragrant. And naked.

'What shall we do today?' she said, with a wide smile.

'I'm going to Indiana,' Reacher said.

HE WALKED north in the heat to the Miami bus depot. Then he leafed through a greasy timetable and planned a route. It wasn't going to be an easy trip. Five different buses, five separate destinations. Beginning to end, it was going to take more than forty-eight hours. He was tempted to fly or rent a car, but he was short of money and he liked buses and he figured nothing was going to happen on the weekend anyway.

WHAT HAPPENED on the weekend was that Rosemary Barr called her firm's investigator at home, ten o'clock in the morning on the Sunday.

'I think I should hire different lawyers,' she said. 'Chapman thinks he's guilty. Doesn't he?'

'I can't comment. He's an employer,' Franklin said. 'How was the hospital?'

'Awful. They've got him handcuffed to the bed. He's in a *coma,* for God's sake. How do they think he's going to escape?'

'What's the legal position?'

'He was arrested but not arraigned. He's in limbo.'

'What would you like to happen?'

'He shouldn't be in handcuffs. And he should be in a Veterans Association hospital. But that won't happen until I find a lawyer who'll help him.'

'He blocked off a parking space,' Franklin said. 'He premeditated this.'

'You think he's guilty too.'

'I work with what I've got. And what I've got doesn't look good.'

Rosemary Barr said nothing.

'I'm sorry,' Franklin said.

'Can you recommend another lawyer?'

'How much money have you got?'

'Not much.'

'How much has *he* got?'

'There's some equity in the house.'

'It won't look good. It'll be a kick in the teeth for the firm you work for.'

'I can't worry about that.'

'You could lose everything, including your job.'

'I'll lose it anyway, unless I help James. If he's convicted, they'll let me go. I'll be notorious. By association. An embarrassment.'

Franklin paused. 'Try Helen Rodin,' he said.

'Rodin?'

'She's the DA's daughter. She's new and she's keen.'

'Is she any good?'

'I think she's going to be.'

ROSEMARY BARR called Helen Rodin at her office. It was like a test. Someone new and keen should be at the office on a Sunday.

Helen Rodin was at the office on a Sunday. She answered the call sitting at her secondhand desk. It sat proudly in a mostly empty two-room suite in the same black glass tower that had NBC as the first-floor tenant. The suite was rented cheap through one of the city's business subsidies.

Rosemary Barr didn't have to tell Helen Rodin about the case because the whole thing had happened right outside her office window.

'Will you help my brother?' Rosemary Barr asked.

Helen Rodin paused. The smart answer would be *No way.* Two reasons. One, she knew a major clash with her father was inevitable at some point, but did she need it *now*? And two, she knew that a new lawyer's early cases defined her. To end up as a when-all-else-fails criminal defence attorney would be OK, she guessed. But to start out by taking a case that had offended the whole city would be a marketing disaster. The shootings were being seen as an *atrocity*. To be the person who tried to excuse it or explain it away would be a fatal mistake.

'Can we sue the jail for letting him get hurt?'

Helen Rodin paused again. Another good reason to say no. *An unrealistic client.*

'Maybe later,' she said. 'Right now he wouldn't generate much sympathy as a plaintiff.'

'Then I can't pay you much,' Rosemary Barr said. 'I don't have money.'

Helen Rodin paused a third time. *Another* good reason to say no.

But. But. But. The accused deserved representation. The Bill of Rights said so. And he was innocent until proven guilty. And if the evidence was as bad as her father said it was, then the whole thing would be little more than a supervisory process. She would verify the case against him, independently. Then she would advise him to plead guilty. Then she would watch his back as her father fed him through the machine. That was all. She hoped.

'OK,' she said.

'He's innocent,' Rosemary Barr said. 'I'm sure of it.'

They always are, Helen Rodin thought.

'OK,' she said again. Then she told her new client to meet her in her office at seven the next morning. It was like a test. A sister who really believed in her brother's innocence would show up for an early appointment.

ROSEMARY BARR showed up right on time, at seven o'clock on Monday morning. Franklin was there, too. He believed in Helen Rodin and was prepared to defer his bills until he saw which way the wind was blowing. Helen Rodin herself had already been at her desk for an hour. She had informed David Chapman of the change in representation on Sunday afternoon and had obtained the audiotape of his initial interview with James Barr. Chapman had been happy to hand it over and wash his hands. She had played the tape to herself a dozen times Sunday night and a dozen more that morning. She had drawn some early conclusions from it.

'Listen,' Helen said.

She had the tape cued up and ready. She pressed play and they all heard a hiss and then David Chapman's voice: *I can't help you if you won't help yourself.* Then James Barr spoke: *They got the wrong guy. They got the wrong guy.* Then Helen spooled forward to Chapman saying: *Denying it is not an option.* Then Barr's voice came through: *Get Jack Reacher for me.* Helen spooled on to Chapman's question: *Is he a doctor?* Then there was nothing on the tape except the sound of Barr beating on the interview room door.

'OK,' Helen said. 'I think he really believes he didn't do it. He gets frustrated and terminates the interview when Chapman doesn't take him seriously. That's clear, isn't it?'

'He *didn't* do it,' Rosemary Barr said.

'I spoke with my father yesterday,' Helen Rodin said. 'The evidence is all there, Ms Barr. He did it, I'm afraid.'

'Is your father telling you the truth about the evidence?'

'He has to,' Helen said. 'We're going to see the evidence anyway.'

Nobody spoke.

'But we can still help your brother,' Helen said, in the silence. 'He believes he didn't do it. Therefore he's delusional now. Therefore perhaps he was delusional on Friday, too.'

'You want to have James declared insane?'

Helen nodded. 'A medical defence is our best shot.'

'He might die. That's what the doctors said. I don't want him to die a criminal. I want to clear his name.'

'He hasn't been tried yet. He hasn't been convicted. He's still an innocent man in the eyes of the law.'

'That's not the same.'

'No,' Helen said. 'I guess it isn't.'

There was another long silence.

'Let's meet back here at ten thirty,' Helen said.

'We need to find this Jack Reacher,' Rosemary Barr said.

Helen nodded. 'I gave his name to Emerson and my father.'

'Why?'

'Because Emerson's people cleared your brother's house out. They might have found an address or a phone number. And my father needed to know because we want this guy on our witness list, not on the prosecution's. Because he might be able to help us.'

'He might be an alibi.'

'Or a link to something we can use, at least.'

'He's out of circulation,' Franklin said.

HE WAS two hours away, in the back of a bus out of Indianapolis. He had spent Saturday night in New Orleans. He had spent Sunday night in Indianapolis. So he had slept and eaten and showered. But mostly he had rocked and swayed and dozed on buses, watching the passing scenes. His life was like that. It was a mosaic of fragments.

The bus stopped in Bloomington. Six people got out. One of them left the Indianapolis paper behind. Reacher picked it up. He saw the headline: SNIPER SUSPECT HURT IN JAIL ATTACK. He read the first three paragraphs: 'Brain injury.' 'Coma.' 'Uncertain prognosis.'

This might complicate things, Reacher thought.

The bus moved out of Bloomington. Reacher folded the paper and propped his head against the window and watched the road. It was a black ribbon, wet with recent rain, and it unspooled beside him with the centre line flashing by like an urgent Morse code message. Reacher wasn't sure what it was saying to him. He couldn't read it.

THE BUS pulled into a covered depot and Reacher came out into the daylight and found himself five blocks west of where a raised highway curled round behind an old stone building. It would be a bank, he thought, or a courthouse, or maybe a library. There was a black glass tower beyond it. It was colder here than in Miami but he was still far enough south that winter felt safely distant. He was in white chino pants and a bright yellow canvas shirt. Both were three days old. He figured he would get another day out of them. Then he would buy replacements. He had brown boat shoes on his feet. No socks. He must look out of place in the city.

He checked his watch. Nine twenty in the morning. The city was one of those heartland places that are neither large nor small, neither new nor old. It wasn't booming and it wasn't decrepit. There was probably some corn and soybean trading. Maybe tobacco. Maybe some manufacturing. There was a small downtown area. He could see it ahead of him. He figured the black glass tower would be the flagship building.

He walked towards it. There was a lot of construction under way, heavy trucks moving slowly. He crossed in front of one and hit a side street and came out along the north side of a half-finished parking garage extension. He recalled Ann Yanni's fevered breaking-news recap and glanced up at it and then away from it to a public square. There was an empty ornamental pool. There was a narrow walkway between the pool and a low wall. The walkway was decorated with makeshift funeral tributes. There were flowers, their stems wrapped in aluminium foil. Photographs, small stuffed animals and candles. He glanced back at the parking garage. Less than thirty-five yards, he thought. Very close.

He stood still. The plaza was silent. The whole city was quiet. It felt stunned, like a limb briefly paralysed after a massive bruising blow. The plaza was the epicentre. It was where the blow had landed. It was like a black hole, with emotion compressed into it too tight to escape.

He walked on. The old limestone building was a library. That's OK, he thought. Librarians tell you things, if you ask them. He asked for the DA's office. A sad woman at the checkout desk gave him directions. It wasn't far. He walked east past a new office building that had signs for the DMV and a military recruitment centre. Behind it was a new courthouse building.

He circled the block until he came to the office wing. He found a door labelled DISTRICT ATTORNEY. Below it on a separate brass plate he found Rodin's name. Rodin's initials were A. A. He had a law degree.

Reacher went in through the door. Asked to see A. A. Rodin himself.

'About what?' the receptionist asked politely. She looked like she had worked behind a desk all her life.

'About James Barr,' Reacher said.

'May I tell Mr Rodin's office your connection to the case?'

'I knew James Barr in the army.'

'May I have your name?'

'Jack Reacher.'

The receptionist dialled a phone and spoke. Reacher guessed she was speaking to a secretary, because both he and Rodin were referred to in the third person. *Can he see a Mr Reacher about the case?* Not the Barr case. Just *the* case. The conversation continued. It was a long one. Mr A. A. Rodin had efficient gatekeepers. That was clear.

The receptionist hung up the phone. 'Please go up,' she said. 'Mr Rodin is on the third floor.'

The receptionist wrote his name on a visitor pass. Reacher clipped it on his shirt and headed for the elevator. Rode it to the third floor. There were three closed doors and one open set of double doors made of polished wood. Behind those was a secretary at a desk. The second gatekeeper.

'Mr Reacher?' she asked.

He nodded and she led him to where the windowed offices started. The third door was labelled A. A. RODIN.

She knocked on the door and a baritone replied from inside. She opened the door and stood aside to let Reacher go in.

Rodin was already on his feet, ready to welcome his visitor. Reacher recognised him from the TV. He was a guy of about fifty, fairly lean, fairly fit, grey hair cut short. He was maybe an inch under six feet and a pound under two hundred. He was dressed in a summer-weight suit, dark blue. He had a blue shirt on, and a blue tie. His eyes were blue. Blue was his colour, no doubt. He was immaculately shaved and wearing cologne. Next to Rodin, Reacher was an unkempt giant. He was six inches taller and fifty pounds heavier. His hair was two inches longer and his clothes were a thousand dollars cheaper. It was like a study in contrasts.

'Mr Reacher?' Rodin said.

Reacher nodded. The office was government-basic, but neat. No real view from the window. Just the DMV office with all the ductwork showing. At right angles to the window there was a trophy wall behind the desk, with college degree certificates and photographs of Rodin with politicians. There were framed newspaper headlines reporting guilty verdicts in seven different cases. On another wall was a photograph of a blonde girl wearing a mortarboard and a gown. She was pretty. Reacher looked at her for a moment longer than he needed to.

'That's my daughter,' Rodin said. 'She's a lawyer, too. You're due to meet with her, I think.'

'Am I?' Reacher said. 'Why?'

'She's defending James Barr.'

'Your daughter? Is that ethical?'

'It might not be sensible, but it's not unethical.'

He said *sensible* with emphasis, hinting at a number of meanings. Not smart to defend a notorious case, not smart for a daughter to take on her father, not smart for *anyone* to take on A. A. Rodin. He sounded like a very competitive guy.

'She put your name on her provisional witness list,' he said.

'Why?'

'She thinks you have information.'

'Where did she get my name?'

'I don't know.'

'From the Pentagon?'

Rodin shrugged. 'I'm not sure. But people have been looking for you.'

'Is that why I got in here?'

'That's exactly why,' Rodin said. 'Sit down, please.'

Reacher sat in the visitor chair and Rodin sat at his desk.

'Naturally I'm interested in why you came to see me first,' he said. 'The prosecution, I mean, rather than the defence.'

'I wanted your personal opinion,' Reacher said.

'On what?'

'On how strong a case you've got against James Barr.'

Rodin didn't answer immediately. There was a short silence and then there was a knock at the door and the secretary came in with coffee. She had a silver tray with the works on it. A cafetière, two cups, two saucers, a sugar bowl, a tiny pitcher of cream, two silver spoons. Rodin likes his coffee done right, Reacher thought. The secretary put the tray on the desk.

'Thanks,' Reacher said.

'You're most welcome,' she said, and left the room.

'Help yourself,' Rodin said. 'Please.'

Reacher pushed the plunger down and poured himself a cup, no cream, no sugar. It smelt dark and strong. Coffee, done right.

'The case against James Barr is exceptionally good.'

'Eyewitnesses?' Reacher asked.

'No,' Rodin said. 'But eyewitness testimony can be of random value. What we've got instead is exceptional physical evidence. And science doesn't lie. It doesn't get confused.'

'Exceptional?' Reacher said.

'A solid evidence chain tying the man to the crime. The best I've seen.'

'I've heard prosecutors say that before.'

'Not this one, Mr Reacher. I'm a very cautious man. I don't prosecute capital cases unless I'm certain of the outcome.'

'Keeping score?'

Rodin gestured above and behind him at his trophy wall.

'Seven for seven,' he said. 'One hundred per cent. James Barr will make it eight for eight. If he ever wakes up.'

'Suppose he wakes up damaged?'

'If he wakes up with any brain function, he's going to trial.'

'OK,' Reacher said. 'You've told me what I wanted to know.'

'You knew James Barr, in the army?'

'Briefly.'

'Tell me about him.'

'Not yet.'

'Mr Reacher, if you have exculpatory information, or anything to add at all, you really need to tell me now.'

'Do I?'

'I'll get it anyway. My daughter will submit it. She'll be looking for plea bargain.'

'What does the A. A. stand for?'

'Excuse me?'

'Your initials.'

'Aleksei Alekseivitch. My family came from Russia. But a long time ago. Before the October Revolution.'

'What do people call you?'

'Alex, of course.'

Reacher stood up. 'Well, thanks for your time, Alex.'

'Are you going to see my daughter now?'

'Is there any point? You seem pretty sure of yourself.'

'I'm an officer of the court, and you're on a witness list,' he said. 'I'm obliged to point out that you're obliged to go. It's a matter of procedure.'

'Where is she?'

'In the glass tower you can see from the window.'

'OK,' Reacher said. 'I guess I could drop by.'

'I still need whatever information you have,' Rodin said.

Reacher shook his head. 'No,' he said. 'You really don't.'

He returned his visitor pass to the reception desk and headed back to the public plaza. Stood in the cold sun getting a sense of the place. All cities have colours. Some are grey. This one was brown. Reacher guessed the brick was made from local clay and had carried the colour of old farmland into the façades. It was a warm place, not busy, but it was surviving. There was progress and optimism. All the new construction proved it.

The new parking garage extension anchored the north end of the downtown strip. It was south and slightly west of the kill zone. Very close. Directly west and maybe twice as distant was a length of the raised highway. It curled in behind the library. Then it passed behind the black glass tower. The tower was due north of the plaza. It had an NBC sign near the door, on a black granite slab. Ann Yanni's workplace, Reacher guessed, as well as Rodin's daughter's. East of the plaza was the office building with the DMV and the recruiting office. That was where the victims had come from. They had hustled west across the plaza and had stumbled into a nightmare.

Reacher walked to the revolving door at the base of the tower. He went in and checked the lobby for a directory. NBC was on the first floor. LAW OFFICES OF HELEN RODIN was listed on three.

He waited for the elevator in a queue of two, him and a pretty blonde woman. She got out on one and he realised it was Ann Yanni. He recognised her from the broadcast.

He found Helen Rodin's suite. It was at the front of the building. Her windows were going to overlook the plaza. He knocked. Heard a muffled reply and went in. There was an empty reception room with an unoccupied secretary's desk. No secretary yet, Reacher thought. Early days.

He knocked on the inner office door. Heard the same voice make a second reply. He went in and found Helen Rodin. He recognised her from her father's photograph. But face to face she looked even better. She was probably no more than thirty, quite tall. Slim, in an athletic sort of a way. She had long blonde hair and her father's blue eyes. There was intelligence behind them. She was dressed all in black, in a trouser suit with a tight stretch top under the jacket.

'Hello,' she said.

'I'm Jack Reacher,' he said.

She stared at him. 'You're kidding. Are you really?'

He nodded. 'Always have been, always will be.'

'Unbelievable.'

'Not really. Everybody's somebody.'

'I mean, how did you know to come? We couldn't find you.'

'I saw it on the TV. Ann Yanni, Saturday morning.'

'Well, thank God for TV,' she said.

'I was in Miami,' he said. 'With a Norwegian dancer.'

He walked to the window and looked out. He was on the third floor and the main shopping street ran away directly south, down a hill, emphasising his elevation. The ornamental pool lined up with the street along its long axis. Beyond it and slightly to the right was the new parking structure. It was slightly downhill from the plaza. Maybe half a storey's difference.

'Were you here?' Reacher asked. 'When it happened?'

'Yes, I was,' Helen Rodin said, quietly.

'Did you see it?'

'Not at first. I heard the first three gunshots. They came very fast. The first, and then a tiny pause, and then the next two. Then another pause, a little longer, but just a split second, really. I stood up in time for the last three. Horrible.'

Reacher nodded. Brave girl, he thought. She hears gunshots, and she stands up. She doesn't dive under the desk. Then he thought: *The first, and then a tiny pause.* That was the sound of a skilled rifleman watching where his first cold shot went.

'Did you see people die?'

'Two of them,' she said behind him. 'It was awful.'

'Three shots and two people?'

'He missed once. Either the fourth or the fifth shot. They found the bullet in the pool. They drained it.'

Reacher said nothing.

'The bullet ties the rifle to the crime,' Helen said.

'Did you know any of the dead people?'

'No. They were just people, I guess. In the wrong place at the wrong time.'

Reacher said nothing.

'I saw flames from the gun,' Helen said. 'Over there.'

'Muzzle flashes,' Reacher said.

He turned back from the window. She held out her hand.

'I'm Helen Rodin,' she said. 'I'm sorry, I should have introduced myself properly.'

Reacher took her hand. It was warm and firm.

'Just Helen?' he said. 'Not Helena Alekseyovna or something?'

She stared at him again. 'How the hell did you know that?'

'I met your dad,' he said. 'In his office, just now.'

'Why did you go to *his* office? *I'm* representing James Barr. And you're a defence witness. You should have been talking to me, not him.'

Reacher said nothing.

'The case against James Barr is very strong.'

'How did you get my name?' Reacher asked.

'From James Barr, of course,' she said. 'How else?'

'From *Barr?* I don't believe it.'

She pressed a key on a cassette player on the desk. Reacher heard a voice he didn't recognise say: *Denying it is not an option.* Helen touched the pause key. 'His first lawyer,' she said. 'We changed representation yesterday.'

'How? He was in a coma yesterday.'

'Technically my client is James Barr's sister. His next of kin.'

She let go of the pause key and Reacher heard room sounds and then a voice he hadn't heard for fourteen years. It was exactly how he remembered it. It was low, and tense, and raspy. It was the voice of a man who rarely spoke. It said: *Get Jack Reacher for me.*

Reacher stood there, stunned.

Helen Rodin pressed the stop key. Then she checked her watch. 'Ten thirty,' she said. 'Stick around and join the client conference.'

SHE UNVEILED him like a conjurer on a stage. Like a rabbit out of a hat. First in was a guy Reacher immediately took for an ex-cop. He was introduced as Franklin, a freelance investigator.

'You're a hard man to find,' Franklin said.

'Wrong,' Reacher said. 'I'm an impossible man to find.'

'Want to tell me why?' There were instant questions in Franklin's eyes. Like, *How much use is this guy going to be as a witness? What is he? A fugitive? Will he have credibility on the stand?*

'Just a hobby,' Reacher said. 'Just a personal choice.'

Then a woman came in. She was in her mid- to late thirties, probably, dressed for an office, and stressed and sleepless. She looked like a kind and decent person. Even pretty. And she was clearly James Barr's sister. She had the same colouring and a softer, feminised version of the same face.

'I'm Rosemary Barr,' she said. 'I'm so glad you found us. It feels providential. Now we're getting somewhere.'

Reacher said nothing.

Helen Rodin's offices didn't run to a conference room. So all four people crowded into the inner office. Helen sat at her desk. Franklin perched on a corner of it. Reacher leaned on the windowsill. Rosemary Barr paced.

'OK,' Helen said. 'Defence strategy. At the minimum we want to pursue a medical plea. But we'll aim higher. How high we eventually get will depend on a number of factors. In which connection, I'm sure we all want to hear what Mr Reacher has to say.'

'I don't think you do,' Reacher said.

'Why wouldn't we?'

'Because you jumped to the wrong conclusion. I didn't come here to help James Barr.'

Nobody spoke.

'I came here to bury him,' Reacher said.

'But why?' Rosemary Barr asked.

'Because he's done this before. And once was enough.'

REACHER PROPPED his back against the window reveal and turned sideways so he could see the plaza. And so he couldn't see his audience.

'Is this a privileged conversation?' he asked.

'Yes,' Helen Rodin said. 'It is. It's a client conference. It's automatically protected. Nothing we say here can be repeated.'

'Is it ethical for you to hear bad news, legally?'

'Are you going to give evidence for the prosecution?' Helen Rodin asked.

'I don't think I'll have to. But I will if necessary.'

'Then we would hear the bad news anyway. We would take a deposition from you before the trial.'

'James Barr was a sniper,' Reacher said. 'Not the best the army had, and not the worst. Just a good, competent rifleman.'

Then he paused and looked out the window. At the new building with the recruitment office in it.

'Four types of people join the military,' he said. 'First, for people like me, it's a family trade. Second, there are patriots, eager to serve their country. Third, there are people who just need a job. And fourth, there are people who want to kill other people. The military is the only place where that's legal. James Barr was the fourth type. Deep down he thought it would be fun to kill.'

Rosemary Barr looked away. Nobody spoke.

'But he never got the chance,' Reacher said. 'I was a very thorough investigator when I was an MP, and I learned all about him. He trained for five years. I went through his log books. I counted a career total of nearly a quarter-million rounds fired, and not one of them at the enemy. He didn't go to Panama in 1989. We required only a small force, so most guys missed out. It burned him up. Then Desert Shield happened in 1990. He went to Saudi. But he wasn't in Desert Storm in 1991. James Barr sat it out in Saudi, cleaning sand out of his rifle. Then after Desert Storm was over, they sent him to Kuwait City for the cleanup.'

'What happened there?' Rosemary Barr asked.

'He snapped,' Reacher said. 'That's what happened there. The Soviets had collapsed. Iraq was back in its box. He looked ahead and saw that war was over. He had trained nearly six years and had never fired his gun in anger and was never going to. A lot of his training had been about visualisation. About seeing himself putting the graticule on the medulla oblongata, where the spinal cord broadens at the base of the brain. About breathing slow and squeezing the trigger. About the split-second pause while the bullet flies. About seeing the puff of pink mist from the back of the head. He had visualised all of that. Many times. But he had never seen it. And he wanted to.'

Silence in the room.

'So he went out in Kuwait City one day, alone,' Reacher said. 'He set up and waited. Then he shot dead four people coming out of an apartment building.'

Helen Rodin was staring at him.

'He fired from the first floor of a parking garage,' Reacher said. 'It was opposite the apartment building's door. The victims were American non-coms, in street clothes.'

'This can't be true,' Rosemary Barr said. 'He wouldn't do it. And if he did, he'd have gone to prison. But he got an honourable discharge instead. And a campaign medal. So it can't have happened.'

'That's why I'm here,' Reacher said. 'There was a serious problem. I followed the trail all the way to your brother. But it was a very tough trail. We took all kinds of wrong turns. And along one of them we found stuff out about the four dead guys. They had been doing things they shouldn't have.'

'What things?' Helen Rodin asked.

'Kuwait City was a hell of a place. Full of rich Arabs. Even the poor ones had Rolexes and Rolls-Royces, and marble bathrooms with solid gold taps. A lot of them had fled temporarily. But they had left all their stuff behind. And some of them had left their families behind. Their wives and daughters.'

'And?'

'Our four dead noncoms had been doing the conquering army thing, just like the Iraqis before them. That's how they saw it, I guess. We saw it as rape and armed robbery. And we found enough loot in their footlockers to start another branch of Tiffany's.'

'So what happened?'

'It got political, inevitably. It went up the chain of command. The Gulf was supposed to be a hundred per cent squeaky clean. And the Kuwaitis were our allies. So ultimately we were told to cover for the four guys. We were told to bury the story. Which also meant letting James Barr walk. If we took Barr to trial, his lawyer would have countered with a justifiable homicide claim. He would have said Barr had been standing up for the honour of the army, in a rough-and-ready sort of a way. All the beans would have spilled in the process. We were told not to risk that.'

'Maybe it *was* justifiable homicide,' Rosemary Barr said. 'Maybe James really did know all along.'

'Ma'am, he didn't know. He was never near any of those guys before. He was just killing people. For fun. He confessed to that, to me personally.'

Silence in the room.

'So we said his four guys had been killed by Palestinians, which was plausible in Kuwait City in 1991. James Barr got away with murder. So I went to see him before he left and I told him to justify his great good fortune by never stepping out of line again, not ever, the whole rest of his life. I told him if he ever did, I would come find him and make him sorry.'

Silence in the room. It lasted minutes.

'So here I am,' Reacher said.

'This must be classified information,' Helen Rodin said.

'Highly classified. It's sealed inside the Pentagon. That's why I asked if this conversation was privileged.'

'You'd get in big trouble if you talked about it.'

'I've been in big trouble before. I came here to find out if I needed to get in big trouble again. As it happens, I don't think I do. But my help is always available if your father needs it.'

Then Helen understood. 'You're here to pressure me, aren't you?' she said.

'I'm here to keep my promise,' Reacher said. 'To James Barr.'

HE LEFT THEM there, three silent and disappointed people. Then he rode down in the elevator, got out in the lobby and headed for the door.

He stood for a moment in the plaza. Deciding. James Barr's medical condition was the complicating factor. He didn't want to stick around until the guy woke up. It might take weeks. And Reacher was not a guy who liked to stick around. Two days in one place was about his limit. But he was stuck for alternatives. He couldn't hint at anything to Alex Rodin. Alex Rodin would make the link to the Pentagon easily enough. Reacher had even asked *Did she get my name from the Pentagon?* That had been a careless mistake. Alex Rodin would put two and two together, eventually. The Pentagon would stonewall him, of course. But Rodin wouldn't like being stonewalled. He wouldn't give up on it.

And Reacher didn't want the story out there. Not unless it was absolutely necessary. Gulf War vets had it hard enough, with the chemical stuff and the uranium poisoning. And it had been a good army.

So he decided to stick around for twenty-four hours. Maybe there would be a clearer prognosis on Barr's condition. Maybe somehow he could check with Emerson and get a better feel for the evidence. Then maybe he could feel OK about leaving things with Alex Rodin's office. If there were problems down the road maybe he would read about them in a newspaper somewhere, and then he could come all the way back again.

So, twenty-four hours in a small heartland city.

He decided to go see if there was a river.

There was a river. It was a broad, slow body of water that moved west to east through an area south of downtown. Some tributary that fed the mighty Ohio, he guessed. Its north bank was straightened and strengthened with massive stone blocks along a 300-yard stretch. They were immaculately chiselled and expertly fitted. They made a quayside. A wharf. They had tall, fat iron mushrooms set into them, to tie off ropes. Stone paving slabs made the wharf thirty feet deep. All along its length were tall wooden sheds, open on the river side, open on the street side. The street was made of cobbles. A hundred years ago there would have been huge river barges tied up and unloading. There would have been horses and carts clattering on the cobbles. But now there was just stillness, and the slow drift of the water. Scabs of rust on the iron mushrooms, clumps of weeds between the stones.

Reacher strolled the 300 yards and looked at the sheds. They were ripe for renovation, he guessed. It was inevitable. There was construction all over town. They would spruce up the waterfront. They would give someone tax breaks to open a riverside café. Maybe a bar. Maybe with live music.

He turned to walk back and came face-to-face with Helen Rodin. She was carrying a briefcase. 'You're not such a hard man to find,' she said.

'Evidently,' he said.

'Tourists always come to the docks,' she said. 'Can I buy you lunch?'

SHE WALKED HIM back north to the edge of the new gentrification, and led him into an eatery. It was the kind of place he usually avoided. White walls, some exposed brick, weird salad combinations.

She led him to a table in the far back corner. An energetic kid came by with menus. Helen Rodin ordered something with oranges and walnuts and Gorgonzola cheese. With a cup of herbal tea. Reacher gave up on reading his menu and ordered the same thing, but with coffee, regular, black.

'I need you to explain something,' Helen said.

She opened her briefcase. Came out with the old tape player. Pressed play. Reacher heard Barr say: *Get Jack Reacher for me.*

'You already played that for me,' he said.

'But why would he say it?' Helen asked.

'That's what you want me to explain?'

She nodded.

'I can't,' he said.

'Could he have been in any doubt about how you felt? Fourteen years ago?'

'I don't think so. I made myself pretty clear.'

The food came, and they started eating. The salad wasn't too bad. And the coffee was OK.

'Play me the whole tape,' he said.

She put her fork down and pressed the rewind key. She had long fingers. No rings. Polished nails. She pressed play. Reacher heard a door open and the thump of a man sitting down. The lawyer started talking. He was old and bored. He didn't want to be there. He knew Barr was guilty. Grew frustrated with Barr's silence. Then he said, full of exasperation: *I can't help you if you won't help yourself.* Then Barr's voice came through: *They got the wrong guy.* He said it again. Then the lawyer started up again, not believing him, saying the evidence was all there. Then Barr asked for Reacher, twice, and the lawyer asked if Reacher was a doctor. Then Barr got up and hammered on the door.

Helen Rodin pressed the stop key. 'So why?' she asked. 'Why say he didn't do it and then call for a guy who knows for sure he did it before?'

Reacher just shrugged his shoulders.

'You know something,' she said. 'Maybe you don't know you know it. But there's got to be something there. Something he thinks can help him.'

'Does it matter? He's in coma. He might never wake up.'

'It matters a lot. He could get better treatment.'

'I don't know anything.'

'Did he claim insanity back then?'

'No, he claimed a perfect score. Four for four.'

'Did you think he was nuts?'

'That's a big word. Was it nuts to shoot four people for fun? Of course. Was *he* nuts, legally? I'm sure he wasn't.'

'You must know something, Reacher,' Helen said.

'Have you actually seen the evidence?' he asked.

'I've seen a summary. It's terrible. There's no question he did it. This is about mitigation, nothing more. And his state of mind.'

'So wait until he wakes up. Run some tests.'

'They won't count. He could wake up like a fruitcake and the prosecution will say that was caused by the blow to the head in the jailhouse fight. They'll say he was perfectly sane at the time of the crime.'

'Is your dad a fair man?'

'He lives to win.'

'Like father, like daughter?'

She paused. 'Somewhat,' she said.

Reacher finished his salad. Chased the last walnut around with his fork and then gave up and used his fingers instead.

'What's on your mind?' Helen asked.

'Just a minor detail,' he said. 'Fourteen years ago it was a very tough case with barely adequate forensics. And he confessed. This time the forensics seem to be a total slam dunk. But he's denying it.'

'What does that mean?'

'I don't know.'

'May I ask you a personal question?' Helen Rodin said.

'Depends how personal,' Reacher said.

'Why were you so untraceable? Normally Franklin can find anyone.'

'I was in the machine,' Reacher said. 'My whole life. Then the machine coughed and spat me out. So I thought, OK, if I'm out, I'm all the way out. I was angry and it was probably an immature reaction. But I got used to it.'

'Like a game?'

'Like an addiction,' Reacher said.

The kid brought the bill. Helen Rodin paid. She and Reacher left together. They walked north. She was heading to her office and he was going to look for a hotel.

A man called Grigor Linsky watched them walk. He was slumped low in a car parked at the kerb. He knew where to wait. He knew where she ate when she had company.

CHAPTER THREE

Reacher checked into a downtown hotel called the Metropole Palace, two blocks east of First Street. He paid cash up front for one night only and used the name Jimmy Reese. He had cycled through all the presidents and vice presidents long ago and was now using second basemen from the Yankees' nonchampionship years. Jimmy Reese had played pretty well during part of 1930 and pretty badly during part of 1931. He had died in California, age ninety-two. But now he was back, with a single room and a bath in the Metropole Palace, for one night only.

The Metropole was a half-empty, faded old place. But it had once been grand. Reacher could see that. His room was old-fashioned and gloomy. The mattress felt like a part of the original inventory.

He lay down on it and put his hands behind his head. Thought back more than fourteen years to Kuwait City. All cities have colours, and KC was white. White stucco, white-painted concrete, white marble. Skies burnt white by the sun. Because of the glare, the four dead guys had all been wearing aviator shades. All four men had been hit in the head, but none of the shades had broken. They had just fallen off. All four bullets had been recovered, and they broke the case. They were an American sniper's bullets, either army or Marines. If Barr had used a regular battle rifle or a submachine gun Reacher would have got nowhere. Because every firearm in theatre except the sniper rifles used standard NATO rounds, which would have cast the net way too wide. But Barr's whole purpose had been to use his own specialist weapon, this time for real. And in so doing, his four thirteen-cent bullets had nailed him.

But it had been a tough case. Maybe Reacher's finest ever. At the end of the trail was James Barr, a man who had finally seen the pink mist and was strangely at peace with his capture.

He had confessed. The confession was voluntary, fast and complete. Then Barr asked questions about the investigation like he was fascinated by the process. Clearly he had not expected to be caught. He was simultaneously aggrieved and admiring.

Fourteen years later he had not confessed.

There was another difference between this time and the last time, too. But Reacher couldn't pin it down.

GRIGOR LINSKY used his cellphone and called the Zec. The Zec was the man he worked for. It wasn't just Zec. It was *the* Zec. It was a question of respect. The Zec was eighty years old, but he still broke arms if he smelled disrespect. He still had his strength and his attitude. He was eighty years old *because* of his strength and his attitude. Without them he would have died at twenty. Or later, at thirty, which was about when he went insane and his real name finally slipped his mind.

'The lawyer went back to her office,' Linsky said. 'Reacher turned east off First Street. I laid back and didn't follow him. But he turned away from the bus depot. My guess is he checked into the Metropole Palace.'

The Zec made no reply.

'Should we do anything?' Linsky asked.

'We should distract him,' the Zec said. 'Or discourage him. I'm told he was a soldier. Therefore he will probably maintain a predictable pattern of behaviour. If he's at the Metropole, he won't stay in tonight. He'll go out somewhere. Probably alone. So there could be an incident. Don't use our own people. And make it look natural.'

'Damage?'

'Broken bones. Maybe he gets a head injury. Maybe he winds up in the coma ward along with his buddy James Barr.'

HELEN RODIN spent an hour at her desk. She took three calls. The first was from Franklin. He was bailing out.

'I'm sorry, but you're going to lose,' the investigator said. 'And I've got a business to run. I can't put in unbilled hours on this any more.'

'Nobody likes hopeless cases,' Helen said, diplomatically. 'If I get a budget, will you come back on board?'

'Sure,' Franklin said. 'Just call me.'

The next call was from her father, who sounded full of concern.

'You shouldn't have taken this case,' he said.

'It wasn't like I was spoilt for choice,' Helen said.

'Losing might be winning, if you know what I mean.'

'Did you ever set out to lose a case?' she asked.

Her father said nothing. Then he went fishing. 'Did Jack Reacher find you?' he asked, meaning: *Should I be worried?*

'He found me,' she said, keeping her voice light.

'Well, should we discuss it?' Meaning: *Please, tell me.*

'I'm sure we will soon. When the time is right.'

They arranged to meet for dinner that night. Then they hung up. Helen smiled. She hadn't lied. Hadn't even bluffed. But she felt she had participated. The law was a game, and like any game it had a psychological component.

The third call was from Rosemary Barr at the hospital.

'James is waking up,' she said.

'Is he talking?'

'The doctors say he might be tomorrow.'

AN HOUR LATER Reacher left the Metropole. He headed north towards the off-brand stores he had seen near the courthouse. He wanted clothes. Something local. Something more appropriate than his Miami gear.

He bought a pair of pants that the label called taupe and he called olive drab. He found a flannel shirt almost the same colour. Plus underwear. And a pair of socks. He changed in the cubicle and threw his old stuff away in the store's own trash bin.

He came out and walked west towards the afternoon sun. The shirt was too thick for the weather, but he figured he might go to Seattle next. It would be fine for Seattle.

He came out into the plaza and saw that the fountain had been restarted. He picked his way among the flowers and sat on the low wall, with the parking garage in front of him. He looked to his left and watched the DMV building's door. Looked to the right and watched the cars on the raised highway. Traffic up there was light, even though First Street itself was already building up to the afternoon rush home. Then he looked to his left again and saw Helen Rodin sitting down beside him. She was out of breath.

'I ran all the way down, hoping you wouldn't wander off. That was a half-hour after calling all the hotels in town and being told you aren't registered anywhere. James Barr is waking up. He might be talking tomorrow.'

'Or he might not.'

'I want you to be my evidence analyst,' she said.

'You've got Franklin for that.'

She shook her head. 'Franklin's too close to his old PD buddies. He won't be critical enough.'

'And I will? I want Barr to go down, remember.'

'Exactly. You want to confirm that they've got an unbreakable case. Then you can leave town and be happy.'

'Franklin quit, didn't he?'

She paused, and then she nodded. 'I'm doing it pro bono. But Franklin's got a business to run.'

'So he won't do it for free, but I will?'

'You *need* to do it. You're a perfectionist. You want to be able to leave town knowing everything is buttoned down tight, by your own standards.'

Reacher said nothing.

'This gets you a real good look,' she said.

A real good look. Leave town and be happy.

'OK,' Reacher said.

She pointed. 'Walk four blocks west and one block south. The PD is right there. I'll go upstairs and call Emerson.'

'We're doing this now?'

'James Barr is waking up. I need this stuff out of the way early. I'm going to be spending tomorrow finding a psychiatrist who will work for free. A medical plea is still our best bet.'

Reacher walked four blocks west and one block south. It took him under the raised highway and brought him to a corner. The police department had the whole block. The building was made of glazed tan brick.

He found Emerson waiting for him behind his desk. Reacher recognised him from his TV spot on Saturday morning. Same guy, pale, quiet, competent, not big, not small. In person he looked like he had been a cop since birth. It was in his pores.

'Welcome to Indiana,' he said.

Reacher said nothing.

'I mean it,' Emerson said. 'Really. We love it when old friends of the accused show up to tear our work to shreds.'

'I'm here for his lawyer,' Reacher said. 'Not as a friend.'

Emerson nodded. 'I'll give you the background myself,' he said. 'Then my crime-scene guy will walk you through the particulars.'

Reacher smiled. The way Emerson spoke told him things. It told him that this was a guy secretly happy to meet with a critic. Because he knew for sure he had a solid gold slam-dunk case.

'You knew James Barr pretty well, am I right?' Emerson asked.

'Did you?' Reacher asked back.

Emerson shook his head. 'Never met him. There were no warning signs.'

'Was his rifle legal?'

Emerson nodded. 'It was registered and unmodified.'

'I spoke with Alex Rodin,' Reacher said. 'He's impressed.'

'He should be. We performed well. Your old buddy was toast six hours after the first shot. It was a textbook case, beginning to end.'

'So is there any point in me walking through it?'

'Sure. I've got a crime-scene guy desperate to show off.'

Emerson walked Reacher to the lab and introduced him as a lawyer's scout, not as James Barr's friend. Which helped a little with the atmosphere. Then he gave Reacher a card with his numbers on it and left him there. The crime-scene guy was a serious forty-year-old called Bellantonio. He was tall, dark, thin and stooped. And he suspected that James Barr was going to plead guilty. He thought he wasn't going to get his day in court. That was clear. He had laid out the evidence in a logical sequence on long tables in a sealed police garage bay, just so that he could give visitors the performance he would never give a jury.

The tables ran all the way round the perimeter of the bay. Above them was a horizontal line of cork boards with hundreds of printed sheets of paper pinned to them. Trapped tight in the square made by the tables was James Barr's beige Dodge Caravan.

Bellantonio started with the traffic cone. Barr had handled it, that was for sure. There were fingerprints and palm prints. There were way more comparison points than any court would demand.

Same for the quarter from the parking meter, same for the shell case. Bellantonio showed Reacher laser-printed stills from the parking garage video, showing the minivan coming in just before the event and going out again just after it. He showed him the interior of the Dodge, showed him the automotive carpet fibres recovered from the raw new concrete, showed him the denim fibres and the raincoat threads. Showed him a square of rug taken from Barr's house, showed him the matching fibres found at the scene. Showed him the desert boots. Showed him the cement dust tracked back into Barr's house and recovered from the garage and the basement and the kitchen and the living room and the bedroom. Showed him a comparison sample taken from the parking garage and a lab report that proved it was the same.

Reacher scanned the transcripts from the 911 calls and the radio chatter between the squad cars. Then he glanced through the crime-scene protocol. The initial sweep by the uniformed officers, the forensic examination by Bellantonio's own people, Emerson's inspiration with the parking meter. Then he read the arrest report. The SWAT tactics, the sleeping suspect, the ID from the wallet in the trouser pocket. The clothes in the closet. The shoes. The guns in the basement. He read the witness reports. A Marine recruiter had heard six shots. A cellphone company had provided a recording. There was a graph attached. A grey smear of sound, with six sharp spikes. *One, two-three, pause, four-five-six.*

Reacher looked at the rifle. It was heat-sealed into a clear plastic sleeve. He read the report pinned above it. A Springfield M1A Super Match, ten-shot box magazine, four cartridges still in it. Barr's prints all over it.

Scratches on the forestock matching varnish scrapings found at the scene. The intact bullet recovered from the pool. A ballistics lab report matching the bullet to the barrel. Another report matching the shell case to the ejector. Case closed.

'It's good, isn't it?' Bellantonio said.

'Best I ever saw,' Reacher said.

'Better than a hundred eyewitnesses.'

Reacher smiled. Crime scene techs loved to say that.

'Anything you're not happy with?' he asked.

'I love it all.'

'Why did he leave the traffic cone behind? And why did he pay to park?'

'I'm forensics,' Bellantonio said. 'Not psychology.'

Then Emerson came back in and stood there, waiting to accept Reacher's surrender. Reacher gave it up, no hesitation. He shook their hands and congratulated them on a well-worked case.

He walked back under the raised highway, heading for the black glass tower. He went in past the NBC sign and rode up in the elevator.

He found Helen Rodin at her secondhand desk.

'Pick your own cliché,' he said. 'It's a cast-iron, solid-gold slam dunk.'

She said nothing.

'See any doubt in my eyes?' he asked.

'No,' she said. 'I don't.'

'So start calling psychiatrists. If that's what you really want to do.'

'He deserves representation, Reacher.'

Reacher nodded. 'The shrink should think about the parking meter. I mean, who pays for ten minutes even if they're *not* shooting people? It strikes me as weird. It's so law-abiding, isn't it? Maybe he really was nuts this time. You know, confused about what he was doing.'

Helen Rodin made a note. 'I'll be sure to mention it.'

'You want to get some dinner?'

She shook her head. 'I'm having dinner with my father.'

Reacher said nothing.

'Maybe we could have a drink after dinner,' she said. 'There's a sports bar six blocks north of here. Monday night, it's about the only place in town. I'll drop by and see if you're there. But I can't promise anything.'

'Neither can I,' Reacher said.

REACHER WENT to the sports bar after a shower at the Metropole Palace. The bar was in a plain square building that could have started out as anything. Maybe a feed store, maybe an automobile showroom, maybe a pool hall.

Inside it was like every other sports bar he had ever been in. It was one tall room with black-painted air-conditioning ducts pinned to the ceiling. It had three dozen TV screens hanging from the walls and the roof. It had all the usual sports-bar stuff all over the place. The TVs were all tuned to football. Inevitable, Reacher guessed, on a Monday night. There were plenty of people in there, but Reacher got a table to himself. A hard-worked waitress ran over to him and he ordered beer and a cheeseburger.

He ate his meal and drank his beer and watched the game. He sat there in a bubble of quiet, with a message plainly displayed: *Stay away from me.*

Then someone ignored the message. It was partly his own fault. He looked away from the screen and saw a girl juggling a bottle of beer and a full plate of tacos. She was quite a sight. She had waved red hair and a red gingham shirt open at the neck and tied off at the navel. She had tight jeans on that looked like denim but had to be spandex. She had the whole hourglass thing going, big-time. Reacher looked at her for a second too long, and she took it as an invitation.

'Can I share your table?' she asked from a yard away.

'Help yourself,' he said.

She sat down in the chair next to him. 'Thanks,' she said. She drank from her bottle and kept her eyes on him. Green eyes, bright, wide open. She leaned close because of the noise. 'Do you like it?'

'Like what?' he said.

'Football,' she said.

'A bit,' he said.

'I'm Sandy,' she said. 'What's your name?'

'Jimmy Reese,' he said.

He saw a flash of surprise in her eyes. He didn't know why. Maybe she had a boyfriend called Jimmy Reese. Or maybe she was a serious fan of the New York Yankees.

'I'm pleased to meet you, Jimmy Reese,' she said.

'Likewise,' he said, and turned back to the game.

'I was wondering,' she said. 'If you only like football a bit, maybe you would like to take me somewhere else. Somewhere quieter.'

He said nothing.

'I've got a car,' she said.

'You old enough to drive?'

'I'm old enough to do lots of things. And I'm pretty good at some of them.'

Reacher said nothing. She pushed her chair out from the table a little way. Turned towards him and looked down.

'Do you like these pants?' she asked.

'I think they suit you very well.'

'They're too tight to wear anything underneath.'

'We all have our cross to bear.'

'Imagine peeling them off.'

'I can't. I doubt if I would have gotten them on.'

The green eyes narrowed. 'Are you a queer?'

'Are you a hooker?'

'No *way*. I work at the auto parts store.'

Then she paused and seemed to reconsider. She came up with a better answer. Which was to jump up from her chair and scream and slap his face.

'He called me a *whore*,' she screamed. 'He called me a damn *whore*!'

Five guys stood up fast. Big guys, in jeans and work boots and plaid shirts. Country boys.

The girl smiled in triumph. 'Those are my brothers,' she said.

Reacher said nothing.

Rule one: Be on your feet and ready.

Rule two: Show them who you're messing with.

Reacher stood up, slow and easy. Six five, 250 pounds, calm eyes, hands held loose by his sides.

Rule three: Identify the ringleader.

There were five guys. Any five guys will have one ringleader, two enthusiastic followers, and two reluctant followers. Put the ringleader down, and both of the keen sidekicks, and it's over. The reluctant pair just run for it.

Rule four: The ringleader is the one who moves first.

A big corn-fed twenty-something with a shock of yellow hair and a round red face moved first. He stepped forward a pace and the others fell in behind him. Reacher stepped forward a pace of his own to meet them.

Because rule five: Never back off.

'Outside,' the big guy said.

'OK,' Reacher said.

The big guy turned round and shooed the others towards the door. The girl called Sandy tagged after them. Reacher put twenty dollars on his table and followed the blue Spandex pants.

They were all waiting for him on the sidewalk, all tensed up in a shallow semicircle. The street was empty. The big guy was round and smooth and heavy, like a bull seal. Maybe ten years out of high school. An unbroken nose, no misshapen knuckles. Not a boxer. Probably just a linebacker. So he would fight like a wrestler. He would start by charging. Head low.

That was Reacher's best guess. And Reacher was right.

The big guy charged, head low, and Reacher turned slightly sideways and bent his knees a little and drove all his weight up and forward off his back foot and through his shoulder straight into the big guy's face.

Kinetic energy is a wonderful thing.

Reacher had hardly moved at all but the big guy bounced off crazily, stunned. Reacher kicked him in the groin, but left-footed. Right-footed, he would have popped bits of the guy's pelvis out through his nose. *Your big soft heart,* an old army instructor had said. *One day it'll get you killed.* But not today, Reacher thought. The big guy went down. He fell on his knees and pitched forward on his face.

Then it got real easy. The next two guys came in together, and Reacher dropped the first with a head butt and the second with an elbow to the jaw. Then it was over, because the last two guys ran. The girl called Sandy ran after them. Reacher turned back and checked her three downed brothers' wallets. Then he turned round because he heard a car pull up behind him.

It was a taxi. It was a taxi with Helen Rodin getting out of it.

She threw a bill at the driver and he took off fast. Helen Rodin stood on the sidewalk and stared at the three inert forms on the ground behind him.

'What the hell is going on?' she asked.

'Let's walk,' Reacher said.

They walked south, fast, and turned a corner and went east. Then south again. Then they slowed a little.

'What happened back there?'

'I was in the bar watching the game, minding my own business. Then some red-haired bimbo started coming on to me. I wasn't playing and she got it to where she found a reason to slap me. Then five guys jumped up. She said they were her brothers. We took it outside.'

'What had you said to her?'

'Doesn't matter what I said to her. It was a set-up.'

'I need a drink,' Helen Rodin said.

'We can't go back there. They probably called the cops. Let's try my hotel,' he said.

They walked together in silence, through quiet, dark streets.

'How was dinner?' Reacher asked.

'My father was fishing. He still thinks you're my witness.'

'Did you tell him?'

'I can't tell him. Your information is classified, thank God. Are you leaving tomorrow?'

'You bet I am. This place is weird.'

'Some girl comes on to you. Why does it have to be a big conspiracy?'

'It was a set-up, Helen. Those guys weren't her brothers. I checked their licences. They all had different last names.'

'Oh.'

'So it was all staged. But why pick on me? They must have known they were going to get their butts kicked.'

'There were five of them. Five guys never think one guy could kick their butts. Especially not in Indiana.'

'Or maybe I was the only stranger at the bar.'

Helen looked ahead, down the street. 'You're at the Metropole Palace?'

He nodded. 'Me and not too many other people.'

'But I called and they said you weren't registered.'

'I use aliases in hotels.'

'Why on earth?'

'Just a bad habit. Like I told you.'

They went up the front steps together. The lobby was deserted. There was a bar in a side room. It was empty, except for a lone barman.

'Beer,' Helen Rodin said.

'Two,' Reacher said.

They took a table near a curtained window and the guy brought two beers in bottles, two napkins, two chilled glasses and a bowl of mixed nuts.

'So who does the Metropole think you are?'

'Jimmy Reese,' Reacher said.

A flash of surprise in her eyes. He didn't know why.

I'm pleased to meet you, Jimmy Reese.

'The girl was looking for me personally,' he said. 'She wasn't looking for some random lone stranger. She was looking for Jack Reacher specifically.'

'She was?'

He nodded. 'She asked my name. I said Jimmy Reese. It knocked her off balance for a second. Like, *You're not Jimmy Reese, you're Jack Reacher, someone just told me.* She paused, then she recovered, fast. Jack Reacher was supposed to get worked over, and she was going to make sure it happened.'

'So who were they?'

'Who knows my name?'

'The police department. Were they *cops*? Protecting their case?'

'I'm not here to attack their case. It's solid gold.'

'Who else has an interest?'

'Rosemary Barr. And she knows why I'm here.'

'That's ridiculous,' Helen said. 'Rosemary Barr is a mousy little legal secretary. She wouldn't try a thing like that. She wouldn't know *how*. And remember, James Barr *asked* for you. He *wanted* you there. Therefore his sister wants you there, too. It's in her best interests to have you here, alive and well and thinking.'

Reacher took a long pull on his beer and nodded.

Helen took a pen from her purse and wrote something on her cocktail napkin. Slid it across the table.

'My cellphone number,' she said. 'You might need it.'

'I don't think anyone will sue me.'

'I'm not worried about you getting sued. I'm worried about you getting arrested. Those three boys went to the hospital, that's for sure. And the girl definitely knows your alias now. So you might be in trouble. If you are, listen to the Miranda and then call me.'

Reacher picked up the napkin. 'Thanks.'

'Are you still going to leave tomorrow?'

'Maybe. Or maybe I'll stick around and think about why someone would use violence to protect a case that's already a hundred per cent watertight.'

GRIGOR LINSKY called the Zec on his cellphone from his car.

'They failed,' he said. 'I'm very sorry.'

The Zec said nothing, which was worse than a tirade.

'They won't be traced to us,' Linsky said. 'No harm, no foul.'

'Unless it served merely to provoke the soldier,' the Zec said. 'Then there would be harm. He is James Barr's friend, after all. A little additional pressure might help. But after that, don't let him see you again.'

REACHER SAW Helen Rodin into a cab, then went upstairs to his room, stretched out on the bed. Questions. There were a lot of questions, but as always the key would be finding the fundamental question. First question: *Was* the case already watertight?

Yes, it was. It was as close to a certainty as human life offers.

But that wasn't the fundamental question.

Helen Rodin's cassette tape was the fundamental question. James Barr's voice, hoarse, frustrated. *Get Jack Reacher for me.* Why would he say that?

Who was Jack Reacher, in James Barr's eyes?

That was the basic question.

Jack Reacher stared at his hotel room ceiling. Five minutes. Ten. Twenty. Then he pulled the cocktail napkin out of his back pocket and dialled the phone. Helen Rodin answered after eight rings. She sounded sleepy.

'It's Reacher,' he said. 'What was the weather like last Friday at five?'

'The weather? Friday? It was kind of dull. Cloudy.'

'Is that normal?'

'No, not really. It's usually sunny. Or else raining. This time of year it's usually one or the other. More likely sunny.'

'Was it warm or cold?'

'Not cold. But not *hot*. It was comfortable, I guess.'

'Have you got a car?'

'A car? Yes, I've got a car. But I use the bus for work.'

'Use your car tomorrow. I'll meet you at eight o'clock in your office.'

'What's this about?'

'Tomorrow,' he said. 'Eight o'clock. Go back to sleep now.'

REACHER WOKE at six and went out for breakfast. He found a working man's diner with a basic menu. He drank coffee and ate eggs. He sat at a window and watched the street. Because if he had been followed the night before it was logical to assume he would be followed again. But he saw nobody.

Then he walked the length of First Street, north. He sat for a moment on the NBC monolith, with his back to the tower, like a guy who was wasting time because he was early. Which he was. It was only 7.45. Reacher looked first at men on their own with newspapers. That was a pretty traditional surveillance cover. Although in his opinion it was due for replacement with a new exiled-smoker cover. Guys standing near doorways and smoking were the new invisibles. Or guys on cellphones.

He settled on a guy who was smoking *and* talking on a cellphone. He was a short man of about sixty. There was a permanent lopsided tension in the way he held himself. An old spinal injury, maybe. He was in a double-breasted suit that had been expensively tailored, but not in the United States. It was square and boxy, too heavy for the weather. Polish, maybe. Or Hungarian. Eastern European, certainly. He had thin grey hair and his eyes were dark. They didn't glance Reacher's way, even once.

Reacher checked his watch: 7.55. He slid off the shiny granite and walked into the tower's lobby.

GRIGOR LINSKY stopped pretending and dialled an actual number on his phone.

'He's here,' he said. 'He just went up.'

'Did he see you?' the Zec asked.

'Yes, I'm sure he did.'

'So make that the last time. Now you stay in the shadows.'

REACHER FOUND Helen Rodin already at her desk. She was in the same black suit, but her shirt was different. It was china blue and matched her eyes. Her hair was tied back in a long pony tail. Her desk was covered with legal books. She had about eight pages of notes going, on a yellow legal pad.

'James Barr is conscious,' she said. 'Rosemary called me.'

'Is he talking?'

'Only to the doctors. They won't let anyone else near him yet.'

'What about the cops?'

'They're waiting. But I'll need to be there first. I can't let him talk to the cops without representation.'

'What is he saying to the doctors?'

'That he doesn't know why he's there. That he doesn't remember anything about Friday. The doctors say that's to be expected.'

'Where does that leave you?'

'With two big problems. First, he might be faking the amnesia. So I'm going to have to find a specialist opinion on *that*, too. And if he isn't faking, we're in a real grey area. If he's sane now, and he was sane before, but he's missing a week, then how can he get a fair trial? He won't be able to participate in his own defence. And the state let him get hurt. It was their jail. They can't do that and then go ahead and try him.'

'What's your father going to think?'

'He's going to fight it tooth and nail. No prosecutor can afford to admit the possibility that amnesia might screw up a trial. Otherwise everyone would be looking to get beat up in pretrial detention.' Helen looked straight at Reacher. 'When you called me last night I thought you were going to walk in here this morning and tell me he's innocent.'

'Dream on,' Reacher said.

She looked away.

'But,' he said.

She looked back. 'There's a but?'

Reacher nodded. 'He's not quite as guilty as I thought he was.'

'How?'

'Get your car and I'll show you.'

They rode down together to a tenants-only underground parking garage. There were NBC broadcast trucks in there and cars and pick-ups and SUVs of various makes. There was a new blue Mustang convertible with an NBC sticker in the windshield. Ann Yanni's, probably, Reacher thought.

Helen Rodin's ride was a small dark-green Saturn sedan, not new.

'Where are we going?' Helen asked.

'South,' Reacher said. He racked his seat back and crunched a lot of stuff in the footwell behind him.

'What do you know?' she asked.

'It's not what I know. It's what James Barr knows. About me.'

She came up out of the garage and started south. The rush-hour traffic was still heavy.

'Barr knew you as an investigator who broke a tough case.'

'A case he thought couldn't be broken. He watched me do it every step of the way. He thought I was an investigative genius.'

'That's why he wanted you here?'

Reacher nodded. 'I spent last night trying to live up to his opinion.'

They crossed the river, on a long iron trestle.

'Go west now,' Reacher said.

She made a right and took a two-lane county road.

'There's more to this case than Emerson saw,' he said. 'Barr wanted someone else to understand that. But his first lawyer wasn't interested.'

'So why didn't he just lay out the facts?'

'Because he couldn't. And because nobody would have believed him.'

There was a highway cloverleaf ahead.

'Take the highway north.'

She powered the little car through the ramp and merged with the traffic flowing north. The city centre was ahead, on the right. The highway rose gently on its stilts.

'Be ready to take the spur that runs behind the library,' Reacher said.

It was going to be a right exit. They passed onto the spur. Reacher checked the rear window. Nobody behind them. Two hundred yards ahead the spur started to curve, behind the library, behind the black glass tower. Traffic engineers had marked out a single lane through the curve. It was a little wider than a normal lane, to allow for misjudgments.

'Go real slow now,' Reacher said.

The car slowed. Way up ahead of them on the left was a crescent-moon shape of white cross-hatching. Right next to them on the right was a long thin triangle of white cross-hatching.

'Pull over,' Reacher said. 'Here, on the right. Like you had a flat.'

Helen braked and steered onto the cross-hatched no-man's-land on their right. She stopped.

'Back up a yard,' Reacher said.

She drove back a yard. Reacher wound his window down. They sat for a whole minute before anyone else came the way they had taken.

'Not busy,' Reacher said.

'It never is,' Helen said.

The highway was raised up on tall stilts. The roadbed was maybe forty feet above ground level. The parapet wall was three feet high. Beyond it, ahead and to their right, was the upper storey of the library building. It felt close enough to touch. Reacher pointed with his thumb and then leaned back so Helen could see across him. Directly to their right was an unobstructed view down into the plaza, with a straight line of sight along the narrow bottleneck between the end of the ornamental pool and the plaza wall. And beyond it was the door of the DMV office.

'James Barr was a sniper,' Reacher said. 'Not the best, not the worst, but he trained for more than five years.'

'I don't understand.'

'*This* is where a trained sniper would have fired from. Because from here he's got his targets walking directly towards him in a straight line. Single file, into a bottleneck. He sets up with one aiming point and never has to vary it. Shooting from the side is much harder.'

'But he didn't fire from here.'

'That's my point. He should have, but he didn't.'

'So?'

'He had a minivan. He should have parked it right where we are now. He should have climbed into the back seat and opened the sliding door. He should have fired from inside the minivan, Helen. It had tinted windows. The few cars that passed him wouldn't have seen a thing. He should have fired his six shots, and the six cartridge cases would have ejected inside the van, and then he should have climbed back into the driver's seat and driven away. It would have been a much better firing position and he would have left nothing behind. No physical evidence of any kind. It would have been a great getaway. In five minutes he would have been five miles away.'

'It's farther away. It's a longer distance to shoot.'

'It's about seventy yards. Barr was reliable at five times that distance.'

Helen Rodin said nothing.

'And he was expecting it to be sunny,' Reacher said. 'You told me it usually is. Five p.m. the sun would have been in the west, behind him. He would have been firing out of the sun. That's a basic preference for a sniper. Every reason in the world says he should have been up here in his van.'

'But he wasn't. Why not?'

'We should get back to your office. You've got a lot of strategising to do.'

HELEN RODIN sat down at her desk. Reacher walked to her window and looked out into the plaza. Looked for the man in the boxy suit. Didn't see him.

'Barr made a choice about where to shoot from, that's all,' Helen said, 'and it wasn't a great choice, according to some fourteen-year-old military theory that he probably forgot all about the day he quit the service,'

'They don't forget,' Reacher said. 'That's why he asked for me.'

'Whatever. How does it make him less guilty?'

'Because if a person chooses a terrible *B* instead of a great *A*, there has to be a good reason for it. He trapped himself inside a building, at street level, in a congested area, with a much harder shot, in a place whose very nature made it the best crime scene a veteran like Emerson has ever seen.'

'OK, tell me why he would do that.'

'Because he was literally going out of his way to leave every last piece of evidence he could.'

She stared at him. 'That's crazy.'

'Everyone was so happy with how great the crime scene was, they never stopped to realise it was *too* great. Me included. It was too good to be true. Everything was wrong with it. Like, why did he wear a raincoat? It was warm and it wasn't raining. He wore it so he could scrape unique fibres off it onto the pillar. Why did he wear those stupid shoes? Why did he shoot out of the dark? So people would see his muzzle flash and pinpoint the location so they could go there afterwards and find the other clues. Why did he scrape his rifle on the wall? Why didn't he take the traffic cone away with him?'

'This is crazy,' Helen said.

'Two clinchers,' Reacher said. 'Why did he pay to park? He wanted to leave a quarter in the meter with his prints on it. To connect it with the shell case, which he probably also left there on purpose.'

Helen Rodin paused. 'What's the other clincher?'

'He wanted to be looking at the pool lengthwise, not sideways.'

'Why?'

'Because he fired into the pool deliberately. He wanted to put a bullet in the water, down the long axis, at a low angle, like a ballistics tank, just so it could be found later, undamaged. Just so it could tie his barrel to the crime. Sideways wouldn't have worked for him. Not enough travel distance. The bullet would have hit the wall too hard. It would have gotten damaged.'

'But why the hell would he do all that?'

'Because he was made to, Helen. Simple as that.'

She stared at him.

'Someone forced him to do it,' Reacher said, 'and forced him to take the blame. He was told to go home afterwards and wait for the arrest. That's why he took the sleeping pill. He was probably going crazy, sitting there waiting.'

Helen Rodin said nothing.

'He wasn't a lone nutcase. He was coerced. That's why he said, *They've got the wrong guy.* He meant they should be looking for the guy who made him do it. The puppet master.' Reacher checked the plaza again.

'I should be turning cartwheels,' Helen said.

'He still killed five people.'

'But if the coercion was substantial, it's going to help him.'

Reacher said nothing.

'Should we take it to Emerson?'

'No,' Reacher said. 'Emerson's got the best done deal he ever saw. He's not going to pick at the seams now. No cop would.'

'So what should we do?'

'We should ask ourselves three basic questions: who, and how, and why. We need to figure out who benefits. Because James Barr certainly didn't.'

'The who was whoever set those guys on you last night. Because he didn't want the boat rocked.'

'Correct,' Reacher said.

'So I need to look for that person.'

'It might get your client killed,' Reacher said.

'He's in the hospital, guarded night and day.'

'Your client isn't James Barr. It's Rosemary Barr. You need to think about what kind of a threat can have made James Barr do what he did. It had to have been one hell of an effective threat, Helen. And what's the only thing Barr's got to lose? No family. Except a sister.'

Helen Rodin said nothing.

'He was told to keep quiet, obviously. That's why he asked for me. It was like a coded communication. Because the puppet can't talk about the puppet master, not now, not ever, because the threat is still out there. I think he might be trading his life for his sister's. Which gives you a big problem. If the puppet master sees you poking around, he'll think the puppet talked. That's why you can't go to Emerson.'

'So what should I do?'

'Nothing,' Reacher said. 'Because the more you try to help James Barr, the more likely you are to get Rosemary Barr killed for it.'

'Can we protect her?' she asked.

'No,' Reacher said. 'We can't. There's only two of us.'

Helen Rodin came out from behind her desk. Stood next to Reacher. She was fragrant. Some clean scent a little like soap.

'You could look for him,' she said.

'Could I?' he answered, nothing in his voice.

She nodded. 'He gave you a reason that's not connected to James Barr. He set those boys on you. You could go after him and he wouldn't necessarily conclude that James Barr had talked.'

'I'm not here to help the defence.'

'Then look at it as helping the prosecution. If two people were involved, then two people deserve to go down.'

Reacher said nothing.

'Just look at it as helping me,' Helen said.

REACHER RODE the elevator to the top of the black glass tower and found a maintenance stairwell that led to the roof. It was only fifteen storeys up, but it felt like the highest place in Indiana. He could see the river to the south. South and west, he could see where the raised highway separated. He walked to the northwest corner. Directly below him the highway spur curled round behind the library and the tower and ran away due east. Far beyond it in the distance the state highway carried on straight and met a cloverleaf about two miles away in the haze. A long straight road came off the cloverleaf and ran back towards him. That was the road he wanted.

He rode down to the lobby and set out walking. At street level the air was warm and still. The road he wanted was straight and wide. Closest to downtown it had small run-down establishments. There was an old-fashioned motor court hotel that once must have stood on the edge of town. He kept on walking and after a mile he passed a fast-food drive-through. Then a tyre store. And a dealership for small cars. He figured he was getting close.

Are you a hooker?

No way. I work at the auto parts store.

Not *an* auto parts store. *The* auto parts store. Maybe the only one. Which in any city is always on the same strip as the tyre stores and the auto dealers. Which in any city is always a wide new strip near a highway cloverleaf.

He spent ten minutes hiking past a Ford dealership with about a thousand new pick-up trucks lined up. Behind the new trucks were old trucks.

And then an auto parts store.

It was a franchise operation, long and low, neat and clean. The parking lot was about a quarter full. There were two cars alone together in the end bays. The store staff's cars, Reacher figured. One was a four-cylinder Chevy, the other a small Toyota SUV. The Chevy had chromed silhouettes of reclining women on the mud flaps, which made the Toyota the redhead's car.

Reacher went inside. There were maybe a half-dozen customers walking around, looking. There was a service corral made of four counters boxed together. There were registers and computers and thick paper manuals. Behind one of the computers was a tall boy in his early twenties. Not someone Reacher had seen before. Not one of the five from the sports bar. He looked to be in charge. He was wearing red overalls. A uniform, Reacher guessed. His name was embroidered on the left of his chest: GARY.

'I need to speak with Sandy,' Reacher said.

'She's in back right now,' the guy called Gary said.

'Shall I go through or do you want to go get her for me?'

'What's this about?'

'It's personal.'

'She's here to work.'

'It's a legal matter.'

'You're not a cop.'

'I'm working with a lawyer.'

'I need to see some ID.'

'No, Gary, you don't. You need to go get Sandy.'

'I can't. I'm short-staffed today.'

Reacher shrugged and bypassed the corral of counters and headed for a door marked NO ADMITTANCE. It would be an office, he guessed, not a stockroom. A place like that, stock was unloaded directly onto the shelves.

It was an office, small, dominated by a large white laminate desk. Sandy was sitting behind it, wearing red overalls. Hers looked a whole lot better than Gary's. They were cinched in tight round her waist with a belt.

'We meet again,' Reacher said.

Sandy just looked up at him. She seemed smaller than Reacher remembered, quieter, less energetic.

'I'm very sorry for what happened,' she said.

'Who set it up?' Reacher asked.

'I don't know.'

'You must know who told *you* about it.'

'Jeb,' she said.

'Jeb?'

'Jeb Oliver,' she said. 'He works here. We hang out sometimes.'

'Is he here today?'

'No, he didn't show.'

Gary had said: *I'm short-staffed today.*

'Where does he live?'

'I don't know. With his mother somewhere. I don't know him that well.'

'What did he tell you?'

'That I could help with something he had to do.'

'How much did he pay you?'

Sandy didn't answer.

'A thing like that, nobody does it for free,' Reacher said.

'Hundred dollars,' she said.

'What about the other four guys?'

'Same for them.'

'Who came up with the plan? The brothers thing?'

'It was Jeb's idea. You were supposed to start pawing me. Only you didn't.'

'You improvised very well.'

She smiled a little, like it had been a small unscripted success in a life that held very few of them.

'How did you know where to find me?' Reacher asked.

'We were cruising in Jeb's truck. Kind of standing by. Then he got word on his cellphone.'

'Who called him?'

'I don't know.'

'You want to lend me your car?'

'My car?'

'I need to go find Jeb.'

'I don't know where Jeb lives.'

'You can leave that part to me.'

'I don't know.'

'I'm old enough to drive,' Reacher said. 'I'm old enough to do lots of things. And I'm pretty good at some of them.'

She half smiled again, because he was using her own line from the night before. She looked away, then looked back at him. 'Is this a big deal?'

'You got a hundred bucks. So did four other guys. My guess is Jeb kept another five. So someone paid a thousand bucks to put me in the hospital. That's a moderately big deal. For me, anyway.'

'Am I in trouble?'

'Maybe,' Reacher said. 'But maybe not. We could deal. You could lend me your car and I could forget all about you.'

She ducked down and lifted her purse off the floor. Rooted around and came out with a set of keys.

'It's a Toyota,' she said.

'I know,' Reacher said.

He took the keys and headed back to the corral of counters.

'I need Jeb Oliver's address,' he said to Gary. 'A legal matter.'

'I want to see some ID.'

'You had a criminal conspiracy running out of your store. If I were you, the less I knew about it, the better.'

The guy paused a moment. Glanced beyond Reacher's shoulder at the line forming behind him. He opened a drawer and took out a file and copied an address onto a slip of paper.

'North of here,' he said. 'About five miles.'

'Thank you,' Reacher said, and took the slip of paper.

THE REDHEAD'S Toyota started on the first turn of the key. Reacher racked the seat back and adjusted the mirror, then propped the slip of paper against the instrument panel. Jeb Oliver's address was nothing more than a house number on a rural route. Easier to find than a road with a name.

Reacher moved out of the parking lot and drove north to the highway cloverleaf. He saw the route number he wanted. It was a dogleg: east along a county road, then north, and the blacktop narrowed. There was agriculture going on to the left and the right. Radial irrigation booms turned slowly.

He drove four more miles through the fields and passed a half-dozen tracks with mailboxes at the end of them, painted with numbers. He watched the numbers and slowed before he got to the Oliver place. The track there was narrow with two muddy ruts. There were sharp tyre tracks in the mud. New, wide treads from a big truck.

Reacher turned the Toyota in and bumped down the track. At the end of it he could see a clapboard farmhouse with a barn behind it and a clean red pick-up truck next to it. He parked in front of it and got out. The truck was a new Dodge Ram, probably worth more than the house, which was about a hundred years old and badly maintained. The barn was no better. But it had new iron clasps on the doors, with a bicycle U-lock through them.

There was no sound except for a distant hiss as the irrigation booms turned slowly in the fields. Reacher walked to the front door and knocked twice. No response. He walked around to the back of the house and found a woman sitting on a porch glider. She was a lean and leathery person, wearing a faded print dress and holding a pint bottle of something golden in colour.

'What do you want?' she said.

'Jeb,' Reacher said.

'Not here.'

'He's not at work, either. Are you his mother?'

'Yes. You think I'm hiding him? Go ahead and search the house.'

'I'll take your word for it. What about the barn?'

'It's locked from the outside. He's got the key.'

Reacher said nothing.

'He went away,' the woman said. 'Disappeared.'

'Is that his truck?'

The woman nodded. Took a small, delicate sip from her bottle.

'So he walked?' Reacher said.

'He was picked up. Late last night.'

'To go where?'

'I have no idea.'

Reacher sat down on the porch step. The glider kept on rocking. He could smell mildew from the cushions, and bourbon from the bottle.

'Cards on the table, whoever the hell you are,' the woman said. 'Jeb got home last night, limping. With his nose busted. And I'm figuring you for the guy who bust it.'

'Why?'

'Who else would come looking for him? I guess he started something he couldn't finish. So he ran.'

'Did you see who picked him up?'

'Some guy in a car. He waited on the road. I didn't see much. It was dark.'

Reacher nodded. He had seen only a single set of tyre marks in the mud, from the pick-up. The car that had waited on the road was probably a sedan, too low-slung to make it down the farm track.

'Did he say how long he would be gone?'

The woman just shook her head.

'OK,' Reacher said. 'Thanks.'

He walked back the way he had come, listening to the glider moving, listening to the hiss of irrigation water. He backed the Toyota all the way to the road and swung the wheel and headed south.

REACHER PUT the car keys on the redhead's desk.

'Thanks for the loan,' he said.

'Did you find him?' she asked.

'He's gone.'

She said nothing.

'Have a nice life, Sandy.'

'You too, Jimmy Reese,' she said.

He turned round and closed the door on her again. Started walking south, back to town.

THERE WERE four people in Helen Rodin's office when he got there. Helen herself, and three strangers. One of them was a guy in an expensive suit. He was sitting in Helen's chair, behind her desk. She was standing next to him, head bent, talking. The other two strangers were standing near the window. One was a man, one was a woman. The woman had long dark hair and glasses. The man had no hair and glasses. Both had lapel badges with their names printed large. The woman had MARY MASON followed by a bunch of letters that had to be medical. The man had WARREN NIEBUHR with the same bunch of letters. Doctors, Reacher figured, probably psychiatrists.

Helen looked up from her discussion. 'Folks, this is Jack Reacher,' she said. 'My investigator dropped out and Mr Reacher agreed to take over his role.' Then she gestured at the guy in her chair. 'This is Alan Danuta. He's a lawyer specialising in veterans' issues. From DC. Probably the best there is.'

'You got here fast,' Reacher said to him.

'I had to,' the guy said back. 'Today is the critical day for Mr Barr.'

'I got lucky,' Helen said. 'Alan could fly right in. And then even luckier, because there's a psychiatric conference in Bloomington all week. So Dr Mason and Dr Niebuhr drove down.'

'I specialise in memory loss,' Dr Mason said.

'And I specialise in coercion,' Dr Niebuhr said.

'We need to talk,' Reacher said, looking at Helen. 'Just for a moment.'

Helen made an excuse-me face to the others and led Reacher into the outer office. 'You get anywhere?' she asked him.

'The bimbo and the four other guys were recruited by a friend of theirs called Jeb Oliver. He paid them a hundred bucks each. I figure he kept another five for his trouble. I went to his house, but he's gone. He was picked up by a guy in a car.'

'Who is he?'

'He works at the store with the bimbo. But he's also a small-time dope dealer. There's a barn behind his house with a fancy lock on it. And he owns a truck that had to cost twice what a store clerk makes in a year.'

Helen said nothing.

'They were all hopped up last night,' Reacher said. 'Speed, judging by the way the bimbo looked today. Really down, like an amphetamine hangover.'

'So you think James Barr was involved with a dope dealer?'

'Not necessarily. But maybe coerced by one for some unknown reason.'

'This raises the stakes,' Helen said. 'What should we do?'

'We should go to the hospital. Let Dr Mason find out if Barr is lying about the amnesia.'

Helen Rodin drove out to the hospital in her Saturn with the lawyer Alan Danuta beside her in the front and Reacher in the back. Mason and Niebuhr followed her in the Taurus they had rented that morning in Bloomington. All five people got out in the visitors' lot and then headed together towards the building's main entrance.

GRIGOR LINSKY watched them walk. He was fifty feet across the lot, in the Cadillac that Jeb Oliver's mother had seen the night before. He dialled his cellphone. The Zec answered on the first ring.

'The soldier is very good,' Linsky said. 'He's already been out to the boy's house.'

'Where is the boy?'

'Under the crushed stone in the new First Street roadbed.'

'What's happening now?'

'The soldier and the lawyer are at the hospital. With three others. Another lawyer and two doctors, I think.'

'Are we relaxed?'

'We should be. They have to try. That's the system here, as you know. But they won't succeed.'

'Make sure they don't,' the Zec said.

THE HOSPITAL was on the outer edge of the city and therefore relatively spacious. But it smelt like any hospital anywhere. Decay, disinfectant, disease. Reacher didn't like hospitals very much. He followed the other four down a long bright corridor to an elevator. It took them up to a fifth-floor lobby that was all blank painted concrete except for a steel-and-wired-glass door that led into a security air lock. Reacher guessed that the whole fifth floor was funded by the state prison service.

A guy in a Board of Corrections uniform met the party at a reception desk. Everyone was searched and everyone signed a liability waiver. Then a doctor showed up and led them to a small waiting area.

'Barr is awake and reasonably lucid,' the doctor said. 'But that doesn't mean he's a well man. So we're restricting his visitors to a maximum of two at any one time, and we want them to keep things brief.'

Reacher saw Helen Rodin smile, and he knew why. The cops would want to come in pairs; Helen's presence as defence counsel would make three at a time. So the medical restrictions were handing her a defence-only day.

'His sister is with him right now,' the doctor said, then he left.

'I'll go first,' Helen said. 'I need to introduce myself and get his consent for the representation. Then Dr Mason should see him, I think.'

They took a chair each and settled in. Everyone seemed to know that they were in for a long, slow process. Reacher sat opposite Mary Mason and watched her. She was young for an expert. She seemed warm and open.

'How do you do this?' he asked her.

'The assessment?' she said. 'I start out assuming it's more likely to be real than fake. A brain injury bad enough for a two-day coma almost always produces amnesia. Then I just watch the patient. True amnesiacs are very unsettled by their condition. They want to remember. Fakers show up different. You can see them avoiding the days in question.'

'Kind of subjective,' Reacher said.

Mason nodded. 'I'm in the opinion business.'

'How much will he have forgotten?'

'Several days, minimum. If the trauma happened Saturday, I'd be surprised if he remembers anything after Wednesday. Before that there'll be a shadowy period about as long where he remembers some things and not others.'

'Will anything come back?'

'From the initial shadowy period, possibly. Working forward, he'll be much more limited. There'll be a hard boundary somewhere. Typically it would be when he went to sleep on the last day he's aware of.'

'Will he remember fourteen years ago?'

She nodded. 'His long-term memory should be unimpaired.'

A door opened halfway down a corridor and Rosemary Barr stepped out of a room. She looked exhausted and ten years older than the day before. She walked slowly towards the waiting area. Helen Rodin got up and went to meet her halfway. They stood together, talking low. Then Rosemary walked on alone towards the security desk.

'I'm going in to see him now,' Helen said, and went into the room Rosemary had come out of.

Reacher turned to Niebuhr. 'Seen this kind of thing before?' he asked.

'Coercion? Have *you* seen it before?'

Reacher smiled. Every psychiatrist he had ever met liked to answer questions with questions. 'I've seen it a lot,' he said.

'But?'

'Usually there was more evidence of a dire threat.'

'A threat against the sister isn't dire? You came up with that hypothesis yourself, I believe.'

'His sister hasn't been kidnapped. She's not a prisoner. He could have told her to get out of town.'

'Exactly,' Niebuhr said. 'We can only conclude that he was instructed not to. Evidently he was told to leave her ignorant, and vulnerable. That demonstrates to us how powerful the coercion must have been. And it demonstrated to *him* how powerless he was in comparison. He must have been living with deep dread, and helplessness, and guilt for his obedience.'

'Ever seen a rational man afraid enough to do what he did?'

'Yes,' Niebuhr said.

'Me too,' Reacher said. 'Once or twice.'

Then the waiting area went quiet again. Danuta stretched his legs out and worked on papers inside an open briefcase on his knees. Mason had her eyes closed and might have been asleep. Niebuhr stared into space.

Helen Rodin came out of James Barr's room fifteen minutes after she went in. She walked straight back to the waiting area.

'Your turn,' she said to Mary Mason.

Mason walked down the corridor.

'I liked him,' Helen said, to nobody in particular.

'How is he?' Niebuhr asked.

'Weak, and smashed up,' Helen said. 'He's coherent. But he doesn't remember anything. And I don't think he's faking.'

'How far back is he blanking?'

'I can't tell. He remembers listening to a baseball game on the radio. Could have been last week or last month.'

'Did he accept your representation?' Danuta asked.

'Verbally,' Helen said. 'He can't sign anything. He's cuffed to the bed.'

'Did you walk him through the charges and the evidence?'

'I had to,' Helen said. 'He wanted to know why I thought he needed a lawyer. He assumes he's guilty.'

Alan Danuta closed his briefcase and put it on the floor. 'We cannot let him go to trial. The government injured him through its own negligence and now it wants to put him on trial for his life? Not if he can't even remember the day in question. What kind of a defence could he conduct? It's a Bill of

Rights issue. Federal, then Appeals, then the Supremes. That's the process.'

'I'm not qualified for this,' Helen said.

'Intellectually? That's not what I heard.'

'Tactically and strategically. And financially.'

'There are veterans' associations that can help with the money. Mr Barr served his country, after all. With honour.'

Helen didn't reply to that. Just glanced Reacher's way.

Reacher said nothing. He turned away, thinking: This guy is going to get away with murder again?

'There is an alternative,' Danuta said.

'What is it?' Helen asked.

'Give your father the puppet master. Half a loaf is better than none. And the puppet master is the better half.'

'Would he go for it?'

'Any prosecutor worth his salt wants the bigger fish.'

Helen glanced at Reacher again. 'The puppet master is only a theory,' she said. 'We don't have anything that even remotely resembles evidence.'

'Your choice,' Danuta said. 'But you can't let Barr go to trial.'

'Let's wait and see what Dr Mason thinks,' Helen said.

Dr Mason came back twenty minutes later. 'Permanent retrograde amnesia,' she said. 'Completely genuine. As clear a case as I ever saw.'

'Duration?' Niebuhr asked.

'Major League baseball will tell us that,' she said. 'The last thing he remembers is a particular Cardinals game. But my bet would be a week, counting backward from today.'

'Which includes Friday,' Helen said.

'I'm afraid so.'

'OK,' Danuta said. 'There it is.'

'Great,' Helen said. She stood up and the others joined her.

For all of them, Reacher thought, Barr had changed from being a man to being a medical specimen and a legal argument.

'You guys go on ahead,' he said. 'I'm going to look in on my old buddy.'

Helen stepped away from the others and came close. 'Why?' she asked.

'Don't worry,' he said. 'I'm not going to switch his machines off.'

She stood still for a moment. Said nothing. Then she stepped back to join the others and they all left together. Reacher walked down the corridor to James Barr's door. Paused a beat and turned the handle and went inside.

CHAPTER FOUR

The room was overheated. You could have roasted chickens in it. There was a wide window with white venetian blinds closed against the sun. They glowed and filled the room with soft white light. There was medical equipment everywhere.

Barr was flat on his back in a bed in the middle of the room. His head was clamped in a brace. His hair was shaved and he had bandages over the holes they had drilled in his skull. His left shoulder was wrapped in bandages that reached to his elbow. His right shoulder was bare and unmarked. His chest and his sides were bandaged. His arms were straight at his sides and his wrists were handcuffed to the cot rails. He had IV needles taped to the back of his left hand. There were red wires leading out from under the bandages on his chest. They led to a machine with a screen showing a rolling patterns of peaks and troughs. The machine made a muted beep every time a peak hit the screen.

'Who's there?' Barr asked. His voice was weak and rusty. And scared.

Reacher leaned over the bed.

'You,' Barr said.

'Me,' Reacher said.

Barr's right hand trembled. 'I guess I let you down.'

'I guess you did.'

'I don't remember anything,' Barr said.

'You clear on what I'll do to you if you're bullshitting me?'

'I just can't remember anything.' Barr's voice was helpless, confused. Not a defence, not a complaint. Not an excuse. Just a statement of fact.

'Tell me about the ball game,' Reacher said.

'It was on the radio.'

'Not the TV?'

'I prefer the radio,' Barr said. 'That's how it always was. When I was a kid. Summer evenings, the sound of baseball on the radio.'

'I'm not here to discuss your media preferences.'

'Do you watch baseball on TV?'

'I don't have a TV,' Reacher said.

'Really? You should get one.'

'I don't have a house.'

'Why not? You're not still in the army.'

'How would you know?'

'Nobody's still in the army. Not from back then. Are you a cop now?'

Reacher shook his head. 'I'm just a citizen.'

'Why are you here?'

Reacher didn't answer.

'Oh,' Barr said. 'To nail me.'

'Tell me about the ball game.'

'It was the Cubs at the Cardinals,' Barr said. 'Close game. Cards won, bottom ninth, walk-off.'

'Home run?'

'No, an error. A walk, a steal, then a groundout to second put the runner on third, one out. Soft grounder to short, check the runner, throw to first, but the throw went in the dugout and the run scored on the error.'

'When was this?'

'I don't even know what day it is today.'

Reacher said nothing.

Barr closed his eyes. 'I can't believe that I did what they say,' he said.

'Plenty of evidence,' Reacher said.

Tears welled out of Barr's closed eyes. 'I thought I'd changed. I was sure I *had*. I tried real hard. Fourteen years, reformed.'

'Why do you own all those guns?'

'They were reminders. They keep me straight.'

'Do you ever use them?'

'Occasionally. At a range.'

'Where? The cops checked.'

'Not here. I go across the line to Kentucky. There's a range there, cheap.'

'Tell me how you did it.'

'I don't remember doing it.'

'So tell me how you *would* do it. Theoretically.'

'What would the targets be?'

'Pedestrians. Coming out of the DMV building.'

Barr closed his eyes again. 'That's who I shot?'

'Five of them,' Reacher said.

Barr started to cry again. 'When?' he said.

'Friday afternoon.'

Barr stayed quiet for a long time.

'I would have waited until just after five. Plenty of people then. I would have stopped on the highway behind the library. Where it's raised. Sun in the west, behind me, no reflection off the scope. I would have opened the passenger window and lined it all up and emptied the mag and hit the gas again. Only way to get caught would be if a state trooper stopped me for speeding and saw the rifle. But I'd have hidden the rifle and driven slow.'

Reacher said nothing.

'What?' Barr said. 'Maybe a trooper stopped to help me. Was that it? While I was parked? Maybe he thought I had a flat.'

'Do you own a traffic cone?' Reacher asked.

Barr started to say no, then stopped. 'I guess I've *got* one,' he said. 'Not sure I own it, exactly. I had my driveway blacktopped. They left a cone on the sidewalk to stop people driving on it. They never came back for it.'

'So what did you do with it?'

'I put it in the garage.'

'You got any friends?'

'A few. Just guys. One or two.'

'Any new friends?'

'I don't think so.'

'Women?'

'They don't like me.'

'Tell me about the ball game. Where were you?'

'Home,' Barr said. 'I was in the kitchen, eating cold chicken.'

'How did you feel? Happy? Sad? Normal?'

'I think I was feeling happy. Like something good was on the horizon.'

'Tell me about your sister. How do you feel about her?' Reacher said.

'She's all I've got.'

'How far would you go to protect her?'

'I would do anything,' Barr said.

'What kind of anything?'

'I'll plead guilty if they let me. She'll still have to move, maybe change her name. But I'll spare her what I can. She bought me the radio. For the baseball. Birthday gift.'

Reacher said nothing.

'Why are you here?' Barr asked him.

'To bury you.'

'I deserve it.'

'You didn't fire from the highway. You were in the new parking garage.'

'That's nuts. Why would I fire from there?'

'You asked your first lawyer to find me. On Saturday.'

'Why would I do that? You ought to be the last person I wanted to see. You know about Kuwait City. Why would I want that brought up?'

'What was the Cards' next game?'

'I can't remember,' Barr said. 'I remember that winning run, and that's all. The announcers were going crazy.'

'What about before the game? What's the next to last thing you remember?'

'I remember going out somewhere,' Barr said.

'Alone?'

'Maybe with people. I'm not sure. Not sure where, either.'

Reacher said nothing. He listened to the quiet beep from the heart machine. It was running pretty fast. Barr's handcuffs were rattling.

Reacher stood up and walked out of the room. He processed out at the security desk and passed through the air lock and rode the elevator down to the street. Helen Rodin's car was gone. She hadn't waited for him. So he set out walking, all the way from the edge of town.

He picked his way past ten blocks of construction. It was getting late in the afternoon, but the library was still open. The woman at the desk told him where the old newspapers were kept. He browsed through the previous week's stack, starting with Thursday, Wednesday and Tuesday, and he got a hit with the second paper he looked at. The Chicago Cubs had played a three-game series in St Louis starting Tuesday. It was the series opener that had ended the way Barr had described. The details were right there in Wednesday morning's paper.

Reacher backtracked to the police station. He went straight to the reception desk and claimed defence counsel's right to another look at the evidence. The desk guy made a call to Emerson and then pointed Reacher to Bellantonio's garage bay.

Bellantonio met him there and unlocked the door.

'Updates?' Reacher asked.

'Always,' Bellantonio said. 'We never sleep.'

'So what's new?'

'More tests on the fibres, and more ballistics. We're beyond definite on everything. The Lake City ammo is relatively rare, and we've confirmed a purchase by Barr less than a year ago. In Kentucky.'

'He used a range down there.'

Bellantonio nodded. 'We found that out, too.'

'Anything else?'

'The traffic cone came from the city's construction department. We don't know how or when. And I think that's about it.'

'You're giving me all the good news. What about the questions that didn't get answered?'

'I don't think there were any.'

'You play poker?' Reacher asked.

'No.'

'Good decision. You're a terrible liar.'

Reacher left the police station and walked all the way back to the black glass tower. Helen Rodin was at her desk. Danuta and Mason and Niebuhr had left. She was alone.

'Rosemary asked her brother about Kuwait City,' she said. 'She told me so, when she came out of his room at the hospital.'

'And?' Reacher said.

'He told her it was all true. Rosemary is pretty devastated. She says James is, too. He can't believe he did it again.'

Reacher said nothing.

'I apologise,' Helen said. 'For telling Danuta we didn't have any evidence for the puppet master.'

'You were right,' Reacher said. 'At the time.'

She looked at him. 'But?'

'We do now. They've been gilding the lily over at the police station. They've got fibres, ballistics, a receipt for the ammunition from Kentucky. They traced the traffic cone to the city. But they haven't got James Barr on tape driving in to place the cone in the garage beforehand.'

'Are you sure?'

Reacher nodded. 'If they had found him, they'd have printed the stills and pinned them up for the world to see. But they didn't. Which means James Barr didn't drive in and leave the cone beforehand.'

'Which means someone else did.'

'The puppet master,' Reacher said. 'Or another of his puppets. Sometime after Tuesday night. Barr thinks the cone was still in his garage Tuesday.'

'Whoever it was must be on the tapes.'

'Correct,' Reacher said.

'But there'll be hundreds of cars.'

'You can narrow it down some. You're looking for a sedan. Something too low-slung to get itself down a farm track.'

'The puppet master really exists, doesn't he?'

'No other explanation for how it went down.'

'Alan Danuta is probably right,' Helen said. 'My father will trade Barr for the puppet master. He'd be a fool not to. So how do we find this guy?'

'Why would I want to?'

'Because I think you want the truth,' Helen said. 'I don't think you like it when the wool gets pulled over your eyes.'

Reacher said nothing.

'Dr Niebuhr expects we'll find a pre-existing relationship. Some new friend. We could go at it that way.'

'Barr told me he doesn't have any new friends,' Reacher said. 'Only has one or two old friends.'

'I'll ask Rosemary. If Niebuhr's wrong about the friend, what do we do?'

'There had to have been a guy following me last night and I know for sure there was one this morning out there in the plaza. So the next time I see him I'll have a word with him. He'll tell me who he's working for.'

'Just like that?'

'People usually tell me what I want to know.'

'Why?'

'Because I ask them nicely.'

Reacher left the black glass tower and walked south, beyond his hotel. He found a cheap place to eat dinner. Then he walked north, slowly, all the way back to the sports bar. Altogether he was on the street the best part of an hour, and he saw nobody behind him.

The sports bar was half empty, and there was baseball on every screen. He found a corner table and watched the Cardinals play the Astros in Houston. During the commercial breaks he watched the door. Saw nobody.

GRIGOR LINSKY dialled his cell.

'He's back in the sports bar,' he said. 'He paraded around for nearly an hour, trying to make me show myself.'

'Leave him there,' the Zec said. 'Come in and we'll talk.'

ALEX RODIN called Emerson at home. Emerson was eating a late dinner with his wife and two daughters. He wasn't thrilled about taking the call.

'We need to do something about this Jack Reacher guy,' Rodin told him.

'I don't see how he's a huge problem,' Emerson said. 'He can't make the facts go away.'

'This is not about facts now,' Rodin said. 'It's about the amnesia. It's about how hard the defence is going to push it.'

'That's up to your daughter.'

'He's a bad influence on her. I've been reading the case law. It's a real gray area. The test isn't really about whether Barr remembers the day in question. It's about whether he understands the process, right now, and whether we've got enough on him to convict without his direct testimony.'

'I would say we do.'

'Me too. But Helen needs to swallow that. She needs to agree. But she's got that guy standing over her all the time, turning her head. I know her. She's not going to suck it up until he's out of the picture.'

'I don't see what I can do.'

'I want you to bring him in.'

'I can't,' Emerson said. 'Not without a complaint.'

'Well, keep an eye on him,' Rodin said. 'He spits on the sidewalk, I want you to bring him in and do something to him.'

'This isn't the Wild West,' Emerson said. 'I can't run him out of town.'

'An arrest might be enough. We need something that breaks the spell. He's pushing Helen. On her own she'll give Barr up, no question.'

LINSKY WAS in pain on the way back to his car. An hour on his feet was all he could take. A long time ago the bones in his spine had been methodically cracked with an engineer's ball-pein hammer, one after the other. Playing the xylophone, they had called it. Playing scales. But he never spoke of it. Worse had happened to the Zec.

The Cadillac had a quiet motor and a soft seat. Cadillacs were the kind of things that made America such a wonderful place, along with the trusting population and the hamstrung police departments.

He drove to the Zec's house, which stood eight miles north and west of town, next to his stone-crushing plant. The house was a big fancy palace built a hundred years ago for a rich dry-goods merchant. Once there had been beautiful gardens, but the Zec had razed the trees and shrubberies to create a flat and open vista all round. There were no fences, because how could the Zec bear to live another day behind wire? For the same reason there were no extra locks, no bolts, no bars. There were surveillance cameras. By day visitors were clearly visible at least 200 yards away, and after dark night-vision enhancement picked them up only a little closer.

Linsky parked and eased himself out of the car. The front door opened. Light spilled out and he saw that Vladimir had come down to welcome him, which meant that Chenko had to be there too, which meant that the Zec had assembled all his top boys, which meant that the Zec was worried.

Linsky walked into the house. Vladimir said nothing, just followed him upstairs. It was a three-storey house. The ground floor was used for nothing at all, except surveillance. All the rooms were completely empty, except one that had four TV screens on a long table, showing wide-angle views north, east, south and west. Sokolov would be in there, watching them. Or Raskin. They alternated shifts. The first floor of the house had a kitchen, a dining room, a living room and an office. The second floor had bedrooms and bathrooms. The first floor was where all the business was done.

Linsky could hear the Zec's voice from the living room, calling him. He went in without knocking. The Zec was in an armchair with a glass of tea between his palms. Chenko was sprawled on a sofa. Vladimir pushed in behind Linsky and sat down next to Chenko. Linsky stood still and waited.

'Sit, Grigor,' the Zec said. 'Nobody's upset at you. It was the boy's failure.'

Linsky nodded and sat down in an armchair, a little closer to the Zec than Chenko was. That maintained the hierarchy in the proper order. The Zec was eighty, and Linsky himself was more than sixty. Chenko and Vladimir were both in their forties. They didn't have the history that the Zec and Linsky shared. Not even close. Chenko was a small man, short, wiry, no bulk at all. He had coarse black hair that stuck up in all directions, cropped short. Vladimir was very tall and heavy and blond. Unbelievably strong.

'We've been talking,' the Zec said. 'We have to confront the fact that we made a mistake. Just one, but it could prove irksome.'

'The cone,' Linsky said.

'Obviously Barr isn't on tape placing it,' the Zec said.

'Your opinion?' Linsky asked, politely.

'The detective Emerson and the DA Rodin won't care about it,' the Zec said. 'It's a minor detail, one they won't feel inclined to pursue.'

'But?'

'But it's still a loose end.'

'The evidence against Barr is indisputable.'

The Zec nodded. 'That's true. But Barr may have permanent retrograde amnesia. It's possible that Rodin won't be able to put him on trial. If so, Rodin will be expected to seek a consolation prize.'

'All this from a videotape?' Linsky said.

'It depends entirely on the tenacity of the soldier,' the Zec said.

'Silencing him now would draw attention,' Linsky said.

'We could use the redhead again,' the Zec said. 'Several people know she tried to set him up for a beating. Perhaps she could be found severely injured. The soldier would be the obvious prime suspect. We could let the police department silence him for us.'

'She would know who attacked her,' Vladimir said.

'Then perhaps she should be left unable to tell anyone anything,' the Zec said. 'Possibly she should be found somewhere suggestive.'

'In his hotel?'

'No, outside his hotel, I think. But close by. Where she can be discovered by someone other than the soldier himself.'

'Why would her body be outside his hotel?'

'Evidently he hit her and she staggered away and collapsed before she got very far.'

'The Metropole Palace,' Linsky said. 'That's where he is.'

THE ASTROS beat the Cardinals 10–7, after a limp defensive performance by both teams. Reacher settled up his tab at the bar and stepped out to the sidewalk. He decided he wouldn't go back to the Metropole Palace. He decided it was time for a change. No real reason. Just his normal restless instinct. And the Metropole was a gloomy old pile. Unpleasant, even by his undemanding standards. He decided to try the motor court instead. The one he had seen on his way to the auto parts store.

CHENKO LEFT the Zec's house at midnight. He took Vladimir with him. If the redhead was to be beaten to death, then Vladimir would have to do it. Chenko was too small to inflict the kind of battering that an enraged six-foot-five, 250-pound ex-soldier might be provoked to. But Vladimir might well be able to do the job with a single blow, which would be convincing on the post-mortem slab. A refusal, a sexual taunt, a big man might lash out once in frustration, a little harder than he intended.

They were both familiar with the girl, because of her connection to Jeb Oliver. They knew where she lived, which was in a rented garden apartment on a barren patch of land in the shadow of the state highway, where it first rose on stilts. And they knew that she lived there alone.

REACHER WALKED a long, aimless three-block circle before approaching the motor court. He listened hard for the gritty crunch of a shadow behind him. He heard nothing.

The motor court was practically an antique. It was well maintained but not updated. It was exactly the kind of place he liked.

He roused the clerk and paid cash for one night only. He used the name Don Heffner, who had played second base and hit .261 during the Yankees' lean year of 1934. The clerk gave him a big brass key and pointed him to room number eight. The room was faded and a little damp. So was the bathroom. But everything worked and the door locked tight.

CHENKO and Vladimir approached the girl's apartment building from the back, unseen. Chenko told Vladimir to keep out of sight. Then he knocked gently. There was no response. So Chenko knocked again, a little louder. He saw a light come on. Heard her voice behind the door.

'Who's there?' she asked.

'It's me,' he said. We need to talk. It's urgent.'

The door opened. She was standing there, clutching a robe around her.

'You need to come with us,' Chenko said.

Vladimir stepped out of the shadow.

'Why is *he* here?' Sandy asked.

'He's helping me tonight,' Chenko said. 'You need to get dressed, look really good. Like for a date. But you just have to be seen, for a minute.'

'How much do I get?'

'Two hundred,' Chenko said. 'Because it's so late.'

'OK,' Sandy said. 'But I'll have to shower. Do my hair.'

'We have time.'

Sandy walked into the living room after an hour, looking, as the Americans would say, like a million dollars. She was wearing a filmy black blouse that was nearly transparent. She had on tight black pants that ended just below the knee. She was wearing black high-heeled shoes. With her red hair and pale skin and green eyes, she looked like a picture in a magazine.

Pity, Chenko thought.

'My money?' Sandy asked.

'It's in the car.'

Chenko led the way. Sandy came next. Vladimir brought up the rear. The car was right there ahead of them. There was no money in it. Chenko stopped six feet short and turned round. Nodded to Vladimir.

Vladimir reached forward with his right hand and put it on Sandy's right shoulder from behind. He used it to turn her upper body sideways and then he crashed his left fist into her right temple, above and in front of her ear. It was a colossal blow. Her head snapped violently sideways and she fell to the ground like an empty suit of clothes slipping off a hanger.

Chenko squatted down and felt her neck for a pulse. There wasn't one.

They unlocked the car and raised the rear armrest and laid the body across the back seat. Then they got in the front together and drove off. They looped well to the east, came up on the Metropole Palace from behind and stopped outside a fire exit. Vladimir slid out and opened the rear door. Pulled the body out and left it where it fell. Then he got back in.

Chenko drove on, not fast, not slow, all the way back to the Zec's house.

CHAPTER FIVE

Reacher got up at 8 a.m. and went out to look for a drugstore. He walked a zigzag half-mile and saw nobody behind him. He found a drugstore and bought a pack of throwaway razors, a can of shaving foam and a tube of toothpaste. He went back by a roundabout route. He showered and shaved, then went out for breakfast to the only place he could find: the drive-through he had seen the day before. He had coffee and an English muffin filled with a round piece of ham and something that might have once been egg. His threshold of culinary acceptability was low, but he felt he might be pushing at it. He followed the muffin with a piece of lemon pie. It was better than the muffin, so he had a second piece, with a second cup of coffee. Then he went to find a barbershop.

THE BODY in the alley had been discovered at 5.30 a.m. by a cleaner coming in to work. The cleaner rushed inside and told the night porter, who dialled 911. Two patrol cars and an ambulance turned up within eight minutes. The paramedics confirmed the DOA and the ambulance went away again.

Emerson got there by 6.25. He brought his number two, a woman called Donna Bianca, and the city ME, and Bellantonio himself to run the crime scene. Technical work occupied the first thirty minutes. Then Emerson ran into his first major problem. The girl had no purse and no ID.

Ann Yanni showed up behind the Metropole at 7.15. She had an NBC crew with her, consisting of a cameraman and a sound guy.

The ME had checked the girl's arms and thighs and found no needle tracks. So she hadn't been there to score. So maybe she was a hooker. Who else would come out of the side door of a downtown hotel in the middle of the night dressed like that? She was young and she still had her looks. Therefore she wouldn't have been cheap. Therefore she would have been carrying a big purse full of twenties that had just come out of some businessman's ATM. She had run into somebody. He had snatched her purse and hit her in the head, a little harder than necessary.

'Nobody leaves,' Emerson said to Bianca. 'We'll talk to all the guests and all the staff. And tell all units to be on the lookout for a guy with more new twenties than he should have.'

'A big guy,' Bianca said.

Emerson nodded. 'A real big guy. That was some punch.'

The ME took the body to the morgue and Donna Bianca commandeered the hotel bar for the interviews, which were finished by 9.20. They gave Emerson absolutely nothing at all.

Then a guy named Gary called, from the auto parts store.

GARY HAD got to work at eight and had found himself *really* short-staffed. There was still no sign of Jeb Oliver, and Sandy hadn't shown, either. He had called her apartment and got no reply. On her way, he had assumed. But she never showed. So he called the cops for information. The desk guy told him there had been no traffic accidents that morning. Then there was a pregnant pause and the desk guy seemed to consider another possibility. He asked for a name and a description. Gary said Alexandra Dupree, known as Sandy, nineteen years old, white, petite, green eyes and red hair. Ten seconds later, Gary was speaking to a detective called Emerson on a cellphone.

GARY AGREED to close the store for the day and Emerson sent a patrol car to pick him up. First stop was the morgue. Gary identified the body and was white and badly shaken when he arrived in Emerson's office. Emerson watched him carefully. No way could a person fake that kind of shock.

So Emerson started in, gently, with all the usual questions. Last time you saw her? Anything unusual over the last couple of days?

And so by 10.15 Emerson knew all about the stranger that had come to the store the day before. Very tall, heavily built, tan, demanding, wearing olive-green pants and an olive-green flannel shirt. He had spent two sessions with Sandy and had borrowed her car, and had demanded Jeb Oliver's address, and Jeb Oliver was missing, too.

Emerson went out to the corridor and used his cellphone to call Alex Rodin in his office.

'Your lucky day,' he said. 'We've got a nineteen-year-old female homicide victim. Someone broke her neck.'

'How does that make me lucky?'

'Her last unexplained contact was yesterday with a guy that sounds a whole lot like our pal Jack Reacher.'

'Really? Who was the girl?'

'A redhead from the auto parts store out towards the highway. There's also a boy missing from the same store.'

'So when are you going to bring Reacher in?'

'As soon as I find him.'

HELEN RODIN called Rosemary Barr at work. She wasn't there. The receptionist sounded embarrassed. So Helen tried Rosemary's home number.

'Did they let you go?' she asked.

'Unpaid leave,' Rosemary said. 'I volunteered for it. Everyone was acting awkward around me.'

'That's awful.'

'It's human nature. I need to make a plan.'

'I need a list of your brother's friends,' Helen said. 'I need to know who he hung out with. Especially anyone new.'

'There wasn't anyone new,' Rosemary said.

'What about old? He must have buddies.'

'A couple I guess. There's a guy called Mike from the neighbourhood. They talk about lawns and baseball. You know, guy stuff.'

'Anyone else?'

'Someone called Charlie,' Rosemary said. 'I don't know much about him. I only saw him once.'

'What does he look like?'

'He's small. He's got weird hair. Like a black toilet brush.'

'What was their point of contact?'

'Guns,' Rosemary said. 'They shared an interest.'

At ten to twelve a courier arrived at Helen Rodin's building with six large cardboard cartons containing the defence's copies of the prosecution's evidence. Helen signed for them and he left. Then she opened them. There was a mass of paperwork and dozens of photographs.

In one of the cartons, Helen discovered a photocopy of a sheet of paper that had been found next to James Barr's telephone. It had three numbers on it. Two were for his sister Rosemary, one at her condo and the other at work. The third number was for Mike. Nothing for anyone called Charlie.

Helen dialled Mike's number. It rang and cut to an answering machine. She asked for a return call on a matter of great importance.

In the next evidence carton, Helen found eleven new VHS cassettes. A notarised sheet described them as faithful and complete copies of the parking garage's security tapes. Helen would have to take them home. She didn't have a VCR in the office. Or a television set.

THERE WAS a television set in the diner where Reacher was eating lunch. The sound was off. Ann Yanni was on. She seemed to be live on location. *In front of the Metropole Palace Hotel.* She talked silently for a moment and then the picture cut to tape of dawn twilight. An alley. Police barriers. A shapeless form under a white sheet. Then the picture cut again. To a driver's licence photograph. Green eyes. Red hair. Just under the chin a caption was superimposed: ALEXANDRA DUPREE.

Alexandra. Sandy.

Now they've gone too far, Reacher thought. Way too far.

EMERSON SPENT an hour with a sketch artist and came up with a pretty good likeness of Jack Reacher's face. The drawing was then scanned into a computer and colourised. Dirty-blond hair, ice-blue eyes, medium-to-dark tan. Emerson then typed the name, and estimated the height at six five, the weight at 250 pounds, the age between thirty-five and forty-five. He put the police department's phone number on the bottom line. Then he emailed it all over the place and set the printer to churn out 200 colour copies. He told every prowl car driver to give one to every hotel clerk and barman in town. Then he added: every diner, restaurant and sandwich shop, too.

JAMES BARR'S friend Mike called Helen Rodin back at three o'clock in the afternoon. He said he was home for the rest of the day. So she called a cab and headed out. Mike lived on James Barr's street. The two houses were similar, 1950s ranches, long and low. Barr's place looked worn. Mike's place looked manicured.

Mike himself was a tired fifty-something who worked the morning shift at a paint wholesaler. His wife arrived home when Helen was still introducing herself. She was also a tired fifty-something. Her name was Tammy, which didn't suit her. She was a part-time dental nurse. She ushered Helen into the living room.

'So what can I tell you?' Mike asked, after an initial awkward silence.

'You were Mr Barr's friend,' Helen said.

'We were neighbourly. We would chat a little if he walked by.'

'Was it a surprise?' Helen asked. 'That he did what he did?'

'Yes,' Tammy said. 'It was.'

'You're trying to get him off?' Mike said.

'Actually I'm not,' Helen said. 'But there's a new theory that he didn't act alone. I'm just trying to make sure that the other man gets punished, too.'

'It wasn't Mike,' Tammy said.

'I didn't think it was,' Helen said. 'But whoever the other man is, you might have heard about him, or even seen him coming and going.

'Barr didn't have friends,' Mike said. 'Not that he spoke about to me.'

'Does the name Charlie mean anything to you?'

Mike just shook his head.

'I've seen a man over there,' Tammy said.

'When?'

'Now and then, ever since we moved here. He comes and goes. I spend more time at home than Mike does. So I notice more.'

'When was the last time you saw this man?'

'Last week, I think. Tuesday and Wednesday.'

'What does he look like?'

'He's small. He's got funny hair. Black, like hog bristles.'

HELEN RODIN walked thirty yards and stood on the street for a moment out-side James Barr's house. It looked forlorn and empty. There was nothing to see. So she used her cellphone to call a cab and had it take her to the hospital. It was after four o'clock in the afternoon when she arrived.

Barr was awake. He was still handcuffed to the cot. He was staring at the ceiling. His arms were trembling slightly and his handcuffs were rattling against the bed frame. 'Who's there?' he said.

Helen leaned into his field of view. 'Tell me about your friend Charlie.'

'Is he here?'

'No, but I don't think they allow visitors. Just lawyers and family.'

Barr said nothing.

'Are those your only friends?' Helen said. 'Mike and Charlie?'

'I guess,' Barr said. 'And Mike's more of a neighbour.'

'What about Jeb Oliver?'

'I never heard of him.'

'Do you use drugs?'

'No,' Barr said. 'Never. I wouldn't do that. Truth is I don't really do much of anything. I just live. That's why this whole thing makes no sense to me. I spent fourteen years in the world. Why would I throw it all away now?'

'Tell me about Charlie,' Helen said.

'We hang out,' Barr said. 'We do stuff.'

'With guns?'

'A little bit.'

'Where does Charlie live?'

'I don't know.'

'How long have you been friends?'

'Five years. Maybe six.'

'And you don't know where he lives?'

'He never told me.'

'You never went to his place?'

'He came to mine instead.'

'Do you have his phone number?'

'No. He just shows up, now and then.'

'Are you close?'

'Close enough.'

'Enough to tell what happened fourteen years ago?'

Barr didn't confirm or deny it. Just closed his eyes.

'I'm surprised that a man doesn't know where his friend lives. Especially a friend as close as Charlie is.'

'I didn't push it,' Barr said. 'I was lucky to have a friend at all. I didn't want to ruin it with questions.'

A POLICE black-and-white crawled north through the building rush-hour traffic. Then it eased right and turned into the motor court. The cop in the passenger seat walked to the office. Gave the clerk a flyer.

'Call us if this guy shows up, OK?' the cop said.

'He's already here,' the clerk said. 'But his name's Heffner, not Reacher. I put him in room eight, last night.'

The cop stood still. 'Is he in there now?'

'I don't know. He's come and gone a few times.'

'How long did he book for?'

'He paid for one night. But he didn't give the key back.'

The cop stepped back to the office door. Signalled his partner. His partner shut the motor down, locked the car and walked over.

'Room eight, false name,' the first cop said.

They took the clerk with them. They made him stand back. They drew their weapons and knocked on room eight's door.

No response.

'Got a master key?' the first cop asked.

The clerk handed him a key. The cop put it in the lock. Opened the door a half-inch, paused and then smashed it all the way open and stepped inside. His partner stepped in right behind him. Their guns traced left and right and up and down, fast and random and tense.

Nothing in the room at all, except a forlorn little sequence of bathroom items lined up on a shelf above the sink. A new pack of throwaway razors, open, one used. A new can of shaving foam, with dried bubbles round the nozzle. A new tube of toothpaste, twice squeezed.

'This guy travels light,' the first cop said.

'But he hasn't checked out,' his partner said. 'So he's coming back.'

EMERSON'S plan was pretty straightforward. He put Donna Bianca in room seven. Told the two patrolmen to stash their car three streets away and walk back and wait in room nine. He told the clerk to stay awake and call Bianca as soon as he saw the guy he knew as Heffner walk in.

THE SIDEWALKS were busy and the traffic lanes were starting to clog. Reacher walked at a normal pace, scanning the middle distance for patrol cars or cops. He checked his watch. Ten to five. He came up on the parking garage's entrance from the west. He walked up the ramps to the first level, headed for the far back corner. The garage was quiet, but full.

Between the old garage and the new construction was a triple barrier of tape strung between pillars. Above and below the standard yellow and black contractor's CAUTION DO NOT ENTER tape were new lengths of blue and white POLICE LINE DO NOT CROSS tape. Using his forearm, Reacher stretched all three lines higher and ducked underneath. No need to drop to one knee. No need to leave fibres. Not even for a guy six inches taller than Barr, and not even with a new tape six inches lower than the original one. Barr had literally gone out of his way to leave every last piece of evidence he could.

Reacher arrived at the new northeast corner after thirty-five paces. He stood six feet back from the perimeter wall and looked down and right. He had a perfectly good view. No need to press up against a pillar.

People were coming out of the government office in increasing numbers. There was quite a flow. None of them walked where Barr's victims had walked. The funeral tributes were a disincentive. A reminder. Therefore it was hard to judge what Friday's scene had looked like. Hard, but not impossible. Reacher watched the walking people and in his mind made them continue straight on, entering the bottleneck right to left.

He closed one eye and extended his arm and pointed his finger. *Click, click-click, click-click-click.* Six aimed shots. Four seconds. Fast.

Six hits, including the deliberate miss. Exceptional shooting.

He dropped his arm to his side. It was cold in the gloom. It had been hot in Kuwait City. Reacher had stood in the parking garage and sweated.

He stood and watched the plaza, looked for anyone not moving. Didn't see anybody. No cops, no old men in boxy suits. He retraced his steps to the street. Turned west, heading for the library.

He made it to the lobby and stepped over to the payphones. Took the cocktail napkin out of his pocket and dialled Helen Rodin's cellphone.

'Are you alone?' he asked.

'Yes,' she said. 'But you're in trouble.'

'I'm coming to see you.'

'There's a cop in the lobby.'

'I figured. I'll come in through the garage.'

'I SHOULD turn you in,' Helen said, when he stepped inside her suite and closed the door behind him.

'But you won't,' Reacher said.

'No,' she said. 'I should, but I won't.'

'Truth is I liked that girl,' Reacher said. 'She was a sweet kid.'

'Somebody didn't like her.'

'She was disposable, that's all. A means to an end.'

'The puppet master really doesn't want you around.'

Reacher nodded. 'That's for sure. But he's out of luck, because I'm not leaving now. He just guaranteed that. But this thing with the redhead is going to slow me down. So you're going to have to do most of the work.'

She led him into the inner office. She sat down at her desk. He stayed well away from the window.

'I already started the work,' Helen said. 'I spoke to Rosemary, talked to Barr's neighbours. Then I went back to the hospital. I think we're looking for a guy called Charlie. Small guy, bristly black hair. Interested in guns. The only long-term friend anyone could name, and the only one Barr owns up to.'

Reacher nodded again. 'That works for me.'

'And Barr doesn't know Jeb Oliver and doesn't use drugs.'

'You believe him?'

'Yes, I do,' Helen said. 'Really. It's like he spent fourteen years turning his life around and now he can't believe he went back.'

'Does this guy Charlie know about Kuwait City?'

'Barr wouldn't say. But I think he does.'

'Where does he live?'

'Barr doesn't know. Charlie just shows up now and then.'

Reacher said nothing.

'Did you find the guy that was following you?'

'No, I didn't see him again. They must have pulled him off.'

'So we're nowhere.'

'We're closer than we were. We can see four guys, at least. One, the old guy in the suit. Two, the guy called Charlie. Three, someone big and strong.'

'Why him?'

'He killed the girl last night. The old guy is too old and it sounds like Charlie might be too small.'

'And number four is the puppet master.'

Reacher nodded. 'In the shadows, making plans, pulling strings.'

'But how can we get to him?'

'We missed something very obvious,' Reacher said. 'We spent all this time looking down the wrong end of the gun. James Barr fired four times in Kuwait City. And he fired six times here.'

'OK,' Helen said. 'He fired two more shots here. So?'

'But he didn't,' Reacher said. 'Not if you think about it laterally. Truth is he fired four *fewer* shots here.'

'That's ridiculous. Six is two more than four. Not four *fewer*.'

'Kuwait City was very hot,' Reacher said. 'Unbearable in the middle of the day. The streets were deserted. In Kuwait City James Barr killed every live human he saw. Our four guys were the only people dumb enough to be out in the heat. And Barr took them all. In Kuwait City, he ran out of targets. But he didn't run out of targets here. There had to have been a dozen people in that bottleneck. And he had a ten-round magazine. But he stopped shooting after six. He left four rounds in the gun. They're listed right there in Bellantonio's dog and pony show.'

Helen Rodin said nothing.

'I asked him,' Reacher said. 'When I saw him in the hospital. I asked him how he would have done it, theoretically. He said he would have parked on the highway. Behind the library. He said he would have buzzed the window down and *emptied the mag.* But he didn't empty the mag. Which makes the psychology different. This wasn't random, Helen. It wasn't psychotic. There was a specific, coherent purpose behind it. We should have seen it. We should have seen that this whole thing is about the victims, not the shooter.'

'They were targets?' Helen said.

'Carefully chosen. This wasn't a spree. It was an assassination.'

Silence in the office.

'We need to look at who the victims were,' Reacher said. 'And we need to look at who wanted them dead. That's what's going to lead us to where we need to be. And we need to do it real fast.'

THE TIRED thirty-year-old doctor on the sixth floor of the county hospital was finishing up his afternoon rounds. He went into Barr's room and picked up the chart. Took out his pen. Glanced at the machines. Glanced at the patient.

'Happy?' he asked.

'Not really,' Barr said.

Responsive, the doctor wrote, and put his pen away.

Barr's right handcuff was rattling against the cot rail. His right hand was trembling and slightly cupped, the thumb and index finger in constant motion, like he was trying to roll an imaginary ball of wax into a perfect sphere.

'Stop that,' the doctor said.

'Stop what?'

'Your hand.'

'I can't.'

'Is that new?'

'A year or two.'

'Do you drink?' the doctor asked.

'Not really,' Barr said. 'Sometimes, to help me sleep.'

The doctor flipped through the chart to the tox screen and the liver function test. But the tox screen was clear and the liver function was healthy.

'Stiffness in your arms and legs?'

'A little.'

'Does your other hand do that, too?'

'Sometimes.'

The doctor took out his pen again and scribbled on the bottom of the chart: *Observed tremor in right hand, not post-traumatic, primary diagnosis alcohol unlikely, stiffness in limbs present, possible early-onset PA?*

THE ZEC had only a thumb and a single finger remaining on each hand. On the right was a stump of an index finger, blackened and gnarled by frostbite. His left hand retained the pinkie. The middle three fingers were missing. They had been amputated by a sadist with garden shears.

Ruined hands. Souvenirs of another time, another place. They made modern life difficult. Cellphones had got so damn *small*. Linsky's number was ten digits long. The Zec never retained a phone long enough to make it worth storing a number.

Eventually he got the number entered. Then he juggled the phone into his other palm and cupped it near his ear.

'Yes?' Linsky said.

'They can't find him,' the Zec said. 'I shouldn't have told you to break off our own surveillance. My mistake.'

'What do you want me to do?'

'I want you to find him. Use Chenko and Vladimir. And I'll send Raskin to you. Work together. Find him tonight and then call me.'

HELEN RODIN searched through the evidence cartons and came out with the formal specification of charges against James Barr. The State of Indiana had listed the five alleged homicide victims by name, sex, age, address and occupation. Helen scanned the page.

'I don't see any obvious connections,' she said.

'I didn't mean they were all targets,' Reacher said. 'Probably only one of them was. Two at most. The others were window dressing.'

'I'll get to work,' she said.

'I'll see you tomorrow,' he said.

He used the fire stairs and got back to the garage unseen. He hustled up the ramp and across the street and under the highway. *The invisible man.*

GRIGOR LINSKY waited in his car in a supermarket parking lot. In his mirror he saw Raskin's old Lincoln Town car coming towards him. It stopped nose-to-tail with him and Raskin got out. He looked exactly like what he was, which was a second-rate Moscow hoodlum. Square build, flat face, cheap leather jacket. Forty-some years old. A stupid man, in Linsky's opinion, but he had survived the Red Army's last hurrah in Afghanistan. Which made Raskin a survivor, the quality that meant more than any other to the Zec.

Raskin opened the rear door and slid into the seat behind Linsky. Handed over four copies of Emerson's *Wanted* poster. A delivery from the Zec. How he had got the posters, Linsky wasn't sure. But he could guess.

'Thank you,' Linsky said, politely.

Chenko and Vladimir showed up two minutes later, in Chenko's Cadillac. Chenko was driving. They got out of their car and got into Linsky's own Cadillac, Chenko in the front, Vladimir in the back next to Raskin. Linsky handed out three copies of the poster. He kept one for himself, even though he had seen Jack Reacher many times.

'We're going to start over,' he said.

CHENKO AND VLADIMIR stayed together and took the north side of town. Linsky took the south side. Raskin took the heart of downtown. He was on foot with the sketch in his hand. He started at the Metropole Palace. The lobby, the bar. No luck. He moved on to a Chinese restaurant two blocks away. In and out, fast and discreet. He figured he was pretty good for this kind of work. He wasn't a very noticeable guy. Just a hole in the air. People looked at him, but they didn't really *see* him. Their eyes slid right on by.

Reacher wasn't in the Chinese place. Or the Irish bar. So Raskin decided to head north. He could check the lawyer's office and then head to the Marriot. Because according to Linsky those places were where the women were. And in Raskin's experience guys who weren't just holes in the air got to hang out with women more than the average.

Suddenly Raskin saw him. He was thirty yards away, walking fast. A stray beam from the streetlight played briefly across the man's face. Just for a split second. But enough for Raskin to be certain. The man was the man in the sketch. Jack Reacher, for sure.

Raskin stepped back into the shadows. Watched. Saw Reacher walking straight ahead, due west, fast and easy.

Raskin counted to three and let Reacher get forty yards ahead. Then he set out following. He dialled Grigor Linsky's number.

'I found him,' Raskin whispered. 'He's walking. He's about level with the courthouse now, two blocks to the north.'

'Where's he going?'

'Wait,' Raskin whispered. 'Hold on.'

Reacher stopped on a corner. Glanced left and turned right.

'He's turned north,' Raskin whispered. 'The sports bar, maybe.'

'OK,' Linsky said. 'We'll wait fifty yards up the street from the sports bar. Call me back in three minutes exactly. Meanwhile, don't let him out of your sight.'

Raskin clicked his phone off but kept it up at his ear. Reacher was still forty yards ahead, still in the centre of the sidewalk, arms swinging, still moving fast. A confident man, Raskin thought.

Then he stopped, because Reacher had stopped forty yards ahead. Raskin stepped back into a shadow and Reacher turned left, into the mouth of a cross-street, out of sight behind a building.

'He's gone west again,' Raskin whispered into the phone.

'Still good for the sports bar?' Linsky asked.

'Or the motor court.'

'Either one works for us. Don't lose him now.'

Raskin sprinted ten paces and slowed at the turn. Pressed himself up against the corner of the building and peered round. The cross-street was long and wide and straight and lit at the far end by bright lights. He had an excellent view. The problem was that Reacher was no longer part of it.

He had disappeared.

CHAPTER SIX

Reacher had seen the guy in the leather jacket blocks earlier. Caucasian, medium height, medium weight, and fair hair tinted orange and yellow by the streetlights. The jacket was a boxy style, made of chestnut-coloured leather. Eastern European, just like the suit the twisted old guy had worn in the plaza.

Reacher had kept his own footsteps quiet and focused on the sounds behind him, forty yards back. This wasn't Charlie. No way would anybody call this guy small. And he didn't have black hair. And this wasn't the guy who had killed the girl. Not big enough. So, add one to the tally. Five of them. At least.

Was this guy armed? Possibly, but only with a handgun. He hadn't been carrying anything longer. And Reacher was sanguine about his chances as a moving target 120 feet in front of a guy with a handgun.

Reacher took a random turn and walked on. He kept his pace steady. He let the guy behind him fall into the rhythm. Left, right, left, right. Like hypnosis. He heard the distant sound of a cellphone being dialled.

He walked on. Heard faint sibilant whispering behind him. Then he stopped on the next corner. Glanced right and turned left into a wide straight cross-street, behind the cover of a four-story building.

Then he ran, fast and silent in his boat shoes, across the street to the right-hand sidewalk, past the first alley he saw, into the second. He crouched back in the shadows, in a grey double doorway. He lay down flat on his front. The guy following him had been used to a vertical target. Instinctively he would be looking six feet off the ground.

Reacher waited. He heard footsteps on the opposite sidewalk. Close now. Then he saw the guy. He was on the left-hand sidewalk, moving slowly. He had a cellphone up at his ear. He stopped. Looked back over his right shoulder, then at the alleys on the other side of the street. *Worth checking? Yes.*

The guy moved sideways and backwards like a crab, diagonally, facing the street ahead of him and searching the right-hand sidewalk all at the same time. He moved out of Reacher's field of view. Reacher stood up silently and moved deeper into the alley into total darkness at its far end.

Then the footsteps came back. On the sidewalk. Into the alley. Slow, soft, careful. The guy came close enough to smell.

Cologne, sweat, leather. He stopped four feet from Reacher and peered hopelessly into the darkness. Reacher thought: Another step and you're history, pal. Just one more and it's game over for you.

The guy turned. Walked back to the street. Reacher stood and followed him, swift and silent.

Now *I'm* behind *you*, he thought. Time to hunt the hunters.

Reacher was big and in some ways quite clumsy, but he could be light on his feet when he needed to be and had always been good at covert pursuit. It was a skill born of long practice.

The guy in the leather jacket searched every alley and every doorway on both sides of the street. He spoke twice on his cellphone. Quietly, but with agitation obvious in his whisper. The guy's searches became faster and more cursory. Hopeless and panicked. He made it to within twenty feet of the next turn and gave up. Just quit, and walked straight ahead. Reacher waited long enough to be certain it wasn't a trick. Then he followed, moving silently from shadow to shadow.

RASKIN WALKED past the sports bar's door and headed up the street. He could see Linsky's car in the distance. And Chenko's. The two Cadillacs were waiting for him. Waiting for the failure. Well, here I am, he thought.

'So what now?' Chenko asked.

'I'll call the Zec,' Linsky said.

'He'll be royally pissed,' Vladimir said.

Linsky dialled his phone. Relayed the bad news and listened to the response. It was a short call. Linsky clicked off.

'We keep on looking,' he said. 'On a half-mile radius of where Raskin last saw him. The Zec is sending us Sokolov. He says we're sure of success with five of us.'

'We're sure of nothing,' Chenko said.

'Take the north, Chenko,' Linsky said. 'Vladimir, the south. Raskin, head back east. I'll take the west. Sokolov can fill in where we need him when he gets here.'

Raskin headed back the way he had come, as fast as he could. He saw the sense in the Zec's plan. He had last seen Reacher about fifteen minutes ago, and a furtive man moving cautiously couldn't cover more than half a mile in fifteen minutes. So he was somewhere inside a circle a mile across. They had found him once; they could find him again.

He made it all the way down the wide, straight cross-street and turned south towards the raised highway. Retracing his steps. He passed through the shadows under the highway and headed for the vacant lot on the next corner. Made the turn.

Then the wall fell on him. At least, that was what it felt like. He was hit a staggering blow from behind and he fell to his knees and pitched forward onto his face. Last thing he felt before he lost consciousness was a hand in his pocket, stealing his cellphone.

REACHER HEADED back under the highway with the cellphone warm in his hand. He leaned his shoulder against a concrete pillar as wide as a motel room and slid around it until he was in the shadow. He took out the card with Emerson's numbers on it and dialled the cell.

'Yes?' Emerson said.

'Guess who?' Reacher said.

'Reacher?'

'You named that tune in one.'

'This isn't a game, Reacher. You need to turn yourself in.'

'Listen up,' Reacher said. 'And take notes.' He recited the plate numbers from the two Cadillacs. 'My guess is one of those cars was in the garage before Friday, leaving the traffic cone. I heard some names. Raskin and Sokolov. Then Chenko and Vladimir. Vladimir looks good for the guy who killed the girl. He's as big as a house. Then there's some kind of a lieutenant whose name I didn't get. He's about sixty and has an old spinal injury. He talked to his boss and referred to him as the Zec.'

'Those are Russian names. Except Zec.'

'It's not Zec. It's *the* Zec. A word, used as a name.'

'You should come in,' Emerson said. 'Talk to me face to face.'

'Do your job and I'll think about it.'

'I am doing my job. I'm hunting a fugitive. You killed that girl. Not some guy whose name you claim you heard, as big as a house.'

'One more thing,' Reacher said. 'I think Chenko also goes by the name of Charlie and is James Barr's friend.'

'Why?'

'The description. Small, dark, with black hair that sticks up like a brush.'

'James Barr has got a Russian friend? Not according to our enquiries.'

'He sounds American. I think Charlie was involved with what happened on Friday, which means maybe this whole crew was involved.'

'Involved how?'

'I don't know. But I plan to find out. I'll call you tomorrow.'

He clicked the phone off and put Emerson's number back in his pocket and took out Helen Rodin's. Dialled it.

'Yes?' Helen Rodin said.

'This is Reacher.'

'Are you OK? The cop is right outside my door now.'

'Don't worry about me. I saw Charlie. I gave Emerson his plate number. Are you making progress?'

'All I've got is five random names. No reason I can see why anybody told James Barr to shoot any one of them.'

'You need Franklin. You need research. I want you to find that address in Kentucky for me.'

'Kentucky?'

'Where James Barr went to shoot.'

Reacher heard her flip through paper. Then she read out an address. 'What's Kentucky got to do with anything?' she asked.

Reacher heard a car on the street. Close by, to his left, fat tyres rolling slow. A PD prowl car. 'Got to go,' he said. He clicked the phone off and put it on the ground at the base of the pillar. Emerson's caller ID would have trapped the number and any cellphone's physical location could be tracked by the recognition pulse it sends to the network, once every fifteen seconds, regular as clockwork. So Reacher left the phone in the dirt and headed west.

Ten minutes later, he was opposite the back of the black glass tower, in the shadows under the highway, facing the vehicle ramp. There was an empty cop car parked on the kerb. The guy outside Helen's door, Reacher thought. He crossed the street and walked down the ramp into the underground garage.

He walked all the way across to the back wall. The garage was dark back there. He threaded between two NBC vans and found the blue Ford Mustang convertible he guessed belonged to Ann Yanni.

He tried the passenger door. Locked. He moved round the hood and tried the driver's door. The handle moved. Unlocked. He glanced around and opened the door. No alarm.

He reached inside and touched the unlock button. There was a triple *thunk* as both door locks and the trunk lock unlatched. He stepped back to the trunk. The spare tyre was under the floor. Nested inside the wheel were the jack and a metal pipe that both worked the jack and undid the wheel nuts. He took the pipe out and closed the trunk. Stepped round to the passenger side and got in the car.

He opened the glove box and found a stack of maps and a small leather folder. Inside were an insurance slip and an auto registration, both made out to Ms Janine Lorna Ann Yanni. He had about three hours to wait. He stretched out in the seat and tried to sleep. *Sleep when you can, because you never know when you're going to sleep again.* That was the old army rule.

FIRST THING Emerson did was contact the phone company. He confirmed that the number his caller ID had caught was a cellphone. The service contract was written out to a business operating under the name Specialised Services of Indiana. The business was owned by an offshore trust in Bermuda and had no local address. But the phone company reported that the cellphone was stationary and was showing up on three cells at once, which meant it had to be downtown and would be easy to triangulate.

The phone company marked the cellphone's location on a large-scale city map and faxed it to Emerson. He had expected to find the three arrows meeting at a hotel, or a bar, or a restaurant. Instead, they met on a vacant lot under the raised highway. Emerson had a brief image in his mind of Reacher sleeping rough in a cardboard box. Then he concluded that the phone was abandoned, which was confirmed ten minutes later by the patrol car he sent out to check.

And then, just for formality's sake, Emerson fired up his computer and entered the plate numbers that Reacher had given him. They came back as late-model Cadillac DeVilles, both black, both registered to Specialised Services of Indiana. Emerson wrote *dead end* on the sheet of paper and dropped it in a file.

ROSEMARY BARR sweet-talked her way past the desk on the fifth floor of the hospital and was granted an out-of-hours visit with her brother. But when she got to his room she found he was deeply asleep. She sat for thirty minutes but James didn't wake up. She checked his chart. She saw the doctor's scribbled note: *possible early-onset PA?* She had no idea what that meant.

REACHER WOKE up every time he heard the elevator motors start. The sound whined down the shaft through the cables and the moving cars rumbled. The first three times were false alarms—just anonymous office people heading home after a long day—and Reacher went back to sleep.

The fourth time, he stayed awake. He heard the elevator start and checked his watch: 11.45. *Showtime.* He waited and heard the elevator doors open. This time, it wasn't just another lone guy in a suit. It was eight or nine people. It was the NBC affiliate's eleven o'clock news team.

Reacher pressed himself down in the Mustang's passenger seat and hid the tyre iron underneath the tails of his shirt.

A heavy guy in baggy jeans passed through the darkness within five feet of the Mustang's front fender. Then came three more people.

Then came Ann Yanni.

She put her hand on her car's door handle and opened the door. She dumped herself in the seat and shut her door. Then she glanced to her right.

'Keep very quiet,' Reacher said to her. 'Or I'll shoot you.'

He jabbed the tyre iron at her, under his shirt. Half-inch wide, long and straight, it looked plausible. She stared at it in shock. Face to face, two feet away, she looked thinner and older than she looked on the television screen. But she was very beautiful.

'Hands where I can see them,' Reacher said. 'In your lap.' He didn't want her to go for the horn. 'Just sit tight, nice and quiet.'

'I know who you are,' she said.

'So do I,' he said.

He kept the tyre iron in place and waited. Yanni sat still, hands in her lap, breathing hard. People drove away, one by one.

'Keep very quiet,' Reacher said again. 'Then we'll be OK.'

'What do you want?' Yanni asked.

'I want you to listen to a story,' Reacher said.

'What story?'

'Watch,' Reacher said. He lifted his shirt. Showed her the tyre iron resting against his stomach. She stared at it. Or at the shrapnel scar he'd picked up years ago. Or both. He held the tyre iron up in the light.

'From your trunk,' he said. 'Not a gun.' He clicked the button on the door and unlocked the car. 'You're free to go,' he said. 'Whenever you want.'

She put her hand on the handle.

'But if you go, I go,' Reacher said. 'You'll miss the story.'

'We've been running your picture all night,' she said. 'You killed Alexandra Dupree.'

Reacher shook his head. 'Actually I didn't, and that's part of the story'

'What story?' she said again.

'Last Friday,' Reacher said. 'It wasn't what it seemed.'

'I'm going to get out of the car now,' Yanni said.

'No,' Reacher said. 'I'll get out. I apologise if I upset you. But I need your help and you need mine. So I'll get out. We'll talk through the window.'

Yanni said nothing. Just stared straight ahead. Reacher opened his door. Slid out and turned and laid the tyre iron gently on the seat. Then he closed the door. He heard the *thunk* of her door locks. He walked round to her window. She buzzed the glass down an inch and a half. He dropped into a crouch, so he could see her face.

'Why do I need your help?' she asked.

'Because Friday was over too soon for you,' he said. 'But you can get it back. There's another layer. It's a big story. You'll win an Emmy, or whatever it is you guys get.'

'You think I'm that ambitious?'

'I think you're a journalist. Journalists like stories. They like the truth.'

She paused, almost a whole minute. 'So tell me the story,' she said finally. 'Tell me the truth.'

He told her the story, and the truth. He sat cross-legged on the concrete floor, so as to appear immobile and unthreatening. He ran through all the events, all the theories. At the end he just stopped talking.

'Where were you when Sandy was killed?' she asked.

'Asleep in the motor court. Room eight. I slept very well.'

'No alibi.'

'You never have an alibi when you need one.'

'What do you want me to do?' she said.

'I want you to research the victims.'

'We could do that,' she said. 'We have researchers.'

'Not good enough,' Reacher said. 'I want you to hire a guy called Franklin. Helen Rodin can tell you about him. She's in this building.'

'Why hasn't she hired this Franklin guy herself?'

'Because she can't afford him. You can. A week of Franklin's time probably costs less than one of your weather guy's haircuts.'

'I don't know,' she said. 'I should turn you in.'

'You can't,' he said. 'You pull out a phone and I'll take off up the ramp. They won't find me. They've been trying all day.'

He took out the napkin with Helen Rodin's number on it. Held it at the crack of the window. Yanni took it.

'Call Helen,' Reacher said. 'She'll vouch for me.'

Yanni took a cellphone out of her handbag and turned it on. Then dialled the number. Listened to the phone.

'Helen Rodin?' she said. Then she buzzed the window all the way up and Reacher didn't hear any of the conversation. He gambled that it was really Helen she was speaking to.

But it was Helen. Yanni buzzed the window down again and passed him her phone through the gap.

'Is this for real?' Helen asked him. 'Is it a good idea?'

'She's got resources,' Reacher said. 'And having the media watching our backs might help us.'

'Put her back on.'

Reacher passed the phone through the window. This time Yanni kept the glass down so that Reacher heard her end of the rest of the conversation. She arranged to meet Helen on the third floor first thing in the morning.

'What exactly are you going to do?' Reacher asked.

'I haven't decided yet,' Yanni said. 'I guess I need to understand where you're coming from first. Obviously you don't care anything about James Barr himself. So is this all for the sister?'

'Partly for Rosemary,' he said. 'But mostly for the puppet master. He's sitting there thinking he's as smart as a whip. I don't like that.'

'Like a challenge?'

'He had a girl killed, Yanni. She was just a dumb, sweet kid looking for a little fun. So he deserves to have something come out at him.'

'OK. NBC will spring for Franklin.'

'Thanks,' Reacher said. 'I appreciate it.'

'You should.'

'I apologise again. For scaring you.'

'Anything else?'

'Yes,' Reacher said. 'I need to borrow your car.'

'My *car*? What for?'

'To sleep in and then to go to Kentucky in.'

Yanni shook her head. 'This is nuts. I'd be aiding and abetting a fugitive.'

'I'm not a fugitive. I'm a suspect, that's all.'

'I can't lend you my car after running your picture all night.'

'You could say you didn't recognise me. It's a sketch, not a photograph.'

'Your hair is different.'

'There you go. I had it cut this morning.'

'But I would recognise your name. I wouldn't lend my car to a stranger without at least knowing his name, would I?'

'Maybe I gave you a false name. You met a guy with a different name who didn't look much like the sketch, that's all.'

'What name?'

'Joe Gordon,' Reacher said. Yankees' second baseman in 1940.

'How would I get home tonight?'

'I'll drive you.'

'I'll call a cab,' she said.

She used her phone again and told a driver to meet her inside the garage. Then she climbed out of the car. 'Go park in a dark corner,' she said. 'Safer for you if you don't leave before the morning rush.'

'Thanks,' Reacher said.

Ann Yanni walked away and stood at the bottom of the ramp. Reacher slid into her seat and racked it back and reversed the car deep into the garage. Five minutes later a green-and-white Crown Vic rolled down the ramp and Ann Yanni climbed into the back. The cab turned and drove out to the street and the garage went quiet.

Reacher stayed in the Mustang but he didn't stay in the garage. Too risky. If Yanni had a change of heart he would be a sitting duck. So three minutes after her cab left he drove out and around to the garage on First Street. He went up to the first level and parked in the slot that James Barr had supposedly used. He didn't put money in the meter. Just pulled out Yanni's stack of maps and planned his route, then reclined the seat and went back to sleep.

He woke himself up five hours later, before dawn, and set out on the drive south to Kentucky.

DAWN HAPPENED about an hour into the drive. The sky changed from black to grey to purple, then orange sunlight came up over the horizon. Reacher kept the car at a nothing-to-hide seventy miles an hour and touched the CD button on the dash. Got a blast of Sheryl Crow. He stayed with it. *Every day is a winding road*, Sheryl told him. I know, he thought. Tell me about it.

He crossed the Ohio River on a long iron trestle with the sun low on his left. For a moment it turned the slow water into molten gold. He kept south on a county road and waited for the Blackford river. Near its source it formed a perfect equilateral triangle about three miles on a side with two rural routes. And according to Helen Rodin's information, James Barr's favoured firing range was somewhere inside that triangle.

But it turned out that the firing range *was* the triangle. Reacher followed the wire fence along two of its sides till he found a gate and a gravel clearing and a complex of huts. The gate was chained. It was hung with a hand-painted sign that read: *Open 8 a.m. Until Dark.* Reacher checked his watch. He was a half-hour too early. On the other side of the road was an aluminium coach diner. He pulled in. He was hungry.

He ate a long, slow breakfast at a window table. By eight o'clock there were three pick-up trucks waiting to get into the range. At 8.05 a guy showed up in a black diesel Humvee and unchained the gate.

By 8.20 Reacher started to hear rifles firing. He listened to the familiar sounds for a spell and then went outside and got back in the Mustang and drove straight in through the range's open gate.

He found the Humvee guy behind a waist-high counter in the main hut. More than fifty, less than sixty, sparse grey hair, lined skin, but ramrod straight. He had the sort of eyes that pegged him as an ex-Marine noncom even without the tattoos on his forearms and the souvenirs on the wall behind him. The centrepiece of the display was a yellowing paper target framed under glass. It had a tight group of five .300 holes inside the inner ring and a sixth just clipping it.

'Help you?' the guy said. He was looking past Reacher's shoulder, out of the window, at the Mustang.

'I just want to ask you some questions.'

The guy paused. 'About James Barr?'

'Good guess.'

'I don't speak to reporters.'

'I'm not a reporter.'

'That's a five-litre Mustang out there. And it's got an NBC sticker in the windshield. Therefore my guess is you're a reporter fixing to gin up a television story about how James Barr used my place to train and prepare.'

'Did he?'

'I told you, I'm not talking.' No hostility in his voice. Just determination.

'I'm not a reporter,' Reacher said again. 'I borrowed a reporter's car, that's all. To get down here.'

'So what are you?'

'Just a guy who knew James Barr way back. I want to know about his friend Charlie. I think Charlie led him astray.'

The guy didn't say: *What friend?* He didn't ask: *Who's Charlie?* He just said, 'Can't help you.'

Reacher switched his gaze to the framed target.

'Is that yours?' he asked. 'Because I'm thinking that if it was six hundred yards, you're pretty good. If it was eight hundred, you're very good. If it was a thousand, you're unbelievable.'

'You shoot?' the guy asked.

'I used to,' Reacher said.

The guy turned around and lifted the frame off its hook. Laid it gently on the counter. There was a handwritten inscription in faded ink across the bottom of the paper: *1978 US Marine Corps 1000 Yard Invitational. Gunny Samuel Cash, third place.*

'You're Sergeant Cash?' Reacher said.

'Retired and scuffling,' the guy said.

'Me too. But army,' Reacher said. 'My dad was a Marine.'

Cash nodded. 'Makes you half-human.'

Reacher traced his fingertip over the glass. 'Good shooting,' he said.

'I'd be lucky to do that at half the range today.'

'Me too,' Reacher said. 'Time marches on.'

'You saying you could have done it back in the day?'

Reacher didn't answer. Truth was he had actually won the Marine Corps 1000 Yard Invitational, exactly ten years after Cash had scraped third place. It had been an exceptional year. He had been at some kind of a peak, physically, mentally. That year, he couldn't miss, literally or metaphorically. But he hadn't defended his title the following year. Looking back, he understood how that decision marked two things: the beginning of his long slow divorce from the army, and the beginning of restlessness. The beginning of always moving on and never looking back. The beginning of never wanting to do the same thing twice.

'Thousand yards is a long way,' Gunny Cash said. 'Truth is since I left the Corps I haven't met a man who could even put a mark on the paper.'

'I might have been able to clip the edge,' Reacher said.

'I don't have a thousand-yard range here,' Cash said. 'But I've got a nice three-hundred that's not being used this morning. You could try it.'

'I guess,' Reacher said.

Cash opened a drawer and took out a new target. 'What's your name?'

'Bobby Richardson,' Reacher said. Robert Clinton Richardson, hit .301 in 1959, 141 hits in 134 games.

Cash wrote *R. Richardson, 300 yards*, and the date and time on the paper.

'Record keeper,' Reacher said.

'Habit,' Cash said. Then he drew an *X* inside the inner ring. It was about half an inch tall and a little less than half an inch wide. He left the paper on the counter and walked away into another room. Came back out a minute later carrying a rifle. It was a Remington M24, with a Leupold Ultra scope and a front bipod. A standard-issue Marine sniper's weapon. It looked to be well used but in excellent condition. Cash detached the magazine and showed Reacher that it was empty. Operated the bolt and showed Reacher that the chamber was empty, too. Reflex, routine, caution, professional courtesy.

'Mine,' he said. 'Zeroed for three hundred yards exactly.'

'Good enough,' Reacher said. Which it was.

'One shot,' Cash said. He took a single cartridge from his pocket. He stood it upright on the *X* on the paper target. It hid it entirely. Then he smiled. Reacher smiled back. He understood the challenge perfectly. *Hit the X and I'll talk to you about James Barr.*

'Let's go,' Reacher said.

Outside, the air was still, and it was neither hot nor cold. Perfect shooting weather. Cash carried the rifle and the target, and Reacher carried the cartridge. They climbed into Cash's Humvee together and Cash fired it up.

'You like this thing?' Reacher asked, over the noise.

'Not really,' Cash said. 'I'd be happier with a sedan. But it's a question of image. Customers like it.'

The landscape was all low hills, covered in grass and stunted trees. Someone had used a bulldozer to carve wide straight paths through it. Each path was a separate rifle range.

'My family's owned this land for ever,' Cash said. 'The range was my idea.'

Reacher saw three pick-up trucks. The guys who had been waiting at eight o'clock were well into their morning sessions.

'It's a living,' Cash said, in answer to a question Reacher hadn't asked.

He pulled the Humvee off the main track and drove 300 yards down the length of an empty range. He got out and clipped the paper target to a frame and got back in and K-turned the truck and headed back. He parked it.

'Good luck,' he said.

Reacher sat still for a moment. He was more nervous than he should have been. Four fast cups of strong coffee were not an ideal preparation for accurate long-distance shooting.

But it was only 300 yards, with a good rifle, no heat, no cold, still air. More or less the same thing as pressing the muzzle into the centre of the target and pulling the trigger. He could do it with his eyes closed. The problem was with the stakes. He wanted the puppet master more than he had wanted the Marines' cup all those years before. He didn't know why.

He slid out of the Humvee. Carried the rifle across rough earth to the coconut mat. Placed it gently with its bipod feet a yard back from the edge. Bent down and loaded it. Stepped back behind it and lined himself up and crouched, knelt, lay full length. He snuggled the stock into his shoulder. He ducked his head. Closed his left eye and moved his right eye to the scope. Draped his left hand over the barrel and pressed down and back. Solid. He spread his legs and turned his feet out so they were flat on the mat. Drew his left leg up a little and dug the sole of his shoe into the mat's fibres so the deadweight of the limb anchored his position. He relaxed.

He breathed out and kept his lungs empty, one second, two. He pulled all his energy downwards, into his gut. Let himself settle. He stared at the target. *Wanting* it. He pulled the trigger. The gun kicked and roared.

Bull's-eye. The *X* was gone. Reacher pushed back and stood up. Cash dropped down in his place and used the scope to check the result.

'Good shooting,' he said.

'Good rifle,' Reacher said.

Cash carried the rifle back towards the Humvee.

'So do I qualify?' Reacher called after him.

'For what?'

'For talking to.'

Cash turned round. 'You think this was a test?'

'I sincerely hope it was.'

'You might not want to hear what I've got to say.'

'Try me,' Reacher said.

They detoured up the length of the range for Cash to retrieve the target. Then they drove back to the huts. Cash filed Reacher's target in a drawer, under *R* for Richardson. Then he danced his fingers forward to *B* for Barr and pulled out a thick sheaf of paper.

'Check these out,' Cash said.

He dealt the filed targets like a deck of cards, all along the length of the counter. Then he started a second row, directly underneath the first. In the end he had thirty-two sheets of paper displayed, all of them marked *J. Barr, 300 yards,* with times and dates stretching back three years.

Every single target showed an expert score.

Reacher stared at them.

'What gun?'

'His own Super Match. Great rifle.'

'Did the cops call you?'

'Guy called Emerson. He was pretty decent about it. I've put in a lot of work here, and this place could get a bad name because Barr trained here.'

'What about his buddy Charlie?' he asked.

'Charlie was hopeless by comparison.'

Cash opened another drawer and ran his fingers back to *S* and took out another sheaf of paper.

'Charlie Smith,' he said. 'He was military too, by the look of him.'

'They always showed up together?' Reacher asked.

'Like peanut butter and jelly,' Cash said.

'Separate ranges?'

'Separate planets,' Cash said.

Reacher nodded. In terms of numerical score, Charlie's targets were much worse than James Barr's. Low, low scores. But his hits weren't precisely random. There was a weird kind of consistency there. He was aiming, but he was missing. Maybe some kind of bad astigmatism.

'What type of a guy was he?' Reacher asked.

'Charlie?' Cash said. 'Couldn't read him at all.'

'Small guy, right?'

'Tiny. Weird hair.'

'Barr bought his ammo here, right?'

'Lake City. Expensive.'

'His gun wasn't cheap, either.'

'He was worth it.'

'What gun did Charlie use?'

'The same thing. Like a matched pair. In his case it was a comedy.'

'Can I take one of James Barr's targets?'

'What the hell for?'

'For a souvenir,' Reacher said.

Cash shrugged and turned back to the file drawer.

'The most recent one,' Reacher said.

Cash pulled a sheet. Reacher took it and put it in his shirt pocket.

'Good luck with your buddy,' Cash said.

'He's not my buddy,' Reacher said. 'But thanks for your help.'

'You're welcome,' Cash said. 'Because I recognised you when you got behind the gun. I never forget the shape of a prone position. You won the Invitational ten years after I was in it. I was watching, from the crowd. Your real name is Reacher.'

Reacher nodded.

'Polite of you,' Cash said, 'not to mention it after I told you I came in third.'

'You had tougher competition,' Reacher said. 'Ten years later it was all a bunch of dead-beats.'

REACHER STOPPED at the last gas station in Kentucky and filled Yanni's tank. Then he called Helen Rodin from a payphone.

'Is the cop still there?' he asked.

'Two of them,' she said.

'Did Franklin start yet?'

'First thing this morning.'

'Where is Franklin's office?'

She gave him an address.

Reacher checked his watch. 'I'll meet you there at four o'clock.'

'How was Kentucky?'

'Confusing,' he said.

BELLANTONIO had been at work in his crime lab since seven o'clock in the morning. He had fingerprinted the cellphone found abandoned under the highway and come up with nothing. Then he had copied the call log. The last number dialled was Helen Rodin's cell. Last-but-one was Emerson's cell. Clearly Reacher had made both of those calls. Then came a long string of calls to several cellphones registered to Specialised Services of Indiana.

He moved on to the garage tapes. The first Cadillac on tape was a bone-white Eldorado. It had parked before ten in the morning on the Wednesday and stayed parked for five hours. The second Cadillac on tape was a new STS. It had parked soon after lunch on the Thursday and stayed there for two hours. The third Cadillac was a black DeVille. It entered the garage just after six o'clock in the morning on the Friday, when the garage would have been more or less empty. The tape showed the DeVille sweeping up the ramp, fast and confident. It showed it leaving again after just four minutes.

Long enough to place the cone.

The driver wasn't really visible in either sequence. There was just a grey blur behind the windshield. Maybe it was Barr, maybe it wasn't. Bellantonio wrote it all up for Emerson.

Then he scanned the forensic sweep through Alexandra Dupree's garden apartment. There was nothing of interest there. Nothing at all. Except the fingerprint evidence. The apartment was a mess of prints, like all apartments are. Most of them were the girl's, but there were four other sets. Three of them were unidentifiable.

The fourth set of prints belonged to James Barr.

James Barr had been in Alexandra Dupree's apartment. In the living room, in the kitchen, in the bathroom. Clear prints, perfect matches.

Bellantonio wrote it up for Emerson.

Then he read a report just in from the medical examiner. Alexandra Dupree had been killed by a single massive blow to the right temple, delivered by a left-handed assailant. She had fallen onto a gravel surface that contained organic matter including grass and dirt. But she had been found in an alley paved with limestone. Therefore her body had been moved between death and discovery. Other physiological evidence confirmed it.

Bellantonio took a new sheet of memo paper and addressed two questions to Emerson: *Is Reacher left-handed? Did he have access to a vehicle?*

THE ZEC spent the morning hours deciding what to do with Raskin. Raskin had failed three separate times. First, with the initial tail, then by getting attacked from behind, and finally by letting his cellphone get stolen. The Zec didn't like failure. He considered pulling Raskin off the street and restricting him to duty in the video room on the ground floor of his house. But why would he want to depend on a failure to monitor his security?

Then Linsky called. They had been searching fourteen straight hours and had found no sign of the soldier. 'Should we keep on looking?' he asked.

'Keep on looking,' the Zec said. 'But send Raskin back to me.'

REACHER COASTED through the silent countryside on Jeb Oliver's rural route. The irrigation booms were turning slowly and the sun was making rainbows in the droplets. He slowed to a stop next to the Olivers' mailbox. No way was the Mustang going to make it down the driveway. So he slid out and picked his way down the rocky track. Jeb Oliver's red Dodge hadn't been moved. The barn was closed and locked.

Reacher walked round the side of the house to the back porch. Jeb's mother was on her glider, scooting it twice as fast as she was before.

'Jeb not back yet?' Reacher said.

She just shook her head.

'Got a gun?' he asked.

'I don't hold with them,' she said.

'Got a phone?'

'Disconnected,' she said. 'I owe them money.'

'Good,' Reacher said. 'I'm going to break into your barn and I don't want you calling the cops while I'm doing it. Or shooting me.'

He turned his back on her and continued down the track. The doors, like the barn itself, were built of old planks alternately baked and rotted by a hundred summers and a hundred winters. The lock was a brand new U-shaped bicycle lock. One leg of the U ran through two black steel hasps that were bolted through the planks of the doors. Reacher shook it. It was pretty solid. But a lock was only as strong as what it was fixed to.

Reacher grabbed the straight end of the lock at the bottom of the U. Pulled on it. The doors sagged and the bolts gave a little. He held the lock with both hands and leaned back like a water-skier. Pulled hard and smashed his heel into the wood under the hasps. The old wood splintered. He jerked hard. The bolts fell out and the whole lock assembly hit the ground and the doors sagged all the way open. Reacher folded the doors back flush with the walls and let the sunlight in. He guessed he was expecting to see a meth lab. Or else a big stash. He saw none of that.

The barn was maybe forty feet by twenty inside. It was completely empty except for a well-used pick-up truck, a light brown Chevy Silverado, several years old. It was a working vehicle. It had no licence plates. The doors were locked and there was no sign of a key.

'What's that?'

Reacher turned and saw Jeb Oliver's mother behind him.

'It's a truck,' Reacher said. 'Is it Jeb's?'

'I never saw it before.'

'How long has this thing been in here?' he asked.

'I don't know.'

'When did he put the lock on the door?'

'Maybe two months ago.'

'Why keep an old truck locked in here and a new one out in the weather?'

'Beats me,' the woman said. 'Jeb always does things his own way.'

Reacher backed out of the barn and walked each door closed. Then he used the balls of his thumbs to press the bolts back into their splintered holes. He got it looking as neat as he could, and then he left it alone and walked away back to the Mustang.

'Is Jeb ever coming back?' the woman called after him.

Reacher didn't answer. He just got in the car and, because it was facing north, he drove north down an arrow-straight road, aiming for a horizon that never arrived. He stared upwards and saw nothing but sky.

He stopped fifteen miles north of the city and parked on the unplanted corner of a field where the radial irrigation boom didn't reach. He checked his watch. He had two hours until his rendezvous at Franklin's office. He took the folded target out of his pocket and looked at it for a long time. Then he put it away again. He stared upwards and saw nothing but sky. He closed his eyes and started to think about ego and motive, and illusion and reality, and guilt and innocence, and the true nature of randomness.

CHAPTER SEVEN

Emerson read through Bellantonio's reports. Saw that Reacher had called Helen Rodin. No big shock there. Then he read Bellantonio's questions: *Is Reacher left-handed? Did he have access to a vehicle?* Answers: *Probably*, and *Probably*. Southpaws weren't rare. Line up twenty people, and four or five of them would be left-handed. And Reacher had access to a vehicle *now*, that was for sure. He wasn't in town, and he hadn't left on a bus. So he had a vehicle, and had probably had one all along.

Then Emerson read the final sheet: James Barr had been in Alexandra Dupree's apartment. What the hell was *that* about?

REACHER MADE it to Franklin's office about ten minutes late. It was a two-storey brick building in the heart of the city. The lower floor looked like a light industrial unit. There was an outside staircase leading to an upper door with a white plastic plate on it: FRANKLIN INVESTIGATIONS. There was a parking apron at street level. Helen Rodin's green Saturn was there, and a blue Honda Civic, and a black Chevy Suburban. The Suburban was Franklin's, Reacher guessed. The Honda was Rosemary Barr's, maybe.

Reacher slotted the Mustang next to the Saturn and got out. Ran up the staircase and went in the door without knocking. He walked along a short hallway to a large room. There he found Franklin at a desk, Helen Rodin and Rosemary Barr in two chairs huddled in conversation, and Ann Yanni looking out of the window at her car. All four turned as he came in.

'Do you know any medical terminology?' Helen asked him.

'Like what?'

'PA,' she said. 'A doctor wrote it. Some kind of abbreviation.'

Reacher glanced at her. Then at Rosemary Barr. 'Let me guess,' he said. 'The hospital diagnosed James Barr. Probably a mild case.'

'Early onset,' Rosemary said. 'Whatever it is.'

'What is it?' Helen asked.

'Later,' Reacher said. 'Let's do this in order.' He turned to Franklin. 'Tell me what you know about the victims.'

'Five random people,' Franklin said. 'No connection between any of them. No connection to James Barr. I think you were absolutely right. He didn't shoot them for any reason of his own.'

'No, I was absolutely wrong,' Reacher said. 'Thing is, James Barr didn't shoot them at all.'

GRIGOR LINSKY stepped into a shadowed doorway and dialled his phone.

'I followed a hunch,' he said.

'Which was?' the Zec asked.

'With the cops at the lawyer's office, I figured the soldier wouldn't be able to go see her. So I thought maybe she would go to him. And she did. I followed her. They're together in the private detective's office. With the sister. And that woman from the television news.'

'Are the others with you?'

'We've got the whole block covered.'

'Sit tight,' the Zec said. 'I'll get back to you.'

HELEN RODIN said, 'You want to explain that statement?'

'The evidence is rock solid,' Franklin said.

Ann Yanni smiled. *A story.*

Rosemary Barr just stared.

'You bought your brother a radio,' Reacher said to her. 'He told me that. Did you ever buy him anything else?'

'Like what?'

'Like clothes.'

'Sometimes,' she said.

'What size pants does your brother wear?'

'Thirty-four waist, thirty-four leg.'

'Exactly,' Reacher said. 'He's relatively tall.'

'How does this help us?' Helen asked.

'You know anything about numbers games?' Reacher asked her. 'What's the hardest part of them?'

'Winning,' Ann Yanni said.

Reacher smiled. 'From the players' point of view, sure. But the hardest part for the organisers is picking truly random numbers. True randomness is very hard for humans to achieve. Nowadays the big lotteries use complicated machines. But you can find mathematicians who can prove the results aren't truly random. Because humans built the machines.'

'How does *this* help us?' Helen said.

'Just a train of thought,' Reacher said. 'I sat all afternoon in Ms Yanni's car, thinking about how hard it is to achieve true randomness.'

'Your train is on the wrong track,' Franklin said. 'The evidence is crushing.'

'You were a cop,' Reacher said. 'You put yourself in danger. Stake-outs, take-downs, high-pressure situations, moments of extreme stress. What's the first thing you did afterwards?'

Franklin glanced at the women. 'Went to the bathroom.'

'Correct,' Reacher said. 'Me too. But James Barr didn't. Bellantonio's report shows cement dust in the garage, the kitchen, the living room, the bedroom, and the basement. But not in the bathroom.'

'Maybe he stopped on the way.'

'He was never there. There is no evidence that says he was there.'

'Are you nuts?'

'There's evidence that says his van was there, and his shoes, and his coat, and his gun, and his ammo, but there's nothing that says *he* was there.'

'Someone *impersonated* him?' Ann Yanni asked.

'Down to the last detail,' Reacher said. 'Drove his car, wore his shoes and his clothes, used his gun.'

'This is fantasy,' Franklin said.

Reacher stood still, then took a single pace forward. 'My pants are thirty-seven-inch legs. I crossed the new part of the garage in thirty-five strides. James Barr has a thirty-four-inch leg, so he should have done it in about thirty-eight strides. But Bellantonio's count shows *forty*-eight strides.'

'A very short person,' Helen said.

'Charlie,' Rosemary said.

'I thought so, too,' Reacher said. 'But then I went to Kentucky. I'd gotten to thinking that maybe James Barr wasn't good enough. Fourteen years ago he was good, but he wasn't great. And when I saw him in the hospital the skin on his right shoulder was unmarked. To shoot as well as he apparently did, a guy's got to practise. And a guy who practises builds up bruising on his shoulder. Like a callus. So I figured a guy who started out average could only have gotten worse with time. Maybe he'd gotten to the point where he *couldn't* have done the thing on Friday. Through a simple lack of ability. So I went down to Kentucky to find out for sure how much worse he'd gotten.'

'And?' Helen asked.

'He'd gotten *bette*r,' Reacher said. '*Way* better. Look at this.' He took the target out of his shirt pocket and unfolded it. 'This is much better than he was shooting in the army fourteen years ago. Which is weird, right?'

'So what does this mean?'

'He went down there with Charlie, every time. And the guy who runs the range is a Marine champion. He files all the used targets. Which means that Barr had at least two witnesses to what he was scoring, every time.'

'I'd *want* witnesses,' Franklin said, 'if I was shooting like that.'

Reacher said, 'I think the truth is he had actually gotten really bad. He couldn't face it, and he wanted to cover it up.'

Franklin pointed at the target. 'Doesn't look lousy to me.'

'This is faked,' Reacher said. 'You're going to give this to Bellantonio and Bellantonio is going to prove it to you.'

'Faked how?'

'I'll bet this was done with a handgun. Nine millimetre, from point-blank range. If Bellantonio measures the holes, my guess is he'll find they're forty-six thousandths of an inch bigger than .308 holes. And if he tests the paper, he'll find gunpowder residue on it. Because my guess is James Barr made these holes from an inch away, not three hundred yards.'

Nobody spoke.

'He must have gotten a lot worse,' Reacher said, 'because if he'd gotten a little worse he'd have owned up to it. To fake the score because of embarrassment proves he couldn't shoot well any more. If he couldn't shoot well any more, he didn't do the thing on Friday.'

'You're just guessing,' Franklin said.

Reacher nodded. 'I was. But I'm not now. I fired a round down in Kentucky. The guy made me, like a rite of passage. I was full of caffeine, twitching like crazy. Now I know James Barr will have been way worse.'

'Why?' Rosemary asked.

'Because he has Parkinson's disease,' Reacher said to her. 'PA means paralysis agitans, and paralysis agitans is what doctors call Parkinson's disease. Your brother is getting sick. And no way on earth can you fire a rifle accurately with Parkinson's disease. My opinion, not only didn't he do the thing on Friday, he *couldn't possibly* have done it.'

Rosemary went quiet. *Good news and bad news.* She looked at the floor. She was dressed like a widow. Black silk blouse, black pencil skirt, black nylons, black patent-leather shoes with a low heel,

'Maybe that's why he was so angry all the time,' she said. 'I moved out because of that. It was no fun living with him. But maybe he felt it coming on. Felt helpless and out of control. He would have hated that.' Then she looked straight at Reacher. 'I told you he was innocent,' she said.

'Ma'am, I apologise unreservedly,' Reacher said. 'You were right. He kept to his bargain. And I'm sorry he's sick.'

'Now you've got to help him. You promised.'

'Since Monday night I haven't done anything else.'

'This is crazy,' Franklin said.

'No, it's exactly the same as it always was,' Reacher said. 'It's someone setting James Barr up for the fall. But instead of actually making him do it, they just made it look like he did it.'

'But is it possible?' Ann Yanni asked.

'Why not? Think it through. *Walk* it through.'

Ann Yanni walked it through. 'He dresses in Barr's clothes, and shoes, and maybe finds a quarter in a pocket. He wears gloves, so as not to mess up Barr's fingerprints. He's already taken the traffic cone from Barr's garage, maybe the day before. He gets the rifle from the basement. It's already been loaded, by Barr himself. He drives to town in Barr's minivan. He leaves all the clues. Covers himself in cement dust. Comes back to the house and puts everything away and leaves. Fast, not even taking the time to use the bathroom. Then James Barr comes home later and walks into a trap.'

'But where was Barr at the time?' Helen said.

'They arranged something to get him out of the way,' Reacher said. 'He remembers going out somewhere. Then being optimistic. Like something good was about to happen. I think he had a date on Friday. Maybe with Sandy.'

'So who really did it?' Helen asked.

'Charlie,' Rosemary said. 'Got to be. He's small. He knew the house.'

'He was a terrible shooter too,' Reacher said. 'That's the other reason why I went to Kentucky. I wanted to test that theory.'

'So who was it?'

'Charlie,' Reacher said. 'His evidence was faked, too. But in a different way. The holes in his targets were all over the place. Except they weren't *really* all over the place. They weren't entirely random. He was trying to disguise how good he actually was. Once in a while he'd get bored, and put one through the inner ring. One time he drilled all four corners. Charlie was a tremendous shot, but he was trying to look like he was missing all the time. But like I said, true randomness is impossible for a human to achieve. There are always patterns.'

'Why would he do that?' Helen asked.

'For an alibi. He noticed that the range master was saving the used targets. He's an ice-cold pro.'

'Who is he?' Franklin asked.

'His real name is Chenko and he hangs with a bunch of Russians. He's probably a Red Army veteran. Probably a sniper.'

'How do we get to him?'

'Through the victim.'

'Square one. The victims are all dead ends. You'll have to come up with something better than that.'

'Chenko's boss calls himself the Zec. In old-time Soviet slang, a *zec* was a labour camp inmate. In the Gulag in Siberia.'

'Those camps are ancient history.'

'Which makes the Zec a very old man. But a very tough old man. Probably way tougher than we can imagine.'

THE ZEC was tired after dealing with Raskin. But he was used to being tired. He had been tired for sixty-three years, since the day the recruiter came to his village, 4,000 miles from anywhere, in the fall of 1942. A brisk, confident Moscow Russian, the recruiter permitted no argument. All males between the ages of sixteen and fifty were to come with him. The Zec was seventeen.

The recruits were locked in a truck, then a train, for a five-week journey. Formal induction into the Red Army happened along the way. Uniforms were issued, thick woollen garments, and a coat, a pair of felt-lined boots and a pay book. But no pay. No weapons. And no training, beyond a brief stop in a snow-covered rail yard, where a commissar brayed over and over again the same twenty-word speech: *The fate of the world is being decided at Stalingrad, where you will fight to the last for the Motherland.*

The journey ended on the eastern bank of the Volga, where the recruits were unloaded onto old ferries and pleasure cruisers. Half a mile away, on the opposite bank, a city, larger than anything the Zec had seen before, was in ruins, burning. The river was exploding with mortar shells. The sky was full of planes, diving, dropping bombs, firing guns. There were corpses everywhere, and screaming wounded. The Zec was forced onto a boat that was crammed tight with soldiers. The crossing lasted fifteen minutes and at the end of it the Zec was slimy with his neighbours' blood.

He was forced off onto a narrow wooden pier and made to run towards the city while a commissar with a megaphone roared at him: *No retreat! If you turn back even one step we will shoot you down!* So the Zec ran helplessly onwards and turned a corner and stepped into a hail of German bullets. He stopped, half turned, and was hit three times in the arms and legs. He was bowled over onto the shattered remains of a brick wall and within minutes was buried under a mounting pile of corpses.

He came to forty-eight hours later in an improvised hospital and made his first acquaintance with Soviet military justice, run strictly in accordance with its own arcane rules. The matter at issue was his having half turned: were his wounds inflicted by the enemy, or had he been retreating towards his own side's guns? Because of the ambiguity he was spared execution and sentenced to a penal battalion instead. Thus began a process of survival that had so far lasted sixty-three years. A process he intended to continue.

He dialled Grigor Linsky's number.

'We can assume the soldier is talking,' he said. 'Whatever he knows, they all know now. Therefore it's time to get ourselves an insurance policy.'

FRANKLIN SAID, 'We're really no further ahead. Are we?'

'So work the victim list,' Reacher said.

'That could take for ever. Five lives, five case histories.'

'So let's focus.'

'Great. Terrific. Just tell me which one you want me to focus on.'

Reacher nodded. Recalled Helen Rodin's description of what she had heard. *The first shot, and then a tiny pause, and then the next two. Then another pause, a little longer, and then the last three.*

'The third,' he said. 'There's a rhythm there. The first cold shot, then a lead-in, and then the money shot. The target. Then a break. He's making sure the target is down. It is. So then the last three.'

'Who was the third?' Helen asked.

'The woman,' Franklin said.

Reacher said, 'Tell me about her.'

Franklin shuffled his notes. 'Her name was Oline Archer,' he said. 'Caucasian female, married, no children, thirty-seven years old.'

'Employed in the DMV building,' Reacher said.

Franklin nodded. 'DMV clerical supervisor. Been there a year and a half. But DMV clerks don't get killed by customers.'

'So what about her personal life?' Helen Rodin asked.

'Nothing jumped out at me,' Franklin said. 'But I'll keep digging.'

'Do it fast,' Rosemary Barr said. 'We have to get my brother out.'

'We need medical opinions for that,' Ann Yanni said. 'Regular doctors now, not psychiatrists.'

'Parkinson's real, isn't it?' Rosemary said. 'Either he's got it or he hasn't.'

'It might work at trial,' Reacher said. 'A plausible reason why Barr couldn't have done it, plus a plausible narrative about someone else doing it?'

'Plausible is a big word,' Franklin said. 'Better to get Alex Rodin to drop the charges altogether. Which means convincing Emerson first.'

'I can't talk to either one of them,' Reacher said.

'I can,' Helen said.

'We all can, apart from you,' Ann Yanni said.

'But you might not want to,' Reacher said, looking at Helen.

'Why not?' she asked.

'Think,' Reacher said. 'The thing with Sandy being killed, and the thing in the sports bar Monday night, why did those two things happen?'

'To tie you up. To prevent you hurting the case.'

'Correct. And the thing Monday night started with me being followed from my hotel. Sandy and Jeb Oliver and his pals were standing by, until someone called them. So really it started with me being followed *to* my hotel, much earlier in the day. But how did the puppet master get my name? How did he even know I was in town? How did he know there was a guy who was a potential problem? Who knew, early in the day on Monday?'

Helen paused a beat. 'My father,' she said. 'And then Emerson, presumably. They'd have talked about the case.'

'Correct,' Reacher said again. 'Then one of those two guys called the puppet master. Well before lunch on Monday.'

Helen said nothing.

'Unless one of those two guys *is* the puppet master,' Reacher said.

'The Zec is the puppet master. You said so yourself.'

'I said he's Charlie's boss. That's all. But someone communicated. Either your father or Emerson. So one of them is bent and the other one won't help us because he already likes the case exactly the way it is.'

The room went quiet.

'I need to get back to work,' Ann Yanni said. 'Call me if there's news.' She crossed the room. Stopped next to Reacher. 'Keys,' she said.

He handed them over. 'Thanks for the loan,' he said. 'Nice car.'

LINSKY WATCHED the Mustang leave. It was audible for a whole block. Then the street went quiet again and Linsky dialled his phone.

'The television woman is out of there,' he said.

'The private detective will stay at work,' the Zec said.

'So what if the others leave together?'

'Take them all.'

ROSEMARY BARR asked, 'Is there a cure? For Parkinson's disease?'

'No,' Reacher said. 'But it can be slowed down. There are drugs for it.'

'I should go to the hospital,' Rosemary said.

'Tell him what really happened on Friday,' Reacher said.

Rosemary nodded and went out of the door. A minute later, Reacher heard her car start up and drive away.

Franklin went out to make coffee. Reacher and Helen Rodin were left alone in the office together. Helen stepped to the window and looked down at the street below. She was dressed the same as Rosemary Barr. Black shirt, black skirt, black patent leather shoes. But she didn't look like a widow. She looked like something from New York or Paris. Her heels were higher and her legs were long and bare and tan.

'These guys we're talking about are Russians,' she said. 'My father is an American.'

'An American called Aleksei Alekseivitch.'

'Our family came here before World War One.'

'What did your father do before he was the DA?'

'He was an assistant DA. He always worked there.'

'On Monday he was wearing a thousand-dollar suit. You don't see many public servants wearing thousand-dollar suits. And his coffee was served in china cups on a silver tray. The county didn't buy them for him.'

'He's got expensive tastes.'

'One more question. Did he pressure you not to take the case?'

Helen turned round. 'He said losing might be winning.'

'Concern for your career?'

'I thought so. He's an honest man.'

Reacher nodded. 'There's a fifty per cent chance you're right.'

Franklin came back in with the coffee. It was served in three nonmatching pottery mugs, with an open carton of milk and a yellow box of sugar, on a cork bar tray. Helen Rodin stared at it, like it was making Reacher's point for him: *This is how coffee is served in an office.*

'David Chapman knew your name on Monday,' Helen said. 'James Barr's first lawyer. He's known about you since Saturday.'

'But he didn't know I ever showed up,' Reacher said.

Nobody spoke.

'I was wrong about Jeb Oliver,' Reacher said. 'He isn't a dope dealer. There was nothing in his barn except an old pick-up truck.'

'I'm glad you can be wrong about something,' Helen said, standing up. 'I'm going back to work.'

'Give me a ride?' Reacher asked. 'Let me out under the highway?'

'No,' Helen said. 'I really don't feel like doing that.'

She picked up her briefcase and walked out of the office alone.

Reacher sat and listened to the sounds out on the street. He heard a car door opening and closing, an engine starting, a car driving away. He sipped his coffee and said, 'I guess I upset her.'

Franklin nodded. 'I guess you did.'

'These guys have got someone on the inside. That's clear.'

'A cop makes more sense than a DA.'

'I don't agree. A cop controls only his own cases. Ultimately a prosecutor controls everything.'

'And I have to say, Alex Rodin kills a lot of cases. People say it's caution, but it could be something else.'

Reacher put his mug down. Stood up to go. 'Check out Oline Archer,' he said. 'The victim. She's what's important now.'

He stepped to the window and checked the street. Saw nothing. So he nodded to Franklin and walked down the hallway and out of the door to the top of the outside staircase.

He paused on the top step and stretched. Rolled his shoulders, flexed his hands, took a deep breath. He was cramped from driving and sitting all day. And oppressed by hiding out. It felt good to just stand still and do nothing, high up and exposed. Out in the open. He started down the stairs.

As he stepped off onto the sidewalk he heard a footfall behind him. Then the unmistakable *crunch-crunch* of a pump-action shotgun racking a round.

Then a voice said: 'Stop right there.'

Reacher stopped. Stood still and stared straight ahead.

Then the voice said: 'Step to your right.'

Reacher stepped to his right. A long sideways shuffle.

The voice said: 'Now turn around real slow.'

Reacher turned around, real slow. Saw a small figure fifteen feet away. Not more than five four, not more than 130 pounds, slight, pale, with cropped black hair that stuck up crazily. Chenko. Or, Charlie. In his right hand was a sawn-off with a pistol grip. In his left hand was some kind of a black thing.

'Catch,' Charlie said.

He tossed the black thing underhand. It was a woman's patent-leather dress shoe, black, with a heel. It was still slightly warm.

'Now toss it back,' Charlie said.

Reacher paused. Whose shoe was it? He stared down at it. *Low heel.* Rosemary Barr's. He soft-tossed the shoe back.

'She's in summer school,' Charlie said. 'Think about it like that. She's going to work on her testimony. About how her brother planned in advance. How he let slip what he was going to do. She's going to be a great witness.

Reacher said nothing.

'Take two steps back,' Charlie said. 'Then turn around.'

Reacher took two steps back. They put him right on the kerb.

'You going to shoot me?' Reacher asked.

'Maybe.'

'You should.'

'Why?'

'Because if you don't, I'm going to find you and make you sorry.'

'Big talk. Now turn around,' Charlie repeated.

Reacher turned around. Faced the street. He strained to hear sounds behind him. Listened for the quiet metallic click of the trigger. Would Charlie shoot? Common sense said no. Homicides were always investigated. But these people were crazy. And there was a fifty per cent chance that they owned a local cop. Or that *he* owned *them*.

Silence. Then a hundred yards away to the east Reacher heard a siren.

Two police cruisers turned into the street simultaneously. One from the east, one from the west. They jammed to a stop. Doors opened. Cops spilled out. Reacher turned his head. Charlie wasn't there any more.

THE ARREST was fast and efficient. Reacher stayed silent throughout. He knew the kind of trouble that talking can get a guy into.

The trip to the station house was mercifully short. Reacher figured he would be taken to Emerson, which gave him a fifty per cent chance of being put in a room with a bad guy. But he ended up a hundred per cent sure he was in a room with a bad guy, because Emerson and Rodin were there together.

'Tell us about the night Alexandra Dupree was killed,' Rodin said.

'Tell us how it felt,' Emerson said. 'When her neck snapped.'

Reacher said, 'Phone call. Call Ann Yanni.'

'From the TV?' Rodin said. 'Why her?'

'I get a phone call,' Reacher said. 'I don't have to explain anything. I say who, you dial the number.'

'She'll be getting ready to go on the air. The local news is at six o'clock.'

'I've got all the time in the world,' Reacher said. He was thinking, Which one of you knows that isn't true?

It turned out the wait wasn't long. Emerson placed the call to NBC and told Ann Yanni's assistant that the police department had arrested Jack Reacher and he was requesting Yanni's presence. Yanni was in Emerson's office less than thirty minutes later. She was a journalist on the scent of a story.

'How can I help?' she asked. She had presence.

'I'm sorry,' Reacher said to her. 'I know I said I would never tell, but under the circumstances you're going to have to confirm an alibi for me.'

He saw confusion cross her face. No reaction. Reacher held his breath. He kept his eyes on hers. *Get with the program, Yanni.*

Then she nodded. Reacher breathed out.

'What alibi?' Emerson said.

Yanni glanced at him. Then at Rodin. 'I thought this was about Jack Reacher,' she said.

'It is,' Emerson said.

'But this is Joe Gordon,' she said.

'He told you his name was Gordon?'

'When I met him. Two days ago.'

'You've been running his picture on your show.'

'That was *his* picture? It looked nothing like him. The hair was different.'

'What alibi?' Emerson said again.

'For when?' Yanni asked.

'The night the girl was killed.'

Rodin said, 'Ma'am, if you know something, you need to tell us now.'

'I'd rather not,' Yanni said.

Reacher smiled to himself. The way she said it absolutely guaranteed that Emerson and Rodin were a minute away from begging to hear the story. She was a hell of an actress. Reacher figured maybe all news anchors were.

'Can't you just take my word?' Yanni said.

'For what?'

'That he didn't do it.'

'We need details,' Rodin said.

Yanni sighed. Looked straight into Emerson's eyes, furious, embarrassed, magnificent. 'We spent that night together,' she said.

Emerson pointed. 'This man?'

Yanni nodded. 'That man. From about eleven forty. When the news was over. Until I got paged the next morning when you guys found the body.'

'Where were you?'

Reacher closed his eyes. Recalled the conversation in the parking garage. The car window open an inch and a half. *Had he told her?*

'The motor court,' Yanni said. 'His room.'

'The clerk didn't say he saw you.'

'Of course the clerk didn't see me. I have to think about things like that.'

'Which room?'

Had he told her?

'Room eight,' Yanni said.

'Can you offer any corroboration?' Emerson asked.

'Like what?' Yanni asked back.

'Distinguishing marks? That I can't see but that someone who had been in your position would have seen?'

'Oh, please.'

Reacher recalled switching on the Mustang's interior light and lifting his shirt to reveal the tyre iron.

'It's important,' Rodin said.

'He has a scar,' Yanni said. 'Low down on his stomach.'

Reacher got to his feet. Pulled his shirt out of his pants. Lifted it.

'OK,' Emerson said.

'Satisfied now?' Reacher asked.

'Ms Yanni will have to put it in writing,' Emerson said.

'You type it, I'll sign it,' Yanni said.

Silence in the office. Emerson dug in his pocket and found a handcuff key. Reacher held his wrists out and waited for Emerson to unlock the cuffs.

Two MINUTES later the Zec took the phone call. A familiar voice, low and hurried. 'It didn't work,' it said. 'He had an alibi.'

'So what next?'

'Just sit tight. He can't be more than one step away now. In which case he'll be coming for you soon. So be locked and loaded and ready for him.'

'THEY DIDN'T fight very hard,' Ann Yanni said. 'Did they?' She started the Mustang's engine before Reacher even got his door closed.

'I didn't expect them to,' he said. 'The innocent one knows the case was weak. And the guilty one knows putting me back on the street takes me off the board about as fast as putting me in a cell right now.'

'Why?'

'Because they've got Rosemary Barr and they know I'll go find her. So they'll be waiting for me, ready to rock and roll. I'll be dead before morning. That's the new plan. Cheaper than jail.'

They drove back to Franklin's office and ran up the outside staircase and found Franklin sitting at his desk, staring blankly at his computer screen.

Reacher broke the news about Rosemary Barr. Franklin went very still.

'What are they going to do to her?' Franklin asked.

'They're going to make her give evidence against her brother. Some kind of a made-up story.'

'Will they hurt her?'

'That depends on how fast she caves.'

'She's not going to cave,' Yanni said. 'She's totally dedicated to clearing her brother's name.'

'Then they're going to hurt her.'

'Where is she?' Franklin asked Reacher. 'Best guess?'

'Wherever they are,' Reacher said. 'But I don't know where that is.'

SHE WAS in the upstairs living room, taped to a chair. The Zec was staring at her. He was fascinated by women. Once he had gone twenty-seven years without seeing one. The penal colony he had joined in 1943 had had a few, but they were a small minority and they died fast.

'Are you comfortable?' the Zec asked.

Rosemary Barr said nothing. Chenko had returned her shoe. He had fitted it to her foot like a store clerk. Then he had sat down next to Vladimir, on the sofa. Sokolov had stayed downstairs. Linsky was pacing the room.

'Does she understand her position?' Linsky asked.

The Zec smiled at him, and Linsky smiled back. It was a private joke between them. Any claim to humane treatment in the camps was always met with a question: *Do you understand your position?* The question was always followed by a statement: *You don't have a position.* The first time Linsky heard the question he had been about to reply, but the Zec had hauled him away. By that point the Zec had eighteen years under his belt, and the intervention was uncharacteristic. But he had taken the kid under his wing. They had been together ever since.

Linsky had been a soldier and a thief. In the west of Europe or in America he would have served time, two years here, three years there, but during the Soviet stealing was an ideological transgression. It showed an uneducated and antisocial preference for private property. Such a preference was answered with a swift and permanent removal from civilised society. In Linsky's case the removal had lasted from 1963 until civilised society had collapsed and Gorbachev had emptied the Gulag.

'She understands her position,' the Zec said. 'Next comes acceptance.'

FRANKLIN CALLED Helen Rodin. Ten minutes later she was back in his office. She was still mad at Reacher. But she was too worried about Rosemary Barr to make a big deal out of it. Franklin stayed at his desk, one eye on his computer screen. Helen and Ann Yanni sat at a table. Reacher stared out the window. The sky was darkening.

'We should call someone,' Helen said.

'Like who?' Reacher asked.

'My father. He's the good guy.'

Reacher turned round. 'Suppose he is. What do we tell him? That we've got a missing person? He'll just call the cops. And if Emerson's the bad guy, the cops will sit on it. Even if Emerson's the good guy, the cops will sit on it. Missing adults don't get anyone excited. And they'll figure she ran away because her brother is a notorious criminal and she couldn't stand the shame.'

'But you saw her get kidnapped. You could tell them.'

'I saw a shoe. That's all I can tell anybody. And I've got no credibility here. I've been playing silly games for two days.'

'So what do we do?'

'We work through the woman who was shot, we get names, we get some kind of a context, we get a place. Then we go there.'

Yanni turned to Franklin and said, 'Tell us more about the woman who was shot.'

'There's nothing more to tell,' Franklin said. 'She was very ordinary.'

'Family?'

'All of them are back East. Where she came from.'

'Friends?'

'Two, basically. A co-worker and a neighbour. Neither of them is interesting. Neither of them is a Russian.'

Then Franklin's eyes lost focus. 'Wait,' he said, turning to his computer. 'Something I forgot.'

'What?' Reacher asked.

'What you said about Rosemary Barr. Missing persons.'

He started clicking and typing. Then he hit his enter key, and waited.

Franklin's screen stayed blank for a long, long time. There was a little graphic in the corner. It was rotating slowly. Then it stopped. The screen wiped down and redrew into a densely printed document.

'OK,' Franklin said. 'At last. Finally we catch a break.'

'What?' Yanni said.

'Oline Archer reported her husband missing two months ago.'

Everyone crowded round the screen. Two months previously Mrs Oline Anne Archer had made a missing persons report concerning her husband, Edward Stratton Archer. He had left for work early on a Monday and had not returned by the end of Wednesday, which was when the report was made.

'Is he still missing?' Helen asked.

'Yes,' Franklin said. He pointed to a letter A buried in the code at the top of the screen. 'It's still active.'

'So let's go talk to Oline's friends,' Reacher said. 'No time to waste.'

Franklin wrote down names and addresses for Oline Archer's co-worker and neighbour. He handed the paper to Ann Yanni, because she was paying his bill. 'I'll stay here,' he said. 'I'll see if the husband shows up in the data bases. This could be a coincidence.'

'I don't believe in coincidences,' Reacher said. 'Find a phone number for me instead. A guy called Cash. He owns the range where James Barr went to shoot. Call him for me.'

'Message?'

'Give him my name. Tell him to drive up here, tonight. Tell him there's a whole new Invitational going on.'

'Invitational?'

'He'll understand. Tell him to bring his M24. With a night scope. And whatever else he's got lying around.'

Reacher followed Ann Yanni and Helen Rodin down the stairs. They got into Helen's Saturn, the women in the front and Reacher in the back.

'Where first?' Helen asked.

'The co-worker.'

Traffic was slow. Daylight was fading. *Time ticking away.*

THE CO-WORKER lived in a plain heartland suburb east of town. She was a harassed woman of about thirty-five. She opened her door and stepped out and pulled the door shut behind her to block out the noise from what sounded like a dozen kids running riot inside. She recognised Ann Yanni immediately. Even glanced beyond her, looking for a camera crew.

'Yes?' she said.

'We need to talk about Oline Archer,' Helen Rodin said.

'OK,' the woman said. 'What do you want to know?'

'We need to know about her husband,' Helen said.

'His name's Ted, I think,' the woman said. 'I never met him.'

'What does he do?'

'He's in business. I'm not sure what kind.'

'Did Oline say anything about him being missing?'

'Missing?'

'Oline reported him missing two months ago.'

'I know she seemed terribly worried. I think he'd been having problems with his business for a year or two. That's why Oline went back to work.'

'But she didn't give you details?' Ann Yanni asked.

'She was a very private person,' the woman said.

'It's important.'

'She would get distracted. That wasn't like her. About a week before she was killed, she was gone most of one afternoon. That wasn't like her either.'

'Do you know what she was doing?'

'No, I really don't.'

'OK, thanks,' Helen said.

She turned and headed back to her car. Yanni and Reacher followed her. The woman stared after them, disappointed, like she had failed an audition.

'Strike one,' Ann Yanni said when they reached the car. 'It always happens. Sometimes I think we should just skip the first person on the list. They never know anything. But don't worry. The neighbour will know more.'

It was already twilight. *Time ticking away.*

ROSEMARY BARR struggled against the tape binding her wrists.

'We know it was Charlie who did it,' she said.

'His name is Chenko,' the Zec said. 'And yes, he did it. He was able to wear his own shoes inside your brother's. But *who* knows?'

'Helen Rodin knows,' Rosemary said.

'You'll dismiss her as your lawyer. Ms Rodin will be unable to repeat anything she learned while your relationship was privileged.'

'Franklin knows,' Rosemary said. 'And Ann Yanni.'

'Hearsay and speculation,' the Zec said. 'They have no evidence, and no credibility. Your deposition will be definitive. You'll go to Rodin and you'll give sworn testimony about how your brother plotted and planned. About how he *told* you what he was intending. In detail. You'll say that to your everlasting regret you didn't take him seriously. Then a public defender will plead your brother guilty and the whole thing will be over.'

'I won't do it,' Rosemary said.

The Zec looked straight at her. 'You will do it,' he said. 'Twenty-four hours from now you'll be *begging* to do it.'

'Reacher knows,' Rosemary said.

'The soldier? The soldier will be dead by morning. He'll come for you tonight. We'll be ready for him.'

Rosemary said nothing.

'When will he come?' the Zec asked.

'I don't know,' Rosemary said.

'Four o'clock in the morning,' Linsky said. 'He's an American. They're trained that four o'clock is the best time for a surprise attack.'

'Direction?'

'From the north would make the most sense. The stone-crushing plant would conceal his staging area and leave him only two hundred yards of open ground to cover. But he'll avoid the north, because he knows it's best.'

'Not from the west,' the Zec said.

'I agree. Not the driveway. Too open. He'll come from the south or east.'

'Put Vladimir in with Sokolov,' the Zec said. 'Tell them to watch the south and the east very carefully. Then put Chenko in the upstairs hallway with his rifle. He can be ready to deploy to whichever window is appropriate. With Chenko, one shot will be enough.'

He turned to Rosemary Barr. 'Meanwhile we'll put you somewhere safe,' he told her. 'Your tutorials will start as soon as the soldier is buried.'

THE OUTER western suburbs were bedroom communities for people who worked in the city, so the traffic stayed bad all the way out. The houses were much grander than in the east. The evening light was fading away to darkness and lamps were coming on behind draped windows. The whole street looked warm and quiet and very satisfied with itself.

Reacher said, '"They sleep safely in their beds because rough men stand ready in the night to visit violence on those who would do them harm."'

'You know George Orwell?' Yanni asked.

'I went to college,' Reacher said. 'West Point is technically a college.'

They drove past the Archer place. The neighbour they were looking for lived across the street, one lot to the north. Helen pulled into a long limestone driveway and parked about twenty feet behind an imported SUV.

'Tight-ass middle class,' Reacher said. 'They won't talk. Not their style.'

'I'm sure these are perfectly nice people,' Helen said.

'But will they talk to us?'

'They'll talk,' Yanni said. 'Everyone talks.'

The front door had an iron knocker shaped like a quoit in a lion's mouth. Helen lifted it and thumped on the door. Then she found a discreet electric bell push and pressed that, too. The door sucked back like a vault. A guy was standing there with his hand on the inside handle.

'Yes?' he said. He was in his forties, solid, prosperous. He was wearing corduroy trousers and a patterned sweater.

'We'd like to speak to your wife about Oline Archer,' Helen said.

'About Oline?' the guy said. He was looking at Ann Yanni.

'I'm here as a journalist,' Yanni said. 'But not on a human interest story. Nothing tacky. There might have been a miscarriage of justice.'

'A miscarriage in what way?'

'They might have arrested the wrong man for the shootings. That's why I'm here. That's why we're all here.'

The guy sighed and stepped back. 'You'd better come in.' He led the way to a spacious living room. 'I'll get my wife,' he said.

He came back a minute later with a handsome woman a little younger than himself. She was wearing pressed jeans and a yellow sweatshirt.

'What's this about?' she asked.

'Ted Archer,' Helen said.

'Ted? I thought you told my husband it was about Oline.'

'We think there may be a connection. Between his situation and hers. We suspect that Oline might have been a specific target.'

'Wouldn't that be a matter for the police?'

Helen paused. 'The police seem satisfied with what they've got.'

The woman glanced at her husband. Then she sat down on a sofa and her husband sat next to her. Yanni perched on the edge of an armchair facing them. Helen took another chair. Reacher went to the window. Used a finger to move the drapes aside. It was dark outside now. *Time ticking away.*

'Tell us about Ted Archer,' Yanni said. 'Please.'

'Ted had business problems,' the woman said. 'He was getting screwed rotten and he was mad as hell about it and he was fighting.'

Her husband leaned forward. 'His principal customer stopped buying from him. So Ted offered to renegotiate. Offered to drop his price. No dice. So he offered to drop it more. Still no dice.'

'What do you think was happening?' Yanni asked.

'Corruption,' the guy said. 'One of Ted's competitors was offering kick-backs. No way for an honest man to compete with that.'

'When did this start?'

'About two years ago. Financially they went downhill very fast. Ted sold his car. Oline had to go out to work.'

'What was Ted doing about it?'

'He was trying to find out which competitor it was.'

'Did he find out?'

'We don't know. He was trying for a long time. Then he went missing.'

'Didn't Oline include this in her report?'

The guy sat back and his wife shook her head. 'Oline didn't want to. Not back then. It was all unproven. All speculation.'

'Did Oline *ever* go to anyone with this? Later, maybe?'

The woman nodded. 'She stewed for two months after he disappeared. We talked. Eventually she decided there had to be a connection. I told her she should call the police.'

'And did she?'

'She didn't call. She went personally. She felt they would take her more seriously face to face. Not that they did, apparently. Nothing happened.'

'When did she go?'

'A week before the thing in the plaza last Friday.'

Kindly, gently, Ann Yanni asked the obvious question: 'You didn't sus-pect a connection?'

The woman shook her head. 'Why would we? The shootings were random, weren't they? You said so yourself. On the television news.'

Reacher turned away from the window. 'What business was Ted Archer in?' he asked.

'I'm sorry, I assumed you knew,' the husband said. 'He owns a quarry. Huge place, forty miles north of here. Cement, concrete, crushed stone.'

'And who was the customer who backed off?'

'The city,' the guy said. 'All this construction going on right now is manna from heaven for people in that business.'

'What car did Ted sell?'

'A Mercedes-Benz.'

'Then what did he drive?'

'He used a pick-up truck from work. A Chevy, I think.'

'An old brown Silverado? Plain steel wheels?'

The guy stared. 'How did you know that?'

'One more question,' Reacher said. 'For your wife.'

She looked at him.

'After Oline went to the cops, did she tell you who it was she talked to? Was it a detective called Emerson?'

The woman was already shaking her head. 'I told Oline if she didn't want to call she should go to the station house, but she said she'd go to the DA instead. His office is much closer to the DMV. And Oline preferred to go straight to the top. So she took it to Alex Rodin himself.'

HELEN RODIN was completely silent on the drive back to town. She drove like a robot, competently, not fast, not slow. She parked on the apron below Franklin's office and said, 'You two go on ahead. I just can't do this.'

Ann Yanni got out and walked over to the staircase.

Reacher leaned forward over the seat. 'It'll be OK,' he said.

'It won't.'

'Helen, get your ass upstairs. You're an officer of the court and you've got a client who's in trouble.' He climbed out of the car, and by the time he had walked round the trunk she was waiting for him at the foot of the stairs.

Franklin was in front of his computer, as always. He told Reacher that Cash was on his way up from Kentucky. Then he noticed the tension.

'What's up?' he asked.

'We're one step away,' Reacher said. 'Ted Archer was in the concrete business and he was frozen out of all these new city construction contracts by a competitor who was offering bribes. He tried to prove it and the competitor offed him.'

'Can you prove that?'

'Only by inference. We'll never find his body without digging up First Street again. But I know where his truck is. It's in Jeb Oliver's barn.'

'Oline Archer didn't suspect anything?'

'She did eventually,' Reacher said. 'She started to go public with it and all kinds of private alarm bells must have gone off because a week later she was dead. Staged the way it was because a missing husband and then a murdered wife two months later would have raised too many flags. But as long as it looked random it was going to be seen as coincidental.'

'Who had Oline taken it to? Emerson?'

'She took it to my father,' Helen Rodin said.

There was silence for a long moment.

'So what now?' Franklin asked.

'You need to hit that keyboard again,' Reacher said. 'Whoever got the city contracts is the bad guy. We need to know who he is. And where he's based.'

Franklin turned away, his fingers pattering over the keys. A minute later he came up with the answer. 'Specialised Services of Indiana,' he said. 'They own all the city contracts for cement, concrete, and crushed stone.'

'Where are they?'

'They're a trust registered in Bermuda.'

'A Bermuda trust needs a local lawyer.' Helen's voice was resigned.

'There's a phone number,' Franklin said. He read it out.

'That's not my father's number,' Helen said.

Franklin clicked his way into a reverse directory. Typed in the number and got a name and business address. 'John Mistrov,' he said.

'Russian name,' Reacher said. 'Do you know him?'

'Vaguely. He's a wills and trusts guy. One-man band.'

'Can you find a home address?'

Franklin went into a regular directory. Typed in the name and came up with a domestic listing. 'Should I call him?' he asked.

Reacher shook his head. 'We'll pay him a visit,' he said.

VLADIMIR made his way down to the ground-floor surveillance room. Sokolov was in a rolling chair in front of the long table that carried the four CCTV monitors. From left to right they were labelled NORTH, EAST, SOUTH and WEST. All four screens were misty and green, because it was dark outside and the thermal imaging had kicked in. Occasionally a bright dot could be seen moving fast in the distance. An animal. Nocturnal. Fox, skunk, raccoon, or a pet cat far from home. The north monitor showed a glow from the crushing plant. It would fade, as the idle machines cooled. Apart from that, there was nothing out there except miles of fields constantly misted with cold water from the always-turning irrigation booms.

Vladimir pulled up a second wheeled chair and sat down on Sokolov's left. He would watch north and east. Sokolov would concentrate on the south and west.

Upstairs in the second-floor hallway, Chenko loaded his own Super Match. He opened all the bedroom doors to speed his access north, south, east or west, as required. He walked to a window and turned his night scope on. Set it for seventy-five yards. He figured he would get the call when the soldier was about 150 yards out. He would step to the right window and acquire the target when it was still more than 100 yards distant. He would let it come to him. When it was seventy-five yards out, he would kill it.

He walked back to the hallway and propped the gun against the wall and sat down in a straight-backed chair to wait.

HELEN RODIN insisted on staying behind in Franklin's office. So Reacher and Yanni went out alone, in the Mustang. Yanni drove. The address they were looking for was a loft building carved out of an old warehouse halfway between the river wharf and the railhead. Yanni slowed as the bulk of a large brick building loomed through the darkness.

'You can ask first,' Reacher said. 'If he doesn't answer, I'll ask second.'

'He'll answer,' Yanni said. 'They all answer.'

But John Mistrov didn't. He was a thin guy of about forty-five. They found him all alone in a big white loft apartment eating Chinese food from paper cartons. Initially he was very pleased to see Ann Yanni. But his enthusiasm disappeared when she ran through her suspicions and insisted on knowing the names behind the Bermuda trust.

'I can't tell you,' he said. 'Surely you understand.'

'I *understand* that serious crimes have been committed,' Yanni said. 'And you need to understand that, too.'

'No comment,' the guy said.

'There's no downside here,' Yanni said, gently. 'These names we want, they'll all be in jail tomorrow. No comebacks.'

'No comment,' the guy said again. Loud and smug.

Yanni gave up, and glanced at Reacher. He stepped up close.

'You got medical insurance?' he asked. 'Dental plan?'

The guy nodded.

Reacher hit him in the mouth. 'Get *that* fixed,' he said.

The guy doubled over and then came up coughing. Cut lips, loose teeth all rimed with red.

'Names,' Reacher said. 'Now.'

The guy hesitated. Reacher hit him again. Then the guy came up with six names, and descriptions, and an address, all from a position flat on the floor.

Reacher glanced at Yanni. 'They all answer,' he said.

In the dark in the Mustang on the way back Ann Yanni said, 'He'll call and warn them.'

'He won't,' Reacher said. 'He just betrayed them. My guess is he'll be going on a long vacation tomorrow.'

'You hope.'

'Doesn't matter anyway. They know I'm coming for them.'

YANNI DICTATED to Franklin the names that John Mistrov had given up. Four of them corresponded with names Reacher had already heard: Charlie Smith, Konstantin Raskin, Vladimir Shumilov and Pavel Sokolov. The fifth was Grigor Linsky, which Reacher figured had to be the damaged man in the boxy suit, because the sixth name had been given simply as Zec Chelovek.

'I thought you said Zec was a word,' Franklin said.

'It is,' Reacher said. 'And so is Chelovek. It's a transliteration of their word for human being. Zec Chelovek means prisoner human being.'

'The others aren't using code names.'

'Neither is the Zec, probably. Maybe he forgot his real name. Maybe we all would, in the Gulag.'

'You sound sorry for him.'

'I'm not sorry for him,' Reacher said. 'Just trying to understand him.'

'No mention of my father,' Helen said.

Reacher nodded. 'The Zec is the puppet master.'

'Which means my father is just an employee.'

'Don't worry about that now. Focus on Rosemary.'

Franklin used an online map and figured out that the address Mistrov had spilled related to a stone-crushing plant built next to a quarry eight miles northwest of the city. Then he searched the tax rolls and confirmed that Specialised Services of Indiana was its registered owner. Then he found that the only other real estate registered to the trust was a house on the lot adjacent to the stone-crushing plant. Yanni said she knew the area.

'OK,' Reacher said. 'That's where Rosemary is.'

He checked his watch. Ten o'clock in the evening.

'Now we wait,' Reacher said.

'For what?' Yanni asked.

'For Cash to get here. Then we wait some more.'

'For what?'

Reacher smiled. 'For the dead of night,' he said.

AT ELEVEN o'clock exactly they heard the rattle of a big diesel engine. Reacher stepped to the window and saw Cash's Humvee.

'The Marines are here,' he said.

They heard Cash's feet on the outside stairs. Heard his knock on the door. Reacher went out to the hallway to open it. Cash came in, brisk, solid, reassuring. He was dressed all in black. Reacher introduced him to everyone. Inside twenty minutes, Cash was up to speed and totally on board.

'Do we have a plan?' he asked.

'We're about to make one,' Reacher said.

Yanni went out to her car for the maps. Franklin cleared away the coffee cups. Yanni chose the right map. Spread it out flat on the table.

'It's like a giant chessboard out there,' she said. 'Every square is a field a hundred yards across. There are roads laid out in a grid, about twenty fields apart.' She pointed. 'But right *here* we've got two roads that meet and southeast of the corner they make we've got an empty space three fields wide and five fields high. The northern part is the stone-crushing plant and the house is south of it. I've seen it and it stands about two hundred yards off the road, all alone in the middle of absolutely nothing. No fence, either.'

'Dark out there,' Cash said.

'As the Earl of Hell's waistcoat,' Reacher said. 'I guess if there's no fence it means they're using some kind of thermal imaging at night.'

'What's the best approach?'

'From the north,' Reacher said. 'Without a doubt. We could get into the stone place straight off the road. Good concealment until the last minute But they'll anticipate that. Too obvious.'

'Presumably the driveway comes in from the west. Probably too straight and too open. South or east would be better.'

'They're going to be thinking the same thing. I kind of like the driveway,' Reacher said. 'Paved?'

'Crushed limestone,' Yanni said. 'They've got plenty to spare.'

'It'll have retained a little daytime heat,' Reacher said. 'It'll be warmer than the dirt. It'll put a stripe of colour down their thermal picture. If the contrast isn't great it'll give a shadow zone either side.'

'Are you kidding?' Cash said. 'You're going to be forty or fifty degrees hotter than ambient temperature. You're going to show up like a road flare.'

'You got a better idea?'

'Cut the power lines? Kill the cameras?'

'Too dangerous,' Reacher said. 'We can't give them a second's warning, or turn the place into a free-fire zone. We've got Rosemary to think about.'

'Your call.'

'I like the driveway,' Reacher said.

'But what about the cameras?' Yanni asked.

'I'll think of something,' Reacher said. He turned back to Cash. 'Does your truck have a CD player?'

Cash nodded. 'Part of the comfort package.'

'Do you mind if Franklin drives it?'

'Franklin can *have* it. I'd prefer a sedan.'

'OK, your Humvee is our approach vehicle. Franklin can drive us there, let us out, and then get straight back here.'

'Us?' Yanni said. 'Are we all going?'

'You bet your ass,' Reacher said. 'Four of us there, with Franklin back here as the comms centre.'

'Good,' Yanni said.

'We need cellphones,' Reacher said. 'I don't have one.'

Franklin took a small Nokia out of his pocket. 'Take mine,' he said.

The others all had their own.

'Can you set up a conference call?' Reacher asked. Four cellphones and your desk phone? As soon as you get back here?'

Franklin nodded. 'Give me your numbers,' he said.

'And turn the ringers off,' Reacher said.

'When are we doing this?' Cash asked.

'Four a.m. is my favourite time,' Reacher said. 'But they'll be expecting that. We learned it from them. Four in the morning is when the KGB went knocking on doors. So we'll surprise them. We'll do it at two thirty.'

'Where am I going to be?' Cash asked.

'Southwest corner of the gravel plant,' Reacher said. 'Looking south and east at the house. You can cover the west and the north sides with your rifle.'

'OK.'

'What did you bring for me?'

Cash dug in the pocket of his windcheater and came out with a knife in a sheath. He tossed it across the room. Reacher caught it. It was a standard-issue Navy SEAL SRK. Seven-inch blade. Not new.

'This is it?' Reacher asked.

'All I've got,' Cash said. 'Only weapons I own are my rifle and that knife.'

'You're kidding.'

'I'm a businessman, not a psycho. You can take a gun from the first one you cut. Face it, if you don't get close enough to cut one of them you aren't going to win anyway.'

Reacher said nothing.

THEY WAITED. Midnight. One o'clock. Reacher went through the plan one more time, so that everyone was clear. Then he started to allow himself to think about the endgame. He turned to Franklin.

'Who is Emerson's number two?' he asked.

'A woman called Donna Bianca,' Franklin said.

'She'll need to be there. Afterwards. It'll be a real three-ring circus. Too much for one pair of hands. Bring Emerson and Donna Bianca out there. And Alex Rodin, of course. Wake them up and get them there. After we win.'

'*If* we win,' Franklin said.

At one forty-five, people started getting restless. Helen Rodin stepped over and squatted down next to Reacher. 'Why are you doing this?' she asked.

'Because I can. And because of the girl.'

'You'll get yourself killed.'

'Unlikely,' Reacher said. 'These are old men and idiots. I've survived worse.' He checked his watch. Stood up. 'Let's do it,' he said.

CHAPTER EIGHT

They stood for a moment in the shadows on the parking apron. Then Yanni went to get the Sheryl Crow CD from her Mustang. She gave it to Cash. Cash unlocked the Humvee and leaned inside and put it in the player. Then he gave the keys to Franklin. Franklin climbed into the driver's seat. Cash got in next to him with his M24 across his knees. Reacher and Helen Rodin and Ann Yanni squeezed together in the back.

'Turn the heater up,' Reacher said.

Cash leaned to his left and dialled in maximum temperature. Franklin started the engine. Backed out into the street. Swung the wheel and took off west. Then he turned north. The heater kicked in and the interior grew warm, and then hot. The drive was a series of long, droning cruises punctuated by sharp right-angle corners. Then they made the final turn.

'This is it,' Yanni said. 'About three miles to go.'

'Start the music,' Reacher said. 'Track eight.'

Cash hit the button. *Every day is a winding road.*

'Louder,' Reacher said.

Cash turned it up. Franklin drove on, sixty miles an hour.

'Two miles,' Yanni called. Then: 'One mile.'

Reacher stared out of the window to his right. Watched the fields flash past. Random scatter from the headlights lit them up. The irrigation booms were turning so slowly they looked stationary. Mist filled the air.

'High beams,' Reacher called. Franklin flicked them on.

'Music all the way up,' Reacher called.

Cash twisted the knob to maximum. *EVERY DAY IS A WINDING ROAD.*

'Half a mile,' Yanni yelled.

'Windows,' Reacher shouted.

Four thumbs hit four buttons and all four windows dropped an inch. Hot air and loud music sucked out into the night. Reacher saw the dark outline of the house flash past, isolated, solid, dimly lit from inside. Flat land all round it. The limestone driveway, pale, long, as straight as an arrow.

'Stop sign in four hundred yards,' Yanni yelled.

'Stand by,' Reacher shouted. 'Showtime.'

'One hundred yards,' Yanni yelled.

'Doors,' Reacher shouted.

Three doors opened an inch. Franklin braked hard. Stopped dead on the line. Reacher and Yanni and Helen and Cash spilled out. Franklin took off again like it was a normal dead-of-night stop sign. Reacher and Yanni and Cash and Helen dusted themselves down and stared north until the glow of lights and the thump of music were lost in the distance and the darkness.

SOKOLOV had picked up the Humvee's heat signature on both the south and west monitors when it was still about half a mile shy of the house. A big powerful vehicle, travelling fast, trailing long plumes of hot air from open windows, what was to miss? Then he heard it too. Big engine, loud music.

Vladimir glanced his way. 'Passer-by?'

It didn't slow down. It hurtled past the house, trailing heat.

'Passer-by,' Sokolov said.

UPSTAIRS on the second floor, Chenko heard it too. He looked out of a west-facing window in an empty bedroom. Saw a big black shape doing about sixty miles an hour, lights bright, music thumping. He opened the window and leaned out and watched the bubble of light track north into the distance. It went behind the stone-crushing plant, but was still visible as a moving glow in the air. After a quarter-mile the glow changed colour. Red now, not white. Brake lights, flaring for the stop sign. The glow paused for a second. Then the red turned back to white and the glow took off again, fast.

The Zec called up from the floor below: 'Was that him?'

'No,' Chenko called back. 'Just some rich kid out for a drive.'

REACHER LED the way through the dark, four people single file on the edge of the blacktop with the gravel plant's high wire fence on their left and huge fields across the road on their right. There was nothing to hear but the hiss of irrigation water. Reacher raised his hand and stopped them where the fence turned a right angle and ran away east. He stepped forward and checked the view. He was on a perfect diagonal from the northwest corner of the house. He had an equal forty-five-degree line of sight to the north façade and the west. There was a glimmer of cloudy moonlight.

He pointed at Cash, pointed at the base of the corner post.

'This is your position,' he whispered. 'Check it out.'

Cash knelt down in the weeds. He switched on his night scope and raised his rifle. Tracked it slowly left and right, up and down.

'Three storeys plus a basement,' he whispered. 'High-pitched shingle roof, many windows, one door visible to the west. No cover *at all* in any direction. You're going to look like a beetle on a bed sheet out there.'

'Cameras?'

'Under the eaves. One on the north side, one on the west. We can assume the same on the sides we can't see.'

'OK, so listen up,' Reacher whispered. 'I'm going to get to my starting position. Then we're all going to wait for Franklin to get back and put the comms net on the air. Then I'm going to make a move. If I don't feel good I'm going to call in fire on those cameras. That'll slow them down.'

'Negative,' Cash said. 'I won't direct live rounds into a wooden structure we know contains a noncombatant hostage.'

'She'll be in the basement,' Reacher said.

'Or the attic.'

'You'd be firing at the eaves.'

'Exactly. She's in the attic, she hears gunfire, she hits the deck, that's exactly where I'm aiming.'

'Gunny, you are one uptight Marine, you know that?'

Cash didn't speak. Reacher stepped forward again and peered round the corner of the fence. Took a long hard look and pulled back.

'OK,' Reacher said. 'New plan. Watch the west windows. You see muzzle flash, you put suppressing fire there. We can assume the hostage won't be in the same room as the sniper.'

'You might be in the house already,' Cash said.

'No wonder you came in third,' Reacher said. 'You need to lighten up.'

'OK,' Cash said. 'I see hostile gunfire, I'll return it.'

'Hostile is about the only kind you're going to see, don't you think? Since you only gave me a damn knife?'

'Army,' Cash said. 'Always bitching about something.'

'What do I do?' Helen asked.

'Keep low, follow the fence round the corner, stop opposite the house. Stay down. They won't pick you up there. It's too far. Listen to your phone. If I need a distraction, I'll ask you to run a little way towards the house and back again. Real fast. Just enough to put a blip on their screen. No danger.'

She nodded.

'And me?' Ann Yanni asked.

'Stay with Cash. He gets cold feet about helping me out, you kick his ass.'

Nobody spoke.

'All set?' Reacher asked.

'Set,' they said, one after the other.

Reacher walked away into the darkness.

HE KEPT on walking off the blacktop, across the shoulder, across the stony margin, right into the field, all the way into the middle of the soaking crop. He waited until the irrigation boom rolled slowly round and caught up with him, then kept pace with it, letting the water rain down and soak his hair and his skin and his clothes. The boom pulled away as it followed its circular path and Reacher walked into the next field. And the next, and the next. When at last he was opposite the driveway entrance he simply walked in a circle, under the last boom, waiting for his cellphone to vibrate, like a man caught in a monsoon.

CASH'S CELLPHONE vibrated against his hip and he pulled it out and clicked it on. Heard Franklin's voice, quiet and cautious in his ear.

'Check in, please,' it said.

Cash heard Helen say: 'Here.'

Yanni said, 'Here,' from three feet below him.

Cash said, 'Here.'

Then he heard Reacher say: 'Here.'

Franklin said, 'OK, you're all loud and clear.'

Reacher said: 'I'm on my way.'

Then there was nothing but silence. Two minutes.

Cash heard Reacher ask: 'Gunny, do you see me?'

Cash lifted the rifle and swept the length of the driveway as far as the house. 'Negative. Where are you?'

'About thirty yards in.'

Cash moved the rifle. Estimated thirty yards from the road and stared through the scope. Saw nothing. 'Good work, soldier.'

'Why don't you see him?' Yanni asked. 'You've got a night scope, right?'

'The best money can buy,' Cash said. 'And it works off heat, just like their cameras. But my guess is Reacher walked through the fields. Soaked himself in water. It's coming from the aquifer, stone cold. So right now he's close to ambient temperature. I can't see him, they can't see him.'

'Smart,' Yanni said.

'Brave,' Cash said. 'But ultimately dumb. Because he's drying out every step of the way. And getting warmer.'

REACHER WALKED through the dark in the dirt ten feet south of the driveway. He was shivering. Which was bad. Shivering is a physiological reaction designed to warm a cold body fast. And he didn't want to be warm. Not yet.

On the map the driveway had looked to be about 200 yards long. On the ground it felt like he had been walking for ever. And he was less than half-way to the house. He walked on. Just kept on going.

He realised his hair wasn't dripping any more. He touched one hand with the other. Dry. Not warm, but no longer cold.

He was tempted to run. Running would get him there faster. But running would heat him up. He was approaching the point of no return. He was right out there in no-man's land. And he wasn't shivering. He raised his phone.

'Helen,' he whispered. 'I need that diversion.'

HELEN TOOK off her heels and left them neatly side by side at the base of the fence. Then she sprinted forward. Just ran crazily, twenty feet, thirty, forty, then stopped dead and stood facing the house with her arms out wide like a target. Then she turned and ran back in a wide zigzag loop. Threw herself down and crawled along the fence again until she found her shoes.

VLADIMIR SAW her on the north monitor. Nothing recognisable. Sokolov sensed the interruption to Vladimir's rhythm and glanced over.

'Fox?' Vladimir said.

'I didn't see it,' Sokolov said. 'But probably.'

'It ran away again.'

'OK.' Sokolov turned back to his own pair of monitors. Glanced at the west view, checked the south, and settled into his regular cadence again.

CASH WAS INCHING his night scope along at what he guessed was the speed of a walking man. But every five seconds he would sweep it forward and back in case his estimate was off. During one of those traverses he picked up a pale green shadow.

'Reacher, I can see you,' he whispered. 'You're visible, soldier.'

REACHER WALKED on. Probably the most unnatural thing a human could force himself to do, to walk slowly and surely towards a building that probably had a rifle in it pointing directly at his centre mass. If Chenko had any sense at all he would wait until his target was pretty close. And Chenko seemed to have plenty of sense. Fifty yards would be good. Or thirty-five, like Chenko's range out of the parking garage. Chenko was pretty good at thirty-five yards. That had been made very clear.

Reacher took the knife out of his pocket and unsheathed it and held it right-handed, low and easy. Transferred the phone to his left hand and held it near his ear. Heard Cash say: 'You're shining like the north star. It's like you're on fire.'

Forty yards to go. Thirty-nine. Thirty-eight.

'Helen?' he said. 'Do it again.'

He heard her voice: 'OK.'

He walked on. Thirty-five yards. Thirty-four. Thirty-three.

He heard panting in his ear. Helen, running. He heard Yanni ask: 'How close is he?' Heard Cash answer: 'Not close enough.'

VLADIMIR LEANED forward and said, 'There it is again.'

Sokolov glanced across. Sokolov had spent many more hours with the screens than Vladimir. 'That's no fox,' he said. 'It's way too big.'

He watched for five more seconds. The image was weaving left and right at the very limit of the camera's range. Recognisable size, recognisable shape, inexplicable motion. Sokolov stood up and walked to the door.

'Chenko!' he called. 'North!'

Behind his back on the west screen a shape as big as his thumb grew larger. It looked like a painting-by-numbers figure done in fluorescent colours. Lime green on the outside, then a band of chrome yellow, with a core of hot red.

CHENKO WALKED through an empty bedroom and opened the window as high as it would go. Then he backed away into the darkness. That way he was invisible from below. He switched on his night scope and raised his rifle.

He saw a woman. She was running crazily, barefoot, darting left and right, out and back. Chenko thought: *What?* He squeezed the slack out of his trigger and tried to anticipate her next pirouette. Then she stopped moving, facing the house, arms out wide like a target.

Chenko pulled the trigger.

Then he understood. He stepped back to the landing.

'Decoy!' he screamed. '*Decoy!*'

CASH SAW the muzzle flash and called, 'Shot fired,' and jumped his scope to the north window. The lower pane was raised, the upper pane was fixed. No point in putting a round in the opening. The upward trajectory would guarantee a miss. So he fired at the glass. He figured if he could get a hail of jagged shards going, then that might ruin somebody's night.

SOKOLOV WAS watching the crazy heat image on Vladimir's screen when he heard Chenko's shot and his shouted warning. He turned to the south monitor. Nothing there. Then he heard return fire and shattering glass upstairs. He pushed back from the table and stepped to the door.

'Are you OK?' he called.

'Decoy,' Chenko called back. 'Has to be.'

Sokolov turned and checked all four screens, very carefully.

'No,' he called. 'Definitely nothing incoming.'

REACHER TOUCHED the front wall of the house. He was ten feet south of the door, near a tall, rectangular sash window that looked into a dark empty room.

Then he heard the shooting. Shattering glass.

Then he heard Cash in his ear: 'Helen? You OK?'

He heard no reply.

Reacher put the phone in his pocket. Worked the blade of his knife up into the gap where the bottom of the upper sash overlapped the top of the lower sash. He moved the blade, feeling for a catch. He found one, dead-centre. Tapped it, gently. Pushed it, left to right. It moved.

He pushed it hard, and knocked it out of its socket.

He lifted the lower sash and rolled over the sill into the room. Then he moved through the empty room to the door. Heard nothing. Opened the door, very slowly. Checked the hallway. Empty.

There was light from an open doorway fifteen feet ahead on his left. He paused. He moved ahead, slowly, silently. *Boat shoes. Good for something.* Reacher stopped in the doorway.

He was looking at two guys from behind. They were seated side by side at a long table with their backs to him. Staring at TV monitors. On the left, Vladimir. On the right, a guy he hadn't seen before. *Sokolov? Must be.* To Sokolov's right, a yard away from him, a handgun rested on the end of the table. A Smith and Wesson Model 60. A five-shooter.

Reacher took a long silent step into the room. Held his breath. Reversed the knife in his hand. Held the blade an inch from its end. Raised his arm. Cocked it behind his head. Snapped it forward. Threw the knife.

It buried itself two inches deep in the back of Sokolov's neck.

Vladimir glanced right, towards the sound. Reacher was already moving. Vladimir glanced back. Saw him. Half rose. Reacher watched him decide to go for the gun. Reacher charged. He buried his shoulder in Vladimir's chest and wrapped both arms round his back and jacked him bodily off his feet. Just lifted him up and turned him away from the table.

And then squeezed.

Best route to a silent kill against a guy as big as Vladimir was simply to crush him to death. As long as his arms and his legs couldn't connect with anything solid there would be no noise. No shouting, no screaming.

Reacher squeezed with all his strength. He crushed Vladimir's chest in a bear hug so vicious and sustained and powerful that no human could have survived it. Vladimir rained desperate blows down on Reacher's back and flailed with his feet at his shins. Reacher tightened his grip. Crushed harder.

Vladimir stopped moving. Reacher kept the pressure full on for another whole minute. Then he eased off and laid the body gently on the floor. Squatted down. Checked for a pulse. No pulse.

He stood up and pulled Cash's knife out of Sokolov's neck and cleaned the blade on Vladimir's shirt. He pulled the phone out of his pocket. Heard Cash say, '*Helen?*'

He whispered: 'What's up?'

Cash answered, 'We took an incoming round. I can't raise Helen.'

'Yanni, move left,' Reacher said. 'Find her. Franklin, you there?'

Franklin said, 'Here.'

'Stand by to call the medics,' Reacher said.

Cash asked, 'Where are you?'

'In the house,' Reacher said. 'Where did the shot come from?'

'Second-floor window, north. They've got the sniper up there. They can direct him based on what they see from the cameras.'

'Not any more,' Reacher said. He put the phone back in his pocket. Picked up the gun. Checked the cylinder. It was fully loaded. Five Smith and Wesson '38 Specials. He moved out to the hallway with the knife in his right hand and the gun in his left. Went looking for the door to the basement.

He soon found it. It took him less than a minute to be certain that Rosemary Barr wasn't in the basement. Then he crept back up the stairs.

CASH HEARD Yanni talking to herself as she moved away. She was saying: 'I'm moving east now, keeping low, staying tight against the fence in the darkness. I'm looking for Helen Rodin. We know they fired at her. Now she's not answering her phone. We're hoping she's OK.'

Cash listened until he couldn't hear her any more.

YANNI FOUND Helen's shoes by literally stumbling over them.

'Helen?' she whispered. '*Helen*? Where are you?'

Then she heard a voice: 'Here. Keep going.'

Yanni walked on. Found a black shape rolled against the base of the fence.

'I dropped my phone,' Helen said. 'Can't find it.'

'Are you OK?'

'He missed me. I was leaping around like a madwoman. But the bullet came real close. I just dropped my phone and ran.'

REACHER CREPT down the hallway. Opened doors and searched rooms to the left and right as he went. They were all empty. All unused. He paused at the bottom of the stairs. Backed away into an empty space that might once have been a parlour. Crouched down and pulled out his phone.

'Gunny?' he whispered.

Cash answered: 'Yanni found Helen. She's OK.'

'Good. The basement and the ground floor are clear. I think you were right after all. Rosemary must be in the attic.'

'Body count?'

'Two down so far.'

'Lots more upstairs, then.'

'I'll be careful.'

Reacher put the phone back in his pocket. Stood up and crept out to the hallway. The staircase was at the back of the house. He went up slowly and quietly. When his head was level with the first floor, he raised the gun. Now he could see the whole of the landing. It was empty. Six closed doors, three on each side. He carried on up. Stepped onto the landing.

He moved slowly towards the front of the house. Listened at the first two doors. Nothing. Before he reached the third door he heard sounds coming through the floor above. *Slide, scrape, crunch, tap. Slide, scrape, crunch, tap.* He stared up at the ceiling. Then the third door opened and Grigor Linsky stepped out onto the landing right in front of him. And froze.

He was wearing his familiar double-breasted suit. Grey colour, boxy shoulders. Reacher stabbed him in the throat. Instantly, right-handedly. He buried the knife and jerked it left. Caught him under the arms from behind and dragged him back into the room he had come out of. It was a kitchen. Linsky had been making tea. Reacher turned out the flame under the kettle. Heard nothing except: *Slide, scrape, crunch, tap.* Then he knew. *Glass.*

Cash had returned fire through Chenko's northern vantage point and like all good snipers had sought maximum damage from his one shot. And in turn, like all good snipers Chenko was keeping his physical environment operational. *He was cleaning up the broken glass.*

Reacher crept to the next staircase. The second-floor landing had the same layout as the one below, but it wasn't carpeted. There was an upright chair in the centre of the corridor. All the doors were open. North was to the right. Reacher could feel night air coming in. He crept onwards. The noises got louder. He pivoted slowly into a doorway.

Chenko was twelve feet from him. Facing the window. Both panes had been blown out. The floor was covered in glass. Chenko was clearing a path from the door towards the window. Skidding on a pebble of glass could cost him precious time in a firefight. His rifle was upright against the wall, six feet from him. He was concentrating hard on his task.

Reacher put the knife in his pocket. Freed his right hand. Stepped forward down the path that Chenko had cleared. Four quiet paces. Chenko sensed it. He straightened. Reacher caught Chenko round the neck from behind. He gripped hard. Took one more long fast stride and stiff-armed the Russian forward and threw him out of the open window, head first.

'I warned you,' he whispered into the darkness below. 'You should have put me down when you had the chance.' Then he took out his phone.

'Gunny?' he whispered.

'Here.'

'Second-floor window, where you returned fire. A guy just fell out. If he gets up again, shoot him.'

Reacher put the phone away and went looking for the attic door. Then he walked quietly up the stairs and found Rosemary Barr sitting upright on the attic floor, unharmed. Her feet were taped, her wrists were taped, her mouth was taped. Reacher put his finger to his lips. She nodded. He cut her free with the bloodstained knife and helped her stand. She shook herself and gave a kind of nod. Reacher guessed that whatever fear she had felt now had been neutralised by some kind of a steely determination to help her brother. If she survived, he would survive. That belief had kept her going.

'Have they gone?' she whispered.

'All except Raskin and the Zec,' Reacher whispered back.

'No, Raskin killed himself. I heard them talking. The Zec made him do it. Because he let you steal his cellphone.'

'Where's the Zec likely to be?'

'He's in the living room. First floor.'

'Which door?'

'Last on the left.'

'OK, stay here,' Reacher whispered. 'I'll be right back.'

'I can't stay here. You have to get me out.'

He paused. 'OK, but you've got to be real quiet.'

Reacher held her arm down the stairs to the second floor. Then he went ahead alone to the first. All quiet. The last door on the left was still closed.

He waved her down. They headed to the ground floor together. To the front of the house. To the room he had entered through. He helped her over the sill and out of the window, to the dirt below. He pointed.

'Follow the driveway to the road,' he said. 'Turn right. I'll tell the others you're coming.'

She bent down and took off her shoes and started running like hell towards the road. Reacher took out his phone.

'Gunny?' he whispered.

'Here.'

'Rosemary Barr is heading your way.'

'Outstanding.'

'Round up the others and meet her halfway. There's no more operational night vision. Then stand by.'

Reacher put the phone away. Backtracked through the silent house, on his way to find the Zec.

IN THE END, it came down to waiting. Wait, and good things come to you. And bad things. Reacher crept back to the first floor. He ducked into the kitchen. Relit the flame under the kettle. Then he walked quietly to the front of the house and leaned on the wall beyond the last door on the left. And waited.

The kettle boiled after five minutes. The whistle started low and quiet, then the note and the volume rose to full blast. Ten seconds later, the door on Reacher's right opened. A small man stepped out. Reacher let him take a pace forward and then spun him around and jammed the Smith 60 hard in the base of his throat. And stared.

The Zec. He was an ancient, stooped, battered old man. He was covered in livid scars and patches of discoloured skin. His face was lined and seething with hatred and cruelty. He was unarmed. His ruined hands didn't seem capable of holding a weapon. Reacher forced him down the hallway. Into the kitchen. To the stove. The noise from the kettle was unbearable. Reacher used his left hand and killed the flame. Then he hauled the Zec back towards the living room.

'It's over,' Reacher said. 'You lost.'

'It's never over,' the Zec replied. Hoarse voice, low, guttural.

'Guess again,' Reacher said. He eased the Smith's hammer back. *Click-click-click-crunch.*

'I'm eighty years old,' the Zec said.

'I don't care if you're a hundred,' Reacher said. 'You're still going down.'

'Idiot,' the Zec said back. 'I meant I've survived things worse than you. Since long before you were born.'

'You know when my birthday is?' Reacher asked.

'Obviously not.'

'It's in October. You know what day?'

'Of course not.'

'You're going to find out the hard way. I'm counting in my head. When I reach my birthday, I'm going to pull the trigger.'

He started counting in his head. *First, second.* He watched the Zec's eyes. *Fifth, sixth, seventh, eighth.* No response. *Tenth, eleventh, twelfth.*

'What do you want?' the Zec said.

'The twelfth,' Reacher said. 'That's how long you lasted. Because you want to survive. It's the deepest instinct you've got. It's *what you are.*'

'So?'

'So we've got ourselves a competition. What you are, against what I am.'

'And what are you?'

'I'm the guy who just threw Chenko out of a second-floor window. After crushing Vladimir to death with my bare hands. Because I didn't like what they did to innocent people. So now you've got to pit *your* strong desire to survive against *my* strong desire to shoot you in the head.'

No response.

'One shot,' Reacher said. 'In the head. That's your choice. Another day, another roll of the dice. Or not. As the case may be.'

He saw the calculation in the Zec's eyes. Assessment, evaluation, speculation. 'What do you want?' the Zec asked again.

'There's an innocent man I need to get out of the prison ward. So I need you to tell the truth to a detective called Emerson. I need you to finger Chenko for the shooting, and Vladimir for the girl, and whoever it was for Ted Archer. And whatever else you've done.'

A flicker in the Zec's eyes. 'Pointless. I'd get the death penalty.'

'Yes, you would,' Reacher said. 'But you'd still be alive tomorrow. And the next day. And the next day. The appeals process lasts for ever here. You might get lucky. There might be a mistrial, there might be an earthquake.'

'Unlikely.'

'Very,' Reacher said. 'But isn't that who you are? A guy who'll take a tiny fragment of a chance to live another minute, as opposed to no chance at all.'

No response.

'Thirteenth,' Reacher said. 'Fourteenth, fifteenth, sixteenth.'

'OK,' the Zec said. 'You win. I'll talk to the detective.'

Reacher pinned him against the wall. Took out his phone. 'Gunny?'

'Here.'

'Come on in, all of you. I'll open the door. And, Franklin? Wake those guys up, like we talked about before. Get them out here.'

Reacher tied the Zec's wrists and ankles with wire torn from table lamps and left him on the living-room floor. Then he went downstairs. Walked down the hallway and opened the front door.

Yanni came in first. Then Cash. Then Rosemary. Then Helen. She was barefoot and carrying her shoes in her hand.

'Are they all dead?' Yanni asked.

'All but one,' Reacher said.

He led the way upstairs. Stopped Rosemary outside the living room.

'The Zec is in there,' he said. 'You OK about seeing him?'

She nodded. 'I want to see him. I want to ask him a question.' She stepped into the living room, stood over the Zec, quiet, dignified, not gloating.

'Why?' she said. 'Why not just use Chenko, from the highway? Why did you have to bring my brother down?'

The Zec didn't answer. He just stared into space.

'There had to be a story,' Reacher said. 'And he had to control that story. If he gave up a shooter, then the story would be about the shooter. No shooter, the story would have been about the victims. And if the story had been about the victims, too many questions would have been asked.'

'So he sacrificed James.'

Reacher kicked the Zec aside and pulled the sofa away from the window about four feet. Hauled the Zec up and dumped him on one end.

He told Cash to perch on the windowsill behind the sofa. Told Yanni to find three dining chairs. Reacher put them in a line facing the sofa. He ended up with a square arrangement, sofa, dining chairs, armchairs off to the sides. Checked his watch. Nearly four in the morning.

'Now we wait,' he said.

THEY WAITED less than thirty minutes. They heard cars crunch on the limestone driveway and Reacher went downstairs to open the door. He saw Franklin's black Suburban. Saw Emerson sliding out of a grey Crown Vic.

Saw a compact woman with short dark hair getting out of a blue Ford Taurus. Donna Bianca, he assumed. He saw Alex Rodin climbing out of a silver BMW. Rodin locked it with his remote. He was the only one who did.

Reacher led them upstairs. He put Alex Rodin and Donna Bianca and Emerson in the dining chairs, left to right. He put Franklin in an armchair next to Yanni. Rosemary Barr and Helen Rodin were in armchairs on the other side of the room. Helen was looking at her father. Cash was on the windowsill. Reacher stepped away and leaned against the doorjamb.

'Start talking,' Reacher said.

The Zec sighed. Started talking. He told a long story. He spilled details of earlier unconnected crimes. Then he got to the bidding process for the city contracts. He named the official he had suborned. It wasn't just about money. There were girls, too. Some of them very young. He talked about Ted Archer's fury, his two-year search, his close approach to the truth. He described the ambush, one Monday morning. Jeb Oliver had been used. The red Dodge Ram had been his payoff. The Zec described the fast decision to get rid of Oline Archer two months later, when she became dangerous. He described Chenko's subterfuge, how they lured James Barr out of the way with a promise of a date with Sandy Dupree. He described the end of Jeb Oliver's usefulness. He told them where to find his body. He told them about Vladimir killing Sandy in an effort to stop Reacher in his tracks. Altogether he talked for thirty-two minutes, then he stopped suddenly.

Donna Bianca said, 'Unbelievable.'

'Something you left out,' Reacher said. 'You need to tell us about your inside man. That's what we're all waiting for.'

The Zec looked at Emerson. Then at Donna Bianca. Then at Alex Rodin. Then back at Reacher.

'You're a survivor,' Reacher said. 'But you're not an idiot. There won't be a mistrial. You won't survive a ten-year appeals process. You know all that. But still you agreed to talk. Why?'

The Zec said nothing.

'Because you knew that sooner or later you'd be talking to a friend. Someone you own. Am I right?'

The Zec didn't move.

'Someone right here, right now, in fact,' Reacher said.

The Zec said nothing.

'One thing always bothered me,' Reacher went on. 'From the start. The thing is, when I was in the service I was a hell of a good investigator. I was maybe the best they ever had. And you know what?'

'What?' Helen Rodin asked.

'I would never have thought of emptying that parking meter. Not in a million years. So was Emerson a better investigator than me? Or did he *know* that quarter was there?'

Nobody spoke.

'Emerson is not better than I was,' Reacher said. 'That's what I decided.' Then he turned to the Zec. 'The coin was one clue too many.'

'This is bullshit,' Emerson said.

Reacher shook his head. 'A lot of things clicked into place after that. I read the 911 transcripts and the squad car call log. Right at the start you were quick to make up your mind. Within twenty seconds you were on the radio telling your guys this was a lone nutcase with an automatic rifle. There was no basis for that conclusion. Six shots fired, ragged sequence. It could have been six kids with a handgun each, firing once. But you knew it wasn't.'

'Bullshit,' Emerson said again.

Reacher shook his head again. 'Final proof was when I told your boss here that he'd have to tell the truth to a detective called Emerson. I said your name specifically, and a little light came on in his eyes. He agreed real fast because he figured he'd be OK as long as you were in charge.'

Silence. Then Cash said, 'But Oline Archer went to Alex Rodin here. *He* buried it. That's what you found out.'

'We found out that Oline went to the DA's *office*. And you know what? Alex here has got himself a couple of real dragon ladies working the door. My guess is they told Oline it was a police matter, and sent her trekking all across town to the station house, where she sat down with Emerson here.'

The Zec squirmed. 'Emerson, *do* something.'

'Nothing he can do,' Reacher said. 'I'm not dumb. I think ahead. I'm sure he's got a Glock under his arm, but he's got me behind him with a .38 and a knife, and he's got Cash facing him with a sniper rifle hidden behind the sofa. I guess he could try to kill us all and say there was some kind of massacre here, but how would that help him with NBC?'

'NBC?' Cash repeated.

'I saw Yanni fiddling with her phone earlier. I'm assuming she's transmitting all of this back to the studios.'

Yanni pulled out her Nokia.

'Open channel,' she said. 'Digital audio recording on three separate hard discs. They've all been running since well before we got in the Humvee.'

Cash stared at her. 'That's why you were talking to yourself like a sports announcer.'

'She's a journalist,' Reacher said. 'She's going to win an Emmy.'

He stepped forward and leaned over the back of Emerson's chair and slid his hand under his coat. Came back out with a Glock nine. Handed it to Bianca. 'You've got arrests to make,' he said.

Then the Zec smiled and Chenko walked into the room.

CHENKO was covered in mud and his right arm was broken, or his shoulder, or his collarbone, or maybe all three. His wrist was jammed into his shirt like a sling. But there was nothing wrong with his left arm. Reacher turned around and saw the sawn-off rock-steady in his left hand. Where did he get that from? he thought irrelevantly.

'Put the gun down, lady,' Chenko said to Bianca.

Bianca laid Emerson's Glock on the floor.

'I guess I was out for a little while,' Chenko said. 'But I got to tell you I feel a whole hell of a lot better now.'

'We survive,' the Zec said, from across the room. 'That's what we do.'

Reacher didn't look back at the old man. He looked at Chenko's gun. It had been a Benelli Nova pump. The stock had been cut off behind the grip.

'Emerson,' the Zec called. 'Untie me.'

Reacher heard Emerson stand up.

'I need a knife here,' Emerson said.

'The soldier's got a knife,' Chenko said.

Reacher moved a little closer to him. A big guy and a little guy directly face to face, separated by about three feet, most of which was occupied by the Benelli.

'Come and get it,' Reacher said.

'I'll shoot,' Chenko said. 'Twelve-gauge, in the gut.'

Reacher thought: And then what? A pump-action shotgun ain't much good to a one-armed man.

'So shoot,' he said.

Chenko did nothing. Just stood there. Reacher knew exactly how the room was laid out. He had arranged it. He pictured it in his mind. He knew where everyone was, and what they were looking at.

'Shoot,' he said. 'Aim at my belt. That'll work. Go ahead.'

Chenko just stared up at him. Reacher was so close and so big he was all Chenko could see.

'I'll help you,' Reacher said. 'I'll count to three. Then you pull the trigger.'

Chenko just stood there.

'One,' Reacher said. 'Two.'

Then he stepped out of the way. Took a long, fast sideways shuffle to his right. Cash fired from behind the sofa at the spot where Reacher's belt had been a split second before, and Chenko's chest blew apart.

Then Cash put his rifle back on the floor as silently as he had picked it up.

TWO NIGHT-SHIFT squad cars came and took the Zec and Emerson away. Then four ambulances arrived for the casualties. Bianca asked Reacher what exactly had happened to the first three. Reacher told her he had no idea. A falling out among thieves, maybe? Bianca didn't push it. Rosemary Barr borrowed Franklin's cellphone and used it to call area hospitals, looking for a safe berth for her brother. Helen and Alex Rodin sat close together, talking. Gunny Cash sat in a chair and dozed. An old soldier's habit. *Sleep when you can.* Yanni stepped up close to Reacher and said, 'Rough men stand ready in the night.' Reacher found himself very aware of the live phone. He just smiled and said, 'I'm usually in bed by twelve o'clock.'

'Me too,' Yanni said. 'Alone. You remember my address?'

Reacher smiled again, and nodded. Then he went downstairs and stepped out to the front porch. Dawn was coming. Black shaded to purple right on the horizon. He turned and watched the last ambulance loading up. He emptied his pockets and left Emerson's card, and Helen Rodin's cocktail napkin, and the motor court's big brass key, and the Smith 60, and Gunny Cash's Navy SEAL SRK, all in a neat little pile beside the front door. Then he asked the paramedics if he could ride with them to town. He figured he could walk east from the hospital and be at the bus depot before the sun was fully up. He could be in Indianapolis before lunch. Then he could buy a pair of shoes and be just about anywhere before the sun went down again.

LEE CHILD

Born: Coventry, 1954
Place of Residence: New York State
Website: www.leechild.com

RD: The bad guys in *One Shot* have links with a mafia-style organisation. Was there any reason why you chose that kind of background?

LC: Well, all thrillers are about conflict, and conflict works best when the opponents are powerful. David and Goliath is better than David and David, right? Given that Reacher is very capable, he had to face a ruthless and connected set of villains.

RD: Did you have to do any particular research for this book?

LC: Only a little—about Russian language, history and customs. And a little about sniper ammunition. The manufacturer of the cartridges I chose even sent me some samples!

RD: You use a number of baseball aliases in *One Shot*—just as, being an avid Villa fan, you used Aston Villa player names in an earlier book, *Die Trying*. Can we take it that living in America has turned you into more of a baseball fan?

LC: It's about equal for me now, but obviously Reacher himself is more familiar with baseball. I think that stuff worked well in suggesting his disconnected, military-brat background—those kids pored over baseball stats to try and get connected with home.

RD: Do you still follow the fortunes of Aston Villa?

LC: You bet. Thank goodness for the internet. Also, a couple of bars here carry some Villa games live on TV.

RD: Reacher's attitude to women seems to have changed since the days of his girlfriend, Jodie, in the earlier novels. Is it our imagination or is he finding it easier to 'love 'em and leave 'em' these days?

LC: That depends on how they measure up to Jodie, the love of his life. If they fall short, which they usually do (despite their many virtues), he moves on without a second thought.

RD: Where next for Reacher? Will he continue to roam America? Or could you see him travelling further afield, to London, for example?

LC: Great question—and as it happens, the next novel, *The Hard Way*, will move from New York City to London halfway through. I thought it was time to send Reacher overseas.

RD: You originally worked in television, for Granada in Manchester. Do you miss that world at all?

LC: Occasionally I do, when big news events are happening. They were fun, viewed from inside a big media organisation. And I miss the collegiate atmosphere. TV was all teamwork, and writing is very lonely by comparison.

RD: You moved to America because you love it so much. What is it about the country that appeals to you?

LC: The size, the diversity, the weather, the recklessness of it all. But my feelings are changing a little, with the current administration. New York City is still untainted, but I must admit I'm spending more time in Europe now—we have a house in the South of France.

RD: *One Shot* is your ninth novel. Does the writing get easier or harder?

LC: I think I reached a plateau with the third book and it hasn't become either easier or harder since then. It's a great job, but fundamentally it will always be quite difficult to assemble the right 100,000 words in the right order.

RD: If you had to name one characteristic that you share with Reacher, and one of his that you'd like to emulate, what would they be?

LC: I share his disgust with injustice. I'd like to have his way of dealing with it.

RD: Do you come back to England much? Anything you miss about it at all?

LC: I come back two or three times a year. I miss the BBC, and Marmite, and the way it stays light so late in May and June.

RD: Life as an international best-selling author must be quite phenomenal, especially the freedom. But what is it you like best about it?

LC: I like the fact that if it doesn't work, it's nobody's fault except mine. I like the fact that I'm not hurting anybody—I make good money but I'm not selling crack or heroin. All book purchases are voluntary. And books touch lives occasionally.

RD: And finally, what's the question you most dread being asked in interviews?

LC: Anything about Reacher's underwear. I still get 10,000 letters a year asking why he doesn't change it more often.

The Valley

Barry Pilton

The inhabitants of the Nant Valley in mid-Wales live sheltered lives, untroubled by the relentless march of progress. So when they're faced with new neighbours, armed with exotic tastes and expectations of rural bliss, there's trouble in store.

Dafydd the postman is among the first to spot the signs. And before long, tongues are wagging from the market square to the local pub, where the landlord fears he might actually have customers to serve.

Chapter 1

'It was the trousers,' said the postman. 'When I saw the dog had got the trousers, I knew something wasn't right.'

Gareth stared gravely at the ground, tapping the tractor wheel with his boot. This was a detail he hadn't known about.

'Dog didn't want to play with them or anything, just dropped them at my feet. They were his best pair too, chapel pair.' With every farm he stopped at, the postman's account of the previous day's events improved in colour and texture. 'Dragged across the yard in the mud.'

Gareth looked up, shocked. 'What, not . . . not the ones he had on when he . . . ?'

The postman nodded grimly.

'Dear God! How did they end up in the farmyard? I mean, if he was already—'

'Yes, took us a while to work that out.' The postman was not keen to take questions, to surrender the thrust of his narrative. 'Anyhow, straight away I said to the dog, "What is it, girl, what's up?" And she ran over to the barn. Well, I knew Hefin wasn't in the house, I'd been knocking, with a parcel. Replacement part for the generator. That's what'd brought the dog out. So I followed her over to the barn.' He paused, ostensibly for composure but betraying a gift for timing. 'And that's where I found him. Hanging.'

'Had he been dead long?'

'All night, I reckon. He was white with frost. White and stiff. Reminded me of a lynching, the way he was dangling there in the gloom.'

'Must have been one hell of a shock.'

'He's my third in two years. At least he had the consideration not to use a shotgun. Not like John Howells up at Ty Mawr. I'll never forget the state of that kitchen, it was—'

'Yes, I remember you saying.'

'Oh. Mind you, the sight of poor old Hefin, all alone, suit and tie and long johns . . . his dog whimpering. That'll stay with me a fair while.'

'Was it you cut him down?'

'No. Police did that. Did you know they got lost? Nine-nine-nine call and they got lost.'

'Apparently the call goes to some central computer somewhere these days.'

'Moscow.'

'I don't understand the business with the suit. Why would he get all dressed up just to . . . just to die?'

'I don't know. Last chance at some dignity, I suppose. There was sod all dignity to be had in the state of that farm. And that was the other strange thing. He'd locked the place up. Half derelict, scarcely worth anything, and he'd locked it up. And then walked out with his best clothes on.'

There was silence as they reflected on this. Neither of them said it, because they were old-fashioned men, but somehow they found this the most moving aspect of all.

'And even they got ruined by the mud. It was the belt, you see. He'd used his belt to . . . to loop round his neck. Jumped off the hay bales and . . . well, the jolt must have . . .' His hands depicted trousers falling from a corpse.

'A week before Harvest Festival,' sighed Gareth, and wondered about the pasture he rented from his late neighbour. 'Who'll look after the dog?'

'Jessie? Don't know. Isn't there a brother?'

'In pigs. Don't need a dog for pigs. And she's a good working bitch.'

There was another long pause. Accidentally, they had strayed off the subject of the tragedy, and they could not find a bridge back.

The postman nodded at the middle distance, in a muted manly way, and restarted his engine. He still had another twenty people to tell the story to.

But he couldn't tell any of them what was really churning round in his mind. As he bumped down the potholed track back towards the valley road, he kept going over and over his interview with the new area manager.

Dafydd used to love his job. 'I'm with social services,' he would say with a laugh. And it was true: he would check whether Mrs Higgins had fallen from her walking frame, assist old Norman to water his flowering baskets, transfer homemade cakes from the Commodore's sister to the village hall, and it all came for the price of a stamp.

As for stray heifers, he'd lost count of the times his van had helped corral the beasts, nudging them back down lanes and onto home territory.

The first warning sign had been the pedometer from Cardiff, special delivery from headquarters. He hadn't even known what a pedometer was then. One of the young sorters, Richie, had known—and told everyone with triumphal glee—because the word had cropped up in his pub quiz. 'A mechanical instrument for counting paces and measuring distance,' he announced. And they had all laughed.

Eight cottages and three farmhouses were removed from his round as a result of that mechanical instrument. In one case, the front door was just six paces over the 'statutory maximum distance from a maintained road necessary to qualify for delivery by Royal Mail'. So the owners all had to put up mailboxes at the end of their tracks. As if they lived in Arizona and were expecting some American mailman to drive by and throw letters in their general direction. These people were old friends, lonely widows and frail, retired farmers who wanted a cheery word as much as any dull brown envelope. Of course, he ignored the ruling.

After the pedometer came an assessor. And he (or perhaps she, for there was no known sighting of the person) calculated the exact time required per property for the satisfactory delivery of mail. Dafydd was one hour fifteen minutes over target. Nor was he the sole offender.

The union promised representations. His own, somewhat petulant, proposals to the branch—that extra time be allowed for 'a savage dog situation', 'a wild bull situation', 'a fallen tree situation', 'a flood situation' and 'a thick mud situation'—were judged by more seasoned negotiators to be 'unhelpful'. Apparently, reference to these normal aspects of rural life would be considered provocative by head office. Diplomacy was to be the chosen channel.

After two months, an unofficial admission was obtained from the authorities that bad weather was 'a grey area'. But still they insisted that rounds be subject to strict timekeeping. And from then on the joy started to go from the job.

Dafydd had been among the more vociferous in mocking the unreason of modern management, but never in his daftest dreams had he considered it

necessary to propose rules for a dead-body situation, with a statutory minimum time to be allowed per corpse during the course of duty.

He had stayed an hour and a half beside the frozen body of fifty-eight-
year-old Hefin, late bachelor of the parish, and watched a misty-red
October dawn rise over the hills. He had helped the police with their questions, had arranged for someone to tend the sheep. As a result some letters
were late.

'Do you not think ninety minutes was excessive? He had been deceased
for some twelve hours, I understand. It's not as if you were applying a
tourniquet.'

'I was a witness.'

'No, you weren't. You found him. That's all.'

Dafydd hated the new area manager, and the fact that the man was
twenty years his junior. Nor did his being an incomer from Swansea help.

'I had to give a statement.'

'Like what? "I found him"? That's three words. That take you an hour
and a half, does it?'

'There were also the sheep to—'

'You're not responsible for sheep. Unless you want to pack this job in,
and become a sheep farmer.'

Dafydd sensed he was close to having a noose slipped round his own
neck, and knew he had to decide between silence or throwing a punch.

As he dropped to second gear for the one-in-six past old St Brynnach's,
he still regretted he had not opted for the punch. He might have been
sacked, but he would have been kept in drinks for a month. Instead, he had
spent the morning catalysing his resentment into a bloody-mindedness—
and his provision of a news update service on the death of Hefin had put
him fifty minutes behind target. Had he been a new man, he would have
claimed he was helping with the valley's grieving process.

Indeed, young Ms Courtney-Stone from the converted barns, who was
struggling to establish herself as a homeopathic vet, had said that dead
bodies in stressful contexts could create a psychological undertow, and
was of the view that Dafydd should ask for counselling. While Dafydd had
no time for such nonsense, he suspected the Post Office was probably just
the sort of organisation to have a detailed policy on post-traumatic stress
disorder, if only because PTSD involved jargon and sounded cutting edge.
The idea did, however, offer one major attraction: if he were entitled to any

sick leave it would cause considerable stress to the area manager.

He was still savouring this fantasy as he accidentally scattered Marjorie Whitelaw's hens with his van. She emerged as turbulently as ever from her caravan, shooing the dozen Buff Orpingtons back to the abandoned VW Beetle that served as their henhouse.

'I hear you've killed somebody else off with all these bloody bills you deliver,' she shouted, and gave a fortissimo laugh. 'Tea?'

'Why not?' He got out of the van and stretched his legs. He thought the detail of the trousers would go down well with her.

Chapter 2

'Twenty-two thousand pounds . . .' Stéfan hesitated. He didn't like hesitating. Dynamic, flamboyant, imperious, these were the adjectives he liked to leave in his wake. Stinking rich was another description he didn't object to. But not patsy. His visceral competitiveness would not allow him to appear a patsy. And to pay a five-figure sum for what should have been his for nothing, put him in patsy territory. In front of 150 strangers, soon to be neighbours. So he hesitated.

Stéfan was, on the other hand, also prey to vanity. And buying Lot 563 could do a great deal for his vanity. Ownership would enable him to feel part of Britain's historic continuum, as the toady from Sotheby's put it. Lot 563 would be the cultural icing on his cake. The cake was the listed, twenty-eight room Jacobean manor house, plus land and outbuildings, whose six-figure purchase had so recently been sealed by his signature. The icing was the archives.

'Against you, at twenty-two thousand pounds . . .'

On all sides, the historic contents of the estate were being murmured over. Woodwormy dining-tables, obscure statues, monstrous tureens made mirror-like by generations of dutiful scullery maids. And outside, in one large, sad clump, stood the old ironware of agriculture, purpose now known to only a few, desired only by the nerdishly romantic. As Stéfan blinked about him, he found himself reflecting that he was younger, by many years, than any item in the catalogue. Younger, probably, than any of the serious buyers.

A large dollop of water suddenly splashed down his neck, putting an end to this satisfying thought. Looking up, he saw a row of heavily pregnant raindrops preparing to ease themselves from the sodden canvas above his head. He made a sideways leap across the coconut matting, just missing a Sloanish lady in jodhpurs, and realised that seven hours of this upper-class clearance sale had rendered him oblivious to the rhythmic drumming of the rain upon the marquee.

The significance of the rain was lost upon Stéfan. Being as yet on little more than nodding terms with the landscape, he believed his new-found family seat was merely suffering the whims of an obsessive cloud. But the long ascent from the foot of the valley up to the high moorland was more than just a scenic glory. For every two miles advanced, the rainfall increased by ten inches a year. At the first bridge over the river, the cottage owners benefited from thirty inches' worth. Fifteen bridges and ten chapels later, the hill-sheep were splashing around in an annual ninety inches.

Crug Caradoc, ancestral home of sundry lords lieutenant of the county, stood in red-creepered and decaying splendour over three-quarters of the way up the River Nant, where the steep-sided valley unexpectedly opened out onto what looked like a Swiss mountain meadow but was actually a flood plain, a fact unmentioned by estate agents. The Jacobean mansion had the oaks of mid-Wales for a backdrop; in the foreground, a generous terrace descended to two lakelets fed by the river and seventy-five inches of rain, jugs of which were now disturbing Stéfan.

'Any advance on twenty-two thousand pounds . . . ?'

He knew he was nearing the final call. Since £10,000 it had been head to head, and the bastard of it was, he knew he was up against a dealer. He had caught sight of him earlier, a cocky, unshaven little man in a hooded zip-up jumper, running suspicious fingers along the private parts of the pricier furniture and making squiggles in a small notebook. But, unlike the other dealers—and there were many—this man affected a public contempt for most of the objects on offer. Were these the traits of a master poker player, or just provocations of an impostor? Stéfan could not decide.

The rival bidder did not sound local, did not dress local . . . yet he looked local and all the locals knew him. And today the locals were out in force, in deference to the house and to its history. The farmers were the most evident—all governed, it would seem, by a nineteenth-century dress code, gathered at the rear in woolly ranks of tweed and Wellington boots.

Present in equal force were the county set who, mysteriously, were never seen in public except at point-to-points or upon dismemberment of a dead relative's assets. Their choice of attire testified that class is not dead. The gentlemen all went for the matching ensemble, with Barbour triumphant in every department except (presumably) underwear, while the ladies opted for the somebody-royal-on-horseback look, but more floral.

Stéfan's choice of clothes was, by contrast, unique. He had turned up in a white cricket sweater, white shirt and a pair of white flannels. No one quite knew why. Had he childhood memories of some dogeared schoolbook on village life in Britain, and not fully grasped the essentials? Or had he heard the role of squire was vacant and confused it with colonial administrator? Or did he not know it was October?

These were among the questions being put to Clydog the Knowledge in the refreshment tent. As chief reporter, indeed only reporter, of the weekly *Mid-Walian*, he had gained what Fleet Street would call 'privileged access'. However, his forty years of births, marriages and deaths and the occasional hay-barn fire had not honed any noted inquisitorial skills. Rather, this old sub placed his trust in more amateur arts: twice a day his portly, tweeded figure would potter round the local market town of Abernant and, just by the raising of his hat, gossip would stick to him as flies to flypaper. In truth, Clydog the Knowledge was not prepared for Stéfan, or anyone foreign. He was certainly not prepared for being driven at 110 miles an hour round the bypass, or being pressed to drink a magnum of champagne—from the bottle—at the traffic lights. Clydog had done his best. He had asked questions as vigorously as his heart condition would allow. But the news that 'Stéfan is a foreign name' was not much by way of a scoop. Asked where he came from, Stéfan had laughed and said 'Nowhere that you could spell!' Then added, 'Home of the Mongol hordes' before laughing again, at unreasonable length, and leaving Clydog unsure what the joke was, or what he should write. At the risk of impertinence, Clydog had tried enquiring as to Stéfan's line of business. And been told rather more about property deals than he could understand, the words nightclub and import–export majoring in the monologue.

Clydog was unused to new money. Like all the valley, he was unused to change. For forty years he had been the chronicler of stasis. And for more than forty years he had been witness to the dynastic decline of Crug Caradoc. Yet even Clydog had not predicted the overthrow of Eryl, its one-time heir, whose absence from the auction spoke such volumes of bitterness; nor had he foretold the murky manoeuvrings of Trystan, who had so undeservedly inherited these spoils of the past. Spoils that he had now put under the hammer.

And when the locals tempted Clydog with a pint or two, he could tell them little of the future either, save that the new owner from afar liked the idea of Welsh country life because 'you got more bricks for your buck'.

Back in the marquee, Stéfan had become bored with the stand-off.

'Oh, fuck it!' he said, in unexpectedly plummy tones for a foreigner. Three rows of moneyed heads turned, and he boomed at full throttle: 'Twenty-five thousand pounds!', then gave vent to a braying, intimidating laugh. He knew from long experience of negotiations that a sudden leap in price was the rabbit punch, the blow that broke the spirit of the opposition.

'Twenty-five and a half,' said the auctioneer, and thirty yards away Stéfan saw a stubbly face smirk at him from beside the tent flaps. At heart, he understood the problem. He wanted the family deed boxes for sentimental reasons, to bask in their heritage. His rival wanted their contents for commercial reasons, to bask in their profits. For Stéfan the bidding was indulgence, for the dealer it was business. This was not an equal contest.

As he pondered on this dilemma, torn between prudence and vengeance, he was smiled at by the Sloanish lady in jodhpurs who he had nearly upended earlier. Haughty and horsy, she wore polished riding boots, breeches so tight that it seemed she enamelled her buttocks, a quilted burgundy top, a chiffon scarf, rainbow-finned glasses, and make-up in bulk. It was hard to tell if she was en route to the pony club or a fancy-dress ball. One suspected that she deludedly thought herself en route to the county set.

Stéfan had watched all her bids fail—her horse was going to be very short on equine leatherwear this winter—and assumed her smile was one of empathy. Had he asked a local, any local, he would have been advised that her smile was strongly related to his ability to lay out £25,000 on a whim. The horsewoman observed him closely through her dark-tinted lenses, and then, after injecting further warmth into her features, took a step towards him. Had he asked a farmer, almost any farmer, Stéfan would have learned why he made her heart beat faster. She liked a man with stabling.

His instinct said caution; he sensed neurosis, a woman who brought trouble. He smiled back.

She touched him on the cricket sweater with her crop. 'Felicity. I'm in the hunt,' she said with practised cut-glass vowels, and then moved away, leaving Stéfan to grapple with rural double meanings.

'Against you at twenty-five thousand, five hundred pounds . . .'

He reassessed. Part of the fun of buying the house was making his townie friends pig-sick with envy, and to have rare historical documents stuck all over the bog walls would make them even pig-sicker. Nonetheless, the main game plan, as he constantly announced to everyone, including complete strangers, was to have a country estate ready for when he retired at forty, that age when all successful men retire and leave London. That was what mattered. And yet, and yet . . . Like many an outsider and exile he hankered after roots, longed to appropriate a past. He had seen the brittle bundles illuminating the history of this seventeenth-century manor house. He had felt them. For it was he who, by chance, had first come across the archive that chronicled four centuries and seventeen generations of ownership by one family, the Llewellyns—who, with the death of ninety-two-year-old Gwendolen, had finally come to the end of a 400-year line.

He vividly remembered the perfect summer afternoon in late August when he had broken into the deserted house. It was, admittedly, not the orthodox way to view a property for sale. He had been at a weekend house-party in the Borders, celebrating his twenty-seventh birthday, when he heard the tale of 'the house that time forgot'. It had the tabloid lure of tragedy and treachery. Even the name Trystan, the usurper, came from the ancient word for 'tumult' and had overtones of dark Celtic deeds.

So, on impulse, Stéfan had driven across the moors to find this ancient manor house. As he told on his return, he had barely gone five yards up the long gravel drive before he felt the cheque of destiny in his hands.

The swallows were swooping through the roofless outbuildings and snatching flies just inches off the surface of the upper lake. Cattle were chomping noisily in the meadow. A pair of iridescent green dragonflies were mating on the wing in the walled garden.

He had found himself spoilt for choice of broken windows—it was years since the family had spent money on such trifles. Decades, even. Neglect of the estate had begun before the war, when a frisky polo pony in India had bounced the colonel on his brain, and the colonel's wife had discovered drink. Thereafter, for Gwendolen, maintenance of the inheritance had come a poor second to upkeep of the cellar. Even the proceeds of a minor Vandyke had gone on Châteauneuf-du-Pape.

Stéfan had eventually squeezed through some sort of scullery window at the back. From there he passed through a panelled anteroom, which in turn led to a grand entrance hall. Oak doors offered promise in every direction and, though the finest artefacts were gone, lost to folly and family vultures, there remained pantechnicons of pickings still to be had. But it was the house itself he wanted.

Stéfan made his way through dusty shuttered room after dusty shuttered room; in one would be rotting carpets, in the next a fading tapestry of the Napoleonic wars, in the next a shrouded four-poster bed. And everywhere a soft silence. Gwendolen's corpse had been gone a month, the last mourners had long left, the house was now breathing to its own rhythms. He wandered from library to study to parlour, pondering on new furnishings and where to show his guitar collection to best advantage.

Eventually, he reached the attic rooms, the servants' floor. From here, too, he could look upon history: the peeling cottages, the overgrown grounds, the fractured glasshouse, the ruins of a tennis court that had not seen a forehand in forty years, the half-dug hole for a swimming pool.

A door was ajar on one of the small rooms. By chance he looked in. A glint of metal drew him to the broken corner cupboard. Inside was a set of First World War ammunition boxes. He dragged the top one out. And that was when he saw the photos. He was there until the light gave out.

A hundred and twelve people worked for the estate in the summer of 1897. And when the harvest was safely gathered in, every one of them— farmers, farriers, gardeners, labourers, butlers, valets, cooks, housekeepers, parlour maids, chambermaids—had put on their one set of simple finery, and lined up on the terrace of Crug Caradoc on either side of the seated Sir Richard and Lady Margaret, their five children and four springer spaniels. And a Mr Dai Williams, photographer of Messrs D. Williams and Sons, formerly of Llanwern, buried his head under his tripod's black cowl, fired the release, and put on record a scene of ramrod formality.

Innumerable moments of such ritual charted years of plenty, years when patriarchs and matriarchs were time and again pictured beside horses, hunting dogs, garden ornaments and vegetable displays, always in their full regalia but rarely smiling, just gazing determinedly towards posterity.

Almost every day, a carriage went fifteen miles to the local station halt, and the guard would unload a hamper from Harrods. Indeed, Harrods hamper upon Harrods hamper cascaded on this far-off family as if each day heralded a picnic for 500. Thanks to exemplary housekeeping, every can of consommé, every jar of caviar, every tin of shortbread, every bottle of vintage wine, was accounted for. As the family gourmandised, so their consumption was itemised, in copperplate, in lined exercise books.

These same books also listed the wages of every person on the payroll. The annual salary of a chambermaid was entered as four shillings and sixpence . . . which put her cost for the year at less than a case of champagne. And in one month alone there were a dozen cases of champagne.

In the third ammunition box was a lifetime of diaries and correspondence, charting the full story of the rise and fall of the House of Llewellyn—fierce rival for four centuries to the House of Powell in the lower valley. It seemed that the hereditary rich adapt uncertainly to poverty. One account described the hard winter of '63. With cavalier eccentricity, it related how a set of dining chairs had been chopped for firewood, thus keeping the family warm even as they dined off Dresden, with a Rubens on the wall.

And in the fourth and final box was the backbone of the dynasty: 400 years of documents. Of property rights, land purchases, farm leases, dowry demands, stock sales, court cases . . . These were the manuscripts integral to the history of the house, dating back even to the day when Crug Caradoc was built—a year when Shakespeare was in full flow. This was a fact not without relevance. For there, almost lost among the scrollwork, was a farmhouse listed as the property of Llewellyn . . . and named in the History Plays. Visited, indeed, by Hotspur. So, somewhere in all these miles of manuscripts was perhaps proof of whether Shakespeare himself ever came to the valley, and with which grand family he had stayed.

'For the last time, at twenty-five thousand, five hundred pounds . . .'

Stéfan stiffened, bit on his lip and tried to forget that he was the prime exhibit of the day.

'Oh, fuck it!' he said, even louder than before. And with bad grace and in a strop, he exited into the rain.

As the hammer landed, Nico, the troublemaker with the stubble, tugged on his hood and smiled. He knew at least three buyers who would be interested in taking parts of the collection, one of whom would pay dollars.

On that wet afternoon in the eighties, the valley was parted from its history. And as new blood started to seep through its world, all the old certainties began to fracture.

Chapter 3

It was the bell-ringers who first noticed the problem. They were thirty-seven minutes into 'Cambridge Surprise Minor' when Mrs Hartford-Stanley felt a draught on her bottom. The night was dark and stormy and she instinctively put it down to the wind. Then, a few more changes rung, she felt it again—a ripple of cold air up her pleated skirt.

Being an experienced ringer, the intense concentration needed was second nature to her. Yet even as she kept her focus fixed on the intricate sequence of bells (5–6–3–4–2), somewhere in her mind was a niggling sense of something odd. She had not heard the ancient oak door of the church creak open. 4–2–6–3–5. And the echoing flagstones were sure to have registered the entrance of even the most discreet visitor. Not that a visitor was likely on so wet a night in such a distant hamlet. 2–3–5–6–4. But wind there was. And then it came a third time. Like a goblin with cold breath.

In a reflex action, she turned her head, looking quickly from the bell-tower into the nave. And saw nobody. And nothing. 6–4–5—

'Oh, shoot! Shoot, shoot, shoot, shoot, shoot!'

The bells tumbled to a discordant halt.

'I'm so sorry, everybody!'

Sympathetic smiles masked the others' disappointment. No one blamed her, they had all done it in their time. Though several of them were not best pleased to have driven up to ten miles through falling branches and flooded lanes only to see their evening's pleasure so soon truncated.

'That's not like you, Rosemary,' said the conductor, a genial old hand in the science of ringing.

'Yes, I'm sorry, I—'

'I thought Mr Chigley's trousers had fallen down again,' said Joanne, a skittish spinster in her fifties, and giggled.

The others joined in the laughter, although old Mr Chigley could only manage a forced smile and a beetroot blush. The night of Mr Chigley's trousers had passed into local bell-ringing legend. Halfway through a 'Kent Treble Bob Major' the top button of his corduroys had ceded victory to his stomach and slowly, inexorably, bell by bell, his trousers had descended to his ankles. Yet such was the discipline of the team that they had managed to continue ringing for nearly two minutes before collective hysteria made progress impossible.

'No,' said Rosemary, 'I was distracted by . . .' By what, exactly? She turned and looked behind her. Then she walked with deliberation across the floor of the old bell-tower.

'What is it?' asked the conductor.

'I'm not sure.'

She stopped, and stared intently at the ancient stone walls in front of her.

No one was to be seen, but everywhere the footprints of the diocesan surveyor were ironed in the dew on the graveyard's grass, and in the high trees that framed the church, the rooks squawked warnings of his presence. By the time the vicar hurried through the lych gate, it was a textbook autumn morning—a brilliant blue sky, a mist rising off the river, and a blood-red sun that had yet to make headway against the cold.

The oldest church in the valley, St Brynnach's nestled almost unnoticed in a dell. At its eastern end curled the river, at its western end rose the woods, and away to the south stood the mountains.

The vicar puffed his way down the path of yews, past the tumbled tombstones and the Llewellyn vault. Prematurely old at thirty-five, he was a Bunteresque figure but with eyes too close together to be jolly. As he rounded the far end of his church he caught sight of the surveyor on his knees.

'You can use the church for that, you know,' he quipped.

The surveyor did not look up. He had pulled back the brambles and was burrowing into the ground near the riverbank. Below him, a dipper bobbed uncertainly then flew low and fast upstream, to seek refuge under a small humpback bridge. He watched the bird go by. As a child, he had watched kingfishers and even otters along this tranquil stretch of the lower Nant.

He pushed himself up a little stiffly, and rubbed at the green smear now on both knees of his navy-blue suit. Then he held out a spadeful of earth. And slowly cascaded its contents onto the ground, an action clearly intended to be of significance.

The vicar looked blank. 'I'm not with you, Euan.'

'Come and look at this.' Euan, the older man by some twenty years, led the vicar back along the side elevation of the church and came to a halt a few yards from the porch, where the great oak door opened into the nave.

He stepped back and gestured towards the building. 'Norman,' he said, pointing up at the squat old tower. 'Victorian,' he said, pointing to the body of the building. 'Silurian,' he said, waving at his pile of excavated earth.

Somewhat to Euan's satisfaction, the vicar still looked blank.

'A geological term.'

'Oh.' The vicar smiled the placebo smile that he used to stave off his parishioners and their crises. But such smiles were wasted on the surveyor. 'Are you saying there's a problem?'

'There's a problem.'

'Is it serious?'

'Put it this way, have you considered a career change?' Confident he had the vicar's attention, Euan moved closer to the church's stonework. 'Look, see here . . . and here . . . and here.' His finger traced a path up the joints. 'This is where the Victorian section was joined to the Norman section.' He paused. 'And now it's saying goodbye.'

As the vicar looked more closely he could discern a definite crack, which steadily widened as it rose up the building. 'Oh God in heaven! So . . . so how far will the church move?'

'Given time? To the sea.' These were moments he cherished in his work for the diocese. Unknown to his colleagues in the religious buildings department, he had for years been a secret subscriber to atheism. And now, at a time of tighter budgets and leakier churches, his specialist field of work afforded him ever more job satisfaction. 'It's falling into the river, nave and all.'

'It must be possible to underpin it or something.'

'Normally, yes. The trouble is, Reverend, whoever built this church hadn't read their Bible.'

Again that bovine look of incomprehension crossed the vicar's face.

'The man who builds his house on sand?' offered Euan. 'That's what the Victorians did with their end of the church. It's just standing on earth. Not a rock in sight. And this lovely river is meandering closer and closer. Eating away at the house of God.'

'Oh dear . . .' As at all moments of crisis, the vicar's hand went straight to the boiled sweets in his cassock. After years in this valley, he was only too aware that the house of God was being eaten away, but up till now he had blamed it on a declining population, materialism, television, apathy and moral decay. Silurian sediment had not been a major worry. Now, in an instant, he saw his livelihood flash before his eyes. Not that spreading divine love was anything but a thankless task. Religion was no longer the social glue of these hills, and to see a couple of 4 x 4s by the lych gate on a wet Sunday was cause for hallelujahs. And that was the combined haul for two churches. All women, all moaning, all gossiping, all worrying about the Sunday joint. The menfolk stayed at home, watching videos.

'I'll put the full details in the report.'

'Oh right.' The vicar didn't want to know details, any more than he would want to pore over X-rays should he be afflicted with cancer. He just stood and stared at the crack in the church wall, sucking noisily.

'But I need to check inside first. Will the Commodore be long?'

'Who knows? Who ever knows?'

The Air Commodore was holder of the church key. Although, technically, this was the most minor of administrative roles, it symbolised a larger truth. His aristocratic, landowning family, had worshipped at St Brynnach's for generations and had the tombs to prove it. With the demise of the rival Llewellyns upriver, no one could now refute the Powells' claim to be the valley's premier dynasty. From their Queen Anne house, whose roof could be seen across the water meadow, came a constant supply of flowers to bedeck the altar and dusters to polish the plaques.

The two men stood a few feet apart in uneasy silence, marking time among the gravestones. Nearby lay the valley's newest grave, Hefin's headstone an interim cross of wood. The sun was edging up over the yews and had begun to cast extravagant shadows across the earth. The vicar pondered his personal tragedy. He felt bitter at the injustice of geology. 'So,' he asked eventually, 'what's to be done?'

'Prayer?' suggested the surveyor.

The vicar sensibly ignored this suggestion. 'This would be the second church I've lost. I was rationalised at Nantgarreg. Three times in one month I was preaching to just the churchwarden. And then he got flu. Is it still safe?'

'This building? For the moment, yes. I wouldn't advise any rousing hymns, though.'

'Little chance of that. Mrs Skinner still plays the organ and she's eighty-nine. One wrong foot on the loud pedal and her head would explode.'

'Is the church ever full?'

'Harvest Festival, of course. Weddings. And funerals. Most of the valley comes to a funeral. Particularly when it's a farmer.'

'I'd steer clear of the altar. Especially if the nave starts to slope.'

'Good . . . morning.' The soft, nervous tones of the Air Commodore took them by surprise. He had appeared behind them, his six-feet-two-inch frame having navigated the stile in the graveyard wall. Despite looking gaunt and tired, he had walked down through the fields, down one of the myriad rights-of-way in the valley that now marked yesteryear's forgotten paths to church. Even more gaunt and tired, and defeated by the stile, was Rupert, his old black labrador.

'You . . . er . . . you wanted the . . . um . . .' Conversation with the Commodore was always difficult.

'Good of you to come, Air Commodore,' said the vicar.

'Some sort of . . . um . . . problem, my sister said.'

'That's right,' replied the surveyor.

'Mmm . . . nasty things, problems. Seen the dipper this morning?'

'Yes, indeed,' said the surveyor.

'Good. Very good.' He stared at the ground.

The Commodore had not had a good war. Invalided out was the whispered word. The exact cause of the problem was not known, but was believed to be all that noise and shouting. Always a delicate child, his life in the rural ruling classes had not prepared him for, well, for anything. A breakdown had ensued in the late 1940s. And 1950s. And, indeed, most succeeding decades. His sister Dilys—who still lived with him—was a noted hostess, and few were the guests who did not have accounts of standing alone with him in front of the hall's life-size oil portrait of his father, unable to discover a single subject of conversation to which he would respond. This awkwardness was compounded by his wife Josephine, who had been in bed with gin for over fifteen years.

'The key.' He held the church key out to the vicar.

It was a monstrous key, nearly a foot in length. Without a religious function, it would have constituted an offensive weapon. The vicar took it from him and creaked the oak door open, a creak given new significance by the eastward march of the nave.

Inside, an echoing mustiness, with a hint of Brasso and fresh-cut flowers, still hung round the pews. The bell-ropes still lay looped over their hooks. The hymn numbers, testimony to the valley's farewell to Hefin, were still displayed on the board.

What was new, however, was that the secular world beyond the church was now visible from within. On the frontier between Norman and Victorian was a clear flicker of daylight—and a crack that explained why Mrs Hartford-Stanley had felt a frisson in her upper thighs for the first time in many years. The surveyor described it as a 'yawning gap' to upset the vicar further, then set about bridging the crack with slivers of glass so that, as they fractured, the pace of movement could be monitored. By such matter-of-fact measures did reality strike home.

The prospect of being left with a third of a church greatly disturbed the Commodore. For generations his family had had a whole church. To the Powells, the provision of spiritual welfare for their community was an historic duty exemplified by the range of embroidered kneelers they had made available. Patronage had long been in their blood, and today was on the headed notepaper of many a local cause. Red Cross, Blue Cross, Green Cross, dogs, cats, lepers—a Powell would usually lend their name, or at least their rose garden.

This sense of duty had been passed down to the Commodore. Although he rarely spoke in whole sentences, he was often heard to mutter individual words of some length, words like obligation, responsibility, integrity. The Commodore also hoped to be on a polished plaque one day, next to his ancestors, and if the church were short of a nave this would be difficult. He was therefore eager to suggest remedies for the impending crisis.

'Bring-and-buy sales.'

'Bring-and-buy sales?' queried the vicar.

'Always a great success.'

'I don't think that—'

'Tombola?'

'Yes, but—'

'Raffles?'

The vicar pressed the surveyor to hazard a guess at the cost of underpinning.

'Impossible to say,' Euan replied. And then said, 'Twenty-five thousand pounds.' And added, 'Plus.' For good measure.

'Twenty-five thousand pounds!' said the vicar, astonished. Extrapolating from an average collection plate of three pounds and fifty pence, this was not cause for optimism. 'Twenty-five thousand pounds?'

The Commodore considered this new information for a while.

And then cried, 'A garden fête!'

Chapter 4

'He may look like some psycho out of a zombie movie,' said the estate agent, 'but he's basically harmless.'

Jane twisted herself sideways in the front passenger seat, and looked back at Mr Probert. Rob, her boyfriend, was struggling to double-declutch the old Morris 1000 Traveller from second to first, a manoeuvre he had never found necessary in England, and this had left Jane in charge of conversation. 'And he'd be our nearest neighbour?' she asked.

'He's a good field away.'

'Oh, that's all right then,' said Jane.

'His trouble is he's lonely. Fifty and never been kissed, I reckon!' he added. Before leaving the office, Mr Probert had decided the best sales strategy was to employ light-hearted witticisms on the subject of Glyn, who, in his attempts to sell the late Hefin's farmhouse, was having the effect of human dry rot. To date, three prospective buyers had not even made it up to the property after they had experienced the leering rustic by his farm gate.

The wheels skidded briefly on wet leaves as the 1,098cc engine over-revved up the steep lane.

'How d'you know we'll see him?' asked Jane.

This was the question to evade. One always saw Glyn. Or rather Glyn always saw one. Harmless he might be, but spy satellites could not have improved on Glyn's detection rate of strangers. And access to the empty old farmhouse on the ridge went via the entrance to his smallholding.

'Oh, I don't know for sure we'll see him,' Mr Probert said, with estate agent honesty. 'Though I guess when your farm's got no power or heating you do like to get out a bit!'

'Is that right?' replied Jane with exaggerated interest. Her tone immediately reminded him why this young pair was able to consider the purchase of remote Pantglas: its absence of all known amenities.

'Your turn to get mucky,' Rob said to her, bringing their car to a halt.

The single-track road, which had wound upwards from the valley bottom, had run out of tarmac at a fork in the track. Two closed farm gates lay ahead. To the left, a rough track followed a stream down to a dilapidated building in a hollow. To the right, a mud slalom climbed up through a copse towards a distant meadow.

The trick, as the estate agent knew, was to leap out of the car, open the gate, race through the gate, close the gate, and leap back into the car before the arrival of Glyn. It was, however, a two-door estate car and he was in the back—along with several dozen well-squeezed tubes of oil paint, a broken oar and a rich crop of unidentified animal hairs. He was deeply regretting that he had chosen today to have the firm's Range Rover serviced.

'Come on, prissy pants! Out!' urged Rob.

'I opened the last gate!'

'If I take my foot off the brake we'll roll back in the ditch.'

'It's raining.'

'It's Wales.'

'Can you fit remote controls to farm gates?' Jane asked, laughing as she forced open the rusty car door with her shoulder.

The car stood at an angle on the slope, which added gravity to the problems of exiting. To keep the door from slamming, Jane swung both legs out together, and the clammy plastic seat made her short skirt rise to the top of her thighs. As she levered her lower body out and up she saw the eager, unshaven face of Glyn arrive panting from his hovel. She squelched across the mud to tackle the gate to Pantglas, struck by the accuracy of the long-forgotten childhood word 'turnip-head'.

'Good morning, Glyn,' called Mr Probert.

'Morning to you, sir,' replied Glyn, his eyes fixed on Jane's crotch.

'Hello, there!' said Rob, smiling through the passenger door.

'How do you do, sir,' replied Glyn, his eyes fixed on Jane's crotch.

'Lovely dog,' said Jane, as his border collie bounded up to join in her struggle with the latch.

'Name's Twm, miss,' replied Glyn, his eyes fixed on Jane's crotch. He leaned low over his rotting gate. A stocky figure, his clothes exuded wafts of wood smoke made malodorous by weeks of sweat and body odour. Even at ten paces one could sense that mains water played little role in his life.

Despite his enthusiasm for company he made no attempt at conversation.

'Not seen you at market lately,' said Mr Probert.

'I've had a problem with phlegm,' replied Glyn.

There was a brief pause in the interchange as he appeared about to illustrate these health problems.

Then, with a sudden tug, the latch was released. The moment he saw this, Rob revved his old banger forward—a move that played havoc with Glyn's eyeline—and bounced the gate open with his bumper. Leaving the gate to clang shut, Jane called 'Goodbye' and leapt back into the car as it yawed noisily up the track.

'Well, that's worth five thousand off at least,' she said, turning to address Mr Probert. 'After all, the risk of impregnation by an alien life form every time you go shopping is not exactly a plus point.'

'Oh, the view's the plus point. Eleven hundred feet. Woods and mountains in every direction. You don't get that in Leeds.'

'Manchester.'

'Right.' His patter faded. The Morris Traveller jolted up the track.

Mr Probert was not happy with houses. Normally he did animals—cows, sheep, pigs, that sort of thing—and to sell those he just had to call out bids and bang a gavel in a huge tin shed, pungent with the odours of animal dung and warmed by the packed bodies of hard-pressed farmers. It was a comforting, if fetid, world that he had known since his schooldays—schooldays that he had shared with many of the buyers and sellers.

Of late, though, the market in animals had hit hard times. So his boss had added house sales to the firm's portfolio, transactions that took place up a flight of rickety stairs, like an afterthought to the real business of the land. For valley people did not move home. They stayed put, resistant to such frivolity. But every passing decade now doubled the acreage needed for survival, and accumulating field after field had left many a farmhouse surplus to requirements. So, today, the homesteads were being picked off like cherries, separated from their land, parted from their purpose, and sold for the value of their views.

And were usually bought by a new breed of country-lover, with whom he had no common language.

'What's that smell?' asked Jane, sniffing the air. 'I can definitely smell something.'

'It's burning rubber!' snapped Rob, cross with her for asking, furious with himself for stalling. The second of the hairpins had been the car's undoing. Its bald tyres were a handicap even on a bypass, but this track was little more than ruts into which a few bricks and slates had been stamped in order to offer some grip. Mostly the surface was mud and sheep shit.

After several minutes of wheelspin and smoke, the three continued on foot.

On first seeing Rob and Jane, Mr Probert had opined in the office that they were hippies, a judgment based on little more than a T-shirt slogan and a packet of Rizlas. Their desire to be property owners had upgraded them to bohemian. What remained undeniable, though, was their unworldliness. Both had failed to ask any of the normal questions about easement rights and drainage. The man, who often smiled when there appeared to be no joke, had asked about the possibility of a duck pond. And a wind turbine. (Twice.) The woman had enquired about low-flying aircraft. Such attitudes had left Mr Probert unsure what constituted a good selling point.

The track wound up through a dingle of wind-stunted hazel and crossed a rivulet that tinkled with treacherous innocence. Even in the dank days of autumn one could not mistake the magic of the landscape. Several times Rob stopped to stare, to admire the fungus on a rock or the ferns in the fork of a branch. This apparent sensitivity was all the more surprising given that he had the sinewy build of a bantamweight and inner-city stubble.

'About the only place sheep don't get, halfway up a tree,' said Mr Probert.

'Whose are the sheep?' asked Jane.

'Gareth's. Field belongs to Gareth Richards now.' He was about to add that it had always been grass-let to Gareth until the tragedy of recent events, but then realised such matters were probably best not aired.

Driven on by their eagerness to view, Rob and Jane were ten yards in front of Mr Probert when they emerged beyond the treeline.

'Jee-sus!' echoed down to him.

Followed by a long whoop.

The storm clouds were just starting to break, and the dramatic contrasts of light and shade were racing across the meadow above them. The grass-land and its battalion of molehills stretched some 200 yards up towards the ridge, where yellow-ochred walls were just visible beyond a hawthorn hedge. A long slate roof was glistening in the day's first rays. A specimen pine tree towered protectively at one end. Broom and gorse and hawthorns were scattered over the surrounding hillside. And no other habitation could be seen for miles.

'THE OWNER was a . . . er . . . a bit of an eccentric.'

'How long's it been like that?'

'About . . . about thirty years, I'm told.'

'Thirty years!'

Estate agent and clients were gathered in the farmyard, gazing at the farmhouse's most unusual feature.

The particulars described the building as a rare 150-year-old long house, once the most traditional of Welsh farm buildings, now much prized and protected. Long and low and narrow, they were designed to keep the elements at bay. Often, as here, the building was L-shaped, and in its lee a rectangular farmyard lay hidden from the world and the worst of the westerlies. Along the short stroke of the 'L' at Pantglas were the stone barns. The long stroke of the 'L' had originally housed the parlour, the lounge, and the four bedrooms, each room the width of the building.

What the particulars did not mention was the combine harvester. Which was parked in the lounge. And in two of the bedrooms.

'This would presumably reduce the value somewhat?' enquired Jane.

To provide this unconventional parking space it had been necessary to demolish an external wall, two internal walls, and a ceiling. The result was a neat excision that exposed a complete cross-section of the building's innards. Indeed, surreally on display some ten feet above the ground was an exquisitely tiled Victorian fireplace, whose fires could only be lit by ladder. The small-paned bedroom windows at the rear also remained intact, though their panoramic view could only be fully appreciated by climbing onto the combine's cab roof.

'Some of these old farmers, they were real characters,' said Mr Probert, clutching at straws. Then he added, 'It's a '57 Massey Ferguson. The old red ones are getting very rare.'

'And it's in excellent condition because it's been kept in the lounge,' observed Jane helpfully.

'That's right.' He knew for a fact it had been used last summer. 'Full working order.' Mr Probert sensed there was still some customer dissatisfaction to defuse. 'The house'll be with full vacant possession, of course.'

'But just a little short on walls.'

In truth, the combine harvester should already have gone. Somehow, though, its vintage value had fallen under the vulturine eye of Nico, the mocking dealer from the marquee. With predatory haste, he had ploughed the profits from Crug Caradoc's archives into purchasing this icon of agriculture. But, as always, there was a catch to deals with Nico. This time, it was the small matter of where to put a '57 Massey Ferguson, given that he lived in town, in a flat above his antiques shop.

And his solution was that, while he sought a collector of geriatric tractors, the two-storey vehicle would stay parked in Pantglas's lounge. Because, like many in the valley, the vendor owed Nico a favour.

'Yes, but the accommodation is as advertised,' said Mr Probert, struggling on. 'Kitchen-parlour, two bedrooms, bathroom, outbuildings and lots—'

'—of potential.' Jane made the word sound dirty as she batted back his ace. Although she had a slightly dippy look to her, and it was easy to be distracted by her thighs, she was the more practical of the two, and busied herself putting pound signs on what Rob called his dreams.

Indeed, he had already wandered off, drawn as if by a magnet into the barns at the end of the farmyard, where he was stood gazing at some of Mr Probert's potential. 'Look at the light!' he called. 'Look at the light!'

Entry was by two vast arches, unbothered by doors, and at the rear the thick stone walls were dramatically pierced by those vertical gashes once essential to Norman bowmen. Even the farthest corners of the barns could not escape the low-angled rays of the winter sun. And if extra natural light were needed, it flooded through the patchwork of missing slates. This was a garret-in-waiting.

Rob paced it out, stepping round an abandoned milk churn, and exulted in the space. The floor was flagstoned, thick, worn, uneven, original. The walls would withstand a battering-ram. In the air was the smell of age, on the eye the sense of craftsmanship. Rob ran his hands along the stonework, as if savouring the unfashionable pleasure of roughness.

Here the pictures would paint themselves. The house was on a ridge and all Wales, it seemed, was visible. It was a landscape in thrall to the wind. The clouds swirled like an eddying sea, the grasses bent as if in prayer, and the bushes crept low for survival. But it was the trees that dared the most. Out beyond the barn against the skyline staggered a defiant row of hawthorns, distorted and deformed as they struggled to obey the laws of growth. Every shoot and every branch grew sideways, the network of twigs and foliage ballooning like a head of hair trapped in the blast of a hairdryer.

'*And* it comes with a house,' said Jane loudly, all too aware of his attention span.

'Oh, I'm sorry!' Rob turned round. 'But you must agree,' and he waved his arm at the cavernous space, 'this does beat our attic!'

She smiled. 'And when it gets dark? What are you going to use, luminous paint?'

The estate agent made a swift intervention. 'Oh, the barn can easily be wired up to the generator. No problem.'

'Who wants light bulbs?' said Rob. 'I could work by hurricane lamp! Now that would be romantic. I could wear a smock and hang the lamps here, in rows!' He reached up and slapped the squat beam that ran the width of the barn, his laughter echoing off the walls.

Even Mr Probert, with his shaky sales sense, knew not to mention that the last object to hang from that beam was the previous owner.

The tour of the long house made it evident that little of decorative significance had happened in the past century. There was a Rayburn, whose blackened oven was testimony to prewar roasts, an iron bath, whose stain raised the possibility of a past life as a sheep dip, and a toilet whose cistern contained a dead rook. Yet the weather had, by and large, remained outside, and the neglect had been broadly benign.

In a perverse way, Jane found such habitability almost a disappointment, a hindrance to her negotiating position.

'Be over ten thousand pounds for mains electricity. At least that again for general modernisation. Then there's the slates off the barn. The guttering. The paintwork. The two-storey car park. The neighbour who becomes a werewolf every full moon. We'd be looking for a considerable reduction.'

'There is considerable interest.' And it was true, there was considerable interest. Mr Probert thought they were all mad. He himself had a very pleasant little bungalow, with mod cons. 'What sort of reduction?'

Jane hesitated. She had yet to qualify as an acupuncturist. So a lot depended on Rob's income, which depended on Rob's sales, which depended on the quality of Rob's inspiration. And, of course, on the quantity of Rob's buyers.

'And then there's the state of the track. Must need five thousand quids' worth of hardcore at least.'

'It's a knack, driving up it, that's all.'

Mr Probert was lying. The most powerful vehicle to attempt the climb recently had been a hearse. Despite being in immaculate working order, it had failed to get past the first hairpin.

'Anyway,' added Mr Probert, trying a bit of hardball, 'I'm afraid the state of the track is not really relevant to the price of the house. You see, you're up against the "second home" market. The sort of people who like skipping through grass twice a month. At premium rates.'

Jane looked across at Rob, who was making a very poor show in his role as reluctant buyer. 'Will you excuse us?' she said.

Mr Probert pretended not to watch as the couple wandered round the wilderness that was once a vegetable garden. Some vicious gooseberry bushes and a few beanpoles strangled by convolvulus were the only remnants of self-sufficiency, but location was all. Set on a lumpy bank beyond the farmyard, it gave views to die for.

After three circuits they were back.

'We think the asking price is too high,' said Jane, 'given that half the house is missing. However, we would like to make an offer.'

'How much for?'

'Twenty-five thousand, five hundred?' said Jane.

'You've got yourself half a house,' said Mr Probert, smiling.

'Good?' said Jane to Rob.

'Pub?' said Rob to Jane.

Chapter 5

There used to be one public house for every two miles of the valley road, making the descent from moors to market town a long-term project. Opening hours were a reflection of the season, insomnia, or just bloody-mindedness. Occasionally, the police would raid, but in a spirit of fair play they would usually telephone to arrange their visit. The longest opening time on record was believed to be ten days, when a blizzard on the moors obliged the trapped clientele to drink the pub dry in the interests of survival. Even the advent of the breathalyser did not immediately impinge on the pursuit of drink. At night, the serious drinker would often arrive on horseback, knowing his nag would safely return his insensate body to the appropriate family bosom.

Remoteness encouraged the more individual breed of landlord, unschooled in modern notions of public service. At the Griffin Inn, Major Watkins, retired, would refuse to serve beer in half-pint glasses to male customers, proclaiming to all drinkers present that this nancy practice encouraged the spread of homosexuality. At the Boar's Head, Edward

Mason, also retired, would refuse to serve anyone employed by the water authorities. (A five-year dispute over billing meant that even mention of the word 'water' could trigger a verbatim account of four court cases.)

All landlords fell victim to that common folly of retired folk, the belief that to run a country pub was a piece of piss. And over time, the long hours and the laws of economics thinned out their numbers. And the pubs became barns. Or second homes.

The pubs that stayed serving were free houses, a sure sign that the brewery chains had done their clinical sums. Three months' tourism and nine months' rain did not amount to break-even point on ploughman's lunches. So only the local landlords kept pulling the pumps. And by the eighties, the valley choice had shrunk to two.

On the edge of the moors was Dolly. Dolly was a legend, almost as old as the century. Originally, the writing above her front door had read 'Dolly and Walter Price', and declared them joint licensees. That inscription had been a source of much pride for it made Dolly the fifth generation of her family to run the tiny alcoholic outpost. Husband Walter, however, always yearned for wider horizons. And one day in the sixties a tour bus of lost Americans unexpectedly stopped to sample the ale. Eager to pass on knowledge of his native Wales, Walter had proposed two days of his services as a free guide. He was never heard from again.

But Dolly just kept on serving, year after year. As a watering hole, the Wheatsheaf was in the Irish tradition: the bar was in the parlour, the pub was a private house. The domesticity of these arrangements made payment seem almost in bad taste. As Dolly aged, she moved her bed downstairs, to the room seen beyond the bar. This had the advantage that she could nap between customers, though the effect on passing trade of a pint poured by a little old lady in a nightdress was harder to determine. Nor did Armond help.

She went nowhere without Armond. The first sight any customer ever had of her, Armond would be in her arms. And always the introduction would be the same. A rendition of Greig's Piano Concerto. 'Would you like to hear Armond play?' she would ask. And then she would take the fluffy paws of her beloved Sealyham and dramatically pound them up and down the length of the bar as she 'mmm'ed the beat with her eyes shut.

The Wheatsheaf appealed to a rather specialist market.

The valley's one remaining hope for drinkers was the Dragon's Head. Its position was promising and it had eighteenth-century beams, low ceilings and a fine view of the mountains. Just twenty minutes from town, it offered the prospect of a fun evening out. There was just one problem. Gwillim.

Gwillim was a surly, brute-sized cattle farmer. His only observable pleasure in life was to block the traffic when he herded his cows for their twice-daily milking. The source of his embitterment was his tenancy. His farm belonged to the now much-shrunk estate of the Commodore. And, as with most tenancies, there was a small explosive device in the sub-clauses. Gwillim's farmhouse had been built onto the public house (or possibly vice versa) and those two professions had become formally intertwined in the lease. He was legally responsible for the Dragon's Head. Should he cease to be a publican he would also cease to be a farmer. And become both homeless and jobless.

He resolved this dilemma by serving beer with the worst possible grace. Sometimes he denied he had any beer to serve. Sometimes, if he had beer to serve, he insisted it was five minutes' walk away in the cellar. Indeed, almost anything was five minutes' walk away in the cellar. Occasionally, he did not come back. But the moment most treasured by the locals was his annual response to the mini-Eisteddfod held in the village hall opposite. This event attracted bourgeois types from up to fifteen miles away, and afterwards their dry throats, parched by an hour of 'Land Of My Fathers', would drive them in their dozens to the Dragon's Head. The cries would go up for spritzers, Cinzano, whisky sour, gin and tonics, sherry, and sometimes—with lunatic hubris—a vodka martini straight up with an olive. The six-foot Gwillim would stand four-square, like Horatio defending the bridge, and to each cry he would bellow 'No!' The record was believed to be seventeen straight 'No's', followed by a refusal to supply free tap water.

A normal Friday lunchtime like today was an altogether quieter affair. Only those locals who had gained respect by years of dogged persistence were present. They totalled four, all men. And a dog.

By the bar stood Gareth, hill-sheep farmer of 120 acres, and Eryl, dispossessed heir of the Crug Caradoc estate; Gareth was much depressed by the height of his wife, and Eryl was much depressed by the loss of a house with twelve bedrooms. Click-clacking in the background were the dominoes of Teg and Ben the molecatchers, both in their seventies and also faced with uncertain futures. The dog was Jessie, who had passed in mysterious ways from Hefin to Gareth.

Although four was only a small sample, they reasonably reflected the perennial concerns of the valley: sex, money and moles.

'About a million pound, I reckon,' said Eryl, for roughly the tenth time. He wiped some slops of bitter from the Zapata moustache that straggled mournfully over his mouth. 'Yes, about a million pound,' he repeated bitterly, 'if you add in the fishing rights and the shooting rights. And the development potential.' He said the words with saloon-bar authority, his attempt at gravitas undercut by the sweatshirt with 'Boogie Baby' on it.

Since prematurely parting company with school—a minor public school—Eryl had not bothered with the irritant of a career. An old-style dropout for most of his twenties, he had now graduated to jobbing carpenter and aspiring playboy and was shacked up with Bryony from the health-food shop. This led to long unhappy lunch hours.

'I could be in the Riviera now. On a yacht. If it wasn't for that conman screwing me out of my inheritance!' He paused, as he had paused a dozen times already that morning, in hope of a sympathetic response to his plight.

'Double six!' came the triumphant cry from the long pine table in the corner. Several dominoes were thrown angrily on the stone floor.

'No wonder he's buggered off and left the country. My lawyer says I could have sued him. It was criminal what he did.'

A million-pound lawsuit would certainly have been an unusual event in the daily life of the valley, but still Gareth said nothing. Indeed, since slouching in some twenty minutes earlier, Gareth had said nothing apart from 'hello'. The scandal of the lost inheritance had made few inroads into his own thoughts. He remained preoccupied with his failure to achieve the erections expected by his young wife, but, being of the old school, felt this was a subject best not shared.

Forty-one-year-old Gareth knew he had never been the best-looking of men—like his stunted father before him, he had inherited the features of a ferret—but he had had high hopes of Moira. Times though, as even he was dimly aware, were changing. In the old days, 120 acres were enough to satisfy a woman. Now they wanted conversation. And those women who came from foreign parts had no end of oddities about them. When he and Moira first met—at a rugby international in Cardiff—he had felt a bond with her Donegal roots. It was a land with similar levels of rainfall, plus a shared history of sheep, and so, his shyness thus eased, he had been lured by her lilt and her hair. Only when he had got her home, some months later, with a ring on her finger, had he realised that the length of her legs could be a problem.

'After all,' Eryl went on, 'I was the nearest blood relative. Almost the only blood relative. Well, not blood. But you know what I mean.'

He meant adopted. It was scarcely a secret, his looks matched no valley profile. Eryl was rugged, barrel-chested with coarse blond hair tied in a dated ponytail—in another life he could have been a *Baywatch* surfer, except that he had poor skin. In this life he was a Llewellyn, but without the DNA. And now without the money.

'No, that's two quid you owe, you bastard!' Behind him, the molecatchers were getting restive. Four pints meant abuse, six pints meant punches, eight pints meant kicking, and after ten pints Teg and Ben could be relied on to provide free entertainment by fighting in a ditch. A wave of self-pity came over Eryl, and he briefly saw his future as a life in moles.

'I was in her will for twenty years.'

'Eighteen,' said Gwillim, unexpectedly appearing from the cellar. He positioned himself and his tankard on their side of the bar, not from comradeship but so that in the event of passing custom he could deny all knowledge of the landlord's whereabouts. 'Eighteen years.' In recent weeks, he had been spared few details of this beery, teary tale and its many reprises. Should there ever be—over Gwillim's dead body—a pub quiz held at the Dragon's Head, all ten rounds could be devoted to the scandal of Great-Aunt Gwendolen's will. For scandal there was.

'Eighteen, twenty, whatever. I was in her will until her marbles were got at by *him*! You knew the old lady, Gareth—bright as a button she was until she hit ninety . . . and Trystan came crawling!'

Gareth just nodded. For some time now, he had felt unable to comment with confidence on women of any age. And that was the key word: confidence. No man can be confident in life when his head only comes up to his wife's neck. And they weren't just ordinary legs, they were sexy legs. Part of a sexy body. None of his farmer friends had ever had to put up with a sexy wife, and he was at a loss. It sapped morale, it sapped the will to farm, and it had certainly sapped his baby-making facilities.

'I mean, Trystan wasn't even a *second* cousin, for God's sake! Fifth, more like it! Go that far back and we're all related to Adam and Eve—you could put a claim in for half the earth. And now he's flogged my birthright to some townie in flannels. As a weekend pad!'

Eryl reached over the bar for another bottle. Since the early death of his adoptive parents, the prospect of being heir to Crug Caradoc had been integral to his career plan, key to his pulling-power. The sudden emergence of a smooth-tongued fortune hunter from the family woodwork, oozing chat and charm into gullible old ears, and guiding shaky hands over bills of sale, had been as life-changing as a boot to the genitals.

'Did you know that even *before* she signed, he tried to remove the Dresden in a horsebox at midnight?'

A pew scraped back across the flagstones. The clatter of violently discarded dominoes reverberated off the cold stone walls, the noise forestalling a catalogue of Trystan's perfidy.

'I'm sick of playing!' said an angry Teg, and he stood up, reaching for his sack of moles.

He was a shambling mass of a man. By nature blessed with endless country courtesy, his temper had been sorely tested that day. For over fifty years he and Ben had tracked and trapped the little gentlemen in velvet, eschewing the crudity of poison and the brutality of gunshot. Instead, they had mined for moles, employing a mix of acoustical subtlety and kindergarten mechanics. Armed only with a spade, a length of pipe and a bucket, they were the true, traditional countrymen, the provisional wing of morris dancing. Their work was an art form, and they could void a field in a day.

And now their life's work was to be municipalised. Their skills were to be rendered redundant. The mighty minds of the council were to create a Mole Operatives Unit, and kit it out with strychnine. The cost-effective kill would soon sound the death knell of Teg and Ben.

'Forget your bloody million,' said Teg, looking pointedly at Eryl. 'A thousand'd be quite nice for most of us.' He had little time for ponytails, except on ponies.

'Be up to do your new field in the New Year,' said Ben to Gareth.

'Hurry up and fuck off,' said Gwillim.

The motley four ignored him. Teg and Ben were born contrary, and Eryl and Gareth were intent on dragging out their drinks (well aware that, by the rules of the house, a glass put down was a glass confiscated, unlikely ever to be replenished). These rural diehards had come to lean on a five-barred gate indoors, the only place for a long moan in the dry. They also knew that the lunchtime session deprived Gwillim of his ultimate sanction, that moment when he appeared behind the bar in his pyjamas, emptying a kettle into his hot-water bottle, and turning out the lights.

'D'you do food?'

All heads turned.

A pretty, dark-haired woman in a short skirt, and a slender man with T-shirt and stubble were standing in the doorway. There was a shocked silence.

'Food?' Gwillim's body tensed. 'You want food?'

'Yes, some pasta perhaps, or a small salad?' said Jane.

'This is not a restaurant, madam. This,' replied Gwillim, 'is a public house.'

'Is it, bollocks!' snorted Ben.

The regulars erupted into laughter, delighted at such a public put-down of mein host. It was the first recorded laughter in the Wheatsheaf for several weeks and the hilarity threatened to develop into full-blown hysteria, much to the bafflement of Rob and Jane who were already nonplussed by the sack of moles.

When the guffaws died down, it was Eryl who spoke. 'Best try town. Abernant. About twenty minutes down the valley.' Then, with what may or may not have been irony: 'That's where it all happens.'

Chapter 6

The Mayoress of Abernant was running late. Half a dozen dresses lying in a heap of civic indecision upon her bed. Myfanwy Edwards was not by nature indecisive (her capacity to give orders—on any subject, to anybody—would have fast-tracked her through the Paras had not God called her to the voluntary sector), but her mind kept drifting back to the Queen. Many citizens have fantasies about the royal family; they fantasise that the Queen requests the pleasure of their company at a royal wedding, or invites them to share a picnic at Balmoral, or an early-morning canter à deux at Sandringham. Myfanwy, however, always fantasised about Her Majesty opening the mail. And it was always a letter about her.

For over thirty years, Myfanwy had been busy raising the artistic consciousness of Abernant's 5,000 inhabitants. Be it the sponsored harpist in the Indian restaurant, the campaign for a love-spoon exhibition in the defunct abattoir, or the production of a Young Farmers' AmDram Night every Christmas, Mrs M. Edwards was always the name in big type on the publicity leaflet. Such were her powers of persuasion that fully grown dignitaries had been known to hide in alleyways at the sight of her fifteen stone in pursuit of a pledge.

Eventually, with a fourth decade of her initiatives looming, the council had bowed to the inevitable and announced that Mrs M. Edwards was to be Mayoress of Abernant. The official statement said this was 'in recognition of her long-standing services to the arts' and made tribute to her energy levels. In private, the councillors' preferred choice was Mr Capstick the butcher, for not only was he male, he also brought credit to the town with his specialist sausages. Myfanwy's popularity was not aided by her acceptance speech—reminiscent of a diva accepting the freedom of the city—and her advocacy of an arts festival caused a mocking rumour that she had plans to twin the town with Salzburg (wherever that was).

The mayoralty attained, however, her thirty-year-old royal fantasy had grown ever stronger. Myfanwy had always envisioned Her Majesty delicately holding her letter-opener, discreetly monogrammed, with a select pile of envelopes laid upon her lap. She would be seated on a chaise longue, open French windows leading onto terraced gardens, a cold drink of crushed lemons by her side, her handbag on a small Edwardian marquetry table. A faint breeze would have tried in vain to ruffle her hair. After taking several sips of drink—there was never a rush—Her Majesty would slice open the pale azure-blue envelope . . . and withdraw a handwritten note.

The mayoress was never able to discern who had recommended her for the OBE. Always at this moment the fantasy would dissolve into an orgasmic haze of satisfaction.

Myfanwy gazed again at the choice of frocks. Today it was the Chamber of Commerce, and she was searching for an ensemble appropriate to the ways of small business. Hers was, after all, the face that had to launch a thousand fêtes.

Her public image was, unfortunately, little helped by Auberon, the local paper's freelance photographer. Dividing his time among weddings, events of municipal record, and his evening job as a petrol-pump attendant, young Auberon had darkroom skills that were not yet cutting edge. In every edition of the *Mid-Walian*, his portraiture transformed the world into a uniform fuzzy grey, depicting a population that was either living underwater or in an earlier century. Myfanwy had twice complained—without success since Auberon was the nephew of the proprietor—arguing that her weekly appearance as a corpse-coloured apparition was a threat to the dignity of her office.

Pink and orange, she decided. She had a ceremony to perform and she wished to convey a mood of dynamism. Insinuating herself into the size eighteen, she rehearsed the sentences of welcome she had prepared earlier. Speeches were her strong point for she had been gifted with lungs undaunted by sub-clauses. Then, having urged her zipper the final yard, she glanced over the guest list, a *Who's Who* of banking and business in Abernant.

At the door she paused in front of her full-length mirror to wonder if the gold chain of office might clash, but dismissed the thought. A gold chain of office went with everything. Her appearance did, however, suffer from another problem, a problem much commented on in the town's bars. Now past fifty, her age at last exceeded her bust size. But it was a bust of such prominence and disproportion that it relocated her centre of gravity—with the consequence that her profile varied from the vertical by several degrees. When on the move—and especially when on the move with a grand décolletage—Mrs M. Edwards bore a quite startling resemblance to a figurehead on the prow of a galleon.

Resplendent in her multicoloured glad rags, the mayoress left for her official car at full tilt, like a ship heading into a severe southwesterly.

'YEEUGH!'

Bryony gingerly juggled the container. She was right, the nuts *were* moving. Independently. Although still only in her first month at the health-food shop, she knew that nuts were meant to be stationary objects. And, *ergo*, that small wiggly creatures were not part of the deal. She looked around for a bin bag.

'What are you after?' A wreath of pipe smoke emerged from a darkened recess nearby.

'Something to put these nuts in. They've got maggots.'

'Maggots?' She heard footsteps and then Hubert appeared behind her in the storeroom. He looked over her shoulder. 'Don't waste good nuts. Put them in the oven for five minutes. Two hundred degrees.'

'You can't do that! You could poison someone,' she insisted.

Hubert raised an eyebrow, a boss's eyebrow. 'I doubt it. Good nutritional value—don't you read survivalist magazines? Juicy maggots, we could put them on special offer for the SAS.'

Despite herself, and despite her wishy-washy 'alternative' views on life, Bryony could not resist a grudging fondness for anyone still an *enfant terrible* at the age of sixty-two. Less admirable was the fact that he was serious about selling his superheated nuts. With a large profit margin.

'Well, I'm not doing it,' she said flatly.

Again he raised an eyebrow. He was a tall, well-preserved man—and he exuded the residue of a once-potent charm.

'I'm not.' She had faced him down once before, and achieved a victory . . . of sorts.

One of her ill-paid functions was that of cook, and her daily creation of *amuse-gueules* was much prized by the local bourgeoisie. Their enthusiasm for such delicacies would, however, have ceased had they known the use-by dates of the ingredients. And this information Bryony had threatened to let slip. As a concession to good housekeeping, Hubert eventually agreed that items such as flour would only be kept for one year after the date they should have been thrown away.

In the battle of the nuts, Hubert blinked first, then took them from her. Shuffling the nuts so the maggots were uppermost, he laid them on a baking tray in the oven. Bryony returned to the till, attributing her calm resolve to her skilful use of essential oils, of which she now knew twenty-three.

The health-food shop had been a runaway success, a place where the word aubergine had been heard in town for the first time in 300 years, where chocolate was to be seen in individual pieces instead of bars, and where occasionally it was possible to buy pitta bread and hummus on the same day. Key to the shop's triumph was Hubert's exquisite calligraphy, which provided labels that enabled him to double the asking price.

Less masterly was his retention of staff, who sometimes lasted a shorter time than the fresh veg, and on average possessed a sack-by date of six weeks. In part, this was down to Hubert's delight in the role of curmudgeon, but credit must also be given to his temperamental wife Gloria, a former leisure-wear model who no longer looked good in colour. Not merely did the pair issue contradictory orders at the speed of ping-pong finalists, but the faded Gloria brought the rules of absolute monarchy to management, driven by the delusion that every female employee had the hots for Hubert.

Hubert reappeared and slipped into his vantage-point, half-hidden in the corner of the shop yet still within sight and sound of money changing hands. There was something indefinably mercantile about his posture as he stood brooding in the shadows by the baguette basket. He stayed almost motionless, like a Dickensian overseer, puffing constantly on his pipe and never losing sight of the High Street.

His old vantage-point by the front door, where he used to play the old-fashioned proprietor and exchange banter with his customers as they came and went, was now a no-go area. It had been so for over three months and the pettifogging lunacy of the ban still enraged him. It was *his* shop, *his* health food, and so whether or not he smoked a pipe in it was nobody's business but *his*—as he had told the Public Health and Hygiene official in simple four-letter words. He had wanted to go to court, but the tyranny of political correctness, now the tide of the times, had captured hygiene as its latest fad, and the certainty of legal failure—with costs—had forced him to retreat. So now he skulked, puffing with phoney defiance, and praying that the gloriously pungent fumes would not be seen by any passing agents of the environmental Stasi.

He had even had a speech ready for his arrest. For this was not the first time he had fallen foul of the men with clipboards and a nose for killer cockroaches. 'Dirt is good for you,' he would have declaimed to the bench. 'Bacteria are an invention of bored bureaucrats.' 'The biggest cause of death in catering is falling over the Hoover.' His attacks on red tape, sell-by dates, smoking bans and hygiene regulations, rang a chord among the small businessmen of the town and, for three years in succession, they had elected him President of the Chamber of Commerce.

'I think you're on soon,' said Bryony, who was nearer the shop window. 'The paparazzi are here.'

He diverted his attention from the High Street and the small crowd gathering outside the bank, and watched a florid Clydog struggle towards the shop, accompanied by young Auberon, the photographer.

Hubert cut and wrapped a portion of Mississippi Mud Pie, in anticipation. Clydog came in and wheezed his way to the counter.

'Not a bad turnout,' he said, with the authority of an expert in local crowd size. 'Rain coming though.' He laid down some change and reached to pick up his treat.

'No eating in the shop!' Hubert warned him fiercely. 'We had dinner with Dr Frost and his wife last night, heard all about your blood pressure. You could go blue at any minute.' Then Hubert twinkled, his face lit up by mischief, and handed over the cake. 'You are looking a bit iffy though, Clydog.'

'I've just been chased by a heifer,' the newspaperman said, irritably. 'What else did he tell you about my medical history?'

'Oh, I couldn't repeat that, it's confidential. I'm sure you understand, being a journalist.'

'It's my mother's fault,' sighed Clydog, who, though fifty-three, had yet to leave home. 'The food she cooks is too rich. Makes me go this colour.'

'What happened with the heifer?' Bryony asked the non-speaking Auberon, whose private education had omitted social skills.

'The usual. Es-esc-escaped from the pen, just as it was going into auction. Then ran halfway round the town,' he said.

'Get a good picture?'

'C-c-camera got c-caught in the c-case.'

'Oh.'

'Thought we might not make the grand opening,' said Clydog. 'Until we saw the mayoral car stuck in the chaos. You down for a speech today?'

Hubert shook his head. 'I'm just there as decoration. An icon of Welsh capitalism.'

'Again?' Clydog fondled his mud pie through the paper bag. A pretty, dark-haired woman in a short skirt and a slender man with T-shirt and stubble had just entered, and Clydog was reluctant to gorge himself in front of strangers. He moved aside to let Bryony show them the allegedly home-made pasta.

'Well, guess Auberon and I'd better get over there, get into position. You coming now, Hubert?'

'Might as well. Abernant calls.'

The other two turned to leave.

As Hubert removed his gastronome's apron, the timer on the oven rang. 'D'you like nuts, Auberon?'

'OF COURSE, I should have realised the bastard wasn't interested in art. I mean, he even used to choose crap Christmas cards! I just thought he wanted to widen his horizons, when all he was after was to widen her legs.'

Mr Blake nodded sympathetically.

'Fruit, he told me. In bowls. He lied from the start! Seems the shit was in the library, getting out of the rain, and he saw a poster for a life class. So he goes off painting some tart in Llanbedr village hall. Hardly the last word in passionate romance, is it? It's even got a corrugated-iron roof! *I* certainly wouldn't want to go lying around naked in there. Not for anybody's art.'

Mr Blake's encouraging silence continued.

'So off my husband trots with his charcoal, week after week. Capturing essences, he says. And apparently one pose leads to another . . .' She paused, suddenly fragile. 'They've been in Cardiff for a year now.'

Mr Blake sensed the possibility of a tear, and moved a pre-emptive hand gently forward across his desk.

'I went and met the class tutor, you know,' she said. 'Wolfgang. Another incomer. Said it's a first. Never happened when he ran the classes in Berlin. According to him, the cultural history of the nude has bypassed mid-Wales. Can't say I'm surprised.'

Mr Blake felt the conversation was in danger of drifting. 'So you found out about them, what, eighteen months ago?'

'Approximately, yes. It was the caretaker. Saw a light still on and came over to investigate. Found them re-enacting Rodin by the boiler. Now it so happens that the caretaker's sister is married to the brother of our postman, Dafydd . . . Just twelve hours, the news took to reach me.'

A sob burst through and Lionel Blake reached across his desk and compassionately squeezed her hand—for perhaps a touch longer than was strictly professional. Yet his was a tall, reassuring presence: the well-cut suit, the authoritatively greying hair, the oak-panelling backdrop.

'She's twenty years younger than him, you know. A psychology student. Hope she's got *his* personality disorder sussed!' Not once had any names passed her lips. 'Seems she modelled because she was struggling to make ends meet! So we have something in common now I've had to sell the house.' She tossed back her shock of frizzed auburn hair, a bitter smile tweaking a physiognomy that would make a fine portrait.

'So the divorce settlement didn't bring a pot of gold, then?'

'Correct. Which is why I currently live in a caravan. A very undes res. And a bastard for dinner parties.'

Lionel Blake smiled. 'But you're still working?'

'Yes. Yes, still supply teaching. History. So there's a sort of income. Oh, and there's the eggs from a dozen Buff Orpingtons,' added Mrs Whitelaw. 'Which I don't declare.'

'I think that's a secret we can share,' replied Lionel. 'So . . .' He made a pretence of leafing through the notes in the file before him. 'Shall we say an overdraft of two thousand pounds and see how we go?'

'Oh, that would be wonderful! Oh, thank you *so* much.' It put Marjorie's teeth on edge to overdo the ingratiating, but she felt it was probably in keeping with the role of vulnerable, tearful divorcee.

Lionel Blake smiled comfortingly in response and before putting the top back on his fountain pen, discreetly scribbled a note for his records. *Breasts 8/10, legs 7/10.*

There was a knock on the door. The senior cashier, a plump, resentful woman in her fifties, intruded her head. 'You've not forgotten the mayoress is due at three, Mr Blake?'

'No, I haven't. Thank you. I'll be there.'

He and Mrs Whitelaw rose together and made their way across his office. As they passed the second potted palm, he said, 'So what sort of eggs do you supply, Mrs Whitelaw?'

'Oh, big and brown,' she replied, rightly sensing this was a moment for direct eye contact.

He was on the verge of jokily suggesting he place a standing order for omelettes when the thought of a cashier within earshot inhibited him and he merely bid her farewell, offering a banker's handshake.

It was the trajectory of the manager's career path that made his head cashier watchful. Depicted as a line on a graph, it rose steadily . . . and then fell with unhealthy detumescence. A high-flier in the Welsh capital until just a few months ago, he had chosen to decamp to a small rural outpost. To locals, he sold the change as a rejection of the rat race, a return to life's truer values. He even joked about it as managerial menopause. But, beneath the carapace of polished charm, the cashier sensed some blotting of a copybook, some faint whiff of scandal, and she rarely missed a chance to count the spoons.

OVER TWO DOZEN had gathered in the narrow High Street outside the bank in the rain, awaiting the arrival of the mayoress. This lacked the drama of an escaped heifer, but still qualified as excitement in Abernant. Various councillors and dignitaries were in attendance, including the Traffic Warden, who was wearing a special sash for the occasion. Unfortunately, because of limited space, there was no opportunity for the town band.

The council factions had assembled on separate pavements. So great was the enmity that the opposing councillors insisted on breathing separate air. Like the Corn Laws and Home Rule, the burning issue was one of human rights: car-parking charges. The *Mid-Walian* called it the Debate of the Day and an entire page of letters was dedicated to the issue of Free *vs* 10p. Today's occasion, though, was without controversy and had widespread support.

All that was lacking was the mayoress. With hindsight, it was unwise to have chosen Friday for it was market day, the day of dawn-to-dusk gridlock along the town's few key streets. Relocation of the market had been under urgent consideration for thirty-five years, but had so far proved too complex a problem for the council's special subcommittee. As a result, the mayoral limo was now victim of a ritual dispute for territory between the town dust-cart, a hay lorry and a cattle truck.

There was little option. Although conscious that her action lacked civic grandeur, the OBE-in-waiting decided to abandon her limousine and walk—in full regalia—through the puddles of the crowded town centre.

A hundred yards away, the official welcoming committee stood waiting. In pole position was the President of the Chamber of Commerce, giving his views on town planners and the use of cattle prods. Behind the committee, lesser mortals of the business world, men who had yet to contribute as fully to the life of the community, shuffled their feet and talked of slides and swings. The more political among them spoke of strengthening the local ordinance against urinating in shop doorways. At the back were some out-of-season tourists and a puzzled Rob and Jane, who were trying to get the measure of their new home town.

Then all were interrupted by a stir in the vicinity of the launderette.

'Here comes Cutty,' murmured Hubert, in a naval *jeu d'esprit* lost on his neighbours.

Suddenly, the wet mayoress hove into view, breathless from her voyage, and docked by the microphone stand in front of the bank.

At the same moment the bank manager emerged from his branch bearing a de luxe pair of kitchen scissors on a small velvet pouffe, protected from sogginess by the head cashier's umbrella. These he offered to the mayoress before guiding her, with ceremonial aplomb, to the waiting red ribbon.

The photographer chose a viewpoint that would minimise the mayoral mammaries, the councillors emitted a ripple of sycophantic applause, and the mayoress made the much-awaited deft cut.

Then, turning to the crowd, the Mayoress of Abernant announced to the world: 'I declare this cash machine open.'

Chapter 7

Stéfan pressed his stubby finger over half an inch into the rotten wood of the window frame. Had there been an audience he would have pressed his finger all the way through the frame and then smashed the window for good measure.

Christmas had come and gone. The window maker had done neither. He had not even acknowledged letters marked 'Urgent'. The occasional painter had wandered by, trailing Dulux drips, and the visit of a plumber was evident from a note outlining his failure to find a stopcock. But the three-month schedule of works was three months behind schedule. And the handmade window frames had yet to become a gleam in their artisan's eye.

Stéfan had been masterminding operations from his London base. Only on his weekend visits did he learn the limits to the power of an absentee squire. Where he came from, people jumped when given orders. And if they didn't jump high enough, or quick enough, they regretted it. They certainly didn't yawn and scratch their buttocks.

'I'm sorry, Mr Griffith Barton is ex-directory.'

'Ex-directory? He can't be!' Stéfan took hold of the phone, cradled in between his shoulder and cheek, and placed its mouthpiece where he could better bellow at the operator. 'You've got that wrong! Check it again!' His annoyance was heightened as his latest status symbol, a mobile phone, had ceased to work the moment it caught sight of a Welsh mountain.

He continued to stand and glare at his offending windows while he waited, his urge to sit curbed by the dustsheets that lay over almost every item of furniture in the house. They constituted the decorators' formal declaration of intent, a time-honoured pretence that work was imminent. But the effect was a house closed down for the duration of a war. So yet again Stéfan had cancelled his plans for a grand housewarming. 'I'm sorry, sir. Definitely ex-directory.'

'It's his business address, for fuck's sake. Why would his business address be ex-directory?'

'Perhaps he's shy, sir.'

The dialling tone returned to the phone.

STÉFAN DISLIKED driving on country lanes. He belonged to the Mr Toad school of roadcraft, and found anything narrow and winding an affront to his freedom. Even the briefest relationship with the backside of a tractor was a test too far of his patience. But anyone's patience would have been tested by the lattice of lanes that led off the Nant Valley into the hills. And of the six miles Stéfan had to negotiate, he had so far driven ten.

The directions to Mr Griffith Barton and his window workshop were scribbled on a strip of wallpaper, courtesy of the decorators, and verged on hieroglyphic. Best advice was that, if lost in them there hills, he should find a local, any local, and simply ask for The Windowman.

But as the Jaguar rattled over a cattle grid and up onto common land it was not merely the replacement of windows that was preoccupying Stéfan.

Although his mansion had twenty-eight rooms and three storeys he frequently worried that it didn't make a big enough statement about him. While he had it on good authority that Jacobean was an historically kosher architectural style, it caused him regret that its key design features were short on triumphalism. If he could be said to have a personal architectural style, it would best be described as Imperial Domestic. He had a penchant for pillars and plinths. Indeed, on a business trip to Athens he had been much taken by the vision of the Parthenon at night, and was currently considering a plan for the permanent floodlighting of Crug Caradoc.

Of course, what he really wanted was for a spotlight to fall on him. Ever since childhood, he had nurtured the need to be treated as a big player in his adopted land. In some countries, being a big shot came, literally as well as metaphorically, from a casually slung AK 47. But in Britain the key to social standing often proved more complicated. And so his mind had turned to statuary. He had the requisite rhododendrons and the Wellingtonia pine, a lakeside walk, a couple of arbours. All he lacked was a set of goddesses. Busty goddesses. The classical look, he reckoned, in white stone. About fifteen deities in varying poses, with labels in Latin, along a woodland way.

He had just crossed a plateau of upland meadows, and was nearing the end of his scribbled directions. He had only seen two people in twenty minutes, but had been reluctant to ask directions since the Stéfan method of cornering had forced their old Morris Traveller to leave the road. The last miles began to wind past, and the land became a mix of windswept bogland and rectilinear pine plantations, a terrain of bleak beauty. A setting tailor-made for Mr Griffith Barton, a man variously described as a recluse, a misanthrope, a mad widower . . . and a genius with wood.

It was a slow, upward trickle of wood smoke that gave Stéfan the clue. Down a forest track and bounded on three sides by a grim symmetry of pine, the plain Victorian cottage was set back in a half-acre clearing. A large prefabricated shed with a corrugated roof stood to one side, half-hidden by the debris of offcuts, and giving little hint that it might be home to an artisan worthy of a Renaissance Kitemark.

The dull fusillade of mud on mudflaps ceased as the Jaguar pulled off the track onto wet grass. Stéfan turned off the engine, and sat and looked in some bemusement at the ex-directory business premises.

Drumming his fingers on the steering wheel, he pondered the matter of Mr Griffith Barton. A matter on which every one of his fitful workmen and even the postman had offered much advice. He was, on all sides, judged to be a temperamental man—so temperamental a man that he had actually been known to *refuse* business, *to turn away* customers if the mood so took him. The consensus held that Mr Griffith Barton should be thought of as a fish, a fish to be slowly, patiently, reeled in over an indefinite period of time, and then given much tickling of the gills.

But Stéfan was not keen on patience—indeed he thought fishing was best done by dynamite—for he knew the persuasiveness of cash. The faint-hearts had counselled caution and cunning but Stéfan decided it was down to price. And so he got out of the car ready to deal—thus ignoring the advice that, upon meeting The Windowman, the recommended cry of greeting should be: 'Hello! I don't want any work done.'

THE FIRST HURDLE came immediately inside the gate, and it was a goat. Typical, no doubt, of its owner, it was not a normal goat. It had just the one horn, and was eating a piece of two by four. Any hope that it was a receptionist goat rather than a guard goat vanished when it charged. Stéfan's resolve to remain in control of his visit was much diminished by having to run to and fro through the triffid stumps of the previous year's nettles.

After some fancy footwork and double shin damage, he managed to grab the goat by the horn. He then had to drag it up the path so that he could ring the doorbell. No one answered.

He rang again. There was still no answer. Unable to let the goat go, Stéfan wrestled it across the clearing towards the workshop, where he could see a light. As he tried to force open the ramshackle garage-sized door, the goat got its teeth round his shoelace. Kicking at the goat and shoulder-charging the door, he stumbled into the workshop.

When he had regained his balance and the goat, he looked about him. The place was stacked with wood of every length and width, the floor awash with shavings, the air redolent with the sweetness of resin. Sheets of papers filled with screeds of figures lay beside lethal cutting machines. And a white dust lay over every surface. But it was empty of human life.

'Pegasus!'

The goat pulled from his grasp and ran towards the cottage. Stéfan turned. A tall figure in military camouflage was standing beside the glass lean-to at the rear of it. Stéfan found it one of the more baffling features of country life that people never emerged from the logical exit to their house, but simply appeared round hedges and walls.

'Hello, there!' called Stéfan, dusting down his brass-buttoned blazer. To his great annoyance, he felt the initiative was slipping from him. And loss of power was what he hated above all else. He dragged the door shut, moved across the scrubland and held out his hand.

'I hope you don't want any bloody work done!' said the man in mottled khaki.

Stéfan paused, putting his plans on hold.

Mr Griffith Barton was not the effete artisan of his imaginings. Clint Eastwood was the Doppelgänger that came to mind. Gaunt, austere, and in his late, great period as lone avenger in the West. As refinements, The Windowman had the charmless lavatory-brush hair of a lapsed marine and was wearing army boots without laces. His appearance was a far cry from the smooth, soft fleshiness of Stéfan. And whereas the older man presented a lined and weathered look to the world, young Stéfan's visage bore all the angst and torment of a puffball.

'Work . . . ?' Stéfan tried his braying laugh. 'No, not at the moment, no. Perhaps later.' But now it had become personal. Even if Crug Caradoc burnt to the ground, he would have his windows made.

There was a brief stand-off, for Mr Griffith Barton was not big on social graces. Then the whistle of a kettle began, and soon its high-pitched insistence could not be ignored.

'I'm making tea,' he said. 'Without sugar.' He turned and went inside.

On the assumption that, technically, this was an invitation, also without sugar, Stéfan followed him.

If Mr Griffith Barton had not been as expected, neither was his cottage. Probably a gamekeeper's cottage when first built, it had the usual extensions for twentieth-century mod cons. Yet, inside, the guiding aesthetic was breeze block—for the work had ceased, *circa* 1975. None of the new internal walls had ever been completed, and they stood like a crude and uncertain art statement. Over the years, a chaos of personal effects had cloaked the stark concrete like flotsam on a rising tide, humanising the dereliction. In the primitive kitchen and glass lean-to the only virgin space was a small white Formica table, on which lay that morning's *Financial Times*, open at the shares page, and a pair of donnish half-moon spectacles on a silver chain.

Stéfan stepped around a two-foot pile of *National Geographics* and unfolded the spare deck chair leaning against the Belling cooker. Of his many skills, there was none he set more store by than his powers of negotiation. The flattery, the bullying, the chivvying, the brinkmanship, the brazen lies, the bear hug, all had been passed down in perfect working condition from father to son, and then fine-tuned some more. Now, for the first time, he felt in need of a manual.

He placed his deck chair to give himself the widest arc of vision, and watched the boiling water make it safely into the two chipped white mugs. As he looked around the lean-to—at the unwashed dishes, the objects left to lie where they dropped, the random profusion of hardbacked books—he felt he was staring at the student digs of a man in his fifties. And then he looked to where there should have been a door into the rest of the house. It had not advanced beyond a very large lumpy hole, but gave a helpful view of the room beyond. The only daylight came via the glass of the lean-to, for the windows at the far end of the room seemed to be either shuttered or thickly curtained. And this light was glinting on gold.

Not gold as in gold bullion or gold robbers, but the almost more surprising gold of gold leaf. In abundance. Along both the walls he could see a series of portraits in oils, with huge and elaborate gold-leaf frames. The portraits were of a type and size that he had not seen since rain once drove him into the National Gallery. And, like them, the imperious subjects in the lounge were posed and grand and formal. But, try as Stéfan might, the gloom of the light and the black of the backdrop made details difficult to discern, except that most were women.

'She's thirty-six. Oldest ever known.' The Windowman put a carton of milk on the small table and handed Stéfan his tea. 'But we never had a birth certificate for her.' He cleared a pile of papers to reveal a foam-topped bench and sat opposite, warming both hands on his mug. 'Otherwise we could put her in *The Guinness Book of Records*.'

Not a word had made sense. Wondering if he were witness to signs of psychosis, Stéfan focused his attention on the milk, which he poured with due deliberation. And sought in vain for a suitable response.

Very discreetly, as he raised the mug to his lips, he ventured a glance again into the lounge, to sneak a second look at the nearest of the portraits. He thought he could just detect the outline of a regal décolletage.

'Bloody miracle, given the rubbish that goat eats,' added The Windowman.

'The goat?'

'Yes. Pegasus.'

'Oh, Pegasus!' Stéfan fell untypically silent for the second time.

'Snuff?'

'I'm sorry?'

'Snuff?'

'Er . . . no. No, thanks.'

The Windowman took a tiny enamelled box from his trouser pocket, clicked it open, and put a pinch of snuff to each nostril. He sneezed twice, then placed the box on the table.

'Buggers your tubes, carpentry.'

The Windowman offered no more thoughts, but sat sniffing deeply. He had a stillness to him, and the inscrutability of a scraggy Buddha.

'So you play the market, then?' said Stéfan, tapping the *FT*. 'What have you got shares in?'

'Nothing. Wouldn't give the bastards the pleasure.'

'Oh. So why—'

'Because it tells you what the smart money's doing—before you see the ripples. Tells you what's *really* going on. That and the court pages. Court pages give you more than all the news stories put together. Who's in town, who's meeting who at what fancy dinner. Then, a few weeks later, you see some dodgy deal's been stitched together, and it all falls into place.'

'Wouldn't have thought it mattered up here.'

'If I'm going to be blown up, I like to know why.'

'If you're going to be blown up, best get shares in the bombs, I say!' And Stéfan tried his first matey laugh of the day.

There was no returning laugh.

'They train up here for World War Three, you know. Paratroopers, SAS, Gurkhas. And they all make the same mistake. They think the next war's going to be between countries. Between governments. It won't be. It'll be between multinationals. Nissan bombing Ford, Nike bombing Reebok. All dying for market share. That's what the new vested interests are about.'

Political philosophy, indeed abstract thought itself, had no designated space within Stéfan's brain. But his normal mockery of such ideas would clearly serve none of his own vested interests. So he just kept nodding.

'System's so rotten the governments act like bloody agents for these companies. Probably be paid commission for running their bloody wars!' This forced a smile from him, his first. And for the first time Stéfan noticed the intense gaze of his deep-set eyes. 'We always used to have private armies in this country. So it wouldn't be such a change. Except this time the armies'd be run by the likes of BT and British Steel. After all, they already have security forces of their own.'

He smiled again, an unexpectedly warm smile. 'Sorry. Hobbyhorse of mine.'

'Understood,' said Stéfan. 'Were you army?'

'Good God, no! Army surplus. I just don't like wasting money on clothes.'

At last! A word familiar to Stéfan had entered the conversation and he lost no time. 'Must be a lot of money in your line of work though. Some classy designs on your workbench. You could build half a palace with what's in your shed.' Although Stéfan would never admit it, the words 'fish' and 'reel' were silently taking up residence in his head. 'Looked like good wood out there. Those architraves were oak, weren't they?'

'Probably. More money than sense, most people. Even had them come by helicopter just to check the grain.'

'Helicopter?' Stéfan felt a surge of pique at being upstaged, even though he had no idea by whom.

'Oh, the aristocracy like their wood. Though lately I've had sheikhs, pop stars, all sorts come here,' he said contemptuously. He glared at Stéfan. 'And I take it you're not just out for a picnic.'

'I have tried writing to you. Don't you reply to your letters?'

'Don't read them. Expect they'll be in that pile over there.' He gestured under the table at the heap of papers he had swept off the bench earlier. 'Anyway, forget it, I've got a nine-month waiting list.'

'Nine months . . . ? Money's not a problem.'

'I'm very pleased for you.'

'It's just some windows, windows for Crug Caradoc.'

'Waste of time, windows.' He reached for his snuffbox a second time.

The comment went unnoticed by Stéfan. 'They're Jacobean windows. Very ornamental. Absolutely beautiful, but rotting.'

'They would be. As I said, waste of time, windows.'

'Waste of time? What do you mean, "waste of time"?'

'Why do people have windows? To close them. What do you get if you close them? Condensation. And then they rot.'

'Well, eventually, yes, but—'

'So if you're going to have windows, have plastic.' At this point, Stéfan noticed that the few window frames he could see were plastic.

'If? What do you mean "if"? You've got to have windows.'

'Of course you don't have to have windows. That's just propaganda. Modern sales nonsense. What you need is free circulation of air.'

'I've got a Jacobean manor house worth over half a million. You want me to take out the windows?'

'If you don't want them to rot.' He sniffed deeply at his pinch of snuff.

'So what would you have people use instead of windows?'

'Sacking.'

He sneezed. And sneezed again.

'*Sacking*? Come off it!'

'Ideal material. It was used for centuries. Allows the air through, keeps the cold out, and you pin it up if you want daylight. And it's cheap.'

Stéfan started to smile at the joke.

'Had it for the first five years of married life.'

Stéfan's smile faded. He allowed no one to take the mick out of him. It was the golden rule of all his relationships. But he could not tell if the mick was being taken or not. 'You had sacking over your windows?'

'Can't beat it for staying healthy. Gives constant fresh air. None of those colds and flus. Because there's none of the fug and condensation you get with windows and central heating. Sacking keeps you in perfect health all year round.' Then he said, almost to himself, 'Though the wife did die.'

He said it so matter-of-factly, as a virtual throwaway, that Stéfan almost doubted he had heard correctly.

The Windowman finished his tea in a single gulp and stood up. 'Nine months,' he said, and walked across to abandon his mug in the kitchen.

This, however, was not the wait needed before he could start work. This was the length of time that he judged necessary to effectively deter a customer. And he judged Stéfan to be the impatient type. For reasonable, patient people, he sometimes found it necessary to say two, or even three, years.

Stéfan, however, always ignored the deadlines of others. And he regarded 'no' as an answer only ever accepted by little people. Admittedly, he had yet to get the full measure of Mr Griffith Barton, whose negotiating strategy he found brilliant in its waywardness, but he felt confident that a second visit would crack him. That he would then reel him in.

Stéfan got to his feet. 'There were some big oil paintings like yours at the place I bought,' he said, trying to build up rapport as he walked towards the kitchen door being held open for his departure. 'Are you a collector?'

'No. No, not at all.'

'Oh. So those . . . ?' His arm waved vaguely behind him.

'They're of the wife, and the wife's family. Well, her ancestors.'

'Oh. Big family?'

'The Habsburgs. Watch out for the goat.'

Chapter 8

Rob and Jane peered down the hole in Gareth's field. It was neatly dug, precisely placed, and about two foot square by two foot deep. Inside it was a bucket full of tap water and beside it lay a section of plastic drainpipe. Several times the couple shifted their stance for a better view of these objects.

'Well?' said Teg.

'No,' said Rob, after a long pause. 'I don't get it.'

Jane shook her head.

Teg smiled, quietly pleased by the stupidity of townsfolk. 'It's an art,' he said. 'Catching moles runs in the family.'

As they stood up, his huge outstretched arm drew the eye down a row of molehills as linear as the Greenwich Meridian. 'That's a run,' he said.

And in the middle of their run he had dug his hole. In the distance, Ben was bearing down on another spade, digging out another hole.

Like a magician with a prop, Teg held up the pipe for them to see. It was a normal pipe of some two foot six, but with a small circular piece cut out. He laid it on the ground, across the hole and raised an enquiring eyebrow.

Rob and Jane peered into the earth again. 'No,' said Rob, shaking his head after another pause. 'I still don't get it.'

'Clickety-clop, clickety-clop, clickety-clop, splosh!' said Teg. With an air of helpfulness.

This time they both shook their heads.

The massive molecatcher eased onto his knees, and pointed out a small aperture that had escaped their notice on two walls of the freshly dug hole.

'The mole,' explained Teg patiently, 'runs along his tunnel . . .' As a visual aid he wiggled two vertical fingers like legs. '. . . and then suddenly the tunnel ends. Because of the hole. But . . .' He flourished the plastic pipe a second time and inserted one end, then the other, into the equal and opposite apertures. '. . . the mole does not realise this. Because of the pipe. Which he now enters . . .' Teg twisted the pipe round, so that the missing piece was on the underside. '. . . and continues running along . . .' The sausage fingers doubled furiously as legs again. '. . . until he reaches the gap and . . .' The legs spiralled downwards. '. . . he falls into the bucket full of water!' Teg impersonated a depth charge. 'And drowns!' He beamed with pleasure. 'Followed by all his friends and family. Clickety-clop, clickety-clop, clickety-clop, splosh!'

There was silence.

'Amazing,' said Jane eventually.

Easing his bulk upright, Teg gave a satisfied smile.

Rob and Jane returned up the meadow to the long house and the warm bosom of the Rayburn. Not a townie word had passed their lips, not a hint of any molist critique, for already they knew enough to observe the rural rules of integration. And being far from socially acceptable in their own habits—environmentally radical, artistically original—they were not about to raise the contentious issue of multiple mole deaths.

Indeed, although the pockmarked meadow was not their property, they had a personal reason to welcome the traditional molecatchers.

On several days of late, the morning mists had evaporated to reveal the wraithlike figure of Gareth standing in the field, armed with a loaded shotgun. It was aimed at the earth, but was held with a neurotic, silent intensity, his body coiled tight in anticipation of the blast. And there he stood an hour at a time, poised and primed, in an act more of therapy than rodent control.

Gareth was an only child, and had waited humiliatingly long to take over the reins of the family's 120-acre farm. His parents had delayed retirement well past three score and ten, and had then erected a bungalow within criticising distance of the farmyard. So Gareth would dutifully tramp the land, and plough the fields, and check the stock, and soak up the rain. And still the older cows deferred first to his father.

It was to make his mark that Gareth had gone out on a limb and bought an unimproved patch of pasture. But this rare burst of derring-do, which had so surprised his neighbours, was not entirely at the prompt of agriculture. Dating a year from his marriage, which had equally surprised his neighbours, such independent action was proof of his manhood, a confused sexual response to the length of Moira's Irish legs. In this remote field he found both a virility symbol and a refuge. Here, it was *his* land, *his* law, and life became simple once more. To be unseen, to act unseen, was primitive and thrilling. The power of the gun, the size of the mole, made him a man again.

Rob and Jane had offered him the occasional cup of tea, but he was not a great conversationalist. His face interested Rob, though only from the technical standpoint of its flatness. This offered an unusual challenge to the art of portraiture. But Rob's friendly words, 'Would you mind if I sketched you?', had merely caused Gareth to make a hasty exit.

BY THE TIME Rob and Jane made it back from their hole and mole inspection, Tinkerbell, their new, miniature Vietnamese potbellied pig, was snuffling the morning mail. Shaped like a barrel, built like a battleship, and inky bristly black all over, she nuzzled all-comers with great charm, managing to square that difficult circle of being both lovably cute and an all-terrain Rotavator.

Quite why purchase of a pig had taken priority over the guttering, the slates and the peeling paintwork was one of those mysteries that make life in the country so different from life in the town.

'Oh jeez! She doesn't eat envelopes as well, does she?' yelped Jane, rescuing the mail from the doorstep.

'Probably just collecting the stamps.' Rob took a brown foolscap envelope from Jane's hand. He pulled out the letter, read its brief contents, and sucked his teeth with what Jane knew to be irritation.

'Is it about the ducks?' she asked.

'No, not about the ducks.'

The six ducks, like the pig, had been a perverse priority.

Mr Probert had neglected to mention that in the event of heavy winter rain (an event of almost hourly occurrence), the source of the Severn would appear in their garden. The first time had been quite entertaining and they had some rather jolly photos of Rob rowing the wheelbarrow across the kitchen. But the joke had soon palled.

The two obvious solutions had been diversion or drainage. Rob and Jane went for the duck-pond option. With ducks. Perhaps less understandable was that they had to be exotic ducks. For Rob fell victim, as so often, to aesthetics. And having seen the brochures, he had elected for their ducks to be Cubist in design (a colour scheme also favoured by the foxes). Now they were waiting for literature on their ducks' special dietary needs.

Not all developments had been of such dubious practical value. Wiring—hence lighting and heating—now reached the studio *né* barn, and a polythene mantle hung over its entrance. The joys of multi-tinted emulsion had created a softer mood in the living quarters, and the Rayburn had been rejuvenated by a D and C of its baking bits. And Nico swore on his chequebook that the Massey Ferguson would be gone any day now.

The couple also still loved each other, a statistical oddity among the records of those who forsake urban comfort for rural fastness. Mid-Wales was hardly the last frontier, but both Rob and Jane got a primitive pleasure from going head to head with the elements. A wind that wrenches doors off, a rain that penetrates the bones, a night that is black without break, here was all they needed to play at pioneering.

'It's about the wind-pump,' said Rob rattily, screwing up the letter. 'That two-thousand-year-old technology yet to arrive in Wales! No wonder the estate agent didn't want to answer questions about wind-pumps.' He scrunched the paper some more and gave it a badminton-type tap towards Tinkerbell.

'Another blank?'

He nodded. 'The fifth.'

'Someone must make wind-pumps!'

'I think they're covered by the Official Secrets Act.'

Mains electricity had long thought better of the journey up to Pantglas, and so the farmhouse had the fitful services of a generator, fed by oil. Noisy and temperamental, it intruded on their rural idyll with the unseemliness of a burbling fart. It also offended their notions of eco-sensitivity, and every day further whetted their desire to give the gales something useful to do.

'Dafydd said we'd be the first. He's never delivered mail to anyone with a wind-pump.' Jane handed him the only other post, a Jiffy bag of paint tubes.

'I reckon he'll have spread the word that we're seriously odd. Special Branch will be mingling with the sheep soon. It is a bugger though. I thought we'd just need to look in Yellow Pages. Under Wind.'

They moved into the warmth of the parlour, Rob struggling with a staple as he tried to reach his cerulean blue. 'I mean, they were even in that old James Dean movie, whirring away. And that was Texas back in the fifties!'

Jane looked at him. 'You sure they weren't oil derricks?'

Rob hesitated, trying to visualise the fading Cinemascope footage. 'Well, they were going round all the time,' he said. 'Or was it up and down?'

'MID-WALES'. The very name itself is the undefined confection of some foreign cartographer. It refers to no known shape. It is a non-name given to an identity crisis. There is felt no need for a 'mid-Ireland' or a 'mid-Scotland', and middle England represents not a geographical location but a state of mind. The place 'mid-Wales' is the bit left over after the coast, the valleys, the Marches and Snowdonia have been ticked off and signed up for tourist duty. Mid-Wales is the bit without the castles, without the singing in fancy dress, without the folk memory of pits. Here are the parts where motorways don't reach. Here they burn no cottages.

Finding it empty, the English used it to store the rain, to build the reservoirs that gave them baths in Birmingham. Then, when these were awash with water, and the desecration done, faraway financiers planted battalions of pines that stretched to infinity across the hazy hills, creating a view that offered only tax breaks and fire breaks. And all because this no-name place was that joy of central government, a giant in-fill site that had no votes and needed no governor-general.

The only hint of a heyday had been in Victorian times, when its municipal springs discovered the secret of eternal youth. All it took was a mineral with polysyllables and you had a spa. Baden-Baden, boyo, boyo, cried the hucksters! So, little town after little town tacked 'Wells' onto its name as proof of miraculous properties. And the charabancs and the parasols poured in. Unfortunately, the Nant Valley had the wrong geology for bubbles, its

THE VALLEY | 219

Old Red Sandstone producing a dishwater that suggested the sludge of death rather than the elixir of life. Elsewhere, however, the bathing in early Perrier paid off, and the inland esplanades linger on to this day.

But this abused and empty landscape is now a challenge to the image consultants. While Hungary boasts its Gypsy violins and Transylvania has Vlad the Impaler, mid-Wales is a land where national characteristics have gone to ground, a hole in the heart of the country that runs true to few stereotypes. Here, the accent is liltless. Not for mid-Wales the adenoidal whine of the north, or the nasal squawk of the south, or the bouncy castle rhythm of the films. The speech is slow, the pauses demoralising, the thought processes opaque. This is country speed, and the mores of the speaker leaning on the post are shaped by remoteness.

Stolidity is his character of choice, and, like his tweed, it has long been out of vogue. The maintenance of respect and dignity when in public, as if on the *qui vive* for a corpse, are the ground rules for parish behaviour. Queen Victoria lives on in the blood and formalised courtesies usefully dull the emotions.

Few here are ready for the cultural melting pot, for the coming together of minds from different postcodes.

Chapter 9

Eddie had been driving his taxi long enough to know when a bird was gagging for it and these two lesboes were. The dikey one was sprawled out on the back seat, while the blonde nympho one sat in the pasenger seat, her huge nipples hard with lust and protruding through her skimpy T-shirt. Eddie stopped the metre and pulled over into a lay-by knowing this fare would be one to remember . . .

'Oh dear God!' Bryony leaned back from the keyboard in weary revulsion. It was not a good way to spend a Sunday.

She pushed away the author's pages of scrawl and gazed out of the old school window at the pouring rain. Across the river, in the churchyard, the fat vicar was showing a few old ladies round the surveyor's latest exploratory holes, prodding at the loose earth as if in search of relics whose magic would save their church. From where Bryony sat, looking out over her winter vegetables, the threat to St Brynnach's seemed increasingly to come from a siege by giant moles.

As she watched, the church clock struck twelve. That it was midday surprised her—and angered her, because it most likely meant that Eryl, her absent lover, was on his way to the Dragon's Head, bypassing her and their home as he staggered back from another late-night party. For a brief moment, the hours of overwork and the weeks of worry made her want to cry.

For several months she had tried to be a potter, but found that clay did not respond to her kneads. Her current enthusiasm was aromatherapy and almost every day she smelt different. Essential oils were her one treat; she felt her emotional problems were much aided by intimate contact with the likes of ylang-ylang. She had even begun to think of aromatherapy as a career path. Her magazines said it was a growth area where your only start-up costs were some oils, a comfortable front room and a certificate. Not a natural student, Bryony was drawn to the idea of a course where taking a long bath could be considered as studying.

Otherwise her résumé was short. At twenty-six, she was keen on growing vegetables and smiled a lot.

But two years of living with Eryl had left her lonely, and with little to smile about. Her man was embittered at ending up a squire *manqué*, and raged at the confiscation of his silver spoon. She, meanwhile, worked six days a week for a pittance and came home to slurred speech and arms that rarely held her. This was hard for a woman who loved to touch and be touched, whose soft body filled up the nooks and crannies of a cuddle. And now, to the shortage of sex was added shortage of money, and she was growing weary of her unfair burden.

The stress of the day was mounting. She had already had a coconut and jojoba shampoo, but to little effect. Bryony reached for her hand-woven Andean shoulder bag and started to roll a joint.

It was a week after the auction at Crug Caradoc that she had put the small ad in. One of the few perks of toiling in the deli was free use of its notice board. First reply to the advert was a nice retired railwayman from the council estate on the edge of town. He had spent fifty years operating signals, had changed the points for just about every steam train you could think of . . . and now felt this would make an interesting 500-page book. Then came a cyclist, who had meticulously bicycled along every B-road in Britain, and he too felt his experiences would be appreciated by a wider public. She had typed up both these seminal works.

And then came the Traffic Warden. Who had written a novel in pencil.

No one liked the Traffic Warden. It was not just because he was a Traffic Warden. It was because he was a crooked Traffic Warden. Touched by the entrepreneurial spirit of the age, he would turn a blind eye to infractions if his palm was crossed with gifts. Hardly a trader in the town had not stumped up a bottle of whisky, a crate of carrots, a transistor radio, even a Moulinex mixer, so that his deliveries might proceed unhindered.

And then one day all the warden's extra income had come to a halt.

A new delivery driver called Rhys had brought the bread to the baker's in Abernant. The hefty young man, a rugby player from another valley, had not been officially advised of the system of traffic tithes. After unloading his order of crates, he came out of the baker's to find the Traffic Warden in the back of his van, helping himself to several square-tinned white loaves. Pretending not to notice him, or his cries for help, Rhys slammed the back door and drove off. He then drove, as fast and erratically as he could, twenty miles over the mountains to his next delivery in Llandulais where, feigning astonishment, he discovered the now bruised and floury Traffic Warden in the back of his van and released him. Though apoplectic, his captive was quite without comeback—in more senses than one, since he had no money upon his person.

Hitchhiking while wearing a Traffic Warden's uniform is a particularly harsh handicap. He took eight hours—and was the subject of much ribald hooting—to cover the twenty miles back to Abernant on foot.

He never again solicited a bribe. But needing another source of income, he had turned his talents elsewhere. And now the outcome of his efforts lay resting on the old trestle table.

Bryony forced herself to look again at the ruled exercise book, a WH Smith Student Special. The prospect of spending her evenings and weekends buried in the fantasies of a pervy Traffic Warden did not appeal. Especially if it were just for the benefit of Eryl's bar bill.

She and Eryl had bought the tiny village school (none up, two down) a couple of years earlier, when small had ceased to be beautiful in the ledgers of the Education Committee. Needing work, it had gone for a song—with a minor mortgage.

It was with that unpaid mortgage on her mind that she reluctantly reopened the Traffic Warden's exercise book, and started leafing through its pages in the forlorn hope that redemption might be a late theme. Everywhere the penny-dreadful luridness of the sex lay heavy upon the paper, struggling to make headway against the absence of grammar and punctuation. (Those, the author had informed her, were down to the publisher. 'They know where to put the commas and stuff,' he had told her, the afternoon that he had slipped his brown-paper parcel into Hubert's shop. 'That's their job.') The text sometimes had six to a taxi, so the shortage of colons and commas left the complex sexual couplings almost impossible to disentangle, the correct attribution of private parts calling out for the skills of a senior editor. She picked up her pen again.

'Have you got a fiver?'

Eryl stood unshaven, bleary-eyed and wet in the doorway of Class 2.

'SALSA?' said Gareth.

'Salsa?' said Gareth's mother.

Gareth's father would also have said 'Salsa' in a baffled, disapproving tone, but he had a new Dralon sofa and kept Sunday lunchtimes for lying down and snoring.

Moira already regretted her impulsiveness at voicing the idea in front of her in-laws. Six months as Gareth's wife, and she had learned that impulsiveness, and indeed ideas, were not part of the Richards's family tradition. Nor likely to be so. Death was probably only ten years off and they did not wish to do, or think, anything untoward in the meantime.

'It's Latin American,' Moira said to Gareth, sliding the Entertainments page of the *Western Mail* across the nest of pine tables.

Gareth picked it up warily. He did not like headlines that contained the words 'The Latest Craze'.

Moira felt this was not the moment to explore the full sensual details of salsa, and merely said, 'It's a new venue. Special offer—course of lessons for beginners. By a real Cuban.'

'Cardiff?' said Gareth. 'That's half a tank of diesel.'

'My hymn book's wet,' said Gareth's mother, laying her gloves to dry in front of the electric fire. 'Thanks to that vicar.' She had never taken to the new vicar, since by putting St Brynnach's last on his list of Sunday services he had ruined her routine for the roast. 'Dragged us round the graveyard in the rain, and talked about nothing but money.' She pursed her lips, a tailor-made expression for her face, and Moira knew the leg of lamb would be consumed to the sound of her sighs.

Moira waited as the old lady fussed her way towards her fitted kitchen, fiddling to no purpose with the table laid by her daughter-in-law, and checking that the room temperature was at its optimum sixty-two degrees. As always, there were just the four place settings. It was both a ritual and a duty, this crossing of the farmyard for Sunday lunch in the new bungalow, and only a medical note would have made absence acceptable.

'I must go and chop the mint up now,' sighed the old lady, disappearing into the kitchen as she added, 'Gareth doesn't like dancing.'

Moira did not respond: she tried to have no opinions on a Sunday. It was also her policy to have no personality within a fifty-yard radius of the bungalow. It helped harmony. The arrival of her easy wit and Irish vivacity had not been seen as a boost to the gene pool of the family. There was distrust of her brain and resentment of the dress sense that enhanced her body. And, although no one mentioned a dowry, Moira sometimes felt she should have come bearing a field.

In a valley where every day was a dress-down day, even her yellow wellies were seen as a provocation. Her hair had not brought approval either, as it reached nearly to her waist and lent itself to tossing in an unseemly manner. And her laugh went a decibel beyond what was decent. The thought was unspoken, but some in the bungalow felt her to be the type of Celt seen in films with jig music.

'You must like dancing,' said Moira. 'Everybody likes dancing!'

Gareth shifted uneasily in his armchair. He hated dancing.

'Come Saturday night, we'd drive halfway across Donegal for a good dance at a ceilidh. Usually in village halls with no licence. The *gardai* would frisk you at the front, so people'd pass drinks in at the back!'

She spoke almost like a woman trying to put a stranger at his ease.

It did not succeed. Gareth remembered his Young Farmers' dances as lonely evenings of anguish, trapped in a body that neither rocked nor rolled. 'Me, I'm not rhythmic,' he muttered.

'Oh, everyone's got a bit of rhythm somewhere!' responded Moira. 'And a few salsa lessons would kick-start it!'

It was not just his rhythm she was hoping to kick-start. Her husband was tense to the touch, resistant to intimacy, reluctant to relax. Moira was a tactile woman who found it puzzling, and not a little hurtful, that his body was as cardboard in her hands. Even when she patted his head, he seemed to flinch. By exposing Gareth to the hot-blooded beat of Latin music she hoped to disinhibit him, to let his lusts run free.

'It's like the tango,' she added encouragingly. 'The woman makes the moves, the man just responds with his body.'

Gareth glanced uneasily at the photo in the *Western Mail*.

His father gurgled in his sleep, his head twitching on the antimacassar.

'It's not like the Gay Gordons. You can improvise,' Moira persisted, with a limited grasp of salsa.

Still he said nothing.

'And anyway the lights will be low.'

Gareth looked like a cornered fox. But he gave no vent to his thoughts, leaving it unclear whether the wattage of the bulbs was a plus point.

Her first sight of Gareth had been upon a packed Cardiff Arms Park terrace, leaping and cheering at a fine, pitch-long three-quarters movement against the Irish. Her heart had been stirred by this passion. It was a short courtship, lasting several games. Eager to be gone from the poverty of Donegal, the list of qualities she sought in a husband fell rather short of the usual requirements for matrimony; the tenth of twelve children, she was prepared to settle just for *joie de vivre*. Unfortunately, this was a degree of animation Gareth was rarely to repeat, as the Welsh national team then entered a decade-long decline.

Over the last few months, Gareth had developed a moodiness that Moira could not explain. He was moody when sober and moody after weaving home drunk. But more often he was simply not to be seen. Although she always knew she would have to share him with hill-sheep, she had not been prepared for the length of his absences. Nor indeed for the force of his silences, and the frequency with which he returned home with moles.

Finally, Gareth handed back the newspaper, and leaned forward in his chair. 'I'd better help to shell the peas.'

'HAVE YOU GOT a fiver?' Eryl asked again, rubbing his stubble and yawning.

In his dealings with the world, he relied on what he liked to think of as a raffish charm. If asked to describe his self-image, he would probably have directed the enquirer to old footage of Spitfire pilots, being rather dashing in the mess. But his power as a charmer had peaked some time ago, eroded by drink and his falling stock, and this left him to operate on a hollow bonhomie and a formulaic smile. It was not a winning combination.

'Have you got a fiver?' he repeated.

For several moments, Bryony did not speak, relying on silence to best convey contempt. Finally, she demanded, 'How would I have a fiver?'

Hungover though he was, Eryl recognised a minefield that he had stumbled into before. 'Forget it.' He shambled past her, making for the newly built staircase in the corner of the room.

'No, I won't forget it. How would I have a fiver?' she persisted, rising from her chair to pursue him. '*Tell me how I would have a fiver!*'

Eryl stopped, turned. By this stage, the correct answer, or at least the one that offered best hope of respite, was, 'Because you do all the work and I'm an idle drunken self-pitying bastard.' Instead of which, he said, 'D'you know how Trystan got the old lady to change her will?'

Bryony let out a groan. 'Left a horse head in her bed? I don't give a fuck what he did! Just stop whingeing! Let it go!'

'Yes, but you know the woman in the lodge at Crug Caradoc? Her son was at the party. He said that Trystan used to—'

'Oh, for God's sake!' she screamed. 'Does it matter *how* you were stitched up? You were stitched up, period. OK?'

Eryl turned away, and the sight of his back was one provocation too many. 'And,' Bryony added, 'with good bloody reason!'

She had said the unsayable. And Eryl had no answer. He stormed up the stairs in search of loose change. The new pine treads shook visibly, an unfortunate commentary on his carpentry—his only tangible achievement in their two years together had been a shaky mezzanine, an open-plan floor space where they slept on a mattress below the V-shaped school roof.

Bryony sensed a victory but she wanted more than a retreat. Despite her ideological commitment to niceness, she wanted to see a white flag and spilt blood . . . though somewhere in her heart she also wanted love to be declared. She pursued him up his stairs, belabouring him with abuse.

Eryl's gene pool was unknown. His late adoptive mother, Gwendolen's great-niece, had never spoken of his origins, though the Commodore—who hated Llewellyns—had once been heard to say that he came from a remainders sale. By the time Eryl developed into an adult Llewellyn, he had come to resemble a family skin graft that had not taken. But if he knew he was a disappointment, he never said. He just leched, drank and spoke loudly of grand plans. And paid no heed to others, with Bryony just the latest to be ignored.

Half a dozen coins fell from his black leather jacket as he raised it from the floor. As Eryl reached down for them, the Traffic Warden's lurid fantasies were thrust in his face.

'That's what I have to do so's you can go down the pub, you bastard!'

He snatched the WH Smith Student Special from her.

'And while you stay out all night getting rat-arsed and boring everyone stupid, I'm here typing that garbage so we can eat! And have a home!'

She dabbed a tear away.

'The Traffic Warden?' laughed Eryl, reading. He started to riffle through the dogeared text. 'What's it about, men in uniforms?'

'No, but it's for sickos. And I'm sick of it!'

'I'm broad-minded. You can do what you like while I'm down the pub.' He paused. 'Have the warden round if you want. Dictating.' He laughed again.

'Oh, you shit!' Bryony snatched *Confessions of a Taxi Driver* from him and hurled it to the floor ten feet below.

Eryl grinned and bent to retrieve his scattered coins as Bryony kicked out at him. He pushed his way past her and back down the stairs. He had found money enough for a pint.

He had always liked Bryony, and had found her easy-going ignorance much to his taste. But since his life had imploded, his grievance had become a mantra, and repeating it was now his greatest source of comfort. As he staggered out to join the Sunday drinkers at the Dragon's Head, he was starting to tire of Bryony's domestic world. Brought up to be squire of all he surveyed, two surplus classrooms offered less and less satisfaction.

Chapter 10

'Lions? It kills lions?'

'Apparently.' The postman was gratified to see his news had scored a direct hit on the world-weary Hubert. In his experience, nothing much short of cannibalism in an outlying village was able to surprise Hubert. Dafydd added, 'He calls it Genghis.'

'So it's not a dog you'd kick, then?'

'It's not a dog I'd try to run over.'

'Is there much of a lion problem round Crug Caradoc?'

'Not now. More of a postman problem.'

Hubert slowly tapped his pipe out on the baguette basket as he mulled on the mystery of a country landowner without a black labrador. 'Clydog, you've had audiences with our Mr Big. Is he mad or bad, or both?'

Clydog struggled to free his mouth of mud pie. 'Give us a tissue!' he said, spluttering, and wiggled his sticky brown fingers in the air as Hubert tore a strip from the paper roll behind the counter.

It was the dead part of the afternoon, when Abernant shoppers wait for a second wind. The three often gathered for some men's talk in what Hubert called his high-cholesterol corner. Here, an off-duty Dafydd had the time to be expansive, Hubert had the freedom to be provocative, and Clydog could indulge his greater intestine.

The old sleuth pondered Hubert's question. 'Well, the man's certainly not very British.' After deeper thought, he went on, 'From one of those countries without proper roads, I reckon. Where the electrics only come on once a day and they bug your hotel room. He made a joke to me about part of his bottom being shot off—except I don't think it was a joke. Sort of place you'd need a big dog.'

Although only fragmentary pieces of information, they pretty much fitted with what Abernant knew about foreigners.

'D'you remember Mary Jenkins?' said Dafydd. 'She married a foreigner. A German. Lasted less than two years. He used to block his lane with dustbins, to try to stop the car rallies.'

'Oh, it wasn't just the dustbins,' said Clydog. 'He broke her leg as well.'

'Düsseldorf,' said Dafydd. 'Different mindset over there.'

'I went out with a Scandinavian once,' said Hubert, keen to preserve his cosmopolitan edge. 'I had no complaints. Well, except that she folded her clothes before sex.'

'But you wouldn't have married her,' said Dafydd.

'Oh, no. Not with their level of taxation.'

'Which is my point,' said Dafydd. 'Cultural nuances. They're the barrier reef of marriage.'

At fifty-three, and still a bachelor, Clydog would have been prepared to risk some damage from cultural nuance, yet he instinctively shared this view of the worrying world beyond. 'And it's not just abroad,' he added.

'What's not just abroad?' asked Hubert, after a short wait.

'This "mindset" thing. You get valleys where people think differently, even just a few miles from here. No rhyme or reason for it. But somehow their attitudes are not the same, not quite normal. For instance, I could never marry anyone from the Cynrig Valley.' He thought some more. 'Or the Grwyne Valley. . . . Or the Llynfi Valley.'

'Have you had to fight off many offers?' asked Hubert.

Clydog ignored him. 'Then again,' he mused, 'how far would you have to go to find someone who'd want to pair off with the sort of man who owns ridgebacks?'

'About a mile and a half!' said Dafydd, and grinned. It always pleased the postman when his grapevine was superior to the reporter's.

'You're not serious? Stéfan's got an admirer? Who?' asked Hubert.

'Hunt secretary.'

'What, Felicity?' Hubert laughed scornfully. 'Part-woman, part-horse? Services to the gentry a speciality?'

'I've heard she's after him. Been practising her Lady Di impressions.'

'I'm sure she has, but that doesn't mean she fancies him. If a bloke's rolling in money and paddocks, he could be a Martian and she'd still be after him.'

'Perhaps that's where he's from, Mars. He's got the dress sense of an alien.'

A sort of communal smirk crossed their faces, and Hubert filled up their glasses again. The postman prepared to tell them about the funny-coloured ducks and the black pig that the other incomers had bought.

STÉFAN WAS DINING alone. At home. He did not like to dine alone. Indeed, he did not like to be alone. Alone, there was no gallery to play to. Alone, there was no hierarchy to be head of, no poor sap to pick on.

Stéfan's taste was for groups. Boisterous groups. He took his pleasures in mateyness and horseplay and raucous laughter, with the unspoken rule that he was the funniest. For he was the matey one with money. And for him an appreciative audience was key. Then again, what was the point of a joke if there was no butt?

Stéfan was dining alone. While to dine alone in your mansion may have a tragic splendour, to do so in your overcoat is more likely seen as pathos. It is not a fun night in for one's hands to be colder than the cutlery.

Even when it functioned, the heating system was deeply moody, distributing its warmth like reluctant sexual favours. Some nights it would reward the attic, on other nights the study. And the panelled dining room had, for reasons that evaded the finest of plumbing minds, become completely estranged from the boiler.

Stéfan's one weekend house-party had therefore gone with a somewhat muffled zing. The party mood had been muted, for though dress was casual, gloves were essential. A Jacobean mansion might be a classy venue, but modern high-rollers had yet to embrace the aristocratic tradition that hypothermia was character building.

Nor had all guests been happy to find their view of the hills was framed by scaffolding—useful though it was for the new section of roof. The dust-sheets might be off, and the decorating might be done, but gradually the go-getting Stéfan was starting to gather what he'd gone and got, and it was the domestic version of the Forth Bridge. From jackdaws who nested without planning permission to seventy years of solidified Llewellyn sewage, Crug Caradoc was maintenance man's heaven. Stéfan did not yet regret his impulse buy, but was straining at the bit for the day he would be squire of more than a listed building site.

His family had once before known such a spacious house, long before he was born. He had known it only from the family photo album—and from a large black and white portrait that had hung for many years in his late father's flat. It was a portrait of a grand city house, adorned with traditional wooden balconies, set in the heat and dust of the Caucasus. The money that built it was made from trade—a skill that had stayed in the genes—and through its doors the A-set regularly came to call. Unfortunately, his father's judgments on money were superior to his judgments on politics. His wartime decision to give fulsome backing to the Germans proved, with the benefit of hindsight in '46, to have been a wrong career move. The war over, the Iron Curtain winching down, their palatial family home was judged ideal for the secret police, who were after something nice and central for their headquarters. It was a very sudden house move, which took place without the customary paperwork.

Sitting alone in Wales under his chandelier, Stéfan reflected that the arrival of armed communists would add interest to his evening. Instead, he had to make do with Mrs Grotichley, bearing meat and one veg.

'The cooker's crap.'

This was her first Saturday night as housekeeper-cum-cook, a post that the *Mid-Walian* classified department had unhelpfully advertised among slaughtermen and water-diviners. Chosen from an extensive shortlist of one, she represented the first of his planned retinue. (Handymen and gardeners were next on his shopping list, plus a live-in plumber for the heating system.) Eager to establish his reputation as a host, Stéfan had hoped for someone who could whip up a roast ox, advise on fine wines and tell risqué after-dinner jokes. The unhappily divorced Mrs Grotichley was a squarish woman, little given to speech, who had formerly been a tractor driver. Following the accidental demolition of a wall, she had decided to turn to domestic service.

Mrs Grotichley made her heavy-footed way to the head of the long table, where Stéfan shivered in state.

'I don't do foreign,' she said, offloading the tray. He took this as an allusion to the recipe books he had placed on her kitchen shelf.

The first delft tureen contained a murky casserole. Uncertain what lay in its depths, Stéfan prodded with his fork and an angry sausage shot Polaris-like to the surface, where it then lay like a truculent turd. The second tureen contained half potato purée, half potato lumps, though of a brazenness that suggested it might be a regional delicacy.

'Almost *francais*!' he cried in mock delight.

It was round about now that Stéfan decided to pay his first visit to the Dragon's Head. Technically it was his local, but for some reason he had never dropped in, partial though he was to drink. And Saturday night should see a bit of local colour.

'French?' she enquired.

'*Cuisine lourde*, I think it's called,' he replied satirically.

'Whatever,' said the housekeeper-cum-cook.

As he watched Mrs Grotichley recede, the words 'lumpy woman, lumpy potatoes' kept repeating in his head.

THE PUB'S LOCAL colour was almost in double figures—much to Gwillim's chagrin. It had been a difficult month for trade, with an increased number of customers insisting on being served. There had even been attempts to introduce amenities. The new gamekeeper on the Commodore's estate had turned up with his own dartboard, possessed by some idea of challenging people to a game. Gwillim had put a stop to that by refusing to allow the fabric of the building to be damaged by a hook. The following week he had been forced to throw out several Young Farmers who had turned bolshie and repeatedly proposed a Quiz Night. There had also been talk of a small executive housing development in the village, and he was gearing up to repulse the sort of outrageous demands that people with porches were likely to make.

Dislike of people is a big handicap in a pub landlord, but perhaps a bigger handicap is an absence of small talk. Or indeed of any size talk. Surly and silent, Gwillim gave away nothing, his mind a permanently closed book even to his regulars.

Tonight the talk at the bar was, as so often, of dynastic disinheritance and sexual dysfunction.

This time Eryl had an audience of two, though to describe Gareth as an audience was perhaps over-ambitious. Synchronised drinking was usually the nearest he got to a sentient response. Eryl had, however, recently widened the area of emotional pain he wished to share, and the word 'woman' had several times caused a flicker in Gareth's frontal lobes.

'It's obvious now, I've been used by her,' confessed Eryl. 'Used for my money.'

The other listener kept his counsel, but gave a nod, the regulation nod in bars the world over.

'If people think you're gonna be rich, they go all smarmy. Abuse your good nature.' Froth quivered on his moustache.

Another nod.

'Two years I've been used by her. And now it's empty-your-pockets time.' Eryl looked for more sympathy from his fellow drinker, several years his junior. 'It's the "show us the colour of your money" spiel, you know? Typical woman! Doesn't want to know me now I've got nothing.' Eryl felt almost cheered at finding someone who had not yet heard his full tale of woe. 'Not even my birthright.'

The young guy allowed a noncommittal smile to flicker politely across his tanned face. It was a face that was faintly familiar to Eryl . . . surely he'd been a lad in the town . . . No, that it was it—he'd recently started work as Nico's assistant.

'Go away then.'

'What?'

'Go away. Start over.'

'Go away where?'

'Anywhere. Travel.'

'What, leave the valley?'

'Why not?'

'Dunno.' Why, Eryl wondered, did he feel defensive? 'Is that how you got your tan? Travelling?'

'Sort of,' admitted Sion, with some reluctance.

'Where d'you go?'

Sion looked uneasy, a state that went well with his beanpole posture. He turned to his pint, emptying the glass with a professional, quasi-hydraulic, suction, and muttered, 'Hot places.'

Eryl, who had known little but rain for most of his adult life, felt his self-pity edged out by curiosity. 'Hot places? What, like Africa, you mean?'

Sion seemed tongue-tied. 'Yeah, suppose.'

His limited speech matched Eryl's vague memory of him, a nerdy misfit standing on street corners, plucking up the nerve to watch the girls go by.

'You must know where you went,' pressed Eryl. 'It's a big country, Africa.'

Sion poured another bottle into his glass, and looked around. Gareth was resting his face on the bar, Gwillim had retired to the cellar, the farmers were arguing about sheep dip. Sion took another giant mouthful of beer and said quietly, 'I can't say. I'm on the run.'

Eryl burst out laughing. 'On the run? Who from?'

'Can't say.'

'You've really got people after you? What, like chasing you?'

'Yes, exactly like that.'

'Woman trouble, is it?' In Eryl's fantasy world, the chances of accidentally sleeping with a Mafia man's moll ranked extremely high.

'No, nothing of that sort! Nothing . . . domestic.'

'Oh . . . So . . . these people, are they dangerous?'

'Very dangerous.'

'And they're in the valley?'

Sion sighed. 'They don't give up. They're famous for not giving up.'

Eryl looked around the bar. 'Will they be in disguise?'

Sion appeared torn between his need to talk and the wisdom of staying silent. Then, perhaps exasperated by not being taken seriously, the need to talk won. 'I joined the Legion,' he said, in a tone both furtive and defiant. 'The French Foreign Legion.'

'You can't do that! You're Welsh.'

'That's bollocks! Anyone can join. *I* did. I ran away to join them.'

'But weren't you too young?'

'Yes. So I lied about my age. And they took me. Really. I'm a trained killer now . . . I think.'

'Bloody hell, you can kill people without having to join the French Foreign Legion! I mean, what on earth made you want to join *them*?'

'I saw this film at the Agora.' This was Latin for fleapit—the local cinema. 'It looked kinda fun. Deserts and castles and things. And sleeping under the stars.'

Whether it was the original *Beau Geste* or a later remake was never established. Sion went on to mention Lawrence of Arabia and belly dancers but his exact motive remained murky. The claustrophobia of a small wet community, an ignorance of the outside world, a yearning for adventure, the urge to be macho, a liking for camels, all was muddled up in his adolescent brain. He might well have thought the Sahara was just to the south of Cardiff. And that the guns were make-believe and the knives were rubber. How he had found the Foreign Legion, and what they had made of him, was an unchronicled mystery. Yet, in the end, his actions had a foolishness that verged on the magnificent.

'So how come they're after you?'

'I left. I did three months and then I went over the wall. You're not allowed to do that. Leaving's against the rules. And now I'm wanted for desertion.' He grimaced.

'Desertion?' said Eryl, incredulous. 'You're a deserter from the French Foreign Legion?'

'Yeah.'

'Wow!' Eryl was impressed. He had never met a deserter before.

'So if you only did three months—how long did you sign up for?'

'I'm not sure.'

'Not sure? How can you not be sure? Didn't you ask?'

Sion did not reply. He would have made a good prisoner of war, his natural instinct being to say no more than name and number, even in a pub. But this ill-equipped him for foreign travel beyond the Nant Valley.

Eryl too was now caught up in the excitement and magic of foreign lands. And he was eager to know more. 'So why did you leave?'

Again Sion did not reply.

'Come on, why did you leave?'

After a pause, an embarrassed Sion began, 'They kept hitting me . . .I'm sure they had a valid reason. Probably part of the training, you know, them making a man out of me. But the trouble was that . . . that, well, I didn't know *why* they did it. Or what I was doing wrong.'

'And you didn't think to ask them? Like "What's with this hitting?"'

'I couldn't,' Sion muttered, and stared at the flagstones. A long silence, long even by Sion's standards, came over him. Until finally he said, 'I don't speak French.'

And of course, 'they', the hitters, did.

This esoteric aspect of the French Foreign Legion had come as a terrible shock. He had travelled thousands of miles to the Sahara Desert, not realising that the choice of Woodwork for his one GCSE could prove a linguistic handicap. Unable to translate the reasons for being punched and kicked, he had become demoralised. Had *Beau Geste* been in subtitles he might have sensed that foreigners sometimes speak a foreign language. But life in the valley offered few such clues to the subtleties of life outside the valley. And now he had returned home, probably for ever.

A serious silence fell. And they went back to their drinks. Sion's load had been shared. And, almost mystically, Eryl's load had been lightened. He too would go and see the world. It was time, he now felt, for *him* to move on, to get out, to be his own man. To check out what all those foreigners were up to. Admittedly, he was more Club Med than trainee killer, but suddenly in travel he saw salvation. And he had the first inklings of a plan.

STÉFAN PUSHED open the door of the Dragon's Head and waited in vain to be hit by a wall of noise. Seven polite nods were his lot. He crossed to the bar, where Gareth and Sion were slumped—Eryl having departed into the pitch darkness of the night—and waited in vain to be served. He called 'Landlord!' . . . and waited in vain to be answered.

'Wrong night for the stripper, then?' He spoke so all could hear, and laughed so all could know he was funny.

The silence was broken only by the clicking of dominoes, and the occasional muttering of the molecatchers. The bar and its nooks were dimly lit, and the cracked Barbours merged with the shadows.

'I hear you've got cesspit problems,' said one of the farmers.

In the countryside, neighbourliness can take unconventional forms.

'So that's what that smell is! Thought it was my neighbours' BO!' Stéfan shot back, with a heavy-duty laugh. It did not surprise, nor displease him that he be recognised, but the speed of the grapevine was decidedly not to his liking and he felt the need to assert control. Especially over strangers unduly familiar with his sewage.

'Rodding's no good,' continued the farmer. 'Need a hand grenade to shift that lot! Backs right up, and come the winter rain that meadow goes whiffy.'

This was said in a tone of helpfulness, but it fell short of the ambience that Stéfan had had in mind. He had hopes that in the Welsh hills of a Saturday night he'd find some riotous cross between a male voice choir and indoor morris dancing.

'Landlord!' he cried again.

'That won't work,' said Gareth, raising his chin.

'What won't work?'

'He won't recognise the voice. He doesn't respond to strangers.'

'What is he, a dog?'

'Gwillim!' shouted Gareth.

Stéfan looked around in vain for a bar stool. There were indeed bar stools near at hand, but they were secretly stacked in the cellar.

'Don't need a password, do I? Or a funny handshake?' Stéfan spoke as if at a public meeting, crowding out all other conversation in the bar. 'Because I do funny handshakes.' He held out his hand to Sion—and as Sion reached to take it, he withdrew it. And then laughed, a manic, machine-gun laugh that made his upper body vibrate. The false handshake was a favourite practical joke of his, and never failed to give him pleasure. That it was childish and churlish seemed not to trouble him; that it gave him the upper hand, literally and metaphorically, was satisfaction enough.

'So, when's it get busy?'

'It is,' replied Gareth.

'Christ!' said Stéfan, pulling a face. 'Not very folkloric, is it?'

The pain of concentration settled briefly on Gareth's face as he wrestled with this. He decided to ignore the remark. 'Are you married?' he asked.

'Married? No. Why?'

But Stéfan was never to learn Gareth's views on married life. For Gwillim's head abruptly rose into vision beyond the bar, his emergence from the cellar lacking only a puff of smoke.

'Yes?' he demanded angrily.

'What beers d'you have?' asked Stéfan.

'None,' retorted Gwillim. 'We're closed.' And his body began its return to the underworld.

A lesser man than Stéfan might have slipped away into the night, deterred by the torpor of the bar, trounced by the quality of the service. But Stéfan stood his ground.

'A tenner to reopen!' he retorted in return. And with a showman's flourish he slapped a ten-pound note onto the bar.

The dominoes fell silent.

As *High Noon* it was no great shakes, but the regulars had yet to see anyone get the better of Gwillim. Even on the matter of crisps. Bribery was a new technique—and a tenner was high stakes.

Gwillim halted on the cellar steps. It was not a good position from which to be imperious or curmudgeonly, for his head was at the level of Stéfan's groin. He climbed back out. He moved to where the money lay and looked hard at Stéfan. Keeping his arms rigid, Gwillim placed his palms either side of the note, and leaned ever so slightly across the bar. His face remained as impassively dour as always, his body language suggesting a man who had problems with his feminine side. 'Have you ever milked a cow?'

This was the one response that Stéfan had not planned for. He was immediately suspicious, wary of a trap. Was it witty? Was it coded? Was it abusive? Was it some kind of rustic challenge? He had no ready reply, for it was a cow that had come completely out of left field. 'No,' he said finally.

'Well, I've got fifty to milk, 5.30 tomorrow morning. So I like all the sleep I can get. This place is not a bloody nightclub!' And Gwillim pushed the ten-pound note back across the bar.

Stéfan looked down at his note, now stained by slops.

The Dragon's Head rarely saw human drama, except when Teg and Ben came to blows over a double six, and a palpable sense of interest was taking hold of its phlegmatic drinkers.

Stéfan considered pointing out that the time was in fact a quarter past nine, but sensed that reason would not prove a potent weapon. He felt both angry and frustrated. That his local was at one social remove from a morgue was not the point. He resented being told 'No' by anybody; he was baffled (yet again) by the failure of money to solve life's problems; and above all he loathed being bested in public. He brought the experience of years to bear. 'Let's make it twenty,' he said. 'And all drinks on me.' With that, he laid down a second tenner.

A murmur indicated that he had caught the mood of the bar. He might be an incomer, he might even be a foreign incomer, indeed he might even be a foreign, weekending incomer, but here he had displayed certain universal values that would ensure he did not lack for friends in the valley. The grapevine would add the word 'prodigal' to his file.

For his part, Stéfan found a certain emotional satisfaction was to be had from the farming community. They offered a muted, unsophisticated audience, their silence providing a perfect counterpoint to his noise, their deference providing a stage on which he could perform. His presence in their midst would, he believed, bring some much-needed zip into their lives.

'I serve who I want, when I want,' snorted Gwillim. 'And as far as you're concerned, I'm closed. And you're barred.'

Both the tenners were slid messily back across the slops. And the burly Gwillim stood back with his arms folded.

The small huddle that had started to gather round the bar were now wrong-footed and empty-glassed. A few embarrassedly swished the odd dreg to and fro and gazed floorward. Sion, the only one who could have vaulted the bar and killed the landlord with a single well-aimed blow, felt it was probably time for bed. Gareth wondered briefly, and to no effect, about his powers of conciliation.

It was Stéfan who remained unabashed. He simply stared back at Gwillim, smiled disarmingly and, taking the ten-pound notes, screwed them up into a sodden ball . . . which he tossed lightly over Gwillim's head to the far corner of the bar. Then he reached slowly inside his velvet jacket, brought out first a silver Biro and then a chequebook. He laid the chequebook carefully on a dry section of bar, clicked his silver Biro, and looked up at Gwillim. 'So, how much do you want for the pub?'

Chapter 11

The mist had lifted a little after ten, and a warm day was gathering strength. Rob finished chivvying the earth along a line of fresh green shoots with a hoe, then put it down and lolloped towards the house. A visitor was due. He had arranged for the chief reporter of the local paper, a Clydog Turner, to pay a visit, to view—and hopefully review—his work.

The taming of the garden, the raising of the animals and the humanising of the house, had not led to any neglect of Rob's other love: painting. Time and again he had been out on the hills, hunched under an umbrella, struggling to meld the sights into something that might be called his vision. Some dozen watercolours now leaned against the walls of the barn. They showed a world where the sky and the land almost merged in angry whorls of wind and grass. The colours were near to monochrome, but it was recognisable as landscape—wild, bleak, lonely landscape pushed to the limits of abstraction.

And now he needed to sell. He needed to flush out the local art-lovers. To spread his name in mid-Wales. Because he needed cash for a wind turbine.

They had agreed on 10.30 but, as Rob could see from the bedroom window, the man from the *Mid-Walian* was in trouble making his deadline. Spring rains had washed away the track's latest helping of hardcore, and Clydog, his office car outwitted by the hairpin bends, was not built for a one in seven gradient. Years of Mississippi Mud Pies, courtesy of Hubert, had made his two legs increasingly unviable. For several minutes Rob watched the reporter struggle up the grassy slope, then he went downstairs and made a jug of lemonade, which he waved cheerily at Clydog as he puffed through their gate.

They sat by the pond for some time, while Clydog got his breath back and was introduced to the pig and the ducks.

'That's my studio,' Rob said, and gestured towards the barn. 'I do landscapes mainly. Not traditional, but more like mood pieces. I'm very influenced by Japanese ideas.'

Clydog stared at the barn and sighed. 'Ten column inches.'

'Ten . . . ?' said Rob uncertainly.

'But then you always get good coverage when you hang yourself.'

'Oh. Hefin.'

'You live a successful life and die from natural causes, you get a couple of lines. But fail, and top yourself, it's news. Sad old world, eh?'

'Yes. Yes, indeed. Very sad.' Rob allowed a few moments for the man's memory. Then, 'I suppose you could say my work is Turner without the kaleidoscope of colour.' He paused, expecting Clydog would want to start taking notes. Instead, the reporter continued to gaze into the middle distance, and then unwrapped a piece of nougat which he gave to the pig.

'Funerals, that's what people read first round here. Who went, who gave flowers, who sent apologies for absence. Who was the vicar, what were the hymns, how big were the attendance figures. All sent in by the relatives. Miss out a name, and you're in trouble. We sometimes even have a funeral supplement. People appreciate that. Because of course the Welsh take death very seriously. They often go to funerals of complete strangers. Just to pay their respects. Mind you, vegetable shows come a close second in the summer.' He turned his gaze on the hoe and the garden. 'You planning to grow anything big?'

Rob smiled. 'I think that's down to the vegetables. Ours seem to have a mind of their own,' he added, wondering if the interview had begun.

'Yes, well you're bound to be late, being this high.' Clydog cast a concerned eye over the rows of windswept seedlings. Reaching down, he crumbled a sample of earth between his fingers. 'And the brick dust won't help.' He looked troubled. 'My mother used to have brick dust.'

Although Rob liked to feel he had left urban brusqueness behind, he could no longer contain a townie's urge to organise the conversation, to give some direction to its sentences. 'So will you be taking photographs?'

'What of?'

'Of the paintings.'

'The paintings? Oh, no.' Clydog seemed surprised by the question. 'No, old Miss Nightingale—her family own the paper, have done for years—she has a very strict rule about photos. She only likes to see people and livestock. And vegetables, in exceptional cases.'

'Oh. Right.' Rob took a moment to absorb this information, and then with seeming gravity asked, 'What about paintings of vegetables? Would she publish photos of those?'

'You paint vegetables?'

'No. No, that's just a hypothetical.'

'Oh. Well, I suppose I'd have to ask her what she thought best.' Clydog looked as though that were an exchange he'd rather not have. 'People holding golf cups, that's her favourite. Especially the Nightingale Cup, for ladies' pairs. You ever painted golfers?'

'No, can't say I've ever had the urge. I'm not really representational.'

'She was. She represented the county for over thirty years. Played off six, till her hips packed up.'

Rob decided to take the initiative and stood up. 'I still reckon you can't beat nature as a subject. Whatever the weather. You ready for a viewing?'

Clydog was reluctant to move from his lemonade and his seat in the sun, but could not see a good reason to turn down the offer, it being the purpose of his visit. 'Guess so.'

He rose slowly to his feet and followed Rob into the barn. The water-colours had yet to be framed or hung and they rested informally against the stone walls. They ranged in size from a foot square, a blur of horizontal sedge, to a yard wide, a vortex of battleship-grey wind. Jane liked to call them the mood music of the mountains, and the energy of the brushwork certainly showed signs of being applied at Force 8. The man from the *Mid-Walian* pottered round the studio looking at the works in silence. Occasionally he would put his head to one side like an owl, and twice he raised a picture to eye level so as to look more closely at textural details.

Eventually Clydog spoke. 'I thought there'd be sheep.'

'Couldn't get them to pose in the wind,' Rob replied, affecting regret.

'It's a pity, though,' Clydog went on. 'Locals like to see sheep over their mantelpiece.'

Rob was not precious about his work, he never thought of it as a calling, but he did find the need to place farm animals in strategic parts of it to be a touch prescriptive. He felt a twinge of worry about his client base.

'But then,' and Clydog sighed, 'what do I know about art? Art's always been a closed book to me. As have books,' he added with a laugh, the pol-ished delivery suggesting this was a punch line that had seen much service.

'I thought you were supposed to be the Arts Correspondent?' said Rob. 'I am, I am.' Clydog was unabashed. 'I'm also the Farming Correspondent, the Crime Correspondent, the Local Authority Correspondent, the Religious Correspondent, the Parking Correspondent, and for many years I used to be Rhiannon on the Women's Page, offering advice on undergar-ments and the like. Doesn't mean I have personal experience of pantihose.'

Rob could already foresee the article. A painting being more elusive to define than a vegetable, he would receive a bland and inoffensive 'B'. The *Mid-Walian* was not a paper that liked to offend or have opinions. Also, unlike the article's author, there would be nothing florid or breathless about the prose. And there would be no mention of the Japanese.

'Are there any other painters in the valley?' asked Rob.

'There's a woman does dogs. Pet dogs. Usually on a cushion.'

'Do they sell?'

'I think so. But they're a bit pricy because you have to have an oval frame with dogs.'

'Oh. That I didn't know.'

Rob felt ambivalent almost every time he listened to Clydog. To an exile from the city, Clydog's world offered the Promised Land of 'local colour', and contained a people whose thinking was free of fashion. However, with this world came an awkward truth—namely, that while the upside of the rural idyll was its absence of urban sophistication, the downside of the rural idyll was, well, its absence of urban sophistication. (This insight had begun with Rob's discovery that Abernant's art exhibitions suffered the visual drawback of being held in the town's launderette.)

'What you need is a patron,' said Clydog. 'Someone with a few contacts. The mayoress is very keen on culture. Very keen. Think it comes from her father, who was the first man to have a personalised number plate in this area. He used to trim his hedge in the shape of musical instruments. Woodwind mainly. And she's got his energy. She's always trying to get the council to spend money on arts projects. Have you come across her?'

'Big bosoms? Wears an orange tent?'

Clydog nodded.

'I've seen her do street theatre. She was pretending to inaugurate a cash machine. Very entertaining.' Rob grinned. 'Now *that* you photographed!'

Clydog chose not to rise to the bait. 'Yes, that's her. Mrs Myfanwy Edwards. Point is, she knows the Abernant art world. All sorts, woman who writes poems and a wonderful chap who makes matchstick models of Cardiff Castle. A little group of them meet in her conservatory—"to help stir the creative juices", she says. It was her that tried to set up the love-spoon exhibition and put Abernant on the map.'

'I'll bear her in mind,' lied Rob. 'More lemonade?'

Clydog looked at his watch. 'No, I've got a council meeting to cover. There's a vote on this new ombudsman.'

'Ombudsman?'

'You are cut off from the world! The parking meter ombudsman. To rule on whether to put meters in the high street. And risk civil war.' He eased himself up.

As the two men walked towards the farm gate Clydog looked over at the missing part of the farmhouse. 'That's a splendid old Massey Ferguson!' he said, much impressed. 'Must be what, early postwar?'

'April 1957,' said Rob, failing to reciprocate the enthusiasm. 'No home should be without one.'

Then they shook hands at the gate, and Clydog set off down the steep meadow with the ponderous caution of a man regretting his taste for smooth-soled brogues.

THREE DAYS later Rob joined the queue at the newsagents and waited for the wheelbarrow that brought the latest copies of the *Mid-Walian* from the printers. But he found that that week's edition did not contain an Arts Page, there having apparently been no art in mid-Wales since the previous Friday. He did, however, find an article on old agricultural machinery. Describing how a young artist had a vintage combine harvester in his bedroom. It was written by the Farming Correspondent.

'PLEASE, BE a sensible chap. Put the chainsaw back.'
  'It's my chainsaw! My home! I can do what I fucking like!'
  'What, cause mayhem? I'm sure you don't really want to do that.'
  'I want what I'm owed. I know my rights.'
  'Yes, I'm sure you do. But is a chainsaw really the best way to get them?'
  'Why the hell not? Because *she* won't like it?'
  Marriage guidance was not one of the postman's stronger suits. He had had some experience before, when Mrs Whitelaw had trapped her errant husband on their flat roof for two days by taking away his ladder. And he had once briefly sheltered a naked woman in his mail van to protect her backside from buckshot, an old farming remedy for adultery. But counselling the warring parties was a specialist task and it was stretching his postal skills to the limit.
  'I'm sure Bryony only wants what's best,' he said.
  'Well, go talk to her again then!' said Eryl.
  'Again' meant 'yet again'. For Dafydd had been in and out of the old school playground like a UN special envoy, relaying back and forth each twist and turn of the parties' negotiating positions. As yet it was still talks about talks about talks, and he was an hour behind his new schedule. Indoors, Eryl stood nursing his chainsaw in the classroom-cum-lounge-cum-bedroom; outdoors, Bryony sat defiantly tearful on a child-sized swing, scuffing her legs on the tarmac as she rocked.
  'Well?' she demanded of the postman, as he emerged once more from the schoolhouse. 'Did you tell him he was a parasite? A useless sleazebag?'
  'Er, not in so many words,' said Dafydd, feeling vindicated in his decision

to separate them. He walked across the faded white lines in the playground. 'But I think you are probably right about the relationship being over.'

'So why doesn't he just go? Just take what's his and go, you tell him!' She waved him back towards the schoolhouse.

Dafydd resisted. He had, after all, only just come out, and he felt there should be more to negotiating than this. 'That's the problem. I fear,' he said, a hint of the portentous in his tone, 'that may be exactly what Eryl is planning to do—take what's his and go.' There was a spare swing, and Dafydd wondered briefly whether a fuller empathy might be achieved if he rocked with her, in harmony with her pain. But he was a tall postman, and felt he could look foolish with his bottom just a foot above the ground. Instead, he stretched his hand out to the iron upright and leaned at a paternal angle. 'You see, there's been a sort of development.'

'What development?'

'He's gone and got a chainsaw.'

'A chainsaw? Good. He can cut his dick off!'

'No, I think he's going to cut his bits of the house off.'

Bryony brought the swing to a jangling halt. 'What bits!?'

'The bedroom and the stairs. He says they're his.'

'His? How can they be his?' Bryony was on her feet, outraged and panicked in equal measure. 'Seriously—he's planning to wreck the place? He must be bluffing. Surely?'

Dafydd shrugged. 'I don't know. Is there any petrol in the chainsaw?'

'No idea. All I know is he's a bastard.' She bit her nails, and tried to think straight, and then said, 'Go back and ask what his demands are.'

When the postman had delivered the phone bill and found the pair exchanging insults in their kitchen, he had thought the avuncular authority of a Royal Mail uniform would be all the balm required. Now, after an hour, Dafydd's mind began to fill with loudhailers and police crouching behind cars. He sneaked a look at his watch. 'Go back? Is that wise?'

'Oh, he likes you,' said Bryony.

'He does?'

'You deliver his Giros. That's a meaningful relationship to him.'

With the reluctance he normally reserved for delivering a suspicious parcel, Dafydd went back, once again, into the schoolhouse.

Bryony sat on the stone wall, her caftanned knees up to her chin, and tried to calm herself by rolling one of her wispy cigarettes. Unfortunately, all her essential oils were inside. She tried to reflect serenely. But her refusal to buy Eryl out of his share of the mortgage—on the grounds that he never paid it—now felt worryingly ill-judged. She was still struggling to light her roll-up when the postman came back out again.

He did not immediately speak.

'Well?'

'He says it was him that built the stairs and the bedroom. *And* it was all his wood. So he reckons he can do what he wants with them. And what he wants to do with them is cut them down and take them away.'

'The stairs and the bedroom?'

'Yes. Unless . . .' The postman hesitated. 'Unless you buy them off him.'

'What? Buy my own stairs and bedroom off him?'

'Provided you offer a fair price.'

'You are joking! Never! No way! Go and tell him to drop dead!'

Public-spirited though he liked to be, Dafydd felt this was possibly a mission too far. But before he could reply, the chainsaw fired up. Then it subsided, but remained idling away in the background, its menacing whine an aural reminder of Eryl's negotiating position.

Bryony blanched, fury tempered by alarm, alarm heightened by impotence. From outside she could see nothing of any drama within. The narrow, arched windows of the Victorians ended at his modern mezzanine flooring, and provided no view of Eryl the home wrecker.

'But he can't do it, surely? I mean, it can't be legal, can it? Destroying your own home?'

'I suspect it's a grey area,' said the postman.

'What about the police? Would the police help?'

'It's market day. They only do escaped heifers.'

Bryony slid down from the wall and began to pace. 'So what should I do? What should I tell him?'

'I guess it's a judgment call,' said Dafydd, using a phrase whose meaning he had often wondered at.

'But he must know I've got no money. Did you tell him I've got no money?'

'He said your parents have got money.'

'Not for me. Not for him. Oh Jesus! Tell him I need time to think. Go and play for time. Please!' She looked at him pleadingly.

The postman frowned. Next thing, Eryl would be sending out for a pizza. And being interviewed from a gantry by the Welsh TV News. And then the lane would be floodlit and blocked by CNN Winnebagos. In the meantime, a dozen copies of *Farmers' Weekly* were still to be delivered, Mrs Wilkins would be fretting about the date of her eighth driving test, and the Commodore's leaflets for the Sinking Church Fund's Musical Afternoon & Spring Fête were going unread. And his job was on the line. He wished he had been on more Post Office training courses. He had done 'Relationships with the Public', but that had covered lost motorists, smudged postcards and difficult cats. Nothing about men with chainsaws. But then again, he had known Eryl since he was about six—and for years used to deliver his birthday cards, until Eryl ran out of friends to send them.

'OK. I'll see what I can do.'

Showered with thanks, the postman trudged off, yet again, into the schoolhouse.

Bryony watched. There was a sordid aptness about their relationship ending with a fight over a bedroom. When they had first met, when he was Eryl the heir, he had promised her a choice of twelve. Enough bedrooms to keep a woman busy for weeks, he said. It was a good chat-up line.

He had a cavalier charm then, of sorts. She had fallen for him because he seemed to be as free as the wind, but in reality he was as free as the windfall, and when faced with poverty he crumpled. She was keen not to crumple. And, though it grieved her, she realised she must find some way to buy him off, some pain-free way to raise money. And then she recalled a chance conversation with her neighbour, also forced into penury by a man. She was pondering the neighbour's solution when she heard a shout.

'Bryony!' Ten minutes gone, and Dafydd was back out once more. But with a difference, for as he crossed the playground the sound of the chainsaw no longer seared the air. He smiled. 'I think we may have a deal.'

'Really?'

'More or less. He just needs a helicopter for his escape.' Dafydd gave her a big smug grin. 'No, I said you'd agreed, but that you'd need a few days to get that sort of money.' And then added with another grin, 'After all, you'll have to find a gun and where the Securicor vans park!'

Bryony stretched up and kissed him on the cheek, a gesture he modestly pretended to resist.

'Well, it's a breathing space,' he said. 'But as for paying him . .' He shrugged. It had not escaped the postman's notice that the phone bill, like all her bills, had been a final demand.

Bryony managed to look upbeat. 'I'm working on it.'

'Good luck.'

'And thank you so much.'

'All part of the service.'

And Dafydd got back in his van and drove off feeling, like Wells Fargo, that the mail always got through.

Bryony went back and sat on her swing. Here she tried to give shape to an action plan. Several times in the past she had considered a bank loan and the response had not been encouraging. It was a colonial tradition that the wages of mid-Wales should be the lowest in Britain—no doubt Hubert was the benchmark—and so banking ears were hard to bend. But when paying in her pittance lately she had found signs of a new mood at her branch. A mood that a grateful Mrs Whitelaw, her divorcee neighbour in the caravan up the hill, had described as 'unusually customer-focused'.

Bryony slowly scuffed up the weeds in the crumbling tarmac as she rocked to and fro. Maybe now was the time to take up the offer of the new bank manager, Mr Blake, to go and discuss her needs with him.

Chapter 12

Small cocktail parties for ten or twelve, the Commodore could cope with. He had a strategy for coping, as the modern world would say. He would shake hands with the guests and then would busy himself with coats until Rupert whined. Rupert would whine because, like any twelve-year-old labrador, he needed to do his number ones on a regular basis—and by locking him in for six hours prior to a cocktail party, the Commodore could ensure the whining came on cue. Dog and master would then excuse themselves and exit into the gardens (leaving sister Dilys at the social helm), and quietly spend the evening in the dovecot folly.

More difficult for the Commodore was the 'open house' invitation, the At Home for the neighbours. He still bore the scars of the Silver Jubilee, when five hours of small talk had almost led him to regrets about the monarchy. His only specialist subjects were escutcheons and fly-fishing, each favoured for its solitary nature and neither amenable to a quick joke.

Moreover, when holding such events, events required by his status and insisted on by his sister, he was always prey to the worry that his wife would escape from her bedroom and appear in public. (An alcoholic and a royalist, she found irresistible the prospect of constant toasts to the Queen. Her solo attempts to sing the National Anthem with gestures had twice caused her to trip on the unevenly paved terrace and roll into the rosebed.)

So, as he forced open the glass of St Brynnach's notice board with a twig, and wrote 'T-O-D-A-Y' in black ink across his personally designed Sinking Church Fund's Musical Afternoon & Spring Fête leaflet, the Commodore would rather have been up to his thighs in the River Nant.

There were not many remarkable facts in the Commodore's long life. One was that he had the largest overdraft in the valley. The other was that he regularly managed to transfer this overdraft—and six figures would not be a wild stab—from bank to bank. This beneficial arrangement owed much to the age of deference. The Powells were one of the oldest life forms in the valley and so occupied the top of the social ladder. The bankers, being middle class, had no known way to countermand the wishes of their betters. And any reluctance of the town's bankers to take on these debts, the fruits of a lifetime's inertia, was easily alleviated by an awareness of the family's assets. Land was land was land, and the Commodore had bits of it all over the place, in the way that lesser folk have loose change down the back of their sofa. Whenever one of his many bills reached bailiff level, he would flog off another farm, tenanted and tumbledown.

Their church was but the latest family institution to slide into the mire. Their estate, their shoot, their hostelry, all were on the skids that lead from colonial grandeur to plastic stacking chairs. Had he the nous to be an enlightened landowner, to think in the future tense, he need not have lived in a home of leaks and drafts, fulfilling a folklore image of feckless gentry. But the Commodore was of the old school, and believed the blame lay with the staff, whose standards had declined steadily since the 1850s.

With much of their estate looked after by the likes of Glyn, whom even Wat Tyler would have hesitated to enlist, the returns from the world of sheep now made a long red smudge in the Powell ledger. And the world of his birds did little better. In his woodland covers, there were rarely enough to shoot, since half the pheasants were going AWOL. Apparently in Volvos. For the third year running, he had had to cull his gamekeeper. Even the returns from the estate's one hostelry, the Dragon's Head, were baffling in their shortfall. It was as if the valley had signed the pledge.

'Three pounds fifty, please.'

Her sensuous Irish accent was almost lost under the big golf umbrella. Sporadic drops of rain were falling on to the tautly stretched nylon, which amplified their pitter-patter. Moira pushed a yellow ticket across the little pine table. 'And raffle tickets are fifty pence a strip.' She added a cheesy smile, and nodded encouragingly towards the giant thermometer beside her, whose blood-red mercury showed that ecclesiastical heritage grants currently stood at £12,500.

Long-legged Moira was seated among the rhododendrons at the entrance to the garden, adding unexpected glamour to the role of ticket-girl. Whenever events took place at 'the big house', it was a much-loved feudal tradition that the local wives help out, leaving the husbands, like Gareth, to do the testing manly tasks, like skittle management. So, rejecting the domestic servitude of jam, and tempted by a wider social whirl than ever populated their parlour, Moira had offered herself up for meeting and greeting and tearing of tickets.

A tenner was tossed casually on to the table. 'Aw, bejesus begorrah, Oi'll be having ten pounds' worth!' The big spender stood back and basked in his funniness.

Moira gave an empty smile and, mindful of the proprieties of the occasion, resisted her desire to propose he shove his money up his arse. 'That'll be twenty strips then,' she replied, and began counting them out.

'And what is that Oi'll be winning?' he demanded.

Moira hesitated, determined not to slip into any response that might be taken as a desire for conversation. She did not know who he was, but she knew she did not like him. She did not like his arrogant body language, nor the character suggested by his brass-buttoned blazer, which managed to be both flash and old-fashioned, while the tennis shorts were plain buffoonish, appropriate only to an escapee from a *Carry On* film. She shrugged. 'Oh you know, Woolworths' leftovers.' She tore off his strips. 'There's your twenty. Good luck.'

'Luck? Now would that be after being the luck of the Oirish?' persisted Stéfan, unabashed.

'The luck of any nationality you want.' She gave him another cold and empty smile. 'Three pounds fifty, please,' she said to the next arrival.

Stéfan turned, and took the man confidentially by the arm. 'You be nice to her,' he boomed. 'She's the only Irish woman never been kissed by the Blarney Stone!' And then he treated them both to his trademark laugh.

Beaming happily, Stéfan made his way past the house-high rhododendrons, down the arrowed path into the rose garden and onto the first of two tiered lawns that held the usual selection of stalls. It was a scene familiar to anyone who had read an Agatha Christie novel. It was the thirties incarnate. It was people impeccably polite, with lives of laudable moderation. It was a world hard to fault on moral grounds. It was a world that made murder irresistible.

Stéfan saw it differently. As he crossed the croquet grass, waving to those he knew and to those he didn't, he almost felt contentment. For him, it was a ready-made community, available off the shelf, its people all pigeonholed. It came with instant respect and built-in deference. It was quaint, it was enduring, it was his, and he only had to be here at weekends.

He scanned the browsing crowd for the Commodore. He had business with the Commodore, though the Commodore did not know it. Nor did the Commodore know him, but that was a detail.

Stéfan stopped to guess the number of beans in a jeroboam. It was 10p a go and he had ten goes. He was a man who could rarely resist a gamble. Beneath the jolly smile and a joke about not wanting to win a year's free farts, he was rapidly calculating cubic capacity and the basic dimensions of a bean, for he was also a sore loser. He would not easily give up on a charity bottle of beans. His calculations over, he picked up his ten ticket stubs and moved on down the line of fun. It was odd, though pleasing, to be nodded at by strangers. No one actually doffed a cap, but a couple of the shepherd class tugged what, in a dim light, could have passed for a forelock. Not for the first time, he regretted the surrender of the archives, for he harboured a suspicion that they might give mention of obscure seigneurial powers. Stéfan did not know quite what such powers would be, though in his fantasies it usually involved the wearing of robes. And, conscious of history, he rather warmed to the idea of supplicants queuing at his study door for the settling of grievances and the dispensing of virgins.

The grass gave way to a flagged path with laburnum arches, and in quick succession, he tried his hand at hoopla, block-bought the sponge cakes, and said no to joining the Bat Society. He was nearing the grand house, where it was rumoured the Commodore might be hiding, when he came upon the nerve centre of the day's good cause: an exhibition in an old family tent.

Stéfan looked in.

It was the fat vicar. He was standing against a backdrop of grainy photographs, numbered one to sixteen, and offering close-ups of the church cracks. A wodge of leaflets in hand, he was busy explaining St Brynnach's predicament to the Traffic Warden.

Stéfan backed out. His devotion to the saving of St Brynnach's had its limits, and proximity to fat clergymen was one of them.

He paused under the tent's awning, and began wondering how to flush out the Commodore.

'Ringalongathon, sir?'

'Do what?'

It was Mrs Hartford-Stanley, owner of the wind-sensitive thighs, and she was clutching a clipboard. 'Sponsored bell-ring,' she said with matronly hauteur. 'We're aiming at twenty-four hours. On the town bells.'

'All night long? Wouldn't you make more money if you were sponsored *not* to ring? Ha-ha-ha!'

Had she not sensed the size of his wallet, Mrs Hartford-Stanley might well have stomped on by. But years of shaking tins for cat sanctuaries had given her a killer instinct and she knew where his jugular would be hidden.

'Mayoress is down for a pound an hour.'

'Put me down for two pounds.' Stéfan seized the Biro and made sure his signature was the bigger. It wouldn't be *his* fault if the bells of St Brynnach's never rang again.

Satisfied, Mrs Hartford-Stanley moved on, leaving Stéfan to take stock of the Commodore's substantial house, which lay before him up a flight of weathered stone steps. Despite the flaking white paint, it was an elegant building, with a portico at the side and grand circular bays to the front, their windows looking out across the valley. Stéfan was pleased to see that it had just the two storeys, where Crug Caradoc technically had three. He also won on the listing, for he had checked and the Commodore's was only Grade II. Admittedly, the Powells had a few hundred years of ancestors, whereas the end of the line for Stéfan was Great-Aunt Ottilia, of no known address. But that was easily solved by a few lies, should the need arise.

As he was looking towards the house and the upper lawn, a straight-backed lady in her sixties walked briskly along the terrace to the public address system. She moved confidently for she had an OBE. She tapped the microphone. It was 3 p.m.

There was a short delay while the sound got some screeching out of its system, then the Commodore's sister started to speak. It was a short speech, and merely informed those in the grounds that music was now available in the house. For anyone who was interested.

As Stéfan glanced over at the ground floor bay—an attractive feature that, to his chagrin, his Jacobeans had omitted—he caught a glimpse of a grey-haired old man gazing through its box-sash windows. Forgoing the chance to guess the weight of a pig, Stéfan moved to join the ranks of music-lovers who were working their way up the terrace steps.

'Hallo-o again!' He felt a hand on his arm, soft yet far from tentative. The voice was sort of Ladies' College, but overdone. Stéfan looked round and saw a woman in jodhpurs whom he recognised but could not place. She was clearly a woman unable to detect fashion overkill.

'The auction. You nearly knocked me over.'

'And you've come for an apology.' He remembered her now. She had been sending out sexual signals, as far as that is possible in a wet marquee.

'Oh, definitely. Cringing and protracted.'

He leered. 'I'm afraid I don't do cringing.'

She tapped him lightly with her riding crop. 'I'm sure that could be arranged.'

He hesitated before he responded, wondering what age lay beneath her make-up.

'Twenty-five thousand pounds, you'd just bid twenty-five thousand pounds.'

'Yes, yes, of course I remember you.' His eyes wandered over her welded-on jodhpurs as he tried to decide whether to invest the Stéfan charm.

'Felicity. I like to hunt,' she said huskily.

'Felicity!' He went for the big, full-on smile. 'How splendid! Been a few months but I was hoping to see those buttocks again!'

AT THE OTHER end of the garden, Moira's two hours of smiling was almost up. She tidied her stubs into little piles and started to total the money.

'Done well?'

She looked up. Silk shirts were rare in the valley, and to all but cover one with cashmere seemed ultra-cool. 'Is over a hundred good?'

'Pounds or people?'

'People.'

'Oh definitely a success then.' And the urbane face creased into a smile, its unseasonal glow hinting at the vanity of a sun lamp. 'Though there are better ways to raise funds.'

'Oh?' She took the brand-new note the man offered and started to sort his change. 'Like what?'

'Like selling a video of the church when it falls into the river.'

Moira burst out laughing, though partly from relief at finding a fellow cynic.

Pleased with the response to his wit, Mr Blake modestly ran a hand over the silver waves of his hair. He enjoyed events such as fêtes. They showed his personality to advantage. Not that he wasn't already pleased with himself. It had been a good week at the bank. His loans had exceeded target for the month and he had brought much pleasure to several of his customers.

A hundred yards away, Stéfan had gained a phone number but lost sight of the Commodore. The man had retreated from the window, like some pallid heroine imprisoned in the tower of a Gothic novel. Stéfan set off up the steps. Pink arrows cut out of card directed the music-lovers along the terrace and round to the front entrance. The porch was framed by an ancient wisteria, its greenery miraculously springing out of trunks that resembled tortured driftwood. Here politeness had led to bunching on the gravel. Ahead of him he could see the ponderous figure of Clydog, whose interviewing skills he still remembered for their power of anaesthesia, and so he briefly hung back.

He was, however, curious about the company Clydog was keeping. On one side was a rather funky young couple; on the other side was an inverted pyramid of a woman, whose dress designer appeared to work in the floral sack industry. She was holding court on the subject of art.

The bottleneck unbunged, and the little group went into the house. Stéfan followed a few paces behind, and was immediately struck by the entrance hall. He had not expected the mêlée of muddy boots and the musty smell—nor the fact that no attempt had been made to tidy up for the day. A couple of fishing rods, wedged inside waders, were leaning against the lincrusta wallpaper; a croquet mallet and a dog bone rested on a pair of waterproofs that lay in disarray; on the windowsill stood a row of rifle cartridges. Although contemptuous of the tattiness of the entrance hall, Stéfan had an uneasy envy of its lived-in quality, an insecurity created by a décor that was the accretion of generations, not the *tabla rasa* of an interior designer.

As he followed the echoing voices down the unlit hall, he listened out for the sound of music.

Dilys, the Commodore's sister, was on the door, being gracious with her hands. Even without its bay, the lounge was the largest of the reception rooms, and had in slower, grander times been waltzed over. It was a room with a view, a room that saw the day dawn and stayed in sunlight till afternoon tea. For today, though, the crinkled chesterfields had been despatched to an anteroom and the potted aspidistras were relegated to the recesses.

Filling the seventeenth-century salon were stacking chairs: grey, plastic and in rows. On them, in neat, cramped rows sat the farmers, the farmers' wives, the vet, the eggman, the pond provider, the fence contractor, the poisons adviser, the turkey breeder, the subpostmistress, and a goodly sample of the agro-bourgeoisie, all rounded off, of course, by the valley elders, wheezy martyrs to a lifetime of agriculture.

There were just two notable absentees. One was the church's atheist surveyor, who had diagnosed the damage to St Brynnach's in such loving detail, who had ordered the digging of the dumper-loads of dirt . . . and who had now failed to attend the fund-raiser. The other was the church's godfather, the Commodore himself.

Stéfan was a restless man, who lost interest on page one of books, and he had no desire to be trapped alive in a concert. He spurned the seats and stood in the claque at the back, the better to observe and escape.

Then, from the corridor outside, came a terrible squealing and grinding. And a piano, pulled by the gamekeeper and pushed by the Commodore, made a late entrance—which might have provoked a round of applause but here it only provided the trigger for a community smile of deference.

Except from Stéfan.

'Heave!' he roared, having once seen the Last Night of the Proms. 'Heave!'

Heads were turned, and an embarrassed titter did the rounds.

The piano and its recalcitrant castor was then pushed to the bay, its rosewood lid was opened, sheets of music put in place, a stool put in front, and for a brief, appalling moment the prospect of rustic male duets seemed imminent. Whereupon Dilys brought on the performers.

Isobel and Arwyn. Aged eleven and twelve. Pianist and violinist. Grades 3 and 4. Dressed by the Fauntleroy family.

Shyly, the two youngsters gave a little bow each, to oohs and aahs from the audience. They then shook hands and turned to take up their playing positions, silhouetted against the Queen Anne windows.

'A minuet in D by Bach,' warned Dilys sternly.

Outside, the two lawns led the eye down to the water meadows where the Welsh Blacks still munched through the rich grasses, and on to where the Norman church tower rose above the yew trees. Indoors, the scrolled pediment rococo arabesques on the ceiling gave visual testament to the house's rich history. And doing the rounds of the acoustics was the tentative tuning of violin strings.

'Ah, now this,' whispered the mayoress to the six nearest seats, 'is just like Jane Austen.'

And, in a way, it was.

Young Isobel flexed her fingers on the keys of the baby grand, young Arwyn pressed the over-polished violin under his chin, then, after pausing briefly for an outbreak of farmer's lung to subside, they set to work on Bach.

As the children lived at opposite ends of the valley, they rarely practised together. So, while their individual notes were excellent, they moved through the music at somewhat different *tempi*. And that perhaps produced the mild artistic tension that could be detected from Arwyn's habit of beating time with his foot. But all agreed it was lovely to watch two such charming children play the classics so delightfully.

A very generous outburst of clapping greeted the end of the minuet. At the back, Stéfan, not to be outdone, and eager in some way to integrate, shouted 'Bravo!' More than once. But even as he applauded, he kept a watching brief on the old Commodore, who throughout had lurked inscrutably by the open salon door.

The applause finally died away, only for Dilys to reappear—and announce a second piece. This time by a lesser known composer.

Stéfan listened for a minute or so more, while the violin tried very hard to be contrapuntal, but his mind was elsewhere. Time, as he so often said, was money. It certainly wasn't music.

There were some dozen people standing along the walls but he had a clear sightline of his target and was fearful the man might vanish again.

'Pssst!' he said. 'Pssst!'

It was one of the few moments that day when the acoustics of the room did full justice to the quality of the sound. Almost everyone turned round— with the exception of the Commodore.

There were two possible reasons for his failure to respond: deafness, or the fact that no one had ever gone 'Pssst!' to a Powell before.

The second composition was more *forte* than *piano*, and the vigorous keywork of eleven-year-old Isobel quickly recaptured the attention of the audience. Stéfan, meanwhile, had still to capture the attention of the Commodore. Elbowing his way through the groupies, he manoeuvred to the door and laid his hand on the man's shoulder.

'Stéfan. Crug Caradoc.'

The Commodore spun round, startled, like a highly strung thoroughbred. Physical touching and the use of forenames were the sort of things he had fought a war against.

The old man stared uncertainly at Stéfan. The blazer in particular foxed him, and he briefly wondered whether, in one of his less lucid moments, he had promised to hold a charity cricket match.

'Wonderful concert. And such a lovely house.' Stéfan had to shout slightly, to be heard above the noise of the young duettists.

'Oh . . . er . . .'

'And such a good cause. Brynnog is one of my favourite saints.'

Heads were beginning to turn, the audience was growing tetchy, and Arwyn's *glissando* skills were starting to suffer. Stéfan took the Commodore by the arm and led him into his hall. 'Business proposition for you, Julian.'

He waited expectantly. In his experience, these were words that brought a flush of excitement to any man's cheeks. . . . But not, apparently, Julian's.

'Oh . . .' He gazed vacantly down the hall, towards the portrait of his father. 'Er . . . no . . . No, not my sort of thing . . . thank you.'

'But you don't know what it is.'

He made a fluttery sort of gesture with his hands. Eventually, if only because it was his turn to speak, he said, 'I don't know what anything is these days.'

'It's a figure with a lot of noughts on, that's what it is!'

'Oh.' If it were possible, the Commodore's gloom increased. He started to look around him. 'Have you seen Rupert?'

'Rupert?'

'He needs to widdle.'

'He can widdle later. I want to buy your pub.'

'Is it for sale?'

'Well, *you* own it!'

'Oh . . . oh, yes. Yes . . . I suppose I do . . .' The Commodore's head began to ache. So much conversation in one day was extremely taxing. He ruminated a while, then said, 'D'you ride?'

'Ride? What, horses? No.'

'Oh.'

The old man fell silent again, leaving Stéfan uncertain whether he was still considering his proposal, or indeed whether his brain had stopped. After a while, he realised the Commodore's slight head movement showed instead that he was listening to the music, whose strains were drifting in and out of the hall's shadows.

'I'd give you a fair price.'

'I used to hide in your attic.'

'Pardon?'

'My record was three and a half hours. Because I could keep quiet. My sister never could.'

'Crug Caradoc?'

'Tea with the Llewellyns, we used to have to come to tea. We hated the Llewellyns. All our family hated the Llewellyns.'

'Well, no dark corners to hide in now. I've spent eighteen thousand pounds on paint and lights alone. And I'd be spending that sort of dosh on the pub as well.'

The Commodore did not appear impressed. Indeed, few expressions ever crossed his face apart from sadness and puzzlement. And now puzzlement seemed to have advanced from the general to the particular, from the mysteries of a baffling world to the strangeness of one inhabitant.

'Why?'

'Why what? Why do I want to buy the pub?' Stéfan struggled for an answer, sensing that temper tantrum would sound an odd motive.

The Commodore mused aloud. 'It makes no money. You'd be out of pocket. I'm out of pocket.'

'And you want to keep it?'

He shrugged, with a vagueness that gave no purchase point for a discussion, and eventually said, 'My father kept it.'

'D'you like it? D'you go to it?'

He shrugged again. 'They tell me it's a dreadful place.'

'Well, I could always reduce my offer.'

'I suppose so. You'd have to talk to my solicitors about that.'

'About what? About . . . Is that a yes?'

Applause burst from the music room, prolonged and enthusiastic. The Commodore, sensing a surge of people might be imminent, started to back off down the hall. 'I wanted to have tombola,' he muttered.

'Is that a yes?' Stéfan asked again, more insistently.

The old man looked flustered . . . but finally nodded agreement. Adding, 'I'm on pills, you know.'

Stéfan gave him a clenched fist salute, for reasons that escaped both of them. The Commodore continued towards his front door, querulously calling for Rupert. He was almost outside when he turned, and said, 'They're all buried in my churchyard, your Llewellyns.' Then he went out, leaving Stéfan to simmer at what he assumed to be one-upmanship.

As he stood alone in the ancestral hall, Stéfan found himself taken by the urge to now buy a church of his own.

'OH, I LOVE *all* art!' declared the mayoress, as her entourage filed out of the concert and back down to the garden.

Rob did not reply. He had replied the first time she had announced this, and the second time, and the third time, but had now realised that the tone was *municipal declamatory*, a debased form of the oratory favoured by the Romans, and required no response other than well-timed nodding.

'My father was forty years in the male voice choir, that's where it comes from. D'you sing? I'd love to sing. I used to sing as a child.' She eased herself respectfully over the camomile and feverfew in the flagstone cracks. 'I've always been good at projecting.'

Clydog had introduced the parties as his contribution to rural networking. He had only a hazy view as to how patronage worked, but knew that Myfanwy Edwards had pull with the sister-in-law of the man who owned the launderette where art exhibitions were sometimes held.

'Welsh National Opera came to Abernant last year. Touring their celebrated production of *Rigoletto*. I went both nights, once as mayoress, once as myself. Wonderful! Quite wonderful! If this were Italy we'd have an opera house. Everywhere in Italy has an opera house. We should have one here!'

'Not a lot of votes in that,' observed Clydog. 'Hubert can't even make money out of pasta.'

'So, Robert!' said the mayoress, turning to him as the four paused at the bottom of the terrace. 'You're an artist, then. Tell me about your work. Who is your muse?'

Rob and Jane exchanged looks, a snigger not far away.

Before he could reply, Jane sighed sadly and said, 'Aah, you know the fickle world of art, Myfanwy. His muse keeps leaving him to fuck someone else. But then that's muses for you!'

Valley people had long noticed that incomers swore more often and more vividly. Some deplored this, but others attributed it to their greater sophistication. The result was a two-speed language zone, the outsiders effing and blinding while the locals listened benignly and replied in the Queen's English. Or in their idea of the Queen's English.

A fuck would never have passed the lady mayor's lips, and not just because word might have got back to the Queen. Nonetheless, as an artistic person herself, she understood that creative types have to be free of the rules that bind ordinary mortals.

'True, very true,' she replied. 'Inspiration's never nine to five, is it?'

'He does Japanese landscapes,' said Clydog.

'Oh, I love Japan,' said the mayoress, who had once been to Cyprus.

Everyone smiled.

'Are you familiar with the art world in Abernant?' she continued.

'Er, no, not . . . er . . . not as such, no.'

'Oh, we must get you along to one of our coffee mornings. I have coffee mornings for people who are artistic. Where we all exchange ideas, cross-fertilise. We're short on painters. Got a lot of potters, though. A potpourri of potters, as I call them.'

Rob avoided Jane's eyes, for a snigger now would be terminal.

'It's like a rural Bloomsbury set, I suppose. Rosie—she's a divorcee—her hedgehog pots go all over. Started out with just mugs, and now she's got an order from Disney. Disney! And apparently they want other animals. It's a great achievement.' The mayoress would have continued her way through the rest of the CVs had she not caught sight of Dilys.

She hated her hostess. Dilys was everything the mayoress wanted to be. She had classier invitations on her mantelpiece, and every time Clydog wrote about her in the *Mid-Walian* he put OBE after her name. And her breasts didn't need stabilisers. Yet the mayoress also knew that a good word from her, a leaf of her scented notepaper, and doors might open—doors to flunkeys and medallions.

'I'll be in touch!' she said, and was off powering up the slippery terrace steps towards her hostess like a fell runner.

Clydog gazed after her. 'Guess it's time to go. I think the fat lady's about to sing,' he said, somewhat unexpectedly.

Rob and Jane were also ready for a quick exit, as they had promised some tea and sympathy to Bryony. The day had been a good crash course in meeting neighbours and, in the interests of community spirit, they had loaded up with jam.

The parting cars crunched down the gravel drive, mud spraying from their wheel arches, and eased out into the lane. Watching them from the junction by the church, seated on a shiny new black motorbike with garish striping, was a biker kitted out in shiny new black leathers. On the back of his bike were two full paniers and a CYMRU sticker. His visor was closed and, although many gave him a second glance, he remained anonymous to them all.

Eryl sat in the rain for some ten minutes, then revved hard and raced away down the valley, the valley that was once to have been all his.

Chapter 13

'In a lay-by?'

'Yes.'

'A lay-by fifty yards from the caravan?'

'Yes.'

'Why would he put it there?'

'Precisely!'

Hubert pondered this information. 'And you saw it two weeks ago?' He puffed his Old Holborn over the profiteroles. 'What time?'

'On my morning round,' replied Dafydd.

'Some time between dawn and dusk, then.'

'About nine thirty,' the postman retorted. Then added, 'And I'm always finished by eleven these days. Well, nearly always.'

'You've no idea if the car was there all night?'

'No—'

'You didn't slip back and feel the bonnet?'

'No, of course I didn't!'

'Call yourself a postman! What use is your bloody gossip if you don't get all the details?' Hubert was enjoying himself.

'You've got enough proof. Why would the bank manager's car be parked fifty yards from her caravan? And how come she wouldn't answer the door to sign for her parcel? *Rare Breeds of Hen*—she's been waiting weeks for those magazines.'

'Oh you managed to find out what was in her parcel, then? That wasn't too much trouble?'

'I just deliver things to people. I don't kick their doors down.'

'Come on, Clydog, you're the pro here, what's your theory?'

So far, Clydog had not spoken, as he had got into trouble with his Mississippi Mud Pie. For several minutes he had been leaning on the counter, trying not to choke. Attempts to speak made him go puce. Gamely, he struggled to get enough air together for a sentence.

'Well,' postulated Hubert helpfully while they waited, 'perhaps Mrs Whitelaw was overdrawn and he's killed her. Banks are getting very strict on loans these days.'

At last Clydog spoke. 'It's not far from the river. He could have gone fishing.'

'*Fishing?*' The other two men spoke as one and turned to stare at him.

'Early morning. Relieving the stress of high finance on his way to work. Make a nice human interest story, that would. 'S got a page seven feel.'

'Except it's bollocks!' said Dafydd.

'You don't know that.'

'I do.' The postman hesitated, glancing around the deserted delicatessen with an almost conspiratorial air. 'I don't know if I should say this . . .'

'Oh you can speak freely in front of Clydog,' said Hubert. 'He's like a priest. Nothing you say to him—no matter how shocking or scandalous—will ever be repeated. Certainly not in print.'

Dafydd lowered his voice mysteriously. 'Guess where else the bank manager's car's been parked at 9.30 in the morning.'

'Hope it's not on double yellows. Council's planning to make that a hanging offence.' Hubert was spearheading the anti-fascist campaign against new parking regulations, and this made him prone to obsessiveness.

'Go on, guess.'

'Outside the nuns.'

'Outside the old schoolhouse. Lived in by,' the postman nodded knowingly towards the back kitchen, where sounds of angry chopping could occasionally be heard, 'your Bryony.'

'Bryony? But he's old enough to be her . . . her . . .'

'Bank manager?'

Hubert was more than shocked. He was miffed. He was only ten years older than Mr Blake, the new bank manager, and this left him wondering whether he too could have successfully tried it on with her. Assuming it was true. That these sightings weren't mere coincidence. 'You're sure . . .?'

'Being a postman,' said Dafydd, 'you get a feel for funny goings-on.'

'The man does wear silk shirts,' admitted Hubert.

'There's no proof he's up to anything,' Clydog said again. 'He could be one of these . . . these new roving bank managers'—Dafydd and Hubert found this very funny—'who do home visits.'

'Go on, then,' said Hubert. 'Tell him you want a home visit and see what happens.'

'Yes, go undercover, Clydog! Say you want to try the home bonking service!' Hubert was on a roll. 'Demand customer satisfaction!'

The laughter took a while to subside, eventually quieted by the fear that Bryony might come out to investigate. Amidst all the joking the postman felt his revelation had not received the credit it deserved.

'Your editor should employ me,' he told Clydog. 'As gossip columnist. Like that Nigel Dempster.'

'Local people don't want to read tittle-tattle. That's not journalism. It's muckraking.'

'I'd have more scoops in a week than your paper has in a year.'

'Like what?' muttered Clydog. 'Cars parked in unusual places?'

'Oh, I've got better than that!' said Dafydd, riled by the mockery.

'What, "the lady mayor seen belly-dancing in the Bombay Garden"?' suggested Hubert. 'Or "Gwillim smiles!"?'

It was Clydog's turn to join in laughter at another's expense. And adding to the merriment, he spluttered, '"Prize pig caught in love triangle"?'

THE HIGHWAY CODE does not have much to say on the subject of cows. Its writers are more exercised by horses and their need to buy taillights and not ride two abreast. This emphasis on the safety of horsy people, though commendable, suggests a rather class-based document, in which the needs of cows—an intellectually slower, more downmarket creature—are neglected. There exists, however, an ancient and somewhat secret law that offers the freedom of the road to the cow. And no rights at all to the motorist.

It was the favourite law of the pub landlord.

Twice a day Gwillim would herd his cows along the lane to their milking parlour, a chore enhanced by the antisocial delight of blocking all traffic. His surly swagger was boosted by his knowledge of this arcane law, which stated simply that the presence of a herdsman conferred immunity on even the most bolshie of his cows. Responsibility for damage to any passing cars—or indeed any politely waiting cars—lay with their drivers.

Threatened with the loss of his lease and his livelihoods, Gwillim had little armoury at his disposal. Had he been more Mediterranean, more swarthy and scarred, he could have initiated a vendetta likely to keep Stéfan's relatives busy for several hundred years. But a wet climate is not conducive to multiple generations of bloodlust. So, instead, Gwillim brooded and kept his cows primed.

Not since the Romans held the valley had such an enthusiastic watch for incomers been mounted. From his yard the landlord had a clear view of the valley road, a B-minus road for much of its length, as it wound down from the headwaters of the Nant. This vantage point would, he reckoned, give him some ten minutes' warning of an advancing Stéfan.

And so it did, mid-morning one Saturday when Gwillim caught a glint of Stéfan's Jaguar. The cows were already back in their field, so Gwillim had to quickly send in his collies to get them out onto the road again. As the dogs nipped and barked at their hoofs, Gwillim snarled and whacked at their rumps, using a holly branch to discourage any docility. By the time all fifty beasts cascaded out of the farm gate, the car was just a few hundred yards away.

Stéfan was on his second journey to The Windowman, listening to Wagner. He had chosen the Valkyrie and was giving them full vocal support, all decibels blazing, when he saw the cows as he rounded the long, fast curve into the village. They were ambling with attitude.

Stéfan braked to a halt by the ditch and waited for them to pass. The ditch narrowed the lane at this point, and the car added to the bottleneck.

As the cows, caked in mud, struggled to squeeze through, Gwillim kept up the barrage of shouts and urged his dogs to greater yapping. Panicking, some animals tried to mount the beast in front, bellowing loudly. The crush intensified and—to the rousing chorus of the warrior-maidens—a trapped Stéfan watched as his wing mirror snapped off. A number of the cows were in calf and their great bellies swung from side to side with a rhythmic and irresistible force that did not regard the bespoke panelling of a luxury car door as an immovable object. With a series of heavy crunches, nearly half a ton of Welsh beef stove in first the front door and then the back door of Stéfan's Jaguar. The car rocked.

And still the Valkyrie sang on.

Stéfan was incandescent and, when the herd had passed, hell-bent on retribution. Unfortunately, he could not open his car door. He began to yell his rage at Gwillim, who was walking blithely by. Unfortunately, he could not open his car window. He crawled across the front seats and opened his passenger door. Unfortunately, it opened onto a ditch. It took several minutes of a muddy struggle before he made it onto the cowpats of the lane.

'Hey!' he yelled after Gwillim. 'Hey!'

Gwillim kept on walking.

'Hey!' Stéfan started running to catch him up. 'Hey!'

Gwillim whistled, an apparently simple whistle. But to the two Welsh sheepdogs, attuned to the subtlest of commands, it meant 'go and bite large lumps out of that unpleasantly rude man behind us'.

Stéfan hesitated, then, faced with the advancing jaws, turned and began to retreat . . . faster and faster as he realised he could not reach safety through his offside doors.

'SEE YOU'RE GETTING used to the countryside then,' said Mr Griffith Barton, The Windowman. 'Not nearly so smartly dressed any more.'

Stéfan looked down ruefully at his muddied trousers, the cowshit on his shoes, and the soaking left arm of his jacket, still rank from where he had tumbled into the ditch. He did not attempt to explain.

He held up a bottle of champagne.

'You've cut your fingers.'

Again Stéfan offered no explanation. 'Drink?'

The Windowman looked doubtful. He showed little sign of asking Stéfan into his lean-to. 'Why, what are you celebrating?'

'Oh, end of another month. Time to wet the project's head.'

'Bollocks!' he said, then turned. 'I'll get a bandage.'

Stéfan followed him in as he disappeared.

The kitchen was as Stéfan remembered it, except the piles of papers and unopened post seemed that little bit higher. The lounge was still in semi-darkness and, as before, the latest *FT* lay open on the table.

Stéfan rinsed the dried blood off his fingers, and watched the pink-tinged water eddy out of sight down the crockery graveyard in the sink.

'You annoy someone, then?' The Windowman handed him a small air-sealed tin of Band-Aids.

Stéfan thought of being wittily offhand, and saying 'cow rage', but felt even that reflected badly on him and so he ignored the enquiry.

'I suppose champagne glasses would be out of the question?'

The Windowman hesitated, then disappeared again, returning with a pair of engraved antique flutes. He watched, stern-faced, as Stéfan opened the highly excitable Bollinger and poured him a very generous measure.

'We're not bonding, you know,' he warned Stéfan sharply, lest gratitude be inferred.

'Of course not. It's just a gesture.'

'A gesture? A gesture of what?'

'To show I'm a serious client.'

'One tax-deductible bottle of posh plonk does that?'

'How do other clients show appreciation?'

'They bugger off.'

Nonetheless, he emptied his glass, and allowed it to be refilled. A blood-ied, mud-covered Stéfan was a not unsatisfying sight.

Silence settled, a silence that Stéfan would normally have colonised. But he felt low on brio, and anger kept taking his mind elsewhere. He knew he needed to do the empathy thing. He had brushed up on the Habsburgs (thanks to 2.5 yards of *Encyclopaedia Britannica*, bulk-bought to bring cultural cred-ibility to his study), but dead people were not really his bag. His gaze drifted round the room's bric-à-brac in search of conversational leverage.

'Bullet holes.'

'Sorry?' said Stéfan.

'They're bullet holes.'

'What are?'

'There. Where you're looking.' The Windowman pointed to the lintel above the would-be doorway. 'Straight through the window, into the wall! Bam-bam-bam. Made four weeks ago.'

'They're fresh?'

As on his previous visit, the agenda was moving away from him. Trying to conceal his doubts, Stéfan inspected the lintel. But, yes, there were holes, round holes, of what he assumed to be bullet size, and, yes, they did seem recent. He did not know what to make of this. He remembered how last time their talk had quickly turned to the violence of the world. And once again his host was dressed in military camouflage.

Stéfan looked from the wall to The Windowman. 'You have a gun then?'

'What? No! That's not *my* doing! *I* don't have a gun.' He spoke as if to a child.

'Oh . . . But I thought . . .' Stéfan gave up on what he thought.

'The house was attacked. In the middle of the night.'

'What, by a dissatisfied customer?'

'No!' But The Windowman allowed himself a grin at the thought. 'No, by the army.'

'Your house was attacked by the *army*? Had you declared war?'

Then Stéfan began to worry whether he was in danger. No one knew he was here, he was miles from any other habitation, and The Windowman was all muscle. The extreme isolation, the antisocial behaviour, the obsessions, were now forming a familiar profile. Stéfan already wished he'd followed Plan B today, and rung the woman from the hunt for a shag.

'The attack seems to have been a mistake. The army has apologised.' The Windowman's face had a tight smirk of triumph. 'A man with lots of stripes has been up and said sorry.'

'I don't understand. Why would the army attack your house?'

'SAS actually. Misread their map references. Good job we're on a bloody island! They could start a damned war with that sort of mistake!' He stretched for the last of the champagne.

'Crack soldiers misread their map references?'

'So they said. Thought this place was some target on the range. Said it looked abandoned, for God's sake!'

'So, er, what happened to all these highly trained soldiers running amok?'

'The goat got them.'

'No, I meant—' He stopped. 'The goat got them?'

'One horn can come in very handy. Straight up the arse.'

Stéfan searched for a twinkle, a hint of a tease. He found nothing. This was not delusional. He was being made a fool of. For the second time in one morning. He geared up for some straight talking.

'And I got to keep a souvenir.' The Windowman stretched over and tossed Stéfan a snuffbox. It was full of used bullets. Wrapped in an official letter of apology from the Ministry of Defence.

Stéfan abandoned the plan for straight talking.

'Biscuit?' The Windowman held out some Hobnobs.

'Please.' Enormously relieved, Stéfan suddenly felt ravenous. The events of the day had done something funny to his stomach.

They munched for a while in silence, Stéfan watching as the other man dipped his biscuits in the champagne, and questioned whether he could have got away with a Reisling. After all, even dinner at the Ritz would not, he now felt, have advanced the business in hand—which so far had not been mentioned once. He had The Windowman's forbearance for just so long as he did not say the word 'windows'.

'So . . . it's not been dull then. Anything else happened?'

'Since you last bothered me?'

Stéfan did not respond.

'They published a letter. Did you see it?' He nodded towards the mound of back *FT* issues.

'No. No, not my paper.'

'Cut it, of course. Cut the reference to the IMF as Vikings.' He rubbed at the stubble on his chin, sighing angrily. 'Sanitised. Everyone wants things sanitised these days. Did you know you can get plastic goat horns now?'

'D'you send many letters?'

'Depends. If I'm angry. Send too many and they have you down as a crank.'

Stéfan saw the chance for bonding, and went for it. 'Think that's how they see me down here. A maverick. Someone who speaks his mind.'

The Windowman ignored him. '*And* I got my views printed on corporate fascism. The State as a bloody pawn. That got up a few important noses! Right up!' He paused. 'So I don't think it was a mistake.' And he looked Stéfan straight in the eyes as he emphasised these last few words.

'What wasn't a mistake?'

'To attack the house.' The Windowman rattled the bullets. 'I think it was deliberate.'

Stéfan felt his heart sink.

'I think it was a warning.'

Chapter 14

'Sky? It doesn't look like sky.'

'It's a stylised sky.'

'Oh . . .' The old lady continued to gently fold her underwear, feeling for damp. 'What's a stylised sky?'

'It's . . . it's a sky done in a certain style. This is done in a sort of Japanese style.'

'Why? Are you Japanese?'

'No,' said Rob.

The old lady stared again at the picture, spinning the drum to check no garments had clung to its sides.

'My husband and I, we like Welsh skies. D'you do Welsh skies?'

'That's my interpretation of a Welsh sky.'

Rob's hunch said he hadn't got a buyer. As she zipped up her laundry bag, he dropped lightly down from the spin dryer on which he was perched. Holding open the launderette door, he smiled politely at her as she left.

The exhibition was on its tenth and final day. There was not a red dot in sight. Ellie, who did the service washes in the morning, said his clouds reminded her of people's laundry swirling round and round behind the glass. She was not a buyer either.

At the age of eight Rob had declared—according to his mother—that when he grew up he was going to live in the country and be a painter. He had no memory of saying this, nor could he even remember thinking it. Only when he announced that he had bought a hovel in the hills did she tell him it was his lifelong ambition. He did not demur for he was more than ready to leave the city. And the chance to turn a sporadically profitable hobby into a proper living had become irresistible.

Jane was his main influence, providing moral support and framing. She did, though, stamp hard on his sentimental dreams of garret life and death in poverty. It had been her idea to exhibit, and the actual display also owed much to her eye, for she had once worked in PR (before majoring in acupuncture) and so knew about presentation. Nonetheless, both agreed that washing machines did not adequately contextualise his work.

Rob was on the hard news section of the *Mid-Walian*, reading the court reports of the meter unrest, when the launderette door opened again.

'D'you reckon you can get the stains off this jacket?'

Rob did not need to look up. Nor did he smile. 'Have you tried a blow-torch?' he said with feeling.

'OK, OK!' Nico eased off on the jokes. 'It'll be gone by next week. I promise. Landed gentry chap wants a birthday present for his son—kid called Trefor—mad keen on old tractors.'

Rob lowered the paper. 'Any relation of the sure-fire cash buyer?'

Nico gave a shrug. 'It's a volatile market.' He turned his attention to the paintings and walked very slowly up and down the launderette, focusing with the screwed-up eyes of a connoisseur. Sion followed two paces behind, with the blank look of a philistine.

Rob went back to his paper. After ten dull days, the background noise of endlessly churning clothes had come to resemble the ambient sounds of deepest space. The place made his mind feel numb, as if he too were living in a sealed tub.

'Don't they do the red dots any more?'

Rob allowed several calming seconds to pass. 'Your point?'

'I'd have thought it was obvious.'

'It's not exactly an ideal venue.'

'Oh, I don't know. At least people *have* to sit and look at the pictures.'

'If they can't afford a Hotpoint, they can hardly afford a painting.'

'Want some advice?'

'From you?' Rob did not try to hide his disdain.

'I know about art.' Disdain was an oddly ineffective weapon against Nico. His skin had grown thick in response to a lifetime's disdain. 'And I know what people want round here.'

'And what do people want?' The question was dipped in sarcasm, but did not quite conceal a desire to know. '"Round here?"'

Nico pulled himself up on to the dryer opposite. 'I've been twenty years in the antiques business. I go round people's homes. I see what they buy. What they put on their walls and their sideboards. What plates they collect. The mugs, the jugs, the bowls, the knick-knacks. So I know their tastes. The pictures they want. I know what will sell.'

'Oh, really?'

Nico nodded, displaying that cockiness which had driven Stéfan out of Sotheby's marquee and into the storm. 'Yep!'

'And . . .' Rob tried to smile patronisingly, 'what would this magic formula be?'

'Farmyard scenes.'

Rob's disdain was muted by a sudden memory of Clydog's response to his work, and he didn't immediately reply.

'Livestock. Well-fed pigs, and cows, and chickens and things. Bit like the Ark—but on land. And farm animals only.'

'All smiling and waving, I suppose,' said Rob. 'Anything else?'

'The animals have to be big. Definitely big. Bugger perspective!'

'Oh, that should make it easier.'

'It's what I call the school of Animal Realism,' said Nico.

'It's what I call kitsch,' said Rob, drawing a line under the discussion. He was about to drop emphatically down to the floor when he realised that, being in charge of the exhibition, he could not exit and would be obliged to wander vaguely about.

Rob did not know it, but Nico had long believed there to be a gap in the farmyard animal sector of the art world. Domestic animals were well catered for, being smaller and often coming with their own cushion. But bigger beasts could be stroppy and muddy and unwilling to hold the same position for hours. Nonetheless, they were much loved by their owners.

'But it's not just the paintings,' continued Nico. 'It's the merchandising. You paint Ferdie the Bull right and you'll have an icon. Probably a tea towel as well. And a coaster.'

'This isn't art, it's business.'

'This is art that makes money. Art with hundreds of red dots.'

Rob shifted uneasily on his dryer. 'I like painting sky and trees. I don't know the first thing about farmyard animals, and I certainly wouldn't know how to "merchandise" them.'

'That's why you need an agent.'

'THIGH BONE,' said the Commodore.

Startled to see him materialise by the yew tree, Gareth twitched upright, abandoning his rest against the gravestone. His mind was elsewhere, wondering whether a hobby would make him more interesting. It was not far short of dusk, and he'd thought that he and his sheep had the churchyard to themselves. With night coming on the Speckled Beulahs were quietly setting up camp beside the lych gate and the giant thermometer saying £18,000. Not even the chimes of the church clock disturbed the animals' Zen-like calm.

'Last time it was a shin bone.' The Commodore gave a rare smile.

Rupert had now slavered into view and was bearing the bone in question. He dropped it on Gareth's Wellington boots, and then lay down.

The two men stood like ill-made statues while the darkening air filled with the cries of the rooks above.

Gareth knew his duty was courteous deference but his thoughts were elsewhere, for his unease about his wife's legs had spread to other parts of her body, like her brain. The Commodore's thoughts were on the dinner party that he had escaped from, yet he felt obliged to grant the farmer a few moments of his presence, in unspoken acknowledgment of the sheep, so kindly offered in St Brynnach's hour of need. (The surveyor's insistence on ever more excavations had caused access problems for the mower, and this required a fresh approach to the Tidy Churchyard Scheme. The community council had voted eight to one in the sheep's favour, the dissenting voice being the churchwarden, Mr Lugley, who stood to lose fifteen pounds a fortnight from his mowing stipend.)

Gareth flicked the sticky and unexpectedly heavy bone off his feet, back to Rupert. He wondered about evening classes, but had heard the choices were usually martial arts or dried-flower arrangements, neither of them an obvious way to create an improved bond with Moira.

'That's why he always likes his number ones. Usually finds something,' said the Commodore.

Lately she had started humming to herself, in a happy sort of way and for no apparent reason. This puzzled him. He had little experience of sustained smiling. He was glad to see her happy since for a while she'd seemed bored. Nonetheless, he felt excluded. Humming was not an activity for couples.

'It's male,' said the Commodore.

She also read books. Gareth did not object in principle, but found this strange after he'd been to the trouble of renting a twenty-four-inch television. Apparently, the Irish were the most well-read people in Europe. She had not taken kindly to his surprise at this fact. She had recently even gone as far as joining the library, and was often out hours choosing just the right book. Occasionally, he wondered if he would enjoy books.

'It's a Llewellyn, you know,' said the Commodore.

Gareth took comfort from the fact that the Commodore did not expect two-way conversations. Even the old boy's sister, blessed with the OBE, had been heard admitting that her brother sometimes made little sense. But then a parallel emerged from the muddle of Gareth's thoughts, and he realised how few two-way conversations there were in his marriage. Lately there was even a shortage of one-way conversations. Cul-de-sac conversations! He warmed to this use of traffic language. But then he tried to extend such analysis of his relationship to roundabouts and indicators, and realised he had stumbled into an intellectual minefield.

'He got a whole hand once.'

Rupert put the bone back on Gareth's boots.

'A hand?' said Gareth, the Commodore's words finally breaking through. 'A human hand?'

'Of course all the rings had gone. Looted years ago.'

Gareth looked down at the dog's bone resting on his boots, and hurriedly kicked it away into a trench.

The Commodore pointed through the fading light to the rusting, broken railings of the Llewellyn's Victorian vault. Inside, broken and upturned slabs, their inscriptions mossed beyond recognition, lay in a giant jumble. 'Dozens of the buggers!' he cried delightedly. For a moment, he became almost animated at the idea of his rivals being dispersed so liberally around the churchyard. 'Go, boy! Fetch!' He urged Rupert on towards the vault, and slowly the old dog set off to cannibalise some more Llewellyns.

'The Commodore gestured to Gareth to accompany him, and the pair followed the retired gun dog across the neatly nibbled grass.

The mysterious supply of bones had begun some months earlier, when the Commodore, unable to bear the thought of hours of unbroken bonhomie on New Year's Eve, had slipped away with the dog and a bottle of Pimm's and seen out the old year on a gravestone. Amidst all that night's number ones, Rupert had, with much snuffling, managed to assemble sufficient skeletal remains for a modest crime scene.

The two men peered down into the murk.

'My sister says they were parvenus,' sniffed the Commodore. Only to slightly weaken his position by adding, 'Sixteenth-century parvenus.'

There was little obvious sign of recent desecration. The damage of the looting seemed to belong to an earlier era, from a time, perhaps, when

Llewellyns had been buried with undue ostentation, flaunting their deaths in the face of their neighbours.

What was new, though, was a collapse in the side wall, some ten feet down. The earth had tumbled away, and taken with it several rotting coffins and their contents. The once whole occupants had burst through the wet blackened wood and come to a new last resting-place, but in a more informal arrangement of bones.

'Doggie heaven!' said the Commodore, who also seemed revivified.

Gareth, the more fleet of the two, made his way along the railings and found a fissure in the earth. It led towards the river end of the church.

As he came round the back of St Brynnach's, the cause was immediately apparent. Euan, the indefatigable diocesan surveyor and closet atheist, was now taking his inspiration from the Somme. In his search for bedrock, he had left no mud unturned. Out of sight from the road, his zeal to underpin the declining church had created a battlefield, zigzagged by trenches that could have hidden a tank company.

'OH, DON'T LIE DOWN! Please! Get up! I want you to look at me!'

Rob's entreaties had little effect, for Tinkerbell was sulking. His emollient tones had failed to move her; she had even refused to acknowledge his offer of potato peelings. Tinkerbell was not a happy pig.

It was the dog collar she had taken exception to. And the dog lead that attached her to the gatepost. Like any sensitive domestic pig, Tinkerbell liked to have a positive self-image: she saw herself as a born-free pig, with roaming in her blood. The idea of portraiture did not come easy.

Rob had been inking her in since dawn. He had left her snout till last, for it had a porcine ambiguity that he found difficult to capture. Doing the body had been a doddle, for the Vietnamese potbellied pig is a creature of simple, if eccentric, layout.

Tinkerbell's belly was almost spherical. To see her whizz around the garden was to watch a cannonball with legs. But unlike most cannonballs she had the soft baby bristles of a nascent Desperate Dan. And as Rob's thick nib filled out her bulk and gave her character, his mind filled with yet another image. He kept seeing her as a barrage balloon, tethered in the sky above the barn. For Tinkerbell had a nimbleness that made her seem weightless, that made one believe pigs really could fly.

As Rob struggled to realign her snout, she suddenly nuzzled him with the sort of sloppy, slimy kiss that set her apart from your normal life models.

'Am I interrupting something?' said the postman, appearing at the gate.

Distracted by art, Rob had for once not heard the engine of the mail van, revved into the red as it struggled up the last few yards of sodden track.

'No, just creativity,' replied Rob with a grin, pushing himself to his feet.

Dafydd looked at the work-in-progress on the easel, cocking his head slightly to one side, in that manner which laypersons believe appropriate to artistic appreciation. 'So it's true, then? You doing animals?'

'Who told you that?'

'Mrs Whitelaw.'

'Who's Mrs Whitelaw?'

'Buff Orpington eggs?' This detail did not aid Rob's understanding. 'Now, her hens would look good, all lined up outside her caravan.'

'Oh, well, I suppose I should be grateful for the way news travels.'

If Rob was philosophical about abandoning his ambitions as an artist, it was because he was essentially a romantic. He was in love with the romance of being a painter, with the romance of the painterly life. He had no artistic demons driving him, no inner urges dictating what he put on canvas. What he liked was the lifestyle, the image and the aura of the artist. If surviving in the valley meant a bit of Animal Realism, then Animal Realism it would be.

'Of course, farmers are very particular in this valley,' commented the postman, with his head at a new angle.

'I might have guessed.'

'They like their pigs to be pink.'

'And on a plate,' said Rob. 'Never mind. It's only a try-out, this one, anyway. 'S not for sale.'

'Oh, right! Looks good, though,' said the postman, backtracking. 'Very . . . er, piglike.'

'Thank you.'

Dafydd turned his attention to the mail and held out a brown foolscap envelope. 'So who d'you know in Aberystwyth, then?'

'Aberystwyth?' Rob shared his puzzlement. 'No one.' He shook the envelope, felt its weight. 'Bumph, I think.' He slid his finger into an unstuck corner and ripped the envelope open, leaving a jagged, black-smudged tear.

Inside the envelope were several photocopied sheets, with pictures of a wind-pump. The address meant nothing. And then he remembered Nico.

Who had said he knew a man who knew a man who . . . Rob instinctively turned away to read the pages, aware his pump was source of much mockery.

'Can I black the rest of your pig in. I used to like art at school.'

'If you want. The arse is a bit patchy. And you can fill in a leg.'

'Right.' The postman reached for the ink.

Rob looked more closely at the photos, and at the diagrams of blades and bolts, and at the accompanying graphs and numbers. As he skimmed across the tech specs he sensed confirmation that this was not a DIY project. He could only 'sense' it because he could not actually read the text. The text was in a language unknown to him. He assumed it was Welsh, but it was short on double 'l's and did not look very lyrical.

Reluctantly, Rob turned to the postman, who was inking away with vigour, and showed him a section of the text. 'Can you translate that, Dafydd? Is it Welsh?'

Dafydd peered at the paper, then admitted defeat. 'Don't know what it is. Looks a bit like German, but it's not. What's it on about?'

'Wind-pumps.'

Before either could say more, Gareth had squelched into the farmyard.

This was unusual. A distant wave of the shotgun was the usual limit of his sociability. His daily check on his sheep was done with eyes well averted from humans. Rob had once joined him in celebrating the rather messy birth of lamb triplets. But even then few words had been exchanged. Jane's theory was that Gareth wanted to talk—or at least his subconscious was keen to—but he didn't know the rules of conversation.

'Got any mail for me?'

A plausible question, but a pretext. An evening in the company of corpses had left even him feeling the need of a few convivial grunts. He had observed Rob from a distance, but didn't know what to say to a man who kept a pig on a lead. Then, when at the far end of the field, he had heard the van. After a lifetime of post he felt comfortable with Dafydd.

'What d'you reckon?' said Dafydd, stepping back from the almost completed pig.

Gareth moved closer and stared hard at the picture. And then thought and stared some more. 'Could do with a bit of tractor behind it.'

'Right,' said Rob.

'And a sheep would look better.'

'Right,' said Rob.

'And maybe some rain.'

'Rob's branching out,' said Dafydd. 'Farm animals.'

'I know,' replied Gareth. He wondered whether telling Moira about the postman helping paint the pig would make her laugh.

'Oh,' said Dafydd, slightly deflated by his answer. 'Did you know about the Dragon's Head?' he asked, by way of revenge.

'That odd bloke's trying to buy it.'

'*Bought* it! Had surveyors in. They told him it'd got dry rot. He told them to sod off. And he bought it anyway.'

Gareth had lived through some changes in his lifetime, but this was one of the biggest. 'D'you reckon he'll allow a dartboard?'

'Topless barmaids, I've heard.'

Gareth failed to spot a wind-up, and his heart raced disconcertingly fast for several moments. But then Dafydd reluctantly admitted he had no details; and the pair fell to speculating about themed Irish pubs and fruit machines. It was broadly agreed that a bar with more than one brand of beer—and probably still on sale after children's bedtime—would be an improvement. As would service without abuse. As would crisps. Even plain. And yet somehow Gareth could not shake off a lingering melancholy. It was as if a stranger had bought his living room.

Meanwhile, Rob's mind had drifted and was on its way to Aberystwyth. In his dreams he was already an eco-pioneer, and fit subject for another Clydog profile. He was eager to tell his news to Jane, but her acupuncture exams were coming and she was down at the old schoolhouse practising on Bryony. The friendship had begun with a shared interest in organic vegetables. During the early days of the vegetable patch, when the hoe kept hitting the leftovers of the lounge, Hubert's delicatessen had been the sole source of life's rarer vitamins. Some days they would see her on the road and give her a lift home, where she would entertain them with the follies of the valley, and occasionally a folksong. Bryony was outside the mainstream, in a sweet-natured if wild-child way, and this was unusual in the land of the Nant. Both Rob and Jane found much to their liking in her freewheeling approach, her eco-friendly habits, her warm-hearted nature.

'I said what d'you reckon, Rob?' repeated the postman.

'Sorry. Reckon to what?'

'I've heard there might be call for some sort of artwork down the new pub. You be interested?'

'Artwork?' Rob laughed. 'They'll have to speak to my agent!'

Dafydd laughed as well, aware the answer was yes. He put the round, dip-pen nib back on the easel, and ruffled Tinkerbell's pliant ears. As he nodded farewell he even forgot to ask, as he always mockingly asked, how long before Rob and Jane could afford to repair their track. And with the wheelspin of a rally driver he was gone.

'Can you give one as a present?'

Rob was caught unawares and he looked blankly at the farmer.

'Can you give one as a present? A painting?' Gareth asked again.

'Of course you can,' said Rob, baffled by the question.

'It wouldn't be odd?'

'It wouldn't be odd at all. It would be a nice thing to do.'

'Right. I just wondered.'

And with that, Gareth too was off down the field.

'WILDEBEEST?' said Hubert incredulously.

Stéfan sighed, trying to hide his exasperation. 'That was just a for instance,' he said, irritated at the man's failure to grasp the bigger picture. 'It could be, I don't know, water buffalo, or bison, or gazelles.'

The President of the Chamber of Commerce toyed with his pipe, avoiding Stéfan's eyes. 'We don't get a lot of demand for water buffalo.'

'You don't get a lot of supply either. That's my point.'

He was making little headway. Even the delicatessen, which had led the county in aubergine, struggled to cater for Stéfan's vaulting ambitions. His latest idea, for a game park and abattoir in his grounds, was everywhere running into the swamp of small minds.

Where Rob blew with the wind, and adapted to the valley in the hope he might survive, Stéfan blew back at the wind, and strove to bend the valley to his will. This was the age-old choice of strategies for incomers, as ever lured on by the chimera of social acceptance. But in the Nant Valley the only true path to acceptance was to be fourth generation. And Stéfan had scarcely patience to be first generation.

So far he had a pub with dry rot and no beer, and a large collection of scaffolding poles with a house attached. He had decided to open a third front, and it was wildebeest. Or water buffalo. Or whatever. The estate had for some time been a thornbush in his side. As planned, he had enhanced his landowner's status with a pair of Rhodesian ridgebacks—but in the absence of local lions they had twice breakfasted on sheep and cows, and a magistrate had judged this unneighbourly.

For a while, his fickle attention span had alighted on rare breeds, but Stéfan could never quite see the need for endless minor variants on goats and sheep and pigs. Apart from some quirks of nature, like a kink in the tail or a toe too many, they all looked the same—and equally dull—as their more successful counterparts.

It was the Pick Your Own fields of strawberries—in more enterprising England—that had given him the idea for a game park. Initially, the concept was Longleat with a difference—various exotic animals roaming his swards, and large placards by the roadside saying Shoot Your Own, with family barbecue sites in a compound. Petty legal minds had sabotaged this idea and now he was exploring more practical options.

'Don't get a lot of supply? I should bloody hope not!' snorted Hubert in response. 'I've not got much room for water buffalo! Would they be sliced ready for sandwiches?'

'You slice venison for sandwiches,' Stéfan replied, skewering his objection. 'What's the difference?'

'Have you researched the water-buffalo market?'

'Look, forget water buffalo. That's just a for instance. I'm talking exotic meats. The top end of the market. Eating like you're on safari.'

'But my customers aren't top end of the market,' retorted Hubert. 'It took three years to interest them in pepperoni.' He grimaced.

'That's just a question of marketing.'

'And how are you going to market wildebeest? Get David Attenborough behind the counter?'

Stéfan was a broad-brushstrokes man and offered no view on the subject. He was beginning to weary of the conversation. His vision had not carried. He needed firmer, more detailed proposals, maybe a visit to the zoo.

The irony of the exchange was that Hubert, too, viewed himself as an adventurous entrepreneur, forever pushing back the boundaries of the Abernantian palate. And in truth Hubert rather took to Stéfan, who, until an hour before, he had only known as a customer—the only one ever to have bulk-bought his quails' eggs. Hubert was tempted to ask if he felt strongly about the proposed car-parking charges, since volunteers were needed for the next round of direct action. Instead, having deftly derailed the plan to bring the veld to the valley, he said, 'Have you thought about olives?'

Stéfan, who was eager to leave Hubert's smoky backroom office, sank down again in his chair, unable to hide his surprise. 'Olives?' he repeated.

Hubert smiled, as befitted a man blessed with the trump card of a special discount. 'You could still make history,' he said. 'First pub in the area with olives.'

IT WAS RAINING heavily when Stéfan arrived at the pub—now his pub—for the second of his three appointments that day. The 200-year-old building was locked and in gloom, almost as if pining for trade. Sheltering in its tiny porch was Rob.

Rob and Stéfan had never quite met. Stéfan had once forced Rob's car off the road when on the way to The Windowman. Rob had once seen Stéfan weighed down with charity sponge cakes at the Commodore's. And the postman had kept each abreast of the other's odder doings. It was not a perfect basis for friendship.

Stéfan shoulder-charged the jammed door after finally getting the key to turn. Inside, the flagstones gave off damp and the air smelt unhealthy. He switched the lights on at the fuse box. The Formica tops were still stained with slops. Behind the bar, the few crates were full of empties; the only sign of alcoholic life was three elderly bottles of tonic in the fridge, probable result of some long-forgotten error in ordering.

'All going to be gutted!' said Stéfan. 'With sensitivity.'

Rob had not been inside since he and Jane had failed to order pasta, on their very first day in the valley. He looked around at the brown, smoke-stained walls, only now aware of the dismal decay of the place.

'Secret ambition, was it? Own a pub?'

'No, bought it because I like a drink. And if I own it, I can't be thrown out of it.'

'Can't fault that logic,' said Rob. 'Perhaps I should buy one.'

Their voices echoed as the dominoes once had.

'Going to have a restaurant. Pub and restaurant. Something a bit special.'

Rob looked around the walls a second time. A few uplighters in the alcoves, and his stylised nimbuses and windswept hills would look almost homely. 'Teg and Ben with ties, eh? That'll be worth seeing.'

'Yeah, well, I'll have to hide the locals. Extend the snug into the farm-yard.' He laughed. 'Or encourage them to go and drink somewhere else!'

Rob glanced across at Stéfan as he boomed with laughter, only to realise he was about 10 per cent joking and 90 per cent serious. Rob went with the 10 per cent, and sniggered uneasily in his wake. 'So. The walls, you having a neutral colour scheme?'

'Ah, all that's still under wraps. But I've told the designer, "Golden rule of décor—no chintz". What it will be is classy. We're having silverware, plus live music, no tapes. And if Clydog does the restaurant review, he'll have a coronary! Now, the mayoress tells me you're a painter. Gather you had an exhibition, full of lifelike pictures of washing machines!' Stéfan burst into laughter at his own wit.

Rob smiled thinly. 'Yes. A collection of my local work, the valley in all weathers. As a group, I think they'd create a good atmosphere in here.'

Stéfan's brow furrowed. 'In here? I don't want any of your paintings!'

'You . . . you don't? Oh.' Rob paused. 'But I thought the postman said—'

'No.' Stéfan took him by the arm and led him back through the bar and out into the rain. He pointed upwards. 'I want a new pub sign.'

Blinking in the downpour, Rob stared up at the paint flaking off the dragon.

'Can you do that?'

'Well . . . er, yes . . . I suppose so.'

'Good.'

'Though I've never done a dragon before.'

'I don't want another fucking dragon! I want a picture of *me*!'

'Of you?' The rain ran in rivulets down Rob's face as he pondered on this latest unexpected development.

'Yes.'

'Outside the pub? On a sign?'

'Yes.'

'Oh . . . Oh, I see . . .'

Rob wondered how to explain to Stéfan that this was not a British tradition. Unless he were both landlord and king. Which of course he might have plans to be. Rob was also wondering how best to advise him of the belly laughs that would ensue. Yet at the same time, he was keen to observe the rules of the painter/patron relationship.

'Is there a problem?' demanded Stéfan rudely. 'You can do portraits?' His final rendezvous of the day was at home in under ten minutes, and he was growing impatient. He was now both late and wet—neither of which is good for a first date. Especially with a predatory horsewoman.

But then again, thought Rob, being a laughing stock is *his* problem. And the commission would help pay for heating their bathwater in an environmentally responsible way. 'Yes, I can do portraits,' he replied.

'Good. I'll send you some photos. My best side. Both of them!' Then Stéfan sealed the deal with a hurried handshake, his mind on haste and lust. A curt farewell, and he started running back towards his car.

'Oh, hang on!' Rob called after him. 'There is a problem!'

Stéfan squelched to a stop. 'What?'

'Won't it look odd to have "The Dragon's Head" written across your face?'

'Oh, sorry!' Stéfan had the grace to grin. Then he shouted through the rain, 'I forgot to say. There's been a change of name.'

'Oh? What's the pub called now?'

'The Stéfan Arms.'

Chapter 15

Felicity warmed her damp buttocks against the study fire. From auction marquee to hearth-rug had taken her longer than she planned, even though she specialised in collecting country toffs. Her last encounter with Stéfan had been in the spring. She had engaged him in libidinous eye contact by the hoopla stand, yet in the absence of further fêtes their weekend worlds had failed to collide. While she went to point-to-points, Stéfan's quality time was occupied by estate management and issuing death threats to workmen. But, as hunt secretary, Felicity knew how to run a quarry to earth. And by leaving answerphone messages that laid coded stress on her love of bareback riding she had at last won a place in his diary.

Felicity was not of the county set, and was acutely conscious that her bloodline was less impressive than that of her horse. This insecurity had led her into a life of overcompensation, overdoing her vowels, her Sloane accessories and her lipstick. As lackey to the hunt, she had a haughtiness worthy of Royal Warrant. Yet still her stock did not pass muster, and the best hope for her future lay with moneyed men who could not tell a fake.

Felicity stretched herself full length along the rug, loosened another button, and let out a languorous sigh as she waited for her new man. Mrs

Grotichley had that morning been given two commands: to produce some assorted *petits fours*, and to bugger off. She had adequately done the latter, and Stéfan was now busy in the kitchen, arranging her eight macaroons in a semblance of artistry upon a plate.

Stéfan did not seduce women so much as overwhelm them, and they usually surrendered. Wherever possible he liked to combine sex with an ulterior motive, making it the sort of dual-purpose activity so highly recommended by time-and-motion studies. So even as he prepared to charm the jodhpurs off Felicity, his motives were no more exclusively carnal than hers. Where her inner desires were for high-quality stabling, he had set his heart on the hunt. And membership thereof. Certainly he had nothing equine in mind, and no desire to fall in hedges, but the social cachet of hunt-ball circles was a nut he wished to crack. For this way lay contacts and contracts, this way lay funny handshakes and old money.

'Macaroons and Bolly!' he announced at the study door.

Felicity had undone another button. As she always did when in doubt.

Stéfan laid the tray on the floor and sat down beside her, leaning against the dark green leather of his chesterfield. As he looked at her reclining in the firelight, he realised for the first time that she had a halfway decent body, apart from the usual horse damage to her bottom.

'So,' she said, in what she believed to be seductive tones, 'Stay-fan. What sort of a name is Stay-fan?'

'Georgian.'

'Georgian?'

'From Georgia.'

'Oh.'

He could tell that, as he'd expected, she was none the wiser. He rarely offered information on his background, but he felt sure any secrets would be safe with her, safeguarded by her incomprehension.

'Near Azerbaijan?' he added, as if helpfully. 'Nagorno-Karabakh?'

She shook her head.

'Armenia . . . ?'

She shook it again.

'How about the Caucasus? . . . You familiar with the Caucasus?'

'Not really,' she replied.

'Well, anyway, that's where I come from. It's where Stalin came from.'

'Oh. Did you know him?'

'Not closely, no.' He poured her a glass of champagne. 'Georgians are famous for being very wild, and poetic, and passionate!'

'Super,' said Felicity.

Outside, the afternoon rain was easing off, the steady patter on the windowpanes giving away to a silence made homely by the crackling of the firewood.

Stéfan made his move. He slid down alongside her on the floor, and murmured (as far as it was possible for him to ever murmur), 'D'you want to drink the Bolly or have it poured over your nipples?'

She giggled, but in the manner of someone who found this a fairly routine choice. 'And what are you going to do with my macaroon?'

He took this as a yes to sex, pausing only to leer and say, 'Oh, I'm sure I'll find a place to put it,' before he set to work on her remaining buttons.

The jodhpurs (which she wore with or without horse) were an advanced obstacle to seduction. Being an old-fashioned sort of man, he felt it was his responsibility to rip a woman's clothing off, but the heavy-duty material cleaved to her limbs like an equestrian wet suit. It defeated his ripping techniques and he had to call for assistance.

But they still made good time and Felicity was down to a small pair of frilly red things in approximately one minute forty-five seconds by his grandfather clock.

She wrapped her legs around him and the pair tussled in erotic mayhem for several moments. These were legs that won rosettes for dressage, restraining stallions from their urge to bolt, and Stéfan soon found himself pinned as if by railings. Whelps of pleasure from Felicity gave a bawdy hint of unconventional tastes to come.

She liked his bulk, and warmed to his arrogance. It turned her on that he showed no sign of inhibitions, and owned an endless number of rooms in which to prove it. Yet there was also a puppy dog chaos to his advances that, with her love of animals, she found engaging.

Stéfan dragged her onto her back and tugged down the last of her lingerie. She began to utter noises that made him glad he had no neighbours for nearly an acre. Convulsively she arched her body into the air, and he was frenziedly kicking off the last of his clothing when there was a tap at the window.

Stéfan looked up over the sofa. The clouds had started to lift and a watery sun was shining on the rain-streaked glass. On the far side of it stood Mr Griffith Barton, The Windowman. Waving a tape measure.

Immediately, Stéfan's heart began to pound.

The Windowman tapped again.

'He's come at last!' cried Stéfan.

'He's what? Who has?'

'The Windowman! He's come to do the windows!'

'Well, tell him to fuck off!'

'I can't!' cried Stéfan, 'I can't!' He scrabbled for his trousers in high excitement. 'I've waited nine months for this!'

'So have I!' she screamed. Although used to rejection, she had never before lost out to a man with a ladder and khaki camouflage.

But Stéfan ignored her. And, still struggling with his zip, he rushed from the room to go and greet his tradesman.

ROB WENT DOWN into town from the Dragon's Head. He wanted a language lesson from Nico, and some explanation of the mystery letter.

Rob always felt uneasy when he met Nico. He knew too many facts and had too much charm. It was a phoney charm, and some of the facts felt false, but Rob had yet to find a way to derail him. How Nico had become his agent still remained unclear to Rob, though his advice so far seemed sound. But Rob had a feeling he was not a good person to annoy.

Nico's antiques shop was on a side street, on the corner of an eighteenth-century alley, and offered the poky promise of an Aladdin's cave. He knew how to dress a shop window with just the right balance of bric-à-brac and treasure trove, tat and promise. Inside was a clutter of farmers' cast-offs. On every side, some glassware, some porcelain, some records, some bookcases, some books. Plus several of that traditional standby, the Welsh dresser.

Nico had his back to Rob, and was negotiating with an attractive woman in her thirties, notable for a shock of frizzed auburn hair. She was carrying a large raffia bag and had laid out its contents on a battered gateleg table. Alerted by the tinkling of the wind chimes, Nico glanced round, and was a little surprised to see Rob. He made a quick apology and hurried over.

'I've got a rock-solid buyer this time,' he said in a confident whisper. 'Vintage tractor dealer in East Anglia. He just needs to clear time to collect it.'

'Oh, damn!' said Rob. 'I'd rather hoped to hang on to it a little longer.'

'You do? Whatever for?'

'Artistic backdrop. Bit of agricultural history behind the animals. In a nice red. Got some definite interest in that idea.'

'Oh. Yes, I can see why . . . could be a good gimmick. OK.'

'OK? But what about your buyer?'

'Oh, I was lying.'

And with that, Nico hurried back to his customer and resumed examination of her items. As Rob wandered round the shop, idly checking out the prices, he could hear snatches of their conversation: Nico, professionally sad, sighing and regretful, the woman, insistent, needy and argumentative. He watched as a carriage clock and an early American flag changed hands. There followed a disagreement over the value of a lava lamp. Several objects, including a garlic crusher, remained unsold. The woman put these back in her bag somewhat disconsolately and threaded her way out of the shop, the door opened and closed by an unctuous Nico.

'Never get divorced!' declared Nico, in worldly summary. 'She's from up your way, that one. Part-time teacher. D'you know her?'

Rob shook his head.

'Lives in a caravan now. Whitelaw, Mrs Whitelaw.'

'Oh, the Buff Orpingtons!'

Nico looked at him as if he were mad, then went on, 'Bank's turned nasty for some reason. Wants its loan back. That's when they all come in here, bank trouble.' He refocused. 'So, people showing interest, you say?'

'In my paintings? Yes. Yes, a few farmers starting to come out the woodwork. Seem to want a family group, most of them. Daddy bull, mummy cow, baby heifers and a duck thrown in!'

'Well, the sooner you start to make your name, the sooner we can get into the spin-offs. You paint 'em cute enough and we can start thinking posters and T-shirts, and—who knows?—mugs, teapots and playing cards!'

Before Rob could plead integrity, the irritating chimes tinkled again and a middle-aged couple came into the shop. He let the issue drop. 'What do you know about Aberystwyth?'

'Let me know if I can help you,' Nico called to the couple, his accent upgraded a notch. He turned back to Rob. 'Er, town on the west coast. Rain tastes of salt. Where university students go to die of boredom.'

Rob held up the letter. 'Why do they speak Swedish there?'

Nico glanced at it. 'Aaah. They don't. It's Dutch.'

'Dutch? OK, why do they speak Dutch?'

'They don't. That's from head office—in Holland.'

'So why am I getting a letter from Holland?

'Lot of wind in Holland.'

'True.'

'And this contact of mine—the one who's into eco-things—he knows a firm sells their wind-pumps in Aberystwyth. So, as a favour, I passed on your name.' (The word 'commission' hovered over that sentence like a ghost at the party.)

'Sounds promising,' Rob confessed.

'Antiques isn't just antiques. It's contacts.' Nico's eyes kept darting away from Rob, following the new customers around the shop like an undercover agent's, sensitive to every nuance that might mean money.

'Guess I'd better get over to Aberystwyth,' said Rob. 'You know, I've spent the best part of a year looking for someone that makes wind-pumps!'

'Oh, they don't actually *make* wind-pumps in Aberystwyth.'

'But I thought—'

'No, the firm just sells them. Supplies them. They come from Holland.'

'So why—'

'Look, I'd better attend to this pair.' Nico's interest in wind-pumps was waning. 'I'm on my own here.' He turned and squeezed past a six-foot wooden hayfork. 'Sion's left me in the lurch.'

'What, that lad who never spoke? With the suntan?'

'That's the one.' Nico pulled a face. 'Supposed adult. Just disappeared last week, not a word of warning. Like he'd been abducted by aliens. Now, you'll have to excuse me a moment. Money calls.'

Rob was not in the mood to wait, and left.

THE SUMMER was just about over, its arrival and departure noticed only by the calendar, its one seasonal concession the warmth of its rain. Now was the time of year when incomers had second thoughts.

Dafydd was more aware than most of the cusp of autumn. This was the season of mists and heavy removal vans, when 'Please Forward' was the leitmotif of letters. To him, a postman, the cycle of life meant the urban idyll-seekers returning like salmon to spawn in the city. For some incomers, the process took one year, for others, it took five. For some, the cause was the absence of street lighting, for others, it was the failure to grow sprouts.

Dafydd claimed to have a nose for those whose dreams would die.

Sometimes it was their words: the wish to 'commune with nature' provides an early hint of trouble. Sometimes it was their actions: strangling a neighbour's cockerel bodes ill for integration. And sometimes it was their attitude: a belief that 'good morning' can be said in under five minutes reveals the irredeemably urban.

Which is why, as the postman drove back down the valley on that last Saturday of summer, fresh from his deliveries to Crug Caradoc and Pantglas, he was pondering on the prospects for their owners. In his twenty-odd years of Royal Mail service, he had consoled many a pining exile. However, there had as yet been no call for a sympathetic shoulder from either Stéfan or Rob. Each had had their little local difficulties and each had seen their best-laid plans go bottom-up. Yet their unorthodoxy had given them resilience, and their battles with the valley were going the distance. Indeed, they were even making headway, as he had witnessed that very morning.

Yet to be a gossip is usually to be a cynic, dependent on the worst in others. So Dafydd and his hunches quietly took the long view, and he stayed host to the thought that their dreams could still end in disaster.

'Is this scaffolding safe?' asked The Windowman.

'Surprised you believe in scaffolding,' retorted Stéfan. 'Thought you'd take the purist approach. Hang by a rope from the gutter.' Now that Stéfan had a pick-up truck full of finished windows in his drive, he felt less constrained in his manner.

If anything, it seemed The Windowman was flattered. He gave a vestige of a smile as he put his foot upon the sill and prepared to climb out of the bedroom window, or rather, out of the space awaiting a window. He did not hurry. The ground floor now done, this was his tenth new window of the week, and the work had put him in reflective mood.

'Tell me something.' He looked at Stéfan. 'I've met a few crowned heads in my time . . .'

Stéfan, who was about to object to the effect of army boots on his freshly painted windowsill, elected to wait for the completion of the sentence.

'Well, pretenders to crowns, mainly. Kings-in-exile, that sort of thing. They used to exchange postcards with my wife. Her being Habsburg. Well, lapsed, of course.'

Stéfan's attention was no longer focused on the army boots.

'And in the old days—when we were first married—we'd take trips, and visit some of these royal pretenders at home. Provide a bit of company for them. Because it's a lonely business, waiting for the call to come from your people. It can sometimes take a lifetime to get your throne back.'

For some reason, Stéfan found it hard not to nod.

'So Helga and I, we were able to see how they lived, these monarchs-in-waiting.' The Windowman pulled himself up on the sill, one hand upon a scaffolding pole, then turned and looked down onto Stéfan. 'And, by and large, they had fewer windows. So tell me. You're a single man. Why do you need a house this size?'

Stéfan showed no signs of a ready answer. Not because he had no answer, but because he was struggling to understand why anyone would ask the question. In the end, he said, 'To keep you in business!'

It was a good answer, and they both laughed. And the moment of human contact was over. The Windowman manoeuvred himself out onto the planks of the scaffolding, and checked the frame was millimetre perfect in its new home.

Stéfan watched from within, running his fingers along the beautifully grained wood of the new window. 'By next spring, they'll be profiling this place in *Country Life*! Hire a few debs with pearls, and I'll be Squire of the Month. Now that's worth splashing out on!'

'If you want to be burgled,' said The Windowman gloomily. 'And I'd be grateful if you said the windows were from MFI. I have quite enough prats turning up, thank you.'

Over the months, The Windowman had discovered one of the few pleasures in working for Stéfan was that his ego made him almost impervious to insults, and The Windowman was able to indulge his innate misanthropy to gratifying lengths.

Not that Stéfan was entirely immune to pique. What did stick in his craw was that he was the employer of a workman who might, had history turned out differently, have inherited Hungary.

This galling thought gave him the urge to go up himself on the scaffolding, for there he could bask in the therapeutic vista of his own estate. He gripped the pole, squeezed past The Windowman, and pulled himself out. The summer rain was pattering gently on his trout lakes, and in the oak woodland the first leaves were giving up their green. He promenaded carefully along the planks and past the bedrooms, looking in a great arc from east to west. Though still short on statuary and beasts of the jungle, he took much pride in his acreage. He was master of all he surveyed for nearly as far as the pub, and a warm glow of vainglory enveloped him.

But most of all Stéfan gloried in the ancient house, whose creepered walls were at last being punctuated by windows worthy of the name. Single-handed, give or take a craftsman, he was now reversing the neglect of decades. And from this he gained a real—and rare—sense of achievement.

'DON'T PAINT lamb chops, do you, mate? Because I'd buy that!' laughed the first wind-pump man, struggling past Rob's easel with a rotor blade.

'Yeah, make mine a leg steak!' laughed the second wind-pump man, following him out of the barn with a coil of wire over his shoulder.

'I'd, er . . . I'd like the middle sheep to have a bit of a smile,' said Gareth, who was nervously observing Rob's brushwork from the barn door.

It was not just the sheep that were short of a smile. These were not ideal circumstances for an artist to carry out his first commissioned painting. Rob had told Gareth that he considered it best to paint generalised sheep, sheep typical of their kind, the common sheep. But Gareth had it in his head to commit to posterity his favourite sheep, sheep whose character marked them out, whose features had meaning for him and Moira. To this end, he had herded three of his finest up from his lowland fields, and proposed their arrangement in a tableau.

At approximately the same moment, the two burly wind-pump men had arrived without warning—and with a multitude of wind-pump parts—after setting off before breakfast from the far side of the Cambrian Mountains. There being a financial nexus between these two events, Rob felt unable to spurn either party.

And now all were busy in the barn, art at one end, wind-pump assembly at the other. One and a half sheep had taken bodily form, and a steel mast was firmly fixed to Rob's chimney.

'Give it a smile?' he repeated. 'Is it a smiley sort of sheep, that one?' Even as he spoke, his attention was being distracted by an extension ladder quivering in the vicinity of his eighteenth-century chimney pots.

'I want her to look homely. Women like homely things, don't they?'

There came a clang, and a shout of 'Steady there!'

'I suppose so,' said Rob, who had never counted homeliness among Jane's virtues. The ladder wobbled under the weight of the man who had the rotor blade, now struggling up the chimney to begin the bolting-on.

'I think of the middle one as mother,' said Gareth.

'Mother?' said Rob, echoing on autopilot. Out of the corner of his eye he could see the man who had the wire, now examining several component parts with the tentative approach of a bomb disposal officer.

'Mother and family. Not real family, obviously. Because they've gone to the abattoir. But make-believe family.' Rarely had Gareth spoken so much.

Rarely had Rob listened so little. 'Everything all right?' he called.

'Fine!' cried the first wind-pump man.

'Fine!' cried the second wind-pump man.

Rob wondered about their grasp of Dutch. He turned back to his painting. 'D'you want the sheepdog in as well?'

'Umm. Not sure,' said Gareth. 'You're the expert. What d'you reckon?'

Rob stepped back in the way artists do when they want a better perspective. With years of shepherding skills at his disposal, Gareth had arranged his three sheep in what art critics might describe as an agricultural triptych: two sheep sitting, the middle one ('Smiler') standing. Given the barn setting, this had oddly biblical overtones, and the half-complete painting suggested how the Nativity would have been portrayed by Stubbs. Except that in the background of the picture, where one might have expected to see a little Lord Jesus, there was a bright red combine harvester.

'Homely,' Rob declared. 'The dog would look homely.'

He reserved a spot for the dog and then went back to fleshing out his three lifelike sheep. He gave them a bulky quality, the muscular armature of sheep wearing a fleece two sizes too big. Were it not for the smile they could have been mistaken for gangster sheep. Rob was finishing off mother when the wireman wandered over from the parts department.

'Not come across a wiring diagram, have you?'

'No, sorry. Is it important?'

'No, no, nothing to worry about.' The wireman was looking over Rob's shoulder at the painting. 'Those animals, should they be that size?'

'It's primitivism.'

'Oh. But aren't sheep normally smaller than tractors?'

'Bloody hell, it was wet and windy on that chimney!' said the rotor-blade man, bursting into the barn to join them.

'You done up there, then?' asked Rob.

'Yeah. It's solid as a rock. Well, solid as glass fibre reinforced polyester. Just got to connect all the bits together now.'

'Not a day too soon either. Be glad to get shot of my old generator!'

The wind-pump men began to rummage through the various parts that lay across the floor of the barn. Through the gaping entrance Rob had a clear view of his virgin turbine, a glistening addition to the skyline. Its profile had elegance and simplicity, like a silver bow tie that was born for the wind. It stood, still tethered to the mast for safety, as if waiting for a giant finger to spin it into action.

'You don't know what an inverter looks like, do you, mate?' asked the wireman.

'A what?' said Rob.

'An inverter.'

'An "inverter"? No idea. What's it do?'

'God knows! Just thought, you being one of these green sorts—'

'Hang on! Hang on! How come you don't know what it does? *Or* what it looks like?'

'Don't get aerated! There's a lot of bits here, mate.'

'And you're supposed to be able to put them together!' snapped Rob.

'I know. And we will. It's just it's the first wind-pump we've done.'

'What if we had a ram in it?' mused Gareth, who had moved further into the barn for a better look at his first commissioned work.

'*The first one you've done?*' said Rob.

'Well, it's the first one we've sold.'

Rob was not normally an angry person, but on this occasion he was prepared to make an exception. Unfortunately, he was angry at Nico, and Nico was not there. Rob felt all interest in art ebbing and he clenched his fists and glowered. He moved away from the painting and paced up and down, taking care to avoid the heating coil, the control unit, the permanent magnet, the brushless generator, the galvanic steel units, and the other lo-tech bric-à-brac which now lay strewn across his flagstoned floor.

The two men waited for him to calm down. The rotor-blade man thrust his cold hands deep into his overalls and wandered over to have a look at the sheep triptych. His partner had another go at connecting the wire that would turn wind into water.

'Should they be that size, those sheep?'

'It's primitivism,' said the wireman.

'So if,' said Rob, returning with improved composure, 'if you don't do wind-pumps, what do you do?'

'It's not we *don't* do them,' said the rotor-blade man, 'it's more that we're diversifying into them.'

'I see. So what do you normally do? I mean, what's your line of work?'

'Oh, that'd be agricultural hardware.'

'Yes, firm's been doing agricultural hardware over twenty years now.'

'What, farm generators and things?'

'Not exactly,' said the rotor-blade man.

'More sort of . . .' The wireman hesitated. 'Milk churns.'

Chapter 16

Two weeks had passed, and Gareth was a happy man, even an excited man. He had just auctioned six heifers at a profit, he was on his fifth pint in the Market Tavern, and at noon the picture framer would be finished. In less than an hour, Moira would be the proud owner of the first framed painting of stock in the family's history. *And* he'd managed to keep it a surprise.

Such was his enthusiasm that he was even ending his drinking early. The all-day licence of market day, the saloon-bar crush of noisy farmers, the post-mortem minutiae of meat sales, this was normally the high point of his week, a heady mix for a man who so often stood alone in wet fields. Usually he would totter out as the empty livestock pens were being hosed down, and go home with early evening coming on. But today he was on a mission.

As he left behind the roar of the bar and the dank Barbour odours, he came across Dafydd, also on his way out. 'You off early too?'

'I wish!' said Dafydd.

'I'm collecting a framed painting of my sheep. For the wife.'

'She'll think Christmas has come early.'

'You're not married, are you?'

'I have my moments. That little red van's a turn-on for some women!'

On a less momentous day, Gareth might have asked for details. After a few more pints, Dafydd might have offered them.

'You're lucky,' said Gareth. 'Don't think a tractor ever turned anyone on.'

They went down the alley that led into town. Behind them, a cow mooed with panic as it was corralled towards the auction ring. Ahead of them, the grey slate roofs managed to look aesthetic and depressing at the same time. Storm clouds were forming over the mountains, and a strong wind was beginning to gust litter into the air.

'It's looking a bit rough,' said Dafydd.

'I've shot moles in worse.'

They walked down along the High Street, navigating around the farmers' wives bursting to spend the cash from the carcasses of market day. It was no longer a high street where spending was easy, for of late, despite the best efforts of the Chamber of Commerce, almost every second shop had become a charity shop. Nor indeed was the navigating easy, for of late, despite the best efforts of Hubert, its President, works were in their final throes for the county's first parking meters. The blight of modernity was gaining ground.

In the distance, they spotted Clydog who struggled to doff his hat in the wind.

'You going for a gossip at the deli?' Gareth asked the postman, almost garrulous amidst the slew of new emotions he was coming across.

'Maybe later. I'm just off to be "appraised".'

'I was appraised last year. Gave me the all clear. Apart from cold sores.'

'No. No, not the Well Man Clinic. My boss.'

'Oh, I see. Glad I don't have a boss.'

'If I owned a gun I wouldn't have! Know his latest bloody idea?' The postman was on to his hobbyhorse. 'Annual "performance monitoring and assessment". Annual bollocks, more like!'

And then they reached the crossroads and went their separate ways.

It was just fifty yards to the picture-framing shop, a shop whose existence Gareth had never known of until a week before. Tucked in the alley opposite Nico's antiques, it was run by a tight-lipped man who had established that 48 inches x 30 inches was the optimum frame size.

The picture was ready for him, leaning against the wall alongside black and white photographs of the mountains and drawings of small hairy dogs in baskets. He hoped the owner would pass approving comment, but he said nothing apart from offering to wrap it. Gareth refused his offer. He had in his head this image of walking into their farmhouse and holding the picture up in front of his face. He did, however, accept the suggestion of temporary brown paper.

It was five minutes of unsteady walk to his empty cattle truck and fifteen minutes of low-gear work to his farm. The farm and its outbuildings stood quite high on the eastern side of the valley, with a view of the river and the church below. Above him on the ridge lay Pantglas and Rob's studio-barn.

Gareth drove the cattle truck slowly into the farmyard, around his Land Rover, and parked in the large barn. He clambered out of the driver's cab, handling his painting like china as he muttered his way through a short speech. Then he slipped softly round to the back of the farm, to the farmhouse kitchen where Moira spent her days. He crouched low as he passed the window and, easing the latch with his bottom, he burst in backwards, spun round and held the painting aloft.

To his surprise she was not there. Her apron was there, and the early stages of the stew were there. But of her there was no sign.

Gareth had choreographed this moment for weeks and now felt cheated of his triumph. A triumph with no back-up plan. He wondered whether to down a sixth beer while he waited for her to return from his parents, from their bungalow just across the yard. . . . And then he heard the tell-tale creak of floorboards above his head. And he suddenly realised the truth. Had he known Moira better, he would have realised it immediately. For him, Friday was market day, but for her, it was the day she changed the sheets.

He set off up the stairs, torn between the desire to run and the need to be silent. The treads were cracked and creaky, and he moved on tiptoe from safe step to safe step, the picture held in outstretched hands.

Fortunately, the bedroom door was ajar. Gareth counted silently to three, like the armed response groups he had seen on TV, then barged open the door, and burst in, the huge painting clutched to his upper body.

Mr Blake's orgasm suffered an immediate setback, but, arguably, it was Gareth Richards who suffered the greater shock. It wasn't just the infidelity. He simply hadn't expected his first-ever encounter with oral sex would involve a third party from the world of banking, and certainly not from a local branch. So shocked was he that initially he forgot to lower the painting, and continued to peer over the top like a visiting voyeur.

Moira decided not to emerge for the moment. Conversation with her husband was difficult at the best of times.

And still no one spoke. Denial seemed, in the circumstances, to be a lost cause. But recrimination required a level of fluency to which Gareth could not rise. He felt he would be verbally outmanoeuvred by a bank manager, as he had been the last time he asked for a loan. And he was a foot too short for a fight. He continued to stare, angry, confused, betrayed, helpless.

Not knowing where he was going, he left.

Not knowing what he was doing, he took Rob's picture with him.

He clattered back down the stairs, through the house, and out into the yard. He leaned against his Land Rover, struggling to regain his thoughts. Then an impulse took him. He threw the painting down in the deepest mud. He got into the 4 x 4, started up—and drove over the painting. Then he reversed over it, went forward over it, reversed again, went forward again, and continued back and forth, back and forth, until its all-terrain tyres had crushed the last piece of canvas from sight.

After that he rested his head upon the steering wheel and slumped in unmanly despair.

Around Gareth the quiet determined patter of the coming storm began to grow in volume, and gusts of wind scuffed the puddles in the yard.

Finally a new impulse overtook him. With mud spraying out behind, he pressed the accelerator to the floor, scattered the remnants of the frame, and roared out up the track and back towards town.

AT AROUND the same time, Stéfan was driving over the mountains on the last lap of his weekly journey. Waiting for him was a completed Crug Caradoc, the battle of the windows won, the facemask of scaffolding finally peeled away. Tomorrow, almost a year to the day since the auction, he would be celebrating in the Stéfan Arms, where the last blobs of emulsion were even now being stippled fashionably into place.

No expense had been spared—the talk of the valley was of inside toilets—and the Stéfan taste had been stamped throughout. The pub now had a décor that belonged to few brewery chains, indeed to few, if any, buildings west of Offa's Dyke. *And* he had created a culinary first for the area: a menu without lamb! The actual cuisine was still a secret. Rumour held it to be exotic and spicy.

The only detail yet to be sorted—apart from the bills—was Gwillim. He still kept cattle on the Commodore's land, but the flat above the pub was his farmhouse home, and the Notice to Quit would shortly see him evicted. Few things in life made Gwillim happy, but one of them was bearing a grudge—ideally of the Albanian format, which endures for generations and fills the cemeteries. As a heavyweight malcontent, his way with cows still caused Stéfan's car engine to miss a beat whenever they rounded a bend. So Stéfan had proposed a meet, and was trying hard to think of offers that Gwillim couldn't refuse.

But first came the bills. Stéfan was a cash man. In his world of import-export (and still the locals could not say if this were cashew nuts or cocaine, guano or guns) it was cash that paid the bills. And his pub bills were no exception. So, despite the worsening weather, Stéfan decided to stop off in Abernant, at the cash point immortalised by the mayoress.

It was not easy to park. A new parking regime was to start the following day; the meters wore hoods like a gang of embarrassed outlaws, the department of tape had run amok, and the white-line men were out in force. But illegality was a trifle that rarely troubled Stéfan, and he crowbarred his resprayed Jaguar into the end of a disabled bay.

Declaring a cash point open is the easy part. Keeping it stocked with money is what takes the years of training. And every week the demands of market day proved beyond the wit of mortal clerks. Stéfan pressed every button in sight but the cash flow was a no-show.

Inside, the bank was almost as full of farmers as the Market Tavern, all paying in their wads and filling out their stubs. On such days the place had the feel of a gossip exchange, like London's early coffee-houses, but without the coffee. There were four queues, and it was all hands to the tills, including those of the senior lady cashier.

So Stéfan reluctantly waited in line

It was an old-world, old-style bank, built at a time when moneymen believed in cornice work. Its double doors opening onto a marble floor of generous proportions, with space that served no financial purpose, and its high ceilings had an echo that added dignity to a cough. Known in its formative years as a banking hall, the building spoke of an age when a starched collar was the prerequisite for an overdraft.

It took some ten minutes for Stéfan to reach the counter, ten minutes of waiting while each transaction was subjected to enquiries re the next of kin, and their health.

The senior cashier was a matronly figure, ten years short of retirement, and, it seemed, a blood relative of all her customers. But she had a brisk efficiency where cash was concerned, and breezed through Stéfan's five-figure request. Like the bank itself, she had an old-fashioned quality, a concern that things be proper, a respect for the niceties.

Mrs Plimpton was counting out the last few hundred pounds when the armed man came in.

It was a low-key entrance, a few people moving to make room, the odd raised voice. It was when he started to push his way to the front of the queue that the mood in the bank changed. Stéfan sensed some sort of mêlée behind him and turned round. And there, in his dingy cap and dungy Barbour, with his shotgun under his arm, was Gareth. Walking like a man who had come via the Market Tavern.

Gareth stopped a couple of yards from the screen-free, customer-friendly counter, held himself steady and yelled, 'Your manager's screwing my wife!'

He now had the full attention of the bank.

There was no immediate response to his cry. Some of the staff exchanged looks, but no one wished to provoke him by saying anything. Some of the farmers exchanged smirks. The only person deriving satisfaction from the drama was Mrs Plimpton, the senior cashier. She was now feeling a warm glow of vindication for her long-held view that Mr Blake was a rogue and a wrong 'un. But she said nothing, well-schooled by a lifetime's training in customer confidentiality.

The silence did not please Gareth, as he wanted understanding of his plight. He yelled again, this time turning around to address the bank's customer base, 'Their manager's screwing my wife!'

It was hard not to be moved by his pain, yet hard not to laugh at his folly. All the rights and wrongs of his marriage had clogged into this moment of madness. He no longer knew how or where to receive relief. But finally he wished his suffering to be shared.

The assembly of customers—and many had known him since childhood—avoided his eye and hid from his pain. They too had wives. Stéfan meanwhile breathed again, sensing his money was safe.

Still yearning desperately for some impossible dream of redress, Gareth raised his gun above his head. To a female chorus of gasps, he fired both barrels into the ceiling. And then he yelled one more time, '*Your manager's screwing my wife!*'

The only immediate consequence of his action was that a section of elaborate stucco fell from the ceiling and unfortunately concussed Mr Probert, the estate agent, who until a few moments earlier had been enjoying a rather successful day as auctioneer.

Seeing the man's body crumple to the floor, Gareth realised his folly had gone too far. All that remained to him was a chance for dignity.

He stepped towards the counter and, with the over-elaborate precision of a drunk, uncocked the shotgun that had done for so many moles and laid it carefully along the counter, its barrel pointing away from the staff. Then, with much conscious effort to display composure, and brushing a little loose plaster from his shoulders, Gareth addressed the senior cashier.

'Excuse me,' he said, with the courtesy that is the hallmark of the valley.

'Yes, Mr Richards?' Mrs Plimpton decided to make no mention of the waiting queue.

'I wish to close my account, please.'

Chapter 17

At first, Stéfan could not tell why he had woken. Indeed, for a second he could not tell where he had awoken. And then he realised he was on the chesterfield in his study.

He had dropped into the study for a late-night Armagnac, to wind down beside the fire. After the tedium of the drive and the drama in the bank had come the drudgery at the pub—where last-minute crises were available on draught. 'Finishing touches' were words he never wished to hear again in the Nant Valley, unless spoken by builders willing to take lie-detector tests twice daily. At last, though, after much late stippling and ad hoc plumbing, the Stéfan Arms was ready to open. Even the live music had finally been booked. *And* he had come to a working arrangement with Gwillim.

Several minutes passed as Stéfan lay yawning on the sofa. He was almost sure that something had woken him. But what it was, he could not tell. He looked across at his grandfather clock. It was well gone midnight. He decided against another brandy, for tomorrow would be a busy day. And then he heard it. Quiet but distinct. Steady but insistent.

Dripping.

The noise of the rain had masked the sound. The house faced southwest, and was taking the force of the wind on its Jacobean chin. The sudden squalls would hit the windows like handfuls of gravel hurled from a sling. And the noise of the rain had misled him, had noisily merged with the dripping. Except for one small detail that had jarred upon the ear. One small detail that betrayed the dreadful truth.

The dripping was on the inside.

Stéfan leapt from the chesterfield and rushed to the window, looking for the dripping. He soon found it. It was not just one drip. When drips come, they come not singly but with fellow drips. Evenly spread and forming little puddles. Pouring from the frame and down the wall. Pouring from the floor above and down the frame. Pouring from God knows where.

Stéfan hurried to the library, and there too he found drips in mass attendance. He hurried to the lounge, to the salon, to the dining room; to the reception room, to the second reception room, to the third reception room, and to a room he had as yet no name for. The scene was the same, give or take some hundred drips. He hurried upstairs, to bedrooms one to seven, and to the room where he and The Windowman had had their epiphany. Everywhere, the unhurried, undiscriminating drip, a chilling remorseless sound. Hours and hours of driving rain had breached millimetre gaps in the frames' hand-tooled defences. Defying gravity, the driven rain had gone up and along and about and around to hunt down the Achilles' heels of carpentry. The raindrops had, like programmed mice, squeezed their way through a hundred hairbreadth holes, only to end their journey on Stéfan's carpets. Which now squelched beneath his feet.

It was at this moment that he recalled Nico's mocking smile on auction day. It had transcended mere sparring over lots. It had been a smile not of transient venom, but of malign certainty that the fates were against him. It was the smirk of experience, the smirk that said he, an outsider, was doomed to fail. Such was Stéfan's temper tantrum that day, he had stormed from the tent. And had determined to succeed.

A year of valley habits had modified this outlook. He had learned that the forces of class and feudalism, of history and apathy, were ranged against him. But only tonight did he fully understand why Nico had such confidence in the forces of reaction. Only now did Stéfan realise that the climate itself was aligned with the enemy, that the seventy-five inches of annual rain were strictly personal.

And then his thoughts turned to Mr Griffith Barton. And what he would say to him (were he not ex-directory). And what he would do to him (were he not miles away). Apart from the violence, he would personally take The Windowman on a grand tour of the house, now, at one o'clock in the morning. And he would show him every last drip. Every pitter-patter, every splish-splosh, every plip-plop, every plink-plonk, that he could possibly find. Several times over.

'OOOH!' cried the little group in unison.

A gargoyle had fallen off, breaking an angel into several parts.

'An architecturally duff gargoyle,' said the surveyor unfeelingly.

Attention switched to the weather vane, which had already had a heavy night of oscillating, and was looking iffy.

'My great-great-grandfather did the gargoyles,' said the Commodore.

There were seven people standing on the humpback bridge, possibly a record for 3 a.m. It was the vicar, on his way home from a Boy Scouts' drinks party, who had noticed that St Brynnach's was inching itself into the river. The crisis was much too serious for prayer and he had rushed at once to the Commodore's.

'Oooh!' came another cry from the bridge as ominous crunching was heard.

'Just a voussoir,' said the surveyor, who took no prisoners when it came to ecclesiastical architecture.

The Commodore had not reacted well to the landslide news; it was this sort of upset that had led him to leave the war early. But his sister was not an OBE for nothing and knew to reach straight for the phone. The 999 call had initially produced an administrative uncertainty as to which service was most appropriate to assist a terminal church, but in time a policeman, two fire officers and a water official were sent.

All were now peering across the river at the church's progress through the graveyard.

'At least it's stopped raining,' said the vicar, who was wishing he belonged to one of those religions that gave you worry beads.

'Too late,' said the surveyor, with suppressed satisfaction. His elaborate trench-work now resembled a miniature Venice, and the river's highest surge had yet to pass through.

Another yard of riverbank collapsed. Undercut from below, the earth and stones slithered from sight. The Nant was a greedy river, at its greediest in spate. Even darkness could not hide its ceaseless scouring of the muddy meadow banks that ordained its course.

With the waters burrowing away beneath the church like a monster vole, the body of the nave had begun to slightly tilt. The Hartford-Stanley crack was widening and letting in enough wind to blow off a corset. Pressure was growing on the tower to say goodbye to the nave, to begin a new life as a ruin.

The vicar continued to lean upon the parapet of the bridge gazing glumly towards his vanishing church.

A yard or two away, the men in uniform were monitoring the situation— by means of looking in the direction of the church and standing around with authoritative posture. At one point, the senior fire officer spoke into his walkie-talkie, updating headquarters on the status of the incident, and the words 'big splash' were heard. But for these people the drama had no personal importance, no deep significance.

'I do find life is odd,' mused the Commodore. 'Very odd. When I was young I used to have dreams that our house would fall into a great big pit, dug by the clergy. And now this . . .' He gestured haplessly downstream.

The vicar struggled with the imagery. 'You were worried about falling down into hell?'

'No, no, no, no, no,' said the Commodore. 'Into the gold mines. Under our sitting room.' He had always found the vicar to be slow on the uptake. 'My sister was forever warning me. "The Church are coming!" she'd shout. "With their shovels."' The childhood memory was vivid in his eyes. 'It's a large house. I never knew which room the vicars would be digging under. All mining away with their cassocks on. Hunting for the gold.'

This was a view of church history with which the Reverend Oliver was not familiar.

It was the surveyor who understood.

'House was first a rectory,' he said *sotto voce* to the vicar. 'And the church likes to keep the mining rights under its old property. Just in case. After all, heaven's still on the gold standard. Souls are just a sideline.'

The dead thud of a belly flop signalled that the first headstone had hit the water. The retaining wall of the graveyard, the last line of defence, was now just token stones.

The surveyor smiled. It was a job Euan loved, bringing repair bills to the bishopric; demolition orders to the archdiocese. It was the perfect revenge for his schooldays. As boarder at a religious school in the hills, his lessons had come from Christians whose teaching aids were leather belts. Euan's one-man programme of church deconstruction had its roots in five formative years of weals and welts.

Bits of a moon were appearing. A couple of clouds were fraying at the edges. The storm was exhausted. But still the water was on its way up. And the river end of the nave was on its way down. The scissor trusses supporting the roof were beginning to buckle. Beneath them, the mosaic friezes on the walls were popping their tiles like podded peas.

Reality and the Commodore appeared to continue on their parallel paths even as the air crackled with the noise of snapping slates. Then the old man slowly raised his arthritic hands to his mouth, watching as a rolling, twisting tree trunk slalomed its way through the giant eddies beyond the bridge. 'What I can't bear is the thought of our own bones . . . all mixed up with Llewellyn bones.'

As if in response to such lack of Christian charity, St Brynnach's shivered with a violent spasm. Beside the round-headed doorway the crack had become a chasm. The stained-glass pictures of Jesus and his Beulah lambs slid from their lead moorings and shattered into shards.

And above, the moon, finally freed of cloud, shone upon a graveyard in turmoil, upon a spray that rose high in the sky as the land hurled its consecrated debris into the muddy depths.

As the nave broke from the tower, it took on the form of an errant railway carriage, decoupled and on end in a pile-up. Then the Victorian nave slid in almost stately slow-motion into the River Nant. The remains of the church entered the dark waters like a rare breed of ecclesiastical liner, launched upon a doomed final voyage.

Chapter 18

Dafydd sighed bitterly and expressively. 'I was "appraised" yesterday. Annually appraised. It's a management word. Typical two-faced management word! Seven letters spell praised. And the "a, p" bit means fuck off, you're sacked.'

'Sacked?' said Clydog and Hubert together.

'What for?' asked Hubert.

Even at a moment this bleak, Dafydd was aware that he had his audience in the palm of his hand, and he did not disappoint.

'Oh, a long list of offences. Crimes against efficiency. First was looking after Hefin after he died. Then it was stopping that yob Eryl from cutting Bryony's house in half. Then it was for helping paint a bit of Tinkerbell, one time up at Rob's with Gareth. And so on. My boss had a long dossier of things like that. Inappropriate use of Royal Mail time, he calls it.'

'But how would he know?' asked Clydog.

'How indeed? Is my van bugged, I ask?'

'So who else knew?'

'Who *could* know?' said Dafydd.

'Lionel Blake,' Hubert said quietly. 'That's who. And, of course, the rest of the Chamber of Commerce. Including the Royal Mail representatives. Entertaining man, the bank manager, especially about you and the pig.'

'Oh my God! But how—'

'Pillow talk, I guess. Via Bryony. And via Moira via Gareth.'

The postman did not need to act dumbfounded. At the last count, the bank manager had slept with thirteen of Dafydd's customers. Who knew every last detail of Dafydd's deliveries. Indeed, in exchange for eggs he had even shown hard-up Mrs Whitelaw how best to remove unfranked stamps.

The ruin of his career was now moving beyond melodrama, and the postman felt sick at heart. 'That's the trouble with this valley,' he said angrily. 'People just don't realise the harm that idle gossip can do.'

'I know,' said Hubert sympathetically. 'It's very unfair. I wish I could do something to help.' He spun his chair round and stood up. 'Look, I'm sorry, Dafydd, it's nearly time, we've got to go. The mayoress awaits.'

Clydog eased his bottom off the desk, and wiped the last of the Wicked Chocolate Fudge Cake from his chin. He gave Dafydd an awkward, repressed pat on the back. Young Auberon did the same, his camera swinging dangerously loose as he leaned across.

Hubert delayed them a second while he reached under his desk and pulled out a rather heavy holdall to take with him.

'So what's she doing this time?' asked Dafydd. 'Our Lady of Good Works.'

'Unveiling the new parking meters,' said Clydog.

'The new unwanted parking meters,' said Hubert, with his Chamber of Commerce hat on.

'Oh, yes,' said Dafydd, trying to raise a smile.

'So we can't be late,' said Clydog. 'Can't miss this one. It'll be our big lead story of the week.'

ERYL REVVED down and eased the big black motorbike off the bypass and into the roundabout. He turned at the sign for Abernant and soon saw the grey slate roofs below him in the late afternoon sun. He pulled into the first lay-by and pushed up his goggles. He laid his heavy black gauntlets along the jazzy red stripe of the fuel tank and rubbed at his tired eyes. Then he stretched out his legs and looked almost fondly at the view ahead.

'There!' he said to his wife. 'Abernant! That's where it all happens!'

'Yes,' said Irina.

'No,' said Eryl. 'A joke. Nothing ever happens there.'

'Yes,' said Irina.

'And beyond,' he said, pointing, 'is the Nant Valley. Where nothing ever changes.'

'Yes,' said Irina.

Eryl pulled down his goggles and tugged his gloves back on. The mileometer registered 24,736 miles. Dank and lonely though the memories were, he already felt nostalgic for a pint at the Dragon's Head.

He rode slowly in through the outskirts and pointed out the few Abernantian items of interest. Irina seemed impressed, for where she came from there were no outskirts. Eryl pointed out the Elim Tabernacle, the new car-wash, the monkey-puzzle tree in the Pensioners' Memorial Garden, the stuffed-animals shop that was always closed. All was as before, apart from an unexpected mini-roundabout, and little had prepared him to see an altar lodged under the bridge at the end of the High Street.

Eryl pointed it out to Irina but could think of no convincing explanation. He also lacked the language skills to convey that submerged altars were not a standard cultural feature of the mid-Wales landscape. Or that the crowd on the bridge were not worshippers. But Irina seemed unfazed and continued to cling trustingly to his expensive leathers as he rode on past.

The High Street was busier than usual and he kept the revs low, looking for friends to wave to, looking for friends—and indeed merest acquaintances—to whom he could introduce his beautiful foreign wife. Abernant on a Saturday is hub of the local universe, and it was not long before he spotted a familiar face. Normally he and Gareth sat glumly on bar stools, bemoaning their lot and their love lives; the sight of him being led handcuffed from the police station to a waiting squad car was therefore hard for Eryl to fathom. He watched as Gareth's head was pressed down to enter the police car, and he rode on past.

All that is important in Abernant is in its hundred yards of high street. Eryl had pointed out the KwikSave, the Woolworths, the Short Cuts hair salon, the cinema where *Beau Geste* had changed Sion's life, and was about to thrill Irina with the deli when he caught sight of the bank.

The blue and white tape of police movies was festooned across its pillared porch. Fluttering and fluorescent, it proclaimed 'Crime Scene' to the world. Two chunky men in uniform stood guard outside, barring entry. Even the historic cash machine was out of bounds. In a region where almost all crimes were animal related, armed bank robbery represented an historic first. Eryl was by now at a bit of a loss, and he rode on past.

Until he saw the meters. And the crowd ahead.

He slowed the bike to walking pace. Rows of taped-off parking meters stretched ahead of him on either side of the High Street. Polished and shiny, their slots at the ready, they stood like symbols of lost innocence. In the distance, on a dais, stood the mayoress, awaiting the official scissors.

To Eryl's Romanian bride, this was yet another thread of the rich capitalist tapestry she had dreamed of so often while under communism. Ever since Eryl, the man of mystery, had ridden into her remote and primitive farm collective, she knew that he offered salvation. Her father knew it too. Never had they seen such a bike, so powerful, so expensive, so stylish. Never had they seen such bikewear, so lavish, so airtight, so imperiously black. Never had they seen such a biker, so aristocratic in his Austro-Hungarian moustache. As Eryl rode into sight trailing wealth from his mighty exhaust, Irina's peasant father had said to her, 'This man will bring us fortune and happiness.'

The romance was whirlwind; the betrothal was a blur; and the marriage was a red-letter day for the village. And thus was Irina granted her entrée to the wonders of the West, to an unknown land of Celtic milk and honey.

'Parking meter ceremony,' said Eryl, by way of explanation.

'Yes,' said Irina. And watched dutifully.

The Traffic Warden, the authority in whom parking was vested, carried forward the velvet pouffe bearing the ceremonial scissors and a 10p coin. The mayoress waved to the crowd, adjusted her centre of gravity, and aimed the scissors at the tape. 'I declare these parking meters—'

'A monstrosity!'

Hubert burst into view, followed by the Free Trade faction, and advanced upon the mayoral dais. To a shaky chant of 'Meters Out!', the parking extremists moved through the crowd handing out protest leaflets. Hubert opened up his holdall, and pulled out several lengths of chain. He and his followers then spent several minutes working out how to handcuff themselves to a row of meters. Once secured, Hubert declared himself available for interviews and Clydog—whose nose for news had given him no warning—moved in with his pad and pencil. To keep it professional, he began by asking Hubert's name.

The climax to the protest, which had been several months in the planning, was for Hubert, President of the Chamber of Commerce, to be very publicly arrested. Unfortunately, the only police on duty were busy guarding a loose piece of stucco at the bank. Equally unfortunately, Auberon had used up all his film on shots of a coffin and had had to return to Boots. And the only authority with statutory powers was the Traffic Warden, whose history of blackmailing traders for gifts rendered him prone to be thumped.

The crowd, who rarely got to see street theatre, tore down the tapes in their excitement, and declared the meters open without the use of scissors. Whereupon the mayoress fled in the mayoral car, fearful that news of the imbroglio might reach the ears of an honours committee.

Eryl judged it was time to move on from the town.

As he was nearing the town limits and the freedom of the valley lay ahead, the 'No Limit' sign came into view.

And then a 'Road Closed' sign.

Eryl steered round it. He was puzzled, not for the first time that day. Only snow ever closed the valley road and it was not snowing. The cause had to be an accident and a bike could always steer round an accident.

He also had the strong motive of thirst, and it was near opening time—or would be if the pub was under new ownership.

'Pub,' said Eryl, pointing to the hills.

'Yes,' said Irina.

The familiar field patterns of mid-Wales now filled the view. The farm animals lay scattered Lowry-like, as static as props. In the sky circled a buzzard, with its usual pretensions to be a vulture. A ferret ran jerkily in front of Eryl, from one verge to the other, the first he had seen since he left. Sometimes, at dusk, you could see a badger crossing this stretch of road on its way down to the river. And sometimes, when rolling home at first light from parties, you would catch sight of a fox, whose timetable of secrecy had not catered for drunks.

Like Sion before him, he had tired of abroad. Like Nico before him, he had felt the need to come home. With the passing of countries, the ebbing of money, Eryl had come to feel there was more comfort in failure at home than failure overseas.

And then he saw the giant crane blocking the road—and that half the church was missing. In what used to be the bit with the pews, demolition men in shiny yellow coats stood directing a killer cannonball to and fro amidst the ruined walls. Eryl almost left the road with shock as a sandstone window arch was hit for six and thundered to the ground.

Ignoring the shouts, he steered his bike up onto the verge and round the crane, and halted on the corner of the lane just beyond. This was where he had sat on the day he left the valley six months before. Here, with his visor down and engine running, he had watched the parish parting for home, serene in the belief that a musical afternoon had saved the church.

He and Irina paused beneath the overhanging yews. Leaning against the lych gate, toppled by the storm, was the mighty thermometer, its mock-mercury stuck at £20,000. Beyond, the men in hard hats crunched through glass where people once had knelt. Around them rose the last of the buttresses, true to the spirit of Victorian ruins. And above them, like a monstrous metronome, swung the relentless wrecking ball.

Eryl glanced over the bridge at the schoolhouse, which he had last left with such acrimony. He wanted, for the most immature of motives, to introduce Bryony to his beautiful bride. He wanted her to see just how well he had done. The visit would, however, have to be another day. For a reason he could not explain, there was a police car parked by the swings.

He turned to kiss Irina—she was a girl who needed regular kissing—before they set off on the final few miles. As they clinched, a beat-up saloon came down the valley road, from the direction of the moors.

'We're lost,' said the driver. 'D'you know a Marjorie?'

Inside the car were three bullet-headed squaddies, that breed of men who were the nemesis of The Windowman. They rarely strayed from the moor and their barracks beyond.

'The teacher?' asked Eryl.

'Teacher?' said the driver.

'Tart in a caravan,' said a passenger.

'Oh,' said Eryl, shocked. 'Over the bridge and up the hill. Follow the hens.'

He watched them go up the lane till they vanished from sight, then he slipped the bike in gear and Irina clasped him tightly round the waist. He rode ever more slowly up the last lap home, for there was trust in those arms and it worried him. It worried him as never before. Eryl had a recess in his brain where he stored those parts of life that he wanted to forget. It was now very full. For weeks he had stored his marriage there, refusing to contemplate the future, refusing to admit to a problem with the past. He was living his life in denial, and he was planning his life in fantasy, if he was planning his life at all. The plum brandy had said that marriage in a foreign language didn't count. But now he had a wife on the back of a bike. And a bike and a wife was all that he had. Plus the price of a couple of rounds. Very soon he would have to explain all this, and to a woman who only said yes.

Beyond the bend, above the hedge, the pub came into sight. It was not the pub as he remembered it.

A lopsided sign hung unhappily from a single hook, victim of nasty, gusty Welsh winds. At the bottom of the sign, in lettering which aimed for the Gothic and achieved Hammer Horror, were the words: THE STÉFAN ARMS. Above this was the new landlord, his teeth bared in a rictus of welcome. The primitive school of art had not been kind to Stéfan. His head was disproportionately large. In his outsize left hand he held a bottle of champagne, in his outsize right hand a glass. And his medium-size body rested above overlong legs that stood rigidly apart, as if he might wish to pee.

Underneath the sign, beside the blackboard that read 'Welcome to Grand Opening!, a row was raging. Teg and Ben the molemen were raising their fists to Gwillim, and Gwillim was roaring 'Bugger off!'

Even from a distance, Eryl could see that Gwillim too was not as he remembered him. Although always surly and eccentric, he had never before dressed as a medieval brigand in black baggy knickerbockers, red gaiters and a fur hat.

'Bugger off and go to Dolly's!'

'What's wrong with how we're dressed?' demanded Teg.

'It's not smart casual. Got to be smart casual.'

'You're not smart casual.'

'I'm a Georgian.'

Eryl parked out of range. Despite the Grand Opening, he was spoilt for space in the newly surfaced, newly lined car park. The crane was as effective as a curfew in cutting the pub off from the town.

He took Irina's hand and walked towards the pub's newly enlarged porch, past the newly rendered front wall.

'Hello, Gwillim!'

'No bikers!' said Gwillim, pleased at his speed of thought.

'But I'm Eryl,' said Eryl.

Gwillim gave no hint of recognition, his body barring the entrance.

'And this is Irina, my wife.'

'Yes,' said Irina.

'And no women-bikers. No bikers, no molers.' He paused, like a slow learner trying to master lines. Then, somehow managing to be both robotic and self-satisfied, he went on, 'No trainers, no jeans, no T-shirts.'

Eryl pointed at the blackboard. 'What happened to "Welcome"?'

Gwillim flicked some imaginary dust off his knickerbockers and smirked. As he smirked, strange sounds drifted through the porch—a rumbling hum intercut with the noise of a wild cry and the stamping of feet. Looking beyond Gwillim to what was once the snug, Eryl could detect a poster on the door, which read 'The First Georgian Pub in Wales'.

Irina slipped away to look through the pub window.

'I'm not paid to do welcomes,' said Gwillim gruffly. 'I'm paid to do dress code. And it's no deviants, no dossers.' He spoke with the tone of a man who considered these categories to embrace most of the human race.

'But you know us!' said Teg, who had wiped his boots and returned to the fray.

Gwillim allowed himself another smirk. It seemed he had been in training all his life for a job such as this. Had he himself written the job description, in which to be antisocial was essential, he could scarcely have bettered the duties of bouncer.

'You've known us for years, you bastard!' said Ben.

'You must take any complaints up with the management.'

The management creaked overhead as the hook bore his weight. The blotchy champagne bottle seemed to have taken on a derisive air, and the rictus had a subtext of sneer. Eryl suddenly felt a great urge to take on Stéfan, this man who lived the life that should be his.

'Right! We'll talk to him!'

'You can't,' replied Gwillim. 'He's gone.'

And this was said in a voice of triumph, to the tune of checkmate.

It was followed by a long and puzzled silence.

'Gone?' repeated Eryl. 'Gone where?'

'For his Grand Opening?' said Teg.

'Gone away. Disappeared. Given up. Buggered off. In the middle of the night.' A broad smile modelled on his master's crossed Gwillim's face.

Then, as they each tried to absorb his revelation, there came a weird, other-worldly sound. Throbbing, alien, like a Gregorian chant on speed, rose the cry '*Yahlagaragoraraaahlaralagor*'.

Irina beckoned him urgently to the pub window. Inside the Stéfan Arms the opening night was gathering force.

A troupe of folk singers and dancers were stomping up a storm. Weird hybrid banjos soared up and down the scale as high-booted long-skirted peasant women slapped their embroidered thighs and moved in purple waves. A line of mountain men in multicoloured waistcoats clapped hands and kicked their legs high, gyrating their bodies into folkloric frenzy.

The performance was greeted by silence. There was no audience. The pub was empty. No one had got past Gwillim.

Eryl and Irina returned to the others on the forecourt.

Gwillim was glowing. After a lifetime as an embittered feudal tenant, he had found the perfect job. He was being paid to bar people from the pub. Whoever they were. For whatever reason took his fancy. In perpetuity. He even had a uniform to give him authority, though the costumiers in Cardiff had been defeated by Stéfan's demand for authentic Georgian bouncer-wear. So it was as a Shakespearean jester cum Transylvanian coachman that burly Gwillim, the proud cowhand, stood guard outside the smartest newest nightspot in mid-Wales. And cried 'Bugger off!' to the valley.

Inside, the Stéfan Arms remained deserted, apart from the vigorous Georgian folk troupe who were booked until midnight. The owner remained absent, destination and date of return unknown. And the customers—two muddy molecatchers well past retirement and a penniless playboy biker with a Romanian wife—remained waiting in vain for a drink.

Eventually Teg broke the silence.

'Well, I guess it's off up to Dolly's then.'

Ben nodded reluctantly. Three miles to the moors was a long walk for a pint, especially when it was full of froth.

'You two coming?'

Eryl shook his head. He was not a fan of Dolly's. He did not fancy drinking in the front room of a little old lady in a nightdress. Or sharing his evening with a small white dog that pretended to play Grieg's Piano Concerto on the bar. It was not the high life he had promised his wife.

'Good night, then.'

Slowly, Ben and Teg set off into the fading light, the drear brown of their moling clothes gradually merging with the hedgerows.

The new bride and groom were left to stand in silence, alone with their fragile dreams and hopes. Irina looked at Eryl expectantly, tenderly, trustingly, waiting for her rich husband finally to make sense of her day.

Eryl was gazing into the distance, towards Crug Caradoc, an idea beginning to form in his head. A twenty-eight-room idea. A homecoming with truth and justice on its side. An heir restored. The rightful squire in place.

As he was pondering, Irina suddenly tugged him by the arm and pointed into the distant meadows, the veld of Stéfan's dreams.

He looked where she was looking.

Something had moved in the dark.

'Yes?' said Irina.

Eryl screwed up his eyes and took a second look.

It was hard to believe, but there seemed little doubt. He did not know how best to explain it to her. The day had already been long and difficult, yet Eryl still had one more surprise in store for her.

Eryl turned to face her.

'Yes?' repeated Irina.

He held her hand to reassure her . . . and then he replied.

'Ostriches.'

BARRY PILTON

Born: Croydon, 1946
Hates: Routine, matching furniture
Loves: France, hairpin bends, deserts

A careers master once asked Barry Pilton what he would like to do. 'Estate management,' he said, and was then asked what he knew about cows. 'Nothing,' he replied, prompting the careers master to move on to the next profession on his list: estate agency. After dismal exam results, Pilton tried that and turned out to be bad at selling houses, failing to shift a single one in an entire year.

It was the sixties and, unlike many of his contemporaries who departed for university, he decided to set off round the world with a backpack. He stopped for a year in Paris and, in May 1968, as student riots broke out, fell head over heels in love. He was now a struggling writer and had acquired all the recommended attributes: a beard, poverty and a garret. Though he and the girl parted company, Pilton later wrote a book about it all titled *An Innocent Abroad*.

Not long after his return home, an article he'd written was published in *Punch*. Then, while he was working as a lift operator, a chance meeting resulted in a job with the *Sunday Post*. It turned out to be terrible, as all jokes were carefully edited out by the dour Scottish editors. As soon as he could, he escaped to King's College, London to do an English degree.

Jobs as a lorry driver, a removals man and a biscuit packer followed before his big break, in 1976, when a sketch he'd written was accepted for Radio 4's *Week Ending* show. Soon he was working on an ever-expanding range of programmes, including *Not the Nine O'Clock News*, *Spitting Image* and ITV's *Shelley*.

In 1984 he moved to Llandefaelog with his partner, Janice. They stayed for fifteen years. Pilton loved being editor of the *Brecon Naturalist* and warden of a local nature reserve, but in the end found 'knowing everyone, from every level of society' oppressive, so the couple moved to Bristol, where they still live today.

As well as *The Valley*, his first novel, Pilton has written a comic account of his experiences as a reluctant walker on the Pennine Way: *One Man and His Bog*. What is it about walking that he doesn't like? 'The uphill bits!'

CAROLINE CARVER

BLACK TIDE

Jimbuku Bay is a pretty little coastal settlement but it looks out of place against the harsh Australian landscape. And there are rumours that it's not a good place to live—too many residents have been stricken by a mystery illness.

Some say it's coincidence, some an environmental blight. Others remember the curse that Albert Jimbuku uttered against the developers who stole the land of his Aboriginal ancestors . . .

PROLOGUE

He couldn't believe his eyes. Right in front of the building site, leaning his broad back against the JCB digger, sat Albert Jimbuku. His face was smeared with clay, his bare torso covered with dots and messy swirls of yellow and white paint. He had opened up a dead rabbit and taken out the guts and was making a weird sound. He seemed oblivious to the watching crowd. Men wearing hard hats, men in overalls, Maisie Wilson and her daughter, the on-site caterers. Some twenty people, all agog.

Albert threw the intestines on the ground. A breeze suddenly picked up, stirring dust around the Aborigine's big dirty feet, and the next instant the stench of burst entrails hit Bobby's nostrils like a blow.

'Jesus, Albert!' He raced across to the man and his bloody carcass. 'What the hell are you doing? Don't you know Jack's due any minute?'

The Aborigine abruptly stopped his chant and sat there in silence. His shoulders were bowed, his head slumped.

It was a freezing day in August, Australia's winter, and although the sun was bright, the sky a vivid blue all the way to the ocean's edge, Bobby felt as though he had an icicle on his face. His eyes were watering, his nose running, and he wished he could leg it for Maisie's van and warm up with a cup of coffee but he knew he couldn't. Not until he'd shifted Albert.

'Come on, Albert,' Bobby urged. 'If Jack sees you here, he'll go nuts. He's already months behind, thanks to you.'

'This is my camp,' Albert said. His baritone carried easily to the crowd. 'You can't build your bloody houses here.'

'Yes, we bloody can,' called out Laurie Harris, Jack's foreman.

A couple of people started to laugh, but stopped when Albert got to his feet. Despite the blubber hanging over the waistband of his jeans, he was an imposing sight. Standing at six foot four, he had thighs the size of railway sleepers, and the hands hanging at his sides were as large as steel couplings. The ghostly clay on his broad face took away any thoughts of a gentle giant and gave him a peculiarly menacing air.

'This is our sacred place. The springs here are holy.'

'Bollocks!' shouted Laurie. 'You're no more the traditional owner of this area than Kylie Minogue. This isn't your camp, Albert, and you know it.'

Oh my God, Bobby thought. What in hell possessed me to come over this morning? All I wanted was to see how the building was coming along, and here I am between a crowd of people who want to work so they get paid and a giant, paint-splattered Aborigine with cockatoo feathers in his hair.

'Albert,' he pleaded, 'think about it. You've got no chance. What about the cops? The council and the local government?'

'You paid 'em off.' Albert's lips tightened. 'Whole place knows what your family get up to. You buy yourselves into or out of anything any time, not caring what mess you leave behind. You shouldn't be here, mate.'

'And nor should you. Or have you forgotten about the restraining order?'

'It is my ancestral right to be here.'

Bobby looked at him in disbelief. 'It's your ancestral right to wreck our diggers? Pour sugar into the fuel tanks and spray red paint all over the site?'

There was a small pause, then Albert turned and addressed the crowd. 'The springs are part of our Dreaming. We are linked to them by our spirit. Our very being . . .'

As Albert started the same old spiel he'd been dishing out over the past six months, Bobby felt panic in the pit of his stomach. He'd have more luck moving the JCB with his bare hands than moving Albert in full flow. In desperation he rang one of his cousins, a cop at Perth's central PD, and asked him to send someone over fast and remove Albert before Jack arrived. His cousin said, no worries, Kuteli's in the area, give him twenty, and hung up.

'You see, long time ago,' Albert was saying, 'a great hero lost his son hunting here, and in his grief his tears fell to the ground. When the tears struck the ground, a spring of fresh water rose, giving my people a supply of water for many generations. These springs are holy. And this is my home.'

'Bullshit,' said Maisie stoutly. 'You've a house in town like the rest of us. You're just making trouble, you are.'

'I want what is mine,' Albert insisted. 'Before Neville came and buggered us about, my lot used to visit this place for important ceremonies. Sacred, secret rituals, at many times of the year. I need to protect my heritage.'

'Why don't you piss off, Albert, and let us get on with our work?' a man yelled from the back.

'Look, Albert,' Bobby said in an undertone, 'why don't you go home and wash that stuff off and I'll meet you down the pub later? I'll sort something out with you, no worries.' He patted his back pocket, which held his wallet.

'You can't buy me off like you did the others,' Albert said loudly, and Bobby flushed. 'This is not about money. It is about my ancestors. I am telling you white people, if you stop this building, things will be all right.'

Bobby felt a moment of utter disbelief. 'Are you *threatening* us?'

The Aborigine turned and looked at him straight. 'Stop breaking my place.'

'Or you'll do what?'

Albert gestured at the sad bundle of eviscerated fur, now crawling with blowflies. 'I didn't want it to come to this.'

Bobby's mouth turned dry as a billabong in drought when he saw Jack's Land Cruiser pull up behind the crowd. 'Shit, Albert. Jack's here.'

Albert gave no indication he'd heard. 'I talked with a sorcerer, a medicine man. He told me to do this. He says this land will turn against any white people who come to live on our sacred ground.'

The cold breeze suddenly increased, making the hairs on the nape of Bobby's neck stand bolt upright. A plastic cup rattled across the ground and a miniature dust devil spiralled across the site's entrance. The crowd had fallen silent.

'You feel the way the wind has heard me?' the Aborigine asked quietly. 'It has begun. Jambuwal, the Thunder Man, is coming.'

The crowd stirred uneasily, looking over their shoulders at the horizon, where a streak of dark clouds had appeared.

'For God's sake, Albert.' Bobby was almost gasping with the effort not to scream at the stubborn Aborigine. 'You know what Jack's like. *Go home.*'

To his horror, he saw the man's eyes fill with tears.

'It is too late. Jambuwal is already angry.'

With great dignity, Albert stepped over the rabbit's corpse and started to walk away. His final words were spoken under his breath, a whisper against the increasing rush of wind, but Bobby heard them.

'Jambuwal will wreak his vengeance.'

ONE

It was the first time in a week that India had been on deck. The howling southerly had finally dropped and the sun had come out, blazing off the green ocean. Scrubbing *Sundancer*'s deck aft to fore alongside the crew, she was humming to herself, glad to be outside at last.

She paused to watch an inquisitive sooty albatross following *Sundancer*'s wake. Here, 500 kilometres from Antarctica, the air was so raw it felt as if it could strip flesh from her face. Strange to think of everyone at home broiling in the midst of the Australian summer. It was January, the only sensible time to head into the Southern Ocean and avoid colliding with icebergs. She had expected better weather, but the trip so far had been rough. Good job she wasn't seasick or the last four weeks would have been unbearable.

The albatross swooped starboard, and that was when she saw it: a speck on the horizon, another ship. Her binoculars confirmed that it was another ship, and her nerves gave a little hop of excitement. It couldn't be a commercial vessel, because the shipping lanes from Perth to Cape Town crossed way north of here. Was it one of the supply ships that serviced the research stations in the area? There was only one way to find out.

India headed for the bridge, taking care to keep 'one hand on ship' in case *Sundancer* gave a sudden roll. Several crew members were already there, along with Cuan, the expedition leader, *Sundancer*'s captain, and her friend Ned, the first mate. They were all studying the speck in silence, expressions intent. She crossed her fingers for luck. She'd been reporting daily to her editor at the *Sydney Morning Herald* about life on board the Greenpeace boat, the continual maintenance, the fire drills, splicing ropes, tightening shackles, and she was sick of trying to be inventive to keep her readers' interest. She wanted evidence of the Japanese fleet hunting illegally in the Southern Ocean Whale Sanctuary and she wanted to make it public. Only last night she had suddenly realised she might return home empty-handed. Boy, did she hate to fail. And boy, had she been naive. She had not realised that the whaling area was around two and a half times the length of Australia. It was mind-bogglingly *huge*, and they were just one boat searching for a fleet of five. The Greenpeace team had made an educated guess based on the whalers' past behaviour and had been hoping they stuck to form, but they may as well have been looking for a single four-leaved clover in a thousand acres of the stuff.

Knees bent to absorb the rock and slide of the boat, she carefully panned her binoculars around the horizon. The sea was relatively calm, for Antarctica that was, and the breeze light. Five minutes later, India spotted another speck off their starboard beam sailing steadily behind the first.

'There!' said Katy, standing beside her.

'Yes!' shouted Ned in delight. 'We'll get the buggers yet!'

India was laughing. Ned's enthusiasm was as catching today as when she'd first met him eight years ago. Which was probably why she hadn't gone completely mad, imprisoned on a ship in the middle of nowhere. Ned was her tonic, her confidant, and without him she'd have lasted twenty seconds before picking a fight with one of the crew. He gave her a grin as the captain spun the wheel and pushed *Sundancer* towards the Japanese boat.

'Oh dear,' said Ned a little later, binos pressed hard against his face. 'I've some really bad news.'

'What? *What?*' pressed India, itchy with excitement.

'It's the *Kagoshima Maru*. The factory ship. And she's got an addition to her stern since we last met—some socking great water cannons.' He sighed. 'I wonder who they're for.'

They realised the factory ship had spotted *Sundancer* when she suddenly picked up speed and started sailing fast in the opposite direction. With Ned's permission, India called them over the VHF.

'Hey, if we didn't know better, we might think you were running away from us. Have you something to hide? We know you're doing some scientific whaling; we're just curious to know what your quota is. And to make sure you're keeping warm because it's very cold out here.'

The radio was silent as the factory ship steamed away with *Sundancer* in pursuit. That was the normal response, Ned said. Catchers, factory ships and scouts fled the second Greenpeace showed up.

'Can you slow down a bit?' India laughingly asked the factory ship a little later. 'We can't keep up!'

To their astonishment, the ship responded.

'Get bigger engine for your boat,' a man said in a thick accent.

'OK, we'll put an order in,' India replied without a beat. 'Which particular engine do you have in mind?'

'More easy to get bigger boat.'

'Next time we'll bring the *QE2*.' She chuckled. 'How does that sound?'

'Ah, this is good. You can have hot bath while you chase us.'

'Now there's a thought.'

'You keep warm also,' said the whaler, and disconnected.

At 7 p.m. the *Kagoshima Maru* reached 60 degrees south, the northern-most edge of the fleet's whaling area, and kept going. To their surprise, it was joined by two catchers.

'I don't believe it,' said Ned. 'It looks like they're headed home.'

'We've chased them off?'

'I'm not sure.' He frowned. 'I'm wondering if they're trying to lure us north to get us out of the way so they can race back here.'

Ned, Cuan and *Sundancer*'s captain started an intense debate about what to do next, and India and Katy left them when they smelt the rich aroma of pizza rising from the mess room.

INDIA REPORTED back to the bridge at five minutes before midnight to find that Cuan had abandoned the chase and set *Sundancer* due south once more.

'Cat and mouse, that's what this is about,' he said with a yawn. 'We never saw the spotter, and I'll bet the *Kagoshima* is speeding back to join her.'

India pulled out the chart and had a look. They were further north than she'd realised. At 53 degrees south, the nearest land was the bleak coast of Heard Island 900 kilometres away, populated by nothing but seals, sea birds and macaroni penguins.

Ned had settled himself on the padded chair at the helm and was peering outside. Although it was the middle of the night, the sky still held a little light. Not that India could see much, thanks to a thick fog. At least it was calm, she thought, and everyone would sleep well tonight.

With another yawn and a wave of his hand, Cuan left the bridge, and India poured herself a cup of black coffee from Ned's Thermos before sitting beside him. Since a mate and a deck hand had to be on watch at all times, and India had undergone a heap of training to enable her to be of use on board, they were on from twelve till four. Sipping coffee, they talked over the minutiae of their day. India noticed that Ned wasn't looking so hot, and she wondered if he was coming down with the flu. She didn't like the sweaty sheen on his face, nor the fact that his breathing was loud and raspy. She asked him if he was sure he shouldn't hand over his watch to someone else.

'I'm not *sick* sick,' he said, shocked. 'It's just the start of a cold, that's all. Besides, I want to keep an eye on this . . .' He indicated an echo on the radar about eight nautical miles to the south and heading directly their way.

India frowned. 'The spotter?'

'Could be, but I'm thinking it's another catcher wanting us to think they've given up. It's just a trick.' Using channel 16, the emergency channel that all ships monitor, he called them up. No response. 'Must be part of the fleet,' he said with a shrug, 'or they'd have answered.'

Their conversation soon turned to home. India talked a little about Mikey and Polly, and Ned talked a lot about Ellie. How much he missed her. His plans for a second honeymoon one day. What he'd like to name the baby.

'Albert?' India said, horrified. 'You can't call the poor kid Albert!'

Ned looked disgruntled. 'That's what Ellie says.'

'Why Albert, for God's sake?'

'He's the guy who protested about the Jimbuku Bay development being built. His ancestors used the springs there for generations, you know. He tried to save it.' His expression grew distant. 'I thought if we named our baby after Albert—well, that they'd be safe.'

'What do you mean, safe?'

Ned remained silent while she studied the sickly glow on his face. Then he glanced at his watch. 'Time for your rounds.'

He was fobbing her off but she didn't mind. She had another four weeks to find out what was going on. Before she left the bridge, she glanced at the radar and saw the echo was closing in.

'Yes, I'm changing course.' Ned gave her a quick grin. 'They won't come within cooee of us, OK? Now, off you go.'

First, India scouted the galley, touching each stove to make sure it was cold. Then the laundry, followed by the engine room, looking for oil leaks, constantly checking for fire hazards. If the ship caught fire they'd have nowhere to go except into the life rafts.

Finally India went out on deck. Made sure the helicopter and the Zodiac and the Avons—rigid inflatables—were secure. Everything looked fine. She would, she thought, have a quick nicotine hit before she rustled up some soup for her and Ned. Resting a hip against a railing, she lit a cigarette and looked into the peculiarly green half-lit mist. There wasn't a lot to see. Visibility had to be down to less than fifty metres now.

Out of nowhere she thought she heard a faint throbbing sound and pushed her head to one side, listening hard. It couldn't be the ship they'd seen on the radar, surely, not if Ned had changed course.

Taking another puff, she looked at her watch: 2.30 a.m. Which made it 5.30 in Sydney. Mikey and Polly would be fast asleep. Mentally she blew them both a kiss and glanced around the ship one last time.

She had just finished her cigarette when she became aware the throbbing sound was louder. A ship. Scanning the rolling waves, the fine curling mist all around, she couldn't see another vessel, but the throb-throbbing was increasing. To her horror she realised the ship was closing in.

India raced for the bridge, adrenaline in full flow. She catapulted onto the bridge, calling urgently, 'There's a ship out there, Ned . . . Oh Jesus . . .'

Ned was sprawled unconscious on the floor.

India sprang for the radar. There were two echoes, but where one was around half a mile away and chugging steadily south, the other was terrifyingly close, heading straight for them from starboard.

She glanced through the windows. Nothing but fog. But the radar told her the ship was on a collision course. She hit the fire button. Alarms hollered.

Oh, please get Cuan here quickly; he'll know what to do. The air horn, you idiot, use the bloody horn.

Fire alarms ringing, air horn blaring, she fumbled for the radio. Called up the ship on channel 16. 'This is *Sundancer*, we're on a collision course, go starboard immediately . . . GO STARBOARD!'

No response. Since *Sundancer* was the give-way vessel, India immediately altered to starboard, trying frantically to pass round the stern of the ship, praying they'd do the same. She could hear voices yelling as the crew raced to their emergency posts. Suddenly Cuan and Katy were beside her, barefoot, slickers over their nightwear.

'India,' gasped Katy. 'Oh God. Ned. What's happened?'

'Christ,' said Cuan, and at the same time India saw a dark shape to starboard. A huge ship, looming out of the mist, steaming straight for them.

No lights, she thought.

'Deploy the Zodiac, the Avons!' yelled Cuan into the ship's Tannoy. He spun round. 'You two, *out*.'

India belted after Katy down the metal staircase, grabbing a couple of life vests at the bottom. She yanked one on, and buckled it up as she ran across the mess room and past the galley. Bursting onto the port deck, she saw the Zodiac already being lowered into the water along with one of the

Avons. A distant part of her mind registered that *Sundancer*'s engines had stopped. The crew were shouting, the air horn still blaring. Katy was staring at something behind India, her face white. India glanced round to see the great white prow of a container ship streaked with rust filling the sea, the sky. They had a handful of seconds before it hit.

India shoved the second life vest at Katy, yelling, 'Put it on!'

Katy caught the vest, got one arm through, then she grabbed India's hand, and they were yelling, tiny sounds lost in the giant bang as the ship smashed straight into *Sundowner*'s starboard flank.

India's hand was wrenched from Katy's as she crashed to the deck. There was a deafening howl of metal tearing, groaning and screeching. *Sundancer* rolled violently starboard and India wrapped her arms round a railing. The next second she was underwater. For a moment she thought the cold might kill her. It made her lungs squeeze and her heart contract. But she wasn't dead, she was just submerged in freezing water, so all she had to do was hang on tight, hold her breath, and wait for *Sundancer* to right herself. But then the boat tilted further.

Oh my God. She's going to flip.

The water was filled with a dull grinding sound that went on and on. Clinging desperately to her railing she prayed that *Sundancer* wouldn't roll.

The grinding sound stopped, and slowly *Sundancer* recovered herself. India crouched on deck, choking and gasping, and watched what appeared to be half an ocean pouring through the scuppers. Gradually she made it to her feet. She looked round. Saw the huge container ship easing past *Sundancer*, just metres of sea between them. It didn't appear to be slowing. It was continuing its steady path as though nothing had happened.

Then she took in the black tide of oil leaking from *Sundancer*'s bowels. The way the ship sat low in the water. She was flooding fast. They had maybe five minutes, no more, before she sank. She could hear Cuan's voice on the Tannoy, but she couldn't make out what he was saying.

Another split-second glance at the container ship as it chugged away. A snapshot image of a dent on its transom, like a footprint, and traces of red-painted lettering. *The Pride of Tang*-something, from . . . Only two letters of the ship's home port were clear. A and A. No registration number.

Shivering violently, she searched frantically for Katy. People were in the water. She saw one of the crew on deck fling a life jacket at a man, shouting for him to GRAB IT! Others were lighting flares and aiming searchlights.

One man clinging to a rope was being slowly hauled from the water up the hull. A woman was shouting HELP! as she drifted away. The Zodiac was powering after her. People were trying to swim for the life rafts. She could hear them choking and sobbing. A shout made her look round. Joe was screaming at the still form of his wife in the freezing ocean, screaming at Emma to SWIM, dammit, SWIM! And then he was leaping overboard.

Where was Katy? Katy had been with her, she'd been *holding her hand*. Leaning over the railings she scanned the mist curling over the greeny-grey waves. Please God, let Katy be all right. To her horror, she caught a glimpse of something shiny and humped floating away from *Sundancer*'s flank. Katy's slicker. No life vest. She was face down. Motionless.

India shouted so hard her voice cracked. 'Katy!'

Sundancer's stern was listing sickeningly, her bow rearing up. The boat was in her death throes, and India could hear Cuan's voice over the Tannoy, instructing everyone to get into the life rafts, the ship was going down.

'Someone get Katy!' she yelled at the Zodiac, but it was on the port side of the bow, pulling two people aboard, and couldn't hear her.

India was trembling. Katy would die unless she went in for her; hauled her to one of the inflatables. Grabbing a horseshoe life buoy, she flung it into the water next to Katy's motionless form.

The instant she hit the water her muscles cramped with cold, but she kicked out determinedly for Katy. Her clothes were dragging her down but she didn't remove anything. She would need every ounce of fibre to hold warm water against her skin and keep her body from freezing. She clawed her way to the glistening shroud of Katy's slicker. Nearly there . . .

A wave broke over her head, flooding her mouth with icy salt water. She coughed and choked, gasping for air, her mind shrieking with panic.

Treading water, she cleared her lungs, steadied herself for a second before lunging through the water for Katy. She got swept past the life buoy, struggled back within reach of it again, and finally hooked her elbow over it. Her muscles were turning rigid but she managed to catch the collar of Katy's slicker. Giving a terrific heave, she hauled Katy's head onto her shoulder. Tried to shake her, but Katy was too heavy.

'Katy!' Her voice was a low croak. 'For God's sake, Katy!'

Exhausted and desperate, she gripped the woman's hair and put all her energy into shaking her head as hard as she could. *If she doesn't come round, I'll have to leave her. I'll never make it to a life raft otherwise.*

'Katy!' Another couple of shakes, then a sudden gasp, a spluttering cough. She was breathing.

With a monumental effort, India took Katy's left arm and hooked it over the plastic rim. 'Katy . . . Hold on to the life buoy! *Hold on!*'

A wave slapped near her face and India wanted to duck away from the spray, but her body was refusing to respond. Hypothermia was creeping through her veins. Must get help, she thought.

Straining her eyes over the waves she saw *Sundancer's* lights go out. Blue sparks arced into the water. The only light cutting through the gloom came from the sweeping dots of searchlights. She and Katy would be invisible to them. They'd drifted too far away to be seen.

I can't die, she thought. I promised to take Polly to the zoo next week.

A wink of light appeared and disappeared behind the swell. It looked as though it was coming their way. Please God, let it be the Zodiac.

Then she realised Katy's grip had slipped. She was drifting away. India grabbed her oilskin but the weight of her was dragging her down.

'Katy! Help me, dammit!'

No response.

India clung on to Katy's unconscious form with one arm, the other round the life buoy, and dragged her knees up to her waist, trying to reduce heat loss. She couldn't feel her hands any more, nor her arms, legs or feet.

'Katy!'

She couldn't feel her heart beat. Her vision started to blur.

Katy. The word wasn't even a whisper, just a thought.

Red light strobed her eyelids. Red was replaced by glaring white. She opened her eyes and was nearly blinded by the searchlight.

A man was shouting but she didn't understand what he said. She stared, transfixed, at the hands reaching for her. Then she was being hauled out of the sea, and she wanted to help, but her body was like a block of concrete. She wanted to tell them to save Katy too, but her mouth wouldn't work.

The next instant men were landing her onto a slippery deck like a big fish. Her nostrils were filled with the putrid reek of blood and fishy entrails and she retched and heaved, bringing up what felt like a gallon of salt water.

A man was barking orders and she tried to work out what he was saying, but it was unintelligible. A moment later she was being carried along corridors and down companionways, then into someone's quarters with a TV set on full blast, an unmade bed, piles of oiled sweaters and socks tossed in one corner. Carefully, the man laid her on the bunk and began cutting off her clothing. 'No need for shyness,' he said briskly. 'Emergency.'

She could feel him patting her dry. 'No rub,' he said. 'Very bad to rub skin now.' He wrapped her limbs in a variety of towels and blankets separately, then covered her with more blankets. Helped her sip a cup of hot, bitter tea. She started to shiver. Gently he raised her thick mane of hair in one hand and wound another towel round her neck.

He said, 'We must be slow. Sometimes the limbs contain blood that is very cold. It is dangerous for you if it gets to the heart.'

India couldn't even manage a nod. She simply lay there for what seemed like an age. Then she felt him touching her as though checking whether she had defrosted and was ready for cooking. He murmured something. His voice was calm and soothing. She didn't say anything back; she was absorbed in trying not to cry out with the pain of her limbs returning to life. White-hot flames were shooting through each vein like bullets from a gun. After a long time she opened her eyes. A pair of dark, expressionless eyes looked back. Ruler-straight eyebrows. Wide mouth, square jaw. Black hair, flecked with white above the ears. If the man hadn't been dressed in filthy oilskins and reeking to high heaven, she might have thought him distinguished.

She managed to say, 'Katy. My friend . . .'

Immediately the eyes brightened. 'Your friend is OK. She asks for you.'

'Ned. What about Ned?'

'He is your captain?'

'No. The first . . . mate.'

Immediately he ducked his head. 'So sorry.'

'Ned's dead?'

'So sorry.'

Her vision began to waver. 'Who . . . are you?'

'I captain of this ship.' He looked uncertain whether to say anything else, then added quietly, 'The *Kagoshima Maru*.'

If she hadn't been so weak, her jaw would have dropped in astonishment. They'd been rescued by the whaling fleet's factory ship.

THE *KAGOSHIMA MARU*'S paramedic checked India several times during the night. When dawn broke he drew back the blind covering the porthole hatch. She looked out at the grey sky and white-crested sea that she knew was as cold as the hand of death and said, 'Could you close it, please?'

She didn't want to see the ocean right now. Pulling the blankets up round her shoulders, she wriggled her toes in the captain's too-large socks, and wondered if she'd ever feel warm again.

Her mind suddenly switched to Ned's unconscious form sprawled on the bridge. Had he regained consciousness after the collision? Had he drowned under a landslide of water as the boat sank? However her friend had died, she hoped it had been fast and that he'd known nothing of it.

India lay there thinking about Ned for a long time, and finally mustered the strength to go and check on Katy. She followed a crew member down mile-long corridors dressed like a whaler: baggy blue trousers held up with string, rubber boots and an oily sweater that smelt of fish.

'Hey, nice outfit,' Katy greeted her.

'Nice outfit, yourself.'

Katy wore a pink robe dotted with yellow pansies. She had black rings round her eyes. India took her hand, glad to feel it was warm.

'How are you?'

'They told me you saved my life.'

India looked away. 'I'm not sure about that.'

'So who held my head out of the water while I was unconscious?'

India smiled and gave Katy's hand a little shake. 'I was hoping you'd come round and offer me a cigarette.'

The faintest smile brushed Katy's face, then her expression sobered. 'Thanks, India.' Katy slumped back on her bunk. 'Sorry, I'm so tired.'

'I'll come back later.'

Hoping to find the rest of the crew, India began walking down a lengthy corridor, thinking about the first time she'd met Katy, how she'd felt like an unkempt and malnourished cart-horse next to Katy's thoroughbred good looks. Talk about opposites. Katy had curves, India had angles. Katy had a shiny blonde bob, India, a black mane that was always tangled into a mass of corkscrews. Katy was outgoing and physically expressive, India was neither. They would never have bonded so quickly if it hadn't been for the fact they were the only smokers among the crew.

She was on her third lengthy corridor when she bumped into Cuan, also dressed like a whaler. He opened his arms and she walked straight into his embrace, hugging him back.

'Good on you,' he said, and she felt him press a kiss on her head. 'You're a bloody star, jumping into that water for a mate.'

Tears leaked down her cheeks.

'Look, love, you ought to know . . . We lost Emma. And Keith, Matt, Vince and Marie.' He leaned back and looked at her straight. 'We lost Ned too.'

'Yes.' She buried her face into his shoulder.

His embrace tightened. 'I'm sorry, India. I know how close you were.'

'How did he die? Did he drown?'

'After the collision—well, the bridge was a mess. He'd hit his head . . .' Cuan cleared his throat. 'He never came round.'

Her fingers spasmed on the rough wool of his whaler's sweater. 'What about *Sundancer*?'

'She stayed afloat long enough to get us all off. But when she went, she sure went. She reared bow-up and went down fast like she was yanked under by a giant squid.' He kissed her hair again. 'You'll feel better if you get something to eat. They're serving brekky, and I think you should give it a go.'

She'd never felt less like eating in her life, but she said obediently, 'OK. But you'd better direct me or I'll never find it.'

'I show you,' a voice said behind them. They turned to see the *Kagoshima Maru*'s captain standing there, looking determined.

Cuan gave the captain a nod and walked away. India watched him head down the corridor, his normally straight back bowed, his shoulders low.

BREAKFAST WAS a bowl of hot, savoury noodles and a mug of green tea.

The captain ('You may call me Shinzo') had given India Ned's watch after Cuan had left. She had taken it gingerly, feeling numb and disbelieving, and knew the tears would come later, when the full force of what had happened sank in. Ned's watch was now on her left wrist above her own, which had stopped. Mikey had given it to her last Christmas as a reminder that she was always late home for supper. Mikey would hit the roof when he heard about the collision; he was always banging on at her to keep out of trouble. But she was more concerned with having to face Ellie.

Ned, killed by an unregistered container ship. Why hadn't the ship answered Ned's radio call? Why hadn't it stopped to help? No lights. They hadn't wanted to be seen. Why? If they'd been hit by a fishing trawler it would make sense, but a *container ship*? The shipping routes were over 2,000 kilometres north of where they'd collided. And they'd been coming from the *south*. Where there was nothing until you hit the desolate snow-bound coastline of Wilkes Land. India couldn't work it out.

Gulping down another mouthful of noodles—her appetite had kicked in as soon as her taste buds informed her that they were remarkably good— she looked at Shinzo sipping his bitter green tea. He'd rescued the entire Greenpeace crew. He'd pulled nine people from the freezing ocean and recovered the bodies of those that hadn't made it. Four people dead from hypothermia, two from injuries suffered when the ship hit them. Shinzo told her that he'd radioed the authorities and prepared the port of Fremantle for their arrival. He was obviously not looking forward to facing the officials and their questions: what had he been doing hunting in the Southern Ocean Sanctuary, a critically protected area for whales? And why did his ship have the meat and blubber of over 100 minkes in its hold?

Before he'd shown her to breakfast, she'd asked for a tour and, to her surprise, he'd agreed. Most of his crew were taking it easy: playing cards, reading or watching videos. There wasn't much for them to do when they weren't actually processing whales. Shinzo had allowed her a glimpse into the ship's freezer: row upon row of flensed flesh the colour of salmon stretched as far as her eye could see.

'What on earth do you do with it all?' she'd asked innocently.

'Scientific purpose,' he'd replied.

'Yeah, right.' India's tone could have stripped an engine. 'I gather your scientific samples retail for over a hundred million bucks a year.'

He had grinned, showing a gold incisor. 'Good business, heya?'

'But they're *endangered*. What happens when you've killed the last whale?'

'Plenty of whales for me.'

'Shinzo, you're *wiping them out*. They don't breed like rabbits! They have a single calf every two years or so and it takes that calf *years* before it can reproduce! They can't keep up with your killing sprees!' She had realised she was shouting, but couldn't seem to stop herself. 'Thanks to you they'll be extinct in the next few years!'

Shinzo had calmly dug in his overalls and passed her a greasy-looking square of cotton. When he pointed to her face she'd realised she had tears on her cheeks and, ignoring his gesture, stalked off. They hadn't spoken since.

Looking at Shinzo now, she felt swamped with guilt. Not only had he saved her life and shown remarkable tenderness and respect as he thawed her frozen body, but he'd offered her his handkerchief for her tears. At that moment he looked up and caught her eye, but she ducked her head, pushing away her noodles. Shinzo was like all whalers. He only cared about the money.

THE *KAGOSHIMA MARU* was twice as fast as *Sundancer*, but it still took them four days before they neared the coast. Four days of numbed disbelief, hushed voices and endless cups of green tea. India was glad she was with people who were physically affectionate; she needed every hug that came her way. She knew it was stupid, but she kept looking for Ned's head of fair hair among the crew members, and when she didn't see him she'd crumple inside.

Not long after dawn on Sunday, Shinzo dropped anchor. The sea was calm, the sky filled with grey cloud. India scanned the horizon but couldn't see any land. Just a fishing trawler speeding their way.

'Friends of yours?' she asked him.

Shinzo didn't answer.

They were on the bridge, Shinzo squinting against the smoke drifting from his cigarette. Ned's body was already on deck along with the other dead crew members, each shrouded in fine muslin-like netting.

India watched the fishing trawler make fast against the factory ship, then a bulky Japanese man in overalls climbed on board and headed their way.

'This man,' said Shinzo, 'will take everybody ashore.'

Overalls came up to Shinzo and they shook hands. India saw Shinzo slip the man a fat, oil-skinned package and realised he'd lied. Shinzo hadn't alerted the authorities in Fremantle at all.

She waited until Overalls was back on his trawler before she confronted Shinzo. 'You bribed him, didn't you?'

'You are alive.' His mouth set in a stern line that indicated she owed him.

Remorse washed over her. He could have ignored *Sundancer*'s pleas for assistance, but he hadn't. He'd then risked the possibility of his ship being reported to the police and Customs in order to bring them safely to shore.

'Shinzo, I'm sorry.'

He gave a formal bow and India held out her hand. His grip was strong and hard as a monkey wrench.

'If you hear of the container ship, or see it at all, could you ring me? It'll have a whacking great dent in its bow from hitting us, and her name is—'

'*The Pride*.' He gave a curt nod.

'Yes. Would you call me at the *Sydney Morning Herald*?'

He blinked. 'You are a reporter?'

'Yup.'

He made a grunting sound at the back of his throat that could have meant anything from gratification to disapproval.

'I know I've been rude.' She softened her tone. 'After all you've done . . . Don't think I don't appreciate it. It's just that my friend died.'

He rested a hand lightly on her shoulder. His voice was gentle. 'May the best of your friend's past follow him to his future.'

Touched, she put her hand over his. 'Thank you,' she said solemnly.

A glint of humour crossed his face. 'Next time you chase me, bring your *QE2*. We have drink on board your ship. I beat you at poker.'

She grinned. 'It's a deal.'

'IT WAS an accident,' Detective Inspector Zhuganov repeated, and glanced at the door as though he wished he could walk away and never return.

'Yes,' India said, 'but there's no way they couldn't see we were in trouble, that we had people overboard. They left us to *die*.'

She was in Fremantle's police station with Cuan and two federal cops. Because the collision had taken place outside Australian waters, the feds had turned up on behalf of AMSA, the Australian Maritime Safety Authority in Canberra. The rest of the crew were making their statements in the squad room, leaving the five of them crammed into a room the size of a walnut. Three chairs, but nobody was sitting.

'Why would they do that?' one of the feds asked.

'Because they had something to hide.'

'Any ideas?'

'Not yet.'

'No ship's come in with a damaged bow,' the other fed said, 'but we'll keep looking. We've put up a couple of planes to see if they can spot her.'

India nodded, but she wasn't holding out much hope.

Detective Inspector Zhuganov briskly rounded off the meeting. As they left, they all agreed to keep the disaster under wraps until the next of kin were informed. India would only phone her editor once she'd been given the go-ahead from Cuan. She didn't want any unsuspecting relatives to learn of the death of their loved ones from her newspaper.

In the squad room, the cops were trying to sort out how to get everyone back home. One constable was handing out ten-dollar notes so the crew could buy themselves sandwiches and coffee; others were making phone calls. The atmosphere was frenetic and tearful, and India felt claustrophobia and panic rush through her. She turned and hastily started for the door.

'India, wait!' Katy scurried after her.

'Got to go.' Her voice was clipped. 'Sorry.'

'Can't we give you a lift? William's on his way.'

India wanted to be alone, to gather her thoughts before she saw Ellie. 'Thanks, but I'll be fine,' she said.

A light rain was falling outside. Dismal weather for a dismal day. Cars splashed past but there were few people on the street. India gulped lungfuls of damp air, pretending she could taste the endless wheat fields from across the expanse of the city, and the deep red desert stretching behind them. Gradually a sense of distance and space trickled through her, and she felt calm.

She wanted to ring Mikey but didn't dare just yet. He'd hear the tears in her voice and then he'd be on the next flight to Perth, and she didn't want that. She wanted to be in the snug haven of their home tonight with Polly when she told him what had happened, not in some bland hotel room.

She was wondering what she should do next when she heard someone exit the police station behind her. Before he put an arm round her shoulders she already knew who it was. She'd only been at sea with the crew for a month, but she felt as though she was linked to them by tensile steel.

'You're going to Ellie?' Cuan asked.

She nodded.

'May as well drive Ned's utility vehicle home for her.'

She didn't have Ned's car keys but it didn't dissuade Cuan. They caught a cab to Victoria Quay where, to her astonishment, he hot-wired the thing, and showed her how.

'You think because I'm expedition leader I'm squeaky clean?' he said, trying to lighten his tone, but it was tight from stress and India quickly said, no, she'd always thought of him as a car thief, and was proud of his speciality.

'Love you too, babe,' he said and kissed her cheek before waving her off. 'Speak soon.'

IT WAS LATE afternoon before India finally arrived at Jimbuku Bay. She parked Ned's car by the beach and lit a cigarette. Her hands were shaking and she knew she had to calm herself before she faced Ellie. An easterly wind punched the side of the car from time to time, making it shudder and India flinch. What she needed was a stiff drink, but she wouldn't get that until she'd broken the news.

She eyed the thundering surf and the plumes spraying off the tops of dunes, then turned her gaze to the artful jumble of designer homes hugging the furthest reaches of the wind-blasted beach. Not for the first time she felt a sense of disbelief as she gazed at the place. Jimbuku Bay, a bunch of houses the colour of Smarties with little turrets and round nautical windows, would sit nicely on the banks of Perth's Swan River, but here, in the middle of this flat, salty wasteland, it looked seriously out of place.

Stubbing out her cigarette, India started up the car and headed for Ellie's. Dread squirmed in her gut. How would she tell Ellie that the man she loved wouldn't be around any more? She could remember the day Ellie met Ned in London, at the Tate, like it was yesterday. Ellie blasting into the flat yelling at the top of her voice, 'We had coffee! And he loves Kitaj as much as I do and I can't believe it! He's perfect!' and then Ned saying to India in the kitchen as he opened a bottle of wine the following week, 'I can't believe she likes Kitaj. She's perfect.'

They'd been married for four years when they decided to return to Australia and have children. They'd set up home near Ellie's parents, who lived in Geraldton, and everything had been perfect. But now Ned was dead.

India halted outside Ellie's cherry-red front door, and concentrated on clamping her emotions. She had to be strong. Her own grief could wait until later. With an unsteady hand, she pressed the bell.

When Ellie opened the fly-screen door, her expression immediately turned into alarm. 'What's happened? Why are you back?' Her gaze swept over India's baggy trousers clinched at the waist with string, her rubber boots, and the blood drained from her face. 'Where's Ned?'

'Let's go inside.'

Stock-still, Ellie stared at India. *'Where is he?'*

India crushed the wave of grief threatening to rise and locked it in a small black box inside her. 'Let's go inside,' she repeated, voice steady. Calm.

'No.' Ellie's stare grew unfocused. 'Oh God, he's in hospital, isn't he?'

'I'm sorry, Ellie. There was an accident—'

No, no. *No.*' Ellie's voice started to rise. 'No, don't tell me he's dead, please, no, not that, please, *please.*'

'We collided with a container ship. We lost six crew . . .' Her voice started to crack but she forced herself to finish. 'Including Ned.'

India held out Ned's watch. 'Ellie, I'm so sorry.'

'NO!'

Ellie's shout came from deep within her heart, and wrenched India so hard that the box she'd locked flew open and she was crying and trying not to, she wanted to be *strong*, and Ellie was falling to her knees, her face contorted as she screamed, her hands balled into fists and smashing the ground. India dropped beside her and tried to hold her, but Ellie fought her off, hitting and punching, her terrible wail piercing India like a knife.

'I'm sorry,' India kept saying over and over. 'I'm so sorry.'

Ellie raised her face to India and for a second India thought she was going to punch her, but then she had her arms round her and was sobbing against her neck. India knew her friend's heart had broken.

A LONG TIME later, when Ellie's sobs quietened, India managed to get her inside. Pushing aside a stack of baby magazines, she sat her on the sofa and took her in her arms again. She tried not to think of how Ellie would get through her pregnancy without Ned. She had another seven months to go. India rocked Ellie and stroked her hair.

'H-how did it happen?' Ellie asked. 'Tell me. Everything.'

'Maybe later,' India said gently.

Ellie twisted upright, her expression suddenly fierce. 'No, India. Now. I want you to tell me everything. His last day. I have to *know*.'

So India told her. When she got to the part where she and Ned had been on watch, talking about naming the baby Albert, Ellie stiffened.

'He mentioned the curse?'

India frowned. 'What curse?'

Ellie stared past her. 'The one on this place.' Her voice was a whisper. 'I never believed it. But Ned did. He wanted to sell up.'

'Why?'

'He was scared. People have been falling ill, some of them even died. Oh God, and now Ned's gone . . .' A fresh storm of weeping overtook her and India held her until it eased.

'I'll ring for a doctor,' India said.

'No,' Ellie managed. 'M-mum and Dad.'

After India had called Ellie's parents, who said they were on their way, hold tight, India stood by the kitchen window, gazing at the carefully planted bottlebrushes and yellow banksias, the feathery bracken ferns lining each endlessly neat pathway.

She went to the fridge to get some orange juice, and paused at a memory of Ned giving her an avid tour of his Ocean Green appliances: fridge-freezer, ice machine and air-conditioning units. 'They came with the house,'

Ned had said gleefully, and she could understand why he was so smug. When CFCs had been banned, the efficiency of refrigeration had plummeted, but Ocean Green found a new way of chilling air effectively without damaging the environment. India wanted an Ocean Green fridge too, but since you had to take a mortgage out to own one she was waiting for the price to drop. Her throat tightened. Ned had been so proud of his goddamn fridge.

India took the juice to Ellie and sat with her until her parents arrived. Faces set with anxiety, Ron and Jill didn't seem to take in the fact that India was dressed like a Japanese whaler. They saw nothing but their daughter's distress.

'RON, DID you know this place was cursed?' India asked Ellie's dad a little later. Ron was making tea in the kitchen and looking miserable.

'Yeah. Ned mentioned it a while back. He was up for moving, but Ellie, well, she doesn't believe in all that mumbo jumbo. She loves the place.'

'She said people had been ill. And that some died.'

'Too right. Sick as parrots a lot of them. They've lost five in the past year.' He put a liver-spotted hand briefly over his eyes. 'And now Ned.'

She let him compose himself before pressing on. 'How did they die?'

'To start with they reckoned it was a virus. But when Bob Jarrett keeled over last October they got real worried. Fit as anything, that bloke. So they started checking stuff out. The water, the electrics, radiation. You name it, they've been over it, OK'd it all, but even so Jilly and I, well, we wanted 'em to move too, but no, not Ellie.'

'Isn't she worried about the baby?'

'Actually, she has been a bit bothered. But she said not to tell Ned or he'd sell the house for nothing, he was so wired up over it.'

She recalled Ned's unconscious form sprawled on the *Sundancer*'s deck.

'You'll make sure she stays with you?' India asked anxiously. 'I don't know what's going on here, but it sounds pretty weird.'

'No worries.' He looked down at the floor. 'She wants to see him, you know. Any chance of giving us a hand with it?'

India immediately rang the Royal Perth Hospital mortuary to be told that yes, they could come down any time after 9 a.m. the following morning.

Ron's relief was palpable when India said she would go with them. 'Thanks, love,' he said.

If she was going to stay overnight she had to ring Mikey. No way could she risk him or Polly hearing about the collision before she told them she was OK. Taking a deep breath, she dialled Mikey's number at the north Sydney cop shop.

'Hey, gorgeous,' he said. 'Caught the bad guys yet?'

'Er . . .' She cleared her throat. 'Actually, they rescued me.'

Silence.

'How's Polly?' she asked.

'Polly can wait, I want to know what happened.'

'I'm absolutely fine. Never better. I just need some new clothes, that's all.' She thought she was getting it just about right. A light tone, inconsequential chatter. 'My whaler's outfit stinks.'

'Whaler's *what*?' he said in a strangled tone.

'We had a little accident and a whaling ship kindly brought us to shore. I'm going to stay overnight with Ellie, then I'll jump on a flight and be home in time for supper tomorrow. How about some steak? I love the way you do it with that pepper cream sauce.'

Another silence, then, 'You're OK?'

'Yup. Cross my heart and hope to die. I'm fine.'

'You don't sound it.'

'Thanks. Next time I'll let you read about it in the papers.'

He made a groaning sound. 'That bad?'

Her lungs contracted and she knew she was going to lose it any second, but she wanted him to stay there, be *at home* for her when she got back.

'See you at supper,' she said brightly and hung up.

INDIA DROVE Ellie's car to Perth. Ellie sat up front, glassy-eyed and pale, her parents buckled up in the back. Nobody spoke.

The autopsy report stated that Ned had died from a blood clot after a massive knock on the head.

'He would have been unconscious at the time,' the woman pathologist said kindly. 'He wouldn't have known a thing.'

While Ellie's parents walked their daughter outside, India stayed behind, saying she'd catch them up in a minute. Turning to the pathologist, she said, 'Would you mind if I ask a couple of quick questions about Ned?'

The pathologist frowned. 'It depends.'

India told her how ill Ned had looked on the bridge of *Sundancer*, describing his rasping breath and sweats, and that he'd lost consciousness while he was on watch and just before the collision.

'I didn't realise,' the pathologist said, running a hand over her eyes.

'No.' India knew the woman probably wouldn't release any sensitive information to her, but she asked anyway. 'Did you find anything that would explain him passing out like that?'

'Well, he suffered from asthma,' she said.

Startled, India said, 'He did?' It was the first she knew about it.

'His lungs were constricted and filled with inflammatory cells.'

'You're saying he died of asthma?'

'No. He died from a blood clot after something hit him very hard on the head. But an asthma attack would explain him losing consciousness.' The pathologist studied her carefully. 'I think it's best if you go now.' Her voice was gentle. 'I'm very sorry for your loss.'

As she walked outside to join Ellie and her parents, India felt a surge of anger ignite beneath her breastbone. If it's the last thing I do, she swore, I'm going to hunt that container ship down.

TWO

The ANZ Bank personnel were kindness personified. India was halfway through her story when she was swept to the manager's office and sat down with a cup of coffee and a plateful of sandwiches. She was being treated as though she'd been shipwrecked and deprived of food for days, but she wasn't complaining. After a diet of noodles and raw fish, she was desperate for some decent carbohydrates.

Eventually she was issued a Visa card along with 700 bucks, and she headed for the shops. She swapped her whaler's outfit for her usual uniform of shirt, jeans and boots, then bought some supplies: cigarettes and a lighter, a cheap watch and a notepad and pen. Coming out of the stationers, she swung right, searching for a taxi, and that was when she saw him.

Her breathing stopped. He was wearing a blue fleece, jeans and deck shoes, and had a blond ponytail. For a second she thought he was Ned.

He was looking in the window of a store opposite, and as she stared at him he turned, and she could have sworn he looked straight at her, but then he was walking down the street, and she realised he wasn't anything like

Ned. He was shorter, for a start, and stocky, nothing like Ned's lean frame. It must have been the ponytail that had caught her out, along with his clothes.

A taxi cruised down her side of the street and she forgot about the man as she waved at it and climbed inside, asking to be taken to Fremantle Port.

The sky was leaden when she arrived, and her senses felt as dull as her surroundings. It had to be in the mid-twenties, but she felt chilled and shivery. She walked to Corkhill Landing, her steps sluggish. Standing next to one of the NO FISHING signs, India looked across the harbour at the main port, North Quay, bristling with containers, cranes and cargo ships.

Sundancer had been moored here before she set sail. India could picture the crew loading boxes of kit on board, could hear their cheerful shouts. She could see Emma ticking off lists and packing away groceries; Keith, the chief engineer, double-checking the engines; Vince helping load a spare helicopter blade on board; Matt and Marie taking blood samples so they'd know who matched who; Ned overseeing, always everywhere.

All six of them dead.

Swallowing hard to ease the ache in her throat, India took a breath, turned round and headed for an eleven-storey blue and white building, topped with a navigation control tower. The Port Authority offices.

'Can I help you?' the receptionist asked.

'Is the harbourmaster around?'

The woman looked dubious until India told her what it was about, and then her demeanour turned brisk. Picking up the phone, she dialled. 'Chief? I've someone here about the Greenpeace incident . . . Sure, I'll bring her up.'

Hank Gregory, known by everyone as the chief, was a giant of a man with wildly curly dark brown hair and laughter lines etched round his bright blue eyes. His shirtsleeves were pushed back to reveal a tattoo on his right forearm of a dove with a banner in its beak.

He took one look at India and grinned. 'Not every day we get a nice surprise like this,' he said, unashamedly raking his eyes up and down her body. 'You a model or something?'

'A reporter.'

His face grew guarded. 'Jenny didn't say anything about that. What do you want?'

He hadn't asked her to sit down, so she stood in his office overlooking the harbour and ranks of cargo ships and fork-lift trucks beetling back and forth like insects in the distance, and told him.

'Holy shit,' he said. 'You're the journo who went into the water after your mate, aren't you? Talk about gutsy. How can I help?'

'I just wanted to know if you'd seen the container ship docked here. She'd have a dent on her bow from—'

'The collision, sure.' The chief was nodding. 'My brief says she's around ninety metres long, fifteen metres wide, four derricks.'

'You haven't seen her?'

The chief shook his head. 'Sorry. She's not in our records. We checked the classification society, our movement schedules, ships in port, that sort of stuff. The feds reckon she never called into Australia.'

'Do you have any idea what a container ship could have been doing in the middle of the Southern Ocean?'

He scratched his chin. 'Can't see any skipper wanting to sail half a million bucks' worth of ship in that place.'

'How would you suggest I track it down?'

'The feds are doing that.'

'Me too.'

He held her eyes a moment. 'I see.'

'She's called *The Pride of Tang*-something,' she prompted.

'Yeah, I know.' He flashed her a grin as he finally waved her to a chair. 'And she's from a port that has two As in its name.'

'Two As that were quite well spread apart,' she told him. 'With maybe three or four letters between them, like Manila.'

The chief took a seat and picked up the phone. 'You fancy a coffee?'

Two minutes later coffee arrived in a pair of china mugs. His had a naked woman with a feather boa on it, hers a kangaroo wearing a pair of boxing gloves emblazoned with the Australian flag. The contradiction of smart and efficient offices against Aussie tat made her smile, and while the chief tapped on his computer, taking great glugs of his coffee, India sipped.

'Only ship coming up on the Lloyd's Register is *The Pride*. She runs out of Hong Kong. Want me to give her a call?'

'But Hong Kong doesn't share the same port letters, AA.'

'You'll want to eliminate her from your enquiries, at least. I'll find out where she's at.' He made a phone call. When he hung up he looked disappointed. 'She's on her way back from the North Pacific. Been delivering stuff to Anchorage. No way could it be her. Sorry.'

India said, more to herself than the chief, 'How on earth will I find her?'

He ran a hand through his wild curls. 'Well, the feds are checking the registers worldwide, so not much point you covering the same stuff. I'd get the word out through the docks. Melbourne, Sydney. Offer a big reward. A seaman might have seen her in another port somewhere. But are you sure you should be messing with this kind of stuff? Could be dangerous.'

Choosing to ignore that, India rose to leave and said, 'Should you hear of a boat with a dent on its bow . . .'

'Sure, I'll let you know.'

THE RECEPTIONIST kindly called India a taxi to take her to the airport, and while she waited for it to arrive she went outside for a cigarette. The second she stepped out of the door she saw him. Blue fleece and ponytail.

He was leaning against a dark blue Ford in the car park but the instant she appeared he hopped inside. India let her eyes wash over him and fixed her gaze on a long, ash-coloured ship moored across the harbour.

What the hell was going on? Was he following her? If so, he wasn't doing a great job of it. But then, if he hadn't reminded her of Ned, she probably wouldn't have noticed him. Nerves tight, she smoked two cigarettes, waiting for him to drive away, but he didn't.

When her taxi turned up, she heard him start his car, watched him pull out behind them as they exited the car park. He followed her all the way to the airport, hanging back as she checked in, drifting behind her through the departure lounge. It was only at the final security check that he let her go. The last she saw he was on a mobile phone and walking briskly outside.

AT KINGSFORD-SMITH airport, India did her best to see if she had another tail, but it was difficult with so many people around. When the taxi dropped her outside her block she studied the street. A woman in her twenties with a boy in tow, a fat kid of about ten. Several suited men and women walking on the path from the city ferry. A window cleaner and a guy walking his retriever. She filed them all as best she could in her memory, along with the two cars that drove past: one white Lexus and a rusting Mini Moke.

In the lift, rattling up to the fifteenth floor, she tried to stop her mind from gnawing at the man she'd spotted in Perth. Who was he reporting to?

No point in worrying about it now, she told herself firmly. You're home, and have more important things to do. Like explain to Mikey what has happened and hope he doesn't hit the roof.

TO HER RELIEF, Mikey was halfway through trimming a pile of sugar snap peas when she arrived, steaks marinating to one side, two bottles of Merlot already decanted. If he was angry with her, he never cooked, let alone cracked open a bottle of wine.

'Polly in bed?' she asked.

'She's waiting for you.'

She'd bought Polly a present at the airport, but as soon as she saw that the little girl was fast asleep, she put it aside. It could wait.

Polly's sheet was twisted round her skinny waist, ribs like sticks no matter how much she ate. A tiny teddy bear the size of a pack of cigarettes lay on the pillow beside her, its tartan bow tie askew. India pulled up the sheet, then brushed a strand of dark curly hair from Polly's forehead before pressing a kiss there.

She'd first met the young Aboriginal girl in a baking outback town slap-bang in the middle of nowhere, and when she and Mikey discovered that Polly had recently been orphaned, they had formally adopted her. India smiled and gave Polly another kiss before heading back to the kitchen.

Mikey poured her a glass of wine and watched while she sipped. Then he said, 'Tell me what happened.'

India went to the window and glanced outside. No Lexus or Mini Moke. No people sitting in parked cars staring at her window. Sipping her wine, she told Mikey about *Sundancer*'s collision, checking the street from time to time, but seeing nothing to alarm her.

Gradually she felt herself relax, and when she had finished he looked at her a long time, expression unreadable. Then he put down the knife and came to her and wrapped her in his arms. Kissed her at length. Led her to their bedroom and slowly undressed her.

'I SHOULD have near-death experiences more often,' she said in his arms a little later.

'It was a tossup between putting you over my knee and spanking the hell out of you for terrifying me so much or—'

'Glad it was the Or,' she said, laughing.

'So.' He peered into her face. 'How do you fancy getting hitched?'

Oh God, she thought, not again.

'What, right now?' India tried to keep the mood light.

He grinned. 'Right now would be perfect.'

'I have no intention of getting married naked,' she protested.

'At least I'd see exactly what I'd be getting.'

She gave him an arch look. 'And what you're getting right now is a cup of nice, hot cocoa.' Climbing out of bed, she reached for his towelling robe, paused. 'Or would you prefer a glass of red?'

'What I'd prefer . . .' Mikey reached up and put his hand round her wrist and pulled her back onto the bed.

THE NEXT MORNING India studied the street and saw commuters walking for the ferry, others driving. Nothing unusual. She couldn't think of a reason why anyone would follow her, but she would keep an eye out, just in case.

After she'd downed her coffee and they'd finished their usual breakfast of scrambled eggs and toast, India gave Polly her present.

'A prezzie?' said Polly, agog. 'But it's not my birthday.'

'It's a missing-you present,' India said. 'Because the second I saw it I wished you were there with me to see it too, and I missed you like mad.'

'Go on, Poll,' urged Mikey. 'Open it.'

Polly unfolded the tissue paper and went absolutely still as she stared at the Aboriginal bracelet. Then she picked it up, carefully inspecting the polished black wood decorated with tiny white and yellow dots, the shadows of brown that could be roos, could be dogs or porcupines, India couldn't tell, but Polly obviously could.

'I can see a camp,' she said breathlessly. 'And a water hole. A flock of cockatoos.' Thrusting it up her skinny arm she appraised it against her skin, and then the little girl's smile burst like the sun from behind a thundercloud. 'It's got a whole story!' She flung her arms round India's neck. 'It's the best prezzie *ever*.'

LATER THAT DAY, after an intense debriefing from Scotto, her editor, and her colleagues, culminating in an extremely long and alcoholic lunch, India was back at her desk, trying not to think about Mikey's light-hearted reference to getting hitched. It was the fifth time in as many months. But why get married? After all, they were living together, and with Polly they were a family already. She didn't think a piece of paper would make any difference, but Mikey obviously thought otherwise. What had he said the last time?

It's the commitment, India. It's saying you love me that much you want me for life too.

She'd thought the life part sounded like a jail sentence but hadn't said anything, just given him a bright smile and said she'd think about it.

Sighing, she picked up her office phone and started making calls to the major Australian ports. Then she began to work her way through the ports that had two As in their name: Dar es Salaam, Auckland, Jakarta, Punta Arenas, Mar del Plata. Much a reporter's life was drudge work like this, and India hoped that if she was thorough enough she'd eventually strike lucky.

With Cuan's go-ahead, the *Sydney Morning Herald* carried her story the following day, offering a reward for anyone who had information about *The Pride*. They received a handful of crank calls after the reward money, but nothing else. The feds kept up their search but had no luck in finding the container ship or the *Kagoshima Maru*.

It wasn't until the end of the week when she spotted her tail.

A woman in her twenties, with a fat kid in tow.

The woman didn't always have the boy with her, which was why India reckoned she hadn't spotted her earlier. The woman wasn't always around either, and India guessed she took her tailing duty in turns with someone else. Who, she couldn't tell. They were obviously much better at the job than the woman because she never saw anyone remotely suspicious.

Her awareness heightened, India began to notice other things. Like when she came into her office on Friday morning her computer keyboard was on the right of her screen when she always pushed it to the left after she'd finished typing. And the papers on her desk weren't quite as she remembered leaving them. But what clinched her concern was when she checked her computer. Under FILE were four documents that had been opened in her absence. All were to do with *Sundancer*'s sinking.

When she told Scotto about her suspicions, he pulled off his little gold-rimmed glasses and rubbed the space between his eyes. 'But we've got security. Nobody can just walk in off the street and go through your stuff.'

'Quite.'

'What do you think they're after?'

India told him about the files that had been opened, adding, 'My guess is they want to see how far I'm getting with finding the container ship.' She gave a long sigh. 'Which is pretty much nowhere.'

'You talked to Mikey about this?'

'Not yet. I don't want to worry him.'

Scotto made a humming sound. 'You want locks installed for your office?'

India thought it over. 'No. I don't want to alert them. I'll keep anything sensitive with me. But if you see anyone in my office—'

'I'll arrest them myself,' Scotto said.

THE NEXT few days were spent going to funerals, and, no matter how hard India looked, she couldn't see any sign of anyone keeping tabs on her. Mind you, they'd have to have huge resources and be incredibly well organised considering she'd flown to Melbourne on Tuesday morning, Brisbane that afternoon, and then to Western Australia on Wednesday. No man with a ponytail was waiting for her in Perth's domestic terminal, and nobody appeared to follow her hire car out of the airport. As she approached Geraldton, India finally felt herself relax.

Her mood lasted until after Ned's funeral and she discovered that Ellie wasn't staying with her parents.

'You can't stay there on your own,' India told her.

'He's all around me at home.' Ellie gestured helplessly. 'I don't want to be anywhere else. Maybe in a few weeks I'll feel differently, but not now.'

The last service was for Emma, held up in the drought-ravaged Northern Territory. Standing ankle-deep in red dust, sweat pouring in the forty-degree heat, India watched Katy park and hop out of her brand-new air-conditioned Land Cruiser.

'What's with the stickers?' India gestured at the GET ACTIVE! logos plastered all over the vehicle. 'I thought you were up here saving the bilby from extinction, not advertising a fitness regime.'

'It's William's new name for his company. He chose it to mean *get active* and support his products and therefore support the environment. He's hoping it'll increase sales.'

India raised her eyebrows. She'd have thought William's sales were doing fine considering he'd been listed as one of the wealthiest men in Australia last year. The biggest producer of green household products in the country, William's ads were on every TV station telling the public that his washing-up liquid and floor polish did the same job as any competitor but with far less harm to the environment. William's company, India seemed to recall, had also recently invented an ecologically perfect, self-disposing package.

'Isn't he involved with Ecopac?'

Katy beamed. 'Isn't he brilliant?'

Brilliant wasn't the half of it, India thought, Ecopac was going to change the world. All those plastic orange juice and milk cartons would no longer clutter landfill spaces but would be turning brittle beneath the Australian sunshine and disintegrating into sand.

'Well done him,' India said, impressed. 'When's it being launched?'

Katy glanced at a dusty airstrip beside the road, then up at the sky. 'He'll tell you himself, when he gets here. He's panting to meet you.'

The faint sound of organ music reached them, and they took one dismayed look at each other before bolting through the simmering heat for the little whitewashed church.

AFTER THE SERVICE, India was walking back to her hire car when she heard her name being called. She turned to see a dark-haired man in his early forties striding towards her. Nice suit, she thought. Bet it's hand tailored.

'India Kane?'

'Yup.'

He held out a hand. 'I'm Katy's husband. William Hughes.'

She covered her surprise that he wasn't nearer Katy's age by shaking his hand enthusiastically and saying, 'Hey! Great to meet you!'

He grinned. 'It's my pleasure, believe me. You saved her life.'

'Well, if I hadn't, I'm sure someone else would have.'

'I doubt it,' William said.

Always uncomfortable with praise, India shrugged.

'I'd like you to join Katy and me for lunch, if you're free. And I'd like to thank you profusely and at great length—'

'I'd love to have lunch,' she interrupted, 'but only if you promise not to thank me any more.'

He gave a small smile. 'Can't I do it once?'

He was teasing her, she realised, and she smiled back.

'OK,' he said, and taking both her hands in his, he studied her gravely, then bent his head and kissed her on each cheek. Then he said solemnly, 'Thank you, India Rose Kane, for saving the life of the woman I love. I owe you a debt that should you ever need to call on me, I swear I will honour.'

BACK IN SYDNEY, India continued watching out to see if she was being followed, but she didn't see anyone, and her office appeared untouched. Finally she allowed herself to think they'd given up. Which was a big relief, aside from the fact that she didn't know who they were or what, precisely, had been their intention. One of life's weirder mysteries, she thought, and wondered if she'd ever discover what it had all been about.

The media coverage of *Sundancer*'s sinking continued steadily through the following months. TV shows interviewed Greenpeace survivors, and the government was calling for international cooperation in finding *The Pride*, but nothing turned up. It was as though the ship had vaporised.

Refusing to be disheartened, India kept plugging away, phoning harbour-masters from Mexico to Madagascar to remind them that she was still searching for the ship that had left thirty crew to die in the Southern Ocean. It wasn't until July, however, that she got her first lead.

She was shaking out her umbrella after dashing out for some lunch. Soaked from the knees down, she kicked off her shoes and dumped her burger on her desk before checking her messages. Excitement rushed through her when she heard a boyish voice asking if there was still a reward out for information on the container ship. India immediately rang him back.

'I've someone who knows your ship,' he said. 'How much will he get?'

God, she thought, he sounds about twelve years old. 'Look, that reward is for real, hard information about the Greenpeace disaster.'

'What will I get?' His voice had turned whiny, but her antenna twitched when she noticed he'd changed the 'he' to 'I'.

'That depends.'

'On what?'

'Whether it's the right ship.'

'How about *The Pride of Tangkuban*, then? It's a dry cargo ship operating in the Indian Ocean. Ninety-one metres of rust bucket with a socking great dent in its bow. Four winches and derricks. Indian master, Filipino crew.'

'OK, OK,' she gasped. 'It sounds like her.'

'So how much?'

'Where is she? Are you with the ship now? Is she in Australia?' India had to make a huge effort to rein herself in when she realised she was giving him no chance to respond. 'Hello?' she asked after a few seconds, heart thudding. Oh God, had she scared him off? 'Are you still there?'

'I'm not answering any questions until I've got the money.'

India did some rapid thinking. 'Where are you?'

'Perth.'

Perth was over 4,000 kilometres away, but she didn't hesitate.

'I'll be there tomorrow. Sixish any good for you?'

'How much will I be getting?' he persisted.

'It depends, but maybe up to say . . . two grand.'

'Is that all?' He tried to sound casual and offhand, but she could hear the excitement in his voice and knew she didn't need to negotiate any further.

'That's all,' she confirmed. 'Where shall we meet?'

'The Dolphin. It's a pub in Fremantle.' His words came out in a rush. 'And come alone. I don't want no cops or AMSA guys. Just you.'

'How will I recognise you?'

'You won't. But I know what you look like from the papers.'

When he hung up, India considered calling the feds and decided against it. They'd only have the pub surrounded and tip the boy off, and she had no intention of losing her only lead. She got the go-ahead from Scotto and was booking her ticket when she realised she hadn't consulted Mikey. Or thought of Polly, for that matter. God, living with people made life so *complicated*.

THAT EVENING, over a late meal of Thai coconut chicken and sticky rice, Polly tucked up in bed with her little teddy bear, India filled Mikey in.

'Scott's up for it. My flight leaves first thing tomorrow.'

He put down his spoon and wiped his chin of coconut juice. 'And Polly?'

'Can't your mum have her after school?'

His jaw tightened. 'Not indefinitely, India. God, you are so single-minded sometimes, you're utterly unaware of anyone's existence aside from yours.'

Refusing to look away and acknowledge the shame spearing her, she said, 'Polly could always come with me.'

His look of horror said it all. 'No way.'

'Your mum it is, then.'

'No.' The word was said very flat. 'I don't want you to go.'

India stared at him. 'I'm sorry?'

Slowly, Mikey got to his feet. He faced her across the table. 'This time get someone else to do your legwork. Last trip you took, you nearly didn't come back. Or have you forgotten that?'

'Jesus, Mikey, the Greenpeace thing was an *accident*.' She pushed her chair back with a screech on linoleum. 'Are you saying I shouldn't investigate what happened? Stay home with all the doors locked?'

'No, I'm just saying you shouldn't put yourself in danger.'

'I want to know what happened,' she said tightly. 'You of all people must understand that.'

'No, India.' His voice started to rise. 'I don't want this again. It's like a drug to you, it takes over your life. Polly and I cease to exist . . .' He turned away as though he couldn't bear to look at her, then he strode outside.

She heard Mikey turn on the TV. I should have warned him first, she thought, asked him if he'd be OK with it, given him a chance to talk it over. How could I have been so *stupid*?

Peering into the living room she saw that Mikey was firmly glued to the TV. She could tell by the way his arms were folded and the set of his mouth that she'd have better luck making peace with a saltwater crocodile, so she washed up, always her way of apologising since she hated any sort of housework, and went to bed.

She was already in the thick of sleep when she felt Mikey climb into bed and lie with his back to her. India shuffled her backside fractionally towards him, but the infinitesimal movement he made told her she wasn't welcome.

Feeling small and shamed, she curled into a ball. She didn't think she'd sleep she felt so miserable, but when she woke it was after dawn, and she felt strong and refreshed. Mikey's breath was on her neck and his right arm hooked round her ribs, the same as usual.

EARLY EVENING, India collected Ned's utility vehicle from the airport, amazed as always at the average Aussie's ability to do favours at the drop of a hat. When she'd called Ellie, asking if she could stay, her friend hadn't asked her about her transport arrangements, just said, 'My neighbour's due in Perth then; I'll ask her to drop Ned's ute off for you. She'll get a lift back, no worries.'

India hadn't argued. A free car was always welcome, and she promised herself she'd buy a gift for Ellie's neighbour as thanks.

Driving out of the airport gates, India checked her rearview mirror. She hadn't seen the man with the ponytail at the airport, and nobody was behind her now—no car, no motorbike, not even a bicycle. She drove straight to Fremantle, and killed some time wandering the art galleries and shops before her meeting. It was dark when she finally headed for the Dolphin.

Sticking her head round the door, she saw a crowded bar filled with smoke and noise and the smell of sweat and beer. Through a room on the right she could see men playing darts and pool, and five scantily clad female bar staff were working flat out behind the counter, serving a queue that was three deep. Although the atmosphere was buoyant, India hesitated. She didn't think she'd seen so many hard-drinking blokes in such a small space before and wasn't too sure of her welcome. She was dithering in the doorway when she heard her name being yelled.

'Yo! India!'

A shot of relief catapulted her through the door. 'Chief!'

Fremantle's harbourmaster was wading through the crowd, face red and shining and split with a grin. 'Well, if it ain't my favourite reporter.' He beamed. 'Can I buy you a drink?'

'A beer would be great.'

The chief did a queue jump that nobody seemed to mind, least of all a pretty girl with breasts the size of footballs who started pouring a schooner of Emu Export for him without being asked.

'You came to see me?' the chief asked India, eyes bright.

'I'm actually here to meet someone who says they've got my ship.' She bit her lip then added, 'I didn't tell the feds. Didn't want him scared off.'

The chief didn't seem to be fazed at her confession and passed over her beer. 'I won't tell if you don't.'

She raised her eyebrows.

'Harbourmasters are meant to be pillars of society.' He glanced at the barmaids and then back at India, expression abashed. 'The management would have a fit if they knew I was here.'

India crossed her heart. 'Your secret is safe with me.'

He chinked his glass against hers before taking a long draught. 'Who's this bloke you're meeting, then?'

India ran through her telephone conversation with the kid.

He straightened up, scanning the room. 'Why don't you stay here where I can keep an eye on you? Check him out. Make sure you're OK.'

Another shot of relief. 'Chief, that would be brilliant.'

'I'll be over there.' He gestured across the room to the far corner, where a dozen or so men were squeezed round several circular tables. 'The guys will be well pissed off that I didn't bring you over. They're always partial to a pretty face.' He gave her a cheerful leer and she laughed.

She watched his broad bulk weave effortlessly through the boisterous crowd before he settled with his mates, back to the wall. He raised his glass to her and sent her a wink. She did the same back. All the guys at his table did the same, which made her laugh again.

Barely five minutes had passed when she felt a hand on her arm. She flinched. The young guy who'd touched her flinched too.

'Shit, sorry,' he said, eyes jumping around the room.

'No worries.'

'Sorry,' he said again. 'You're the reporter, right?'

'India.' She held out her hand and they shook. He had a surprisingly strong grip, even if it was slick with sweat.

'Danny.'

Danny was barely twenty and could have been the archetypal surfer, aside from his hair. Tanned and skinny, long hazel eyes. Black curly hair the same texture as a water spaniel's. Eyes belonging to the same spaniel. She didn't think he'd be any trouble but she still glanced across the room. The chief was nowhere to be seen.

'Where's the money?' Danny demanded.

'Somewhere safe.'

The spaniel eyes watered in dismay. 'Didn't you bring it?'

She was about to respond when a man in overalls lurched into her, making her spill her beer. She said, 'It's too crowded here. Let's go—'

'Next door's quieter. Hi, I'm Hank.' The chief pushed a paw out to Danny. 'Hank Gregory. Friend of India's.'

Danny looked taken aback, but he shook.

'Couldn't have a pretty woman unchaperoned in a place like this,' the chief told Danny smoothly. 'I'm sure you understand.'

'But I thought—'

'I won't say a word. Pretend I'm not there.'

With a hand on her elbow, another on Danny's shoulder, the chief ushered them into the room next door, which was fractionally quieter, and took a corner table. India sat opposite Danny with the chief between them.

'Off you go, then,' the chief prompted.

Danny ran a tongue over his lips. 'Where's the money?'

India reached into her coat pocket and withdrew the envelope. She put it on the table. 'Two grand.'

Two emotions crossed his face in quick succession: greed, then fear.

'So, Danny, how come you know *The Pride of Tangkuban*?'

'I crewed for her.'

'When was this?'

'January.' Danny glued his eyes on the table then muttered, 'Sorry.'

What felt like a cold drop of water splashed down India's back. He'd been on board *The Pride* when they'd collided.

Keeping her voice calm, she said, 'Tell me who owns the ship.'

'Dunno.'

'What about the master or ship's agent? Where can I find them?'

'Dunno.'

'OK. What port does *The Pride* come from?'

He chewed his lip for a while, then said, 'Jakarta.'

At last, she thought, something concrete. 'That's great, Danny. Now, what were you doing in the Southern Ocean?'

'I never said we were there!' He looked horrified.

She was going to say that he'd practically admitted it by saying sorry, but took a breath instead and rearranged her thoughts. 'OK. Tell me how long you crewed for *The Pride*.'

'Just the once. The master was four crew short in Sydney. Four of the Filipinos did a bunk just before they were due to sail.'

'Did a bunk?' India frowned. 'I take it you're suggesting that they're now illegal immigrants in Australia.'

'Damn right I am.'

'And the master took you and another three crew on from Sydney.'

'Two. We're a bit more expensive than your average Filipino.'

'I see. So what was the master's name?'

He shook his head.

She tried again. 'Where's *The Pride* now?'

'Dunno.' He took in the look on her face and hastily added, 'She dropped me at Chennai and I got work on to Port Elizabeth. Worked the South Atlantic a bit before coming home.'

Chennai, India knew, used to be known as Madras. It was an enormous, teeming city with a huge port to match.

'What cargo were you carrying on *The Pride*?'

'Cargo?' The horrified look was back, and he was shaking his head. 'Dunno. Dunno nothing about any cargo.'

'Surely you must have some idea,' she insisted.

'Honest, I don't know.' Danny's tone turned desperate, spaniel eyes on hers, pleading. 'I swear it. I was just employed for a couple of weeks. Help out, fill in for those blokes who let their master down. That's *all*. I don't know nothing about any cargo, OK?'

'So, what's the problem?'

'Nothing!'

Like hell, she thought. The second she'd mentioned the word cargo he'd acted as though he'd sat on a firecracker.

'Danny, give me a name. A broker, a company shipping with you, anything you saw on a lading bill, *any name*.'

He made to stand, but the chief put a hand on the boy's shoulder and pushed him back down. 'Let me go,' Danny begged.

'No,' said the chief quietly.

Danny was practically quivering with anxiety, and India doubted she'd get any more out of him. She was about to give him 200 bucks and let him go when he said, 'Harris and . . . I can't remember the second part.'

'It's a company?' She leaned close, tone urgent. 'Where did you see it?'

He dragged a hand down his face, trying desperately not to look at her. 'Look, we took some stuff of theirs on here in Fremantle. Will that do?'

He made to grab the envelope but India was faster.

'Sorry, Danny,' she said, 'but what you've given me is hardly two grand's worth of information.'

She gave him 600 bucks and watched him stuff it into his back pocket. The chief raised his eyebrows at her and she shook her head and let Danny leave. Shoulders hunched and without looking right or left, he scurried outside like a terrified rabbit.

'Thanks, Chief,' she said and, grabbing her coat, pelted after him.

THE WIND was bitingly cold and she pulled her coat collar close round her throat as she followed Danny down the empty street. Her footsteps sounded as loud as machine-gun fire on the pavement, but Danny didn't seem to hear. He was walking fast, head down, oblivious to everything but his urge to get away. He turned right and then left at a crossroads. A car drove past, music booming, and disappeared.

India reckoned that Danny was going home. Home would be temporary digs until he got another job on another ship, and all she wanted was to see where he was staying so she could let the feds know. They would lean hard on Danny and squeeze a lot more information out of him than she had.

Another couple of turns, then she saw a sign that told her exactly where Danny was headed. The Flying Angel Club. Every major port around the world had one. Owned by the Church of England, it was a Mission to Seamen, nicknamed because of its symbol of an angel. She should have known he'd be staying there. It was the perfect place for a seaman to rest up, among people who knew which ships were in port, and where to find work.

A car drove past, and as it approached Danny it showed down almost alongside him. Then it accelerated past him and she didn't think anything of it until it stopped and two guys got out and started walking Danny's way.

India felt a surge of apprehension. Were they muggers? Or was she over-reacting? She thought she saw a metallic glint in one of the men's hands. Oh God. Was it a gun? Apprehension abruptly turned to alarm.

'Danny!' she yelled.

His body jerked round at her shout and the two men paused.

'Look out!'

He was still looking at her when one guy lunged at him, bringing him to the ground. Danny was struggling, but the guy was punching, hitting him, and she was backing away, fumbling for her mobile in her pocket, when the other guy peeled away and sprinted straight for her.

Oh shit. No time to phone—

India turned and tore back the way she'd come, racing for the safety of the pub and the chief. She charged to the end of the street and swung left, then left again. She could hear the man's footsteps pounding behind her, and prayed that she could keep the distance between them constant.

As she pelted right at the crossroads her boots skidded on wet leaves, and the next instant she was falling. Slamming onto her hip she felt the breath rush out of her body, but her hands were pushing her upright, her feet scrambling, and she was trying to take a lungful of air when she saw the man rushing at her, saw the glint of metal in his hand.

The man had a knife.

Fear rocketed a rush of oxygen into her lungs and propelled her down the street. Legs and arms going at full pelt. She spun left at the next junction and could see the pub brightly lit at the end of the street, but nobody was around. She was running as hard as she could, but his footsteps were closing in.

She heard the man behind her say something that sounded like, 'You . . .' And felt him slam into her from behind. His hands went round her thighs, her knees, bringing her crashing to the pavement.

All her breath was gone. She was struggling, wriggling beneath the huge weight of him, and she could smell his breath as his head aligned with hers. Bitter and antiseptic, like crushed herbs.

She could see light spilling from the pub door. A handful of people fell outside and her gaze was fixed on them. They were her saviours but she couldn't speak, couldn't shout. She could feel the man's arm drawing back and she thought, He's going to stab me! Jesus, no!

She grabbed a lungful of air but his hand pressed against her mouth, stifling her shouts, his body on top of her, heavy as a bear, and she was trying to fight him, yelling against his hand and bucking against his weight.

'Shut it, or I'll sodding suffocate you,' he gasped into her ear.

She tried to bite his hand but he simply pressed his palm harder against her face, so she could barely move her head, let alone make a sound.

'Chill out, bitch,' he murmured.

The men from the pub were walking away. Two heading north together, three south, a single man tottering unsteadily towards them.

'You try and bite me again, and I'll hit you so hard your ears will ring for a week. Get it?'

She nodded and the weight of him rose off her. His hands pulled her upright, then slid over her stomach and came to rest beneath her ribs, his chin nestled on her shoulder as though they were lovers.

The man from the pub was nearing. Maybe twenty metres away, muttering, half singing to himself.

'You shout at that bloke for help,' he murmured, 'and I'll slip this knife beneath your ribs quicker than a snake slips underground.'

The man weaved his way along the pavement. As he approached, India bunched her muscles and felt her captor do the same. She felt the cold press of steel against the side of her neck. His knife. Hidden by handfuls of hair.

'Don't,' he hissed.

He was breathing hard and she could feel his breath against her cheek. The smell of rosemary and thyme crushed underfoot. Bitter and sharp.

The man from the pub shambled past them with barely a glance, mumbling incoherently.

India turned her head, trying to follow where he went, but her attacker said, 'Don't even think about it,' and held her even more tightly against him.

Concentrate, she told herself. She stared at the pub door, praying for it to open, but she knew it might be another half-hour until the next mob spilt out.

'You make a run for it,' he said, 'and I'll split you wide open with this knife of mine. You know that, don't you, bitch?'

India forced herself to give a nod.

'I just want a little chat, that's all. Maybe about our pal Danny boy. So let's keep it chilled, bitch . . .'

She felt the knife ease slowly away, his grip slacken from her waist and she heard him say again, 'Bitch,' in such a satisfied tone that she nearly turned on him then, but she forced herself to wait. Wait until the weight and heat of him fell from her back and in that instant, fast as a cat, she planted her right foot forward and swung her body round, till she was face to face with him, his mouth opening in shock as her right knee connected high and deep in the space between his thighs. He went down like a stone.

India watched his gasping and writhing for five seconds or so, then she bent over his ashen form and said, 'See you around, *bitch*.'

THREE

It was well after midnight when India arrived at Jimbuku Bay. The wind was up, but for once she didn't care. It smelt sharp as fresh-cut limes, sliced green and clean and edged with salt, and she welcomed the sensation of purity after the past few hours.

Luckily Ellie was already in bed, so India opened a bottle of red and took it to the bathroom. She turned on the taps, peeled off her clothes and dumped them on the floor. Her right hip and knee were aching and her thigh was already turning an ugly blue-black. She had a bloody graze on her cheek, but once she'd bathed the blood away it didn't look as though she'd been slammed face down onto the pavement; it resembled a rash.

She sank into the bath, letting her mind drift over the evening's events. After kneeing Knife-man to the ground, she'd raced to the pub and, ignoring the startled stares of his mates, dragged the chief outside.

'You were attacked?' he'd said, looking appalled. 'You OK?'

'I'm fine, Chief, but I'm more worried about Danny. Would you mind coming with me to check out his digs?'

The Flying Angel Club had told them that Danny hadn't been there all evening. India had talked over what Danny had said with the chief, who told her that *The Pride* was probably running under a flag of convenience.

'Jakarta doesn't have the regulations we do here. If you're registered in Jakarta you can do pretty much whatever you want.' He chewed his lip then added, 'What I can't understand is how *The Pride* came into port. Danny said they'd picked up cargo from Freo but it doesn't make sense. We only accept ships that have been designated safe and seaworthy, and from what I've heard *The Pride* doesn't fit that particular bill. I don't get it.'

Nor did India.

When the chief escorted her back to her car, he suggested they went to the cops and India reluctantly agreed, praying it wouldn't take long. She was bruised and sore and could already feel her muscles stiffening.

They were dealt with by a meticulously polite Sergeant Kuteli. Late thirties, tanned and athletic-looking, dressed in a well-cut woollen jacket and grey trousers, he recorded their statements with an air of brisk efficiency.

Danny's description would be circulated, Kuteli told them, and the department would do all they could to find him. India suggested informing the federal police about the evening's events, including the fact that *The Pride* came from Jakarta, and Kuteli said he'd add that to his report, no worries.

THE FOLLOWING morning, India's body was stiff and achy. She checked herself over and saw that the bruises had multiplied and were turning a spectacular purple-blue down the length of one thigh. Mikey would have palpitations. After downing a couple of painkillers she made a call on her mobile.

'Hey, India, got your scoop yet?'

'Er . . . Not quite. Actually, I need a favour to achieve that little goal.'

'How big a favour?' Scotto sounded guarded.

'Do you know anyone in Jakarta?'

'Why?'

'That's where the ship that rammed *Sundancer* comes from. She's called *The Pride of Tangkuban*.'

Silence.

'I'd go myself, but she's probably at sea and could be there for months. I need someone who lives in Jakarta, who can scout around and ring us when she turns up.'

'I'll find someone.' Scotto sounded determined. 'I'll get onto it today.'

PROPPED BY the kettle, which Ellie knew was India's first port of call in the morning, she found a note saying that Ellie had had to leave early and would be staying overnight with her parents. She would be back for supper the following day, around 6 p.m. A PS informed her that Katy and William had invited them both to a barbecue the following week.

Smiling at the prospect of seeing her friends again, India made herself a pot of coffee, then checked out the Yellow Pages. Danny had mentioned taking some stuff on board *The Pride* at Freo from a company with Harris in its name, and she hoped she'd get a clue. Five minutes later she gave a groan and shoved the Yellow Pages aside.

There had to be over thirty companies containing the name Harris in the area, covering anything from clothing stores to motor accessories. She'd be driving around the state for the next two weeks if she did her job properly, making sure all those companies were who they said they were. India reread Ellie's note and wrote one back.

Gone for days if I do what I'm meant to do. Don't send out a search party until the end of the week, just send supplies. A case of Bombay Sapphire wouldn't go amiss.

Feeling slightly depressed, she stood by the kitchen window and stared outside. Three rosellas sped past, flashing red and green, and as she followed their flight she saw a cop car cruise down the street. There were two cops up front, and they were craning their necks left and right, looking at house numbers. To her dismay the car parked right outside. Her heartbeat went into overdrive when both cops put on their caps, walked up the front pathway and rang the doorbell.

'Ms Kane?' the taller officer asked.

'Yes.'

'You've a couple of minutes?'

Her mind was speeding, evaluating and absorbing the two cops. Faces neutral. No tension. Guns in their holsters. No handcuffs.

'Sure,' she said. 'Come in.'

She led them into the kitchen and offered chairs. Both preferred to stand. Voice calm, polite as can be, she said, 'How can I help you?'

The taller one introduced himself. Sergeant Block: middle-aged, medium height and build, a plain face scored by lines that suggested he'd been biffed around by life a bit. The shorter officer was Constable Thomas, young and muscular with sandy hair and a tentative handshake.

Block consulted a notebook. 'We've a statement from you in which you say you were at the Dolphin last night.'

A sense of dread uncurled like a snake awakening in her belly.

'Yes, that's right.'

'You spoke with Danny Fawcett.'

'Danny . . .' She swallowed. 'Is he all right?'

'Er . . . did you know him well?'

'Oh God,' she said, and briefly closed her eyes. 'He's dead, isn't he?'

Small silence. Then Block said, 'Why would you think that?'

Her eyes snapped open. 'You said *did*. Past tense.'

There was a pause while the two cops cleared their throats and shuffled their feet, then Block spoke. 'I'm very sorry.'

'Me too.' She lit a cigarette. She'd promised Ellie she wouldn't smoke in the house, but this was an emergency.

'How did he die?' she asked.

'He was stabbed.'

The snake awoke, writhing into coils of nausea. 'Oh Jesus,' she said.

'Would you like to sit down?' the constable asked, watching her anxiously.

'I'm OK, thanks.' She took an unsteady pull on her cigarette.

'I know you've made a statement,' Block said, 'but if you wouldn't mind, we'd like to run over it with you. When was the last time you saw Danny?'

India knew the drill. First, establish the movements of the victim until their death. Second, confirm the last positive sighting of the victim. She was probably the last person to see Danny alive. Aside from his killers.

'Last night, at seven p.m. On his way to the Flying Angel Club.'

'You walked home with him?'

'No. I just wanted to see where he was staying, for the Maritime Safety Authority guys in Canberra. You see, I'd been talking with Danny about the Greenpeace incident . . .'

As she spoke, the constable made copious notes while Block interjected with the odd question.

'Tell me about the man who attacked you.'

She described Knife-man in as much detail as she could. His jeans and fleece, neat brown hair, big boots, maybe Timberlands. Clean-shaven. Mid-forties or so and fairly fit. A squashy-looking face, no angles. Pale eyes, not brown, maybe blue or grey. A mole on his right cheekbone.

The constable seemed impressed. 'You've a good eye for detail.'

India nodded, saying it certainly helped her in her job, but Block was studying her intently.

'Mid-forties, you say.'

'Yes.'

'Not early twenties?'

She shook her head. 'No way.'

Block was staring at her so hard that she decided to change the subject. 'Where was Danny's body found?'

He ignored her question. 'You say he had brown hair.'

'Dark brown. It was difficult to tell with the streetlights. But it wasn't black like an Asian guy might have, and it wasn't grey.'

'Not blond?'

It was her turn to stare back at him. 'Absolutely not.'

Short silence.

'Can you remember who took your statement?'

She felt her eyes narrow. 'Don't tell me you can't.'

'I just want to confirm who you spoke to, that's all.'

'Sergeant Kuteli.'

The constable started and glanced across at Block, who looked as though he'd bitten on a stinging nettle.

'Is there a problem with Sergeant Kuteli?' she asked.

Huge pause while Block stared at the piece of paper in his hand and the constable chewed his lip.

'No problem,' the sergeant said, and then he ran through what else she could remember about the car she'd seen, other vehicles in the street, and when he ran out of questions she repeated her own about where they'd found Danny's body, not really expecting an answer.

To her surprise he said, 'It was unearthed on a municipal dump out of town.'

'When did he die?'

'The forensic department reckons he was killed last night. Between eight and two.'

She tried to hide her shudder, but Block caught it. 'Those two men,' she managed.

'Yes,' he said. 'I'd like to talk to them.'

AFTER THE COPS had gone, India washed the ashtray, opened the windows, and went and smoked another couple of cigarettes on the porch.

She hadn't liked the way the sergeant had intimated that Knife-man was a totally different guy from the one who had attacked her. Rolling her cigarette between her fingers she considered their response to her asking if there was a problem with Sergeant Kuteli. Both cops had been extremely uncomfortable with her question. Which meant what? That they didn't like the guy? That there was some internal politics between them? Or was it something else, something deeper?

India turned her mind to poor Danny, murdered by Knife-man and his mate. Why? Because they had seen Danny talking to her in the pub? Or were they going to kill him and, when she'd yelled, decided to come after her?

She took a pull on her cigarette and exhaled. Why had Knife-man wanted to talk? To find out who she'd confided in and maybe go after them as well before killing her? God, talk about stepping into a pit of vipers. Would Knife-man come after her again?

Wind blew hair across her mouth and she pulled it free, turning her head into the wind. Across the street she saw a flock of cockatoos being buffeted past the trees, and a dishevelled old woman emerge unsteadily from a house. Then she took in the lean woman's tan, the cropped salon-streaked hair and thought, Jesus, she's the same age as me. Is she ill? India was watching anxiously when the woman stumbled and fell to her knees.

India immediately flicked her cigarette aside and raced across to help. Bending over the woman, she said, 'Hey. Are you OK?'

The woman didn't respond. Tears were leaking down her cheeks. Her clothes were clean but rumpled, and her hair a tangled mess.

'Can I help you?'

'I can't . . . want . . .' The woman seemed to have trouble speaking. 'I need some milk.'

'I can always run down and get it for you,' India suggested. 'You should be indoors.'

'Kind,' the woman said. 'That would be very kind. My husband should be home soon but we've run out of milk. Sam wants Weetabix, you see—'

'Here.' Holding both the woman's hands, India heaved her upright. India watched her walk into her house then said, 'How many litres?'

'Two. And . . . I don't want to trouble you?'

'It's no trouble, what else?'

'Orange juice. Without the lumps. Sam hates lumps.'

'So do I,' said India with a smile. 'See you in a tick.'

When she returned she pressed the doorbell, but nobody answered. She pressed again. A little boy, maybe five, opened the door.

'Hi, are you Sam?'

He nodded.

'Is your mum in?'

'She's in the bathroom.'

'I brought you some milk. And orange juice, without the lumps.'

He eyed her intently, and said, 'Are you a friend of Mummy's?'

'Yes, I am.'

He opened the door wide, but she remained on the doorstep.

'Can you carry this inside?' She handed him a litre of milk.

Clutching the carton with both hands, he trotted off, came back.

'Is your mum still in the bathroom?'

He stared at her, eyes big and serious. 'She spends a lot of time in the bathroom. She cries a lot.'

'I'm sorry to hear that,' India said gently, and handed him the next carton, watched him do the next relay. When he returned she said, 'Has Mummy told you why she cries?'

'Because Pippa died. She's my sister.'

He trotted off with the orange juice, leaving India running a hand back and forth over her face, as though she could rub out what little Sam had told her.

I thought if we named our baby after Albert—well, that they'd be safe.

Jesus Christ, what the hell was going on with this estate?

INDIA WENT BACK to the milk bar and asked the guy behind the counter where Albert lived.

'Shoalhaven,' he said. 'Three, Waratah Road. But you won't have any luck. He hasn't been around for yonks.'

India went there anyway. It was better than sitting in a wind-blasted porch smoking cigarette after cigarette and thinking about poor Danny.

Shoalhaven, like most of the towns on this stretch of coast, was originally settled by whalers, pearlers and crayfishers. It was a collection of weatherboard houses set between the sea and drifting white dunes. The sand was speckled with bain, a succulent, ground-hugging plant currently in full bloom. Bright pinky-mauve petals shivered in the stiff breeze, their centres reminding India of glorious globs of clotted cream.

The main street was a dusty thoroughfare lined with a handful of fishing and grocery stores, and she drove along until she found Waratah Road. She parked the car in front of number three, which was now a tour company, offering everything from bushwalks and fishing trips to windsurfer hire. There was an alley on one side and a café on the other.

A young woman looked up from her computer when India entered. Slim as a wand, she had short, curly black hair, caramel-coloured skin and enormous brown eyes that made India think of Polly.

'Hi,' said the girl with a bright smile. 'We're not usually open Sundays, but if you want to book a tour I'd be happy—'

'Actually, I'm looking for Albert Jimbuku.'

The smile faded. 'Look, you ought to talk to my grandmother, Ginny. She's fishing on the jetty. You can't miss her. Just look for an old biddy dressed in orange.'

Before India could ask where the jetty was, the phone rang. When the girl answered, she swivelled her chair round, pointedly turning her back.

India backtracked to the main street and cruised along the seafront. She'd only gone half a kilometre when she saw a handful of motorboats moored close to shore and hey presto, there was the jetty, a line of fishermen dotted along it. Parking beneath a Norfolk Island pine, India went to look for an old biddy dressed in orange.

The wooden jetty looked as though it had been there a while, but it was strong and firm underfoot, and stretched maybe a hundred metres over the water. She passed a pair of blokes in their late teens with beers in one hand, fishing rods in the other, and a couple of kids with their parents. Halfway along, she saw a skinny old black woman flick a small fish out of the water. In two swift movements she had removed the hook and plopped the fish into a plastic tub on her right. She was dressed in a pair of baggy shorts the colour of marigolds and a bright orange overshirt.

'Hi,' said India. 'My name's India Kane. Your granddaughter said you know Albert Jimbuku.'

'What you be doing asking for Albert?'

'I have a friend who lives at Jimbuku Bay,' India said.

The old woman stared at her, the wrinkles on her face deepening. Then she patted the salt-crusted wood beside her, and India hunkered down to sit with her feet dangling over the mottled water, deep blue, almost black, a splash of turquoise indicating a shallow just ahead. Ginny studied India some more, then took a strip of fish intestine from the block of bloody wood beside her, popped it on a hook and chucked the line into the water.

'So, you'll be wanting to know about Albert's curse,' she said.

'Yes.'

Another silence. The old woman shifted her body closer to India.

'Dreamtime,' the old woman said intently. 'You know what it means?'

'A spiritual linking,' India responded. 'The unity of man and nature. The essence of life and man's continued existence.'

The old woman gave a sigh—of satisfaction, India thought—and said, 'Albert was trying to protect his Dreamtime, is all. You know about Neville? That bloke who ran us off our place years back?'

India felt her spirits sag. Yes, she knew all about Neville. She'd read enough about him. Despite having no Aboriginal knowledge whatsoever, A. O. Neville had been designated Chief Protector of Aborigines in 1905. During the next twenty-five years, Aborigines were rounded up and stuck into settlements, children isolated from their parents in order to bring them up to follow a European lifestyle, and by the 1930s they'd gone from being economically independent, living in the bush or on station land, to become outcasts in their own country. India sighed. She'd bet Jimbuku Bay wasn't the only place in Australia that had been cursed by an Aborigine.

'You all right?' Ginny was watching her closely.

'Yes,' India said quietly. 'Neville didn't do us any favours, did he?'

'It's a wonder nobody shot the bloke. Nobody liked him.'

They both fell silent, watching the water.

'So if you know about Neville,' Ginny eventually said, 'you'll know none of us have been about Perth much since.'

India nodded.

'Well, that's why Albert kicked up such a stink. It's a long story . . .' Ginny squinted at the sky. 'But what it comes down to is Albert's finding his roots after years of looking. His mum died giving birth to him, see, so Albert never got to ask her about his family. He was a mixed-race baby and spent his childhood in various foster homes. All he had was his surname, Jimbuku.

'He managed to track his granddad down, and his granddad told him about the springs at Jimbuku Bay, and how their lot had been celebrating them springs that had given them fresh water from the time man was born. Soon as he heard that, Albert set off there like a rocket, and when he saw a bunch of diggers messing up his spiritual home, well, it kind of did his head in.'

Ginny's right arm suddenly jerked, and a fish with a yellow stripe along its flank popped from the water. Two seconds later it was released into the plastic tub to join the other dozen yellowtail. Rebaiting her hook, Ginny tossed it with an expert flick into the turquoise shallow.

'The authorities wouldn't help. He reckoned they'd been bribed, so he went back to his granddad, who's a *maban* man, a type of medicine bloke-cum-sorcerer, and he told Albert to call in Jambuwal, the Thunder Man. He's a bit of a bugger, Jambuwal.' Ginny gave a low chuckle. 'He gets really pissed off if you harm him or his people.'

India held herself still, not wanting to disturb the old woman as she relived her memories.

'Most of us stayed away that day, reckoning we'd get banged up for disturbing the peace or something. But I wish I'd had his balls and been there, 'cause when he chucked those intestines to the ground, old Jambuwal bloody heard him.' She gave a dry laugh. 'Bugger me if a bloody great storm didn't blow up out of nowhere. Gutters got torn off roofs, trees fell over the roads and we all hid like kids beneath the bloody bedclothes. Including Jack and his whole bloody family.'

Frowning, India said, 'Who's Jack?'

'The bloke who built them bloody houses.' Ginny spat into the water.

'Where can I find him?'

The old woman didn't look at her, just made a sweeping gesture across her torso that India recognised. It was a sign to keep away evil spirits.

'What is it?' India asked, her skin prickling.

There was a long silence, then the old woman gave her a searching look. 'You're the first person to ask about Jack. Most just want Albert.'

'But Albert isn't around.'

'Don't we know it.' Ginny gave a shudder. When she next spoke, she leaned close, her voice a whisper. 'His name's Zhuganov.'

'Zhuganov?' India repeated, startled. The Detective Inspector who took her and Cuan's statements after they'd been dropped ashore had the same surname. She asked Ginny if they were related.

Again Ginny made the sign against evil spirits. 'They're all related to bloody everybody. Can't move for the buggers.'

'Where can I find Jack?'

The old woman raised her head and fixed her gaze on a cormorant flying just above the sea. 'He retired out Bulimba way. Place called Goondari.'

'When did he—?'

'That's all you get.' Ginny jerked her wrinkled old knees away from her as if India had suddenly become contaminated. 'Just go away, will you? Let me get on with my fishing.'

As India left the old woman flipping out another fish, she heard Ginny call out after her, 'For Chrissakes don't tell him it was me who sent you!'

IT TOOK INDIA two hours to get to Bulimba, a one-street town with one garage, a small supermarket and a hotel, and in that time she saw just three other cars and a single road train. Despite the lack of traffic, she'd had her headlights on for the entire trip. A southerly had screamed in just after she'd left Shoalhaven, filling the air with sand and salt spray, and it was like driving through patchy fog. She drove into the garage and asked for directions.

'Keep going through town,' the garage guy said, 'you'll find Jack's place thirty Ks on, to the left. Goondari. Can't miss it.'

He was right. Jack obviously didn't believe in discretion; the sign for Goondari was the size of a billboard poster. GOONDARI STUD.

She swung down the smooth, graded track. For some time the road followed the sea, and India slowed a while to watch the surf, which, like the wind, had risen fast. India loved the outback, but she wasn't sure she'd cope with living out here, in the teeth of the wind.

Gradually the coastal scrub fell away to sheep pasture snarled with limestone. There were thick clumps of bloodwoods, majestic spreading eucalyptus trees that exuded a dark red gum, for stock to shelter beneath, and to her right a dark streak of forest crawled into the distance. When she had to stop and open a couple of gates, she realised the wind had begun to drop.

Ten minutes later she came upon Jack Zhuganov's house, and the second she took it in, her foot faltered on the accelerator. Holy cow, she thought, her jaw dropping.

She saw a monolith growing from the earth with angles on the north and south sides and multiple geometric layerings in between. Earth-bermed on its west side, the building had a strangely humped form, like the shoulders of a bull. Three massive square chimneys dominated the horizon, and a shiny roof reflected the dusty colour of the sky. Acres of walls were painted a harsh, cold white, reminding India of Spain, not Australia.

It's like Jimbuku Bay all over again, she thought. It wasn't that it hadn't been well designed, but it *didn't fit in*.

She drove on, feeling Ned's ute rattle over a cattle grid, seeing smart, white-painted fences lining the smoothly tended track. She passed banksias ghosted with dust, horses in the paddocks on either side, backsides facing into the wind. Beneath a patch of trees was a row of immaculate-looking stables. Everything was neat and orderly, except for the rubbish tip encroaching from the near-side paddock and into the front yard.

It was like seeing a pile of bin bags splitting their rotting contents across the front steps of the Sydney Opera House. There was two JCBs, countless stacks of tyres, empty oil drums, old cars, sheets of corrugated iron and, right in front of the unsightly mess, a shiny red five-ton Isuzu truck with a pair of silver horns on its snout.

Typical Aussie mentality, she thought with a disgusted sigh. They've got so much space they never think of disposing of their rubbish the way normal people do. Just chuck it aside to rot.

Still shaking her head, India parked at the end of a row of new-looking Nissan Patrol traybacks, and headed for a dramatic processional stairway leading to the front entrance.

She was halfway up the steps when five dogs appeared at the top, took one look at her, and broke into a run, hackles high, barking and growling. India wouldn't have minded facing down the spaniel, but no way was she going to mess with four German shepherds. She turned and sprinted for her car.

She slammed the door shut just as a German shepherd launched himself at her, smacking his face against her window with a thud. Undaunted, he and his pals leapt and scrabbled at her door, barking dementedly. Boy, what a welcome, she thought.

A few minutes later a woman appeared and yelled at the dogs, who fell quiet. She came across, and India cracked open her window.

'Is Jack around?'

'Yeah. He's gone to give BB a shot of antibiotics. Just look for a mean black bastard, you can't miss him.'

Unsure whether the woman was talking about a horse or Jack, India opened her door cautiously and climbed out. One of the shepherds drew back its lips and snarled. The woman turned to kick it but it scooted sideways.

'Do that again, Satan, I'll bloody murder you,' the woman warned. 'Sorry,' she added, turning back to India. 'They won't bother you now. And tell Jack I'm off, would you? I'll catch him at the barbie later.'

India thanked the woman, and with the five dogs trailing her at a distance like a gang of recalcitrant yobs, she headed for the stables. The light was hard and bright, and she pulled her sunnies from her daypack and popped them on.

The stable block was the antithesis of the rubbish tip. Dotted with giant tubs of geraniums, the yard was well tended and clean, and the smart green and white paintwork on the doors fresh. Although the air was thick with the smell of manure, it was only because of the wheelbarrow overflowing with the stuff at the end of the yard, just cleared from one of the stables.

Half India's childhood had been spent mucking out her aunt Sarah's horses. Not that she'd minded, since in return she was eventually given her own pony. When her parents died, the only relative the social services had been able to dig up—and who'd been willing to take on a seven-year-old Aussie—was her aunt who, as it turned out, wasn't an aunt at all but a distant cousin of her father's.

Aunt Sarah was a brisk, toughened old bird of fifty who lived in a sprawling farmhouse north of Oxford with eleven cats, five labradors, and no central heating. Aunt Sarah had paid for India's education, her school trips, the deposit on her first rented flat in London, but the first thing she'd done had been to teach her how to ride.

Once India had mastered the basics and was hankering to be allowed to jump, Aunt Sarah had whipped away the saddle and made her do it bareback, with her arms folded. India fell off so many times she lost count, but by the time she was ten she was bombing bareback around the countryside on her pony and had never been happier. India made a mental note to ring Sarah sometime—they hadn't spoken for a while.

As she walked along the yard she heard a horse's enraged squeal from a stable to her left, and then there was a clatter of hoofs followed by a crash. Cautiously she peered into the stable, letting her eyes adjust to the gloom. Skittering on concrete and straw, head taut against a thick rope, was a huge, dusty black horse with a white splash on its near foreleg.

A thickset man was holding what looked like a syringe, and as he neared the horse's head it tried to bite him, but the rope was too tight and it couldn't reach. Despite its dirty coat, she knew she was looking at a prime piece of horseflesh. A stallion, no less. Perfectly proportioned, he had an arrogant carriage, and beneath his fine, thoroughbred's skin, she could see the great muscles bunching and flexing with enormous power.

She could feel her throat closing in an automatic Sarah-murmur to gentle the horse as the man approached. Hey, sweetheart, settle down, she said silently, wanting to soothe the animal, and suddenly it stopped its thrashing and stilled, swung its head her way as though it had heard her. The next instant the man gave the injection and slapped the creature's neck. The horse promptly swung its rear round and lashed out with both feet, but he'd tied it well and the hoofs didn't come anywhere near.

With a single twitch, the man released the slipknot and the horse was free. It stood there for a second as though stunned, while the man dashed outside and bolted the door behind him. He turned to face India, expression smoothly neutral, and she realised he'd been aware of her all the time.

A greasy hat topped a square brown face, chequered with sun spots. Grey stubble. Muscular forearms and hands covered in coarse grey hair. Solid chest, strong neck and sloping shoulders, like a professional boxer might have. Probably in his sixties, but still attractive in a blunt kind of way. He wore a padded red-check overshirt and, even though it was winter, a pair of shorts, and the usual pair of large, dusty boots every outback farmer wore.

Wearing her most cheerful expression she said, 'I'm India Kane,' and stuck out a hand. He didn't take it. Nor did he offer his name.

Letting her hand fall by her side, she ploughed on. 'I'm a journalist, and I'd love to talk to you about your horses.'

His expression remained the same, but something cold crawled from the back of his eyes and settled there, watching her.

'I'm a farmer,' he said, 'and I don't talk to journalists.'

All the hairs on the nape of her neck stood on end. She felt as though she'd come across an innocuous house spider that had metamorphosed into a deadly black funnel-web.

'I'm sorry,' she said, trying not to flounder. 'But you've some terrific animals here. Especially your stallion. And some of the brood mares in the paddock are seriously stunning. Are they all racehorses?'

He continued to stare at her with a stillness that was unnerving.

She flinched when he spoke.

'Which magazine?' he asked, tone coldly polite.

'Oh, it's not a magazine,' she lied. 'I work for a publisher who has commissioned me to do a book. A big coffee-table book, with lots of pictures covering the history of horseracing. Owners, trainers, that sort of thing, from the last century up to today.'

She thought she caught a flash of amusement on his face and her stomach went cold. Had he seen through her?

'I see,' he said, his voice gravelly and deep. 'Why the cold call?'

'Because until I'd seen it, I didn't know if the place would be photogenic enough. People hate being contacted and then rejected.'

'Why me?'

Still that hint of amusement that kept her entrails squirming in ice.

'Oh, *Horse Australia* magazine. They said I shouldn't miss out on you. They were right.'

He appraised her a little longer while she held her breath, and eventually he said, 'You fancy a beer?'

'I'd love one.' She was almost gasping with relief. 'Oh, I nearly forgot . . .'

He was already walking to the mansion, obviously expecting her to follow.

'Er . . . a lady at your house said she had to go. And that she'd see you at the barbecue later.'

She saw him slide her a sideways glance, but he didn't say anything. She gave a careless shrug and concentrated on appearing relaxed so he wouldn't see how much he was unsettling her.

He led her to the back of the house and through a landscaped enclosure with sculpted patio furniture and an enormous pool with a swim-up bar under the shade of palm trees and thatched umbrellas.

Feeling as though she was on a film set, she copied Jack when he shucked off his boots, and padded after him along a tiled corridor and into a room she took to be his den. Lots of heavy furniture and thick carpets, stacks of magazines and newspapers, but the chief eye-catcher was the pictures taking up almost the whole of one wall. Horses walking, trotting, galloping in races, but India wasn't interested in them. She was staring at the array of ornately framed social photographs, strategically placed where they couldn't be missed.

Gone was the rough outback farmer and in his place was a man in tailored suits and dinner jackets, looking urbane and charming, shaking hands with important-looking people . . . Good grief, Jack was with Bob Hawke in this one, Australia's ex-Prime Minister. And there he was at a barbie with the disgraced Alan Bond, who'd defrauded Bell Resources of 1.2 billion dollars. Interesting social contacts. She leaned closer to one in a hideous bronze frame to see Jack dining with a family somewhere tropical. At the head of the table, on Jack's left, sat Indonesia's former president, Suharto.

Amazed, completely absorbed, her gaze latched on to a photograph way down, below waist height. Her heart gave a leap.

The picture was faded, quite old, and showed a container ship chugging across a still, blue sea. It had a white accommodation block, one big hatch and four derricks . . . My God, she thought, it could be the same ship that had run them down. This ship looked new, but if the photograph was as old as it looked . . .

Jack had vanished ahead, and she ducked down and tried to see the ship's name, but the print was too small. She was trying to find something else to identify it when she heard the distinctive rubber snap of a fridge opening. Hurriedly she rejoined Jack. He was standing in a broad kitchen adjacent to his den and pulling out a couple of stubbies from a fridge.

Ushering her outside, Jack sat beside her on a giant, tiled verandah overlooking the front paddocks. They were tucked well out of the wind, but the gum trees round the house swung and swayed, the sound of their rattling dry leaves like pebbles being poured into an enamel sink.

Jack chinked his bottle against hers. 'So, Ms Kane,' he said, 'fire away.'

Still unsure of him, she decided to tread carefully. Taking her cassette recorder from her bag, she popped it between them and opened up her notebook. She was longing to ask him about the photograph of the ship but reckoned on softening him up first by talking about his horses, which he seemed happy to do. He told her that they were a hobby he'd come into late in life. He'd backed BB at the Boulder Cup races as an outsider, and when he won, Jack had bought him, built the stables, and shipped him over.

BB was the stallion Jack had given the injection to, and was called officially Grafton Statesman, but after he'd bitten a stable hand so badly he'd had to be hospitalised, the horse had been nicknamed bloody bastard.

She found herself tuning out as he talked about the first mares he had bought, which dams were producing the best colts, but nearly jumped out of her skin when he said the name Harris.

'Harris?' she repeated.

'And Hewitt. The only livestock insurers in the area worth dealing with.'

'They're local?'

He paused as though thinking over whether to answer or not, and after a long moment said, 'Down Moora way. Local enough.'

She'd check them out later, she decided, although quite what a livestock insurance company had to do with a container ship, she wasn't sure.

She took a small sip of beer. Good old Swan Lager, a full five per cent alcohol, guaranteed to put her over the limit if she had the whole bottle. Turning her eyes to the paddocks she saw that a couple of horses had moved broadside to the wind and were cropping the grass.

'So, before you retired happily with your horses, what did you do?'

His face grew guarded.

'I just need an example, that's all,' she said as if it didn't matter. 'I'm not trying to pry, but the readers need something to identify with. You know, Jack Zhuganov, the owner of Grafton Statesman and ex-builder or architect or whatever. How about we include a couple of pictures of that fantastic place you built on the coast, Jimbuku Bay?'

He didn't say a word.

'I heard there was a big storm around that time,' India kept plugging away. 'There were rumours it had something to do with a curse. Now that would be a terrific human-interest story.'

His eyes scuttled. India started to sweat.

Desperately wanting Mr Jack I-love-my-horses to return, she hurriedly pointed at an elegant yellow mare in the nearest paddock that had her rump still turned to the breeze. 'She looks Arabian.'

He clicked his eyes to the mare then back. 'Top drawer for my boy.'

'Lucky BB,' she said, and she felt the muscles in her back relax when the scuttling stopped. With a crack of his knees, Jack got to his feet and waved his empty beer bottle at her. 'You fancy another?'

'I'd love one, but I'm driving,' she said. 'Sorry.'

Jack gave a derisive snort. 'The only bloke on patrol along the coast is a cousin of mine. He won't dob you in if you say you know me.'

Without a beat, India said, 'In that case, I'd love another beer.'

While he was inside, India tried to calm herself. Jack had extraordinary charisma, she realised, but when he did that creepy thing with his eyes she wanted to jump in her car and never return. Still, she had to push a bit further.

When he returned she let him talk some more about his horses then she pulled up her courage and said, calm as can be, 'What's with the photograph of a container ship in your house? Were you in shipping?'

He didn't blink or show any surprise at her question. Just said, very quietly, 'I think it's time you were going, don't you?'

FOUR

India drove back down the coast slick with sweat. She knew she'd been treading a fine line when she asked Jack about the ship, and although he'd ushered her to her ute with meticulous politeness, she'd felt as though she'd got away with poking a grizzly bear on the muzzle.

At least she'd learned two things: Jack Zhuganov didn't want to talk about Jimbuku Bay or the ship in the photograph. Was it the ship that had run them down? After all, Danny said it came from Jakarta, and Jack had that photo of himself dining with Indonesia's former president, Suharto. Perhaps Suharto owned the thing, or one of his children. From what she knew, they owned just about everything in Indonesia's capital.

She tried to think more laterally but her mind felt fuzzy from the beer sloshing round her system. She knew that if she'd refused Jack's beer he wouldn't have allowed her to stay for as long. It was the way things were out here. You drank what they drank, you were a mate. Not that he considered her a mate, she thought, especially not after her questions.

India was coming into Shoalhaven, bang on the sixty-K speed limit, when a cop car cruised past her from the opposite direction. She double-checked the speedometer, then her eyes were on the rearview mirror as she watched the cop car go. And just as she turned her gaze forward, a ute pulled out from a driveway, right in front of her. The driver wore a stock-man's hat, his passenger a frizz of grey hair, and a car was in the other lane, no hard shoulder, she had no choice but to slam on the brakes.

With a screech of rubber her vehicle fishtailed towards the rear of the ute, and at the last second she raised her foot off the brake and twitched the steering wheel right, regained control for an instant but it was too late. She slammed into a streetlight.

'Shit,' she said.

The ute continued down the road, the driver oblivious.

Unbuckling her seat belt, she checked her rearview mirror.

'Shit,' she said again.

The police car had done a U-turn and was heading her way, lights flashing. She was busted.

India was outside and calmly surveying the damage when two cops approached. 'Hi, Officers,' she said.

One was large and bulky with an alcohol-reddened face, the other looked like he was just out of school.

'Licence and reg please,' said the Schoolboy.

She handed them over. 'A ute with two old folk pulled out right in front of me, no warning. I don't think they even saw me. Since there was traffic coming the other way, I took evasive action.' India gestured at the street-light, which would need a small lick of paint.

'You been drinking at all?' asked the Schoolboy.

She knew that if either of them took one step closer they'd smell the beer on her breath, so she said, 'I shared a beer over lunch, that's all.'

'Just the one?' His voice was sarcastic.

'Yes. I shared it with a friend.' She took a breath and decided to go for broke. 'Jack Zhuganov. He had half, I had the other.'

Huge silence.

'You agree to be breathalysed, ma'am?' asked the bulky cop, a hard edge to his tone.

Deep breath. She knew she'd lost her licence.

'No need for that.' The Schoolboy handed back her papers. 'Half a beer isn't a problem,' he said with a smile. 'So long as you and your car are OK, we don't have a problem either.'

'We do have a problem,' his colleague said violently. 'I'll bet you a hundred bucks she's over the limit and I don't care if she's sleeping with your whole family, I'm going to breathalyse her and—'

The Schoolboy grabbed the bulky guy's arm and twisted him aside, said something India couldn't hear.

Bulky guy was muttering loudly, cursing mothers and dogs and a whole lot of wildlife in between, but in the end he backed down.

The Schoolboy turned and came to her, raised a forefinger to his hat and flicked a salute, saying, 'Safe journey now, Ms Kane.'

'India, please,' she said, and stepped forward to shake.

'Bryce Zhuganov,' he supplied, and gave her a wink as he added, 'Always glad to help a friend of the family.'

THE NEXT MORNING, after an unsettled night back at Jimbuku Bay, India booted up Ned's computer to discover he'd put in a password she couldn't break. She tried everything from Albert and Jimbuku to Ellie, whales, minke and *Sundancer*. Intensely frustrated, she headed for Shoalhaven, which apparently had the only Internet café within a fifty-kilometre radius.

Set on the beach front, the Whizz Internet Café was a crumbling single-storey building with a four-inch-thick drift of sand on the front step. Inside it smelt of fresh coffee, and India was pleased to see that she was the only customer. The young guy at the counter poured her a coffee and set her up at a computer overlooking the beach. The first useful thing to pop up was a five-year-old newspaper report. Apparently, Regent Enterprises, owned by Jack Zhuganov, had been given several government building contracts and a rival firm had accused the development commissioner of cronyism. Which wasn't surprising, India thought, considering the commissioner was married to Frank Zhuganov, Jack's elder brother. Frank, she read on, was in the transport business and had two sons, Jimmy and Bobby, who were 'angry' and 'upset' at the allegations against their mother.

Several more newspaper pieces followed, all in the same vein, accusing the family of corruption and nepotism, but nothing ever came of them.

India dug a little more into Regent to discover that the company had interests right across the state, from Zhuganov-owned skyscrapers in Perth to a Zhuganov-owned taxi firm in Broome. She learned that Jack had never married, had no kids, which was surprising given the fact he was one of seven himself. Jack's brothers and sisters had produced seventeen children between them and, if the information was accurate, those seventeen children had produced twelve more kids, all under the age of eleven. Two of Jack's brothers had emigrated to the United States, but the rest of the family members were firmly rooted in Western Australia.

India leaned back, her mind reeling from the dynastic proportions of the Zhuganov family. No wonder they're being accused of monopolising the state's business, she thought. They couldn't help it; they practically had a relative in every town across Western Australia. Which reminded her. She searched for Harris & Hewitt, Jack's livestock insurance agents, and after a lot of digging around, gleaned that David Harris was third cousin once removed from Jack, and nephew to Steve Harris, the state's health minister.

The café door slammed and she glanced up to see a leathery old bloke in a work shirt and bush hat come in and take the computer next to her. He was tanned the colour of jarrah and the lines around his eyes were scored from a lifetime of squinting into the sun and wind.

'G'day,' he said.

'Hi.'

India rubbed her eyes, and glanced at the clock. She'd been at it for over two hours. She went to get herself more coffee, did some stretches, and settled down again, a pile of doughnuts to hand. This time, she changed tack.

An hour later, India sat back, her shoulders aching, her neck like a block of wood, her mind buzzing. What a family! Talk about fingers in every sort of pie imaginable. There was a Zhuganov industrial cleaning service, a Zhuganov bottling company, and even a Zhuganov at the top of the pile in governmental safety checks on manufactured products.

They were heavily into regional and local government, with Jack's youngest brother, Don, leader of the state's Liberal party. From what she'd read, Don looked poised to topple the current Labour leader at the next election. A Zhuganov as the Premier of the state. The thought of it didn't sit well with her. Not after all those allegations of cronyism.

'Friends of yours?'

India turned to see that the young guy behind the counter had disappeared and the old man was watching her.

'I'm sorry?'

He gestured at her screen. 'The Zhugs.' He pronounced it *Zoogs*.

'Not particularly.'

'What does that mean in English?'

India considered him briefly, noted the curiosity in his eyes, and smiled. 'That I wouldn't trust them as far as I can throw them.'

He gave a dry laugh that ended up in a hacking cough. 'Too right. Jack stiffed my son-in-law a couple of weeks back, the bastard.'

'Stiffed?' she prompted.

'Yeah, poor bugger owed Jack sixty grand but Jack wouldn't wait for him to raise the cash, so he ended up giving him the cars off his own forecourt. Worth two hundred grand, not sixty.'

She stared at the old guy. 'They weren't Nissan traybacks, were they?'

He frowned. 'How'd you know that? You in the transport biz too?'

India shook her head and was going to tell him, no, but something he'd said had stuck in her brain like a bur. Transport, *transport*. Jack's brother Frank was in the transport business. Maybe this included ships.

'What do you know about Jack's brother, Frank?'

A blink of surprise. 'Frank's dead,' he said.

'How did he die?'

'Cancer.' His voice had dropped to a rasping murmur.

'I heard Frank had a transport business.'

'Never thought of it like that, but he had loads of trucks. Made his money dealing with our rubbish, see. Collecting and disposing, even got into recycling at one point. Did all right, too, considering he was worth twenty-one million bucks before he kicked the bucket.'

Danny's body, she thought. *It was unearthed on a municipal dump.*

She asked him about Albert, and she heard another tale of gutters ripped from walls, cars spun in circles and trees toppled.

'Where's Albert now?'

'Nobody knows.' He shook his head. 'Last time I saw him, it was at the Nelson. Right after he'd called in that bloody storm. Wearing one of his godawful floral shirts.'

'Did he go home when he left?'

'Home? Nah. He left when Jimmy turned up . . .' To her annoyance he paused when the young guy reappeared.

'Jimmy?'

He flicked a glance at the guy behind the counter and turned back to his screen. 'Wrong time to be asking questions,' he murmured.

'Who is he?' she whispered.

He waited until the waiter ducked behind the counter and was making clattering sounds with mugs and plates. 'Steve Marsdon,' he whispered back.

Disappointed, she said, 'He's not a Zhug?'

The old bloke leaned close, eyes fixed on the counter. 'One hundred per cent. That mob have changed their names all over the place. Don't like being thought foreign. You've Reillys, Grants, Marsdons—they're all related.'

'Thanks.'

When Marsdon straightened up, the older man swung back to his keyboard, then paused when she pushed back her chair.

'Nice meeting you,' he said.

'You too.'

India walked out of the café and kicked at the pile of sand on the step. Despite the mountain of information she'd gathered, she hadn't found a single reference to Suharto or Jack or any of their relatives owning or having anything to do with a container ship.

IT WAS DARK when India parked outside Ellie's and walked up the little path, searching in her daypack for her keys. One day, she thought, I'll have a bag the size of a matchbox so I can bloody *find* things in it.

Her fingers had just brushed her mobile phone and she was thinking she must ring Mikey as soon as she got inside when she heard footsteps behind her. As she started to swing round a man launched himself at her, smacking her against the door, forcing her left arm high between her shoulder blades. She opened her mouth to yell but a hand clamped over her mouth.

'Hi, bitch,' he whispered into her ear. 'You been missing me?'

India shook her head.

'Oh, but I think you have. Why else have you been sniffing around, asking about stuff that isn't any of your business?'

She rolled her eyes left and right, looking for help, but she was in the porch with her face jammed against the door and she couldn't see a thing.

'Now, listen carefully. I was pretty restrained last time we met, but my patience is wearing thin. So if I hear you chatting to AMSA, the chief or the feds about any sort of ship, I'll be back and I won't be so polite.'

She could smell the bitter antiseptic of rosemary as his words punctured the air. 'Oh, and no more going down to Shoalhaven and pumping the general population about things that don't concern you. My family's got nothing to do with you, and I want you to fuck off home. Message understood?'

She nodded furiously. How did he know so much?

Keeping his hand against her mouth, he dropped her arm and yanked her against him, sliding a hand down the front of her jeans. As she struggled he pulled her even closer.

'I'll miss you, bitch,' he whispered, and licked the back of her neck.

'Bastard!' she muffled against his hand and jabbed an elbow for his sternum, hoping to wind him. Amazingly, it connected.

Quick as a flash she opened her mouth and grabbed the fleshy part of his thumb between her teeth. She bit down, hard. He yelled, his other hand coming up to hit her. She dropped his thumb and spun round and for a split second they were facing each other and she did something she'd never done for real, although she'd been shown how. She headbutted him in the face.

There was a dull *crunch* and he staggered back, and then he was yelling, 'You bitch!' and she was running for the street when a shadow materialised from behind the banksia and something whacked her behind the ear. Pain exploded behind her eyes and she was folding to the ground, dizzy, blinded, her hands fumbling for a rock, a stick, *anything*.

A boot thudded into her ribs, another in her kidneys, and she was groaning, curling into a ball, trying to protect herself against the assault.

'Christ, Jimmy,' a man said. 'Not now. Let's get out of here.'

Thud. 'Bitch.' Thud.

'Jimmy, let's *go*. It was meant to be a *warning*. Jesus, Jimmy—'

'Forget warning her.' Jimmy gave a hysterical laugh. 'She'll only be back. You've seen what she's like.'

Where was everyone? India wondered frantically. Surely someone must have heard them.

'But Bobby told us *not* to.'

'What does he know? He's nothing but a wet rag.'

India desperately tried to clear her head and gather her energy. She had to get enough strength to scream. She squinted through her pain to see a man lit by streetlights standing beside Jimmy, fists clenched. A man she hadn't expected to see. A neatly dressed, athletic-looking man. Sergeant Kuteli. Sweet Jesus. No wonder her description of Jimmy hadn't added up. Jimmy sure had friends in the right places.

'She's recognised you,' Jimmy said, sounding pleased. 'You really want to let her go now?'

'*Shit*.' Kuteli ran his hands over his head.

India pulled a lungful of air against the agony and opened her mouth to scream. She caught a movement out of the corner of her eye and pulled her head round just in time to miss getting mashed by Jimmy's boot. Her shoulder took the brunt of it but the shock of pain sucked the breath from her.

'See?' said Jimmy. 'She's never gives up.'

'OK,' said Kuteli, sounding brisk. 'Let's do it.'

He jogged away then came back. Hands grabbed her and she tried to fight, but she was too weak against their double strength. They lifted her up and carried her to the open boot of a car, threw her in and slammed the lid shut.

With a jolt, the car started to move. India writhed onto her side in the pitch black. Groped with her fingers for the lock, but the mechanism was hidden behind a wall of plastic and the boot lining was screwed into the metalwork. She had no chance of accessing the lock without tools.

She lay there, panting and sweating, aware that the air was already turning stale. She closed her eyes. There had to be a way of surviving this.

The car gave a bounce and she groaned as her hip smacked into something metal beneath her. Feeling around, she recognised the hard rim of the spare tyre. And usually where there were spare tyres, there were tool kits.

India started groping around the tyre. Yes, there it was, tucked inside: one plastic-bound tool kit. Unrolling it, she could feel a couple of spanners, a screwdriver and a wrench. OK, she'd better make a plan. She'd prise the boot open, jump out and run like hell.

The air was hot and heavy, like sucking in a wet flannel. Rest for a bit first, she told herself, just a bit . . .

When she came to, the car was lurching from side to side. They must have turned off the main road onto a dirt track. God, how long had she been asleep? They might have travelled hundreds of kilometres by now. The thought galvanised her.

Screwdriver in hand, India tackled the first screw holding the boot lining in place, but with the lurching of the car and unable to see, unscrewing more than two was going to be impossible. Plan B: Rip the boot lining off.

Hunched up in a tortured position that had her muscles screaming, India wedged the screwdriver between the lip of the plastic and the metalwork and yanked down hard. The plastic gave a little and to her amazement the first screw popped. India grabbed the plastic rim with both hands and pulled. Out popped another screw and she forced her hand into the two-inch gap, searching for the lock, the release cable, *anything*, but all she felt was air.

She shifted her concentration to the near side of the boot, the driver's side, and the screws there. Her hands were sore, her muscles aching, but she kept heaving and tugging . . . She almost gave a shout when she felt the plastic give. At last the lining gaped open.

India thrust her arm inside, searching for cable that would pop the lock from the driver's position. There! She hooked her fingers round the slender wire and pulled it towards her. There was a small clunk, and for an instant she couldn't believe it. The boot lid slowly swung open and stayed there, bobbing up and down with the motion of the car.

India snatched her arm painfully back through the taillight hole, waiting for the car to screech to a halt, but it didn't. Whoever was driving wasn't looking in their rearview mirror. Why should they? It was dark and they weren't on a major highway, so there wouldn't be much to see.

Shoving a handful of smaller tools in her pockets, she glanced outside. In a single second she saw scrubby bush on either side of the dirt track. The stars were out. The wind was freezing, desert cold. She peered down at the ground. It seemed to be going past terribly fast . . .

Don't think. Just do it.

She manoeuvred herself onto the rim of the boot, her breathing coming fast. Tucked her head in. Crossed her arms across her chest. And tumbled outside, shoulder first.

Almost immediately, despite the breath being knocked right out of her, she was scrambling up again, ignoring the pain roaring through her shoulder, and moving fast towards the bush. She crashed through the undergrowth. She couldn't see any details, just an outline of obstacles, lit by starlight. And for an amazing, wonderful second she heard the engine note still cruising away and thought she'd got away with it, but suddenly there was a violent squirt of gravel and then the whine as the car reversed. Fast.

India tried to get as far as she could before they got out of the car. Once they were outside, she'd have to remain utterly quiet, utterly still. Branches tore at her clothes, thorns scratched her skin. Would they see her tracks? No time to worry; the engine had stopped. She fell onto her front and wriggled behind a tree truck. A ghost gum. She heard two doors slam.

'When?' Jimmy demanded. His voice carried easily in the still air.

'I only just noticed.'

'Jesus! Are you telling me she could have jumped out twenty Ks back?' Silence, which Jimmy obviously took for assent.

'You stupid idiot!'

'Shouldn't we look around here, just in case?'

'What's the point? It's dark, in case you hadn't noticed. You got a torch?'

'Sorry.'

Jimmy let rip with a stream of curses. 'Turn the car round, then. Use the headlights instead. Let's see if we can find where she got out.'

'If we can't find her . . .' Kuteli said hesitantly. 'Well, it's not like she's got a survival pack or anything . . . you think she'll survive out here?'

'You'd better hope not.'

Both doors slammed again and slowly, infinitely slowly, they began driving back the way they'd come.

India lay there. She was alive. She had no food or drink, her body felt wrecked, but, for the moment, she was alive.

FIVE

India limped back down the dirt track. She didn't think Jimmy and Kuteli would return, and besides, she had no intention of getting lost out here. She'd follow the track until she hit the bitumen, and then she'd flag down a car and take it from there. What had Jimmy said? Twenty Ks? It wasn't that far. She should be there by morning.

Occasionally she checked her watch in the starlight, trying to gauge the distance she'd covered. A couple of times she heard a crash in the bush and she'd jump a mile, only to relax a couple of seconds later at the soft thud-thudding of startled kangaroos. Her limp eventually became a slow hobble. Her shoulder was throbbing, her ribs sore, and she felt shivery and ill. Come 2 a.m. she stopped for a rest. Moving well off the track she tucked herself in a sandy gully and fell asleep immediately.

India awoke after an hour, shuddering with cold, layered with dew. Morning seemed such a long way away, but she was still petrified that Jimmy might come back, so she forced herself to get up. As she shuffled along the track, she hugged herself, trying to get warm. The track suddenly started to climb. She was sweating and staggering when she got to the top. Time for another rest, she thought, and slumped onto a rock. In the distance, a hair's-breadth strip of crimson split the blue-black of the sky.

India sat and waited for the sun to rise, so she could get her bearings. She was thirsty and hungry and in need of a soft bed and some super-strength painkillers. A knot of anxiety tightened in her chest. Why hadn't she seen any lights from towns or homesteads? Swivelling her head 360 degrees, she realised with horror that there were no lights whatsoever. In her exhaustion, she must have missed a turning.

You think she'll survive out here?

She refused to give in to the tide of fear gushing through her, and hurriedly turned her mind to practical things. First up, water. As the horizon broadened into blue, she studied the endless stretches of desert and scrub, looking for any sign of life. There! A flock of cockatoos flying low, heading west, towards the sun. India followed their steady flight until she could no longer see them, and then she got up and followed them.

She didn't find any water that morning, but she did find some djuk bushes. Blessing God that she'd learned a bit about bush tucker a couple of years back, she stripped the bushes of their tiny orange-red berries, eating half immediately, and pocketing the other half.

Her spirits lifted, she walked on, watching the flight of any birds she saw, tracking the sun, making sure she was on a trail that headed west all the time. She certainly didn't want to walk east, and into the baking interior. Towards the west she at least had a hope of coming across a homestead. God willing. And she wasn't that thirsty yet. So long as she found water by tomorrow, she thought cheerfully, she'd be fine.

It didn't take long for her hopes to crash to earth. She remembered the flippant note she'd left Ellie, telling her not to send out a search party until the end of the week. Nobody would be looking for her, not that they even knew where to look. She pictured her bones being found by some bush walker, picked clean by bush animals and ants.

Get a grip, she told herself. Look, the sun's going down, so concentrate. Sure enough, twenty minutes later a bunch of little brown birds scooted past, chattering. Cementing her bearings firmly in her mind, India followed them off the track and into the undergrowth.

A few minutes later she came across a creek. A small creek, hardly flowing, but there was plenty of water in the rocky pool. On all fours, India bent her head and scooped handfuls of water into her mouth. Water dripping down her neck, she put her little remaining energy into gouging out a hollow in the sand to sleep in, and collecting dry grass to crawl under for warmth.

It was getting dark, so she snuggled into her bush bed and tried to ignore her stomach's growls, her crushed muscles and aching ribs. You will get out of here, she promised herself. And you will make Jimmy pay.

THE NEXT MORNING she found another creek heading west. Occasionally it disappeared underground, but not for long enough for her to lose it. She followed its winding course across the scrub, praying it would lead her to some human habitation, but then it disappeared. She searched for hours but couldn't find it. She wanted to scream but knew it wouldn't help, so she sat on a rock and tried to think what to do. There was no point following it back to where she'd come from; she had to go on, and hope she'd find more water.

By midafternoon the next day, India was frantically thirsty, so she sucked on a stone as she walked. Got to keep going, she told herself. The first indication that she was nearing the coast was a straggly spreading shrub with succulent grey-green leaves. A sea berry saltbush. The ground turned soft, into grey sand, draining each step, but when she came upon some wheel ruts she followed them west. Always west.

The sun had set and was draining light from the sky when the wheel ruts split. One went right, the other dead ahead. She went dead ahead where she could hear the roar of surf, and came to a beach. She skidded down a dune, shucked off her boots and went and bathed her poor, blistered feet in the sea. Scooped salt water against her face, then looked up and down the coastline. No creeks spilling fresh water onto the beach. No people, no shacks in the hollows. She clambered back up the dune and followed the wheel ruts to where they turned left. The sand was cool beneath her feet.

A fence line. A grove of tuarts. The wheel ruts joined a gravel track. Wagtails and honeyeaters fluttered and hopped in the fading shadows of paperbarks. She stumbled on. And then she saw it. A house.

The back door was closed behind the insect screen. She went round to the front. No car in the gravel driveway. No sign of life.

On the verandah was a tattered, overstuffed armchair and a wooden table covered in plates, beer bottles and cigarette ends. She limped to the front door and knocked, even though she was pretty sure nobody was home. Tried the door handle. Unlocked.

She staggered into the kitchen and turned the ancient rusty tap. Oh, thank God. She dipped her head and drank straight from the cool, clear flow.

Switching on the lights she began opening cupboards. Found tins of soup and beans, packs of tea, coffee and cocoa, packets of cereal. She ripped open a box of cornflakes and ate handfuls as she checked out the house. An old dresser with cracked china plates. Aluminium tables and chairs. Fishing gear and a chart by the back door. Band-Aids and sunscreen in the bathroom. It felt like a house abandoned in a hurry. Her legs were softening, ready to collapse, as she came to the last room: a mattress on the floor.

Fear of trespassing didn't enter her head. The last thing she heard was the distant, lonely moan of a crow.

INDIA CRAWLED awake when the sun was high in the sky. She blinked several times until the room came into focus: weatherboard walls, a threadbare rug, curling posters of motorbikes, big trucks and large-breasted women.

She lay there a long time, thinking about what she knew.

Jimmy had come to warn her off her investigation into *The Pride* and talking to people about his family. He'd told her not to talk to the chief, AMSA and the feds. Jimmy had to be Jack's nephew.

The Zhuganovs must have followed her initially, searching her office to see what she had found out about the container ship, but dropped their surveillance when she hadn't had any luck. Witnessing Danny's snatch had brought the Zhuganov searchlights to focus back on her. Jimmy had killed Danny. He didn't want Danny to talk about the ship he'd crewed on, the ship that had rammed *Sundancer*.

Jack had a picture of the guilty container ship in his house. Jack and his family were growing more and more powerful in Western Australia, even preparing themselves to win the next election.

It was, she thought, little wonder that if they owned the ship they wanted it kept quiet. Once it came out that *The Pride*'s master hadn't stopped to help *Sundancer*'s crew, that they hadn't come clean and compensated the families of those who had died, nobody would vote for the Zhuganovs.

India wondered why they hadn't owned up to the collision. Maybe they were protecting something else, something that would explain why *The Pride* had been so far away from the normal shipping routes, and had ignored Ned's calls on channel 16.

Pushing back the blankets, India limped for the boiler, switched on the hot water and waited for it to heat. Then she went to the bathroom, stripped off her clothes, and stood under the shower. Lots of hot water, shampoo and shower gel. Bliss, aside from the fact her ribs still hurt like hell.

When she was clean, she went back to the bedroom and opened cupboards and drawers. She put on a big baggy sloppy joe and shorts that were too big for her. She tied them round the waist with string from the laundry. She washed her clothes and put them out to dry. Then she went and studied the fishing chart stuck to the wall beside the back door. The scuffed mark on the paper, from having a finger prodded at it over time, indicated the house. The nearest settlement was a little scattering of houses just outside the thumb mark. Cape Cray, north of Perth.

Exhausted and in need of another twelve-hour sleep, she took a bowl of Weetabix drowned in long-life milk onto the verandah and sank into the tattered armchair.

She was just finishing up when a guy in his twenties came into sight, walking barefoot for the house. There was no point trying to hide; he'd already seen her. She'd have to brazen it out.

'You a mate of Stewie's?' he asked, looking puzzled.

'Not really.'

He looked at her nearly empty bowl, then at the scratches and bruises all over her legs and on her arms, and gave a disgusted grimace. 'No respect for women,' he said. 'Makes me sick.'

It took her a second to understand. He obviously thought she'd been beaten up by some guy, probably her husband, and was hiding out.

'You all right?'

'Yes,' she said. 'Thank you.'

He nodded then said, 'You wanna rent it for a bit?'

God, she thought, *brilliant*. Jimmy would never find her here.

'I'd love to,' she told him. 'But what about Stewie, won't he mind?'

'Na. Took off a few weeks back under not very favourable circumstances. He won't be coming back for a while.' He raised a hand and had a quick chew at the corner of his thumbnail. 'If ever.'

'I see.'

'He was always getting into trouble. It's been real quiet without him.' He sighed. 'I'm his brother. Everyone calls me Chew.'

'Jenny,' she said.

They shook, and Chew said she could have the house for a hundred bucks a week. If she wanted she could use Stewie's ute, since he'd taken the Valiant. For a hundred bucks a week, of course. Cash.

'Deal,' she said.

CHEW DROPPED OFF the ute late afternoon, when the sun had just hit the water. With a fleece of Stewie's over a pair of his trackies, she drove barefoot to Cape Cray, parked outside the roadhouse. She got out and looked around at the settlement wedged between the sea and sand dunes. A bunch of tin sheds near the water. Weatherboard houses, a bait shop, and from somewhere she could hear the drone of a diesel generator. Down on the jetty a couple of boats were being winched onto trailers. No pub, no café.

Inside the roadhouse, freezers rumbled and heavy metal played on the radio. A man in a pair of greasy overalls gave her a wave and she asked him where the phone was. He pointed behind her.

'Scotto?' She spoke quietly, not wanting to be overheard. 'It's me. Could you do me a favour?'

INDIA SIGNED for Scotto's parcel at the roadhouse two days later, and took it to her home in the dunes before she opened it. There was a list of useful phone numbers, fifteen hundred dollars in cash, her passport for identification, and a mobile phone and charger. But the best surprise was a company credit card. Once she'd set up the phone she rang Scotto and thanked him.

'No staying at the Hyatt, OK?' he told her. 'It's too expensive.'

'Two hundred bucks a week all right by you?'

'So long as you don't bring any bed bugs back to the office.' He gave a little cough that she knew meant he was worried. 'You sure you're OK?'

She wasn't going to tell him she'd spent the last forty-eight hours munching aspirin and sleeping, and assured him she was fine.

'Right.' His tone turned brisk. 'I've found you the contact you asked for. His name's Greg Elsden. He's an ex-boyfriend of our new receptionist, Sally. They met backpacking last year, and when Sally came home, he didn't. He now lives in Jakarta, teaching English. He said he'll check the docks twice a week for us, starting today. We've worked out a rough fee for him, and he gets a pretty nice bonus if he gets one of us over to see *The Pride*, so he's pretty keen. He's got your number, but I'd better give you his.'

She hastily punched it into her mobile.

'That's brilliant, Scotto,' she told him.

'Even more brilliant if we actually get to catch the sucker.'

INDIA RANG Mikey and gave him an abbreviated account of the past few days. She didn't say a word about Jimmy's plan to kill her. Mikey would only demand that she drop her investigation and come home, and since Jimmy probably thought she was dead, she had no intention of giving up the opportunity to do some digging around when he wasn't looking for her. Despite her best efforts, however, Mikey knew something was up, and it took her five minutes of hearty reassurances before he let her hang up.

Lighting a cigarette, India tried to work out what to do next. She wondered how to link the Zhuganovs to *The Pride* without tipping Jimmy off. Danny had said that they'd loaded gear from a company with Harris in its name on board *The Pride* at Fremantle, and the only Harris she could link to Jack for sure was his livestock insurer, Harris & Hewitt, which was run by a distant cousin. It was a pretty tenuous connection but it was the only one she had, so she may as well start there.

The tyres on Stewie's ute weren't great, but otherwise the car looked in pretty good shape. She picked up the highway south, listening to the radio fade in and out. At the first gas station she filled two forty-litre jerry cans with unleaded and managed to get a guy filling his car to help her strap them in the back. Then she went to a sports store across the road and bought a pair of binoculars, some rope and a torch. Next store along, a daypack, notebook and pens, a baseball cap, bottled water, chocolate and biscuits.

Swallowing another couple of aspirin, she pulled the map onto her lap and had a quick look. Fifteen minutes later, she was driving through the gates of Harris & Hewitt, Veterinary Group and Livestock Insurers.

Since the visitor spaces were full, India parked round the back, between two utes emblazoned with H & H VETERINARY GROUP. It was a pretty big outfit all up, and included a pet-food warehouse and a bunch of smaller stores specialising in anything from pet crematoria to pet-sitting services.

The receptionist—Linda, according to the badge on her lapel—greeted India with a cheerful smile. 'How can I help?'

India introduced herself as Jenny Morris from *Your Little Treasure* magazine, and told her she was doing an article on pet insurance. 'I don't suppose Mr Harris is around, is he?'

'Nah. Dave's gone to see a client out at Dundilla. Lost a bunch of alpacas; we don't know why yet.' She pulled a face. 'Shouldn't be farming them things over here; it's too bloody hot.'

India murmured a neutral agreement. 'If Dave's out . . .' she said, purposely hesitant. 'I've a deadline, you see. I don't suppose you might be able to help?'

Linda looked dubious, but said, 'I'll give it a go.'

'You insure horses?' India asked.

'Along with everything else. We had anaconda last week . . .' A truck rumbled past, making the office shudder. Both India and Linda glanced outside to see an enormous lorry grinding down its gears, and right behind it was a bright red Isuzu truck with a pair of silver horns on its snout. India stared at it, stunned, and watched it turn the corner of the building. It was the truck she'd seen at the front of Jack's rubbish tip.

'Linda, I'm sorry,' she said, lunging for the door, 'but my dog's jumped out of my car . . .'

Linda said something, but India didn't hear what it was because she was already racing outside. She belted round the corner, then screeched to a halt when she saw the Isuzu back up to a roller-door at the rear of the veterinary surgery fifty metres down. India watched as the driver climbed out and went through a rear door. A couple of minutes later the roller-door clattered up.

The man began loading what looked like sacks of rubbish into the back of the Isuzu. The plastic bags were tagged with bright yellow strips.

When he'd disappeared inside the loading bay for more bags, she climbed into her ute and watched the truck in her rearview mirror. Finally, with another five bags loaded on board, the truck drove off.

It wasn't difficult to follow him, since he didn't appear to be in any sort of hurry. He went to another veterinary surgery to pick up some more bags flashed with yellow, then the rear of a company called Pharmacy Plus. The truck stopped a few more times, once at a reprographics firm, and by the time they trailed into the centre of Perth, it was late afternoon.

Buzzing down her windows, India let the air tug at her hair. She could smell the briny scent of the sea and what she took to be chicken frying. What an incredible city, she thought. I'm on a major arterial road striking right through its heart and the traffic is light and I can smell the sea. Maybe I should move out here. It would help my stress levels heaps, and it sure would help Mikey's.

When the truck started to slow, indicating left for an industrial park, she slowed too and waited for it to turn. As it turned, her mobile rang.

'Hello?' she said, her eyes fixed on the truck.

'Hey, India.' It was Scotto. 'Look, Ellie's been doing her nut trying to get hold of you. Ring her, would you?'

'God, sorry, I should have done it before. Thanks, Scotto.'

Hanging up, she immediately dialled Ellie's mobile.

'India! Where the hell have you been?'

'Oh, working. You know how it is. Sorry I haven't rung.'

'I assume you're on your way. I mean, I told William and Katy that you were still coming. You are still coming, aren't you?'

India's mind did a scrambled backtrack. Oh hell. Katy was hosting a barbie for them all tonight.

'Hello? India?'

'Give me a sec. Traffic's gone mad.'

Could she go to the barbecue? She couldn't see why not. After all, it wasn't being held at Ellie's, but at Katy and William's, well south of the city. Even so, she dithered. She didn't want to bring the Zhuganovs to her friends' doorstep.

'India? India?' Her mobile was squawking.

'Yup.'

'We've done a pig spit.'

India's mouth watered. She'd been so glad of the cupboards of canned foods when she'd arrived at her house in the dunes, but a pig spit? She could almost taste the crackling now. 'I'm on my way.'

Three minutes later the red Isuzu pulled into a forecourt. As she drove past, the driver climbed out and stretched. She headed to the end of the street and did a U-turn. On her way back she saw three men in overalls unloading the van. The sign at the forecourt's entrance read: KEMBLE ENVIRONMENTAL SERVICES. She drove past slowly, but when she hit the highway she gunned the engine. She'd better get a hoof on. She was kilometres away.

INDIA'S EYES kept flicking to her rearview mirror the whole way. She even stopped at one point on a length of empty road for a good ten minutes to make sure nobody was following her. Two vehicles drove past, one oil truck and a ute overflowing with straw, but otherwise there was no traffic. Relieved, she stepped on the gas, suddenly looking forward to seeing friends. It felt like weeks rather than days since she'd been in safe company.

When she arrived, the sun was lowering and turning the sky pink, the air cooling rapidly. She climbed out of her car and all at once she was surrounded by six dogs of intermingled breeds with wagging tails and shrieks of delight from Katy that India told her could be heard in Darwin.

'Who cares? I can't believe you're here!'

'Neither can I,' she admitted, looking around and trying not to show her amazement. Penselwood Farm wasn't a farm at all, but a zoo. There were lush green paddocks with oxen, donkeys, water buffalo and camels. A handful of antelopes with black stripes down their faces stood beneath a clump of gum trees, swishing their tails.

'This is Billy,' Katy told her as she gave her the tour. Billy was a koala who'd suffered from a nasty virus but had luckily made a full recovery.

'And this is Digger and family.' She pointed out several wombat earths in the ground.

Wild birds were everywhere: currawongs and galahs, pigeons, parrots and white-tailed black cockatoos. It was like being in a different country. Here the ground was red, nothing like the white sandy soil up north, and instead of coastal scrub there were turf farms and dozens of horses grazing on the hills beyond. And the house . . . India tried not to turn green, and failed. Beautifully renovated, the traditional old Aussie building was raised on stumps, to take advantage of the circulating cool breezes in the summer, and had spacious verandahs, shutters on every window, and a long, sloping roof of green, newly painted, corrugated iron.

She could hear William's voice as they approached the back yard, and she tried to drag her fingers through her hair but it was a tangled mess after having the car windows open. She had no make-up on, and was sure she looked as grubby and untidy as she felt. Some guest, she thought. She might have washed her jeans and shirt, but after her trek in the desert they looked as though they'd been dragged behind a galloping horse for a week. She was glad Jimmy hadn't managed to hit her face. At least nobody could see the cuts and bruises under her clothes.

'Sorry I'm late,' she announced, taking in the heated pool, gazebo, and riots of native plants: orange and yellow wattles, pink rainbows, red kangaroo paws. It was chaotic and colourful and, like the house, gorgeous.

'You're always late,' Ellie grumbled, and India was smiling, walking to meet her friend, when William rushed at her and hugged her. It took all her effort not to shout as her ribs howled in protest.

'So good to see you,' he said, voice muffled against her shoulder.

'Hey, good to see you too, William,' she said, disentangling herself, patting his back like she would an over-friendly labrador.

'Sorry.' He stepped back, looking abashed. Flicked a glance at Katy, who was approaching with a glass of wine. 'I'm not normally so . . .'

'Demonstrative,' Katy finished for him. 'But considering you worship the ground she walks on since she saved my life, I'll forgive you.'

William managed a weak grin.

India and Ellie hugged, both checking the other over. Ellie looked great, big belly and all, and India was smiling at the thought of Ellie's baby, *Ned's baby*, until she caught the look in Ellie's eye. Ellie knew something was wrong, and India was glad that her friend didn't say anything, not even when she told her that she wouldn't be staying with her for a while. Just put a hand against her cheek and told her to be careful.

'You've an amazing place,' she said to William as he handed her a glass of wine, glad to feel herself winding down. God, it was good to be with friends. 'A *zoo*, for heaven's sake,' she added.

'I call it my financial big black hole,' William grinned. 'But it makes me laugh. Like when a python broke in last week and ate one of the birds, but couldn't get out because his body was so bloated.'

Dying to know how he came to be so wealthy, she decided on the direct approach. 'You're obviously incredibly successful,' she said. 'Do you mind me asking how you got started?'

'Officially,' he said, eyes creasing at the corners, 'I was curious why eco cleaning products didn't do the job as well as normal brands and were twice the price, so I hired a scientist, Brian Derry, to create our competitively priced, eco-friendly Get Active range.'

'Unofficially?'

'It's a gravy train.'

She gave a snort of half-shocked laughter. 'Are you telling me you're not Mr Green after all?'

'Don't tell Katy.' He rolled his eyes dramatically. 'She'd divorce me.'

'You're as green as the jolly green giant,' she told him tartly. 'Stop denying it. You invented Ecopac.'

'Brian invented it, not me. I just stumped up the funds for his research.'

'You obviously have a thing for big black holes,' she laughed. 'Research is a classic financial bloodsucker. How did you get the money to fund it?'

William's hand paused midair. His whole body went still.

'God, sorry,' she said, cringing at her relentless curiosity. 'It's the journo in me, I'm afraid. Inherently nosy. Just ignore me.'

He took a long pull of beer, then raised his head to watch a handful of black-crested cockatoos fly past, screeching.

'Since you ask,' he said in an even tone, 'I got a loan.'

Holy cow, she thought. It must have been huge. Squillions at least.

'I take it you've repaid it. I mean, God, William, I'm sorry. It's the wine. I'm not normally so intrusive.'

He was still staring at the space where the cockatoos had flown, and India's scalp crawled at the withdrawn, fearful look on his face.

'No,' he said quietly. 'I still owe them.'

'Food's up!' The magic words broke the spell between them. William abruptly turned away and, seeing the tension in his shoulders, India decided to let him be and get her priorities straight. Like leaping for the pig spit and piling her plate high.

When Katy ushered them all inside, India made a beeline for the open fireplace, where great logs of jarrah were burning. The lights were low, the sitting room warm and welcoming with plump couches, thick colourful rugs over old wooden floors and pictures of wildlife on the walls. Munching on tender, juicy pork, she latched on to a collection of photographs of horses displayed on a baby grand piano: sleek horses in parade rings, horses with their necks stretched out as they crossed the finishing line; horses steaming in the winner's enclosure.

'You own racehorses?' she asked Katy.

'William's hoping to win the Melbourne Cup next year.'

Where William's horse pictures were beautifully framed in silver, Jack's had been a haphazard collection in heavy, ornate frames, but there was the same pride, the same passion in their display. When Katy and Ellie cleared the plates into the kitchen, India glanced at William, sipping wine on the sofa. He looked as contented as only a happily married man with a full stomach could. Would he know Jack? she wondered. Could William give her the lever to open another avenue she could follow? The Melbourne Cup was in a different league from the races Jack entered, but you never knew.

'I was talking horses with someone last week,' she ventured. William turned his head in polite enquiry. 'Heard about one that sounded pretty hot. A stallion called Grafton Statesman.'

If she'd shot him in the foot, she couldn't have been more surprised at his reaction. He bolted across the room at her, expression frantic.

'Not here, India,' he pleaded.

'You know him, don't you?' she said, stunned. 'You know Jack.'

'Shhh.' William was making urgent dampening motions with his hands. 'I don't want Katy to hear, OK?'

'OK,' she whispered.

William hunkered beside her, eyes flicking towards the kitchen door. 'How the hell do you know about that horse? What's going on?'

'I think Jack's the owner of the cargo ship that hit *Sundancer*.'

The blood left his face. 'Are you sure?' he asked. '*Absolutely* sure?'

She wasn't at all, but she made her tone firm. 'Yup.'

'What are you going to do? You can't go after him . . . People have tried in the past and regretted it big time. Can't you drop it?'

'I'll be careful, I promise.'

'India, I know you want justice for *Sundancer*, but . . .' William swallowed. 'Jack's ruthless. He'll crush you like a bug beneath his shoe.'

'William,' she said gently, 'how do you know Jack?'

He turned his head aside so she couldn't read his face. 'Business,' he said dully. 'Just business.'

And then Katy and Ellie were coming in with coffee and cake, and William went to his wife and put his arms round her waist, kissing her neck, her hair, and Katy was laughing, protesting because they had guests, but melting all the same and kissing him back.

India smiled as she watched them, but something inside her felt cold and uncertain. She couldn't help hearing herself badgering William earlier in the evening, asking him how he'd got the money to fund the research for his Get Active range and Ecopac.

I got a loan.

I take it you've repaid it.

No. I still owe them.

SIX

Back at her house in the dunes, India was smoking her first cigarette of the day in the kitchen when her mobile rang.

'Is that India Kane?' a man with a high-pitched voice asked.

'Who's calling?'

'Oh, Greg. Greg Elsden. Scotto passed me your number. I'm in Jakarta. I've got your ship here.'

She nearly dropped her Marlboro onto the floor. 'You *what*?'

'*The Pride of Tangkuban*. She's here getting some repairs done.'

'What does she look like?'

'Er . . . well, she's pretty big, a container ship. Looks old. Lots of rust.'

'I'll be on the next flight out. I'll ring you when I get there.'

India punched the line free and stood there, her mind a frantic jumble. Could she ring AMSA now? Tip them off? What if Kuteli found out? She'd bet he had contacts in the feds. With a shudder she realised she couldn't tell anyone official without the Zhuganovs discovering that she was alive.

She had to go to Jakarta alone.

Ringing Scotto, she got his go-ahead. After all, he was the guy who paid her expenses, and she knew he'd never breathe a word. And nor would Mikey. He might hate it when she was on a mission, but you'd have to rip out his fingernails before he'd give her away. And more.

'I know you hate it when I say this,' he said when she had filled him in, 'but *please* be careful. The Foreign Office is advising all nationals not to travel there and the way you attract trouble . . .' Mikey trailed off and she knew he was biting his lip to stop himself from having a go at her. 'Sorry,' he added. 'I can't help myself sometimes. I happen to quite like you. Sometimes.'

'I think you're OK too. Sometimes.'

'Enough to tie the knot?'

'Sorry, Mikey. I've got to go. Love to Polly.'

Pushing all thoughts of marriage aside, she went and rigged up a system that would tell her if anyone had come to the house while she was away. Then she packed her daypack with minimum supplies, grabbed her passport, and drove to the airport.

THE GUIDEBOOK India bought warned her that Jakarta was a dirty, overpopulated city that most travellers tried to avoid, and she could see why. The heat was incredible, as were the pollution and the noise. People shouted, dogs barked and pop music blared from every rickety roadside shop.

Through the open windows of her taxi, she could smell frying garlic, and then the air was full of diesel exhaust and the cloying undertone of human excrement. But India felt her spirits rise. She loved being somewhere new, and her nerves were tingling in curiosity and expectation.

India paid off her taxi at the docks. She had originally hoped that Greg might have come along to be her interpreter, but had changed her mind once she met him. She'd gone to his apartment and, without even saying hello, he'd demanded the money, counted it laboriously, then demanded to be her guide for a fee that would have paid for Polly's entire education. Greedy wasn't the word for it.

At the entrance to the dock were two army lorries. A soldier in camouflage uniform checked her passport and spat a fat red gob of betel juice onto the ground as he handed it back.

'Kelapa office, over there.' He waved a hand at a low-slung building blurred to brown by pollution. 'They book your ship.'

The Kelapa office had advertisements for berths on commercial ships plastered all over its windows. Inside, three Swedish-looking backpackers were discussing whether they should take a tanker to Sumatra or go straight to Singapore. India went back out and walked on. The heat and humidity made her clothes stick to her skin. Swigging mineral water as she walked, India passed a ship loading up and dockworkers shouting to one another as derricks swung containers inside its holds. No one took any notice of her; they were obviously used to seeing foreigners searching for a cheap ride.

India had been walking for well over two hours when she saw a container ship with rust streaking her flanks like bloody claw marks. She had a four-storey block, painted white and topped with filthy windows—that was the bridge. There was no ensign, nobody around that she could see.

Heartbeat picking up, she moved towards the ship, studying the bow, but her port side was clean, *too* clean. It could have been repaired.

Going to the rear of the ship, she saw a dent in the transom, like the footprint of a man's boot in mud. Her stomach swooped and for a second her ears were filled with alarms sounding, the air horn blaring, Cuan's voice over the Tannoy, instructing everyone to get into the inflatables, the life rafts, the ship was going down . . . The deafening screech of tearing metal, the icy water closing over her head, the grinding sound going on and on.

Sweat drenched her neck and shoulders as she studied the ship's name above the dent. Although there was barely any paint, the letters were carved, standing proud of the metal, and in the sunshine it was as clear as day.

THE PRIDE OF TANGKUBAN.

She'd found the ship that had rammed *Sundancer*.

'HELLO, MISSUS,' an excruciatingly thin Indian man greeted her as she stepped inside the Kelapa office. He was smoking a long, thin cigarette resembling rolled bay leaves, and had a smile yellow with nicotine. 'You are looking to go to Singapore? Maybe Pedang?'

She hadn't a clue where Pedang was, but she gave a vague nod.

'You are wanting to see the boat? Meet the captain?'

'Oh, yes, please.' India took the plunge. 'I'd like to look at the ship called *The Pride of Tangkuban*.'

The man placed his skinny cylinder of bay leaves on an overflowing ashtray and flicked through a large folder on his desk. 'I am not knowing this ship,' he said, frowning. 'She is taking passengers?'

'So I've heard.'

He lifted the receiver of a phone and dialled. He spoke in Hindi, quite fast, waited a while, listened some more, then hung up.

'This ship is not taking passengers. You would like to take another?'

'No. I'd like to see *The Pride*. And if it's possible, meet with one of the crew.' Delving into her money belt she withdrew a US $100 bill and placed it on his desk. 'Obviously,' she said, 'if I talk with someone like the chief officer, or the master, if would benefit you further.'

She saw his gaze flick to the note, and his eyes lit up. Immediately he got to his feet and shook her hand vigorously. 'I am Batuan. I am very happy to be helping you in this matter.'

Three phone calls later he hung up, beaming. 'I am having a very good success for you . . .'

He paused when the phone rang, picked it up. His beam vanished. Another fast conversation, and then he did a lot of listening, turning away from her as he finished the conversation in rapid Hindi.

Hanging up, his smile returned. 'So,' he said cheerfully, 'you shall be meeting with a representative of the ship. He will be here shortly.'

THE PRIDE's representative was a young Indonesian man dressed in shorts and an orange T-shirt. He introduced himself as Halim, then they were walking down acres of concrete, which wavered in the heat. In the distance, India caught the faint chanting wail of an *azan*, calling the faithful to prayer.

'*Panas*,' Halim said with a smile. 'Very hot.'

'Very,' she agreed.

Halim asked her where she was staying, and when she said she hadn't booked anywhere, suggested a cheap, family-run hotel. 'The Puri Mango,' he said. 'Very small *losmen*, but very nice, very clean.'

He told her where he lived, and that he didn't work at the docks, but his cousin was the boatswain of *The Pride*. 'I will translate for you,' he said. 'His English is not so good.'

Wow, thought India. A hundred bucks went quite a way here.

Halim's cousin was ten years older, with wary black eyes and muscles that were hard and twisted like knotted rope. A wrench was sticking out of his rear pocket. When he shook Halim's hand, India caught the flash of cash palmed between the two men, and she wondered if he was a cousin at all.

Flakes of rust crunched under her feet as she followed the men along the narrow steel deck and headed for the white-painted block at the stern. The boatswain dragged open the door at the bottom of the block with a screech of exhausted metal, and they went up a flight of stairs through the stale odours of ancient cooking and sweat. She was shown the galley, thick with years of grease, then some of the crew cabins. Each had copious clippings from porn magazines taped to the walls, and reeked of filthy toilets and disinfectant. All the portholes were wide open.

'Do you have air conditioning?' she asked the boatswain.

'Not for a long time,' Halim translated. 'The generators are broken.'

She thought of the icy wastes of the Southern Ocean. 'Heating?'

The boatswain laughed, showing two gold teeth before answering.

'He says no, but he hopes it will be working for their next voyage. This is why the ship is now in port. For repairs.'

They headed for the bridge, a long, dark room running the width of the ship, with a wheel, a radar and radio. A sextant sat on the far port side of the bridge, next to the chart table. Most of the equipment was filthy and looked as neglected as the rest of the ship. Indicating the radar, India raised her eyebrows into a question. The boatswain picked up a pair of binoculars, shook them at her.

'You're kidding,' she said, unable to keep the horror from her face.

The boatswain grinned and shook his head.

India pointed at the autopilot and the boatswain gave another grin. 'Also broken,' he said, beaming. 'I am autopilot!'

In disbelief, she said, 'Does the radio work?'

Halim smoothly stepped back into his translator's role. 'Of course. How else would we know when to move?'

'Who instructs him?'

'The owner.'

'And who is that?'

'He doesn't know.'

'What about the ship's agent, would they know the owner?'

'He says the agent is only responsible for servicing the ship in port. The owner's representative would be better. He would know.'

Before she could ask her next question the boatswain interjected and Halim added, 'No, he doesn't know the owner's representative.'

'OK.'

India watched a seagull alight on one of the derricks. 'What is this ship's registration number?'

'He doesn't know.'

'Is he saying it's unregistered?'

Silence while the boatswain picked at his oil-blackened fingernails and Halim studied his feet. India took this as, 'Yes.'

No wonder the boatswain was looking abashed, she thought. Unregistered meant unregulated and unclassed. No safety inspections. No checks run on the seaworthiness of the vessel.

'Could you ask your cousin when and where he sailed in January?'

The boatswain gave Halim a narrowed look, then studied India.

'Chennai,' translated Halim. 'Madras.'

'I don't believe him. I *saw* this ship. It rammed us in the Southern Ocean and left us to sink.'

When the translation came through the boatswain flinched and glued his eyes to the floor. His whole posture reeked of guilt.

'I see.' India took a deep breath, wrestling to keep her anger under control. 'What cargo was the ship carrying?'

The boatswain was hesitating, so she brought out a twenty-dollar bill and his expression perked up. 'What cargo?' she said to him.

He glanced at Halim then back at the floor. He shook his head.

She gave the boatswain the note anyway and was rewarded with a smile that warmed his eyes. He said something, but Halim didn't translate.

'What did he say?'

'It is his daughter's birthday tomorrow.'

'Tell her happy birthday from me.'

Another smile from the boatswain while India lined up her next questions. 'Is *The Pride* part of a fleet? Does her owner have other ships?'

'Oh, very many. There is *The Pearl of Kupang*, who is at sea at present, and her sister ship, *The Glory of Surakata. The Prince of San Diego* and *The King of New York. The Monarch of Miami.*'

She said, 'The last three are American names.'

'That is because they are American ships, operating out of America.'

A chill swept over her. If Jack owned this shipping company, his business was not just contained to Jakarta and the Southern Ocean; it stretched to the other side of the globe.

'Can't he tell me anything about the cargo on the last trip?'

Long consultation.

'He thinks they had some machine parts. Maybe some chemicals.'

'Can he remember a company name? Any name will do.'

The boatswain studied Halim for a second, then shook his head firmly.

She changed tack. 'I'd like to meet the master. Where can I find him?'

The boatswain gave another firm shake of the head.

'The master is away,' Halim said. 'This is impossible.'

Halim was glancing at his watch and heading for the stairs, so India thanked the boatswain and made to follow him, but stopped when the boatswain put an oil-stained hand on her arm.

'Thank you,' he said very carefully, smiling, patting his front pocket where the twenty-dollar bill lay. He glanced over to the stairwell and the smile left his face. He said quietly, 'Reenpeese. I very sorry.'

Despite the heat she felt a rush of cold over her skin. Every hair on her body stood on end. *Greenpeace?*

'Greenpeace?' she said out loud, her heart beating fast.

'Shhh.' The boatswain put an urgent finger to his lips.

'You know what happened?' she whispered.

He gestured at the binoculars and looked miserable. 'No good. Not see . . . How you say . . .?' He put both hands over his eyes.

Blindfolded, she thought and said, 'Fog.'

'Fog,' he repeated, nodding. 'No radar. I autopilot.'

'But we radioed you. Didn't you hear?'

'I hear radio.' He looked ready to weep. 'You see me. I not see you.'

Sweet Jesus, she thought. He'd heard Ned's radio call and realised there was another ship nearby, and assumed, quite reasonably, that since he'd been called up his ship was on their radar, and that *Sundancer* would take evasive action. But Ned had collapsed before he could change course.

She put a hand on his arm. 'It was an accident.'

He gulped. 'Master not want stop. People in water. Many people.'

India refused to give in to the vision he was now reliving. Emma thrown into the sea and Joe diving for her. Others lying in the freezing ocean unconscious, the Zodiac desperately trying to save them all.

'Master is boss,' she said. 'You boatswain.'

He gave a wan smile, but the misery didn't leave his face.

Both of them flinched when they thought they heard a tap on the metal staircase. Not a footstep, just a tap, like someone had knocked their watch against a railing. Distant. Nothing to worry about.

'Tell me, cargo? Any name of client.' She quickly passed him another twenty bucks and he pocketed it fast, expression earnest.

''Stralia?'

'Yes, from Australia. Your biggest client.'

'Kemmal,' he said. 'How you say? Enronment . . . Like Reenpeese.'

A swoop of excitement. 'You mean Kemble Environmental Services?'

He nodded vigorously.

'What were you doing out there? In the Southern Ocean?'

He looked blank.

'What you do,' she amended, 'before hit Greenpeace?'

His brow cleared.

'Cargo,' he said, and took a breath to continue—

A *crack* like a bullwhip lashed past her ear, and at the same time the boatswain's head disintegrated into a bloody pulp. For a second she stood, motionless with shock, but then, as his body began to crumple, she was yelling, flinging herself sideways.

Shoulder down to absorb the blow of the deck, she hit the floor and gave another yell as pain wrapped round her ribs. She heard another *crack* but she hadn't been hit, and she forced herself towards the boatswain, wriggling behind his body for cover, and there was another *crack*, and a stinging sensation on her upper arm as though someone had sliced her with a knife.

Her eyes went round the bridge. Only one escape route: the stairwell. A man was advancing on her, pistol in hand. He had a thick black moustache and a stripe of grey hair running from his forehead to the crown. Batuan was behind him making terrified moaning sounds, his face ashen.

'Rajiv!' Batuan cried. 'No, Rajiv!'

Rajiv didn't respond to Batuan's pleas. He looked her straight in the eyes. His hands had blood on them and his shirt was soaked with sweat, and the ripe stench of him made her want to gag, but time was slowing to a pinpoint and he was stepping close, pistol aimed at her head, his whole posture and expression telling her he had won.

'I know all about your cargo,' she said. 'I told the police about it.'

Rajiv swung round to yell at Batuan.

That was all she needed. In one movement she grabbed the wrench from the boatswain's back pocket and launched herself at Rajiv. She heard him shout something but it was too late. The wrench connected with his head and she didn't wait to see if he dropped; she was going for the stairwell. For freedom.

Batuan was blocking her exit. Wrench still in her hand, she charged him, screaming at the top of her voice like a banshee.

He dived sideways and vanished, she didn't know where, because she was suddenly in the stairwell with the smell of stale cooking in her lungs, belting down the narrow metal steps, slipping, skidding. She let the wrench drop with a clank. Five floors to go, she told herself, her breathing frantic, her ribs lancing white-hot. Just five.

At the bottom she hurdled Halim's body. No point in stopping. His head had been almost severed with a piece of wire.

She burst outside and raced along the narrow deck, then she was on the dock, a glorious runway of long, smooth concrete that she could run along for ever without tripping, and she could see startled dockworkers follow her flight but she didn't care; she had to get away.

She heard a man shouting behind her, urgent and angry.

Frantic look over her shoulder. Rajiv was coming after her. But what filled her with horror was that he wasn't alone. Dockworkers were joining him, running in pursuit.

Desperately India looked for somewhere to hide, and spotted a line of army trucks ahead. Each had a canopy over its back. A handful of soldiers were up front, leaning against the bodywork of the lead truck, rifles over their shoulders. None of them seemed to hear her, or look her way. She swung out of their line of vision and sprinted for the last truck in the line. There was nowhere else she could go. No other cover.

Fingers fumbling, she undid four toggles and pushed back the canvas. She placed her foot on the towbar and heaved herself into the back of the truck, then pulled the canvas back into place. Inside it was dark and hot and airless, and smelt of gasoline. Gasping and wheezing, she leaned forward, desperately trying to ease the pain in her ribs, but she forgot all about it when she heard the sound of running footsteps.

She held her breath, heart hammering. She heard voices calling to each other, and then they faded a little. But not far. They were talking to the soldiers. What if they searched the trucks? To her horror, she heard footsteps approaching. There was a click and the truck gave a small shudder as the door was slammed shut. Someone was inside the cab.

She heard the rumble of a truck ahead, then other engines started up. With a rough, choking roar, her driver started his truck, and moved forward with a crunching of gears. Just behind them, a man gave a shout. Footsteps ran their way, the man still shouting.

Her mind flew into panic. It sounded like Rajiv. Oh God. Had he seen that the toggles of the canvas were undone? Guessed she was inside?

India readied herself to bolt from cover should the soldier decide to let Rajiv check the back of his vehicle. The truck started to slow. Rajiv was still yelling. And then she heard the driver hit his horn and yell back. He yelled at the top of his voice, well and truly pissed off. Metal was thumped, as though Rajiv was pounding the bodywork.

The driver blasted his horn again and, still yelling furiously, shoved his foot on the accelerator. India careered backwards, hitting her elbow on metal. Above the roar of the diesel engine she heard Rajiv still shouting, but her driver wasn't stopping.

Clunk, the truck was in fourth gear. Doing maybe thirty kilometres.

India peeked through a gap in the canvas. Rajiv and his mob were the size of ants in the distance. After five minutes or so, she peered out again to see that they were passing the Kelapa office and approaching the dock gates. Then, to her dismay, the truck slowed down and stopped. The engine was switched off and the driver got out of the cab and slammed the door. Walked away. She heard more doors slamming. The convoy had come to a halt.

Heart in overdrive, she wondered what to do next. She couldn't stay here and wait for Rajiv to catch up with her. She had to get away.

She took a quick look outside. A couple of dockworkers were walking her way, but nobody else. She waited until they'd passed, then clambered outside. Her nerves were strung tight, but nobody shouted, nobody came for her. Sliding to the edge of the truck she peered round, saw soldiers talking and lighting cigarettes, relaxed, unhurried.

India took a deep breath and walked for the checkpoint, forcing herself not to run, to stay calm. She covered her bloody right arm with her hand and kept walking. One of the soldiers raised his head and she recognised him from earlier, the guard who had spat betel juice onto the ground. She gave him a nod. He nodded back, and she was through.

The *bajaj* driver who picked her up charged her twice the going rate, but she didn't argue. She sat in the back of the three-wheeled scooter cab, clutching her upper arm, blood wet between her fingers, as he beeped and swerved his way to the centre of town. She had everything of value in her money belt: money, passport and airline ticket. Her daypack, however, was still on *The Pride*, so she stopped off at a general store and bought an overshirt to put over her bloody clothes, then got her driver to take her to a shopping mall. She did a quick shop in a pharmacy, then bought clothes and other supplies. Finally, she asked her driver to take her to the Puri Mango *losmen*.

As Halim had said, the Puri Mango was clean and pretty. It had a tiny dining room, and an Internet café comprising a bar, a small pond filled with carp, and a computer.

Rajiv wouldn't look for her here. He'd expect her to go straight to a big Western-style hotel. She booked a double room under the name of Mr and Mrs Drew, and gave the girl behind reception a cash deposit.

Once inside her small, simple room, she gritted her teeth and peeled off her shirt, half expecting to see a massive bullet-shaped hole on her arm. But all she had was an inch-long gouge, as though she'd been raked by a lion's claw. The bullet must have just skimmed her. She washed the wound with mineral water from a bottle on the bedside table, then fixed it up with a sterile dressing and some crepe bandage.

India sagged onto the bed, suddenly feeling weak, and guessed it was her body's reaction to the stress. After all, she hadn't lost much blood. She wondered whether to call the Indonesian police, and decided against it. Not only did she want to avoid being overheard by anyone on reception, but she didn't trust the cops not to shove her in a police station for days of questioning while *The Pride* sailed away scot-free. She needed someone with political weight in Australia, and decided on Cuan, *Sundancer's* expedition leader. The Australian government would have to respond to information from Greenpeace, and get working with the Indonesian authorities.

After she'd set up a Hotmail address and emailed Cuan, she went and washed away the reek of sweat and fear in the communal bathroom. In clean, new clothes, she checked her Hotmail to see that Cuan had responded.

All systems go. Keep in touch.

She spent the rest of the afternoon dozing, aches and pains preventing her from falling into a deep sleep. As evening drew in she forced herself to get up, and although her nerves had taken away her appetite, she managed to eat a plate of *nasi goreng*, fried rice with vegetables and chicken, topped with two fried eggs. Fresh Indonesian coffee followed, thick and tangy.

Returning to her room, she found a gas lamp on the floor, casting a warm glow over her narrow bed. The mosquito net had been released from its knot in the ceiling, and a single frangipani flower sat on her pillow. Although she was pretty sure that Rajiv wouldn't track her to the *losmen*, she went to bed in her trousers and shirt.

SHE AWOKE with a jerk, eyes wide, unsure where she was. Scrambling upright she saw a tangle of sheets round her feet, then took in the light spilling through the slatted window. It was barely dawn but the air was humid and sticky and her mouth felt as though it was packed with sand. She fell back on the bed feeling flat and tired, her limbs barely able to move.

Ten minutes passed before she clambered out of bed, downed a couple of Panadol and stumbled to the Internet café. A new message from Cuan:

It's sorted. We've the equivalent of a police commissioner on our side. Where can he pick you up? He's ready to go now!

India checked the city map on the reception wall. It was conveniently marked with shopping centres and accommodation. She chose a place away from her *losmen* in case she needed a bolt hole to return to.

Outside the Karya guesthouse in forty minutes. It's on the corner of Jalan Jaksa and Jalan Cikini.

In the bathroom she saw that her wound had scabbed over nicely and she washed carefully, keeping it dry. As she combed out the knots in her hair, she realised that she felt brighter, much less tired, and knew the painkillers were doing their stuff. More energised, she got changed into clean clothes: loose oyster-coloured linen trousers and matching shirt, soft leather shoes, nice and flat should she have to make a run for it.

The second she stepped outside the hotel she saw them: two uniforms on motorbikes. They started up their engines and followed her. A handful of cars slowed and parted round them like a cautious shoal of fish with a pair of sharks. They wore green uniforms and round white helmets. Military cops. Her stomach cramped. She knew she'd stirred up a hornet's nest, but this was scary. How long had they known where she was staying? The instant Greenpeace stuck a rocket up their government's backside they must have phoned every hotel and *losmen* asking about a tall, wild-haired woman. Not for the first time she wished her looks weren't so distinctive.

When she reached the Karya guesthouse, firmly shut at 6.30 a.m., she watched the bikers swing in a circle, checking out the area. A weary *becak* driver trundled his three-wheeled pedicab slowly past. A flock of grey Java sparrows squabbled in a clump of banana trees nearby, and suddenly, way in the distance, she heard sirens wailing. Lots of sirens.

A cyclist glanced over his shoulder and wobbled so violently he nearly fell off. She could see why. A motorcade of black, dark-windowed Mercedes saloons was approaching. For a second she considered legging it, but she'd get ten metres before one of the bikes got her. Best stick to her guns.

The stream of shiny black cars braked to a hard stop. Dozens of soldiers jumped out, all armed. She could feel her heart thumping, strong and hard, but she didn't move. Whoever the top dog was in the middle of all this hardware, they could bloody well come to her.

Finally, a man stepped out of one of the middle cars, a limo with blackened windows and a miniature red-and-white flag of Indonesia fluttering on its bonnet. He wore an olive-green uniform with lots of gold braid and medal ribbons. Reflective sunglasses and shoes so shiny she could use them to put on her mascara. With two guys in uniform on either side, he walked briskly towards her. He was a foot shorter than India, and she knew he hated it by the way his mouth pursed when he looked up at her.

The guy on his right asked, 'You are Miss Kane?' He had a slight lisp and a mole on his cheek.

She said she was and looked straight at Medals's sunglasses, waiting for an introduction.

'We go now,' said Lisp.

No intros, no explanation, no small talk, no mention of Greenpeace or government cooperation, but the Indonesian authorities were here, and that was, after all, what she had wanted. Wasn't it?

As Lisp gestured her towards the limo, a rocket of panic blasted through her. What if I get inside and they shoot me and dump my body in one of their stinking canals? Mikey'd never find me, and I can't leave Polly, I *can't*.

She was desperately trying to think what to do next when she heard her name being yelled. As she looked to the rear of the motorcade, her spirits soared. TV cameras and reporters were jostling with military police. Her relief was cosmic. If the press were here, she'd be OK, she had to be.

She gave Lisp a slight nod, a bare inclination of agreement that she was ready to go, and as Medals turned and walked for his car, Lisp and the other uniform took up position on either side of her and escorted her in his wake.

Climbing inside the limo, icy-cold with air conditioning, she sat on the back seat with Medals. Lisp took the bench seat opposite.

Then someone hit the siren button and they were off. Nobody said a word the entire journey. They arrived at the docks and roared past the soldiers at the barrier, sirens still blaring.

'Where is this ship?' asked Lisp. 'Please, show us.'

Marines in powerful inflatables bobbed about in the harbour along with a couple of cop boats. She couldn't see a single dockworker. The entire place had been cleared. And when they came to *The Pride*'s berth, India didn't feel a prick of surprise to see she had gone.

The motorcade came to a stop and they all climbed out. Medals and India stood on the dock where *The Pride* had been moored. The cameras and mikes were close now. She could see a mike labelled CNN and one from Channel 7.

'The ship was here, you say?' Lisp asked. '*The Pride of Tangkuban*?'

'Yes. She was here yesterday, at one p.m.'

'There is no record of this ship being in this port. Could you mean the *Tangub*? The names are all very similar and—'

'No,' India interrupted firmly. 'She was called *Tangkuban*.'

Lisp talked her through what had happened. When they reached the part when the boatswain had been murdered he gave a little sneer.

'And you do not know his name.'

'No. But it should be easy to find out who the boatswain—'

'Of course. If the ship was here'—Lisp loaded the word *here* with disbelief—'everything would be so much easier.' He gestured at the cop boats and the marines. 'They have been searching ever since we heard you thought you had identified the ship that sunk the Greenpeace boat. They have found nothing.'

'I didn't *think* I'd found the ship,' India said fiercely. '*I had found her.*'

Medals murmured something to Lisp, turned his blank gaze on her. 'You said there was a man from the Kelapa office on board this ship.'

'Yes. A man called Batuan.'

'Nobody works there of that name.' Lisp gestured a terrified-looking Indonesian forward. 'This is the manager.'

The terrified manager confirmed that nobody called Batuan had ever worked in his office, that he didn't know anybody of that name, never had, and at the first opportunity, bolted out of sight.

Lisp said, 'We take you to the airport now.'

And off they went again. When they arrived at the airport, Lisp rapped on the driver's window and clicked his fingers. The driver passed Lisp a plastic carrier bag, which he then passed to India. Her stuff from the *losmen*. Bandages, bloody shirt and all. The motorcade halted. Lisp opened the door and India climbed out, followed by the entire entourage.

In the departure lounge, Lisp handed her a one-way ticket back to Perth, told her it had been a pleasure meeting her, and not to worry, they had settled her bill at the *losmen*. Medals didn't say a word.

Turning to the media, Lisp added, 'We shall be making every effort to find this ship, *The Pride of Tangkuban*. Just because we had no luck today, does not mean we will stop looking.' He continued in the same vein for another few minutes, a load of waffle about international cooperation and government resources, while India stood there grinding her teeth.

She was almost glad to get on board the plane. The instant the plane door was closed, the captain came on the address system, apologising for the delay, but now they had their VIP on board, they were at last ready to go.

As the aircraft pushed back, her neighbour gave her a curious look. 'Hi. I'm Howard. Just wondering what—'

'Sorry,' she said, and pointedly picked up the in-flight magazine. 'I don't mean to be rude, but I really don't feel like talking.'

WHEN INDIA disembarked at Perth clutching her paltry plastic carrier bag of bloody clothes, she was as jumpy as a cat. She'd seen a Channel 7 mike in Java, and one from CNN, and she could almost hear the reports in her mind.

India Kane left for Perth at four fifteen today.

Would Jimmy be waiting for her? She kept looking over her shoulder and if anyone bumped into her she flinched as though she'd been stuck with an electric cattle prod.

A gaggle of journalists greeted her in the arrivals hall along with a small group of greenies, who gave her a cheer. She scanned the area. No Jimmy, no Kuteli, no man with a ponytail that she could see. But she had no doubt they'd be here somewhere, waiting.

She gave the journos a good ten minutes, reiterating that she had found the right ship but it had vanished and she doubted they'd now find it. '*The Pride* is the ship that hit *Sundancer*,' she repeated, 'but what she was doing all the way out in the Southern Ocean still remains a mystery.'

As the journos departed, the greenies moved in. India answered lots more questions, her eyes darting round the arrivals hall all the while. Still nothing, but it didn't mean they weren't there.

One of the greenies, dreadlocks, pierced eyebrow, pushed a small tissue-wrapped parcel into India's hand. 'For you,' she said. 'A prezzie.' And then the girl pushed her way back through the crowd, head ducked, embarrassed.

Startled, India called out, 'Thank you,' but the girl didn't acknowledge her and India slid the gift into her plastic bag.

The greenies didn't look as though they would depart of their own volition, so India took the initiative and walked for the door, stepped outside.

Dare she head for Stewie's ute? Would they be watching her? Of course they would. She looked around for a taxi, but then a car pulled up right in front of her with a squeak of brakes, a grey Holden station wagon, and the passenger door was flung open, and she was backing away when she saw a man leaning across the passenger seat and waving an arm urgently at her.

'For God's sake, woman, get in.' It was Hank Gregory, the harbourmaster.

India chucked her plastic bag into the footwell and jumped inside. The instant she slammed the door shut, he gunned the engine.

'Hi, Chief,' she said.

'Hi.'

He drove fast to the gate, fed a prepaid ticket into the machine, then barrelled down the road, eyes clicking to his mirrors, to the road, and back again.

'Well,' she said, and cleared her throat, 'this is a nice surprise.'

He gave a grunt, and at the next intersection jumped a red light and swerved left, narrowly missing a black saloon, which blared its horn at them. India belatedly buckled up. She sat with muscles tense as iron as the chief conducted a set of fast, extremely worrying manoeuvres, and then they were charging into a garage forecourt full of cars and sliding to a stop.

The chief sprang out of the car saying, 'Quick! Get in the white Shogun!'

India did as he said, and then they were whizzing past the garage show-room and taking the rear exit. The chief swung the Shogun north and stepped on the gas, still checking his rearview mirror, fists tense on the steering wheel. India kept quiet.

After they'd made a couple of turns and spent a tense ten kilometres threading their way through the suburbs, the chief pulled over outside a nondescript red-brick house. He was sweating and breathing hard.

'Sorry,' he said.

'But I love being picked up at airports,' India said.

'Sorry,' he said again, and reached out a hand.

India took it and gripped it hard. He was trembling.

'I'm not brave,' he said. His words were jerky. 'I may be big, but I'm pretty useless really.' He pulled his hand free and ran it over his forehead. 'Two blokes came to see me a while back. Jumped me when I was walking home from the pub. One of them had a knife. He scared the crap out of me.'

Jimmy, she thought.

'They killed Danny, didn't they?' he stated.

'Yes.'

They both looked through the windscreen at a woman hanging out her washing, then the chief continued. 'They told me if you ever contacted me, I was to let them know immediately. And if they found out I hadn't dobbed you in, they'd . . . Well, put it this way, I wouldn't be walking for a while, if ever.'

'I'm sorry, Chief.'

'I didn't report it. I just hoped I wouldn't see you again. Which went against the grain since not seeing you wasn't exactly on my wish list.' He managed a faint smile. 'But there you were on my goddamn TV, and I knew if I'd seen you, they would have too.'

'Hmm,' she agreed.

'So I thought I'd get to you first.'

She looked across at him and said simply, 'Thanks.'

I<small>T WAS AFTER</small> midnight when the chief dropped her back at the airport, to pick up Stewie's ute. The car park was still, silent.

As they'd arranged, the chief followed her to the Brand Highway, to keep an eye out should anyone be following her. Nobody did. When it came time for them to part, India for her house in the dunes, the chief for his semi in Fremantle, they beeped one another, flashed their lights. She felt sad to see him go. What a friend he'd turned out to be.

It had been his idea to wait until the airport was quiet before she collected her car, so it would be easier to spot a tail, and when he'd suggested supper at his place to kill time, she'd happily complied.

The second she was inside the chief's house—lots of polished wooden floors and luxurious rugs, golf trophies on the mantelpiece—she asked if she could use the phone and was passed a hands-free unit, which she took outside. Mikey would be going mad for news of her.

She'd dialled Mikey's mobile, got his answering machine. She left a message, reassuring him she was fine, then amended it to she was exhausted and in need of a stiff drink, because she knew it would settle his concern more than if she was 'just fine'.

'I'll be home as soon as I can,' she finished up. 'I've a couple of things to do first.' She wanted to add something warm and loving but knew that if she did her voice would give her away and he'd know that everything wasn't fine at all, and the next second he'd be out here putting himself in danger, so she hung up.

Sipping a delicious chardonnay that the chief had whipped out of the fridge, India had popped herself on a stool in his kitchen and watched him cook. It felt strange being cooked for by another man. Mikey did all the cooking at home, and she felt a deep pang inside her as she thought of him.

The chief eyed her narrowly. 'You OK?'

'Once you get that food on my plate.' She pointed at the lobster tails sizzling under the grill.

'Coming right up.'

India eyed the perfectly tender lobster, the olive-oil-dressed wild leaf salad with Parmesan shavings, the tiny new potatoes drenched in butter and finely chopped flat-leaf parsley. Then she looked up at him. His statuesque physique, bright blue eyes and wild curly hair. She cleared her throat, said, 'Is there a Mrs Chief?'

He paused. 'Not yet. Haven't found anyone I wanted to ask.'

INDIA PARKED on the wheel tracks in the scrub, well away from the house, and approached it barefoot. It was cloudy and as dark as the inside of a broom cupboard. She clicked on her torch, shielding it as best she could, and studied the tyre marks in the sand, looking for fresh tracks. There were none.

Slowly, carefully, India padded to the gravel approach to the house and checked the little shreds of paper she'd torn from brown paper bags and wedged into the back and front doors, which would drop to the ground when the doors opened. All were just as she'd left them.

She moved into the house, her footsteps creaking on the floorboards, but nobody jumped out at her. Lights blazing, she made herself a soothing cup of cocoa. She took it outside and smoked a cigarette, looking into the half-circle of scrub and sand the house lights illuminated. When she finally collapsed on her mattress, she slept as though anaesthetised.

THE SUN woke her the next morning, slanting across her eyelids where she lay. She got up slowly, taking her coffee to the verandah, and collapsed onto Stewie's comfy chair. She knew she'd need another couple of nights' sleep before she recovered from her Indonesian sojourn.

Come 8 a.m. she felt clean and slightly more energised. I need to do some washing, sort myself out, she told herself. She grabbed the plastic carrier bag with her bloody clothes inside that Lisp had given her, and trailed to the laundry. Upended the bag on top of the washing machine. Jeans, shirts, undies and shampoo and soap tumbled out, and she lunged for something falling to the floor, caught it just in time.

A small tissue-wrapped parcel. The present from the girl at the airport with the dreadlocks and the pierced eyebrow. She'd forgotten about it. Unceremoniously, India tore open the tissue to find a small wooden bracelet, decorated with white and yellow dots, shadows of brown that could be roos, could be dogs or porcupines. It had been snapped in half.

She grabbed her mobile, dialled Mikey's number. 'Mikey?' She tried to temper her tone, keep the panic from it, but he still heard.

'What's wrong?'

'Where's Polly?'

'Right here. Just getting ready for school.'

She slumped against the wall and closed her eyes. Thank you, God.

'Mikey? Does she still have her bracelet?'

Small silence, then, 'How the hell did you know about that?'

'She lost it?'

'No. Some fat kid came up to her after school and demanded she give it to him. Clever girl didn't argue, just handed it over.'

The woman who'd followed her. She'd had a fat kid in tow.

'What's going on?' he demanded.

There was no way she could keep this from Mikey. Not when Polly's safety was involved. She told him.

Shocked pause, 'They're *threatening* us?' There was a roar of rage followed by what sounded like the side of his fist hitting the wall.

'I'm going to bring them down,' she told him.

'No, India. You take the next flight home—'

'Take Polly somewhere safe. I'll ring you soon.'

She rang off before she could change her mind and headed straight to the ute, her tiredness swallowed beneath a wave of resolve, her anger burning bright and hard as sunlight falling on polished steel.

SEVEN

India cruised slowly past Kemble Environmental Services, searching for the perfect surveillance point. She had to watch the place, gather details and routines, and maybe get evidence of a connection with *The Pride*. Opposite the warehouse was a cemetery. There were rows of white headstones, and a little rise crowded with trees and dense thickets of shrubs that looked perfect for her needs.

She parked the ute in the cemetery car park, one of seven vehicles there. No one would think anything of it. Just a grieving relative visiting. Checking around to make sure she was alone, she walked casually to the thicket.

India pushed her way through thick clumps of parrot-bush, the spiky fan-shaped leaves snatching at her clothes. When she was comfortably settled against a white gum, she allowed herself a mental pat on the back. Dressed in neutral-coloured clothing, she would be well hidden in the gloom of foliage, and she had a terrific vantage point, almost opposite the warehouse and where she could see vehicles approaching from half a kilometre away.

Using her binos, she saw that the two-storey building looked relatively new, made of pinky-grey brick, and was surrounded by eucalyptus trees. Out front was a car park, filled with delivery trucks, and a loading bay, where a couple of guys were fork-lifting crates out of the trucks and into the building. Jack's red Isuzu was there, along with a Diahatsu, a Subaru and two Toyotas. Nothing flash, just normal cars for normal people.

She made notes of trucks delivering to the warehouse, the cars parked in the forecourt. She should have hit the Internet first, she realised, and found out exactly what Kemble Environmental Services did, but she'd been so filled with anger she hadn't been thinking straight. After a while, however, she realised that the trucks delivering to the warehouse were all unmarked. A whole fleet of anonymous-looking trucks from all over Australia.

She swung her binos to a Nissan Patrol pulling up. A man got out. Beeped on his alarm. Walked inside. Easy, long-legged stride. Nice suit.

India felt as though the breath had been sucked from her lungs.

It was Jimmy.

Chest aching with tension, India stared at the door through which he'd vanished as if it were about to explode, but adrenaline only lasts for so long, and soon she had shaken off her initial shock and was taking down his Nissan's registration. She rang Mikey's mobile.

When he answered she said, 'Hi,' but he didn't respond. 'Mikey?'

'What, India?' he snapped.

'Could you run some registration plates for me?'

He mumbled something that sounded like, God give me strength.

She cringed, remembering her last call when she'd asked him to look after Polly. 'Sorry,' she said, pleading. 'But could you?'

Small silence, and then he said OK, and repeated the numbers back to her. His voice was unnaturally cold. His cop voice.

'Where are you?' she asked him.

'Where do you think?'

Her mind went blank.

Then he said in the same hard voice, 'Can I have your number? Your other one doesn't work.'

She gave it to him and she was about to ask him how he was, how Polly was, maybe apologise for messing up his life and Polly's while she went after Jimmy, but he'd hung up.

India watched trucks coming and going through her binos, and it was only when a thread of spider's web floated past her lens that it clicked. She knew where Mikey had taken Polly. The safest haven they all knew. A weather-board house on the edge of an outback town deep in the desert, where a friend of theirs kept a tarantula as a pet. It was where they'd all first met. She gave a sigh of relief, wondering why she hadn't thought of it immediately. Of course that's where they were. No one would ever find them there.

More trucks arrived and departed, and just after lunchtime Jimmy came out and drove off in his Nissan.

At three p.m. Mikey rang her, his voice very cold. 'All the trucks are owned by Jack Zhuganov. The Nissan, James Zhuganov.'

'Mikey, that's brilliant, thanks—'

'When you've finished whatever you're doing,' Mikey interrupted, tone like ice, 'perhaps you and I can have a talk. See how we feel about each other.' Without another word, he hung up.

India felt as though she'd been slugged with a sandbag. She tried to ring Mikey all afternoon but he had left it on message receive. Mikey didn't want to marry her any more, and who could blame him?

Tears scalded her eyes. Tears of rage, of love, and grief. She couldn't stop now. She had a crowd of people living in her soul. They stood in a ragged line, watching her every minute of the day. Ned and Emma and the other four Greenpeace crew. To the side were the boatswain and Halim, and always, right in the middle, stood Danny with his spaniel eyes.

She couldn't let them down. Not even for Mikey.

BEFORE SHE HEADED back to her house in the dunes, she ducked into the city and checked the Internet. Kemble Environmental Services' website informed her that it was a recycling firm with procedures and regulations in place to ensure that it met its statutory obligations.

'Where possible,' she read, 'we seek to reclaim or recycle material for reuse. When disposal is the only option we will explore all available routes to remove your waste at the most competitive cost.' They recovered scrap metal, recycled glass, plastic and paper, and were signed up to lists of legislation, including the Environmental Protection Act.

India then went for the company's records and business portfolio, share-holders, board members, and eventually found what she wanted.

She let out a 'Yes!' and punched the air with her fist. Kemble Environmental Services used to be owned by Frank Zhuganov, and when he died, his brother Jack had taken it over, along with Frank's son, Jimmy.

THE NEXT MORNING she woke to rain lashing the windows—a violent southerly in full flow. The roof was leaking in five places.

She didn't rush to leave. It was a Saturday, so she thought the industrial estate would be quiet, but when she got there she found she was wrong. Kemble Environmental Services were flat out. Trucks were arriving like ants homing in on an open jar of honey. They didn't seem to be picking anything up, just delivering. Hoping to see something unusual, India parked the ute just inside the cemetery gates and glued her binos to her face.

The weather worsened. Wind blew in horizontal gusts and trees groaned. By 5 p.m. India was cramped, cold and bored, and when a skinny bloke in overalls started up Jack's red Isuzu truck, she decided to follow it. Hurriedly she scraped back her hair and stuffed it into a baseball cap, then pulled on an old padded jacket of Stewie's and turned up the collar. It wasn't much of a disguise but it was better than nothing.

They were barely fifteen kilometres from the city centre when, to India's surprise, the truck swung off the highway and gunned for the countryside. Ahead were damp green hills and paddocks filled with huddles of sheep, and when she glanced at her map she saw they were nearing Bickley's Brook.

The light had left the sky, and because she was so far behind she nearly missed the truck turning down a private road. She dithered briefly, wondering if it was safe to follow. She'd stick out like a sore thumb and there was no way she could drive without headlights now.

She decided to wait and see if he returned, and, if he didn't, do a recce in daylight. She bumped her ute off the road and splashed into a rough field. Parked behind a bunch of trees. Swollen raindrops lashed against her windows, sending the trees into a shivering frenzy. In the distance she could see a scattering of tiny lights flickering on what she reckoned was a hill. People's homes. She pictured them making dinner, chatting, watching TV.

She glanced at the luminous digital clock on the dash: 7.10. She listened to some jazz on the radio. Unwrapped a Violet Crumble and ate it more out of boredom than hunger. By 8.15 she was wondering who on earth would want to be a private eye. Sitting around waiting was so *dull*.

Ten minutes on and a pair of headlights appeared on her left. She waited until the taillights winked out of view, then followed the truck back onto the highway. Realising it was returning to base, she peeled away to take another route. Map on her lap, interior light on, she belted west on Orrong Road, eventually picking up Leach Highway, which took her straight to the cemetery, and she was already parked, lights out, when the truck arrived.

Despite the foul weather and the lateness of the hour, the place was busy. The forecourt and warehouse were brightly lit, and she counted five guys in rain slickers helping four trucks unload. Jack's truck had eight crates that needed a fork-lift to handle them into the warehouse. Two crates had a big red X marked on each side, but the others were plain.

India watched until the last crate had been shifted and the guys were heading home in their own cars before she did the same.

After a shower, she took a packet of nuts and a bottle of red to the window by the verandah, rain drip-dripping into the bowls she'd placed around the house. The southerly was still blowing strong and she could hear the dull boom of waves breaking against the dunes. Mikey and Polly loved storms. If they were here they'd be on the lip of the dunes, watching the sea crash in.

FIRST THING on Monday, India retraced the route that Jack's truck had taken. She glanced at the dashboard clock as she splashed her way down the private road: 9.10. A large, modern complex loomed into view in the distance. White sign with royal-blue letters. Blue Park PLC.

The name suited the place, given that it was built out of blue brick. Lots of glass and steel poles gave the buildings a smart and efficient air. There was a little park with a stream running prettily beside it, and tables and benches set along its banks. Lots of trees and shrubs. Not a bad place to work, out of the city and where you could hear the sounds of the bush.

A security guy took her details and directed her towards reception. Obediently she did as he said and parked in the space provided. Reception was small but smart, and the girl behind the desk small and smart as well. India apologised that she'd mislaid her press card, and handed the girl her *Sydney Morning Herald* credit card as identification instead.

'You don't have an appointment?'

'Sorry, no.'

Frowning, the girl said, 'They're all very busy, but I'll ring round and see if someone can see you.'

While the receptionist made calls, India flicked through a glossy brochure. *Blue Park PLC manufactures high-quality plastics . . . Over forty years of experience . . . Stringent specification product lines . . .*

A limited company that made plastics. Her stomach sank. How in the hell was she going to wing this one?

The girl said, 'Leo's on his way. He's our disposal manager.'

'Thanks.'

Eventually a harassed-looking man in his early thirties came in. He cheered up a bit when he saw India.

'Beth tells me you want to do a feature on us?' Unsurprisingly, he looked puzzled. Plastics weren't the most exciting thing to write about, but then a sudden flash of inspiration hit her so hard she felt her face split into a huge grin. He grinned back.

'What I'm interested in is today's plastic against tomorrow's. You've heard of William Hughes's invention? Ecopac?'

His face cleared. 'Ah, I see. Let's go to my office. Would you like a tea or something? Beth will bring it in for us.'

'Coffee would be great. Black, two sugars.'

Leo led her to a cramped office and waved her into a chair, taking up position behind his desk.

She took out her notebook. 'Thanks,' she said. 'I really appreciate this.'

He gave a nod, his expression serious.

'Do you mind if I start with a bit of background on your company? What it is you produce, where it goes, what it's used for.'

Leo went off like a clockwork toy. She learned that Blue Park supplied the industrial market as well as making accessories. They produced conservatories and fascia boards, polycarbonate roofing and guttering. Silicones and cladding. He took a breath when Beth arrived with coffee. Instant, in two mugs with the company logo on their sides.

'Thanks,' India said as Beth disappeared. Taking a sip, she tried her best not to grimace. It was disgusting coffee.

'You've a lot of plastic on the market. Do you think William Hughes could be a threat to your business?'

'Not really. He's going to produce cartons, as far as I know. For milk, orange juice, wine. That's not our field.'

She asked him a bunch of questions about his clients, and quickly ascertained that Blue Park delivered all their products.

'You don't have any clients who collect?'

He blinked. Leaned back in his chair. 'I can't see what these questions have to do with William Hughes and Ecopac.'

He was more switched on than she'd thought. Rapidly she weighed up her options. She could go the nice route, which would lead her nowhere, slowly, or she could take the direct route, which might get her thrown off the property, but if she was on the right track, and if this was the up-front, honest guy he appeared to be . . . she may as well be bold.

Closing her notebook she leaned forward, turned her tone low. 'Look, Leo, I'm not supposed to do this, but . . . I like you, so I'm going to put my cards on the table. I'm also going to trust you with what I'm about to say, because if it gets out—'

Alarmed, he said, 'If what gets out?'

She took a theatrically deep breath. 'We've a big investigation going on. An exposé about Kemble Environmental Services.'

Leo stared at her. 'KES? You're *investigating KES*?'

'Yes.' She kept her face serious, sombre. 'And although we know you, Leo, aren't personally involved, things are moving really fast here and the cops are itching to bust in and take everyone down.'

'You're kidding me.' His jaw was almost on the ground. 'They're in trouble? KES? I mean, what's going on?' He frowned.

'Look, Leo, we saw an unmarked truck pick up eight crates from here on Saturday, seven thirty p.m. Two crates were marked with red crosses.'

'No, that's not possible.' He shook his head. 'We don't work Saturday.'

'Believe me, it happened.'

'No, no. You must be mistaken.'

'Leo, we *filmed it*.'

'Jesus,' he whispered. His hands were trembling.

'Look, if you could tell me what was in those crates, it'll help you . . . well, when it comes to court.'

Leo gulped. 'Well, I've got a pretty good idea, but . . . OK.' Swinging to his computer he tapped on the keyboard.

'Eight crates, you say.' He was tapping away, expression tense. 'I've got them,' he said after a while. 'It says "Picked up by KES on Monday". Signed and sealed.' He leaned back, looking relieved.

'What was in them?'

'Waste.'

A brush of apprehension made the back of her neck tighten.

'What sort of waste?'

'Stuff that can't go down the drain or be thrown out with the garbage.'

'You're saying it's toxic?'

'Well, not necessarily toxic.' He shifted uncomfortably. 'But we have to dispose of it responsibly. There are dozens of regulations, you know, and one thing you must realise is that we meet all our statutory obligations. We know exactly where our waste is at any time, and although it costs us over half a million dollars a year, we dot every i and cross every t.'

'So where are those eight crates now?'

Small pause before he picked up the phone, dialled. 'Hi, Nicky. It's me. Look, the eight lots of waste you collected on Monday, could you tell me where they are now? . . . Sure, I'll wait.' Leo covered the mouthpiece as he spoke to India. 'We've total batch traceability. I'm sure it's just some sort of mix-up . . .' He turned back to the phone. 'Oh, hi . . . Right. I see . . . No, er, that's fine.' He gave a slightly hysterical laugh. 'Sorry to bother you.'

He hung up, looking sick.

'Leo,' she said, 'what did Nicky say?'

His Adam's apple bobbed up and down. When he spoke it was almost a whisper. 'She doesn't have any record of them.'

India let a long silence develop. 'So where did they go?' she asked eventually. 'You're the disposal manager; you should know.'

The look in his eyes turned wild. 'They can't dump that shit anywhere. Not P24. It's got to be contained. They *can't*.'

'Leo, have you ever had to follow up any waste with KES before?'

'There's no need! They're fully regulated in transportation and disposal.' He gulped, adding, 'The only time I check is when the inspectors turn up. We tally KES's records with mine . . .'

'And they've always been accurate?'

'Totally!'

'Hmm,' India said, and took a pretend sip of disgusting coffee, trying to give a sense of normality, calm him down. 'If your records are in sync with KES's, then my guess is that someone's pulling a fast one in the middle. Somebody from your company, and someone from KES.'

Both of them jumped when the door opened and a woman stepped inside. 'Sorry, Leo,' she said, not sounding sorry at all. 'I thought you said you were going to be a couple of minutes.'

India quickly slipped her notebook and pen into Stewie's daypack. Leo looked at her like a wallaby fixed in the glare of a roo-hunter's spotlight.

'I was just going,' said India, standing up. 'And thanks for the advice, Leo. You're a great friend.' She patted her flat belly. 'My little one thinks so too. Thanks.'

She left his office to the woman's blink of surprise, Leo's shoulders slumping with relief, and walked towards reception.

Giving Beth a smile, she went over, saying, 'Thanks for the coffee.'

'No worries.'

'Look, I wanted to write Leo a thankyou card. Could you let me have his address?'

India left with not only Leo's address, but with his home telephone number and his mobile number as well.

DRIVING BACK into the city, she felt the familiar roll of excitement as everything started to fall into place. Jack's brother, Frank, had made his millions in the rubbish business, and either he or Jimmy had obviously expanded into the illegitimate market. Jack's trucks were collecting waste from companies who didn't want to go the official, expensive route of disposing it legally, and she'd bet her last dollar Jack and Jimmy were shipping the lot off to Chennai at half the expense. She thought of Greenpeace's fight against dumping the world's toxic waste in Asia, and gave a shudder.

India stopped to refuel the ute, then headed back to her shrubby rise in the cemetery. She watched a couple of trucks unloading crates into KES's warehouse, and an hour later Jimmy turned up—natty suit, shiny shoes. He stayed for exactly two hours and twelve minutes, then left.

A little later, India saw a blue truck pull into the loading bay. It had a big white logo on its sides, OG, the letters formed by dolphins swimming nose-to-tail. She made a note of its registration. Crossing her fingers, she called Mikey and left a message, pleading for him to check the truck's registration number, she'd owe him big time, and she was sorry for being such a pain in the backside . . . She hung up as she felt her throat start to close.

Barely twenty minutes later, he called back. 'Got your truck owner.'

His tone was arctic. India swallowed, and said, 'That was quick.'

'Bobynin Zhuganov.'

Interesting, she thought. Bobynin was the first Russian-sounding Christian name she had come across.

Mikey hadn't hung up, so she said, 'Thanks, Mikey.'

Small silence, then he said, 'I take it he's a relative of Jack's. The guy who owns all those trucks.'

'Correct. And you ought to know there's a Detective Inspector Zhuganov along with a constable called Bryce Zhuganov.'

'Christ, India.' The cold tone melted. 'Don't tell me you've unearthed some Australian mafia. Look, do you want to fill me in?'

Did she ever. But just as she began to talk, she saw the blue truck back up to the dock. 'Mikey, hang on a sec.'

Raising her binos, she could see two crates being loaded inside. Both had red crosses on their sides. They were Blue Park's waste. Boy, did she want to see where they ended up. The next second the blue truck started up.

'Look, I've got to go,' she hurriedly told Mikey. 'I'll ring you tonight.'

She'd been following the truck for twenty minutes when she checked her rearview mirror. Her stomach swooped. There was a cop car right on her tail. Sweat sprang onto her skin and she indicated right, intending to overtake the truck, accelerate and disappear.

Please God, she prayed, don't let it be Bryce.

She checked the rearview mirror again and saw that the cop car was indicating left. *It was exiting the highway.*

Limp with relief, India decelerated and edged behind the truck again. Just past a sign for the Cannington Greyhound Racetrack, the truck turned into another industrial estate, and India followed it down a long street with parked cars on either side. Five hundred metres on, the truck turned through a set of factory gates belonging to a company she recognised: Ocean Green, producers of the most eco-kind and expensive refrigerator known to man.

She paused at the gates, engine running, eyes clicking from her mirrors and back in case she was holding up traffic, and watched as the truck reversed to a dock at the far end of a huge forecourt. Within seconds, Leo's crates had been fork-lifted inside.

Swinging right, India pulled over and inched her ute between two sedans. Then she picked up her mobile. 'Leo? India Kane here.'

'Er . . . Hi.' He swallowed audibly.

'Look, a quick question. Those crates of yours with red crosses on the sides—what use could that waste be to a refrigerator firm?'

Silence.

'Leo?'

'*They're using P24 in refrigerators?*'

'Well, nothing's confirmed, but—'

'Oh my God. They can't do that!'

'Leo, please, I need you to be *calm*. Talk me through what P24 is and how it could be used in refrigerators.'

'OK.' He cleared his throat a couple of times. 'Right. Um . . . well, do you know how a fridge works?'

'Not really.'

'Well, there's a gas inside the fridge, and as it expands it uses energy, making everything around it cold. Refrigerators used to use CFCs as they were efficient in absorbing the heat, but since they're ozone eaters they were banned. I guess P24 could be used to produce a more efficient gas, but it's *illegal* . . .' He trailed off, and she had no doubt he had his head buried in his hands. 'What if it *leaks*? You wouldn't even know! It could *kill* you.'

A rush of ice swept over her. 'Say that again?'

'P24 attacks the lungs,' he said, and he was talking about masks and protective clothing but India wasn't listening. She was hearing the pathologist's voice. *His lungs were constricted and filled with inflammatory cells.*

Ellie's dad. *Sick as parrots a lot of them. They've lost five in the past year.*

It wasn't Albert's curse killing the residents of Jimbuku Bay, she realised. It was Ocean Green's ecologically sound refrigerators. *They had to be leaking.*

INDIA HUNG UP, her mind whirling and already planning ahead. She'd ring Mikey first and then the feds. Between them they'd get a team of cops here within minutes and they'd have hard evidence to use in an official investigation, thanks to two crates of P24 on site. What a story! Trembling with excitement, India reached for her phone, and then decided she'd better get the hell out of here first. She could call everyone once she was under way.

Her fingers were on the ignition key when she became aware of a vehicle pulling up alongside. She looked over to ask it to let her out and her heart-beat froze with shock. It was a cop car.

The muscles in her stomach contracted as the sour taste of fear rose to her mouth. Two uniformed cops stepped out. One was Bryce Zhuganov.

Fingers trembling, she quickly pressed the central-locking button and was about to start the car, then realised she had nowhere to go. They'd boxed her in. Bryce came to her window, indicated she open it.

India buzzed it down a couple of centimetres.

'G'day, Ms Kane,' he said.

'Hi.' Her voice was scratchy with fear.

Bryce's smile broadened. 'Would you step out of your car, please?'

'Why?'

'Please, step out of your car.'

'Not until you give me a reason.'

To her horror he unholstered his gun. She lunged to close the window but he had already slid the barrel through. Tilted it so it pointed at her lap.

'This reason enough?'

Desperately she glanced across at the other cop. He was standing back from the car, both hands on his pistol, ready for action.

Sweat streaming, India reached for her mobile.

'Don't. Or I might have to shoot you for reaching for a weapon.'

She dropped her hand.

'Out of the car. *Now.*'

Frantically she scanned the street for help. A couple of cars drove past slowly, and there were two people at the far end of the street, staring, but they were too far away.

'You've five seconds,' he warned. 'Five. Four . . .'

'OK, OK.' Her voice was trembling. 'I'll come out.'

The second India unlocked the car, Bryce pulled open her door and hauled her outside, spinning her round and ramming her face-down against the bonnet. He patted her down, then said, 'Get in the back of my vehicle.'

'Where are you taking me?'

He didn't reply, simply yanked her backwards and, with his gun jammed against her neck, marched her to his car and forced her inside. A Plexiglas partition with heavy-gauge metal mesh separated her from the front two seats. Her doors had no handles on the inside. The windows were tinted. No point in gesticulating to pedestrians.

She saw the other cop hop into Stewie's ute. What was he going to do with it? Burn it to a husk so there wouldn't be any lead for Mikey or the feds to follow? Oh God, this was looking really bad.

They drove for over half an hour back through the city. India wondered how Bryce had found her, whether someone had spotted her with her binos outside KES. Perhaps someone in Cape Cray had mentioned her to someone who was related to the Zhuganovs. Ginny's voice: *They're all related to bloody everybody. Can't move for the buggers.*

The kilometres slipped away as they headed north, and then she saw a green and white road sign: SHOALHAVEN 84. BULIMBA 145. Dread drenched her. They were headed for Jack's place.

Struggling to be calm, she turned her mind to Ellie. If she didn't escape, Ellie would return to her Smartie-coloured house, and she and her baby might die. *P24 attacks the lungs.* And hadn't Western Australia's health minister promised every hospital new Ocean Green refrigerators?

She wondered how Ocean Green could get away with using a poison and her mind jumped back to when she'd first trawled the Internet, and the Zhuganov at the top of the pile in governmental safety checks on manufactured products. Always one of the family in just the right position with the right power to help another relative.

As she'd predicted, Bryce turned left at the sign: GOONDARI STUD. When he came to the first gate and got out, India immediately leaned back on the seat and punched at the rear window with both feet. Nothing happened. No doubt it was reinforced glass.

She glanced up front to see that Bryce was returning to the car. Hurriedly, she took up her seat again. She wanted him to think she was too scared to move, so she could catch him off guard.

He drove through the gate, but he didn't stop and close it behind him. Did this mean he'd be returning shortly?

They approached the second gate. This time when he got out to open it, India lashed her boots at the side windows, but again the glass held. She wanted to scream with fright and frustration as he hopped back inside and continued along the track, but she kept quiet. The only way she could maintain her strength was to keep her fear bottled up. She saw the huge white monstrosity of the mansion, then heard a rattle as they passed over the cattle grid. She saw horses in paddocks on either side, grazing peacefully. Then she saw the rubbish tip.

A Nissan Patrol was parked in front of the mansion and she felt a whimper flutter in her throat. Jimmy was here.

Bryce parked next to the Nissan, hopped out. The second he slammed his door, the five dogs rocketed down the ceremonial stairway and tore straight for him, barking madly. Then she saw them slow and wag their tails. The cop bent over and petted one of the German shepherds, then the spaniel.

She watched him wave a greeting, and Jimmy came into view. Jeans, blue denim shirt, big leather boots, carrying what looked like a baseball bat. He came to Bryce and clapped him on the shoulder. They started to talk. They weren't looking at the car. India started kicking again at the side window. Thud-thud-thud. There! It had cracked! Just one more kick . . .

Her boots were about to smash through the glass, she was sure, when a figure appeared and the door suddenly opened. India's feet hit nothing but air and she toppled backwards for a second, but then she was rolling onto her side and charging out, uncaring about Bryce's gun. She'd rather be shot trying to escape than have Jimmy slash her throat.

But he'd been ready for her. As she exploded from the car, something hit her very hard on her shoulders and she went sprawling to the ground. Another whack and pain blasted through her. It felt as though her shoulder blades had shattered. Her lungs were rasping.

'You really don't know when to give up.'

He was going to kill her. She had nothing to lose. So she lay there and tried to get her breath back, thinking about how to hurt him.

'Get up.'

She moaned and pretended to try to get to her feet, slumping back onto the ground as though it were too painful. In that brief effort she'd seen that Bryce was behind Jimmy, pistol in hand. Jimmy was tapping his baseball bat against the ankle of his boots.

'Get up,' he repeated.

She put out a hand as though she needed help and moaned some more. Waited for him to come closer. But she'd read him wrong. He raised his bat and whacked it against her shoulders again, and this time she screamed.

'I'm not stupid,' he said.

She was shuddering and shaking, her shoulders pulsing red-hot. She couldn't stop the groans jerking from her throat.

'Now get up before I hit you again.'

India put her palms on the ground and forced herself to her knees. Made it to her feet. Stood there swaying. She heard a horse whinny and she could smell dried grasses and manure.

'Walk to the stables.'

Almost crippled with pain, she walked unsteadily ahead of him, towards the stable block. Jimmy jabbed her between her shoulder blades with the bat, prodding her past a couple of stables. As they approached the third, there was a clatter of hoofs, and a big black head snaked out and snapped at them with yellow teeth. Through her blur of pain she recognised Jack's pride and joy, Grafton Statesman. Aka BB. Bloody Bastard.

India was looking at the horse and wondering if she could let him out, create a diversion, when an iron railing thudded against her skull.

She folded slowly to the ground. Her head was buzzing like a swarm of bees and then everything went quiet and dark.

EIGHT

When she came round, she was lying on her side, her head aching so hard she wondered whether Jimmy had cracked her skull. Her shoulders and back were throbbing mercilessly, and she hurt so much she wasn't sure if she was glad to be alive or not.

After a while, a sharp, pungent smell of ammonia seeped into her senses and she opened her eyes. She was lying on dirty straw in a stable. Her mouth was stuffed with cloth, kept in place by more cloth tied round her lower face. Her feet were bound with rope, her wrists tied behind her back.

Up shit creek without a paddle, she thought.

She pictured Polly helping Mikey make bread, her skinny arms coated in white flour. Polly had nicknamed her after Damala the eagle hawk because she thought India was so brave. She'd be horrified if she could see her now, lying on dirty straw, waiting to die.

A trickle of energy returned. She had a family to return to.

Bracing herself against the pain, she started to roll onto her front, but stopped at a violent clatter to her right. Slowly, she turned her head to see a huge black form against the wall of the stable, head collar strung tight and tied to a ring in the wall.

Oh shit. It was BB, Jack's psychopathic stallion. At least he was tied up. So long as she kept clear of his hoofs, she should be OK.

Hauling herself to her knees, India dragged her bound wrists down over her hips. Then she sat back, and eased her hands forward under her legs and feet until they were in front of her. She looked around the stable but knew there'd be nothing sharp in here. Not with a valuable stallion inside. She concentrated on untying the ropes binding her feet. They were tight, but she persevered until they were free. Shuffling through the straw and away from the increasingly restless stallion, she used the wall to get to her feet. Feeling sick and dizzy, she willed herself not to pass out.

She started to wonder where Jimmy was, but forced her mind away from him and began to pick at the knot at the back of her head that held her gag in place. He'd tied it so tightly she wasn't sure if she could undo it, and hurriedly tried to get her woozy mind into gear.

Hands free first or gag? Hands.

She looked around for something, anything, to cut the ropes with, but all she saw was a black horse jerking his head and rolling his body against the waist-high manger. Turning her concentration back to her gag, she paused when she heard a man's voice outside.

'Hey,' Jimmy said. 'How's it going?'

'Pissed off, since you ask,' another man said. 'I've meetings back to back in Melbourne and Sydney, but no, I can't live my own life. I have to be here when he asks.'

It sounded like Katy's William. But what would William be doing here?

'Ever think there might be a reason for it?' Jimmy responded.

'Oh, there's always a reason. But I'm sick of it. I want out.'

It *was* William. She was shouting, *William, William, William*, but she made no sound apart from a faint gargling noise behind her gag, so she lunged for the door and battered her wrists against it.

'What the hell's that?' William said.

'BB. He's been a pain in the backside so I shut his door.'

India was making so much noise she couldn't hear what they were saying, but no way did she sound like a horse. William would have to investigate, he *had to*. She began kicking at the door.

She heard BB's enraged squeal behind her, but she was riveted to the sound of a bolt snapping open. The next instant the top half of the door swung wide, and William was staring at her, expression appalled.

'India? What the hell . . .?' He started to fumble with the second bolt but Jimmy appeared and put a hand on William's arm.

'Don't even think of it, Bobby-boy,' he said.

'But she's *gagged*!'

'That's the least I'm going to do to her, believe me.'

'*You can't!* We agreed, Jimmy. You scared her off . . . she went *home*!'

'I lied.'

India was fighting to loosen the knot at the back of her head.

'Let her go.'

'NO.'

The deep, gravelly voice smashed between the two men like a block of concrete dropped from a great height. She saw the solid breadth of chest, the sloping fighter's shoulders. Jack was here.

Small silence, then William's voice, sounding fierce. 'Her boyfriend's a *cop*. Just *think*. If she disappears we'll have half the Australian police force on our doorstep.'

'Shut it,' Jack said.

William went quiet.

'It's all sorted,' said Jimmy. 'I swear.'

Another silence. Then, 'Tell me.'

'It's all being dealt with as we speak. The offices are being cleared. Trucks, paperwork. We can't help the ship being where she is at the moment, but it's her last pick-up. Hammond says she'll be gone in twenty-four hours. There'll be nothing for them to find. *Nothing*, so long as this interfering bitch is out of the way.'

'No,' William said again, voice hard.

Jack moved to William and put an arm round his shoulder. Spoke quietly. 'Bobby. You want to know where we picked her up?'

'I don't care. I don't want her hurt. I want you to *let her go*.'

Eyes fixed on the men, she increased her efforts to rid herself of the gag. Life or death. *She had to talk to William*.

'We found her outside Ocean Green.' Jack's voice was gentle, almost as though breaking the news of the death of a loved one. 'She followed a certain delivery there. You know the one.'

William swayed so violently she thought he was going to pass out.

'She . . . she knows about the P24?' His voice was faint.

'Why else was she there?' Jimmy interjected harshly. 'Picking up a brochure so she could order a new fridge?'

'I *told* you it was a mistake to use it,' William bleated, his face ashen. 'Cutting costs like that . . . but you wouldn't *listen*.'

'The second it gets out, you'll be finished,' Jimmy sneered. 'No one will want to buy your precious eco-rubbish any more.'

William looked as though he was going to be sick.

Suddenly the knot gave way and she spat out the wad. 'William,' she croaked. Desperately she rubbed her lips with the back of her hand, working her tongue against her gums until she felt the relief of saliva flood her dry mouth. 'They're going to kill me. Please, you've got to *help me*!'

'I don't want her hurt,' said William, but his voice had lost its edge.

'So you said,' Jimmy snapped. 'Now piss off and let me get on with it.'

'Don't let him kill me!' she shouted. 'Please, William. I saved Katy, *remember*? What about your oath?'

Her words seemed to have an effect. William reached determinedly for the stable-door bolt, but Jack stopped him with a hand on his arm.

'Bobby,' his voice was soft, 'what will happen when Katy finds out? You really think she'll still want you?'

William looked desperately at India, and it was then that she saw the worm of fear writhing at the back of his eyes.

'William, my cop friends know everything,' she spoke fast. 'And when Katy discovers you stood back and let this man *kill* me?'

'They know fuck all,' Jimmy interrupted. 'She's bullshitting.' He abruptly swung the upper half of the stable door shut with a bang, and bolted it shut.

She heard William say chokingly, 'I don't want this.'

'Then you'd better leave us, little brother. Since your fragile sensibilities can't take it.'

India stumbled back. William was Jimmy's *brother*?

Oh my God. She almost flinched when more thoughts crashed through. Jimmy had called William Bobby-boy. Was he Bobynin Zhuganov, owner of the blue truck and Ocean Green? William was Jack's nephew. She had a flashback to Ellie's front yard, Jimmy kicking her, Kuteli protesting.

It was meant to be a warning . . . Bobby told us not to.

William had been trying to protect her. But what about his surname? Of course, he'd changed it. *That mob . . . don't like being thought foreign.*

Her vision swimming, she tuned her senses to the stable door and realised she couldn't hear any voices outside. Had William gone?

She thumped the door and yelled for help, then stopped. BB was lashing his hind feet furiously at the manger behind him, squealing with rage.

I hope his head collar holds, she thought. Frantically, she worked at the knot holding her wrists with her teeth, then wondered, could she use BB to her advantage? How could she use a half-maddened horse? He wouldn't let her near him, and if she let him free, he'd probably kill her.

Her mind racing through various scenarios, she took a step towards the horse, and he reared up as far as his head collar would allow. No way could she approach him, she decided, and the, mercifully, she felt the rope round her wrists loosen. It took her just moments to untie herself.

As she was massaging her wrists, he heard the clunk of a bolt being shot back on the other side of the stable door.

'William!' she yelled. Had he gone against his brother's wishes?

A dry laugh. 'Sorry,' said Jimmy. 'It's just me.'

India didn't even think. In eight paces she was crouching in the manger, alongside the surging, maddened form of BB. His hindquarters were pumping as he continued to kick and she knew that, if she misjudged it, one blow from his hoofs could kill her.

BB jerked his head as the top part of the stable door opened, and as he did so, his body swung next to her, and stilled.

Another clunk as Jimmy shot the bolt to the lower door.

Crooning softly to the horse, just as Aunt Sarah had taught her, she put a hand on his withers, but he didn't flinch or seem to feel her. His attention appeared to be riveted on the stable door.

India raised herself on the manger's lip, hand still on the horse's neck. BB was snorting but he wasn't kicking; he was shifting *towards her*.

'OK, boy,' she whispered. 'Be nice, now.'

Murmuring softly under her breath, she raised her leg over his back, expecting him to rear or buck when he felt the weight of it. But he didn't, and she pushed off from the manger with her other foot and slithered into position. She could feel BB's tension, his muscles quivering, and she kept crooning gently to him as she leaned past his neck and felt along the rope for the knot tying him to the metal ring in the wall.

Daylight flooded the stable as both doors swung wide, but she didn't look round. She was concentrating on the rope and she saw that it was a slipknot, and she was practically halfway along BB's sweating and twitching neck as her fingers reached for the free end.

'What the . . .?'

India gripped the end of the rope and pulled. The knot unravelled and the rope spilled free. Grabbing it in both hands, she hung on to a handful of mane and dug her boots into BB's ribs.

'Go, boy, go!' she yelled.

It was as though the racehorse had seen the tape lift in front of his eyes. She felt him stiffen beneath her, and then he surged for the stable door.

Ducking low against the horse's neck, India saw the silhouette of Jimmy with a pistol in his hand and she put another desperate boot into the horse's ribs. She didn't want BB to baulk or shy away; she wanted to *run him down*.

But BB didn't hesitate. He charged for the door as though Jimmy didn't exist, and India closed her eyes, hearing Jimmy yell as the horse crashed into him like an out-of-control truck. Then she felt her mount slip, start to lose his balance, and BB was skidding, his hoofs lashing wildly as he tried to right himself, and Jimmy was entangled, and he was *screaming*.

India was urging BB not to fall, and he was twisting, desperately kicking his hind legs, trying to find a purchase when Jimmy suddenly went quiet. BB heaved himself upright, India still astride, arms practically round the horse's neck, and in the second before BB bolted, she glanced down.

Jimmy's arms were unnaturally splayed, and his hair was thick with blood.

And then they were off, India clinging to BB's neck. They were careering past the mansion when she heard the shots. She glanced over her shoulder to see Jack's sturdy shape with a shotgun, firing from the hip, but they were too far away, and the horse hadn't been hit, she hadn't been hit, and BB was swinging right down the main track, away from the homestead and the rubbish tip, and the sound of the shots diminished with every second.

It had to be the most incredible, most terrifying experience of her life. Astride a racehorse, bareback, with her hands wound into his mane. He was doing at least forty Ks and she prayed that he wouldn't stumble.

Rucking the rope from BB's head collar until it was taut, she increased the pressure, trying to slow him down.

'Hey, boy,' she tried. 'Ease up now. Easy.'

He tossed his head to one side against the rope and, amazingly, increased his pace. India immediately eased the pressure on the rope, but BB carried on galloping at full speed, blowing easily, his head and neck bobbing in a steady rhythm. Sand and dust sprayed beneath his hoofs.

A handful of mane in each hand, she glanced ahead and her heart just about stopped. They were heading straight for the cattle grid. It would snap his legs like matchsticks and she would be thrown to the ground.

India let go of his mane, leaned back and hauled on the rope. She was digging her backside into his spine, legs clamped hard with her heels well clear of his ribs, giving him all the signals she could that it was time to check his pace, but he wasn't taking any notice.

With all her strength she heaved the rope to the right, wanting to bring his head round, but he was too strong and it barely budged at all.

The grid was a few paces away when the horse saw it, but it was too late. BB was like an express train with its brake cables cut, and they were going to crash. At the last second BB flung his head high and began to rear, his forelegs reaching. Although the huge body beneath her was bunching, he was off-balance and uncoordinated and she thought, No, please don't try and jump . . . But BB was already hurling himself into the biggest kangaroo hop a horse had ever attempted, and India had no choice but to go with him.

Suddenly weightless, she found herself hovering above his back. All that connected her to the horse were her hands, gripping his mane. The power from his hindquarters had shot her into the air. Then she was yelling as they descended. Waiting for the cattle grid to break his legs, shatter every bone in her body . . .

BB crashed to the ground with horrifying force. India slammed onto his spine and felt him start to go down. She was still clutching his mane as he fell, trying to work out which way to go to avoid being crushed, but then BB skewed and rose, staggered a couple of steps.

And suddenly, with a lurch, he broke into an unsteady trot, India still clinging on. He was blowing hard, his ribs pumping in and out, but he wasn't limping.

India reached down and hugged his neck. 'You star,' she told him, tears of relief and gratitude on her cheeks. 'You star.'

He gave a snort. Although she wanted to think that he was responding to her, she knew it was nothing but his body reacting from stress and relief.

'Snort all you like,' she said. 'I think you're brilliant.'

She let him trot gently at his own pace for a while, and after half a kilometre or so he dropped into a polite walk.

Listening to his hoofs thudding gently on the dusty track, India tried to work out what to do next. Should she ride BB to the coast road, where she could flag down a car and get help? She didn't fancy riding the horse on the road through the night. Not only would she not be able to see but, thanks to his black coat, nobody would see *him* and they might get hit by a car.

As she was wondering if she should tie BB up before it got dark and hide until daylight, she thought she heard an engine. She swivelled round to see two plumes of dust along the track. Two Toyota traybacks were going flat out and headed straight for her.

India barely had to touch her boots to BB's flanks before he broke into a canter. Neck-reining him off the track, she headed for the thicket of trees stretching across the hills to her near left. It would slow her down, but even the best ute on the market wouldn't be able to follow her in a forest.

Leaning close to the stallion's neck, all she could hear was the thudding of hoofs and BB's hot breathing, and then she took in the sound of an engine roaring. A quick glance over her shoulder and she saw that the ute was catching up.

'Come on, boy,' she said, kicking his ribs as hard as she could.

She wasn't sure what she expected, but it wasn't this sudden surge of power. It was like pushing the gas of a Ferrari. India held on for dear life, threads of black mane stinging her eyes. She didn't dare risk a look to see where the ute was, in case she unbalanced the horse, or herself. She had to go for it, no holds barred.

She could hear the engine above BB's thundering hoofs and knew that the car was closing in, but the trees were coming up fast. She pulled hard on the rope and, to her astonishment, felt BB slacken his pace. She yanked harder, but he'd done all the slowing he felt was necessary. She was hoping he knew something she didn't when suddenly they plunged into the forest.

Flattening herself along his neck, she heard crashing and smashing of foliage around them. A low branch whipped over her head, just missing her. Slowing into a canter, BB swerved wildly to the right and she nearly came off, but when she saw he'd jigged round a large rock she forgave him.

They threaded their way through the forest as fast as they could. The ground rose into a steep hill but BB didn't slacken his pace, and India gripped his mane as he wound his way round boulders and bushes.

Half an hour later they broke free of the forest. They were on top of an escarpment with the sun sinking behind a band of hills to the west. She could see the shadow of a valley below, and what looked like a dry riverbed, shining silver with sand. India looked at the steep slope of loose shale. No one with any sense would ride a horse down that. But in the distance she heard men's shouts and what sounded like the clatter of bike engines. They were beating the forest, heading her way. She couldn't go back.

Heart in her mouth, she gently tapped BB's flanks. He gave a snort, and suddenly they were scrambling down the scree of rocks, India leaning so far back her shoulders almost brushed his rump. She hung on, gasping with fear, until they hit the bottom of the scree.

The horse started trotting downhill, his flanks heaving and soaked with sweat. When they reached the bottom of the valley the moon was high in the sky, a sliver of mercury the size and shape of a nail clipping that lit everything pale grey. The night was still and silent aside from the soft shambling of BB's hoofs and the occasional thud-thud of a startled kangaroo.

India brought him to a halt and slid from his back. Her legs trembled when they touched the ground. Clutching BB's collar, she used his solid form to prop herself upright until she felt some strength return.

When she went to pick up his rope, BB swung his head towards her and nickered, brushing her fingers with his soft velvet nose as though checking on her too. 'Oh, but you're a beautiful beastie,' she murmured, 'not a bastard at all. How could they have called you that all this time?'

He nosed her hand very gently and then, without her asking him to, he walked on. India hugged her arms round herself, trying to keep warm. She put a hand on BB's shoulder, telling him that she'd look after him when they got to wherever he was taking her. The rope was slung across his withers and he was free to do what he wanted. She just followed.

BB led India through the bush, occasionally stopping to sniff the air, and then he'd nose India's hand gently and start walking again. It was just after 10 p.m. when they came to a fence. A horse gave a whinny nearby and then there was the sound of snorting and a small grey mare trotted into view. India saw a huddle of sheep beneath a tree, and at the far end of the paddock, a darkened homestead.

She led BB round the fence, the grey mare following, until she came to a gate, and popped him inside. He touched noses with the mare, who gave a little squeal, which India took to be delight since she was touching noses back, ears pricked. In return BB gave a long, groaning sigh that sounded like satisfaction. Horse romance, she thought.

With a final grateful pat, India left BB and cautiously approached the homestead. Set in front of the verandah was the biggest dog kennel she'd ever seen but, luckily, no dog. Just two vehicles. A white Toyota ute and a tractor. The ute was unlocked and she glanced inside. No keys.

'Strange sort of swap you be making,' a voice said behind her.

India swung round.

'Jack's horse is worth ten times my ute.'

Slowly India put up her hands, her gaze travelling from the shotgun levelled at her chest to the tiny old woman behind it. Stick-thin shins stuck out below a T-shirt five sizes too large. Long grey hair floated around her head like seaweed in shallow sea. Next to her was an enormous dog—a dark brindled Great Dane. He must weigh over 200 pounds, she thought.

'I don't mean any harm,' said India.

'What you be doing with Jack's horse, then?'

'I, er . . . borrowed him.'

Long silence and then the woman chuckled. '*Borrowing* Jack's horse. They didn't say anything about that. Just that if I saw you, to ring them straight up. Sounds like they're pretty keen to get their hands on you.'

India stood quite still. 'And are you going to ring them?'

'Don't be so bloody stupid.' She broke the shotgun and hooked it over her elbow. 'I wouldn't piss on Jack if he was on fire.' She looked at India with interest. 'Let's go in. It's brass monkeys out here,' she said.

India looked at the dog.

'Don't mind Ricky. He may be big but he's got no brains to bite anyone. All he does is eat and sleep.'

The old woman walked towards her house, her pace surprisingly fast, and India followed. Perhaps she could persuade the woman to loan her ute to her. And if not, grab the keys and just steal the thing. Inside, lights were snapped on and India saw a neat home with green patterned carpet, faded prints of Australian landscapes and silk flower arrangements.

'Let's have a beer while you tell me the story,' the woman said.

'Just some water, thanks.'

The woman went to the fridge and popped herself a beer, then filled a glass from the tap and handed it to India. 'I'm Maggie, by the way,' she said.

'India.'

'And you're in trouble with them.'

'I guess I am. A bit.'

'You're not the first to run here.' Maggie looked away, uncomfortable. 'There was another, three years back. Still gives me nightmares.'

But India was only half listening. She was looking around the room, searching for the ute's keys. She spotted a massive plastic bowl by the phone, filled with newspaper clippings, old envelopes, and mail. She walked over, hoping Maggie kept her keys in there as well.

'I saw this bloke running for my house, see. Right up my front drive. Big bugger he was, an Aborigine, going like hell. But he didn't stand a chance. They had dirt bikes and utes. Jimmy shot him in the back.'

India forgot all about the car keys and swung round. 'Jesus.'

'I couldn't report it,' Maggie said sadly, 'or I'd have ended up in the same grave. Typical of them to bury the poor sod on my property. I planted a tree on the grave.'

India's memory was spiralling backwards and she was in the Internet café listening to the old man talking about Albert. *Last time I saw him, it was at the Nelson . . . Wearing one of his godawful floral shirts . . . He left when Jimmy turned up . . .*

'Maggie, what was he wearing? The guy Jimmy shot?'

Maggie stared at her.

'It wasn't a Hawaiian shirt, was it?'

Long silence. Maggie's expression was horrified. 'You knew him?'

But India didn't have time to talk it through. She turned her attention back to the plastic bowl and saw she'd been right. Three sets of keys, one with a Toyota tag. She began to reach for it.

'No point in running,' Maggie said firmly. 'They'll have all the tracks covered. You'd be better off resting up here with me a few hours. They'll be here in a bit anyhow. They said they would.'

India rushed to the window. No cars, no headlights that she could see.

'I've got the perfect hiding place,' Maggie told her.

Muscles aching, wishing she could just get in the car and drive, India started to make for the door. 'I think I'll take my chances on foot.'

'The state you're in? You'd last three seconds. Maggie's eyes started to twinkle. 'I've got a much better idea.'

TUCKED UP at the rear of the massive dog kennel, India nestled on Ricky's bed and waited to see what would happen next. She hadn't wanted to hide so close to the house but Maggie had insisted.

'Safest place in the world. They won't be looking for you on my doorstep. And with Ricky there, who'd have the guts to put his head inside?'

India reached out and patted Ricky. He hadn't appreciated being dragged outside and chained inside his kennel and he ignored her. She tried to peer round his huge bulk and look through the door but he filled the space and she couldn't see a thing. Which, she supposed, was the point.

It had taken Maggie a good ten minutes to persuade India not to run. Not that she didn't trust the old woman; she just wasn't sure if Maggie could hold her own against Jack or Bryce if they turned up here.

'Ha!' Maggie roared with laughter. 'I've known Jack since he was in shorts. Little brute. Had him over my knee for bullying my daughter Becky one time. Wouldn't mind giving him the strap today if he wasn't so big.'

Curled on her side, India lay her head on her arm and tried to ignore the pain still groaning through her shoulders. She thought over other things that Maggie had told her about Jimmy chasing that man down and shooting him in the back. An Aborigine. Had it been Albert? Well, if she got out of here alive, she'd have the cops dig up the grave on Maggie's land and find out.

INDIA AWOKE with a start when Ricky lifted his head with a slap of chops. Barely two minutes later she heard engines roaring, then tyres were crunching on stones, doors were opening and slamming shut. Her skin bristled at the next sound: metallic clicks of guns being loaded.

Thumping on the front door.

'Maggie! Maggie, open up! It's the police.'

A slight squeak as the door opened.

'Maggie, Jack's horse is in your paddock.'

'Is he? Well, blow me down if all my dreams haven't come true. I've always wanted a nice foal by him.'

'Are you saying you haven't seen that woman round here?'

'The one you rang up about? Nah. Haven't seen a thing. Why do you want her?'

'She killed Jimmy.'

'She killed Jimmy?' Maggie repeated, sounding more disbelieving than shocked.

'Yeah. She ran him down with that goddamn horse. Jack's doing his nut. He wants her on a plate.'

India felt goose bumps rise all over her skin as she listened.

'Steve, you go round the back,' a man said quietly. 'Phil, you scout the perimeter. Check every chook house and shed. I'll do the inner circle.'

Sound of boots scrunching on grit, then silence. Ricky gave a low growl.

'Hey, big boy,' the man said in a gentle undertone. 'You got anyone hiding in there with you?'

Ricky's growl grew to a subdued roar.

'Dennis,' Maggie called out. 'I wouldn't if I was you.'

'It's OK, Mags, we all know your dog may be big but he's nothing but hot air. I just want to check—'

To India's horror, Ricky launched himself outside. The kennel gave a creaking, tearing sound and then there was a metallic *snap* and the dog stopped short, quivering and snarling and frustrated at the end of his chain.

'Jeez,' the man said, gasping. 'He nearly got me.'

'For goodness' sake, Dennis.' Maggie's voice came near. 'Don't you know not to mess with a dog when they're on their home turf?'

Ricky was still lunging against his chain, barking furiously, and the kennel was shaking and India prayed it wouldn't break apart under pressure.

'Leave him alone,' Maggie said. 'And come inside and have a drink.'

'OK, thanks, Maggie. That bloody dog . . .'

It was only after Dennis had left that India realised she was covered in sweat. Shivering and shaking all over, she knew she was near the point of collapse. Ricky had stopped growling and was standing there, sniffing the air. India counted the minutes passing. Five, ten, fifteen.

Then a lot of boots on gravel. Men murmuring.

'Listen up, guys,' a man said. She recognised Dennis's voice. 'Phil, I want you to cover the coast road. Tony, there's a track that leads off Narooma . . .' He paused when a mobile chirruped. 'Yeah,' he said, and then, 'Oh Jesus . . . I'm sorry, boss . . . Yeah, yeah. We'll bring her to you. Alive. I swear it.'

'That was Jack.' His tone was tense. 'He just found Bobby. He's hanged himself in one of the stables. Dead as a doornail.'

India felt a wave of dizziness. She could see William the first time she'd met him, wearing his beautifully tailored suit.

'Kuteli's team are covering the highway,' Dennis was saying. 'Jack's put a chopper in the sky. He'll give us what we need. The rest of you, let's go.'

Car doors slammed, engines roared, and then they were gone. Ricky sniffed the air, then came inside and flopped down, landing his head on her lap.

'REST UP for a while,' Maggie told her. 'You're safe here.'

They were sitting at the kitchen table, eating a reheated lamb pot roast accompanied by bottles of cold beer. India's hair was still wet from her shower, and since her clothes were in the wash, she was wearing a pair of Maggie's shorts and an oversized fleece.

'And when you're feeling up to it,' Maggie continued brightly, 'you can stick Jack behind bars, where he belongs. You've got to do it. He won't stop, not now you've killed Jimmy. He'll spend the rest of his days tracking you down. And anyone you care for. You've got to get him first.'

India knew that Maggie was right, but she felt so inadequate, so *small* against the prodigious Zhuganov family. Like an ant attempting to fight off a dozen cockroaches. There was no way she was going to survive.

After a four-hour sleep, India drove Maggie's ute into Perth. She might be an ant, but an ant could deliver a nasty bite before it died.

Come 9 a.m. she was crossing the Swan River ready to face Perth's rush hour. Cracking open her window, she lit a cigarette. Bless Maggie, she thought. She had given her not only two packs of Silk Cut but also a flask of coffee and a stack of sandwiches that would keep her going for a week.

Swinging southwest on Queen Victoria Street, she took Phillimore to Cliff Street, bounced over the railway tracks and pulled into the car park on the left. Her heart squeezed when she saw the familiar NO FISHING signs ahead. She was here again. Fremantle Port.

'SAY THAT AGAIN?' The chief stared at her in amazement.

'The ship's here,' she repeated. 'Jimmy mentioned someone called Hammond, who said she'll be gone in twenty-four hours.'

'Hammond?' he repeated.

'You know him?'

The chief tapped on his computer keyboard. He scrolled down a page and pointed out a name: Geoff Hammond, Minang & Company, ship's representatives. 'You've cracked it, sweetheart,' he said, grinning. 'You've found someone who knows who owns the goddamn ship. Now all we have to do is get him to admit it in court, and we've got the bastards by the balls.'

'But what if he scarpers first? We've got to get the ship. Then we've *evidence* to stick the guys who sank *Sundancer* behind bars.'

He started to tap on his computer keyboard again. India went and stood by the window and looked out at the wind-chopped harbour.

'Take a look,' the chief said, swinging his screen round. 'There's no *Pride* listed. She might have used a false name . . .'

India ran her eyes down the list. Nothing jumped out at her and the chief scrolled on. Halfway down the third page she saw it.

'The *Prize*?' she said.

He checked it out. 'Not your ship. She's from Singapore. *Prize Oldendorff*. Got her Lloyd's rego and all.'

India studied the list and saw three ships that might fit the bill. She asked if she could see them, and also the *Prize*, to satisfy her curiosity.

The chief looked hesitant.

'Please, Chief.'

He rolled his eyes. 'God, I'm a sucker for a pretty face.'

THEY DROVE down Victoria Quay, past a passenger terminal, then ducked beneath a railway bridge and swung left over the Swan River, then left again to North Quay. Deep in the heart of the docks, the chief swung round various fork-lift trucks, accelerating hard when it was clear, sounding his horn regularly, waving to people as he drove. India ducked low in her seat, a yellow hard hat hiding her face. If Jack came after the chief she'd never forgive herself. After five minutes or so, she felt the ute slow.

'Here's one of them,' he said.

India shuffled upright to see a gleaming new ship the size of the Empire State Building toppled on its side. *Source of Taupo*, from Auckland. Nothing about her was familiar. 'Nope,' she said.

The chief showed her two more ships, one from Fiji, the other from Cape Town. She shook her head at both.

'This one's the last on your list. Any good?'

The breath stopped in her throat. The ship was around 100 metres long and had four winches and derricks, one big hold. She had fresh paint on the port side of her bow, where the damage sustained from ramming *Sundancer* had been repaired. It was the ship she'd been on in Jakarta.

'Chief,' her voice was trembling with excitement. 'This is it.'

As she climbed out of the ute, she could barely believe it. The ship that had sunk *Sundancer* sat almost opposite the jetty where the Greenpeace boat had been prepped all those months ago. The hatch was open and a crane was lowering a container inside.

'What the hell . . .?'

The chief was staring at the ship's name, *Prize Oldendorff*. Like all ship's names it stood proud of the metal, but if you were looking for it you could see the D through the Z, and that the rest of the name had been altered.

'It's not possible.' His mouth hung open. 'She shouldn't be here. I mean, we've security arrangements, checks.'

'I'll bet someone in your office has been altering your records,' said India. 'Someone related to the Zhuganovs. Someone open to bribes.'

He paled. 'It would take more than one person to pull this off.'

'It's a big family.'

She watched a second truck move forward and the crane lock on. The driver walked round and uncoupled the container, and the crane bore it up and across and down into the hold.

'Those containers are full of illegal waste,' she told him. 'They're taking it from all over Australia and shipping it off to Chennai.'

'What sort of waste?'

'Industrial, chemical, stuff you have to wear protective clothing for.'

The chief looked at her. 'And she never even lodged a form thirteen, telling me she was transporting dangerous cargo. Fancy that.'

'We've got to contact Customs. Get her cargo inspected.'

'Forget Customs, I'm calling the cops. And I'd better alert the FESA guys—'

'FESA?'

'Fire and emergency services. What if the stuff's leaking?' He began to head for his ute. 'I'd better place an exclusion zone round her.'

He'd just put a hand on the door handle when he paused. 'Shit,' he said. He was looking at a ute driving towards them. 'Best if you get out of sight. I don't want anyone pegging you. Soon as I get rid of these guys, we'll hit the emergency buttons, OK?'

More than OK, she thought, hopping into his ute. Not only did they have a ship's representative who could testify, God willing, that the Zhuganovs owned the ship, but they also *had the ship*!

Pulling off her hard hat, she crouched in the passenger footwell. She heard the sound of an engine slowing alongside, then it was switched off. A car door slammed and a man spoke, but she didn't hear the chief's reply. Go away, she willed the man. The chief's busy.

The chief said a few words, but his tone sent a flurry of cockroaches over her skin. He sounded angry, but it was tinged with fear. What was going on? Cautiously she peeked through the window.

The chief was standing between the two utes, his face white as bleached bone. India felt her own face tighten when she took in the pistol jammed in the chief's stomach, then the man holding the gun.

He had a thick black moustache and a stripe of grey hair running from his forehead to the crown. It was the man who'd shot the boatswain. The man who had tried to kill her. Rajiv.

NINE

What the hell was Rajiv doing here? No time to ponder it; she had to do something, and *fast*. Heart pumping, she twisted her head and saw that the chief had left his keys in the ignition. She took a deep breath. Counted, one, two, three . . . and leapt up and across into the driver's seat. She didn't dare look at Rajiv or the chief for fear she might falter. Cowering and sweating, dreading a bullet smashing into her, she released the handbrake and turned the ignition.

The engine roared into life, and she jammed the stick into drive and stuck her foot hard down on the gas.

Bang! The passenger window exploded into a spray of glass, but she didn't slow down. She wasn't hurt, hadn't been shot, thank God . . .

She barrelled past lines of ships and trucks, gripping the steering wheel so tightly she almost expected it to buckle. How was she going to rescue the chief? Chuck a U-turn and run Rajiv down? The idea held quite a lot of appeal, since she couldn't think of anything else.

India glanced into her rearview mirror. A hollow opened up inside her. The chief was down on the ground, sprawled and unmoving between two other guys. Had they shot him?

Jamming her foot on the brake she spun the wheel hard to the left. With a howl of tyres, the ute swung full circle and India gunned the engine.

So help me God, she thought, charging back down the quay towards the men leaning over the still form of the chief, I'll have one of you smacked onto my bonnet in the next few seconds, come what may.

With one hand on the wheel, she managed to click her seat belt in place as she bore down on the men, swearing under her breath. Shit, shit, shit.

At the last minute, they looked up. One of the men rushed aside but the other man stuck his hand in the air, three fingers raised. She didn't know what it meant, didn't care. Only one man to run down now, and as she tore towards him she saw it was Rajiv.

She belted past a truck, and was just metres away from Rajiv when he took two steps, and stopped. He was astride the chief's body. If she hit Rajiv, she'd pulverise the chief as well.

India hauled the steering wheel to the right. There was a hideous screech of rubber as the weight of the ute shifted wildly to the left, and she swung past Rajiv and the chief. There was a brief, eerie silence. The ute's right tyres had lost their grip and were slipping. She'd hit a patch of oil.

She lifted her foot off the accelerator and pressured the steering wheel into the skid. The ute's rear was already sliding left and she wasn't breathing, just praying not to be tipped into the harbour, when she felt the ute react and begin to reduce speed. She was feeding the steering wheel further into the skid when a fork-lift truck suddenly appeared in front of her and she couldn't help it; she pulled the steering wheel to the right.

She promptly lost all control.

'Oh, no,' she said, and her voice wasn't loud or filled with alarm. It was simply resigned. She knew she'd lost the battle and she braced herself as the side of the ute swung straight for the fork-lift.

INDIA AWOKE with a vibration beneath her cheek, a cold metal shuddering that reminded her of something. She lay there in total darkness, trying to think what it was, but then the pain in her body took over. Her shoulders and neck felt as though they had red-hot knives sawing their tendons.

She concentrated past her pain for clues as to where she might be. She could smell traces of chemical and vomit. Had she been sick? It wouldn't surprise her. She felt like throwing up from the pain pounding through her body more than the rolling beneath the metal floor.

A blast of realisation hit her. She was on a ship. A big ship, given the motion against the waves. She had no doubt she was on *The Pride*.

As she climbed painfully to her feet she felt as though she'd been beaten with a telegraph pole, but at least she hadn't broken anything. Knees bent to absorb the rolling of the ship, she shuffled forward, hands outstretched, unable to see even a pinprick of light. What felt like an hour later, her finger-tips connected with what she thought was a wall, a rough metal wall that was ribbed every metre or so. Walking carefully, she followed the ribbed wall, and when it fell away she realised it turned left. She followed its flank another six metres or so, and then it fell away and she turned left again.

Hell, she thought. It wasn't a wall, but a container. She was in one of the cargo holds. She swallowed hard, trying to keep her panic under control, but it was growing every second. So she yelled, '*Shit!*' and felt better.

'India?' a man's voice called. 'You OK?'

She peered in the direction of the voice. 'Chief?'

'Christ, you just about gave me a heart attack. Hang on a tick.'

A tiny white light flicked on, like the glow from a firefly. She started towards it, her hopes leaping. *She wasn't alone!*

'Take it slow, 'cause there's crap all over the place, ropes and stuff.'

India edged her way towards him. Now she could see they were in a hold the size of a lecture theatre, with a hatch cover for a ceiling, steel floors and rows of containers.

'Hey, how's my favourite reporter?'

'Alive. I think.'

The chief was grinning, but she could see a runnel of blood darkening his shirt collar and he was standing slightly off-balance, as though one side of him was wounded, like his hip or leg.

'Are you all right?' she asked.

'All the better for seeing you, believe me.' He came over and gently tucked her into an embrace. 'You're a real trouper, you know? I saw you bugger off in my ute and I thought: That's the last I'll see of her, then the next second, you're back, aiming straight for that bastard.'

She felt his chest rise and fall.

'You mind if I turn off the torch? Got to save batteries.'

'God, no. Where did you find it?'

'It's attached to my car keys. They didn't do a very good job of searching me. I've a screwdriver too.' He clicked off the torch.

The instant darkness made her sway, but the chief's arm was round her shoulders and holding her close, so she didn't stumble.

'You OK?' he said, and the way he held her against his big, solid girth, the tone of his voice, anxious but not crazed with worry, reminded her of Mikey so much that she gave a choked sob.

The chief held her a little tighter and said, 'It's OK, India, I'm here,' and she closed her eyes, and it wasn't the chief who was holding her with his quiet reassurance, but Mikey.

Mikey, who had taken Polly and vanished into the outback so she could bring Jimmy down. Mikey, who ran rego plates when she asked, and worried himself sick about her.

She had wanted a neon-bright sign to crash on top of her to tell her whether she ought to marry him or not, but it was in the reeking darkness of a steel-hulled ship that it came to her.

She was scared of dying, but she was more scared of living without Mikey. Why she hadn't seen it before, she couldn't think.

She pulled the chief close, wishing he was Mikey, and although he wasn't she hugged him just the same.

'You thirsty?' he asked gently.

'Very,' she said.

'There's a tap over here. Take my hand. It's not far.'

It took a while for them to get there, but it was worth it. Fresh water ran over her mouth and down her neck, into her shirt. It tasted as sweet as syrup against the chemical smell hanging in the air.

The chief led her away from the puddle of water. 'I've done a tour of the place,' he said. 'I've some rope and a bucket.'

'Great. You tie them up and I'll drown them.'

He chuckled. 'It's a deal.'

The ship's motion began to change as the sea picked up. There was a lift to the bow and then a giant *bang* as it came down hard.

'We're well into open water,' said the chief.

India shivered. Rajiv no doubt planned to chuck them overboard once they were well clear of the coast. There'd be no evidence of foul play for a forensics team should their bodies wash up on shore.

'You up for an escape attempt?' the chief asked.

'God, yes.' India carefully pushed herself to her feet, trying to muffle her groan. 'What's the plan?'

'It's a bit risky, but I'm going to light a fire and bank on someone coming down to investigate.'

India thought of *The Pride*'s broken generators and autopilot. 'I bet their fire alarms don't work.'

'Don't worry, they'll smell the smoke pretty quick. Seamen are always paranoid about fires on board.'

'You've got some matches?'

'Yeah. One of those little booklets I picked up somewhere. Didn't realise I carried so much shit in my pockets till now.'

India followed him to the far end of the hold, where he'd made a pile of rags, rope, sandwich wrappers and pieces of oily newspaper, and watched him put the bucket close by before lighting it. Within two minutes, it was blazing away and the hold was bathed in an eerie, flickering orange light.

'This way.' The chief led her towards a metal door at the opposite end of the hold to the fire. 'You hide behind there.' He indicated a rusting container.

'What about you?'

He brought out his screwdriver. 'Come out only when I say so, OK?'

She swallowed. 'Shouldn't I be there with you? In case a whole lot of them come down?'

'Let's keep it simple. I don't want to stab you by mistake.'

India did as he said and hid behind the container, praying that the fire wouldn't take over the hold and burn them to death. Barely five minutes had passed when she heard an almighty great *clang*.

The door was opening.

INDIA DESPERATELY wanted to have a look but didn't dare in case she was spotted. Listening hard, all she could hear was the rumble of the engines, but then there was a man's exclamation, followed by two panicky voices in a language she didn't understand, then footsteps running away from her.

'India, *quick.*'

She bolted from behind the container to see the chief beckoning urgently. A brief glance to her right showed her two guys in overalls. One was racing for the bucket, the other the tap. They were shouting.

Then she was through the door and the chief followed her, banging it shut behind them and slamming the bolts into place.

'That was brilliant,' she panted.

He grinned. 'Two down, maybe six or so to go.'

They were in a long, evil-smelling corridor, lined on either side by rusting walls. She followed the chief until he halted in front of an iron ladder, the screwdriver glinting dully in his hand.

'I'll go first. If anything happens, scoot out of sight and hide.'

To her relief, nobody was waiting for them at the top, and she kept following the chief along endless badly lit alleyways. When they passed a porthole she was surprised to see daylight. She'd thought it was night. She had a quick glance outside and saw that it was raining. Acres of grey sea churned under a darkening sky. They came to an ancient, rasping metal door, and the chief had to put his shoulder to it and shove, and almost fell through. India was right behind him and smacked into his back when he stopped dead.

A squat brown man stood facing them. He held a pistol and it was pointed at the chief's chest. He jerked the pistol at the screwdriver and the chief obediently dropped it to the floor with a clatter. Another jerk of his pistol indicated that they should move ahead of him.

'G'day, mate,' said the chief, sounding amazingly calm. 'How's it going?'

The man barked something incomprehensible.

'Distract him,' the chief murmured to India.

When the chief walked forward, the man screamed. The chief just shrugged. 'Don't understand you, mate. Sorry.'

The chief was closing in on the man when he yelled again and pulled back the hammer of his pistol, priming the gun.

'Hey, you!' India shouted at him and lunged to her right.

Crack! There was a clank as a bullet hit metal, and India dived to the ground. Another shot blasted through the air. Her ears were ringing, her right knee screaming with pain, but she wriggled round to see that the chief had his hands round the man's throat and was slamming his head against the wall. The man went limp. India scrambled across and grabbed the pistol. Trembling, she checked the chamber. Four bullets left.

The chief was breathing hard and sweat ran down his face, but he wasted no time in outlining his plan.

India gave a nod. 'Let's go for it.'

'You mind if I have the gun?'

India handed it over. He passed her his screwdriver. Not the greatest swap in the world, she was thinking, when he suddenly ducked his head and planted a kiss on her lips. She didn't have time to react; she just stared at him.

'I've wanted to do that ever since we met,' he grinned. 'For good luck, eh?'

'Good luck, Chief.' She smiled back.

Inside the accommodation block the air was hot and heavy with the smell of frying onions and cigarette smoke. She could hear the blare of a TV, gunshots, explosions; they were watching a video. The crew's mess-room door was open when they approached, but the crew were so absorbed in the film that nobody saw them scoot past the door. She followed the chief along another corridor and up an iron staircase, using both hands to steady herself against the increasing roll. They halted outside the bridge door. It was ajar, and she could hear a radio playing inside.

Clutching the screwdriver, she waited behind the chief. He gave her a quick glance and mouthed, 'OK?' and she nodded back.

She saw him take a breath. Steeling himself for what was to come. Then he raised a foot, smashed the door open and sprang inside.

'Nobody move! You move, I shoot you!'

Silence.

'What is it you are wanting?' It was Rajiv's voice.

'Get on your knees. Put your hands behind your head. Tell your friend to do the same. And do it *slow*.'

A smatter of Indonesian.

India stood outside, trembling and gripping her paltry screwdriver.

'That's right, no sudden moves, and keep your hands where I can see them . . . Hey!'

Bang!

India leapt into the air. Who had shot who? Was the chief OK?

Bang! Bang! God, what was going on?

Another gunshot. The chief had only four bullets, she had to *act*.

India moved to the door and peered round. Her breathing jammed.

The chief and another guy were on the floor. But Rajiv seemed to be OK; he was standing over the chief with his gun and she heard the wet, metallic *snick* as he primed it.

She went straight for him. She didn't know if she had the guts to stab a man and simply rushed at him, wanted to stop him from killing the chief. He started to spin round but she was faster and she rammed him with her shoulder and then they were falling on top of the chief and she was beneath Rajiv, and she was yelling, trying to bring the screwdriver up, but it was immovable against the weight of his body. She lashed out with her feet, heaving her torso, but it was like trying to shift a sack of wet sand. She felt something warm seep through her shirt but she couldn't think what it was in her fight to free herself. His breath reeked of nicotine and garlic and she was scrabbling, trying to free her legs, pushing against his shoulders. With a final, huge effort, she shoved him aside, then was on her feet, gasping.

Neither Rajiv nor the chief moved. The guy in the corner had half his head blown away. He wouldn't be going anywhere.

In the distance she heard a man's shout, which galvanised her. She locked all the bridge doors. Rain was rattling against the windows. A man crooned on the radio. It sounded like Frank Sinatra. Surreal.

India grabbed Rajiv's gun, which had fallen to the floor, and that was when she saw where the screwdriver had gone.

She couldn't see any steel. Just the yellow plastic hilt sticking out of his upper stomach, about four inches above where his bellybutton would be. She could see his chest moving slightly and realised that he was alive. Hurriedly she checked his gun, three bullets left, and stuck it in her waist-band. She put the chief's on the bridge.

'Oh God,' she said aloud. The chief was covered in blood.

She bent over him and pressed her fingers against the underside of his wrist, desperately searching for a pulse. Her face was close to his and she was looking at her fingers on his wrist, trying to discern if she could feel his breath against her cheek when he said, 'I'm in heaven already?'

Still holding his wrist, she said, 'I'm not sure about that.'

'Help me up, would you?' He was pale and sweating and breathing hard.

'I'm not sure if that's a good idea.'

'Just do it, woman.'

The chief put an arm round her shoulders and she helped him drag himself to his knees towards a padded chair.

'Good stuff,' he gasped, as he fell onto the chair.

'Where are you shot? Can I—?'

'Hand me the radio.' He then turned his wrist, looked at his watch. Said, 'Fuckin' A.'

'What?' she demanded. 'What is it?'

But the chief had already set the frequency—2182 kHz—and was speaking into the handset. 'Mayday, mayday, mayday. This is Hank Gregory, harbourmaster of Fremantle Port. I am with India Kane and we are being held captive on board *The Pride of Tangkuban*, sailing under the name *Prize Oldendorff*.' He rattled off their position, his voice remarkably clear and strong. 'Our lives are in danger, please send help.'

He listened for a bit, but nothing was forthcoming, so he repeated the message several times. The radio remained silent but the chief didn't look too down about it.

'We caught it.' Despite the white sheen on his face, he looked pleased. 'All shipping stops radio communications from the hour to three minutes past the hour, and the half-hour to three minutes past the half-hour. The time is set aside for emergency calls. Someone must have heard us.'

India frowned. 'What about the crew? Wouldn't they have heard you too?'

'Well, yes.'

'What if they call back and pretend it was a hoax? What—?'

She didn't continue, because at that moment the lights went out. One second the bridge had been aglow with red and green dots, the next it was completely dark.

'Shit,' the chief gasped. 'They've blown the fuses.'

There was an almighty *thud* against the port door of the bridge. It sounded like a wrecking ball. Her heartbeat picked up into a gallop. The door wouldn't hold up for long against a prolonged assault.

'India,' the chief managed, 'open the door and shoot them, would you? We have to get control. I don't want them stopping the engines.'

Another metallic *bang*, and then another, near the lock. Hands slick with sweat, she pulled out Rajiv's pistol from her waistband and primed it.

'Are you sure?' Her voice trembled.

'Do it, India. For God's sake . . .'

Don't think. Just do it.

She spun round, shot back the bolts and yanked open the door.

The man outside froze. Overalls, brown skin, flat black hair, a sledge-hammer at his side. She had the gun in both hands and she was bringing it up, aiming for his chest, when she saw the white of his teeth as he opened his mouth to yell and she hesitated.

Do it, India.

The man seemed to sense her hesitation and he was moving towards her, swinging the hammer to strike . . .

She pulled the trigger.

He paused, his body motionless. The sledgehammer dropped to the ground with a clank.

India primed the gun again.

He slumped against the railing, and she was lowering the pistol, wanting to shut the door against the man she'd shot, but out of the corner of her eye she saw another man rushing for her.

This time she didn't hesitate. She simply pointed the gun at him and squeezed the trigger.

He dropped like a stone and she slammed the door shut and backed away from it, pistol in both hands, ready in case they suddenly blasted through the door and came for her. She was shaking.

'India. Come here.'

She walked to the chief, feeling as though her legs were on stilts and she wasn't fully in control of them. Her fingers felt numb, her skin cold.

He took the pistol from her, and chambered a round. Then he hooked an arm round her waist and pulled her close. 'You did good, OK?'

She stood there a long time, the chief's arm a band of warmth against the chill inside her. After a while the chief leaned his head against her ribs and she absent-mindedly stroked his hair.

'Chief?' she asked. 'What's next?'

The chief didn't answer. She felt a jet of alarm and looked down to see that his eyes were shut, and his head lolled to one side.

'Chief?' India patted his cheek, but he didn't respond. '*Chief!*'

SHE STRAINED to see past the water crashing against the windows, and she was glad she couldn't see much outside because she reckoned that if she did she might panic. They were in the middle of a storm, she knew, but the ship, rearing like a demented sea horse, seemed to be doing OK.

She knew that if she left the bridge they would kill her. Her only chance was to stay where she was, and get the ship safely to a harbour. She could do that, surely. The engines were still going, obviously on autopilot. Thank God it's been fixed, she thought, and although I haven't a clue how to switch it off and turn the ship around, I'm sure something will come to me. What I need is a map and some light. She felt the chief's pockets, searching for his book of matches. Running her hands over the chief's shirt, she felt the small, flat square in his breast pocket. Sliding it free, she lit a match, raising it high as she moved around the bridge. Her heart lifted when she saw a pair of clips holding a flashlight just beneath the chart table.

She grabbed the flashlight, turned it on and swung its pool of white light to the chief. His shirt was drenched with blood. India started to search the bridge for a first-aid kit. Loose gear was sliding back and forth as the ship rolled. She found a bunch of lading bills and pushed them aside. In the third cabinet she found a cheerful red box with a white cross on its lid.

Torch between her teeth, India used the scissors from the kit and cut the chief's shirt away. The bullet had smashed through his left breast and she could see splinters of white bone through the mouth of the wound, but the first thing she had to do was stem the bleeding.

She packed the lacerated flesh with sterile pads and taped them in place. It wasn't much, but she hoped it would be better than nothing. Praying he'd be OK, she turned her attention to the chart. She wasn't sure what she expected, but it wasn't this blank of nothing with contours spreading across it. Where was any indication of land? She looked at the chart below, recognising the outline of Western Australia, then flipped the other chart back.

For goodness' sake, you're at sea, she told herself. Of course there's nothing. Use the compass. Use your *brain*.

A gust hit the ship and she staggered to the wheel, hung on. *The Pride* heeled starboard, bow digging down low, then rose and settled again.

I have no idea what the hell I'm doing, she thought. I could be trying to land Concorde for all the effect I'm having. OK, keep calm. She took a couple of deep breaths and lined the ship on the compass, due east.

'No, you've got it all wrong.'

'Chief?' She almost chucked the charts in his face. 'Well, you do it.'

'Keep . . . hair on.'

'I'm sorry.' India could feel tears on her face, not of sorrow but of anger, borne of fright. She pulled over the chart and shone the flashlight down.

'Unless you want to go to Antarctica . . . disengage the autopilot.'

The chief talked her through it, then told her to spin the wheel.

'We've got to risk it,' he said. 'Try and pick a lull between the waves and hope she doesn't broach.'

The muscles in her cheeks were aching from gritting her teeth for so long, but she did as he said.

The Pride gradually turned and, as she did, her keel dug in and waves were crashing over her decks, and then they were broadside to the waves and a blast of wind slammed into them and she heeled sharply to starboard.

'Hold it,' the chief said.

India held it. Another wave came, but *The Pride* let it crash over her fore-deck, and although she slewed further starboard, rolling steeply, the hull lifted, and she was still sailing, powering forward.

The chief shifted up to check their progress.

'Port,' he told her.

They were slanting across a trough, almost diagonal, and the chief repeated the command, but much louder.

She spun the wheel and brought the ship straight.

'Port, dammit!'

She wound furiously and the chief yelled, 'Enough!' And the ship settled herself to take the next wave straight, and the one following.

Then the chief was plotting and drawing vectors, measuring angles. Without any electronics, he told her, he had to estimate their position by what, in the old days, was called dead reckoning: basing their position on the compass card, forward speed and wind conditions. His breathing was loud and rasping as he ran through what she should do if he lost conscious-ness again, where to keep the compass to maintain their course, how to stop the ship and drop the anchor, and when.

She had no intention of sailing a giant metal shoebox through a storm on her own. Surely, there had to be another radio somewhere? Then they could talk her in. Glancing at Rajiv, she saw that he'd moved. Her skin prickled. She'd better find some rope and tie him up. Torch in hand, she rummaged through the bridge again, then moved into the master's cabin, a shambolic mess reeking of dirty bedding. To her delight, she unearthed a sturdy roll of duct tape, and then, in a drawer beneath the bunk, a handheld VHF radio.

Clutching the radio, India shot back to the bridge. 'Chief, look!'

His face split into a lopsided grin. 'Aren't you my ray of sunshine? Get us within twenty Ks of the coast, and we'll have the troops on board, no worries.'

India checked the compass and corrected their course a fraction. Then she took the roll of duct tape to Rajiv. She wanted to bind his hands behind his back but doubted that she could move him, so she settled on taping not just his hands together but also his feet.

Returning to stand by the chief, she pulled out a bandage from the first-aid kit. She saw that the chief had plotted their course on the chart.

'Chief, I want to bandage you, put some pressure on that wound. OK?'

He leaned forward and let her slide her arms round him along with the crepe, until she'd used up all the bandage and he resembled an untidy mummy.

'Nurse India,' he murmured.

She gave a snort.

He smiled into her eyes. 'Marry me.'

She touched his cheek. 'I'm already hitched.'

'Lucky bugger.' He closed his eyes.

After downing a couple of painkillers from the first-aid kit, India went back to the wheel. Ahead, a big wave was looming for the bow. *The Pride* rose for it, up and up, then plunged into the crest, hesitated, and launched out the far side, spray streaming off her deck before she fell into the following gully with an almighty *bang* that had the whole infrastructure shuddering. Christ, India thought. I hope she hangs together for the ride.

INDIA SPENT the night at the wheel, checking their course and trying to keep alert, exhaustion and pain racking her body. The waves increased until she reckoned they were three storeys high.

Occasionally the chief would come to and blearily check that she was doing OK before slumping back into his stupor. She thought a lot about Mikey as the ship churned through the wild darkness of sky and ocean. How much she loved him. How stupid she'd been. Whether he'd still marry her. She hoped so. And if not? Well, she'd face that when the time came.

It was around 2 a.m. when a wave slammed into the bow and India jerked upright. She'd almost been asleep on her feet. Hurriedly she checked the compass. Altered their direction to align their course.

Concentrate, you silly cow. Keep awake . . . She searched for something to occupy her, and her gaze alighted on the charts. The chief's mathematics didn't make any sense to her, but as she flipped through them a bell was ringing in her head and then she remembered what the chief had said.

Unless you want to go to Antarctica . . .

She groaned out loud at the confirmation she'd been dreading. The Zhuganovs weren't shipping the waste to Chennai and Southeast Asia; they were dumping it. That was why they'd been so far south, where there were no witnesses, except a few million penguins.

The skin all over her body contracted as she remembered the fleet of ships operating out of the United States. This was an international operation. No wonder they wanted her dead.

THE CONDITIONS had gone from bad to horrendous. Instead of abating, the storm kept getting worse. The seas grew into ten-metre swells and the winds were moaning around the ship.

India clutched the wheel as *The Pride* climbed to the crest of a gigantic wave. A sudden weightlessness, a swoop in her stomach, and she held her breath as the ship plunged down the back of the wave. As it hit the bottom of the trough, there was a *boom* and the port-side window of the bridge blew out with the sound of a cannon going off. Water gushed inside. Wind screamed through the blown-out window. Pieces of metal, screws and bolts, things that shouldn't move on a boat, were flying everywhere.

Eyes squinting, head ducked against the flying debris, she fought to keep *The Pride* steady into the wind. How long do storms last? she wondered, wet and huddled, shivering against the wind shrieking through the window. A day? Two days? God, she'd never last that long.

A couple of minutes later, to her astonishment, the lights came on. Red and green dots sprang up on the bridge and the overhead bulbs gave a couple of flickers, then steadied. 'No, no,' she wailed. *Turn them off!* If any more windows had blown out and enough water had got in, then it could have worked its way into the engine room, soaked the wiring, and then the entire boat would be electrified. All the circuits would go. The VHF, the radar, everything would be inoperable. But more frightening was the fact that anyone standing in water could get electrocuted.

India desperately looked around, wondering what she could climb onto to avoid getting zapped. She wasn't sure if it worked like that, but she still looked. She saw that the blood on the chief's shirt had watered down, turned to pink, but the crepe on his breast was a sodden, deep, dark red.

She wanted to check his wound, but she didn't dare leave the helm.

Bracing herself against the wheel, she felt her initial panic subside. She hadn't been electrocuted. Not yet, anyway. As another wave shoved them over on one side, she checked her watch to see that she was right in the middle of the emergency radio communication on the half-hour. Hitching the radio out of its cradle, she sent another mayday. It wasn't quite as coherent as the chief's, and involved a lot of urgent pleading, but she thought she'd got her message across.

She was concentrating so hard on the radio that it took her a couple of minutes to realise that something had changed. The ship wasn't heading straight into the waves any more but was slamming from side to side, lurching forward, then rolling back. The sea had turned into a confused mass of energy, and the waves were coming from all directions.

India struggled to turn *The Pride* round, face the waves head on, but as soon as she got the ship straight the wind would shift along with the waves, and they'd slam into her broadside again. At some point, no matter how much she tried, she knew a wave could come that would flip the boat over onto her side, and then the water would gush in through the shattered windows, and drown the ship from inside. There were no life vests, no survival suits. If the ship went down, she'd go down with it.

TEN

India was sweating in the calm of a trough and fighting to keep the ship straight when she heard an engine's howl. She felt her whole body tense, not knowing what it was, wondering if the ship wasn't about to blow up. The sound increased, then abruptly vanished.

What the hell . . .?

Before she could think any further, it came at her again. A shriek through the storm. Blasting past and then away.

Holy mother of God, please let it be what I think it is.

India lunged frantically for the bridge windows, but she couldn't see anything except black and the occasional flash of white as a wave crashed across the bow.

The radio crackled. A man's voice broke through. '*Pride*, do you read?'

The next second the unmistakable roar of a plane shot past.

India grabbed the radio. 'Yes, oh, yes. I'm here.'

Short pause while static crackled.

'I take it you're India Kane?'

'Yes, it's me. I mean, I'm India.'

'Hi, India. We're from the Customs Service of the civil maritime surveillance, Broome. We hear you've a problem.'

'Just a bit.'

'Maritime Emergency Response C called us at one hundred hours. Had a bit of trouble locating you. We heard you've a little problem with the crew.'

'They want to kill us,' she said, thinking how understated the conversation was. Long static pause.

'Is Hank Gregory there? Can we talk with him?'

'He's here but he's wounded. Unconscious.'

'Right.' The pilot explained that the plane was on a surveillance operation, not a rescue mission. 'We'll be covering you until dawn breaks. Then a couple of helicopters will be here with the cops. They'll sort you out.'

'Cops?' she repeated. Her mind became a blur of panicked memories. Constable Bryce pointing his gun at her as she sat in her car. Sergeant Kuteli and Detective Inspector Zhuganov. She wasn't sure she wanted the cops to sort her out and said so.

'Sorry, I should have been more specific. They're from the TRG, the Australian Tactical Response Group. They'll look after you, no worries.'

That was more like it, she thought. The Zhuganov family wouldn't stand a chance against that lot.

As he circled *The Pride*, the pilot reassured India that she was doing fine, and despite the fact that she knew the plane couldn't do much except watch the ship battle through the storm, its presence was enormously comforting.

By 4 a.m. India felt brave enough to reset *The Pride*'s autopilot for the coast of Western Australia. The ship had picked up speed and the wind had changed its deep groan to a high-pitched wail. Waves eased from tower blocks into neater, more well-behaved semidetached houses.

She engaged the autopilot, then scrambled for Rajiv's cabin and grabbed what she could. Raced back to the bridge and heaved two blankets over the chief. Put a pillow under his head. Then she pulled off her sodden clothes and put on some of Rajiv's: track-suit pants, thick socks, two T-shirts and a fleece. They reeked of his sour, bitter sweat, but she didn't care. They were warm, and they were *dry*.

For a couple of hours she struggled to keep awake. Then the rain started to ease. To the east she could see a pale strip of grey on the horizon and realised that they were leaving the storm behind.

As the light grew, she finally saw the plane. A red-and-white-striped Dash 8-200 with CUSTOMS emblazoned on its flank. The radio crackled into life as the pilot wished her good morning.

'The choppers are here, India. Time for us to say goodbye.'

She thanked him, and watched the helicopters take up position on each side of the ship. The plane banked steeply to its right and quickly vanished.

'We docking yet?' The chief's voice was faint and his skin was pale and waxy-looking.

More and more worried, she pleaded with one of the choppers to airlift him to hospital. Sorry, they said, but they had to secure the ship first.

Two minutes later a rope snaked out from one of the helicopter's loading ramps and soldiers abseiled down, like drops of oil speeding down a dipstick.

Things happened fast after that. When the soldiers reached the bridge, the second chopper came in to send down a basket. The chief was strapped inside and sent aloft. Then Rajiv. Next, it was India's turn. Swinging wildly in the wind, she clutched the sides of the basket and looked down. Saw a bunch of crew members huddled miserably at the bottom of the accommodation block, wrists handcuffed behind their backs. Four soldiers stood watch over them, assault rifles cradled. The chopper accelerated away.

India watched the paramedics work. One on Rajiv, the other on the chief. The chief's face was already in a plastic mask as the medic took off her untidy blood-soaked bandages and replaced them with smart new ones. Then he pushed needles into veins in the chief's arms, hooked up various bags to various monitors. His movements were practised and assured, but his face was tense and worried.

'Will he be OK?' she called over the rotors.

The medic didn't look up. India looked across at the paramedic working on Rajiv and yelled, 'Can't he pitch in? Two hands better than one? I mean, that guy tried to *kill us*.'

'They're doing their best,' one of the marines said gently.

She sank back into her seat. Concentrated on gripping the chief's hand and trying to instil it with warmth and life and well-being. Please, God, don't let him die, she begged. Just make him better, will you? He says he's a coward but he's not. He's as brave as a lion.

THE ROTORS eased to a roaring clatter as the helicopter settled on the hospital's landing apron. A blur of white coats and cops in uniform rushed to greet them, clothes snatching in the downdraught. The chief was bundled outside first, shifted into a trolley, and then they were inside the hospital, careering along the corridor when, amazingly, the chief came round. Probably all the commotion, she thought, and gave him a grin.

'Hey, my hero,' she panted.

She watched his lips move beneath the mask. Heard his voice, muffled and raspy. 'Hey . . . my favourite—'

'Save it, Chief. Save your energy. They'll have you fixed up and playing golf by next week, no worries.'

They burst through a pair of rubber doors and a woman was yelling, '*Gunshot wound!*' and there were people in green gowns and bright lights and someone was pulling her away and she shouted, 'Don't you bloody die on me!' and he gave a grimace that she knew was meant to be a smile and he whispered, 'Wouldn't . . . dare,' and he was smiling in a face so white it was almost blue and hands were tugging at her and he'd gone so still she wasn't sure if he was breathing, but then she heard his voice, so faint, rasping, and he said, 'Kiss me.'

India pushed the hands off and went to him and bent over and pulled the mask away and pressed her mouth on his, warming his lips, giving them moisture, tenderly trying to kiss him to life.

'Heav . . .' he murmured against her mouth.

She didn't know what he meant, didn't care, she just wanted to keep him conscious, keep him *alive*, and she shut out the people who were shouting and tugging at his body, and it was just her and the chief, his eyes on hers, and she cradled his face between her palms, brushing her thumbs over his thick, curly eyebrows, and kissed his forehead, the stubble on his chin.

'. . . en,' he said. *Heaven.*

'Me too,' she said.

And then he died.

INDIA SAT on a bench outside the operating theatre, unable to cry. Perhaps she was too exhausted. Perhaps it was because she'd heard that Rajiv was, according to the hospital staff, *doing well*. She didn't want Rajiv to do well. She wanted him dead. She wanted him buried in a coffin fifty feet under and the chief alive, with his feet planted in grass on top, playing golf.

Hey, how's my favourite reporter?

Already missing you, she told him.

The corridor was swaying, rolling from side to side, forward and back, but she didn't fight it. She closed her eyes, sinking in the sensation of being back on *The Pride*, battling that monster of a storm.

A hand on her shoulder. 'India?'

She gave a nod. Didn't open her eyes.

'You know an Ellie Sharpe?'

Her eyes opened. Saw acres of blank white hospital wall. Smelt antiseptic and, faintly, the stale scent of adrenaline from the soldier at her shoulder.

'She's left messages all over the place,' the soldier said. 'Apparently she's having a baby and wants you there.'

'Ellie?' India repeated, tone blank, as though she'd never heard the name.

'Yeah. She's here. In the other wing. You want me to take you to her?'

She couldn't seem to engage her mind in any sort of gear, but she said, 'Of course.'

ELLIE'S HAIR was plastered in sweaty strings against her scalp, and she looked exhausted. She was also beaming from ear to ear and clutching a yelling blob of baby to her chest.

'We did it without you,' Ellie said smugly, glancing at a nurse standing to one side, looking just as smug.

'Well done,' India said, emotions flat as an ocean without wind.

'It's a girl,' Ellie added.

Wrinkled as hell, red-faced and squalling, India didn't think she'd ever seen anything so ugly.

'Do you want to hold her?' Ellie asked, making a little shove of the bawling bundle towards her.

Without thinking, India took a step back.

'Oh, come on, India,' Ellie scolded. 'You are her godmother, you know.'

Reluctantly India took the howling creature in her arms, felt the small head flop and hurriedly brought her hand up to support it. Feeling awkward, she scooped the baby close to her chest. She was as warm as freshly baked bread. Pink and red and wrinkled, with tufts of curly dark brown hair on her head. India brushed a filament from the baby's warm forehead and pressed her lips where the curl had been. The baby promptly stopped squalling and stared up at her with milky-blue eyes.

'What are you going to call her?' India asked, still looking into the baby's eyes. Her voice was husky and filled with unshed tears.

'Well,' said Ellie, sounding remarkably brisk, 'at least we can't call her Albert. That's a saving grace.'

Albert, who'd cursed Jimbuku Bay and who Ned had wanted to appease.

'So I've called her Rose,' Ellie continued. 'As in India Rose Kane. But her middle name's up for grabs if you've got one.'

'Leone,' said India without hesitation. 'The lion.'

'Rose Leone Sharpe she is, then,' Ellie said with satisfaction.

India closed her eyes and pressed another kiss on the baby's forehead. Her skin was softer than BB's velvet nose, softer than anything she'd known before. 'We got them, sweetheart,' she murmured softly as she rocked the baby close. 'Me and the chief. We got the men who killed your daddy.'

BABY ROSE was lying face down on Ellie's chest, arms and legs splayed, little face squashed against Ellie's left breast, and while Ellie interrogated India about why she was wearing two sets of track-suit pants and a fleece that was stinking out the entire wing of the hospital, and India was looking longingly at Rose and wishing that she was lying face down and fast asleep, someone came into the room.

'I was wondering when you'd turn up,' Ellie said.

'Sorry,' a man gasped. 'I tried to get here earlier . . .'

'At least you made the effort.' Ellie was astringent. 'Whereas India only managed to be here by accident, though that's nothing particularly unusual, as both you and I know. But Rose and I coped OK without you guys. Honest.'

India slowly turned her head. Filled her eyes with the man standing at the foot of Ellie's bed. A man who was tall and broad with a dumper-truck shovel of a jaw and a wary expression.

She felt a wave of love so strong she nearly fell over.

He was looking at her as though she might have contracted leprosy and she was looking at the abyss that had separated them, wondering if he'd dare cross the chasm for her or if he'd turn his back.

She was yelling in her head: *Please still love me, please.*

Tentatively she went to him and touched his face. He didn't move. Her throat was aching as she looked him in the eyes and said, clearly, 'I do.'

He opened his arms.

EPILOGUE

Mikey and India were sipping sundowners on the third evening of their honeymoon when Scotto's newspaper clippings arrived. He'd couriered them up with a little card telling them that Polly was fine, and so were Ellie and little Rose. His house had never been so noisy, he added ruefully, but he wouldn't have it any other way.

They read the clippings on their balcony overlooking Hayman Island and the Coral Sea. The first was from the *West Australian*, page three, and head-lined, PRIVATE ZOO OPENS EMERGENCY CLINIC. It detailed the story of Penselwood Farm building a state-of-the-art veterinary surgery for bush-fire victims; they were set up to take any kind of animal from cattle and sheep to wombats and emus. There was no mention of William or his sui-cide. There was a picture of Katy holding a baby wallaby wrapped in ban-dages. India could see she'd lost a lot of weight, but the haunted expression was fading and the shadows under her eyes had gone. She was smiling.

India turned to the *Sydney Morning Herald*. Front page, headline news.

FAMILY CHARGED WITH TOXIC WASTE DUMPING
by Scotto Kennedy

Six months after being arrested for dumping toxic waste in the South-ern Ocean, the owners of a recycling and waste management company face twenty years in prison each and a collective fine of $60 million.

Jack Zhuganov, of Kemble Environmental Services, has been held without bail. He was charged with eleven felony counts of hazardous waste being dumped improperly, posing a threat to the environment. Also arrested were fifteen other members of the family who helped the Australia-wide operation.

Greenpeace, with the help of the Australian Maritime Safety Authority, has brought the case of the sinking of their ship, *Sundancer*, before the court. Further charges are expected.

Arrests have also been made in Los Angeles, and further investiga-tions are being undertaken in other parts of the world, including Ukraine, Kazakhstan, Turkey and Bulgaria.

'Kazakhstan?' she said. 'God, I'm glad I didn't have to go all the way over there to stick them behind bars.'

'Me too.' Mikey took the clippings from her and put them inside their room. He returned with two pairs of flippers and snorkels.

'Let's go see if that wrasse is still about.'

IT WAS EXACTLY two hours later when it happened, and India thanked God when the news came through that all her friends were safe.

She was sprawled on a beach of soft white sand, her snorkel and flippers beside Mikey's as they studied a sky smudged with the Milky Way. They'd been snorkelling with underwater torches, and were drying off in the warm, tropical air and trying to spot shooting stars.

India reckoned that it was just as she kissed Mikey when the freak king wave hit Jimbuku Bay. She spent days working it out, and she wasn't quite sure why she wanted to know the second it happened, but she did.

Created in the Indian Ocean by an underground tremor, the wave hit the town at 11 p.m. Queensland time. It came from nowhere, and nobody had predicted it. Like an unstoppable ocean liner, cresting at a run-up height of over thirty metres and thundering at over 200 kilometres per hour, the towering wall of water had swallowed the Smartie-coloured houses in a gigantic blast and the estate had been annihilated.

No one died, because nobody was living there any more, but Shoalhaven had been flooded out, and one woman found a salmon the size of a labrador flapping in her back yard.

Experts from around the world held intense debates and studied ocean floors and weather patterns and said it was an inexplicable freak of nature, but the locals knew differently. They remembered Albert. And they knew that, finally, Jambuwal had wrought his vengeance.

CAROLINE CARVER

Childhood home: Buckinghamshire
Passion: Adventure of all kinds
Website: www.carolinecarver.com

'Writing thrillers is right up my street,' says Caroline Carver. 'Not just because of my love of adventure but also because I've been scared witless a few times and know exactly how it feels. I've been lost in the desert, survived sandstorms and cyclones, driven through storm-swollen rivers, and each time I think I might not make it, but I do. I'm still here. Amazing!'

She blames her love of adventure—which has taken her, among other things, on two long-distance car rallies—on her parents. Her mother set a land-speed record in Australia in the 1950s, and her Australian father was a jet-fighter pilot who fought in Korea. With such a background, it is perhaps no surprise that she has made her fictional heroine, India Kane, equally adventurous. 'India walked into my life one evening and sat down on the sofa next to me, fully formed. She is nothing like any of my friends and, even though I

'I've been scared witless a few times and know exactly how it feels.'

created her, not much like me either—I'm not half as brave! However, we are both fiercely independent and share a love of big spaces, especially oceans and deserts. India never responds as I would in the situations I set her in, so I never get bored. She's gutsy and impatient and can be as prickly as a porcupine, and I love it when she's on the page.'

In *Black Tide*, Carver takes on the controversial theme of toxic-waste disposal. It first began to intrigue her when she was horrified by an article about the amount of toxic waste being dumped in Australia. 'I write about what interests me or what frightens me, because I have to admit that I get the most out of issues that make my blood boil. I guess it's my way of making sense of what's going on in the world. In real life everything isn't fair, but in fiction I can stack the cards the other way.'

Caroline Carver was brought up on a farm in Buckinghamshire and it was there that she learned to shoot, skin rabbits, make butter and cheese, and ride horses—

something she still enjoys. 'The last thing I rode was a camel in the Thar Desert in India. The great thing about being brought up with horses is that it means you can ride pretty much anything, even if it is bad-tempered and bites!'

When she was twenty-two, Carver went out to Australia for a holiday and ended up staying away for ten years. She back-packed her way round the continent and went on to Southeast Asia, doing a variety of jobs along the way. The chance to enter the 1992 London-to-Saigon Motoring Challenge brought her back to the UK, where she put together a female team and entered the race. Afterwards, *Autocar* magazine asked her to write an article about the rally— which resulted in the beginning of her career as a travel writer.

When choosing a setting for her first novel, *Blood Junction*, Carver, who now lives outside Bath, couldn't resist escaping to Australia in her imagination. 'It was mid-winter when I started the book, wet and windy and cold. Being homesick for Australia, that seemed the natural place to go in my mind.' Last year, research for *Black Tide* gave her a good excuse to pay a return visit down under. 'I wanted to make sure my references to Perth were right. I couldn't have India driving the wrong way down a one-way street in Freo!'

True to character, she has recently been tempted to enter another rally, but decided in the end it would be financial madness. 'So I've decided to take flying lessons instead. I had to have something to look forward to in the summer!'

AUSTRALIA'S SACRED LANDSCAPES

Black Tide touches on the traditional Australian Aboriginal belief in the Dreamtime, when creation spirits roamed the earth and conjured everything into being. Places where these spirits rest, such as Uluru (Ayers Rock), are sacred to the people of the land who recognise their power in ancient and unchanged rituals. Tribal songs, dances and ceremonies are performed on sacred sites to keep the web of existence, the Dreaming, and thus the land itself, seamlessly alive from the past to the present.

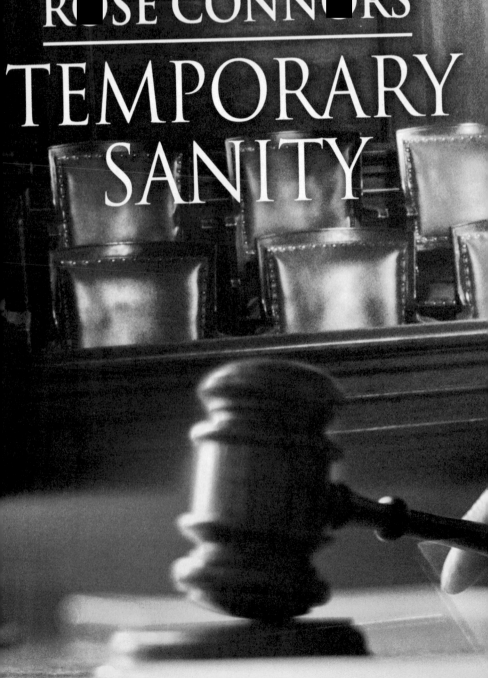

ROSE CONNORS

TEMPORARY SANITY

It's not easy for a lawyer to claim
that a client was temporarily insane.
Especially if the crime is the
most sane thing that the client
has ever done.

PROLOGUE

1879. I asked Janet, the law librarian, where I might find a thorough discussion of the temporary-insanity plea, and she referred me to a case decided in January of 1879.

'That's too old,' I told her. 'I'm looking for a more recent decision—one that explains why we preserve the defence, one that addresses the current philosophy supporting it.'

Janet herself climbed the ladder then, to the top shelf, and pulled out a book so decrepit that portions of its dark brown binding fell in flakes to the library floor as she descended. She opened the yellowed pages to a case already flagged with a sheet of folded notepad paper. Apparently, she'd been asked this question before.

She flipped through the first portion of the decision, then pointed to the centre of a page and handed the fragile book to me. 'Mr Justice Paxson gave it a lot of thought,' she said. 'Read.' And so I did.

We are obliged by the force of authority to say to you that there is such a disease known to the law as homicidal insanity. What it is, or in what it consists, no lawyer or judge has ever yet been able to explain with precision.

Janet was heading back to her desk when I looked up, but she paused to cast a meaningful glance over her shoulder. I got the message: A hundred and twenty-five years have passed. And nothing's changed.

CHAPTER ONE

Monday, December 20

'Your client is a vigilante, Martha. He blew a man away on live television. We'll get murder one at trial; the jury won't have any choice. Murder two is a gift. I can't do any better than that.'

Geraldine Schilling is the newly elected district attorney in Barnstable County, a jurisdiction that includes all the towns on Cape Cod. She won the election by a landslide with her 'tough on crime' campaign. She plans to improve her margin the next time around. And she thinks this case will help her do it.

Geraldine was the first assistant for eighteen years; I worked with her for ten of them, until six months ago. This is the first time I've looked at her from the opposite side of the table. She's formidable.

'Why did you call me, Geraldine? What is there to discuss?'

She's been on her feet throughout our meeting; Geraldine almost never sits down. She folds her thin arms across her tailored jacket, tilts her blonde head to one side, and half smiles. She doesn't answer, though. Her pale green eyes dart over my shoulder.

I don't have to turn around to know that Geraldine's new sidekick, the first assistant DA, is about to join us. J. Stanley Edgarton III always clears his throat before he speaks. It's an annoying practice designed to alert us that his words are coming, lest we miss one of them.

'Reality, Attorney Nickerson,' he drones at my back. 'Perhaps we should discuss reality.'

Geraldine hired Stanley a month ago—stole him, actually, from the New Bedford office—to replace me. A meticulous, prissy sort of man, he leaves behind an enviable track record. Stanley tried a dozen homicide cases during his eight-year career in New Bedford. He won them all. He doesn't intend to lose this one.

Stanley positions himself so that the tips of his tasselled shoes almost touch my boots, making me feel there isn't enough oxygen in the room for both of us.

I move away from him and head for the door. 'If that's the best you can do, Geraldine, we're going to trial.'

Stanley inserts himself in my path. 'And your client's defence, Attorney Nickerson? What might that be?' He picks up a videotape from the edge of Geraldine's orderly desk. He holds it in front of my face for a moment before he moves towards the VCR. 'Perhaps it's, *Gee, I didn't mean to gun him down in front of so many people.* That's a good defence.'

Stanley pops the tape into the slot and watches intently, a savage glee in his eyes as the television screen lights up. He's seen this tape before, of course. We all have.

An olive-green military chopper appears on the small screen, descending to the only runway at Chatham Municipal Airport. A half-dozen squad cars and press vans greet the chopper. Its door opens, and Hector Monteros emerges, hands cuffed behind his back. He begins his descent to the runway, an armed guard on the steps ahead of him, another right behind. The first hint of dawn is on the horizon.

In the lower-right corner of the screen, behind the wall of police cruisers and press vans, Buck Hammond steps from the hangar's shadow. He's my client. He stands perfectly still until Monteros and his escorts reach the runway. Then he raises a hunting rifle and fires. Monteros drops like a felled tree.

Stanley is smiling. 'Or maybe it's, *Darn, I didn't realise those TV cameras were rolling.* Now, there's a defence.'

Stanley is shorter than I am—he's shorter than most people, for that matter—and I examine the top of his bulbous head before I respond. Sparse, almost colourless hair parts just above his right ear, long strands of it combed over his pink scalp, the wispy ends just touching the top of his left ear. Beneath his vast forehead sit small brown eyes, too dark for the pasty skin that surrounds them.

'You people . . .' he says, shaking his head, a thick vein pulsing across his brow. I've noticed that vein before; it turns blue when he's mad. And J. Stanley Edgarton III seems to get mad a lot.

Stanley has been calling us 'you people' since he got here. New Bedford is only about thirty miles away, but Stanley seems to regard Cape Codders—some of us, anyway—as an alien species. He turns his back to me and flicks off the TV. I'm dismissed.

Members of the New Bedford defence bar warned us about Stanley. He's an odd one. He takes pride in being the first person in the courtroom each day, they report. He greets all trial participants upon their arrival, establishing himself as the man in charge. He is, in his own mind, one powerful fellow.

It's going to be a long week.

'See you tomorrow,' I tell him.

Stanley faces me again, still shaking his head. 'Looking forward to it.' His forehead vein throbs steadily.

Geraldine leans across her desk towards Stanley as I head for her office door. I catch her words just before the door slams shut behind me. 'Don't underestimate her,' she says. I can't help but smile. Coming from Geraldine Schilling, that's high praise indeed.

HARRY MADIGAN'S last day with the Barnstable County Public Defender's Office was November 1. After twenty years, he was opening a private practice.

Barnstable County's troubled residents—those who live on the edge when they're not confined to county facilities—know Harry well. Some have been with him his entire career. They trust him. They filled his office, and his filing cabinets, before he hung out his shingle.

I wasn't eager to return to practice after my years with the DA's office, and Harry knew that. But when he approached me about Buck Hammond's case, I had no choice. Harry knew that too.

Sometimes I think Harry knows me better than I do. He knew I'd fight Buck's battle, knew I'd view Buck's act as justifiable homicide. We have a problem, though. Our criminal-justice system doesn't view it that way. Our only hope is that a jury of Buck's peers will rise to the occasion—set the rules aside, if necessary—to reach a just result. Juries do that sometimes.

Hector Monteros raped and murdered Buck Hammond's seven-year-old son. Monteros was in police custody, charged with the crimes, when Buck fired the now infamous shot that took Monteros down. And he did it while two dozen people looked on, half of them police officers.

It shouldn't have happened, of course. Buck Hammond shouldn't have taken matters into his own hands. He should have let the system work, should have allowed Monteros to stand trial for his crimes. Monteros would have been convicted. He'd have spent the rest of his miserable days in a maximum-security penitentiary.

That's what should have happened. That's the way our society should function. But I'm not prepared to condemn Buck Hammond for what he did. It wasn't my son in the morgue.

Harry was appointed to defend Buck Hammond on the day of the shooting. Buck was assigned a new lawyer when Harry announced his resignation from the Public Defender's Office, but Buck and his family wanted Harry back; no one else would do. They met at his new law office. Harry said yes, of course; he's never been able to say no to an underdog.

Harry called late that night. He couldn't do it, he said. No one could. He had more files than any solo practitioner could handle. He would have to call Buck Hammond's relatives and reverse his decision. He couldn't possibly carry this workload and try a murder case in six weeks. Unless, of course, he had a partner.

I knew Harry was playing a trump card. He'd been hounding me for weeks about joining the practice. I wasn't ready, I kept telling him. I didn't think I'd be any good at defence work. I didn't want to be pressured into a decision. In Buck Hammond's case, though, there was no decision to make. I showed up for work the next day.

Within the week, we lured Kevin Kydd away from the district attorney's office. Geraldine is still sore about it. The Kydd, as we call him, is a year and a half out of law school and probably the hardest-working young lawyer in Massachusetts. Any firm in the Commonwealth would hire him in a heartbeat. But Harry and I made him an offer he couldn't refuse: long hours, longer headaches, and a salary with no way to go but up.

The Kydd went straight to work on the misdemeanours. Harry focused on the felonies. And I took on Buck Hammond.

HARRY AND I will try Buck's case together—the relatives wanted him, after all—but I will take the labouring oar. Now, the day before trial, Buck is as ready as he's ever going to be to face the first-degree-murder charge against him. So am I. I head back to the office anyway, though, to think it all through again, and again after that.

Harry is holed up with a client. The Kydd has two clients seated in folding chairs in the front office, waiting to see him, but he's fielding phone calls when I arrive. The cash flow won't support a secretary yet, so the attorneys here answer their own phones, type their own pleadings and open their own mail. It's a no-frills operation. Lean and mean, Harry calls it.

Our practice is housed in an antique farmhouse on Main Street in South Chatham, a seaside community of quaint shingled cottages and owner-occupied small businesses. Harry's farmhouse was built in 1840, and it wears all the charm of that era. Its original wide-pine floors are still in place, uneven and sloping through every room. Our clients are comfortable here in a way they would not be in the wealthier areas of Chatham.

Harry and the Kydd both have offices on the ground floor, on either side of our only conference room. I work in a small pine-panelled office on the west end of the first floor, a rustic, airy room with a view over the tree tops to Taylor's Pond and, beyond that, to Nantucket Sound. Harry lives in the rest of the first-floor space.

I'm barely seated, when the Kydd clambers up the steep staircase and bursts into the room. 'What'd ole Geraldine have to offer?' His grin expands when he mentions his former boss.

The Kydd's speech drops no hint that he ever left Georgia. He's slender and tall, but his posture is poor, his shoulders stooped. 'Stand up straight,' I always tell him, but he never does.

'Murder two,' I tell him now.

'What does Buck say?'

'Buck says no.'

He grins again, pointing his pen at me. 'What do you say?'

I take off my glasses and consider the Kydd's question. 'I don't know,' I tell him honestly. 'My crystal ball is cloudy this week.'

'Well, are you ready?' he asks, turning back towards the staircase.

'Nobody's ever ready for trial, Kydd. You know that. But I'm as close as I'm going to get.'

The Kydd grins from the top step. 'You're ready,' he tells me. 'My crystal ball says Stanley's about to meet his match.'

I start to thank him for his vote of confidence, but the look on his face stops me. His eyes dart from me to the ground floor and back to me again. He utters one word before he disappears. 'Trouble.'

THE KYDD takes the entire staircase in three strides. I follow as fast as I can. The door to the front office is wide open, a raw northeast wind blowing snow inside, papers flying everywhere.

The waiting clients are on their feet, easing a tall, wafer-thin woman into the Kydd's high-backed leather desk chair. She's coatless, and it's freezing. Her face is swollen and bruised. Her white blouse is blood-spattered and open in front, the top buttons torn off. Her lower lip bleeds profusely.

The men part to let me through, and I see at once that her right arm is broken. It hangs from her shoulder at a tortured angle, the wrist taking a brutal bend. I take off my suit jacket and cover her chest, press my handkerchief against her lips.

'Who did this to you?' My own hands suddenly tremble.

Her eyes meet mine, but she doesn't answer.

The Kydd reappears with a makeshift ice pack in a kitchen towel, and an old blanket from the hallway closet. I replace my saturated handkerchief with the ice pack and cover the thin woman up to her neck with the worn blanket.

'Who did this to you?' I ask again, holding the ice pack away from her mouth so she can answer.

Her eyes dart around the room. 'My husband,' she whispers finally. 'But he didn't mean it. It was the drink. He didn't mean it.'

Swell. That's great. This scenario had walked into the DA's office more than once during the years I worked there. She defends the bastard even before she's sewn up. By sunset, she remembers falling down a flight of stairs.

'How did you get here?' I ask, pressing the ice to her lips. She points behind me with her good hand, the left one, and I turn to see a skinny teenage girl wearing silver hoop earrings and a faded denim outfit, gnawing a thumbnail. She can't possibly be old enough to drive—not legally, anyway. I decide not to enquire. 'Your father did this?' I ask instead.

The skinny girl gives up her thumbnail reluctantly. 'He's not my father.' She shakes her head. 'And he's not her husband either. She just says that. Like he's some kind of prize.'

Harry rushes into the front office. He moves his six-foot frame to the woman's side without a word and takes her pulse, one of the skills career criminal-defence lawyers master somehow. 'She's not in shock, but she's got to get to a hospital.' He looks to the Kydd. 'I'm due in court. Can you take her?'

The Kydd gestures helplessly to the two men who've been waiting to see him since I got here. Harry's eyes move to mine, but he doesn't ask. He knows how anxious I am about tomorrow's trial.

'I'll call the rescue squad,' he says.

The woman pushes the kitchen-towel compress away. 'No!' she cries. 'No ambulance. No rescue squad. I won't go with them.'

'She won't go in an ambulance,' the teenage daughter confirms, her eyes rolling to the ceiling. She sighs. 'Forget it. I'll take her.'

The mother sobs now, leaning to one side in the chair, her good arm over her eyes. 'He didn't mean it,' she repeats. 'He didn't. He had too much to drink, that's all. He loses his temper when he drinks that much. He probably won't even remember.'

'I'll take her,' I tell Harry. 'To Cape Cod Hospital. But I can't do any more than that. Not with Buck's trial starting tomorrow.'

'OK,' Harry says. 'I'll call and tell them you're coming.'

The Kydd and his two clients struggle to raise the thin woman from the chair without hurting her arm. My suit jacket falls to the floor, but the men wrap the blanket carefully around her shoulders before guiding her out to the porch, down the front steps, and across the snow-covered lawn towards my ancient Thunderbird.

The teenage daughter follows, her thin jacket wide open in the winter wind. She looks back at me from the bottom step, and when our eyes meet, it hits me. Something is wrong with this picture.

The young girl brought her bleeding mother to a law office. Not a hospital, not even a doctor's office. A law office.

I hurry up the old staircase, grab my parka from the hook at the top, and head back down. I'm almost out of the door when Harry catches up with me. 'Marty,' he says.

I pause in the doorway. Harry's rugged features are worried. He feels it too. Something isn't right here. There's a reason this skinny teenage girl brought her battered mother to us.

He cups the side of my face in his big hand, the way he always does. 'Be careful,' is all he says.

THE KYDD and his helpers install the woman in a prone position on the back seat of the Thunderbird, leaving her sullen daughter with no choice but to ride shotgun. When I get behind the wheel, she moves to the far edge of her seat and stares out of the side window. I look to the rear, where the mother has her eyes closed, her left arm once again slung over her face.

If we don't hit traffic, we'll reach Cape Cod Hospital in little more than half an hour. For the first ten minutes, the teenager beside me doesn't utter a word. She keeps her face turned away, her thumbnail back between her teeth. Her limp dirty-blonde hair hangs forward, almost covering the fine features of her profile.

'I'm Marty Nickerson,' I say to her. 'What's your name?'

She turns towards me. 'I know who you are,' she says so quietly I can barely hear. 'I saw you on the news all weekend.'

The news. Stanley and I had argued pretrial motions in Buck Hammond's case on Friday. The press was all over us.

'I'm Maggie,' my soft-spoken passenger says. 'Maggie Baker.' She turns towards the rear seat. 'That's my mother, Sonia Baker.'

'Where do you and your mom live?'

Maggie twirls one long strand of fine hair around her right index finger. 'On Bayview Road,' she says. 'You know where it is.'

I nod. Maggie's response was a statement, not a question.

Bayview Road intersects with the east end of Forest Beach Road, just a stone's throw from Buck Hammond's cottage. I've been there at least a dozen times during the past six weeks, visiting Buck's wife, Patty, eliciting the awful, necessary details. Preparing her for Buck's trial, for the ordeal she will have to endure on the witness stand.

'You must know Buck Hammond, then,' I say to Maggie. 'You're practically neighbours.'

'We know Patty and Buck. He's in big trouble, isn't he?'

'Yes, he is.'

'It's not fair,' she says, her small voice growing strong for the first time. 'After what that creep did to their little boy.'

Minutes pass before I summon the courage to broach the matter at hand. 'Maggie,' I ask, 'who did this to your mother?'

'Howard,' she says to the dashboard. 'Howard Davis.'

I catch my breath, but Maggie doesn't notice. I know Howard Davis; he's been a Barnstable County parole officer for two decades. He's an enormous hulk with a booming voice and an intimidating stance. He handles the most dangerous of the county's parolees; he's the only employee on staff with any chance of keeping them in line. The first time I saw Howard Davis in the courthouse hallway with one of his clients, I was at a complete loss. There was no way to tell which one was the ex-con.

Sonia Baker is lucky she's breathing. And Howard Davis is going to jail, parole officer or not.

'Does Howard Davis live with you?' I ask.

Maggie stares at me, tears in her eyes. 'Yes,' she whispers.

'Has he done this before?'

Maggie opens her mouth, but no sound comes out. She nods her head up and down, though, hard enough to dislodge her tears. 'When he drinks,' she says at last. 'And he drinks a lot. He was drinking again before we left.'

'Maggie,' I ask, 'how old are you?'

She squirms a little at this, and I'm charmed by her innocence. Under the circumstances, even Geraldine Schilling wouldn't press charges against Maggie for driving without a licence.

'Are you asking as my lawyer?'

I laugh. 'Do you think you need one?'

Maggie speaks to the dashboard again. 'Maybe.'

'OK, then,' I tell her. 'I'm asking as your lawyer.'

'Fourteen.'

'When did you learn to drive?'

'Today.'

I pull to the curb in front of the emergency entrance, and an orderly pushes a wheelchair up to the back seat almost immediately. Harry called ahead, as promised. Sonia Baker lifts herself from the car with help from the orderly, pressing the blanket to her chest and clutching the bloody kitchen towel to her mouth. The orderly slams the back door and whisks her away.

'Maggie, go ahead with your mother. I'll park the car, then come and find you.'

Maggie does as she's told, but her eyes are like pinwheels. Her hands tremble when she closes the car door, and a wave of guilt rushes through me. I had to send her ahead with her mother; I need a few minutes alone to make a phone call. But I should have given her some idea of what to expect. The unknown is a terrifying thing.

CHAPTER TWO

Cape Cod Hospital's parking lot is just about full. It takes ten minutes to find a vacant spot, and even that one is partially blocked by a drift from yesterday's snowfall. I manoeuvre the Thunderbird into it anyway, cut the engine, and dial the district attorney's office on my cellphone. I need to alert them. One of the ADAs will have to appear before a district court judge with Sonia Baker and secure a restraining order against Howard Davis.

Geraldine is in a meeting. Stanley, though, is available. He picks up at once. 'Attorney Nickerson, so good to hear from you. May I assume you've come to your senses?'

Stanley is probably about thirty-five. I wonder how many times he's been decked.

'No,' I tell him. 'I'm still daft. Listen, Stanley. One of you needs to be in the office at the end of the day. I'm at the hospital right now with a woman who's been roughed up big-time by her live-in. And her live-in happens to be Howard Davis, the parole officer.'

'Jeez,' Stanley mutters.

'Yeah. Sounds like he drank himself stupid and lost it. She can't go home with him there; he was drinking again when she left. I'll bring her straight to the courthouse from here, but it might be a while. She's in rough shape.'

'Not a problem. We'll be here.'

Those might be the kindest words J. Stanley Edgarton III has ever said to me. I cut the connection, not wanting to press my luck.

I hurry towards the emergency room, my hood useless against the unrelenting wind. It's about two thirty. This morning's sunshine is gone, blanketed by a thick bank of darkening clouds. More snow is headed our way.

The hospital's automatic doors open as I approach. Signs are posted every three feet or so on the white walls. Some direct patients to have their insurance cards ready. Others inform us that seriously injured patients will be given priority. Still others warn that cellphone use may interfere with the functioning of diagnostic equipment. I reach into my jacket pocket and shut down my phone. There's no sign of Sonia or Maggie in the crowded waiting area.

'Sonia Baker?' I ask the young nurse at the desk.

'We took her straight back for stitches,' she says. 'Her daughter went with her. You're free to join them.' She points down the brightly lit corridor behind the desk. 'The young girl seems upset.'

'Thanks,' I call back to her, already heading down the hallway. I hear Sonia even before I reach her small curtained cubicle. 'He didn't mean it,' she's repeating, this time to a young surgeon who's pleading with her to be still. 'He didn't. He'll feel awful about it. I know he will.'

I wish she'd stop that.

Maggie sits alone in the area outside the cubicle, her tears gone. She rocks back and forth on her plastic chair, shaking her head each time her mother speaks on Howard Davis's behalf.

'Maggie, there are a few things that have to happen now. I want you to know what to expect.'

She stops rocking and stares at me. 'What do you mean?'

'I mean, certain steps have to be taken. The hospital has obligations under the law. All hospitals do.'

'Like what?' she whispers, panic in her eyes.

'Like the police have to be called.'

'No,' Maggie insists. 'No cops.' She jumps to her feet.

I sink into an orange plastic chair across from hers and tell myself to answer calmly. 'You don't have a choice, Maggie. The hospital has to report this to the police. It's the law.'

Maggie drops into her chair, and her tears begin again.

'Maggie, you shouldn't be afraid. You didn't do anything wrong. Neither did your mom. Howard Davis is the only one in trouble here.'

A look of disbelief seizes her wet face, and she gets up again. 'You don't get it, do you?' Her voice is desperate. 'I thought you could help, but you don't even get it.'

'Get what, Maggie? Get what?'

She leans over me. 'He knows them,' she whispers in my face. 'He knows all of them. He tells us that all the time. He knows every cop in the county. And every cop in the county knows him.'

'That's probably true. He's been a parole officer for twenty years. But that doesn't mean he gets away with beating your mom.'

'They won't touch him.'

'But they will, Maggie. They have to. They're probably on their way to your house as we speak, because of the hospital's report.'

'Oh, sure, they might pick him up. They'll have to now, I guess. But he'll be out in no time. The cops are his friends.'

'The cops have nothing to say about it. A judge will decide.'

Maggie straightens up. 'But he'll get out on bail first. He'll be out before any judge decides anything. And you know what will happen then? He'll kill her,' she spits. 'He'll just plain kill her.' She turns away and buries her face in her hands.

I lower my voice. 'Maggie, did Howard Davis say that? Did he say he would kill your mother if she turned him in?'

'Yeah,' she whispers. 'He says he'll break her neck with his bare hands. Right after she watches him break mine.'

CAPE COD HOSPITAL'S parking lot is emptying, the seven-to-three nurses and technicians just off their shifts. The snow is falling in sheets. I insert myself and my cellphone into a crevice of the building's granite wall and punch in my office number.

Sonia Baker needs more than a restraining order. She needs a lawyer to walk her through the process of swearing out a criminal complaint; to convince the district attorney's office to charge Davis not only with domestic violence but with threatening to commit double homicide as well; to persuade a Barnstable County judge to put one of his own parole officers behind bars.

I can't do it; I've already taken too much time from Buck Hammond's case. Harry can't either. He's in court right now. Sonia Baker needs help today, not tomorrow. The Kydd will have to do it. It's a serious matter—he's never handled one of these before—but I know the Kydd. He's up to it.

He answers the phone on the first ring and starts talking as soon as he hears my voice. 'Marty, where the hell have you been? I've been trying to reach you for half an hour. Your cellphone's been shut down.'

'I know that, Kydd. What's going on?'

'Where's Sonia Baker?'

A shiver runs down my spine. The Kydd knows Sonia Baker's name now. He didn't when we left the office.

'She's on her way to X-ray,' I tell him. 'Why?'

He takes a deep breath. 'Chatham police are headed your way.'

'Good. They can take her statement, then pick up the murderous boyfriend. The boyfriend is Howard Davis. You know, that giant parole officer. Can you believe that?'

'Marty . . .' The Kydd takes another deep breath. 'Howard Davis is dead.'

My vision blurs. 'Dead?'

'Stabbed to death with a steak knife,' the Kydd says. 'One from a set in Sonia Baker's kitchen.'

CHATHAM'S CHIEF OF POLICE pulls into the hospital parking lot just as I snap my cellphone shut. I race across the slippery lot to the Thunderbird, grab my camera and a roll of film from the glove compartment, then head back to the ER.

Sonia Baker is reciting her litany all over again, this time to an X-ray technician. I wish I had a muzzle.

I find Maggie in the waiting area. 'Forget everything I said about talking to the police,' I tell her. 'Don't answer any questions. Not for the cops. Not for anybody else. Do you understand me?'

Maggie nods her head yes, but her terrified eyes say no. Of course she doesn't understand me.

'Maggie,' I tell her, 'give them your name. But that's it. Tell them those are my instructions.'

I rush into the X-ray suite and lean over Sonia. The technician scolds me from his booth. 'Hey,' he yells, 'what are you doing?'

I ignore him.

'Sonia'—my hand moves above her stitched lips to stop her recital—'be quiet. I mean it. Don't say another word.'

Sonia stares at me while I load my camera, her expression suggesting she's never seen me before. 'I provoked him,' she mutters.

'Shut up,' I tell her. 'For God's sake, shut up.'

'Sonia Baker?'

The sound echoes through the hallway, a voice I know well. It's Tommy Fitzpatrick, Chatham's chief of police. Two uniformed Chatham detectives are with him.

'This is Sonia Baker,' I tell him. 'She doesn't want to answer any questions. She doesn't want to talk to you.'

The chief gives me a friendly nod with his full head of strawberry-blond hair. 'OK,' he says. 'But she needs to listen.'

I know what's coming. I wish I'd warned her.

'Sonia Baker,' the chief recites, towering over her, 'you're under arrest for the murder of one Howard Andrew Davis.'

Sonia gasps and raises her upper body from the table.

'You have the right to remain silent,' the chief continues. 'Anything you say can and will be used against you in a court of law.'

Maggie Baker leans through the doorway, dwarfed behind the uniforms. I drop my hand to my side and wave her out of the room. She hesitates for just an instant and then disappears as the chief wraps it up. Sonia shakes her head, her mouth open.

The X-ray room is full of hospital personnel, and not just technicians. Nurses and doctors came to see the show too.

'We'll get out of your way,' the chief tells them. 'We know you've got work to do.' He turns his attention to me and my camera. 'You on this one?'

'I guess I am.'

'When she leaves here, she goes to lockup. Arraignment's tomorrow morning. Judge Gould says eight o'clock sharp, before the regular docket.'

'No waiver,' I tell him. 'Don't even ask her what time it is unless I'm with her.'

Sonia leans forward and stares at me while I photograph her face, focusing first on her stitched lip, then on her swollen right eye. 'Howie's dead?' she whispers.

'I'm sorry, Sonia,' I tell her, lowering the camera. And I mean it. The anguish in her eyes now is worse than anything I saw when her pain was just physical. During my years with the district attorney's office, I saw enough of these cases to know she probably loved him. No matter what he did to her, she probably loved him.

'There's a child,' the chief says, sorting out his paperwork on the bedside tray. 'A young girl. She'll need to go to the Service.'

I scan the room, relieved to see no sign of Maggie Baker. No child should be entrusted to the Massachusetts Department of Social Services. A child from Chatham would be safer on the streets.

'I don't know where she is,' I tell the chief. 'But I'll find her, and she can stay with me. No need to involve the Service.'

'You a relative?' the chief asks, not looking at me.

'Yes. A second cousin.'

The chief snorts at his paperwork. 'Sure you are. And my cousin's the Queen of England.' But he balls up the Department of Social Services referral form and tosses it into the wastebasket. He and the uniforms leave the X-ray suite without another word.

I'm relieved and grateful. It's good to know that on some issues at least, Chief Tommy Fitzpatrick and I are still on the same side.

THAT EVENING, I leave Maggie Baker at the office with Harry and the Kydd and drive to the Barnstable County House of Correction. The female violent-offenders unit is an austere, forbidding place. Nonstop grey breeze blocks serve as walls. Cement slabs—the same dull grey—make up the ceiling. The narrow hallway is poorly lit by yellow bulbs protruding overhead, protected by wire cages.

My escort is a well-endowed, gum-chewing matron with wide hips bulging under a heavy holster. She stops in front of a white metal door on our right and selects a key from dozens on her oval ring. She shoves the door open and, with a toss of her head, directs me inside. The door slams shut behind me.

The space has all the comforts of a telephone booth. Sonia Baker is already seated here, staring at me through a pane of bulletproof glass. She's dressed in a prison-issue bright orange jumpsuit.

I sit down in the solitary plastic chair that faces hers and pick up the black telephone on my side. She winces when she lifts her receiver, the movement apparently exacerbating some ache or pain.

Sonia Baker looks like she barely survived a train wreck. The cast starts just below her shoulder, bends at the elbow, and extends to her wrist. Her lips look somewhat better than they did earlier, but her right eye is much worse. We never iced it, I realise. It's turned a deep purple, swollen completely shut.

'He's really dead?' Her voice is brittle.

'Yes, he is,' I report.

Her eyes fill. She lowers her head but says nothing.

'Sonia, you need to tell me what happened to you.'

'What difference does that make? Howard's dead. I'm not.'

'It matters. What happened before you came to my office?'

'Sunday night poker,' she says. 'Howie plays poker on Sunday nights. Every week it's the same thing. He stays out too late, drinks too much, wakes up hung over. Mondays are always bad.'

'But this one was worse than usual,' I venture.

'Yes.' She looks up at me, tears streaming down both cheeks. 'This time he did it up big. He was out all night. It was after five when he came crashing through the door. And he's supposed to be at work at eight. He passed out on the couch.'

I nod.

'I tried to wake him at seven. I really did. When he wouldn't get up, I called in for him. Told them he was sick. That doesn't usually happen. Howie almost never misses work.'

A man with a work ethic. What a catch.

Sonia rests her cast on the counter and wipes her face with her sleeve. 'He woke up around noon, really mad. It was my fault he missed work, he said. It was my fault because I didn't get him up. I told him I tried. I swore I tried, but he didn't believe me. When I told him I called in for him, called in sick, he got even madder.'

I stare at her. She doesn't recognise the insanity she's describing.

'He started drinking again,' she continues. 'He was storming around the living room; he was so mad, his eyes were bulging. I went into the kitchen to get away from him, but he came in and grabbed me and slammed me against the refrigerator. He kept slamming me. When he let go, I fell. He kicked me then.'

She points to her swollen eye. 'I thought he was finished. Maggie was already outside and—' Sonia catches her breath. 'Maggie—where is she?'

'At my office. She can stay with me until things get sorted out.'

Sonia takes a deep breath. 'Thank you,' she whispers.

'It's no problem. But Sonia, today's Monday. Why wasn't Maggie in school this morning?'

She drops her head onto her cast. After a while, she looks up at me, embarrassed. 'Maggie misses a lot of Mondays,' she says.

Of course. Mondays are always bad. She told me that.

'OK, Sonia, so you thought he was finished.'

'Yeah. Usually it's just one fit; once he takes a break, it's over.'

'But not this time.'

'No, not this time. I tried to get to the kitchen door. Maggie left it open and was calling for me to come out. She'd started the car. But Howie grabbed me from behind. He threw his arm around my neck, really tight. I couldn't breathe. When I tried to pull away, he grabbed my arm with his other hand.' She pats her cast. 'He bent my arm back, and he kept bending it. I heard a bone snap. He heard it too. He had to. But he wouldn't stop.'

I close my eyes, picturing the physical disparity between Howard Davis and Sonia Baker.

She cries harder with the memory. 'When he let go, I tried to get out again. Maggie was screaming outside. But I wasn't fast enough. He smacked me in the face with the back of his hand.'

'That's when your lip split.'

'I think so. Anyway, I fell into the kitchen table.'

I nod, encouraging her to continue, but she falls silent. We're just getting to the hard part, I realise. 'What happened next, Sonia?'

'Nothing happened next. He was done. I got into the car with Maggie, and she drove to your office. She said it was time to put an end to this, and that you could help. She'd seen you on the news. I wasn't in any shape to argue.'

I stare at her. She's composed now. I lean forward and look into her only open eye. 'Listen, Sonia. I'm your lawyer. You need to tell me what happened to Howard.'

She stares at me and shakes her head. 'I don't know. I thought maybe you'd tell me.'

If she's lying, she's damn good at it.

'Do you know where he was when you ran from the cottage?'

'Of course I do. I didn't dare take my eyes off him. He was headed back to the living room. Back to his couch and his bottle.'

She looks off into space. She's used up.

'Sonia, I'm going to ask the court for funding to have you evaluated by a psychiatrist, OK?'

'OK.' The look on Sonia's face tells me it's not OK, though. She's starting to wonder about me.

'I'm going to say some things you don't want to hear. I want you to be prepared. I'm going to raise a legal issue known as battered-woman's syndrome. I'm also going to raise a self-defence claim.'

Sonia stares at me but says nothing.

'Try to sleep,' I tell her. I start to hang up my phone, but she raises a hand to stop me.

'You think I killed him,' she says.

'The Commonwealth thinks you killed him, Sonia. And until we know how much evidence the prosecutor has to back that up, we can't leave any stone unturned.'

'I didn't.'

'OK.'

'Can you tell me—are you allowed to tell me—how he died?'

I look hard into her open eye. 'He was stabbed.'

No words. Just a sharp intake of breath.

'Sonia.'

She looks at me, her eyes running like faucets.

'Maggie wanted me to tell you she loves you.'

Sonia smiles through her tears and hangs up the phone.

That wasn't exactly what Maggie wanted me to tell her mother. She wanted me to tell her that we'll straighten out this mess, that everything will be OK. I just couldn't bring myself to say that.

WHEN WE GOT the footage of Buck Hammond from the local news station, Harry moved his television and VCR out of his apartment and into the conference room. The next day, the Kydd had stocked us with video games.

The Kydd and Maggie are engrossed in animated warfare when I get back to the office at ten thirty. Harry is slumped in a chair, watching the action. His baffled expression suggests he might as well be reading hieroglyphics.

'One of you surrender,' I tell them. 'Maggie and I have to go.'

The Kydd looks up, but Maggie doesn't. 'Hah!' she shouts as the sounds of explosions fill the room. 'You're dead!'

'Hey, not fair,' the Kydd whines.

'War is an ugly thing,' I tell him.

Maggie dons her little denim jacket, pats the Kydd on the shoulder and heads out into the winter night. 'Rematch tomorrow,' she calls from the doorway, 'if you're not too scared.'

I head out behind Maggie, Harry on my heels.

'How'd it go?' he asks.

'She says she didn't do it.'

'Maybe she didn't. This guy's been a parole officer most of his adult life. He's probably got enemies.'

'Maybe. I can't think about it any more tonight. I need some sleep. Arraignment's tomorrow morning, before Buck's trial.'

Harry stops in the shadows on the porch and pulls me towards him, his big arms pressing me close. 'OK,' he says. 'I'll see you tomorrow.'

His kiss is soft and long. I'm warmer than I've been all day, and I'd just as soon not move, but I pull myself away. 'My house guest is waiting.'

Harry laughs. 'Good luck with that one,' he says.

She's already seated in the Thunderbird. 'What should I call you?' she asks as soon as I join her.

'Marty.'

'OK. Thanks for doing this, Marty. If you didn't let me stay with you, I'd have to go to Social Services. Howard's always threatening to call Social Services, have them come get me.' She leans towards me. 'And he tells me about all the terrible things that happen to teenage girls at Social Services.'

Someone should have slapped Howard Davis before he died.

'He's a real bully, that Howard,' Maggie adds.

Her use of the present tense concerns me. 'Maggie, you realise Howard's dead, don't you?'

She sits back again. 'Yeah,' she says. 'I got that.'

'And you understand your mom is charged with killing him?'

'Yeah,' she repeats. 'But she didn't. I was there. He beat her up, but all she did was run away. She didn't do anything to him.' The darkness swallows Maggie's features as we leave the driveway. 'You'll get her out, won't you?' she whispers.

'I'll do everything I can, Maggie, but your mom's not coming home anytime soon. This process will take months. And it's not going to be easy. You and your mom are in for tough times.'

'That's not how I see it,' she says. 'My mom's in jail, and that's awful. But Howard won't ever hit her again. So the way I see it, the toughest times are over. I'm sorry Howard got killed, but I'm not sorry that we'll never see him again.'

I PULLED the book with Mr Justice Paxson's decision from my briefcase late that night. I was desperate for wisdom, desperate to understand and believe in the only viable defence the law allows Buck Hammond.

When I opened to the bookmark, my eyes fell at once on a question posed in the text.

What, then, is that form of disease—denominated homicidal mania—which will excuse one for having committed a murder?

Chief Justice Gibson calls it that unseen ligament pressing on the mind and drawing it to consequences which it sees but cannot avoid, and placing it under a coercion which, while its results are clearly perceived, is incapable of resistance—an irresistible inclination to kill.

An irresistible inclination to kill. I found this answer inadequate, unsettling even, and I was disappointed. Because the question, penned more than a century ago by a man long dead and buried, was precisely mine.

CHAPTER THREE

Tuesday, December 21

Maggie Baker is a freshman at Chatham High School. My son, Luke, is a senior and a member of the varsity basketball team. When Maggie and I got to the cottage, it was close to eleven, and Luke apparently had abandoned hope of his mother coming home to make dinner. He was outside paying the pizza delivery boy.

Maggie all but fainted. 'That's your son?' She looked stunned.

'That's him.'

'Your son is Luke Ellis?'

'Last time I checked.'

'Why didn't you tell me?' she snapped, fixing her hair in the rearview mirror.

The next hour was comical. Luke was his usual affable self. He didn't ask why Maggie was with us; he acted as if we'd been expecting her. He shared his pepperoni pizza as well as his senior-year wisdom. She hung on every word.

Heavy winds kept the cottage chilly in spite of a blazing fire in the woodstove. I gave Maggie a pair of flannel pyjamas and a fisherman's sweater. She looked at me as if I'd lost my mind. I made a mental note to arrange to pick up her clothes from Bayview Road.

At midnight, Luke set up the sofa bed for Maggie and dug two heavy quilts out of our cedar chest. Luke headed upstairs with Danny Boy, our Irish setter. Maggie Baker had stars in her eyes.

I DROP Maggie and Luke at the high school at seven fifteen. The roads are ploughed and sanded, but traffic is thin, and I reach the Barnstable County Complex in just half an hour. The parking lot is almost full, even though most courthouse proceedings don't begin until nine. The combination of Sonia Baker's arraignment and Buck Hammond's trial has drawn a crowd.

The district courtroom is packed. All of the benches are filled. A dozen court officers stand guard in the back of the room, guns on their hips. For the first time in my career, I take a seat at the defence table. Geraldine is on the opposite side of the room, covering for Stanley. He's not a multitask employee, it seems.

Just before eight, Sonia Baker enters the courtroom through its side door, her ankles shackled, her good wrist cuffed to one of the two armed matrons escorting her. Her purple eye is still swollen shut. She keeps the other one focused on the floor.

A matron removes Sonia's solitary cuff but leaves the shackles in place. Sonia drops into the seat next to mine. It's obvious she hasn't slept much, if at all. Her open eye is bloodshot.

The bailiff shouts 'Court!' and we all rise. Judge Richard Gould emerges from chambers and strides to the bench. When the judge sits, the rest of us

488 | ROSE CONNORS

do too, all but Dottie Bearse, the district court's veteran clerk. Dottie, holding a copy of the criminal complaint, recites the docket number and announces, '*The Commonwealth of Massachusetts* versus *Sonia Louise Baker.*' Geraldine is on.

'Your Honour, the defendant is charged with the first-degree murder of one Howard Andrew Davis.'

Geraldine hands me a thick document—the medical examiner's report, no doubt—before delivering an identical package to Judge Gould. She remains close to the bench, facing the judge.

'The deceased was found yesterday on his living-room couch, Your Honour, in what can only be described as a blood bath.'

I'm on my feet. This is arraignment, for God's sake. Geraldine is acting as if we're in trial.

Judge Gould is way ahead of me. He bangs his gavel hard. 'Attorney Schilling, please. No need for drama. Stick to the facts.'

I sink back to my chair.

Geraldine gives me the slightest of smiles before facing the judge again. 'Of course, Your Honour. I'll be happy to.'

The packed courtroom grows silent. The gory details of Howard Davis's death are what everyone came to hear, after all.

'Howard Andrew Davis was stabbed eleven times.'

Sonia's gasp is the only sound in the room. She raises her head and gapes at Geraldine, horrified. I've met more than a few criminal defendants over the years. I've seen more than a few emotions—real and contrived—displayed on their faces. And I know one thing for sure at this moment: Sonia didn't kill Howard Davis.

'Five of the lacerations were to major organs,' Geraldine continues. 'Not to mention a fatal puncture wound that reached the aorta. There's no question there was a physical altercation between the deceased and the defendant. Howard Davis lost the fight.'

Once again, I get to my feet, but I hold my tongue. Judge Gould isn't looking at Geraldine. He's not looking at me either. He's reading the medical examiner's report, his expression troubled.

The judge looks up. 'I remember Mr Davis, Ms Schilling. He was an unusually large man.' Judge Gould removes his glasses and taps them on the medical report. 'Six feet four, two hundred and sixty pounds.' The judge looks over at Sonia and shakes his head. 'It doesn't seem physically possible.'

I sink to my chair again. Never argue with opposing counsel if the judge will do it for you.

Geraldine nods at Judge Gould, apparently having expected his reaction. 'Your Honour, if you'll turn to page four of the report, you'll see that the victim's blood alcohol content at the time of death was point three three. He would have been just about comatose when he was stabbed.'

Judge Gould's gaze falls on me while he absorbs this information. 'Attorney Nickerson,' he says, 'how does your client plead?'

I'm up again. 'Not guilty, Your Honour.' I hand my written request first to Geraldine, then to the judge. 'The defence moves for a psychiatric assessment pursuant to Massachusetts General Laws, chapter 123, section 15(a).'

Judge Gould puts his glasses back on. 'Battered-woman's syndrome,' he says.

'We reserve the right to raise that defence if necessary. But there's also no doubt in my mind that she's innocent. Sonia Baker didn't kill Howard Davis.'

Judge Gould reads from my written motion as he rules. 'The defendant's request for a court-appointed expert is granted. The defendant, Sonia Louise Baker, will be examined by a mental-health professional—at the expense of the Commonwealth—to determine whether or not she suffers from battered-woman's syndrome. If she does, the expert should discern whether she is capable of assisting her attorney with her defence, and whether she has a rational and factual understanding of the proceedings against her.' The judge looks out at the crowded gallery. 'We're adjourned until the assessment is complete.'

He escapes from the bench as the bailiff instructs us to rise.

'I don't want that battered-woman thing,' Sonia says, looking at me for the first time today.

'I know you don't. But we had to keep our options open.'

Sonia gets to her feet, surrendering her wrist to the metal cuff attached to a matron. 'Thank you,' she says. 'For telling the judge I didn't do it. I know you probably don't believe me, but I didn't.'

Sonia disappears with the matrons through the side door.

The district courtroom is empty when I leave. Snow is falling. I head out into the frigid morning, steeling myself for the day ahead. In ten minutes, jury selection for *Commonwealth* v. *Hammond* will begin in superior court, Judge Leon Long presiding.

The County Complex looks almost festive in its new white blanket. Small, heavy flakes drift down as I cross the parking lot. It occurs to me, as I reach the back door of the superior courthouse, that my new career is off to a humble beginning. I have two clients, and neither one is much interested in being defended.

JUDGE LEON LONG is the only black judge ever to sit in Barnstable County. He has been on the superior court bench for more than eighteen years. A liberal Democrat who began his legal training during the turbulent '60s, he is the favourite draw among criminal-defence lawyers. To Judge Long, the presumption of innocence is more than a constitutional protection. It's a sacred guarantee. That means Buck Hammond has a fighting chance.

In some courtrooms, jury selection in a case like Buck Hammond's would take days. In Judge Leon Long's courtroom, we'll wrap it up before lunch. I know this from experience. 'People are fundamentally decent,' Judge Long is fond of announcing. 'No need to search for skeletons in the average citizen's closet. Old bones won't tell you anything about a person's ability to be fair and impartial.'

During my decade as a prosecutor, I tried at least a dozen cases before Judge Long. I am used to his rapid-fire approach to jury empanelment. And I tend to agree with his assessment of the average person's ability to judge fairly. J. Stanley Edgarton III, though, does not. The scowl he wears this morning makes that abundantly clear.

We all agreed there was no need to interrogate the potential jurors about what they've seen on television or read in newspapers. They've all seen the footage and read the reports and the editorials for weeks. Instead, Judge Leon Long asks the first prospective juror if he can disregard what he has heard from the press and base his verdict solely on the evidence presented in this courtroom. Of course he can, the juror claims.

Judge Long asks the next candidate in the box if she understands that Buck Hammond is presumed to be innocent as he sits here in the courtroom today. She is dumbfounded. 'But he isn't,' she blurts out. 'We all saw him do it.'

Buck stiffens between Harry and me. 'Thank you, Mrs Holway,' the judge says. 'Thank you for your candour. You are excused with the sincere thanks of the court.'

Mrs Holway leaves the courtroom in a huff.

Harry and I agreed that I would handle jury selection and he would deliver the opening statement. That way, the jurors will hear from both of us on day one. Judge Long's courtroom clerk, Wanda Morgan, selects a new name from the glass bowl on her desk. The new potential juror comes from the gallery to replace Mrs Holway. His juror résumé identifies him as a fifty-six-year-old restaurant owner. More important, he is the father of three adult sons.

We will select fourteen jurors this morning, including two who will be told—only at the close of the case—that they are substitutes. Judge Long addresses the panel. 'Ladies and gentlemen,' he says, smiling, 'the lawyers handling this case have assured me that this trial will take three days, no longer. That means they'll finish not later than Thursday afternoon, at which time the case will be turned over to you. No one can predict how long your deliberations may take. But I believe we'll all be home for Christmas on Saturday.'

The judge points at Stanley, then at Harry and me, and we all nod our acquiescence.

Next the judge conducts a general inquiry into matters such as the presumption of innocence, the burden of proof and reasonable doubt, then asks each potential juror a series of more specific and more personal questions. Only then do Stanley and I get our turns.

Each of us is allowed two follow-up questions per juror. Stanley begins a third question with every candidate, and the judge cuts him off every time. After our questions are asked and answered, the judge calls upon Stanley and me to state our challenges for cause. I have none. Stanley has just one. Juror number nine should be excused, he says, because she has a seven-year-old son.

'Denied.' Judge Long rules while Stanley is still talking.

'But Your Honour,' Stanley protests, 'I'm not finished.'

'But Mr Edgarton,' the judge replies, 'you most certainly are.'

The jurors laugh at this exchange, and Stanley glares at Judge Long. No prosecutor wants a panel laughing during a murder trial.

'But Judge—' Stanley persists.

'Mr Edgarton, no juror will be removed from this panel—or from any panel in my courtroom—because she is a parent.'

'But her child happens to be a seven-year-old boy.'

'Denied, Mr Edgarton.'

'But Judge . . .'

My gut tells me Stanley just uttered one 'But Judge' too many. Judge Leon Long dons his half-glasses, lifts Stanley's trial brief from the bench, and pretends to examine the signature line. Judge Long has done this before. Harry and I both know what's coming.

'Oh, pardon me,' the judge bellows, his voice thick with sarcasm. 'I must be using the wrong name, sir. You don't seem to understand that I'm talking to you. Mr J. Stanley Ed-gar-ton the Third,' the judge roars, 'your challenge for cause is dee-nied.'

If he is true to past pattern, the judge will call Stanley 'Mr Ed-gar-ton the Third' for the rest of the trial. I swallow a laugh. Harry, of course, looks like the Cheshire cat.

In the end, Stanley gets rid of juror number nine by using one of his three peremptory strikes—challenges each side may exercise without cause, without explanation. The new juror number nine is a young construction worker who does not have a seven-year-old son. But he does have a three-year-old daughter.

Stanley's concerns about the first juror number nine tell me that Harry and I are on the right track. We agreed weeks ago to keep as many parents as we could on the panel, more men than women, if possible. We use all of our peremptory challenges to oust three of the four candidates who don't have children. The one we keep is an elderly woman who never married. She did teach English literature, though, at a private girls' school, for thirty-eight years.

We empanel nine men and five women. These fourteen people will be outraged by what happened to Buck's son, by Hector Monteros's crimes. But they'll be outraged by Buck's crime as well. And his is the only one they will watch played out in living colour.

We're satisfied with our panel. We explain all of this to Buck Hammond before the guards lead him away for the one-o'clock lunch break, but he doesn't seem to care.

I WAS GONE only ten minutes. I stood on the courthouse steps for thirty seconds of fresh air. That was all I could stand. But back in Judge Long's courtroom, it's clear that I've missed something.

Court's in recess. The room is quiet. Harry is seated in the front row of the gallery, surrounded by Buck Hammond's family: his wife, his parents, two brothers, even his in-laws. They all look up at me expectantly, then turn their eyes to Harry. He's supposed to do the talking, it seems.

'You have to open,' he says.

'What?'

Harry arches his eyebrows. He knows I heard him.

'I can't open,' I tell the family members. 'I'm not prepared to open. Harry's ready. He'll open.'

'They think you should open,' Harry says. 'And I think they're right.' He paces the front of the courtroom. 'Judge Long has always liked you. Jurors have always liked Judge Long. And we need every point we can score in this trial.'

Buck's mother steps forward, a petite grey-haired woman with tears in her eyes. 'Please,' she says. 'It might make a difference.'

The pendulum clock on the wall behind the jury box says it's almost one thirty. I have half an hour to prepare the opening statement for the most difficult trial I've ever faced.

'OK. I'll open. That means I'd better get to work.'

The family members head down the aisle, and I set up at the defence table. Harry waits until the last of the relatives is gone, then leans over and brushes his lips against the back of my neck.

The tingle down my spine isn't going to do anything good for my opening statement.

'Get lost, Harry.' I swat at him. 'I have work to do.'

'OK.' He laughs. 'Lucky for you, this old dog needs food. What can I bring you?'

'Coffee.'

'Nothing to eat?'

I turn around to face him, and his expression makes me laugh. Not eating when offered the opportunity is a concept Harry can't grasp.

'Oh, I get it,' he says, headed for the courtroom doors. 'You're every bit as hungry as I am.' He smiles at me over his shoulder, then narrows his eyes. 'But it's the hungry lioness who kills.'

JURY NULLIFICATION. I knew the day it happened that Buck Hammond's defence attorney would ask the jury to nullify the law, to acquit Buck Hammond even though the facts that prove his guilt are uncontroverted. I felt sorry that day for the poor lawyer who would end up in that unfortunate position. I would have felt sorrier if I'd known I was that lawyer.

That's not our stated defence, of course. Officially, we're relying on a temporary-insanity plea. These jurors may conclude that Buck Hammond was insane when he pulled the trigger. We'll present expert testimony to that effect. The jurors might find that Buck was unable, during that isolated time span, to distinguish right from wrong, to conform his behaviour to the requirements of the law.

But generally speaking, jurors don't like the temporary-insanity defence. It's too convenient, too tidy. More important, Buck Hammond doesn't like it. He won't cooperate with that portion of our defence, he says. He'll tell the jurors he knew exactly what he was doing. He'll say that, given the opportunity, he'd do it again tomorrow. Further evidence of insanity, I might have to argue.

Not now, though. Now it's my job to paint with broad strokes, to give these jurors the gut-wrenching facts they should bear in mind as they listen to the prosecution's witnesses. It's my job to invite each one of them to stand in Buck Hammond's shoes as they evaluate the testimony against him. It's my job to help them reach a conclusion they almost certainly won't want to accept: put in Buck's circumstances, any one of us is capable of pulling the trigger.

Stanley ended his opening statement with the television footage of the predawn shooting. The panel sat in silence as they watched the chopper land at Chatham Municipal Airport. The jurors were motionless as Hector Monteros emerged, cuffed, flanked by US marshals. The panel held its collective breath when Buck Hammond stepped from the shadows of the airport's only hangar, six feet away. Not one juror blinked when Buck Hammond raised his hunting rifle and took aim. They flinched, though, when Buck fired and the bullet found Monteros's temple. Not one of them breathed, it seemed, as Monteros bled to death on the airport runway.

Stanley would have shown that videotape a hundred times if he could have. In the pretrial motions, the judge limited him to two runs during the course of the trial. Stanley used the first one today, and my bet is, he'll wrap up his closing argument with the second.

When Stanley sits down, I leave my seat and roll the television table away from the jury box. I station myself in front of the panel.

'Seven-year-old Billy Hammond lived near the beach his entire short life,' I tell them quietly. 'He loved to fish.'

Twenty-eight eyes are glued to mine. These eyes remind me why I once loved the practice of law, why I once believed there was no higher calling. Even now, jaded as I am, I stand in awe of this particular piece of the puzzle that is our criminal-justice system. Whatever failings the system may have—and they are legion—the jury is its jewel. These fourteen conscientious people will struggle with every fibre of their beings to do the right thing.

'On June the nineteenth,' I tell them, 'just six months ago, seven-year-old Billy Hammond went into the kitchen with his fishing pole and bait bucket. He told his mom he was headed to the beach.'

I gesture towards Patty Hammond, who is seated in the front row, behind her husband. The jurors all look in her direction. She's a striking woman, with classic cheekbones and thick brown hair cropped close in a boyish cut. But at the edges of her eyes and the corners of her mouth, the ravages of grief are evident. She is much older than her twenty-nine years, much older than she was on June 18.

'You'll hear from Patty Hammond during this trial,' I tell the panel. Their gazes leave Patty—reluctantly, it seems—and return to me. 'She'll tell you she gave Billy a Popsicle and a kiss that morning.' I pause. 'She never saw him again. And she never will.'

The creak of Stanley's chair tells me he's getting to his feet even before he clears his throat. 'Your Honour,' he whines, 'I hate to interrupt my sister counsel's opening statement. But we're getting off track, I'm afraid. Heading awfully far afield.'

Stanley's objection is bogus. Having raised a temporary-insanity defence, we're entitled to discuss almost everything that had an impact on Buck Hammond's state of mind during the days leading up to the shooting. The objection makes me wonder if Stanley is more worried about the possibility of nullification than I thought.

'I'll allow it,' Judge Long says. 'It goes to the defendant's state of mind, an issue that's paramount in this trial.'

I resume my opening statement. I never uttered a word in response to Stanley's objection, never even looked in his direction. My ignoring him sent a message to the jurors, I hope. J. Stanley Edgarton III doesn't matter, people. Listen to the wise judge. And then listen to me.

'There's a reason Patty Hammond will never see her little boy again, a reason Billy Hammond will never go fishing again.' I cross the room and position myself behind Buck's chair, careful that the jurors can still see both him and Patty. 'There's a reason Billy Hammond will never celebrate his eighth birthday.'

Patty lets out a single sob, and Stanley jumps to his feet, looking personally wounded.

'Sit down, Mr Ed-gar-ton the Third,' the judge says.

Stanley does so with a thud, shaking his oversized head at the jurors, and their eyes move from Patty to him. I had wanted to let their gazes linger on Patty a little longer, but Stanley's theatrics are effective; he's in the spotlight again. I walk toward them slowly and wait until their attention shifts to me.

'Hector Monteros is that reason.'

Stanley jumps up again. 'Your Honour, once more I apologise for interrupting. But my sister counsel is assuming facts that won't ever be in evidence.'

'Not so, Judge,' I tell him. 'Not so.'

Harry knew the day it happened that Buck Hammond's defence would necessitate a post-mortem attack on Hector Monteros. Stanley knows that. So does the judge. Buck Hammond won't necessarily walk if we prove Monteros's guilt, but he doesn't stand a chance if we don't.

Judge Long raises his hands to silence Stanley and me, then turns to the jurors. Instantly he has their undivided attention.

'Ladies and gentlemen,' he says, 'it seems I should explain to you what an opening statement is. But first'—he flashes his smile at them—'I'm going to tell you what it isn't.'

I slip into my seat beside Buck and pour a glass of water. When Judge Leon Long has the stage, there are no co-stars. Stanley, though, seems to expect a supporting role. He remains on his feet.

'Opening statement is not an argument,' the judge says, glancing first at Stanley, then at me. 'Though you wouldn't know that from what you've heard so far.' The jurors laugh, and Judge Long leans back in his leather chair, relaxed and smiling. 'Opening statement isn't evidence either. It's nothing more than each lawyer's opportunity to talk to you.' The judge leans towards them in a conspiratorial pose. 'And we all know how lawyers love to talk.'

The panel laughs again, and so does the judge. Stanley, though, shifts on his feet and runs a nervous hand across his sizable scalp.

Harry leans forward on the defence table to whisper, 'Defer.'

'Defer?' I stare at him.

His return gaze is steady. He's serious.

No defendant, civil or criminal, has to give his opening statement at the beginning of the trial. He can defer until the close of the plaintiff's—or prosecutor's—case. In criminal cases especially, there are distinct advantages to waiting. It leaves the prosecutor in the dark, unsure of the defence strategy until after the Commonwealth rests its case. More important, it allows the defendant to hammer twice on the weaknesses in the evidence against him: after the prosecutor rests and again at the end, in closing argument.

But rarely does a criminal defendant opt to defer. The stakes are too high. If he waits that long to give the jurors a glimpse of his side of the story, it may be too late. The prosecutor may have been too persuasive. Too many jurors may have already made up their minds. Harry knows that at least as well as I do.

'Why defer?'

'You can't do any more.' Harry leans closer. 'You told them enough about Monteros to whet their appetites. The judge told them that Buck's mental state is the key issue in this trial. What else can you accomplish at this point?'

The answer, of course, is nothing. Harry's right.

'But we can't defer now. We've already started. It's too late.'

Harry shakes his head. 'Stanley hasn't let you finish a thought without objecting. Tell the judge you've been interrupted enough for one day. Tell him at this point you'd just as soon defer.'

Judge Long isn't talking to the jurors anymore. He's facing our table, waiting for our whispering session to end. 'Attorney Nickerson,' he says when I look up, 'we're ready when you are.'

I steal a final glance at Harry. 'It's worth a shot,' he says.

Stanley drops into his seat as I get out of mine. 'With all due respect to the court, Your Honour,' I say to Judge Long, 'the defence opts to defer its opening statement.'

Stanley jumps up so fast his chair topples backwards. 'Defer? She can't defer. She's already started her opening statement.'

'Barely. I tried twice, and twice I was silenced. We're not up for strike three. We'll defer.'

I turn towards Stanley, but my attention is on the jury box behind him. They're listening intently to this exchange, some eyes on the judge, others on me. Their expressions are impossible to read.

'Don't believe her,' Stanley sputters. He points his pen at me, then at the judge and the jurors. His forehead vein turns blue. 'I didn't silence her. The National Guard couldn't silence her.'

I'm flattered.

Judge Long peers at me over his glasses. 'Attorney Nickerson,' he says, 'this *is* unusual.'

'It is, Judge. I can't remember another case when I was shut down twice without getting a single fact in front of the jury.'

That wasn't what he meant. But he nods, conceding the point.

'We haven't been able to start, Judge. Not in any meaningful way. And now we opt to defer.'

The judge nods again. 'All right,' he says.

Stanley runs up to the bench. 'You can't be serious.' He points at me again. 'You're not going to let her get away with this.'

'Nobody's getting away with anything. The defendant has the right to defer. It's in the Rules of Criminal Procedure.'

'Not now. Not after his lawyer has already addressed the jury.'

'I've ruled, Mr Ed-gar-ton the Third.'

'But Your Honour'—Stanley is on tiptoe, his eyes barely clearing the judge's bench—'she wants an extra bite of the apple.'

Judge Long leans forward and stares down at him. 'Apple?'

Stanley grabs the edge of the bench with both hands and his knuckles turn white. 'She wants to have her cake and eat it too.'

The judge looks as if he's about to laugh. 'Cake?'

I take my seat. 'I'm no match for this legal argument, Judge. I don't even cook.'

'Enough, Ms Nickerson. Mr Ed-gar-ton,' he says, 'sit down.' Stanley returns to his table and rights his chair. He shakes his head and mutters a barely audible 'you people' before he sits.

Silence. For a moment, it seems no one knows what to do next. Finally Judge Long breaks the quiet. 'Mr Ed-gar-ton the Third,' he says, 'call your first witness.'

'OUR FIRST WITNESS is Chief Fitzpatrick, Your Honour, of the Chatham Police Department.'

Tommy Fitzpatrick strides to the front of the room. Tommy has participated in more trials than most lawyers. He's confident. And he's the consummate straight shooter.

Wanda Morgan, the courtroom clerk, approaches the witness box and holds a Bible in front of the chief. He smiles at her, then puts his left hand on the Good Book and raises his right in the air.

'Do you swear that the testimony you are about to give in this court will be the truth, the whole truth and nothing but the truth, so help you God?'

'I do.'

'You may be seated,' Judge Long tells him.

The chief settles into the witness box and faces the jurors.

Stanley is up. 'Would you state your full name for the record.'

'Thomas Francis Fitzpatrick.'

'And your occupation?'

'Chief of police, Chatham, Massachusetts.'

'Were you on duty in that capacity during the early morning hours of September twenty-first?' Stanley isn't wasting time with preliminaries. There's little more than half an hour left in the trial day. He wants to end with Tommy Fitzpatrick's most damning testimony echoing in the jurors' minds throughout the night.

'I was,' the chief says.

'Tell us, if you would, sir, where you were at approximately four o'clock that morning.'

'At the Chatham Municipal Airport.'

'Who was with you?'

'A half dozen of my own officers and four from the state barracks, two more from a neighbouring town—canine handlers.'

'Anyone else?'

'Just the press. I'm not sure how many reporters and photographers were there.'

'Why was it, sir, that so many law-enforcement officers converged on the Chatham Municipal Airport that morning?'

'We were there to receive Hector Monteros. He was coming in on a military chopper. He'd been picked up at the North Carolina border just before midnight. Federal authorities were escorting him back to Chatham at our request.'

'And why did you make that request, sir?'

Stanley looks at me. He wants to be sure I realise he's raising the issue first—diffusing, to some extent, the impact of this testimony.

'Hector Monteros was the chief suspect in the disappearance of Billy

Hammond, a seven-year-old boy from South Chatham.'

'The boy was the son of the defendant—is that correct, sir?'

The chief looks across the room at Buck before he answers. There is, I think, genuine sympathy in his eyes. 'Yes.'

'And you wanted Monteros for questioning?'

'Well, yes. Initially, we were hoping he'd lead us to the boy—or to his remains.' Again, a sympathetic glance in Buck's direction.

'Did you ever get a chance to question Hector Monteros, sir?'

'No. He was shot as soon as he deplaned. He died on the runway.'

'Who shot him?'

The chief looks towards Buck, not unkindly. 'Mr Hammond.'

'Are you certain?'

He nods. 'Yes.'

Stanley makes eye contact with the jurors. They're with him.

'Were you aware, sir, prior to the shooting, that the defendant was present at the airport that morning?'

'No.'

'What happened after Mr Hammond shot Mr Monteros?'

'Four of us backed Mr Hammond up against the hangar, with our weapons drawn, to prevent him from fleeing the scene.'

'And what did he do?'

'He bent down, laid his rifle on the tarmac, then stood up straight and put his hands in the air.'

'What happened next?' Stanley walks closer to the jury box.

'One of my men seized the weapon. Another cuffed him. He didn't resist. I read him his rights.'

'Did he seem to understand what was going on?'

'Yes.'

'Did he seem to know where he was?'

'Yes.'

'Did he seem to know who you were?'

'Yes.'

Stanley stares at the panel again. He wants them to understand that these one-word responses are important. He'll ask them to recall these answers at the end of the trial, when they evaluate our defence in general, our temporary-insanity claim in particular.

'Did the defendant say anything to you, sir, after you read him his rights?'

Again, the chief looks at Buck before answering. 'Yes.'

Stanley clasps his hands together. 'What did he say?'

The chief takes a deep breath and looks at the panel. ' "I wish he'd get up so I could kill him again." '

THE MOON is almost full tonight. Beams of light shimmer on the salt water at the end of Bayview Road. They light up the beach and the narrow lane, reflecting off the newly fallen foot of snow.

Sonia Baker's cottage, crime-scene tape and all, is bathed in a soft yellow glow. Geraldine's Buick is parked at the curb. Soft lamplight peeks out from behind ivory lace curtains. If it weren't wrapped in that black-lettered tape, the small shingled house would look cosy and inviting on this frigid night.

Geraldine agreed to meet me here. The front door is unlocked. I let myself in, tapping on the inlaid glass to announce my arrival. A white, powdery film covers every surface in the living room—the furniture, the doorknobs, even the windowsills—residue from the print search.

'In here, Martha.'

I follow Geraldine's voice to Maggie's back bedroom. It holds only a single bed, an oval braided rug and an old pine chest of drawers. The walls are covered with the predictable tattered posters of movie stars and rock singers, but otherwise the space is surprisingly neat.

Geraldine doesn't look up when I join her. She's busy filling two shopping bags she's positioned on Maggie's bed, selecting items from the chest's open drawers without hesitation.

'How do you know what to choose, Geraldine?'

She gives me a look and gestures towards the drawers; they're just about empty. No choosing necessary.

'Divine inspiration.' Geraldine empties the last few items from the chest of drawers. She heads for the bedroom door. 'Funny,' she says, walking in front of me, 'you never struck me as the foster-parent type.'

'It's temporary, Geraldine.'

'Temporary?' She throws a sceptical look over her shoulder at me. 'As in until-her-mother-serves-a-life-sentence temporary?'

'No,' I tell her. 'As in until-we-figure-out-who-the-hell-killed-Howard-Davis temporary.'

She shakes her blonde bangs at me. 'Your client killed Howard Davis, Martha. We both know that.'

'I don't think so, Geraldine.'

'He had it coming.' She flicks her bangs again. 'I won't fight you there. If any woman's been battered, she has. And we'll plead it out. But your client's doing time, Martha. Real time.'

Suddenly I'm exhausted. I can't help wondering why it is that Geraldine is always certain of her position and I—no matter which side of the aisle I find myself on—am not.

I take the two shopping bags. 'Thanks for these,' I tell her.

She shakes her head again. I'm apparently a lost cause.

CHAPTER FOUR

Wednesday, December 22

We're delayed this morning. Yarmouth police picked up Dominic 'Nicky' Patterson last night, and he's scheduled to face the music here before our trial resumes. Nicky is one of the Cape's better-known deadbeat dads. He gets hauled in every year or two, signs off on a payment schedule, makes a few instalments, then disappears again. This time the Kydd has been appointed to defend him.

Deadbeat dads are usually handled across the parking lot in family court. There's only one way this particular deadbeat ended up in superior court. Judge Leon Long requested him. One of the county's chronic deadbeat dads is about to face a judge who views supporting one's children as a sacred moral mandate.

The errant father comes through the side door, cuffed, shackled and flanked by armed guards. He looks like he had a rough night. He doesn't know it, but his morning will be worse.

Harry and I move back to the row of seats at the bar. The guards deposit Nicky at the defence table, and the Kydd starts talking to him at once. Nicky isn't listening. He'll regret that in a few minutes.

The bailiff intones his morning litany, and Judge Long strides to the bench. His expression is stern, and he bangs his gavel three times. The room falls instantly silent. The judge glares at Nicky Patterson over the top of his half-glasses.

Geraldine and Stanley are both here. Stanley is leafing through his notes, preparing for today's witnesses, paying no attention at all to the deadbeat dad. Geraldine's on her feet, smiling at Judge Long.

'Mr Dominic Patterson.' Geraldine holds both hands out towards the defendant. 'Need I say more?'

The Kydd gets to his feet. 'Your Honour—'

Judge Long silences him with one hand. 'The charges, Attorney Schilling. Read the charges.'

She does. Nicky has two daughters, now ten and eight. He's been estranged from his wife and the girls for five years. He met his support obligations during the first two, but his contributions since then have been spotty at best. All totalled, he's in arrears more than twenty-two thousand dollars, exclusive of interest.

The Kydd does what he can. There are only so many responses one can make to this sort of charge. Out of work . . . hard times . . . looking for a job . . . The Kydd asks the judge to approve a new payment plan.

'Thank you, Mr Kydd,' Judge Long says, his eyes focused on Nicky. 'Stand up, Mr Patterson.' The judge's voice is uncharacteristically quiet. Nicky gets to his feet, looking like he's about to make excuses. 'I'll tell you what we're going to do, Mr Patterson. We're going to send you home.'

Nicky leans forward, eager to please.

'You're going to be back here tomorrow morning at nine o'clock with a bank cheque for twenty-two thousand dollars.'

Nicky swallows his smile. 'I ain't got that kind of money, Judge.'

'Then get it, Mr Patterson. After you deliver the bank cheque, I'll enter an order that allows you to pay off the interest over time.'

The Kydd is trying to bring an end to this session, but Nicky won't budge. He's shaking his head at Judge Long. 'Get it where?'

'What do you drive, Mr Patterson?'

'Chevy pick-up. Two-fifty diesel.'

'Old?'

Nicky hesitates. 'Not really. A year.'

'Sell it.'

The Kydd elbows Nicky Patterson out from behind the table and shepherds him towards the centre aisle.

'Nine o'clock sharp,' the judge says to Nicky's back. 'Oh, and one more thing, Mr Patterson. You show up without that cheque, you'd better bring your toothbrush.'

OUR JURY is sequestered. From now until the verdict is returned, the members of the panel will hear none of the media hype. The press will try its case in the court of public opinion, but I will try mine only in this courtroom, before the men and women who will decide Buck's fate.

Sequestered jurors seem to meld. Twelve strangers, with nothing in common but the case before them, somehow take on a single personality as soon as they are quarantined. Some panels are reserved and distant. Some are angry. Others are warm, sympathetic.

Ours is worried. Worried about convicting a man who has already suffered so much. Equally worried about not convicting a man who shot another in cold blood. It's all written on their faces.

They file through the side door, their expressions tense, sober. Judge Long greets each of them, his radiant smile back where it belongs. He invites them to take their seats, and the crowd in the gallery sits as well. Every bench in the courtroom is full.

Chief Tommy Fitzpatrick reclaims the witness box. The judge reminds him that he is still under oath, and the chief nods.

The jurors have had all night to reflect on the testimony Stanley elicited yesterday. No doubt Buck's words—'I wish he'd get up so I could kill him again'—echoed in their minds throughout the night. Now it's my job to make the jurors understand those words. It's my job to make them feel what Buck felt that morning. None of us can, of course. But the chief of police is going to help.

'Chief Fitzpatrick, tell us what happened to Billy Hammond.'

Stanley clears his throat and stands, then heads for the bench. 'Your Honour, this isn't about the boy.'

I turn to the judge. 'That's *all* it's about, Your Honour.'

Judge Long puts his hands in the air to silence us. 'I'll allow the testimony, but I'm going to give them a limiting instruction.'

I return to my seat. A limiting instruction is fine with me as long as the facts come in. By the time the chief of police tells the story of Billy Hammond's death, the limiting instruction should be a distant memory. And the jurors, I hope, will use the evidence to conclude that justice, albeit a rough justice, has already been served.

Stanley pauses at our table on the way back to his seat. 'This judge,' he whispers, glaring at me as if I had personally appointed Judge Long to the bench, 'is despicable.'

'Ladies and gentlemen,' the judge says, 'the defendant has raised a temporary-insanity defence. The testimony you are about to hear is relevant to the defendant's state of mind and should be considered by you when you evaluate that defence. It should not be considered for any other purpose.'

Buck lowers his head to his arms on the table, and Harry rests a hand on his shoulder. Buck and Patty will have to listen to this testimony too. The chief's words—essential for Buck's defence—will bring him and Patty to their knees. Again.

'Chief Fitzpatrick, you led the investigation into the disappearance of Billy Hammond, did you not?'

'I did.'

'Tell us, sir, what prompted that investigation.'

'The nine-one-one dispatcher got a call from a woman at about eleven o'clock that morning. It was a Saturday—June nineteenth. The caller was hysterical. Turned out to be a summer neighbour of the Hammonds. She'd been weeding her garden, she said, and had spoken with Billy as he passed her house on his way to the beach.'

Stanley stands and clears his throat. 'Your Honour, we're headed for unadulterated hearsay.'

There are twenty-three exceptions to the hearsay rule, and this testimony arguably falls within three of them. One, though, is a perfect fit. I face Judge Long again.

'Excited utterance, Your Honour. The statement is admissible if it relates to a startling event, made while the speaker was still under the stress of the moment.'

Judge Long looks at the jurors, then at Stanley, and finally at me. 'I'll allow it.'

I face the witness box. 'Chief, you were telling us about a conversation between Billy Hammond and his neighbour.'

The chief looks comfortable in the witness chair. He enjoys the ease of a man who plans to tell the truth.

'Yes,' he says. 'The neighbour told Billy he looked like he'd grown three inches since she'd seen him last. Billy laughed and said he probably had. She turned back to her weeding but stood up a few moments later to stretch. She was facing the beach at the time. She saw Billy approach a van idling at the far end of the parking lot. He was reaching out to pat a dog in the front seat. Then Billy vanished. She ran to the beach, but the van peeled off before she got there. She found a fishing pole where the van had been.'

'Billy Hammond's fishing pole?'

'Yes. His mother identified it.'

The members of the panel turn towards Patty. Her eyes are wide, tear-filled, all the horror of that moment written on her face.

'What happened next?'

'Well, as I said, it was a Saturday. One of my men called me at home, and I joined the officers at the scene. The neighbour had the presence of mind to memorise the van's licence plate. We traced the plate immediately. Then I alerted the state barracks, and they set up checkpoints. We didn't want that van leaving Cape Cod.'

'Did it?'

The chief shakes his head. 'No. A state trooper found it the next day in a thicket of bushes at the Cape Cod Canal. Empty.'

'Let's back up a moment, Chief. You say you traced the plate. What did you learn?'

'The van was registered to a Hector Monteros. We did a background check on him, then put out an APB.'

'What did the background check tell you about Monteros?'

Stanley jumps up. 'Objection, Your Honour!'

'Counsel'—Judge Long waves his arms like a traffic cop— 'approach.'

Stanley and I hurry to the judge's bench.

'Where are you going with this, Counsel?' Judge Long directs his question to me in a whisper.

'Monteros was on the county's registry of known sex offenders, a repeat paedophile. State of mind, Judge. That information was conveyed to the parents—to the defendant—before Monteros was arrested. Surely it goes to state of mind.'

Judge Long shakes his head. 'No way. I'll allow testimony about what happened to this child. That's all. No prior acts.'

Stanley sits, and I return to my post in front of the jury box. Twenty-eight eyes search mine. They want to know what information I'm being forced to swallow. They want to know what I know—what Buck Hammond knew—about Hector Monteros.

I'd like to tell them to remember this moment as they listen to the chief's testimony. I'd like to tell them to read between the lines, to fill in the blanks, to figure it out for themselves.

I can't say any of those things. Not now. Not ever.

'You told us yesterday, Chief, that Hector Monteros was the main suspect in the disappearance of Billy Hammond.'

'That's right,' he answers.

'Who were the other suspects?'

'There weren't any other suspects,' he says.

'Never? To this day?'

He nods. 'To this day.'

'You also told us you were hoping—initially, at least—that Monteros would lead you to Billy Hammond, correct?'

'Yes.'

'That wasn't necessary, though, was it?'

'No. We found the boy,' the chief says. 'We found his body. Early Monday morning, the twenty-first, at about half past one.'

'Where did you find Billy Hammond's body?'

Water pouring from pitcher to glass is the only sound in the room. Silence surrounds us, weighs on us, while the chief sets the pitcher down and pauses for a drink. 'We had canine units working the canal, two of them—one on each side. They started combing the area late in the day Sunday, as soon as the van was located. One of them found the boy's body. It was buried in a shallow grave, under thick brush, about a hundred yards behind the power plant.'

The jurors are silent, their eyes riveted to the witness box.

'Tell us about Billy's body, Chief. What condition was it in?'

Stanley's creaking chair tells me he's getting up again. 'Your Honour, please. This is nothing but inflammatory.'

Judge Long shakes his head. 'I've already ruled on this, Mr Ed-gar-ton the Third. The information is relevant to the defendant's state of mind, and I'll allow it for that limited purpose.' The judge turns towards the witness box. 'Chief Fitzpatrick, keep it brief. Just the facts.'

The chief nods up at the judge. His eyes rest on Buck before he faces the panel. 'The boy was bound and gagged,' he tells them. 'Naked. An oil-stained towel was stuffed in his mouth. Thin metal cables were twisted around his ankles and wrists.' The chief takes a deep breath. 'There were no other marks on his body.'

Two jurors in the front row close their eyes. The other twelve don't move a muscle. I wait until all eyes are open and on me; then I turn to face Buck and Patty. Buck's head rests in his arms on the table, his body rigid. Patty lifts her face skyward, eyes closed, cheeks drenched. Neither one of them makes a sound.

The chief wipes his eyes. 'Twenty-seven years I've been on the force. I've never seen anything worse.'

'Objection!' Stanley's face is beet red, his forehead vein bulging.

'Sustained!' Judge Long isn't happy either. 'Chief Fitzpatrick, answer only the question asked. Give us the facts, nothing more.'

The chief looks up at the judge, wiping his eyes again. 'I'm sorry, Your Honour. I apologise.'

Judge Long turns to the panel. 'The jury will disregard the witness's last statement.'

They nod at him, compliant.

'How did you know the dead child behind the power plant was Billy Hammond, Chief?' I ask Tommy Fitzpatrick

'Well, we felt pretty confident about it from the start. Everything fitted. We couldn't say for sure, of course'—the chief gestures towards Buck—'until his father identified the body.'

I cross the room again to stand behind Buck, who manages to lift his head from the table to face the chief. 'When did he do that?'

'Right away,' the chief says, looking back at Buck. 'Mr Hammond was waiting at the morgue when the body arrived—at about two forty-five that morning. We'd called from the road and asked him to meet us there so we could get a positive ID as quickly as possible. We'd also called the coroner in to do an immediate autopsy. Mr Hammond identified his boy before it started.'

'Were you present when Mr Hammond identified his son?'

'I was.'

'Describe for us Mr Hammond's demeanour at that time.'

The chief speaks directly to the panel. 'He collapsed. Fell to his knees, then put his face down on the floor, his cheek pressed against the linoleum. I knelt beside him, said I was sorry. Hell of a thing to say to a man at a time like that. Words are no good sometimes.'

'What did Mr Hammond say?'

'Mr Hammond didn't say anything. Banged his head against the floor. Kept banging it, harder each time. It took three of us to stop him.'

'What happened next?'

'He quieted. He got up and sat on a bench in the hallway outside the autopsy suite. Said he wanted to wait. To wait for Billy, he said. I assumed he meant wait for the coroner's report on Billy. He was still sitting on that bench when I left the building.'

'Chief Fitzpatrick, why did you leave the morgue?'

'I'd just gotten a call from my dispatcher. The army chopper transporting Monteros was in transit, due in Chatham a little before five. I needed to call in extra officers, make preparations.'

'And when was the next time you saw Mr Hammond?'

'When I went back. He was sitting in that same spot on the bench outside the autopsy suite. I don't think he'd moved.'

'Why did you go back to the morgue, Chief?'

'To talk to the coroner. I wanted to issue charges before Monteros landed. Didn't want to wait for the written autopsy report.'

Buck lowers his head to the defence table again. I leave his side and walk towards the jury box. 'Charges against Hector Monteros?'

'Yes.'

I lean against the wooden railing, facing the jurors. 'After speaking with the coroner, Chief, how many charges did you file?'

'Three.'

I study the jurors as they stare at the chief. 'What were they?'

'First-degree murder. Kidnapping. Forcible rape of a child.'

I travel the length of the courtroom again, back to Buck's side, and face the jurors in silence. I want them to look at me. Then I turn my eyes to Buck.

They do too.

Silence. I want them to look hard at this man, to digest the fact that on the morning of June 21, he received the same information they just did. I want them to imagine what it was like for him, receiving that information about his little boy. I want them to react.

But they don't.

'Chief, what was the cause of Billy Hammond's death?'

'Asphyxia. The medical examiner found minute haemorrhages in the lungs and heart, meaning death was caused by a lack of oxygen. The boy suffocated.'

'Did you give Mr Hammond that information while you were both at the morgue?'

'Yes.'

'Did you tell him what specific charges you planned to file?'

The chief nods and turns back towards the jurors. 'Yes, I did. I felt I owed him that much. Otherwise he and his wife—they'd hear it on the radio. Or on TV. I couldn't let that happen.'

'How did Mr Hammond respond?'

The chief shakes his head. 'He didn't. He never said a word.'

'Your office later received the results of DNA tests conducted on both Monteros and Billy Hammond, is that right, Chief?'

'Yes.'

'Tell the panel what was found beneath Billy's fingernails.'

'Skin fragments,' he says. 'The coroner scraped skin fragments from under the boy's fingernails. DNA testing established that Hector Monteros was the source. The boy fought for his life.'

At least half of the jurors shift in their seats, look away from the chief. Their faces are closed; they don't want to hear any more.

But I have one final, burning point to hammer home.

'When Billy Hammond disappeared, Chief, did you open a file? A file you'd need to consult until the investigation ended?'

He seems surprised by the question. 'Well, of course.'

'What's the current status of that file?'

The chief stares at me for a moment, a glimmer of understanding in his eyes. Then he turns to the panel and looks slowly at each person. 'It's closed.'

THE CONFERENCE ROOM looks like a paper-recycling centre gone amok. Documents, manila folders and legal pads litter the table, chairs and floor. A half-dozen courthouse-generated printouts hang from the ceiling-high bookcases, thumbtacked at eye level.

The Kydd sits in the midst of it all, sleeves of his wrinkled shirt rolled up to his elbows. He's immersed in a file and doesn't look up when I join him.

'A little light reading, Kydd?'

He points with his file towards the printouts. 'Any of these guys could've done Howard Davis. They all had trouble with him. And they're all up to the job. I started with the most recent releases.'

That makes sense. Whoever murdered Howard Davis was enraged. If it was one of his parolees, it was almost certainly a recent release. Not someone who wasted much time planning; not someone who weighed the pros and cons in any detail.

I sink into an old chair, and the Kydd leans back in his. 'Howard Davis got six new assignments during the past four weeks.'

I look towards the printouts. 'Anybody interesting?'

The Kydd leans forward and points to one of the shorter printouts. I recognise the intensity in his eyes. He's onto something.

'Yep,' he says. 'Frank Sebastian. Out three weeks and hauled in for violating parole. Failed to check in with Davis when he was supposed to. Got off with a warning. He screwed up again, though—big this time. Knocked over a gas station with two other thugs late Sunday night. The station owner fingered them in a photo line-up on Monday. Old Frank's going back to the big house. Trouble is, he hasn't been picked up yet. He's running.'

A low whistle sails into the room. Harry fills the doorway. 'You're good, Kydd,' he says, throwing his jacket and briefcase on top of the cluttered table. 'You're damn good.'

The Kydd grins. 'Damn good' is Harry's highest praise.

'Anything from the lab?' Harry drops into the chair next to mine, loosening his tie.

'Not yet,' I tell him. 'Geraldine says we'll have everything by the end of tomorrow.'

The chance of finding a match with Frank Sebastian is slim to none. Pointing a finger at a third party to create reasonable doubt is one thing. Proving that the third party is guilty is another. It happens only in Hollywood scripts and *Perry Mason* reruns.

'We do have a small problem,' the Kydd says, his tone apologetic. 'When Sebastian got hauled in the first time, for failing to report, our friend Stanley wanted to lock him up. It was Howard Davis who convinced Judge Long to give Sebastian another shot. Davis told the judge to ignore Stanley, said Stanley would lock up every last Boy Scout in the county if he could.'

Harry and the Kydd laugh, and I reluctantly join them. It's really not funny, though. The prosecution will have a party with that information. We'll end up arguing that Frank Sebastian murdered the one guy who spoke up for him. Sometimes I hate this business.

Harry leans over and gives me a pretend punch on the arm. 'Not a big deal,' he says. 'Davis wasn't going to give Sebastian a break on this one. And Sebastian knew that. That's why he's on the run.'

'Listen to this.' The Kydd's grinning again, holding up the transcript. 'Stanley told Judge Long that he had no discretion. Stanley said the judge was duty-bound to send Sebastian back to prison; the rules don't allow for anything else.'

Harry laughs again. 'The rules according to Stanley?'

'He told the judge he shouldn't listen to Davis, that Davis is a disgrace to the criminal-justice system.'

Harry leans back in his chair, hands behind his head. 'I hate to agree with Stanley about anything, but he's got a point there.'

'What was the ruling on that one?' I ask.

The Kydd shakes his head, his grin growing wider. 'Judge Long didn't respond. But Howard Davis did. Davis asked the judge, "Where the hell'd you find this little guy?"'

We're all laughing again. Harry looks sympathetically at the Kydd. 'You know you've had a bad day,' he says, 'when you feel a kinship with Howard Davis at the end of it.'

'End of it?' the Kydd says. 'I've got two more files to review.'

'Not tonight, you don't.' Harry stands and takes his wallet from his back pocket. 'You look like hell,' he says, pushing a fifty into the Kydd's shirt pocket. 'Go get a steak.'

'What? I don't want a steak.'

'Then get a lobster,' Harry says. 'You look like hell,' he repeats. 'Get out of here.'

The Kydd puts his hands in the air, surrendering. 'OK, OK.'

Harry slaps him on the back and heads for the steep staircase that leads to his first-floor apartment. The Kydd starts packing his briefcase. I head up to my office to do the same.

The Kydd's car is barely out of the driveway when the door between my office and Harry's living space opens a crack. 'Hey, Marty,' Harry whispers. 'Come here a minute.'

I open the door, and Harry whisks me inside, closing it behind us.

Harry's living room, normally something of a mess, is transformed. It's uncluttered, lit only by the glowing logs in the fireplace. On the coffee table is an ice bucket, a fine Fumé Blanc perspiring in its cubes, and two wineglasses. A long-stemmed yellow rose (my favourite colour) stands tall in a vase between them. The mellow sounds of a saxophone drift softly through the room.

'One hour,' Harry says, slipping both arms around my waist and pulling me close. 'Let's take one hour . . . for us.'

My mind jumps back to the image of Harry stuffing a fifty in the Kydd's shirt pocket. I feel like a high-school senior whose prom date just bought off the little brother. I look up into Harry's hazel eyes. 'You're good,' I tell him. 'You're damn good.'

CHAPTER FIVE

Thursday, December 23

By the time Buck's trial was a week away, I had almost convinced myself that my misgivings about the temporary-insanity plea were irrelevant. The only meaningful thoughts on the matter, I told myself, are those of the experts: members of the medical and psychiatric community. Surely Mr Justice Paxson would agree.

He didn't.

Physicians, especially those having charge of the insane, it would seem, have come to the conclusion that all wicked men are mad, and many of the judges have so far fallen into the same error as to render it possible for any man to escape the penalty which the law affixes to crime.

We do not intend to be understood as expressing the opinion that in some instances human beings are not afflicted with a homicidal mania, but we do intend to say that a defence consisting exclusively of this species of insanity has frequently been made the means by which an offender has escaped punishment.

One thing seemed certain the night I read those words. Harry should handle the experts.

THE JUDGE is missing. Buck Hammond is seated, and the attorneys are ready. Today's witnesses are present, and the press is hyperactive. The jurors aren't here yet, though. There's no judge to call for them. It's almost nine thirty.

Stanley is agitated. He must have arrived later than usual this morning; his hair is still wet from his morning shower. Even so, he beat Harry and me to the courtroom.

The crowd in the gallery has grown impatient and noisy. Harry and I are seated at the defence table, leaning back in our chairs and laughing. Stanley fires an admonishing stare in our direction, mouthing 'you people' before averting his eyes. It seems that J. Stanley Edgarton III disapproves of our lack of decorum.

But Harry and I have good reason to laugh. We know where Judge Leon Long is. It's Thursday morning before Christmas. He's in traffic court, ripping up parking tickets, bestowing his annual gift upon the citizens of Barnstable County. And Geraldine, no doubt, is enduring the festivities. Too bad Stanley couldn't join them.

Stanley did, though, receive a small surprise of his own this morning. When Harry and I set up at the defence table, Stanley was flustered. He informed us that he had arrived early, though not as early as usual, and had found the courtroom dark, as it always is when he arrives. But when he flipped the switch that lights the old courtroom's four ornate chandeliers, he found Nicky Patterson already seated on the front bench, waiting in the darkness.

'He made himself right at home,' Stanley complained. 'You'd think he owned the place.'

I wondered who Stanley thinks does own the place.

'It's OK,' Harry consoled him. 'He doesn't look like he's having a good time.'

And he doesn't. Nicky is still seated on the front bench, biting his nails and pulling an envelope from the inside pocket of his jacket, checking its contents. The Kydd isn't here yet, and it's clear from the darting of Nicky's eyes—from the clock to the back doors to the clock again—that he doesn't want to face Judge Leon Long alone. Whatever he's got in that envelope, it isn't enough.

The Kydd rushes into the courtroom. He nods at Nicky, and Nicky waves to him as if greeting the Messiah. The Kydd stares at the empty judge's bench as he heads for our table. 'He's not here?'

'Not yet,' I tell him.

'The electricity went out. My alarm didn't go off,' the Kydd says.

This happened more than once last winter. I explained to him several times that ocean winds wreak havoc with overhead wires. On Cape Cod, I told him, wintertime electricity is a gamble. A battery-operated alarm clock is a must. Obviously, he wasn't listening.

Harry tosses his head towards Nicky. 'Does he have the twenty-two thousand?'

The Kydd pulls a chair up to our table and drops into it, leaning forward and lowering his voice. 'Turns out child support isn't the only unpaid bill. He owes more on the damned truck than it's worth.'

Harry laughs. 'That's a shock,' he says. 'So what's he got?'

'Half.'

'Judge Leon Long isn't going to like this.'

The Kydd points his pen at the empty bench. 'Speaking of Judge Leon Long, where the hell is he?'

Harry grins. 'Think, Kydd. And take a look at your calendar.'

The Kydd pulls a monthly planner from his briefcase, opens to December, then laughs. 'Damn,' he says, 'I wanted to watch.'

'Don't worry,' I tell him. 'Geraldine will memorise the details, and it'll be May before she stops raving about Judge Leon Long's annual obstruction of justice.'

As if on cue, Geraldine blasts through the doors and strides down the centre aisle. She stops at the defence table and points out of the window, towards the district courthouse. 'I need a judge.'

Harry leans back in his chair, smiling at her. 'Get in line.'

'I'm not kidding,' she says. 'If he's going to play this little game every year, he needs to show up. It's standing room only in that courtroom, and there's no judge.'

Harry straightens in his chair, his smile erased. My stomach tightens, and I get to my feet, though I'm not sure why.

Geraldine heads towards chambers, Stanley on her heels like a nervous poodle. She pounds on the door. No answer.

Geraldine opens the door and disappears, but Stanley doesn't follow. He freezes in the doorway and screams.

I'm in chambers before I realise I've moved. The judge's desk chair is swivelled towards the door. Judge Leon Long is sprawled on the floor in front of it. Face-down on the plush carpeting. A knife in his back.

GERALDINE slams the phone into its cradle. Help should be here in minutes.

Harry and the Kydd stand side by side in the doorway to Judge Leon Long's chambers, forming a blockade against the press corps. Even so, bright lights from television cameras and erupting flashbulbs flood the room. Photographers strain against each other for a shot of Judge Long's prostrate form. From behind them, reporters shout questions to Geraldine and me.

'Is the judge dead?'

He's not, but we don't say so.

'Is he breathing?'

He is. I'm on my knees beside him, holding his hand in both of mine. His pulse is weak but detectable 'You're going to be OK,' I whisper. 'Help is coming. You're going to be fine.'

I hope I sound more certain than I am.

Seconds later, four emergency medical technicians appear. They crowd into the small chambers, two of them steering a stainless-steel gurney, the others carting sacks of equipment into the room, unpacking as they move.

Geraldine and I emerge into the courtroom to find Harry, the Kydd and Stanley lined up at the judge's bench in stunned silence. A barrage of Barnstable police officers has arrived, and they've pushed the noisy onlookers into the gallery.

Two court officers lead Buck Hammond towards the side door. Buck's gaze meets mine as he approaches the doorway. His eyes ask, Why Judge Long? And why now?

The police clear a path down the centre aisle just in time. The EMTs hustle through with Judge Long's motionless body. They disappear into the hallway, and the courtroom's back doors slam shut behind them.

Abruptly the room is silent, its occupants still.

Stanley is the first to emerge from paralysis. He walks slowly from the judge's bench towards the gallery. He raises one hand and points a stubby index finger at Nicky Patterson.

'You,' Stanley whispers. 'It was you.'

Nicky is still in his original front-row seat. His eyes grow wide as Stanley approaches, and he clutches his envelope, as if he thinks Stanley might take it from him.

A police officer materialises at Stanley's side. SERGEANT D. B. BRIGGS, his badge says. Geraldine joins the pair, her pale green eyes fixed first on Stanley, then on Nicky Patterson.

'Officer,' Stanley calls out, 'arrest this man.'

The Kydd snaps out of his trance next. He rushes towards the gallery, glaring at Stanley. 'Arrest him? For what?'

'For the murder of a superior court judge who was about to put him behind bars.'

'Judge Long isn't dead,' I say. No one pays attention.

The Kydd grabs Stanley by one elbow and spins him around. 'What the hell are you talking about?'

'He was the only one here.' Stanley's answer isn't directed towards the Kydd. He's speaking to Geraldine and Sergeant Briggs.

'What do you mean?' The Kydd gestures to the crowd. 'There are hundreds of people in this room.'

Stanley shakes his big head. 'Early this morning,' he says, still addressing Geraldine and Sergeant Briggs, 'I found him sitting on this bench in the darkness when I arrived. Alone. He was alone with the judge—the same judge who told him to bring his toothbrush, I might add—and now the judge has been murdered.'

'Judge Long isn't dead,' I repeat. Still, no one seems to hear.

Stanley wheels back towards Nicky, pointing again. 'You don't have it, do you? You don't have the twenty-two thousand dollars. Judge Long was going to put you away, and you knew it.'

The Kydd towers over Stanley. 'That's ridiculous,' he says, looking down at Stanley's comb-over. 'If he'd murdered the judge, he'd have gotten the hell out of here. He wouldn't have sat on the front bench waiting for the rest of us to find the body.'

Stanley doesn't look at the Kydd. He faces the half-dozen uniforms now surrounding Nicky. 'What are you waiting for? I just told you people that this man attacked a superior court judge. Arrest him.'

Nicky gapes at the cops. Sergeant Briggs turns a questioning eye towards Geraldine. No one's taking orders from Stanley.

'You people,' Stanley says, folding his arms across his chest.

Geraldine stares at Nicky. 'Take him in,' she says.

'You can't be serious.' The Kydd faces Geraldine. This is his first battle with our former boss.

Geraldine almost smiles. 'Your client had motive, Mr Kydd. He had opportunity. And his opportunity was exclusive.'

Geraldine turns to Nicky, who's now cuffed, then looks back at the Kydd. 'I'm quite serious, Mr Kydd. Quite.'

JUDGE BEATRICE NOLAN was appointed to the superior court bench fifteen years ago. She brought along a fiery temper. She's a narrow woman— truly. Her shoulder-length dark grey hair is the texture of steel wool. Severe features—pinched eyes and anaemic lips—punctuate her long face. Her complexion, though, is uncommonly smooth for a woman her age. Not a laugh line in sight.

The chief judge called upon Beatrice this morning to preside over the remainder of *Commonwealth v. Hammond*. He postponed a civil suit that was scheduled to begin in her courtroom today. I'm certain she didn't appreciate his meddling with her schedule. Beatrice Nolan doesn't like criminal cases. They're messy.

The chief judge gave Beatrice our trial briefs and the list of exhibits already admitted into evidence. He asked her to spend the balance of the morning reviewing them. Then he directed the court reporter to begin printing the transcript of the testimony received so far. And he told the rest of us to stay put.

After lunch, the chief judge moved our entourage into Judge Nolan's cramped courtroom. It's a former storage area, windowless and dank, at the back of the ground floor. The only real courtroom in the building is off-limits. It's a crime scene.

Stanley rolled his TV table into our new venue at once. He positioned his star witness against the judge's bench, facing the jury box. Stanley can barely wait to show his videotape again.

Judge Nolan emerges from chambers in a huff, and her bird eyes dart around the room before settling on our table. They confirm what Harry and I already know: She's not happy about her new assignment. And she knows we're not either.

Harry and Beatrice have a history.

When young Harry Madigan arrived in Barnstable County fresh out of law school, Beatrice Nolan took notice. That was twenty years ago. Beatrice was already ten years into her private practice. She offered to take Harry under her wing. Show him the ropes. Harry says she scared the daylights out of him. Even then, when her hair was brown.

Turns out, the ropes Beatrice wanted to show Harry had nothing to do with the practice of law. She began cornering him at county bar association meetings. She started monopolising him at the local watering hole, the Jailhouse. She stood too close, Harry says, touched him too often.

Twenty-six-year-old Harry Madigan was mature about it, of course. He hid.

Harry quit going to county bar association meetings. At the Jailhouse, he switched chairs as soon as Beatrice sat down. But Beatrice Nolan was not deterred. She left messages with his secretary, proposing coffee, lunch. She plastered notes on his windscreen, suggesting after-work cocktails, a movie, perhaps.

Harry admits he didn't handle it very well in the end.

He went to the Jailhouse one night. He scanned the place for Beatrice. He didn't see her, so he settled on a stool at the bar.

Another newly graduated attorney, a young woman Harry had noticed around the courthouse more than once, sat a few stools away. She smiled at him when he arrived. He was planning his opening line when Beatrice approached from behind.

Beatrice latched onto his shoulders and massaged, Harry says, until he squirmed off the stool and out from under her grasp. The young attorney disappeared into the crowd.

That's when he lost it. Harry claims not to remember his exact words, but he told Beatrice Nolan to keep her hands to herself. Then he told her to get lost. And he wasn't quiet about it. The bar crowd hushed. Beatrice froze. He blasted her.

And she hasn't spoken a civil word to him since.

Most county employees don't know about the scene at the Jailhouse. Even old-timers have forgotten about it. But Beatrice hasn't.

When I first started working at the DA's office, my co-workers routinely referred to Harry as 'that big guy Judge Nolan throws in jail all the time.' I didn't believe it. Not until I saw it for myself. I've tried a half-dozen cases before her. In half of them, Harry Madigan was my opponent. All three times, he landed in jail.

We're stuck. Beatrice Nolan is our judge. Worse, she's Buck Hammond's judge. And there's not a thing we can do about it.

JUDGE NOLAN issued a stern greeting to our jurors as they took their seats and surveyed their new surroundings. She told them Judge Long had fallen ill and would be unable to continue the trial. Their faces registered concern for Judge Long, disappointment for themselves. The atmosphere in this courtroom is decidedly darker than that in Judge Long's. And it's not only because the room has no windows.

Stanley could barely wait to begin. Beatrice Nolan is his kind of judge, a courtroom drill sergeant. She consistently handles criminal defendants by the book. And then she throws it at them.

The meat of Stanley's case came into evidence on Tuesday. He got all he needed to establish the elements of first-degree murder: A man is dead. The defendant killed him. The killing was premeditated. Stanley also got a prosecutorial bonus—it all happened on TV.

Today Stanley needed to establish one final element: sanity. Because we've raised the issue, it's incumbent upon the Commonwealth to prove that Buck Hammond was sane at the moment he pulled the trigger. Stanley closed his case this afternoon with two expert witnesses—Malcolm Post, a Johns Hopkins-educated psychologist; and Dr Sheldon Turner, Professor of Psychiatry at Tufts Medical School—who said exactly that.

Harry cross-examined both men, which didn't take long. No lawyer can do much with an adverse witness who's a competent expert. Both experts conceded that Buck Hammond had suffered the ultimate human tragedy just hours before the shooting.

Stanley declined redirect and thanked both experts repeatedly for their testimony. Then, with his tiny eyes beaming and his stance triumphant, he rested his case. It's time—at last—for my deferred opening.

I walk towards the jury box. 'Ladies and gentlemen.'

Beatrice's gavel pounds a half-dozen times. It sounds like an angry woodpecker. 'Counsel,' she barks, 'what are you doing?'

'Getting started on our case,' I say. 'The Commonwealth just rested.'

'I'm well aware of that, Counsel.' The judge leans back, arms folded across her robe. 'Call your first witness, Ms Nickerson.'

'But Your Honour, we haven't opened.'

'You most certainly have.'

'No, we haven't, Judge. We deferred.'

Beatrice holds up her copy of the trial transcript. 'You did no such thing.'

'Your Honour, if you'll give me a moment'—I move to the bench and reach up for the printout—'I'll show you the spot. The defence opted to defer opening. Judge Long allowed it.'

Beatrice yanks the transcript backwards with both hands. 'Judge Long is not presiding over this trial, Counsel.' She enunciates each word carefully, as if she's speaking to a dull-witted child. 'I am.'

I stare at her, and I realise this isn't about me. And it's not about Buck Hammond. It's about Judge Nolan. She holds the reins in this courtroom. She wants us to know that her power is absolute.

'You addressed the jury, Counsel. If you didn't say everything you should have said, that's too bad. But it's your problem, not mine. You don't get a second shot.' She leans towards me and bangs her gavel, just once, for emphasis. 'Not in *my* courtroom.'

Harry gets to his feet. He shakes his head at me. There's no point in trying to reason with Beatrice. Let's get on with the case.

Harry buttons his suit coat as he leaves the table. 'Your Honour, the defence calls Dr Martin Simmons to the stand.'

The doctor heads for the witness box. Harry moves towards the front of the room and leans towards me. 'I could be wrong,' he whispers, 'but I don't think she likes you.'

DR MARTIN SIMMONS is chief of psychiatry at Massachusetts General Hospital. He's a handsome man in his mid-sixties, with a friendly manner. His sympathy for Buck and Patty is genuine.

The doctor told the panel that Buck was in the midst of a psychotic episode when he shot Hector Monteros. 'An individual suffering a psychotic episode experiences impaired contact with reality during a specific period of time. The individual's mind is severed from the real world.'

'Before we get into the specifics, Doctor, can you tell the jury what precipitated his psychotic episode?'

Stanley stands. 'Your Honour, we've heard all this before.'

'Approach.' Judge Nolan shakes her head at Harry as he and Stanley near the bench. She leans towards them. Her pinched expression says she doesn't know what Harry's up to, but she's sure it's nothing good. 'Mr Madigan, where are you going with this?'

I wonder why the judge bothered to call a sidebar. She hasn't lowered her voice at all. If I can hear her, then the jurors can too.

'Where am I going?' Harry doesn't lower his voice either. 'My client has raised a temporary-insanity defence, Your Honour. This is our expert psychiatrist. I'm *going* into the relevant facts.'

Stanley clears his throat. 'Your Honour, the chief of police testified at considerable length about the boy. We don't need to hear it again. Besides, it's inflammatory.'

'Inflammatory?' Harry's shouting now. 'Of course it's inflammatory.' Harry wheels around and points at Buck, then looks at the jury. 'This man's son—an innocent seven-year-old child—was raped and murdered. You bet it's inflammatory. Inflammatory enough to push a reasonable man over the edge. That, Judge'—Harry turns and glares at Beatrice again—'is the point.'

Judge Nolan sits up straight. 'Lower your voice, Counsel.'

'I'll do no such thing, Judge.' Harry turns and points at Buck again. 'You have no right to shut down this man's defence.'

Now he's done it.

The judge holds up both hands, palms out, to call for silence. She removes her bifocals, leans on her elbows, eyes closed, and massages first the bridge of her nose, then her right temple. Harry Madigan, not ten minutes into his direct, has given her a migraine.

Finally the judge opens her eyes. 'Mr Madigan,' she says, 'no one is shutting down this man's defence. But I will shut you down, sir, if you get on your soapbox again.' She points at Dr Simmons. 'If your witness has a medical opinion, Mr Madigan, you'd better get to it. This case is about the shooting dead of Hector Monteros. We're not here to belabour the details of an unrelated murder.'

'Belabour the details? Unrelated murder?' Harry's bellowing now.

He turns to look at me, and it's my turn to give him a sign—an index finger pressed vertically against my lips. It means shut up and go where she's pushing you; we need the medical opinion. Continue this argument later.

Harry frowns at my signal and clenches his teeth. After a moment, though, he nods and sighs. He turns and walks towards the witness box. 'Dr Simmons, did you examine Mr Hammond at my request?' Harry's voice is almost normal now; he's working at it.

'I did.' The doctor looks puzzled, then relieved. He doesn't know why the battle ended, but he's glad it did.

'When did you examine him, sir?'

The doctor opens his chart on the ledge of the witness box. 'September the tenth, sixteenth and twenty-fourth of this year, for about two hours each time. October eighth, a little longer that day.'

'More than eight hours of clinical evaluation?'

'That's right.' The doctor leans back in the chair.

'Did you reach a conclusion about Mr Hammond's mental state on the morning of June twenty-first, the morning of the shooting?'

'I did. As I said, Mr Hammond suffered a psychotic episode that morning. It was a limited episode in that he lost contact with a fragment of reality—and had a jumbled perspective on other fragments—but he didn't lose everything. He was still functioning.'

'Which fragment did he lose?'

'His son's death. Mr Hammond's mind rejected it outright.'

'Denial?'

Dr Simmons shakes his head. 'No. It wasn't that. Denial is a normal reaction to death—particularly a death so unexpected. What Mr Hammond experienced that morning was an actual break from reality. In his world, the boy's death hadn't happened.'

'And which fragments were jumbled?'

'The events of the prior forty hours. With the exception of his son's death, every event was clear in Mr Hammond's mind when he stood beside the airport hangar that morning. But the timeline was mixed up; the occurrences were out of order.'

'For example?'

'The most obvious example was also the most significant: his son's abduction. Mr Hammond knew Billy had been grabbed by a dangerous man. He knew his boy's life was in jeopardy. But he had no handle on how long the boy had been gone.'

'And he didn't know his son was dead?'

'No.' Dr Simmons takes a deep breath. 'When Mr Hammond raised his rifle that morning, he believed he was fighting for his son's life. It's hard to understand. I know that.' He gestures towards the defence table, as if the best evidence of what he's telling them is seated here. The jurors' eyes follow, settle on Buck.

He's sitting upright, dry-eyed, staring straight ahead. He looks like a man whose mental universe is nowhere near this courtroom.

Harry paces in front of the witness box, one fist against his mouth. The expression on his face worries me. If I'm reading him correctly, he's about to buy a one-way ticket to lockup.

He stops pacing, and his face registers a decision. 'Doctor, you say Mr Hammond knew the man who abducted his son was dangerous. Can you be more specific?'

Dr Simmons looks surprised. He wasn't in the courtroom when Judge Long excluded the evidence. He assumed the jury already knew. 'The police told him,' he says.

Stanley rouses, but not fast enough.

'They told him they'd traced the van's licence plate to a Hector Monteros. They told him Monteros was a violent sex offender.'

Stanley erupts. 'Objection, Your Honour! Objection!'

The doctor keeps talking. 'On the mandatory registry,' he explains. 'A repeat paedophile.'

'Your Honour! Objection!' Stanley stamps both feet repeatedly. A bona fide temper tantrum. Everyone else in the room is quiet. The jurors appear frozen, their eyes locked on the witness box.

Beatrice pounds her gavel. Stanley's blue forehead vein is pounding. He's shrieking at Beatrice, his voice an octave higher than usual. But Beatrice is on her feet, pointing her gavel at Harry.

'Mr Madigan, your examination of this witness is over. One more word, and I'll hold you in contempt. You can spend Christmas behind bars. And I wouldn't make plans for New Year's Eve.' The judge turns her icy stare on Dr Simmons. 'The county can provide accommodation for you as well, Doctor, if need be.'

The doctor's eyes grow wide. 'Me? What did I do?'

This is a first. Beatrice sends Harry to the pokey with a great deal of ease, but as far as I know, she's never threatened to throw his witness in with him.

Harry looks at me—that look that always takes my breath away—as he takes his seat. He's satisfied, happy even. He'll gladly serve whatever time Beatrice metes out, holidays or not.

STANLEY'S CROSS-EXAMINATION of Dr Simmons was by the book. Stanley scored a few points, but lost a few too. This doctor has been cross-examined before. He's pretty good at it.

A few minutes past four, Judge Nolan excuses Dr Simmons, and he heads for the side door, keeping his eyes at all times on the judge. Good instincts.

It was a decent day for the defence. The expert witnesses cancelled each other out. One side's experts said Buck knew what he was doing; the other side's said he didn't. This is usually the way it plays out in insanity cases. The jurors will probably disregard the psychiatric testimony. They will decide Buck's fate based on other factors and hang their hats on the insanity plea only if necessary.

Harry is packing his day's trial notes. He uses a schoolbag to cart his files back and forth to the courthouse, and he has it open on our table. I give him an elbow. When he looks up at me, I move my eyes to the judge. She's glaring at him.

'What are you doing, Mr Madigan?' Beatrice leans forward.

'Packing up?' Harry looks down at his schoolbag, checking to make sure he's not doing something criminal instead.

'And why would you be packing up, Mr Madigan?'

Harry stares at Beatrice, waiting for her to identify his misstep.

'This courtroom adjourns at five thirty, Mr Madigan, not a moment sooner.'

Her message is clear: She calls the shots now. We're not in Judge Leon Long's courtroom anymore.

'Call your next witness,' she says.

Our next witness is Patty Hammond, but I had planned to call her in the morning. I don't want to call her now. I need to walk her through the testimony one more time before she takes the stand. Aside from Buck, she's our most important witness. She shouldn't be called so abruptly; she shouldn't be rattled.

Stanley wheels around in his chair and stares at me, a savage glee in his eyes. He knows I'm sweating.

I'm searching the recesses of my brain for a reason to delay, one old Beatrice will at least consider, when I feel a hand on my arm. It's Patty, on her feet and leaning over from the front row. 'It's OK,' she says, her eyes dry, her voice calm. 'I'm ready.'

CHAPTER SIX

The room is silent while Patty Hammond makes the trip from the front row to the witness box. She's wearing black slacks, a white turtleneck and a grey sweater. Small coral starfish rest on her ear lobes, and a pewter locket hangs from a chain around her neck. Her short auburn hair is brushed back away from her face. She has a fresh-scrubbed look—fair skin with a few freckles, no make-up.

Patty takes the oath, then perches on the edge of the witness seat. She faces the jurors and nods, then turns to me. Her gaze is steady. She looks sad, as always, but at ease. She really is ready.

We walk through the preliminaries smoothly. She is Patricia Lowell

Hammond, and she lives on Bayview Road in South Chatham. She was born and raised here on the Cape. She is the wife of the accused and the mother of the deceased child. 'Billy,' she tells them, fingering her locket. 'His name is Billy.'

All of the women on the panel nod at Patty; then most of the men do too. The boy's name is important; he's real. They understand that. Finally, a genuine reaction.

I have always been of two minds about Patty Hammond's testimony. On the one hand, I want to prolong it, keep her on the stand as long as possible so the jurors can get to know her. I want them to care so deeply about Patty Hammond that they will be unable to subtract her husband from her world, a world already diminished.

On the other hand, I know that Patty's composure is fragile. And she needs to be clear when she tells the jury about the hours before and after the shooting. She needs to be certain about what Buck did—and didn't—say. She needs to be strong when she faces Stanley's cross-examination.

Better to get to the heart of the matter.

'Let's start on Sunday, Patty, June twentieth, the day after Billy disappeared. Where were you that Sunday evening?'

'Home,' she says. 'Sitting at the kitchen table. I'd been there since . . .' Patty swallows. 'Since it happened.'

'Doing what?'

She shrugs. 'Staring at the phone.'

'And your husband?'

'Searching. He'd been searching for Billy since the police left the day before. They told him not to, but Buck had to go, had to try. He came home around nine on Sunday evening for just a few minutes. Then he left again, to search some more.'

'Did you hear from your husband later that night?'

Patty nods. 'Twice. He called first around midnight to ask if I'd heard from the police.'

'Had you?'

She shakes her head. 'No.'

'He called again after that?'

'Yes,' she says. 'At one thirty.'

'One thirty Monday morning? You're certain of the time?'

'I am.' Patty turns to the panel. 'I looked at the clock as I picked up the phone. When I checked again, the minute hand had barely moved. It seemed like hours had passed.'

'What did Buck tell you during that call? The second one.'

Patty swallows and cups each hand around the opposite elbow, pressing her arms against her stomach. These aren't the most difficult questions, but we're moving in that direction. She's bracing herself.

'He was at the Chatham police station. He said he'd driven back into town to ask the police for an update. He was hoping they'd unearthed some clue. He said he needed to look someone in the eye, to ask his questions in person.'

'Did he?'

'He did go to the station, but he didn't ask any questions.'

'Tell the jury why not.'

Patty takes a deep breath. 'Turns out the sergeant in charge was dialling our number when Buck walked up to the front desk. The chief had called in from the road. They'd found the body of a young boy near the bridge, behind the power plant. They thought it might be Billy.' She looks down at her lap and shakes her head, then continues. 'The truth is, they were pretty confident that it was. The chief wanted Buck at the county morgue as soon as he could get there.'

'To identify the body?'

Patty bites her lower lip. 'Yes.'

I pause to fill a water glass and set it on the ledge in front of her. She mouths a silent thankyou.

'Did you know at the time how long it would take to drive from the station to the county morgue?'

She shrugs. 'Forty minutes, maybe.'

'Was Buck leaving the station as soon as he finished talking with you?'

Patty shakes her head. 'He'd already left. He called from the truck phone. He was on the Mid-Cape Highway.'

I walk towards the jury box and face the panel. 'Patty, when was the next time you spoke to your husband?'

'He was in jail. They let me in around noon.'

I pause so the jurors can do the maths. 'Ten hours later?'

'That's right.'

I turn to face her but stay close to the jury box, my back to the panel. When Patty looks at me to answer these next few questions, she will necessarily face the jurors as well. And that's important.

'He didn't call in the interim?'

She's quiet for just a moment. 'No. He was arrested a little before five.'

'But you didn't know that at the time.'

'That's right. I got a call from Chief Fitzpatrick at ten thirty. He'd just learned that Buck had refused to phone anyone. He called to tell me what happened. He thought I should know, he said.'

'Did you try to reach your husband between one thirty and ten thirty?'

She's perfectly still. 'No.'

'Nine hours. What did you do during that time?'

Patty blinks, looking as if she's never considered this question. 'I'm not sure. I don't think I did anything. I don't think I moved.'

'Patty, your husband went to the county morgue to view the body of a little boy. You knew it might be Billy. You knew the cops thought it was. But you let nine hours go by without so much as a phone call.' I pause. 'Why?' Patty returns my stare for just a moment, her eyes brimming, then sets her jaw and shifts her gaze to the jurors. 'Because I knew.'

'Knew what?'

'I knew the little boy in the morgue was Billy.' Patty bites her lip again and fingers her locket. Her tears flow freely. 'I don't know how I knew. But I did. I knew as soon as I hung up the phone at one thirty. My heart ached. I knew.'

I scan the panel. They're frozen.

Patty takes a deep breath. 'I also knew time was running out. The time when it wasn't certain. The time when there was some part of me that could pretend it wasn't Billy. I clung to that.' She raises a hand towards the jurors, then presses it against her forehead. She wants them to understand. 'I knew that once I talked to Buck, the uncertainty would be gone. And I clung to the uncertainty like a life ring; it was all I had.'

I scan the panel again. No visible reaction.

Stanley clears his throat. 'Your Honour, the defendant's wife isn't on trial. Is counsel trying to prove that she was insane too?'

The juror's eyes move from Patty to Stanley. The courtroom is quiet while Beatrice waits for me to respond to Stanley's objection. It takes a few moments for her to realise I won't.

'Counsel,' she says, 'move on.' Even Beatrice Nolan has enough common sense not to bully Patty Hammond in front of the panel.

'Patty, what did Buck say when you saw him in jail at noon?'

'He didn't say anything. We just looked at each other through the glass. Neither one of us said anything. There weren't words.'

'When was the next time the two of you spoke?'

Patty tilts her head to the side. 'A few days later. I visited every day, but a few days went by before we spoke.'

'Did you ask your husband why he shot Monteros?'

Stanley gets to his feet.

'No,' Patty says. 'I didn't have to.'

'Your Honour . . .' Stanley wants to shut this down. The judge does too, apparently. She has her gavel in hand.

I nod at Patty, hoping she'll finish her thought. She turns to the panel, her eyes wide, but says nothing.

'You didn't have to?'

'No. I knew why.' Patty looks at the jurors as if she just realised something important. 'My husband isn't a murderer.'

'Your Honour!' Stanley's forehead erupts.

The gavel descends, but I ignore it.

The jurors seem to ignore it too. They're zeroed in on Patty. She stares back and speaks directly to them, as if no one else is in the room. 'Buck had to do it. Don't you see?'

More than a few heads shake in the box. Maybe they find it all too hard to take in. Or maybe they don't see.

'Your Honour!' Stanley's holding both hands up to halt Patty's words.

'He didn't have a choice,' Patty says, speaking to the jurors as if Stanley doesn't exist. 'He had to help Billy. Had to try.'

The gavel descends again, on the edge of the bench closest to the witness box. Patty jumps. Her eyes look up at the judge. The jurors' do too.

Beatrice isn't facing Patty or the jury, though. Her gavel pounds again, near the top of Patty's head, but she's glaring at me. 'Ms. Nickerson, this examination is over.'

She's right, of course. We're finished. I couldn't have scripted better testimony to end the day. Better, though, to let Beatrice think it's her idea. 'Whatever you say, Judge. You're the boss.'

LUKE AND MAGGIE, who had been shopping, were in the back row of the courtroom during all of Patty Hammond's direct testimony. It wasn't by design. When I asked them to be here at four o'clock—with the

Thunderbird—I thought we'd all be ready to leave the courthouse by then. But that was this morning, when Judge Leon Long was in charge. Everything is different now.

Buck is gone, en route to his cell with the regular prison escorts. Harry and I will meet with him before we go home tonight, to review his testimony one last time. We had planned to go back to our office first, to run through it a time or two without Buck. We wanted one last search for an inconsistency Stanley might see before we do.

But Judge Nolan just left the bench, and it's almost six o'clock. Harry and I will have to do our consistency check while we prepare Buck. We're running out of time.

Patty is at our table, seated in Buck's chair between Harry and me. She looks dazed now, exhausted. Her cheeks are flushed.

Luke and Maggie wait in their seats while the stragglers in the crowd move through the back door. When they head up front to join us, Geraldine strides through the back door and follows them down the wide aisle. She sets her briefcase on the edge of our table.

'Good news,' she says, 'about the judge.'

'She's stepping down?' Harry bolts from his chair. 'Early retirement?' He faces Geraldine. 'Not a health problem, I hope.'

She frowns at him. 'Not that judge. No, she's not stepping down. And no, there's no health problem.' Geraldine's frown flips into a wicked smile. 'But Judge Nolan would be touched if she knew you were so concerned.'

Harry shrugs. 'She's touched, all right.'

'Judge Long,' I prompt. 'He's OK?'

'Looks like it. They're moving him to the intensive-care unit now. The doctors expect to move him to a regular surgical unit sometime next week. He should make a full recovery.'

Patty leaves her chair and moves in front of our table to hug Maggie. Maggie hugs her back, hard. I'd almost forgotten—they're neighbours. Maggie leans into her, welcoming the support.

'He was stabbed twice,' Geraldine continues. 'The first wound was deep—it missed a kidney by little more than an inch. The surgeon says it needed extensive repair.' She stares at me, her eyes troubled. 'The second cut wasn't, though. It was superficial.'

Geraldine's brows knit. I know that look. The information she's giving us bothers her somehow. Something doesn't add up.

'The surgeon says it looks like whoever attacked Judge Long was interrupted,' she says. 'Prevented from finishing the job.'

Harry narrows his eyes at her. 'And it's your theory that Nicky Patterson stabbed the judge twice, stopped when Stanley arrived, then sat calmly in the front row until the rest of us found out?'

Geraldine doesn't let on that she hears Harry's question. 'I'm headed to the hospital now,' she tells us.

'Is he awake?'

'Not yet,' she says. 'But I want to ask him a few questions as soon as he is. Find out if he saw anything, heard anything.'

'The nurses might not let you in, though.'

'The nurses and what army?'

Luke and Maggie head out as soon as Geraldine leaves. Patty does too. She'll follow them to Chatham, she says, in case Luke has trouble driving on the snowy highway. Or in case she does, she adds. It will be at least a few hours before I can join Luke and Maggie at home. It feels as if this day will never end.

Snow falls steadily as Harry and I trudge through drifts in the parking lot, then climb the steps to the Barnstable County House of Correction. Harry's arm around my shoulders is the best thing I've felt all day. When I lean into him, he rests his chin on the top of my head. If only I could spend this evening with Harry—alone.

But we part company. Harry heads to the men's ward, and I turn towards the women's. Harry will start the process with Buck while I spend some time with Sonia. I'll join them when I can.

Harry has always thought the temporary-insanity plea was Buck's best bet. True jury nullification, he says, is rare. And he's right. For our jurors to return an outright acquittal, they'll have to be willing to say that the law in this particular case is just plain wrong. Rare is the juror willing to adopt that notion. Rarer yet is the juror willing to say so. The odds of an entire panel taking that route are slim. Even I have to admit that.

If the jurors accept the temporary-insanity plea, on the other hand, they can have it both ways. They can send Buck home, even though they acknowledge he committed the crime. They know he's not innocent, but they can find him not guilty—the law allows that.

Harry and I have known from the beginning that Buck should testify. It's critical that the jury hear from him. If he had opted to keep quiet, we would have done our level best to change his mind. But that wasn't necessary. From day one, Buck insisted he would take the stand, insisted he would tell the jurors what happened that morning from where he stood in the shadow of the airport hangar. And he never wavered from that decision.

I'm glad. Glad it's Buck's decision. Glad he's so sure about it. It's Buck, after all, who will live with the outcome.

IT'S ALMOST ten o'clock by the time Harry and I reach Cape Cod Hospital. Two security guards eye us from the front desk, then exchange wary glances. It's plain from their expressions that they don't like what they see. And I don't blame them.

Harry looks like an unusually well-fed refugee. An old tan coat hides his suit. A day's worth of salt-and-pepper stubble covers his cheeks and chin, and dark half-moons underline his bloodshot eyes.

I don't need a mirror to tell me I look every bit as bedraggled as Harry does. Even my soul is tired.

One of the guards checks our IDs. The other one rides the elevator with us to the second floor, clutching a two-way radio.

Geraldine sits in the small waiting area outside the intensive-care unit, writing in a notebook. It's a rare sight—Geraldine in a chair. She looks no different now than she did at nine o'clock this morning. Her dark grey suit and starched white blouse are unwrinkled, and every blond hair is in place. I don't know how she does it.

She stops writing as we approach. 'Good of you to drop in,' she tells us, 'but His Honour isn't receiving guests at the moment.'

Harry drops into a chair next to Geraldine's. 'Is he awake?'

'No. But he was a couple of hours ago—for a few minutes.'

'Did he say anything?'

'Not a word. But he tried. He couldn't get anything out. His throat is sore from the tubes or whatever they put down there during surgery. The poor guy's dying of thirst. He kept reaching towards the water pitcher, but the nurse—she'd only give him ice chips. So he went back to sleep.'

She gets to her feet and starts pacing. Her expression suggests she's shifting gears.

'The lab work,' Geraldine says. 'It's back.'

I take a few steps towards her. 'The blood?'

'All Sonia Baker's,' she says.

Harry arches his eyebrows at me. This is good news.

I turn my attention back to Geraldine. 'And the prints?'

She smiles. 'All Sonia Baker's.'

This news is not so good.

A large woman in white fills the small entry to the waiting area. She folds her arms beneath her substantial bosom and frowns. Her nametag reads ALICE BARRYMORE, RN. 'The judge is awake again,' she says in a full baritone. 'But I'm not taking a crowd in there.'

Geraldine stares at her. 'Crowd? What crowd?'

Nurse Barrymore tips her grey bouffant towards Harry and me.

Geraldine looks over her shoulder at us as if she hadn't realised we were in the room. 'Oh, them.' She flicks one hand at the giant nurse, directing her out of the doorway. 'They won't say a word.'

For reasons I've never been able to articulate, people obey Geraldine. Nurse Barrymore follows as Geraldine leads the way down the brightly lit corridor. Harry and I bring up the rear.

It's high noon in Judge Long's small compartment. Fluorescent tubes beam down from above. Machines hiss and beep from every direction. A brightly lit monitor displays four lines of constantly changing graphics. And it must be eighty degrees. It's hard to imagine anyone sleeping here.

Judge Long lies perfectly still on his hospital bed, his head and shoulders elevated, a thin white blanket pulled up to his chest. Two IV bags drip from a pole at his bedside. He turns his face towards us as we approach, his eyes open and pleading. He lifts his left hand just an inch, towards the opposite side of his bed, towards the water pitcher.

'No water,' the nurse says. She takes a small paper cup and scoops a spoonful of ice chips between her patient's parched lips.

Geraldine is all business. 'Try,' she says to the judge. 'Try to tell us what you know.'

Judge Long makes a guttural sound. It sounds like 'Hndt.'

Harry moves to the head of the bed and squats so his face is level with Judge Long's, and the judge gives it another shot. It sounds no different to me, but it's clear at once that Harry gets it. 'Hand,' he says. 'He saw a hand.'

Judge Long nods, then lifts his head from the pillow. 'Mnz.'

'A man's hand,' Harry translates.

The judge nods again. 'White.'

We all got that.

With considerable effort, the judge raises one arm and presses his hand against his shoulder, forcing his upper body farther down on the pillow. His assailant must have braced him from behind with one hand, stabbed with the other.

'Anything else?' Geraldine has her notebook open, pen poised, but so far there's not much to write.

We all stare at Judge Long. 'Tis,' he says. He points to the bottom of his bed, wiggles his foot.

'Shoes?' Harry asks. 'You saw his shoes?'

The judge nods.

Geraldine clicks the pen, tucks it in her pocket, and rolls her eyes to the ceiling. 'So we're looking for a white guy with shoes.'

'That narrows it down.' Harry grins at her. He turns back towards Judge Long. 'Attorney Schilling has Nicky Patterson in custody. The deadbeat dad,' Harry tells him. 'She thinks he's the perp.'

The judge squints at Geraldine, shakes his head.

'Nicky Patterson was there,' Geraldine answers. 'He's a white male. And I'm pretty sure he was wearing shoes. I haven't heard anything here tonight that rules him out.'

'You don't have anything to rule him in,' Harry says.

'Keep your voices down.' The nurse intends to usher us out.

'Everything rules him in,' Geraldine hisses.

'Shut up. All of you.' The three of them turn my way. Their eyes follow my index finger to Judge Long. He's silent, but his eyes aren't. He shakes his head at Geraldine, mouths 'No.'

'Never argue with opposing counsel,' I tell Harry, 'if the judge will do it for you.'

LATE AS IT IS when I get back to the cottage, I am unable to resist the allure of Mr Justice Paxson. Once more, I centre his words under my desk lamp, the only light on in the house. I flip ahead to his discussion of the defendant.

Orfila has said that the mind is always greatly troubled when it is agitated by anger, overcome by despair, haunted by terror, or corrupted by an unconquerable desire for vengeance. Then a man is no longer master of himself. His reason is affected; he is like a madman.

But in all these cases a man does not lose his knowledge of the real relations of things. His misfortune is real, and if it carry him to commit a criminal act, this act is perfectly well motivated.

And in the near darkness of my bedroom, I realise that this is precisely my concern. One truth about Buck Hammond is beyond debate. His misfortune is real, and if it carry him to commit a criminal act, this act is perfectly well motivated.

CHAPTER SEVEN

Friday, December 24

J. Stanley Edgarton III's cross-examination of Patty Hammond, so far, has been matter-of-fact. Patty admitted that she had no contact with her husband between the moment he viewed their son's body and the moment he shot Hector Monteros.

Stanley should leave it at that. He has all he needs to argue that her testimony is irrelevant. But Stanley wants more. He paces the front of the courtroom, hands clasped behind his back, his blue forehead vein throbbing.

'So you have no personal knowledge, Mrs Hammond, regarding your husband's state of mind during those early morning hours?'

Patty stares at him as if he couldn't possibly mean what he just said.

'Oh, but I do,' she says, turning to the jurors. 'I may be the only person who does.'

'Objection!' Stanley's outburst is so loud, Patty jumps.

I'm up. 'To what? Your own question?'

Stanley turns towards the bench, his back to the jurors. 'The witness's answer is nonresponsive! Move to strike!'

Beatrice nods.

'Motion opposed.' I stay planted behind the counsel table. 'Counsel asked a question, and the witness answered. He doesn't get to strike her response because he doesn't like it.'

The jurors look from me to the judge, their faces blank.

Beatrice fixes her gaze on me. 'The motion is granted, Counsel. Your witness's answer was indeed nonresponsive.'

'Let's have it read back—the question and the answer.' I direct my suggestion to the court reporter, a pale, pencil-thin man in black suit, white shirt and string tie.

'We'll do no such thing!' Beatrice bangs her gavel, her bird-like eyes darting from me to String Tie and back again. 'Ms Nickerson, whose courtroom is this?'

This is a fact I don't mind pointing out to the jury. A reminder. 'This courtroom, Judge, belongs to the citizens of the Commonwealth of Massachusetts.'

'Who is *in charge* in this courtroom, Ms Nickerson?'

'Oh'—I smile up at her—'that would be you.'

She swivels her chair to face the jury box. Apparently, my read-back suggestion is rejected. And I'm dismissed. 'Ladies and gentlemen, you will disregard the witness's last answer.'

The jurors stare at the judge, their expressions still unreadable.

Judge Nolan turns towards Patty. 'Henceforth, the witness will confine her answers to respond to the questions posed. No extraneous comments. Do you understand me, Mrs Hammond?'

Patty shakes her head. 'I guess not,' she says.

Judge Beatrice Nolan doesn't like that answer. She clamps her lips together and leans towards the witness box, nostrils flaring.

Patty actually recoils.

Beatrice opens her mouth to speak, but Stanley intervenes. 'Your Honour,' he says, 'I have no further questions for this witness.'

Beatrice looks at me, her eyebrows knitted into one.

'No further questions from us, Judge. Patty Hammond said it all.'

Beatrice fires a threatening look in my direction before announcing a recess. She's off the bench even before the bailiff tells us to rise.

Harry saunters the length of our table, stops when he reaches my chair, and points at the bench. 'I could be wrong again,' he says, shaking his head, 'but I think you're headed for the cell block.'

IT DOESN'T APPEAR that the break did anything good for Beatrice Nolan's disposition. She ascends to the bench wearing a sour expression. She swivels her chair towards the jury box and studies the wall behind it as the jurors file in and take their seats.

At least she's not staring at us. Buck is sitting up straight, composed, hands folded and steady on the defence table. He's ready to testify. He doesn't need eye contact with our ill-tempered judge.

'Ladies and gentlemen of the jury . . .' Beatrice leans back in her chair, one hand on an armrest, the other fingering her gavel, just in case. 'It's time for the attorneys to deliver their closing arguments.'

Harry and I jump up. For a split second, we're both speechless.

Harry recovers first. 'Whoa,' he says.

It's not much of a recovery. 'Whoa' isn't a word normally bandied about in the courtroom.

Beatrice bolts forward. 'Whoa?' She lifts her gavel from the bench and holds it midair, like a tomahawk she might hurl at any moment. 'Did you say 'whoa', Mr Madigan?'

Harry winces. 'I did, Judge. But that's not what I meant.'

Beatrice lowers the gavel slightly, cupping its head in her hand. 'I'm glad to hear that, Mr Madigan.' She glares at Harry. 'Enlighten us, Counsel. What *did* you mean?'

'What I meant to say was: Excuse me, Your Honour, but the defence didn't rest.' Harry takes a step towards the bench. 'We have one more witness, Judge. Mr Hammond, our last witness.'

'Mr Hammond?' Beatrice looks like she's just been told a potted plant will testify.

'The defendant.' Harry points at Buck, and Buck raises his hand, as if the judge might not know who he is.

Beatrice grimaces. 'Counsel, approach.'

Stanley and Harry get to the bench before I do, but Judge Nolan doesn't feel compelled to wait. It doesn't matter. She's loud enough to be heard in the far corners of the small courtroom. It's becoming pretty clear that Beatrice calls these sidebars to keep her comments off the record, not to conduct any sort of private discussion.

'What's going on here, Counsel?'

'What's going *on* here?' Harry looks mystified. 'The defendant is ready to take the stand. That's what's going *on* here.'

Beatrice's nostrils flare. 'What does he plan to say?'

'You can't ask me that.' Harry's steaming.

'I most certainly can. I'm the judge.'

'I don't give a damn who you are. I'm the defence lawyer,' Harry booms. He points a thumb over his shoulder at Buck. 'And he's the defendant. That means he has a right to testify on his own behalf without giving a sneak preview to the prosecutor.'

Beatrice leans forward. 'He has no right to commit perjury.'

'Perjury?' The word escapes Harry and me simultaneously.

'And you people have no right to suborn it.'

'You people?' Again, we're in unison.

'Did you explain the penalties for perjury to your client, Counsel?' Beatrice's eyes shift from Harry and lock with mine.

'Why would we do that, Judge?'

Beatrice stands, leans completely over her bench, and pats the top of Stanley's television set. She holds my stare, her eyes fierce. 'I've seen this videotape, Counsel. Pictures don't lie. If your client plans to contradict the content of this film on the witness stand, then he plans to commit perjury. And I won't allow it.'

She folds her arms but doesn't wait for a response. 'And if he doesn't plan to contradict the content of the videotape, then his taking the witness stand is foolhardy. Have you so advised him? If you haven't advised against his taking the stand, you're incompetent. I'll remove you from this case.'

'Remove—'

'If you have, and he's not listening, you're ineffective. I'll remove you from this case.'

Beatrice has thought this through.

Hundreds of people are crammed into this room, and not one of them moves. The only sound to be heard is Beatrice's laboured breathing. Her eyes invite me—dare me—to fight.

I turn away from her and walk towards old String Tie. His eyes meet mine for just a second. *Leave me out of this*, they say.

'The defence calls Mr William 'Buck' Hammond to the stand.'

No one moves, not even String Tie. I stand in front of his machine and point my pen at him. 'You were supposed to type that.'

He looks from me to the judge, uncertain, then starts tapping the keys. She may be the judge, but I'm close enough to hurt him.

'Ms Nickerson, did you not hear my questions?'

'I did, Judge. I heard your questions, and I heard your threats.'

Beatrice takes an audible breath as I turn to face her. 'There were no threats, Ms Nickerson, but I'd like to hear answers to my questions, if that's not too much trouble.'

I take my time walking back to the bench. 'You just did. The defence calls William 'Buck' Hammond to the stand.' I signal Buck to his feet and point towards the witness box before fixing my gaze on Beatrice. 'That's our answer, Judge, to all your questions.'

Buck is halfway across the courtroom before Beatrice bellows again. 'Just a minute, Mr Hammond.'

He pauses, looks at me; I tell him with my eyes to continue.

Beatrice bangs her gavel, but Buck pays no attention. He finishes his trip and settles quietly in the box.

'Counsel, what are you doing?'

'I'm calling my client to the witness stand, Judge.' I move away and walk towards the jury. 'You want to stop Mr Hammond from taking the stand in his own defence, go ahead and do it. But I won't let you do it in a fictional sidebar.' I point at Buck in the witness box. 'You want to shut this man down, Judge, you're damn well going to do it on the record.'

Beatrice's mouth opens, but no sound emerges. I move towards the bench and lower my voice, confident that the jurors can hear. 'And you'll be reversed before you call your next case.'

Beatrice straightens in her chair and purses her lips. 'It was never my intention to shut Mr Hammond down, Counsel.'

This is news. I turn and raise my eyebrows at the jurors, but they don't react. When I look back at the judge, she's waiting for me. Her lips barely move when she speaks.

'The courtroom clerk will swear the witness.'

Beatrice's eyes speak volumes. She'll give me this battle, they say, but the war is a hell of a long way from over.

EVERYTHING about Buck Hammond says he has nothing left to lose. He's allowed to wear his own clothes during trial, but they don't fit anymore. His grey suit jacket hangs loosely, its cuffs too wide for his wrists. His black trousers are baggy. He's not permitted a belt; no shoelaces or tie either. He wears an old pair of scuffed loafers and a white starched shirt, unbuttoned at the neck. A dark shadow of stubble covers his cheeks, chin and neck. His black hair is ragged at the edges. Dark circles underline his eyes.

Buck could be a physically imposing presence—he's taller than Harry by a couple of inches—but his shoulders, a match for any linebacker's, sag as if taxed by a burden the rest of us can't see. His light grey eyes, wide and moist, reveal little and ask less. It's not that he has no questions. It's that the questions—the few that still matter to Buck Hammond—have no answers.

He will ask to go home, though. Buck will ask these jurors, in his own muted way, to send him back to his South Chatham cottage. He'll make that request for Patty's sake, not his own, but he'll make it just the same. And it's my job to give him the opportunity.

The task is simple. We'll start with questions that allow Buck to describe his life before June 19. The jurors will hear about a solid family man who went to work every day and ate dinner with his wife and son every night. They'll hear about a man born and raised on Cape Cod who, until six months ago, never had a single encounter with the law. And then they'll hear how all of that changed.

Stanley, of course, is a problem. His forehead vein is throbbing and he's perched on the edge of his chair, prepared to pounce. He might object, it seems, before I ask my first question.

Judge Beatrice Nolan will be all too eager to sustain Stanley's objections. She's another problem.

'Mr Hammond, please state your full name for the record.'

'William Francis Hammond. People call me Buck.'

Stanley's chair creaks, and he clears his throat. When I turn to look at him, he mouths the word 'hearsay'.

He can't be serious.

He flutters his fingers in the air. He'll let it slide, he's telling all of us. Just this once. He's a reasonable guy.

When I turn away from Stanley and face the witness box again, Buck's expression is calm. He's waiting patiently for my next question, unconcerned with his prosecutor's posturing.

Buck is right. Stanley is irrelevant. His petty antics don't matter. And my preliminary questions don't matter either.

These jurors know who Buck Hammond is. They know where he lives; they've met his wife. They can guess his age, and they don't give a damn how he makes his living. They know what he did to Hector Monteros. The only thing that matters now is why.

I head to our table and take two photographs from my briefcase. Eight-by-ten laminated glossies of Billy. One before. One after.

Buck hasn't seen either one of these photos. He took the before shot but was jailed before it was developed. The after shot was taken during Billy Hammond's autopsy. Standard procedure.

Ordinarily, it's not a good idea to surprise your own witness on the stand.

But this was no ordinary murder; it's no ordinary trial. The rules—most of them, anyway—don't apply here.

Harry sets up an easel where both Buck and the jurors can see it. I tuck the autopsy shot under my arm, careful that only its white backing is visible against my jacket. I set the other photo on the easel and pause so they can take it in: Billy on the beach, beaming, a glorious sunset behind him. He holds a surf-casting rod in one hand, a three-foot-long shimmering fish in the other.

'Can you identify this photograph?'

Buck stares at the glossy and blinks repeatedly as his eyes fill. 'Yes,' he says finally. 'That's my son, Billy.'

'Who took the photo?'

'I did. We'd been fishing for stripers at Potter's Landing.' Buck points towards the glistening fish. 'Billy caught a few earlier in the season, but they weren't big enough. This one was his first keeper.'

'When was that?'

'Saturday, June twelfth. A week before . . .'

'Before what?'

'Your Honour—'

Beatrice had her gavel in hand even before Stanley spoke.

'Before what, Buck?'

'Your Honour!'

The gavel descends.

I knew this would happen, but I thought it would take a little longer. I thought I'd get at least a half-dozen questions out before the prosecutor–judge team began its power play. But I'm ready. I've planned this moment. I intend to shut my opponents down. Both of them.

'Before what, Buck?'

'Your Honour!'

Beatrice leans towards me, but I don't turn. I fix my gaze on Buck. 'Counsel,' she barks, 'there's an objection pending.'

'I haven't heard one, Judge. Before what, Buck?'

Beatrice bangs her gavel and then points it at Buck. 'The witness will remain silent. Counsel, Mr Edgarton has raised an objection.'

She inhales audibly when I wheel around to face her. 'No, he hasn't, Judge. There's no objection pending.'

I turn my back to her and point my pen at String Tie. His eyes grow wide, but his fingers keep tapping.

'It seems *you* have an objection, though, Judge. So let's hear it.'

When I face her again, her mouth is a perfect oval, as if she's about to begin an aria.

'Go ahead, Judge. Put your objection on the record. And we'll ask the Big Boys to rule on it.'

My irreverent reference to the appellate panel is more than Beatrice can bear. 'Now just a minute, Counsel.'

'No, Judge. You don't get a minute now. *Now* is my client's time to testify, my time to question him. And nobody interrupts, not even you, unless *this* man'—Stanley takes a step back when I aim my pen in his direction—'voices a coherent objection.'

Now Stanley's mouth is circular. Maybe they plan a duet.

'You're not the prosecutor, Judge. He is. It's his job to raise viable objections. 'Your Honour' doesn't cut it. Those words don't appear in the Rules of Evidence. If the prosecutor can't state a legal basis for his objection, then the judge can't rule on it.'

The gavel pauses midair. Beatrice looks like she might reach out and pound it on the top of my head.

'And if you've got nothing to rule on, then *this* man'—Buck stares into his lap when my pen finds him—'keeps talking.'

Buck looks up, and I turn to the jury. They're gaping at me.

'The Constitution says Buck Hammond is entitled to his turn.'

Stanley remains on his feet but says nothing. Beatrice sets her gavel on the bench and folds her hands into her sleeves.

I'll take that as a go.

'Let's get to the point, Buck—while we still can.'

'Counsel, that's enough.' Beatrice pounds her gavel again. 'One more editorial comment from you, Ms Nickerson, and you'll take a break—a long one.'

I block them out: the judge, Stanley, String Tie. What happens now is between Buck and the jurors. No one else.

'What did Hector Monteros do to Billy?'

In the silence that follows, I study the jurors. Their gazes move from Buck to the easel, then back to Buck again.

'Took him, took him from the beach.' Buck grasps the arms of his chair. 'And hurt him.'

'How?'

Now a few of the jurors grasp the arms of their chairs too. They don't want to hear the story again from anyone, but certainly not the boy's father. Once was more than enough.

'He . . . did terrible things, and then . . . and then he killed Billy.'

'How did he kill Billy?'

Buck lowers his head. For a moment, he seems unable to lift it.

'Take your time,' I say to Buck, and I mean it. Every minute he spends on this witness stand should take us one step closer to a decent result. To me, his agony is apparent, his grief tangible. I can't tell, though, if the jurors feel it. Their faces reveal nothing.

Buck lifts his brimming eyes and turns to the jury.

We practised this testimony. Not because we doctored the answer, but because Buck couldn't address the question at all, at first. He couldn't say it out loud. Even now, he has to say the words quickly, or he won't get through the answer.

'He bound Billy with metal cables. . . .' Buck lets go of the chair arms and presses his wrists together. 'At the wrists and ankles. And he smothered him.'

That's all Buck can say on that topic. He's reached his limit.

'And what did you do, Buck, to Hector Monteros?'

Stanley objects. 'Your Honour, please, these jurors watched the videotape. They heard from the chief of police. They know what the defendant did.'

Stanley knows better. His objection is nothing more than a ploy, a manufactured opportunity to make a speech.

Beatrice stares at me—grimaces—when I look up. I'm tempted to smile. She won't dare prevent Buck from telling the jury what he did. There isn't an appellate panel in the country that would uphold that ruling. Stanley knows that. And Beatrice does too.

'Ladies and gentlemen,' she says, 'I remind you of the limiting instruction you were given on the first day of this trial. I caution you now—that instruction is still in full force and effect.'

Funny, that's the only ruling of Judge Long's that Beatrice has acknowledged. The jurors nod, though, almost as one.

'Buck, what did you do to Hector Monteros?'

'I tried to stop him.' Buck faces the jurors. 'I shot him.'

'Were you able to stop him?'

'No.' He closes his eyes. 'I tried. But I failed. I was too late.'

I move to the easel and set the photo—Billy beaming with his striped fish—to one side. Next to it, I position the other photo.

Buck keeps his face averted, towards the jury box, his eyes still closed. The jurors, though, look first at me, then at the easel. One by one, their gazes settle on the photo. The awful one.

It's a close-up of Billy, from the chest up, on the autopsy table. His arms are bent at the elbows, hands open, palms up, on either side of his head. His eyes are closed, and his freckled face looks as if he might be sleeping. But on his wrists, the ligature marks are plain.

Finally Buck follows the jurors' gazes and stares at the autopsy shot. 'You see?' he asks them through clenched teeth. 'I couldn't stop him. I was too late.'

'TOO LATE?' Stanley scrutinises Buck Hammond as if he's a still life about to be auctioned. 'That was your testimony, was it not, sir? That you were too late?'

Buck leans forward in his chair and nods. 'Yes.'

'You were too late long before you fired the shot that killed Hector Monteros, weren't you, Mr Hammond?'

'I don't know what you mean.' Buck shakes his head.

'Your boy was dead, was he not, when you pulled the trigger?'

Buck nods, agreeing. 'He was.'

'And you knew that to be the case, didn't you?'

'I know it now.'

'And you knew it then!'

I'm tempted to get up, but I don't. I shouldn't act like Stanley. Besides, we've got a long way to go. Stanley's just getting started.

He waits for a response, but he won't get one. Buck and I went over this a thousand times. If there's no question pending, Buck's not to say a word. And he's good at not saying a word.

A moment of silence, then Stanley gets it. 'You knew your son was dead, didn't you, when you fired that fatal shot?'

'I'm not sure.'

'Not sure?'

Stanley walks towards the jury, a slight smile on his lips.

'You were in the courtroom, were you not, Mr Hammond, when Chief Thomas Fitzpatrick testified?' he asks.

'Yes.'

'You heard him tell us then that you identified your son's body at the morgue?'

'Yes.'

'Do you remember identifying the body, sir?'

'Do I remember . . . ?'

Buck looks as if he thinks Stanley might be temporarily insane. 'Of course I do,' he replies.

'And you did that, Mr Hammond—identified your son's body—more than *two hours* before the chopper transporting Monteros reached Chatham. Isn't that correct?'

'I don't know.'

'Did you hear Chief Fitzpatrick tell us exactly that?'

'I did.'

'Is it your testimony, then, that Chief Fitzpatrick was lying?'

The question is improper, but it's not worth an objection. And we anticipated a few cheap shots from Stanley. Buck is as well prepared to deflect them as any witness can be.

'No,' Buck says evenly, 'that's not my testimony.'

'You agree, then, that you identified the body more than two hours before killing Monteros?'

Buck takes a deep breath and answers the panel. 'The chief said more than two hours, so it must have been.'

'But you don't have personal knowledge of that fact—is that your testimony, Mr Hammond?'

Buck faces Stanley again. 'Yes.'

'You don't remember?'

'That's right.'

Stanley strides to the side wall, flips off the overhead lights, then makes a beeline for his star witness.

He holds the videotape in front of Buck for a moment—a dramatic pause—before popping it into the VCR. 'Let's find out, Mr Hammond, what you *do* remember.'

Harry and I exchange surprised glances. We were certain Stanley would save his second run of the video for closing, certain he'd want the bloody runway to be the final scene emblazoned on the jurors' minds.

The glow from the TV screen illuminates Stanley's silhouette and Buck's profile. The rest of us sit in inky blackness. Stanley retrieves a wooden pointer from his table. It has a white rubber tip. He waits patiently while the military chopper comes into view on-screen. He watches silently as the chopper descends to the runway. Then he presses a controller, freezes the frame.

I leave my chair and walk across the room to lean against the wall beside the jury box. I want to keep an eye on Stanley's pointer.

'You've seen this helicopter before, have you not, Mr Hammond?'

Buck nods. 'Yes. I've seen this tape.'

'I'm not asking about the tape. I'm asking about the military helicopter, the real one—'US Army' printed on its sides. You saw it on June twenty-first, did you not?'

There it is. A question I didn't ask. It never fails.

Buck tilts his head towards one shoulder. 'I'm not sure.'

Stanley plasters an incredulous look on his dimly lit face, then turns it towards the jurors. 'You're not sure?'

'I know I must have,' Buck says. 'But I don't remember looking at it then. I don't think I realised it was an army aircraft.'

Stanley presses the controller. 'You don't remember,' he mutters.

On-screen, a uniformed marshal emerges from the chopper, his side arm drawn. Behind him is Monteros, handcuffed and shackled loosely so he can negotiate the stairs. Another guard follows, his weapon pointed up, as if he might fire into the air at any moment.

Stanley freezes the frame again. 'Do you remember these men?' He moves his pointer from the first guard to the second.

That's question number two I didn't ask.

Buck frowns, as if even he doesn't like the answer he's about to give. 'No,' he says, 'I don't.'

Stanley smirks, presses his controller, and the action on-screen resumes. He stops it as soon as Monteros's feet reach the runway.

'And I don't suppose you have any memory of this gentleman either, Mr Hammond.' Stanley's pointer rests on Monteros. 'Is that your testimony?'

This question I didn't overlook. I shift my position against the wall so I can watch the jury as well as Buck.

He sits perfectly still in the witness box, his eyes on the white tip of Stanley's pointer. 'No,' he says, 'that's not my testimony.'

Stanley turns to the jurors, mock surprise on his face. 'Do tell us,' he says. 'What do you remember about Mr Monteros?'

Buck's eyes leave the screen, and he turns towards the jury. 'I remember everything,' he says.

'Everything? Perhaps you could be more specific.'

'The tattoo on his arm, the scar on his chin, the sneer on his face. I remember everything.'

Stanley appears satisfied with this answer. He starts the tape again. 'And tell us, Mr Hammond . . .' Stanley presses his controller and points the tip of his pointer at Buck on the screen, one step from the shadow of the hangar. 'Who is this?'

'That's me.'

'So it is.' Stanley presses twice, turning on the volume.

The shot thunders through the courtroom. Most of the jurors jump in their seats; a few cover their mouths. Buck doesn't move.

On-screen, Monteros collapses, and police officers scatter. A pool of red seeps from Monteros's head onto the runway.

Stanley freezes the frame and moves close to the witness box. 'You fired that shot, Mr Hammond?'

'I did.'

'Whose rifle?'

'Mine.'

'You hunt?'

'Yes.'

'What for?'

'Deer.'

Stanley walks away from the witness box, and Buck exhales. Stanley's pointer taps against Monteros on-screen. 'You intended to kill this man, didn't you, Mr Hammond?'

'I did.'

'You sighted his temple, and your shot was on target, correct?'

'Yes.'

'Pretty good aim. For a man who's insane.'

Harry swivels his chair out from the table, meets my eyes, and shakes his head. He's afraid I might make the objection. He shouldn't be. Jurors don't like sarcasm—from either side of the aisle. We'll let Stanley's caustic comment stand.

Buck says nothing.

Silence appears to unnerve Stanley. He hurries back towards the witness box, his pointer directed at Buck, the rubber tip almost touching his white shirt. 'Is it your testimony, Mr Hammond, that on the morning of June twenty-first, you drove your truck to the Chatham Municipal Airport, loaded your hunting rifle, took aim, fired a single shot, hit your target, all the while insane?'

So much for passing on objections. I move towards the bench. 'Just a minute, Judge. This witness isn't an expert.'

Beatrice doesn't respond.

'Mr Hammond offered no opinion on his own mental state during direct, Judge, and there's a reason for that. He's not qualified. The prosecutor already cross-examined our psychiatrist. He doesn't get to put the same questions to a lay witness.'

'I'll allow it, Counsel.'

'On what grounds? The Commonwealth called two experts on this topic, Judge. How can it ask now for a lay opinion?'

'I've *ruled*, Counsel.'

Harry's right. She doesn't like me.

Stanley leans over towards Buck. 'So tell us, Mr Hammond . . .' Stanley extends his pointer backwards, towards the frozen scene on the television screen. 'Your lawyers claim this was a moment of temporary insanity. Was it?'

'I'm no expert,' Buck says. 'I've no business agreeing or disagreeing with the doctors who testified. But I do know one thing.'

All fourteen jurors sit completely still, their eyes riveted to Buck.

For the first time today, Buck's voice cracks. His eyes fill as he points towards the TV, his arm parallel with Stanley's pointer. 'If that man were alive today, I'd hunt him down and kill him.'

CHAPTER EIGHT

'Hunt him down and kill him', of course, was not in the cross-examination script. We passed on redirect. That way Stanley had no opportunity to recross, no chance to get Buck to repeat those words. Stanley will undoubtedly quote them during his closing. No need for Buck to help the Commonwealth again.

Stanley finished with Buck at two o'clock, whereupon Beatrice called a one-hour lunch break. Closing arguments would begin promptly at three, she promised.

The jurors look a little more relaxed after their lunch break. They're settled into their chairs, a few with notebooks and pens on their laps. I stand before them and wait until the gallery is quiet.

'There are two sides to our judicial system: the civil and the criminal. And there are important distinctions between the two. Most are differences of degree.

'The burden of proof, for example. In a civil matter, the complaining party must prove his case by a preponderance of the evidence. But in a criminal proceeding, the burden of proof is far more steep. The complaining party, the Commonwealth, must prove its case—every element of it—beyond a reasonable doubt.'

Widespread nods. They know this, of course. They read the paper; they watch TV.

'Punishment is another example. A losing defendant is penalised no matter which system he's in. On the civil side, we take his assets. But in the criminal-justice system, we take something far more valuable, far more precious. We take his freedom.'

More nods. They know this as well.

'There is one difference between our civil system and our criminal system that is *not* a matter of degree. It's a matter of substance. And it's important. In Buck Hammond's case, it's critical.'

A few of them pick up pens and open notebooks. As I walk to the jury box and lean on the railing, their faces are focused.

'In our civil system, it's incumbent upon the judge to direct a verdict when the evidence is uncontroverted. If the controlling facts of a civil suit are not in dispute, the judge must take the case away from the jury—decide it himself—as a matter of law.

'Not so in our criminal-justice system. In fact, the opposite is true. In a criminal case, the defendant is *entitled* to a decision rendered by a panel of his peers. Our Constitution guarantees it. The jury has the final word in criminal trials. Always.'

The jurors haven't taken their eyes from me.

'Most of the important facts in this case aren't contested. The Commonwealth told you Buck Hammond shot and killed Hector Monteros.

Buck Hammond took the witness stand and said the same thing. The Commonwealth told you he intended to kill Monteros. Buck took the witness stand and said the same thing—more emphatically than Mr Madigan and I would have liked.'

Most of the jurors look towards the defence table, at Harry and Buck; a few almost smile. I pause a moment before directing their attention to the easel. The few near smiles disappear.

'Some of the evidence in this case was difficult to present. And I know it was difficult to receive. It was gut-wrenching to listen to Chief Fitzpatrick's testimony. It was awful to look at the two photographs of Billy—and it still is.'

Their eyes remain on the easel.

'We had trouble listening to the details of Billy Hammond's unspeakable suffering, his unimaginable death. Those details made us angry, outraged even. And not one of us ever met Billy Hammond.'

Their gazes stray from the easel. Some eyes rest on me; others stare across the room again towards Buck. The retired schoolteacher shakes her head in his direction; her face reveals nothing.

'If the details of Billy's ordeal—of his suffering and his death—made you and me angry, outraged, what did those details do to the child's father? To decide this case, you must answer that question.'

Most jurors drop their gazes from me to their laps, considering the question, I hope.

'Dr Simmons told you that Buck Hammond was in the midst of a psychotic episode—a break from reality—when he pulled the trigger of his rifle on the morning of June twenty-first. Even the Commonwealth's expert psychiatrists agreed that Buck was in the throes of severe trauma. Was he insane?'

I let the question hang for a moment.

'That's for you to decide.'

I turn and point towards Buck. 'Should he spend the rest of his life at Walpole—in the penitentiary—for what he did?'

Another pause.

'That's also for you to decide. And that'—I wait until their eyes return to mine—'is as it should be. This, people, is what's *right* about our criminal-justice system: you, twelve of Buck Hammond's peers, are the final arbiters of justice. You decide what happens next. You and your consciences.'

Stanley drums his fingers on the prosecution table. I stare at him until he stops. I turn back to the jurors.

'This is my final opportunity to speak to you. When I'm finished, the prosecutor will address you. My guess is that he will spend at least some time discussing the need for you to send a message. He might tell you to convict so that our streets won't be overrun with men taking the law into their own hands. He might tell you to convict so that other would-be killers will think twice before slaying their victims. He might say your failure to convict will unravel the very fabric of our society.

'I tell you now, because it's my last chance to do so, don't buy it.' I turn and cross the courtroom to stand beside Buck's chair.

'Your verdict is about one man and only one man. This one. You are seated in that jury box for one reason and one reason alone. Not to send a message to the masses. Not to predict the future of crime control. Not to theorise about the fabric of our society. You're here because you are Buck Hammond's peers. This is his trial. He's entitled to it. Don't let the prosecutor convince you to make it about anyone—or anything—else.'

Not one juror moves as I leave Buck's side and cross the silent courtroom towards them.

'In recent weeks, I've spent more than a few evenings in the Hammonds' living room, talking with Buck's wife, Patty. We talked about Billy and about Buck. We talked about Hector Monteros. And we talked a lot about this trial, about all that would happen in this courtroom.

'One night, about two weeks ago, Patty asked a question she'd never raised before. It was a question I'm sure she'd thought about often during the past six months. But until two weeks ago, she'd never said the words—not out loud, anyway.

'Patty asked if I'd be able to send Buck home, give them the opportunity to piece together the shards of their shattered lives. She asked if I could bring a close to this seemingly endless tragedy, to make this chapter of their pain-filled saga end the way it should.

'I was honest with Patty Hammond that night, people. I told her I couldn't do that.

'But you can.'

'CONVENIENT, isn't it, this temporary-insanity plea? Love it or hate it— believe it or not—you have to admit it's convenient.' Stanley steps out from behind his table and shoves both hands in his trouser pockets. He saunters across the front of the courtroom, head down, his back to the jury.

When he reaches our table, he stops as if he hit a brick wall.

For a moment, he says nothing, stares at the tassels of his shiny black shoes. He looks sideways then and sneers at Buck before pivoting to face the jury. 'It's not only convenient. It's clever.'

He takes his hands from his pockets, folds his arms across his chest, and stands still in front of our table. 'Yes, it's downright clever for this man to claim he was temporarily insane when he took a human life. Insane at that moment, mind you, but not now.'

Stanley smiles at the jurors, as if they share a secret. 'That's the part that's so clever—the temporary part. It's perfect. There's no need to commit him, you see, no need even for psychiatric care. Just send him home. As if it never happened.'

Stanley shakes his head at the jurors. 'Don't fall for it.' His gaze remains focused on the panel as he raises one arm and points into Buck's face. 'Because if you fall for it, he gets away with murder.'

Buck leans as far back in his chair as he can without tipping. Still, Stanley's index finger is only a few inches from Buck's chin. I have a powerful urge to push Stanley's arm away, to get his hand out of our space so we can breathe.

I don't have to, though. He hustles across the room towards the jury box, all the while pointing backwards at Buck.

'Judge Nolan will instruct you that this man is guilty of first-degree murder if he acted with malice aforethought. And this'—Stanley bangs the top of the TV—'is malice aforethought.'

He flips off the lights and presses his remote control.

Harry and I both leap up in the dark.

'Hold on.' My voice is so loud it startles me. My word choice is surprising as well. It wasn't 'whoa', but it wasn't much better.

Harry's already at the bench. His silhouette joins Stanley's in the glow from the screen.

'He's already run the videotape twice, Judge. He doesn't get a third shot.' Harry flips off the TV. Now everyone's invisible.

'Says who?' Beatrice's voice booms from the blackness above the bench.

'This was decided during pretrial motions. There's an order.'

'Whose order?'

'Judge Long's.'

'Judge Long no longer presides over this trial.'

Stanley flips the TV back on.

Harry turns it off again. 'It doesn't matter who presides over this trial, Judge.'

'Doesn't matter?' Beatrice doesn't like being told she doesn't matter.

'No. This issue was decided on motion—before trial. The defendant relied on the court's ruling. And he had every right to rely on it. It doesn't matter which judge signed the order.'

'Tell me, Counsel, what difference does it make? What would you have done differently? Changed your strategy somehow?'

'That's not the point, Judge. The issue here is prejudicial impact. Probative value versus prejudicial impact.'

'Your partner used photographs during her closing.'

'But this videotape was the subject of a pretrial motion, Judge. There's an order.'

'I'll vacate it.'

'You can't do that.'

'I just did. The prosecutor is entitled to use demonstrative evidence during closing, Counsel. Just as your partner did.'

Stanley hits the button, and the blue glow from the screen illuminates his satisfied smirk. He shoos Harry away.

Harry gives up, and he should. Fighting too long about this won't sit well with the jury. He returns to our table, drops into his chair and shrugs an apology towards Buck.

'It doesn't matter,' Buck whispers. 'They've already seen it. They won't see anything this time they haven't seen before.'

Stanley stops the videotape soon after it starts. Buck isn't even on-screen yet. 'One can only assume,' Stanley says, 'that Mr Hammond was in the throes of what his lawyers now call temporary insanity at this point in time—a minute before he shot Hector Monteros.'

Stanley retrieves the pointer from his table and points at the hangar's shadow. 'And what was Mr Hammond doing at this particular moment? Acting insane, perhaps? Ranting like a lunatic?'

Stanley's footsteps move towards the jury box. 'No, not at all. He was hiding, lying in wait. Quietly. Patiently. Sound insane to you?' Stanley hiccups, just barely. 'Sounds like a plan to me. A calculated plan. The plan of a man thinking clearly.'

He presses the button, and the screen comes back to life. He freezes the action again when Buck steps into view.

'And what have we here? Ah, it's Mr Hammond. Acting insane yet? No, not at all. He's moving into position to take a clear shot, aligning himself—and his weapon—with his prey.'

Stanley's footsteps start up again, back towards the TV. 'Sound insane to you?' he asks.

He hits the remote control, hits it again when Buck raises his hunting rifle. 'Here's Mr Hammond again, taking aim. Perfect aim, don't forget. See any sign of insanity here? I don't. Not a trace.'

Stanley plants himself beside the TV, its screen frozen, and faces the panel. He intends to deliver his closing argument in the dark.

'Let's be candid, ladies and gentlemen. We're all horrified by what happened to this man's son. That murder was an ungodly act.'

Stanley hits another button, and the sound kicks in—the single shot heard round the Commonwealth.

'And so was this one.'

No one breathes while Monteros dies again. Stanley waits until a pool of blood collects on the runway; then he freezes the scene.

'What will happen, ladies and gentlemen, if you accept this man's claim of temporary-insanity? He'll go home, that's what. He'll be a free man.'

Stanley moves towards the jury box. 'What will happen then?'

He stands still and waits, as if he expects one of them to volunteer. 'I'll tell you what will happen. Someone else will set him off, send him into a rage. Maybe next week. Maybe next year. I can't tell you when. But I can tell you, it will happen. I guarantee it.'

Stanley looks through the darkness in our direction. 'And what then? Well, Mr Hammond told us himself. He'll hunt down the person who enrages him. He'll hunt him down and kill him.'

Stanley's footsteps tell me he's pacing slowly in front of the jury box. I wish he'd turn on the damned lights.

'I wondered about Mr Hammond's mental state today,' he continues. 'One wonders about a man who would utter those words in a court of law. But his mental state today isn't my concern. His mental state most days isn't my concern. It isn't yours either. Your concern is this moment.' Stanley extends his pointer towards the bloody scene on TV.

'Frankly, I don't care if you think Mr Hammond was insane on every other day of his life, today included. It doesn't matter.'

He moves closer to the TV, taps his pointer on the glass. 'This fragment of time is the only one that matters. In this moment, Mr Hammond was in control. At this moment, he was methodical, he was purposeful.'

Stanley bangs his pointer against the pool of Monteros's blood.

'We all know, ladies and gentlemen, that at this moment, William Francis Hammond was sane. Maybe—just maybe—it was a moment of temporary sanity.'

BEATRICE'S jury instructions were lengthy but by the book. Most members of the panel lost interest in the instructions, and their eyes glazed over about halfway through. The Commonwealth's Uniform Jury Instructions teem with boilerplate directives and unqualified commands. The judge may as well read aloud from the phone book.

She's wrapping it up now. It's almost seven o'clock. The jurors look exhausted, but they rally when the judge tells them she's through. They shift in their seats, stretch their tight limbs. A few even rub their eyes, as if waking from a nap.

Late as it is, they seem ready. Ready to get to work. Ready to take on *Commonwealth* v. *Hammond.* Ready to decide Buck's fate.

'At this point in time, ladies and gentlemen'—Beatrice stifles a yawn—'it's my intention to dismiss you for the holiday.'

Harry shoots up, as if fired from a cannon. 'Dismiss them?'

'That's right, Mr Madigan. Dismiss them.'

I'm up too. 'But they're sequestered.'

'Not tonight, they're not, Ms Nickerson. It's Christmas Eve.'

'Christmas Eve?' Harry's at the bench in a flash. Stanley follows on Harry's heels, as if he thinks Beatrice might need assistance.

Harry points backwards to our table, to Buck. 'You think it's Christmas Eve for Mr Hammond, Judge? You want him to go back to his cell and decorate a tree? His life is on the line here.'

The judge stares through Harry as if he's not there. 'Spare us your melodrama, Mr Madigan. The Commonwealth of Massachusetts doesn't impose the death penalty—not even in capital murder cases. No one's life is on the line here.' She faces the jury again. 'We'll reconvene on Monday morning, December twenty-seventh, at nine o'clock.'

'No, we won't.' Harry's voice is low, controlled. I know that tone. It means, this is war.

'Pardon me, Mr Madigan?' Beatrice glowers at Harry.

'You heard me, Judge. We're not going to reconvene, because we're not going to unconvene. You're not sending them home, Judge. Not until we have a verdict.'

'Are you giving me an *order*, Mr Madigan?'

'No. I'm not giving anybody an order.' Harry turns to the jury. 'Judge Long gave the order. These jurors are sequestered until they reach a verdict. Sheltered from the media blitz. That's been the standing order of this court since trial began.' Harry faces Beatrice again. 'You can't change it now.'

'I *can't?*'

'No, you can't.' Harry's still addressing the panel, not Beatrice. 'It's one more order Mr Hammond relied upon. It's an order that guarantees Mr Hammond a trial by jury—not by the press. You can't take that away from him now. We won't let you.'

'We?' Beatrice glares at the back of Harry's head.

The jurors look as if they might agree with Harry. One by one, they nod up at him, then check in with each other. More than a few look up at the judge, as if they'd like to be heard on the matter.

Beatrice straightens in her chair. She sends a silent signal to one of her two court officers, a burly man with a red beard. Big Red signals back, then heads for the side door.

Harry and I both know where he's going. He's rounding up the troops, preparing for battle. Big Red has been involved in removing Harry from this courtroom before. It's not an easy task.

Beatrice leans across her bench towards Harry and takes a deep breath. 'I'll instruct them to avoid the press, Counsel. No TV. No radio. No newspapers. And no discussion of the case with anyone.'

Harry turns to the packed gallery and lifts his arms towards the crowd. TV-camera lights focus on him, and flashbulbs explode. He'll almost certainly be the top story on tonight's late news, the front-page photo on tomorrow morning's *Cape Cod Times*.

'Avoid the press?' Harry laughs out loud. 'How the hell are they supposed to do that? Spend the weekend in space, maybe?'

Beatrice leans back in her chair, lips clamped. 'Mr Madigan, you are in contempt of this court.'

'You bet I am.' Harry hustles across the courtroom, staring up at her. 'This court is contemptible.'

Beatrice pounds her gavel.

Harry keeps moving. When he reaches our table, he rests his hands on Buck's shoulders and faces the jury again. He's flushed, sweating. He's running out of time, and he knows it.

'This man deserves your verdict before you leave this building, before you're bombarded with the opinions of those who *think* they know what happened here. No fair-minded person would say otherwise.'

Big Red is back with reinforcements. He looks up at the bench, checks in with Beatrice, and she gives him the go-ahead. They surround Harry—four court officers in all—but Harry keeps talking to the jury as if he doesn't notice.

'Don't let her railroad you. She doesn't get the final word. Tell her you want to stay, want to deliberate now, tonight. If she says no, we go straight to the court of appeals, Christmas Eve or not.'

Two of the officers take Harry's arms and try to move him towards the door. He drops to his knees on the worn carpeting instead.

I get to my feet. 'Absolutely,' I tell the jury. 'We'll call in an appellate panel.' As if to confirm my promise, the Kydd emerges from the crowd and stands with me at the defence table.

The jurors' eyes are glued to Harry and the struggling court officers. It's hard to move Harry when he's on his knees.

The retired schoolteacher turns to the man beside her, the restaurant owner, and whispers. He looks back at her and nods once, then again. Whatever it is she said, he agrees.

Big Red slaps a handcuff on one of Harry's wrists but can't get hold of the other one. He orders Harry to stand.

Harry sits. A few jurors snicker.

'Enough!' Stanley's losing it. He points at Harry. 'This man is vile! Reprehensible! Get him out of here!'

All eyes move to Stanley. He's frozen in front of the jury box, still pointing at Harry.

Harry starts laughing—howling, actually—and tosses his head towards his captors. 'What do you think they're *trying* to do, pal?'

The elderly schoolteacher twists round in her seat, whispers to the juror behind her. That juror, in turn, passes a message down the back row. The restaurant owner does the same in row one.

The guards have Harry in hand now—literally. His wrists are cuffed behind his back. And he's still talking. 'You're in charge,' he tells the jurors. 'Don't forget that.'

With a good deal of effort, the court officers drag Harry, still talking, across the worn carpeting and through the side door. When it closes behind them, the room falls abruptly still, silent.

I lean towards the Kydd. 'Follow them. See where they put him. Then get him the hell out.' The Kydd heads for the door.

Our retired schoolteacher raises her hand, but Beatrice doesn't notice. The older woman clears her throat and gets to her feet. 'Excuse me, Your Honour.'

Beatrice looks startled.

'We've discussed it, you see.'

'Discussed what?' Beatrice looks annoyed.

'We'd like to deliberate.' She looks apologetic. 'Now.'

'Now?' Beatrice takes hold of her gavel again, as if she might use it on the elderly juror.

'Yes, Your Honour. No disrespect intended. We feel it's the right thing to do. It's what we all expected to do. And it's what Mr Hammond expected of us. It was planned that way from the start, you see. We're in agreement on this. It's unanimous.' She gives the judge a slight bow, then sits again.

Beatrice turns away from the impudent juror and glares at me. She looks as if she's certain I orchestrated this. I'm flattered.

Big Red returns to the courtroom. The others must have Harry under control. That means he's in a cell. And it's locked.

I pull my phone from my briefcase and place it in the centre of the defence table, then drop into my chair and smile up at Beatrice.

She scowls at the phone, so I know she gets it. Either she allows these jurors to deliberate, or I place a call to the court of appeal's emergency line. And the appellate panel won't like that. The judges on call won't appreciate being summoned on Christmas Eve. Far better that Beatrice work the holiday than the Big Boys.

Beatrice's face turns to stone. She signals Big Red. He tells the panel to stand and follow him, and they do. Just like that, they're gone. Deliberating. Beginning their draft of the final chapter.

The bailiff approaches our table to escort Buck Hammond back to the House of Correction. Buck turns towards me. 'Thank you. And thank Harry too.' He smiles. 'If you ever see him again.'

I laugh. 'Don't worry. We'll see him again. But don't thank us yet. It's too soon.'

Buck leaves his seat, shakes his head. 'It's not too soon,' he says. 'I mean it. No matter what happens. Thank you.' He stares for a moment at Patty, then allows the bailiff to lead him away.

Beatrice looks at me. 'Well, Counsel, I trust you'll enjoy your evening. I'm going home.' She leaves the bench.

'Home?' Beatrice lives in Provincetown, a solid hour from here.

She pauses at the chambers door. 'That's right, Ms Nickerson. Home. These jurors want to bring in their verdict on the holiday, they can damn well wait for me to get back.'

CHAPTER NINE

Santa Claus spends Christmas Eve—every Christmas Eve—in Chatham. At the Main Street Elementary School, the Cape Cod Carolers and the Chatham Band greet one and all with holiday music, home-baked cookies and mulled cider. Santa sits enthroned on the gymnasium stage, chatting leisurely with every good boy and girl in town. The naughty ones usually stop by for a few words as well.

My son and his friends still attend the Christmas Eve festivities. This year Maggie plans to join them. Luke actually invited her, she told me breathlessly this morning.

She and Luke had appeared in the courtroom's back row at five, expecting we'd all head to Chatham shortly thereafter. It didn't work out, of course. It's almost eight now. Santa and his entourage are well into the festivities at the elementary school.

'Can we *please* get out of here?' Luke drapes one arm across his forehead, to show me how gravely he suffers, as he and Maggie approach the defence table.

My plan was to drive them to Chatham, then return to the courthouse to await the verdict or, more likely, the jurors' departure for their hotel rooms. That way, I'd have the car. Luke and Maggie can hitch rides with any number of Luke's friends. Inherent in my plan, though, was an expectation that Harry would sit here, at the defence table, while I was gone. It doesn't seem right to leave our table unmanned. Especially not with Stanley entrenched at his.

The Kydd returns to the courtroom, grinning. He drops into the chair next to mine and laughs. 'He wants to stay.'

'What?'

'Harry wants to stay in lockup. He says if Buck's convicted, the judge's bias will make a decent appealable issue. We'll argue ole Beatrice had a conflict of interest—a huge one—and she should have recused herself at the outset. With that argument in mind, he says, the longer he spends locked up, the better.'

Sometimes I think Harry's pretty damn smart.

The Kydd laughs again. 'He also says he's beat. Says he could use a few hours' sleep. It's quiet, and the cots are comfortable.'

And sometimes I think Harry's certifiable.

'Can we *please* get out of here?' Luke repeats his plea.

'Go ahead,' the Kydd says. 'I'll stay.' He taps the phone in his jacket pocket. 'I'll call you if there's even a peep.'

'OK.'

Luke and Maggie dash for the back door.

The gallery is all but empty as I head down the centre aisle. Only one spectator remains: Patty Hammond. She traded her front-row seat for the back bench, where the lighting is dim.

'I'll be back,' I tell her. 'I'm taking Luke and Maggie to Chatham, to the elementary school.'

She looks at me, her eyes moist. Billy should be at the elementary school tonight. No doubt he was there last year.

'Why don't you come with us? We'll be back in an hour. It'll probably take the jury that long to elect a foreperson.'

She looks uncertain.

'Come on. Let's get some fresh air. You can keep me awake on the ride back.'

'OK,' she says, reaching for her coat.

The snow, it seems, will never end. But the old Thunderbird starts without a problem, as it always does. In minutes, we're travelling towards Chatham, the defrost and the heat at full blast.

Patty turns in the seat beside me to face Maggie. 'How's your mom doing?'

'She's OK.' Maggie leans forward between Patty and me, and the dashboard lights illuminate her face. 'She says it's not too bad in there. I want to go back tomorrow, see her on Christmas Day, if that's OK with you, Marty. Luke says he'll drive me.'

'Sounds like a plan.' I'm fairly certain I'll be coming back myself, though, to pace the hallways and wait for Buck's verdict.

'I have a present for her. A necklace. I know she won't be allowed to wear it in there, but I want to show it to her anyhow.'

Presents. Guilt. This year, I have only a handful of packages for Luke. And half of those, the items that aren't strictly male, I'll cull out for Maggie. They're small things, trinkets I purchased during early fall, when I was unemployed. Lucky for me, Luke's been saving for a pick-up truck, a used one he spotted for sale at the local gas station. I'll write a cheque in the morning, one hefty enough to bump up the total in his passbook to almost match the asking price.

I look into the rearview mirror, catch Luke's eye, and fire a silent reminder into the back seat. He nods. His assignment is to find out what Maggie's saving for. Let's hope it's not a condo on the Riviera.

'It's beautiful, Maggie.' Patty holds a small white box, a glittering necklace dangling from its dark blue velvet lining.

'It is,' I agree. And it is. 'Where in the world did you get it?'

'Luke and I found it today in Hyannis.'

Patty snaps the box shut and returns it to Maggie. 'Well, your mom is going to love it. What a nice present to have waiting when she comes home.'

Silence. The coming-home idea shuts us all down for a beat.

Patty recovers first. 'He's intense, isn't he, that prosecutor?'

I laugh. 'Stanley Edgarton the Third? Intense? What gives you that idea?'

Patty laughs too. 'Does he do all the murder cases?'

I shake my head. 'Not yet. But eventually he will. He used to work in the New Bedford office; he was their lead homicide attorney. He's only been here about a month.'

'So for now, he's specialising in Forest Beach, I guess.'

I don't get it. 'Forest Beach?'

'Buck and Sonia. Probably the only two Forest Beach people in history to be accused of murder.'

I still don't get it. 'And?'

'And the intense guy is prosecuting both of them. Seems like a speciality, doesn't it?' Patty smiles over at me.

I glance at her, but I can't return the smile. I pull onto the shoulder, stop the Thunderbird under the ENTERING CHATHAM sign.

'Patty, listen to me. It's important.'

Her eyes grow wide.

'Why did you say Stanley's prosecuting both of them?'

She shrugs. 'Because he is.'

'Sonia Baker?'

'Sure,' she says. 'I saw him there on Monday, shortly after'—she glances sideways at Maggie—'it all happened.'

I have an enormous urge to grab her by the shoulders, but I resist. 'You saw him where?'

'At Sonia's cottage.'

'When?'

'Right around two. I know because the kindergarten school bus went by, the one Billy rode last year.'

'Why were you at their cottage?'

Patty looks at Maggie again. 'I heard the commotion earlier, so I thought I'd check in. Make sure Sonia and Maggie were all right.'

'Did you go inside?'

'No. I didn't dare. Sonia's car was gone, and Howard's truck was in the driveway, so I figured he was in there alone. Lord knows I didn't want to deal with him.'

Good instincts. 'So how did you see Stanley?'

'I saw him leaving. I thought Howard had been arrested, thought Sonia had finally turned him in. I had no idea about . . . you know.'

'How did you know who he was?'

'Stanley? I attended pretrial motions on Friday.'

THE THUNDERBIRD does a U-turn on its own and retraces its tyre tracks in the snow. I flip open my phone.

The hospital operator connects me to the nurses' station in the ICU. I ask for Alice Barrymore. The unit secretary puts me through. I press on the accelerator.

'Nurse Barrymore, are you in Judge Long's room?'

'Yes, I am. He's sitting up nicely, having a bit of broth.'

'Listen, Ms Barrymore. I need a favour. Ask the judge, please, if he was trying to say the word 'tassel' last night.'

'Now *you* listen,' she says. 'You lawyers have got to leave this man alone—all of you.'

'What?'

'The three of you in here carrying on late last night, and then another one here before dawn. When is the judge supposed to rest?'

'Before dawn? Who was there before dawn?'

'An entirely new one. Short, balding fellow.'

'Did he say what he wanted—the short, balding fellow?'

'Certainly. The same thing you all want. He wanted to ask more questions. Marched into the room as if he were the chief of surgery, telling me he'd need a few moments alone with the judge.'

Panic tightens my grip on the phone. 'And?'

'And I told him he'd be spending more than a few moments alone with security if he didn't turn around and march right out again. The judge was sound asleep. I think that lawyer would have wakened him if I hadn't been there.'

My gut tells me she is wrong about that. Terribly wrong.

'Nurse Barrymore, please. One question. From you to the judge. It's important. Ask if he was trying to say the word 'tassel' last night. Remember? It sounded like "tis".'

'Oh, for the love of Peter.'

'Please.'

She covers the mouthpiece, but I can still decipher her words. 'Judge,' she says, 'it's the woman from last night, the younger one. Damned if I understand it, but she wants to know if you were trying to tell them about a tassel of some sort . . .'

Her words trail off. 'Oh, for the love of Peter,' she says again, speaking into the receiver once more. 'Listen, Miss, I enjoy a good word game as much as the next person . . .'

'What did he say?'

'Not a blessed thing. But his head's bobbing up and down like one of those little statues people put in the backs of their cars.'

'Thank you, thank you.' I snap the phone shut.

I press harder on the accelerator, concentrate on negotiating the curves. My three passengers remain silent as the Thunderbird tears through the black night.

When the pieces come together, I take a deep breath and open the phone again. Three more calls: One to the state dispatcher. One to the Barnstable County police station. And one to the Kydd.

Howard Davis was a disgrace to the criminal-justice system. J. Stanley Edgarton III said so. On a normal day, Stanley wouldn't have stood a chance against Davis. But on Monday, Davis was drinking himself into oblivion, and Stanley knew it. He knew because I told him. I told him when I called from the hospital parking lot.

Judge Long is despicable. Stanley said so. Nicky Patterson interrupted Stanley on Thursday morning. Not the other way around.

Harry Madigan is vile, reprehensible. Stanley said so a few hours ago. Now Harry's asleep in a cell at the all-but-empty Barnstable County Superior Courthouse. Stanley's in the courthouse too.

And Harry sleeps like a dead man.

SWIRLING BLUE and white lights from a dozen police cruisers bathe the superior courthouse. Uniforms pepper the courthouse steps, most holding two-way radios close to their faces. Inside, the building is lit as if it's nine in the morning instead of nine at night.

The Thunderbird rolls silently down the snow-packed road, past the County Complex and the courthouse. I pull over in the darkness on historic Route 6A, under an ancient, leafless oak tree. There's no way I can get back into the county lot; the cops have blockades set up at both entrances. I'll have to go on foot from here.

Patty Hammond takes the wheel. I motion for her to wait while I trudge through the snow to the trunk and retrieve the tyre iron. I wave to Luke and Maggie, both still in the back seat. When they're out of sight, I grab the LadySmith from my jacket pocket, release the safety and hurry across the street. I know how to use it. Geraldine Schilling trained me personally.

The cops have the north and east sides of the courthouse heavily covered, because that's where the doors are. I approach from the west. At the top of a knoll on the west side of the building is a window I can reach. I stop a few steps away from it, tuck the LadySmith back into my pocket and brace the tyre iron with both hands.

I hurl the heavy tool through the window and hear what I knew I would hear: the whoops and shrieks of the security system. I wonder, as I pull myself up on the outer sill and kick out more of the glass, if the alarm will unnerve Stanley, make him slip just enough for Harry to react.

Inside, I find myself in a crowded storage area, a small room adjacent to Beatrice Nolan's makeshift courtroom. The room is lit only by the bulbs in the hallway. No one's here.

No one's in the corridor either. I hurry next door to check Beatrice's courtroom. Another uninhabited space. Our table—strewn with briefcases and legal pads—is abandoned. So is Stanley's.

I hurry out to the hallway again, towards the stairway that leads down to the basement, to the holding cells. I take the steps two at a time and lean against the wall at the bottom to catch my breath. Then I realise that the alarm has been silenced. The building is quiet. Quiet and dark. Someone flipped the main breaker. I've little doubt who that someone is.

Down here, in the subterranean hallway that leads to the four holding cells, it's not merely dark: it's black. Stanley wants it this way. I flash back to the closing argument he delivered just hours ago—he's at ease in the blackness.

A half-dozen polka dots of white light erupt along the hallway. The cops are already here, and they have penlights. The polka dots, and presumably the officers holding them, move steadily, silently, towards the cells. With all of my being, I will them to reach Harry before Stanley does. Harry's odds improve with each step they take. But if I can see their locations, their progress, then Stanley can too.

I press myself against the darkness of the wall and trail them, the LadySmith pointed into the emptiness ahead. The wall extends only half the length of the corridor: that's where the cells begin. The first three are empty. Harry must be in the last one.

A deep voice shatters the silence. The words reverberate through a bullhorn. 'Mr Edgarton, this is Sergeant Briggs. We can help you, Mr Edgarton. Step into the hallway. Drop any weapons you have on the floor in front of you. Kick them away, towards the staircase. Then put your hands behind your head. No one—I repeat, no one—will get hurt. We're here to help.'

If nothing else, the sergeant's announcement might wake Harry. Even with a knife, Stanley isn't likely to overpower Harry.

My boot brushes against something as I reach the bars of the first cell, just after Sergeant Briggs finishes his plea. I drop to my knees to find it. It's metal. A knife. Stanley already dropped one weapon, it seems. I wonder how many he has.

I drop it into my parka pocket and slip past the first two cells. They're empty, as promised. I inch halfway across the bars of the third cell, careful to stay a few steps behind the tiny dots of light, hoping that at least one of us will take Stanley by surprise.

We don't, though.

'Drop them, gentlemen.' Stanley takes us by surprise instead. 'Now.'

There's a click, then a shaft of bright light from Harry's cell.

First the penlights clatter to the concrete floor in front of me. Then the weapons—all of them. I almost drop my own. The light from Harry's cell floods the hallway and illuminates the police officers' faces. There are a dozen of them; half weren't carrying lights. They stare into the cell—all of them—eyes wide, mouths open.

Sergeant Briggs, first in line, is the only one who moves. He lowers the bullhorn to his side, then squats and sets it quietly on the concrete floor. His eyes never leave the cell. He comes up with both hands in front of his chest, palms out. 'Mr Edgarton, what is it you want? Tell us. We'll do everything we can to meet your demands.'

I can't see inside the cell. But the sergeant's offer tells me Harry's alive. And that could change in a heartbeat.

Silence for a moment, then the scraping of metal against metal. The sound of a round being chambered in a semiautomatic weapon.

'A car.' Stanley's voice sounds no different than it does on an ordinary day in the courtroom. 'Unlock this door and have the car outside, running.'

Sergeant Briggs raises his hands. 'We'll have to get the key—'

A hailstorm of bullets blows the padlock and chain off the fire exit at the end of the hallway. Stanley isn't willing to wait for the key, it seems. The hailstorm pelts the top of the door, then shatters the EXIT sign. The door swings open, its top hinge decimated.

Cold wind carries snow into the corridor. Pieces of plaster and shards of the EXIT sign fall to the floor amid the flakes. Sergeant Briggs turns to the officer beside him, the only woman in the line-up. 'Go,' he says. 'Get a car. Radio when it's outside this door.'

She takes off, almost slipping on the debris underfoot.

'Make sure it's an unmarked car,' Stanley calls after her. 'And no wires either. No tricks. I'll know.'

I know something too. Stanley emptied the chamber. And he didn't do it smoothly. He's used to knives, not guns. He can't fire again until he pulls the slide and resets. The process takes about thirty seconds. Not a lot of time, but it'll have to do.

I step out from the bars into the centre of the hallway, both arms outstretched, the LadySmith aimed into the cell at Stanley's eye level. Harry is on his knees, bent down towards the floor, hands clasped behind his head. Stanley holds a 9-mm semiautomatic handgun against Harry's left temple. A low-voltage work light sits on top of the dishevelled cot, its beam aimed directly at Harry's head. For once, it seems Stanley wants to see what he's doing.

He doesn't see me, though. He's still facing the exit, keeping the line of cops in his peripheral vision. He presses his weapon harder against Harry's temple and lets out one of his hiccup-laughs. Then he lifts the handgun up to pull the slide.

In a millisecond, I make the decision to lower the LadySmith before I fire. Stanley howls, topples forward, and his handgun hits the floor just before he does. Police officers storm the cell. Harry drops to the floor and reaches out for Stanley's weapon. Stanley gropes for it too. And the cops, I realise, can't get there in time.

Harry's fingertips brush the handgun's barrel, push it in the wrong direction, towards Stanley. Stanley's fingers reach the butt of the gun and—without hesitation—I aim at his head. But Harry lunges forward, into my line of fire.

Harry smacks the semiautomatic across the cell, and it clatters against the iron bars, out of Stanley's reach. One of the cops dives to retrieve it while the others surround Stanley and cuff him. He wails and writhes like a wounded animal as they shackle his ankles. Instantly, it seems, an ambulance pulls up outside the bullet-riddled fire exit, and a team of paramedics rushes through the door.

Harry gets to his knees and turns his astonished face towards me. I start towards him, but my knees give out. I fall against the wall and slide down to sit on the concrete floor amid the rubble, still clutching the LadySmith in both hands.

Geraldine appears out of nowhere, the Kydd right behind her. They stare at the ruins on the floor, then shift their gazes to the battle-scarred fire exit and the crowded cell.

Geraldine looks down at me, nodding towards Stanley. 'You missed,' she says.

I might strangle Geraldine.

The paramedics wheel the gurney out of the cell, Stanley strapped to it and still wailing, towards the open doorway. Harry emerges behind them. On hands and knees, he crosses the hallway and presses his face into my neck, breathing hard. Minutes pass, it seems, and neither one of us moves. Then Harry lifts his face up to mine. 'Told you you'd end up on the cell block,' he says.

I might strangle Harry too.

The bailiff appears in the hallway and walks towards us. He stops dead in his tracks before he reaches us, surveying the battlefield. After a moment, he shakes his head as if to clear it. It seems to work. 'I'm sorry to bother you.'

He addresses Geraldine as if the rest of us aren't here. It's pretty clear she's the only one he's sorry to bother.

'But those jurors . . .' He shifts from one foot to the other. 'The ones who wouldn't leave? They're done now.'

CHAPTER TEN

Saturday, December 25

Bailiff Joey Kelsey doesn't normally work in Judge Beatrice Nolan's courtroom. And that's a good thing for Joey. Beatrice doesn't have a positive impact on anyone's nervous system. But Joey's seems more fragile than most. He's the new guy, the rookie.

It's 8 a.m. When Joey called Beatrice at midnight to tell her the jury was ready, she informed him that she was not. Judge Beatrice Nolan doesn't drive in the dark. She'd leave her house at daybreak, she told him. Not a minute sooner.

Joey didn't seem to remember that Beatrice had somehow managed to drive home in the dark, and I didn't mention it.

Harry and I spent the wee hours in Geraldine's office, the three of us drafting the documents necessary to secure Sonia Baker's release. By four o'clock, Geraldine left to track down the required signatures. She was back by six, mission accomplished, whereupon Harry and I hand-delivered Sonia Baker's freedom to the Barnstable County House of Correction.

The jail has its own formal exit rituals and paperwork, of course, but Sonia Baker should be out soon. One of the matrons offered to bring her to our courtroom when she's ready. Maggie is twisted round in her front-row seat between Patty Hammond and Luke, watching the back door with all the anticipation of a child on Christmas morning. Which, of course, she is.

The Kydd went home as soon as he heard about Beatrice's aversion to night driving. He's back now, though, looking thoroughly refreshed. It's obvious he's had a few hours' sleep and a hot shower. I feel a twinge of envy. He grins at Harry and me, then slips into the aisle seat of the front bench, next to Patty.

Reporters and photographers roam the courtroom in search of a scoop. Most of them were hanging round the hallways, waiting for the verdict, when the police evacuated the building. They want to know what happened in the superior court holding cells. They all heard the gunfire from the parking lot, and they all saw the ambulance leave the County Complex. They also see that Harry and I are dishevelled, to put it mildly. And with the reading of the verdict imminent, more and more of them are questioning the whereabouts of J. Stanley Edgarton III.

The steady rumble from the gallery rises a notch when Geraldine Schilling arrives. The reporters pelt her with questions about Stanley. Has he been taken ill? Called to another crime scene? Found to have a conflict?

If Geraldine were inclined to answer, she could say 'all of the above'. She's not, though. She ignores them with a thoroughness honed over almost two decades.

Geraldine crosses the front of the courtroom and pauses at our table to scowl. More than ten years I've known Geraldine Schilling. She's never looked worse. 'You're a lousy shot,' she says.

'How can you say that? My shot took him down. I hit him.'

'In the *thigh*,' she fires back.

'That's where I wanted to hit him.'

She rolls her green eyes at me.

'Geraldine, I wasn't trying to kill the man.'

Another eye roll.

I turn to Harry. 'She thinks I was trying to kill him.'

Harry nods knowingly. 'Would've been better that way,' he says. 'Now he'll probably enter an insanity plea.'

THE COURTROOM grows louder when two prison guards arrive with Buck Hammond in tow. He settles into the chair between Harry and me. He eyes Harry with obvious concern. 'You OK?' Buck asks.

'Me?' Harry turns towards him. 'Of course I'm OK.'

'Did you have to stay in jail very long?'

'No,' Harry says. 'Marty shot the place up and got me out.'

Buck laughs.

The noise in the courtroom subsides when the chambers door opens and Judge Nolan emerges. She climbs to the bench, her expression on this Christmas morning even more dour than usual. Joey speed-reads through his litany. He wants to get this over with.

Beatrice stares down at Geraldine. 'Attorney Schilling,' she says, 'you're here for the Commonwealth?'

Geraldine stands. 'That's right, Your Honour.'

'And Mr Edgarton,' the judge asks, 'where might he be?'

Geraldine searches for words. 'Mr Edgarton is indisposed at the moment, Your Honour.'

'Yes,' the judge replies idly, erect in her chair. 'Aren't we all?'

With that, Beatrice nods at Joey, and he scrambles through the side door. He returns moments later with the jurors in a single line behind him, every one of them scrutinising the courtroom floor.

In my peripheral vision, I spot Geraldine casting a satisfied glance over her shoulder at the press. My knees go weak. Popular wisdom among criminal-law practitioners holds that jurors who've acquitted look the defendant in the eye when they return to the courtroom with their verdict. Those who've convicted don't.

The jurors take their seats, and everyone else does too. Everyone except Harry, Buck Hammond and me. We stand side by side at our table, Buck in the middle, facing the panel. We're close enough to each other that I can feel him taking slow, deliberate breaths. Harry rests a steady hand on his shoulder.

Judge Nolan swivels in her chair to face the jurors. 'Ladies and gentlemen of the jury,' she says, 'have you reached a verdict?'

Juror number five, the fifty-something restaurant owner, stands in the front row, and I feel a small wave of disappointment. He wasn't high on my list of candidates for foreman. 'We have, Your Honour.' The foreman's voice is a deep baritone; his eyes are fixed on the judge.

Joey Kelsey scurries to the jury box. He fetches the verdict slip and almost runs to the bench with it. Judge Nolan reads, expressionless, then returns the slip to Joey, who ferries it back across the courtroom to the foreman.

The judge doesn't glance in our direction. She turns to the panel again. 'Mr Foreman, what say you?'

Trials are unpredictable. But certain aspects of them are not. The delivery of the verdict, for instance, follows a pattern. The juror announcing the fate of the accused always stares at the verdict slip and reads. And it's not because he forgets what's written there.

The verdict slip is a crutch. It allows the foreperson to avoid eye contact with the defendant. In a courtroom pregnant with anxiety, even the most stalwart juror needs a mechanism to control his emotions, his voice. The verdict slip provides it.

But our middle-aged restaurateur defies the pattern. He folds the verdict slip in half and palms it, lowering his hands to his sides. He shifts in the jury box and faces our table. He stares at Buck. I've never seen a foreperson look directly at the defendant. I don't know what it means.

'We, the jury . . .' the foreman begins.

My mouth goes desperately dry.

'. . . in the matter of *Commonwealth* versus *Hammond* . . .'

Buck isn't breathing any more. I guess I'm not either.

'. . . on the charge of murder in the first degree of one Hector Monteros, do find this defendant, William Francis Hammond . . .'

Buck grasps the edge of our table with both hands and leans into it until his fingertips turn white. His eyes remain on the foreman, though. The two men seem unable to move, frozen in this moment of judgment.

Finally, the foreman blinks and shakes his head. 'Mr Hammond,' he says.

This is unheard-of. No foreperson addresses the defendant by name.

'The truth is . . .'

The foreman's voice breaks, and Buck looks sympathetic. He nods repeatedly, encouraging the weary restaurant owner to continue. I can take it, Buck's eyes say. Whatever it is you have to tell me, I can take it.

'We agree with Attorney Edgarton.'

Eleven heads nod in the jury box.

'We're disappointed,' the foreman continues, 'that Mr Edgarton isn't here. We wanted to tell him—face to face—that we agree with him.'

I've practised law for more than a decade, tried more than a hundred cases. I've lost before. More than once, the reading of a verdict made my eyes fill, left my vision blurry.

But not this time. This time my eyes are dry. And I'm going to be sick. I sink to my chair. I can't help it; my knees are about to quit again.

'What Mr Edgarton said was true, Mr Hammond.' The foreman is still speaking directly to Buck. 'When you shot Hector Monteros, it was, in fact, a moment of temporary sanity.'

A low rumble emanates from the crowd.

The foreman looks at his verdict slip for the first time. 'We find that the defendant, William Buck Hammond, knew exactly what he was doing when he shot Hector Monteros. He was *not* insane then, and he's *not* insane now.'

I tell myself to take deep breaths, to focus on the appeal. The appeal of a capital-murder conviction is automatic. We'll farm it out. An experienced appellate attorney can argue ineffective assistance of counsel. I've got ineffective assistance written all over me. I never even gave an opening statement, for God's sake.

The foreman pauses again. His eyes don't budge from Buck's.

Without making a sound, the grey-haired schoolteacher gets to her feet in the front row. Then the young pharmacist rises behind her. So does the juror next to him. And the one next to her. The rest of the panel then stands too, in unison.

For a split second, I don't get it. I look up at Harry and Buck. Buck's face is unchanged. Harry's mouth is open; he's not sure what's happening. But his hand starts thumping Buck's shoulder.

The foreman pauses to look at each of his fellow jurors. Their show of solidarity spurs him on. He turns back to Buck and takes a deep breath. 'We also find Mr Hammond . . .'

He shakes his head, his eyes again locked with Buck's.

No one breathes.

'Not guilty.'

Silence.

THE STUNNED COURTROOM stands mute for a full ten seconds. And then Joey Kelsey begins to clap.

Beatrice bangs her gavel, and Joey pauses, but now Harry and the Kydd are clapping too. Buck's prison escorts join in, and Joey watches them before staring back at Beatrice and resuming his applause. The whole room explodes then. A spontaneous, thunderous standing ovation.

The Kydd takes Patty Hammond by the hand and leads her through the crowd to our table. Buck and Patty melt into each other, and the rest of the Hammonds rush forward and embrace them as one.

Luke and Maggie jump to their feet in the front row, whooping and pounding their palms together over their heads. Maggie twists towards the back door, lets out a shriek, and pushes her way into the centre aisle. 'Mom!' she shouts, fighting against the tide of humanity moving against her. 'Let me through. Please. It's my mom!'

The crowd parts to let Maggie pass, even the press. Sonia Baker stands just inside the back door, waiflike in street clothes undoubtedly borrowed from the Barnstable County House of Correction. Her eyes grow wide as she surveys the unruly mob in the courtroom, then fill as she spots Maggie hurtling towards her. She bends to embrace her daughter, but Maggie seems to have other plans.

Maggie allows her mother only the briefest of hugs, then pulls away and presents the small white box. Sonia hesitates, so Maggie opens it for her and stands on tiptoe to clasp the glittering necklace at the back of her mother's neck.

It's Patty who begins the applause this time. Patty, then Buck, then the rest of us. The TV-camera lights and flashbulbs shift to the back of the room. Sonia looks confused. Maggie takes a bow.

Harry appears at my side, and I reach up to brush my fingertips over his left temple. A light blue bruise is taking shape there, the result of pressure from Stanley's gun. All at once, I realise how close I came to losing Harry, and I'm overwhelmed by the thought of it. Hot tears slide down my cheeks.

Harry leans over and cups my face in his hands, brushing my tears away with his thumbs. 'Oh, no you don't,' he says, pressing his forehead against mine. 'You don't get to fall apart yet.'

He's right, of course. We'll both fall apart later. When we can.

'Break it up, you two'—it's Geraldine—'or I'll have you taken into protective custody.' She pauses at our table on her way out of the courtroom and takes me aside.

'Stanley confessed,' she says to me, 'before going into surgery.'

'Confessed to what?'

'All of it: Howard Davis, Judge Long.' She tilts her head back towards Harry. 'Him.'

She leans closer. 'He told me he didn't have a choice. He'd been sworn to uphold and protect the system. And they were destroying it, one case at a time. He said he knew I'd understand.' She tosses her head at the Kydd. 'Tell him I'll have Nicky Patterson out by noon.'

'He'll be glad to hear it.'

Geraldine heads for the door, and as I watch her exit, I realise the bench is empty. I catch Joey Kelsey's eye. 'Where's the judge?'

'Gone,' he says, smiling.

'Did she call a recess?'

'Nope. She just got up and left.' Joey's smile expands, as if the judge's departure is exactly what he wanted for Christmas.

So Beatrice Nolan just got up and left. She didn't bother to tell us we're adjourned, didn't bother to tell Buck Hammond he's free to go. She didn't thank the jurors for their dedicated service. She didn't even wish them a happy holiday.

We will.

If by moral insanity it be understood only a disordered or perverted state of the affections or moral powers of the mind, it cannot be too soon discarded as affording any shield from punishment for crime; if it can be truly said that one who indulges in violent emotions, such as remorse, anger, grief and the like, is afflicted with homicidal insanity, it will be difficult, yes, impossible, to say where sanity ends, and insanity begins.

We say to you, as the result of our reflections on this branch of the subject, that if the prisoner was actuated by an irresistible inclination to kill, and was utterly unable to control his will or subjugate his intellect . . . he is entitled to an acquittal.

Mr Justice Paxson

88 PA 291

January 20, 1879

ROSE CONNORS

Place of Residence: Massachusetts
Profession: Lawyer
Hobbies: Walking, shellfishing

Rose Connors is an American lawyer who turned to crime writing in 1997 because, she says, 'the story insisted.' The story she's referring to started life as an impassioned closing argument for a murder case. When it grew to a hundred pages, Connors decided she had the basis for a novel. Eventually titled *Absolute Certainty*, it introduced her series character, Marty Nickerson, and went on to win the 2003 Mary Higgins Clark Award for suspense fiction.

Connors has been a trial lawyer for two decades, working on both the defence and prosecution sides. Although she has cut back on her legal work to make time for writing, she can't see herself giving it up completely. 'I need my regular courtroom fix. I guess I enjoy high stakes,' she says. 'And anyone searching for drama need go no further than the local courthouse.'

Like her heroine, she lives on Cape Cod with her lawyer husband and two teenage sons. 'I love it here during the summer—pristine beaches and Cape League Baseball—but I love it even more the rest of the year. Aside from July and August, having dinner at a local restaurant is like dining at a private club—you know everyone, including the bartenders and servers. And working the locale into the books is great fun. My idea of a perfect morning is a few hours of writing followed by a walk wherever the current scene takes place. The walk never fails to inspire more writing.'

When she's not walking or working on a book, she spends her summers shellfishing with her sons, Dave and Sam. 'My sons and I motor out to the Monomoy Flats and clam throughout the summer. That means my writing schedule changes with the tides. The boys make more money than they would at any other summer job, and I—well, the shellfish warden accuses me of writing scenes in my head while I'm out there. He's right, but I never admit it!'

Printed and bound by GGP Media GmbH, Pössneck, Germany

235/05